MIKE ASHLEY is an author and editor of over seventy books, including many Mammoth titles. He worked for over thirty years in local government but is now a full-time writer and researcher specializing in ancient history, historical fiction and fantasy, crime and science fiction. He lives in Kent with his wife and over 20,000 books.

The Mammoth Book of

# *Historical Whodunnits*

*Third New Collection*

Edited by Mike Ashley

**ROBINSON**
London

Constable & Robinson Ltd
3 The Lanchesters
162 Fulham Palace Road
London W6 9ER
www.constablerobinson.com

First published in the UK by Robinson,
an imprint of Constable & Robinson Ltd 2005

A copy of the British Library Cataloguing in
Publication Data is available from the British Library.

ISBN 1-84529-004-6

Printed and bound in the EU

1 3 5 7 9 10 8 6 4 2

# Contents

# Foreword

## Three Thousand Years of Crime

The title may be the same but the contents are all different. Here is an entirely new selection of historical whodunnits and period puzzles covering over 3,000 years, from the Queen of Sheba to the *Titanic*. Twenty-six stories, fifteen of them entirely new and specially written for this collection.

As always I've looked for stories that cover as wide a range of history as possible, but also a wide geographical spread. So we have stories from ancient Assyria to colonial Australia, from the Crusades to Revolutionary America and from Pisa to Old Manhattan.

We have several characters returning from past anthologies so you will find Herodotus trying to solve a puzzle in Egypt, Claudia up to her tricks again in ancient Rome, Chaucer trying to avert a war, Dame Frevisse bringing her sleuthing techniques to the monastic world, and Sister Fidelma solving an unusual crime in seventh century Ireland.

But we also have a lot of new characters and settings. They range from such renowned historical individuals as Prince Henry the Navigator and Hildegarde of Bingen to those whom history overlooked such as Theophilus the Fool, Jasper Shrig, the Bow Street Runner and Ian Rankin's creation, Cully the Caddy in Old Edinburgh.

So let's part the mists of time to reveal the mysteries of the past.

*Mike Ashley*
December 2004

# Acknowledgments

All of the stories are copyright in the name of the individual authors or their estates as follows. Every effort has been made to trace the holders of copyright. In the event of any inadvertent transgression of copyright please contact the editor via the publisher. My thanks to David Sutton of Copyright Watch and Bill Pronzini for their help in tracing authors' estates.

"The Duke's Tale" © 2005 by Cherith Baldry. First publication; original to this anthology. Printed by permission of the author.

"His Master's Servant" © 2005 by Philip Boast. First publication; original to this anthology. Printed by permission of the author and the author's agent, Dorian Literary Agency.

"Murder in Old Manhattan" © 1945 by McCall Corporation. First published in *Blue Book Magazine*, January 1946. Copyright © renewed 1973 by Frank Bonham. Reprinted by arrangement with Golden West Literary Agency. All rights reserved.

"The Living and the Dead" © 2005 by Judith Cutler. First publication; original to this anthology. Printed by permission of the author.

"Death in the Desert" © 2005 by Jean Davidson. First publication; original to this anthology. Printed by permission of the author and the author's agent, Dorian Literary Agency.

"The Witching Hour" © 2005 by Martin Edwards. First publication; original to this anthology. Printed by permission of the author.

"If Serpents Envious" © 1998 by Clayton Emery. First published in *Ellery Queen's Mystery Magazine*, July 1998. Reprinted by permission of the author.

"Footprints" © 1929 by Jeffery Farnol. First published in *Collier's Weekly*, 11 May 1929. Reprinted by permission of the author's estate.

"The Stone-Worker's Tale" © 2005 by Margaret Frazer. First publication; original to this anthology. Printed by permission of the author.

"The Jester and the Mathematician" © 2000 by Alan R. Gordon. First published in *Ellery Queen's Mystery Magazine*, February 2000. Reprinted by permission of the author.

"Threads of Scarlet" © 2005 by Claire Griffen. First publication; original to this anthology. Printed by permission of the author.

"The Uninvited Guest" © 1996 by Edward D. Hoch. First published in *Ellery Queen's Mystery Magazine*, November 1996. Reprinted by permission of the author.

"Sea of Darkness" © 2005 by Sarah A. Hoyt. First publication; original to this anthology. Printed by permission of the author.

"Poisoned with Politeness" © 1997 by Gillian Linscott. First published in *Ellery Queen's Mystery Magazine*, September/October 1997. Reprinted by permission of the author.

"The Gentleman on the Titanic" © 1999 by John Lutz. First published in *Ellery Queen's Mystery Magazine*, November 1999. Reprinted by permission of the author.

"Botanist at Bay" © 2005 by Edward Marston. First publication, original to this anthology. Printed by permission of the author.

"The Dutchman and the Wrongful Heir" © 2005 by Annette and Martin Meyers. First publication; original to this anthology. Printed by permission of the authors.

"Benjamin's Trap" © 1994 by Richard W. Moquist. First published in *The Franklin Mysteries* (Salt Lake City, Northwest Publishing Inc, 1994). Reprinted by permission of the author.

"Catherine and the Sybil" © 2005 by Sharan Newman. First publication; original to this anthology. Printed by permission of the author.

"The Tenth Commandment" originally © 1912 by Melville Davisson Post. First published in *Saturday Evening Post*, 2 March 1912. Copyright expired in 2001.

"The Serpent's Back" © 1998 by John Rebus Ltd. First published in *Ellery Queen's Mystery Magazine*, April 1998. Reprinted by permission of the author and the author's agent, Curtis Brown Ltd.

"The Oracle of Amun" © 2005 by Mary Reed and Eric Mayer. First publication; original to this anthology. Printed by permission of the authors.

"The Judgment of the Gods" © 2005 by Robert Reginald. First publication; original to this anthology. Printed by permission of the author.

"The Abolitionist" © 2005 by Lynda S. Robinson. First publication; original to this anthology. Printed by permission of the author.

"Cupid's Arrow" © 2003 by Marilyn Todd. First published in *Ellery Queen's Mystery Magazine*, September/October 2003. Reprinted by permission of the author.

"The Spiteful Shadow" © 2005 by Peter Tremayne. First publication; original to this anthology. Printed by permission of the author and the author's agent, A. M. Heath & Co.

# His Master's Servant

## Philip Boast

*For once I shall part with convention. In all my previous anthologies I have set out the stories in chronological order from the earliest setting to the most recent. Although the rest of the anthology follows that format I wanted this story to open the book because it contains a theme which will keep recurring. It is set during the Crusades when the European and Arabian cultures clashed, something we are still all too familiar with today, and the basis of this story prepares us both to look further back in time and to consider the present. You will find the theme of prejudice throughout this anthology, whether it be religious, racial, sexual or philosophical.*

*Philip Boast has written a number of historical epics, often with a fantasy or religious theme, including* Sion *(1999), the story of Jesus and Mary Magdalene, and* Deus *(1997), which also has links with the Crusades and deals with the legacy of a crime committed in London in the thirteenth century.*

### The Templar fortress, Jaffa, the Holy Land, October 1192

"Hear your servant, O Lord!"

I waited. Darkness. The single candle flame. The stone walls of my prayer-cell.

"Your humble servant begs you to hear, Lord."

Silence.

"Lord, give me strength to slaughter the infidels," I prayed. "Guide my sword to the throats of the Saracen demons. Give me grace to kill those spawn of Hell, their women, and children, and their animals, and burn their buildings and blasphemous books, to make a world fit for your holy Cross."

I whispered prayers until I was hoarse. Not a sound in the great fortress; the ninth hour of the night, the soul's darkest hour between Matins and Lauds. My aching knees bled into my chain mail, my hair-shirt burned and itched my flesh. I rested my forehead on my sword-hilt shaped like the Cross. "Lord, give us back Jerusalem." Jerusalem, City of God, that we call *Hierosolyma*. "Let me die seizing your holy City from the devils. Show me a sign."

But my master, the one true God, did not reply.

I groaned, falling on my face. What earthly master notices his servant? None. The servant performs his duties or is whipped. But to be ignored is worse.

I grasped the whip-handle that lay on the stone bed, tore my back bare of my hair-shirt, raised the whip high.

"Grant my eyes one last sight of Jerusalem, O Lord," I prayed.

"Sir Roger," said a small voice.

I brought down the whip upon my back, *in flagellante delicto*, the agony both startling and familiar.

Know me, Christian: I am Sir Roger de Belcourt, servant and slave of the One True God, Knight of the Order of the Poor Soldiers of Christ and the Temple of Solomon. I am Knight Templar, soldier of God, warrior-priest. My life is God and death.

The healing blood trickled on my spine. More, more, I cried. Hear your loyal servant, O Lord. I was dizzy with prayer.

"Sir, 'tis me!" That small voice again, mouse-small, frightened.

I paused, panting and rose to my knees. The boy stood in the doorway, sixteen years at most, head bowed over the candle in his hand, peeping eyes terrified. He was small because starved as a child, abandoned at Temple Gate in London; I am six feet tall, my sword longer than he. I stared at the lad through my sweat, the lead tails of the whip dripping my blood, trying to think.

"Sir Roger," he quavered, "'Tis I, Dickon-a-Ferret, your servant."

"Ah," I croaked. "You. It's wrong for a master to forget his servant." I tousled his hair. "Dickon, yes."

"For the last five years," he said eagerly, "since I was a child and Jerusalem was lost to Satan, I serve you night and day."

I'd hardly noticed the boy; why should I, my weapons and armour are always oiled ready, my war-horse saddled; on campaign he turns up wine, a cockerel leg, a loaf, something; a good servant.

"Well, boy, goodnight." I threw myself on the straw. "I'll sleep now. Wake me for Lauds."

In chapel we thousand knights pray as one man, brothers all. There are no women here, not one. No female contaminates our purity. The only female flesh I have touched, to my knowledge, is my mother when I was born. My war-horse is a stallion, to ride a meek small mare would disgrace me. Hen, or sow, or ewe, or cow meat, has never passed my lips. No milk, ever. The boy coughed, still waiting. I sighed. "What?"

"Sir," he burst out. "'Tis someone!"

I opened my eyes.

"The Master sent me, sir. He commands your presence."

"The Master?" I blinked, fully awake. "De Gondemar commands me?"

"Himself!" squeaked the boy. "Quick, sir." He covered my torn hair-shirt with a linen vest (permitted in hot climates), jumped on the bed to pull my tabard over my head, lifted my sword from the rack with both hands and strapped it around my waist. "He commands no delay!"

There's no mirror in my cell lest the sin of vanity claim me, but there was a water trough in the stone corridor. I glimpsed my face as I plunged my head beneath the surface: my blue eyes in blistered sunburnt cheeks, lips split by weeks of thirst

on campaign, black beard matted to my chest, unkempt hair
to my shoulders.

My tabard was blazoned with the Holy Cross, red on
white, in God's fresh blood.

I walked fast. "Is the castle attacked?"

He ran behind me, not my equal. "All's quiet, sir."

It was too quiet. The king's men snored. I stepped over
them in the shadows. None woke. Where were the sentries?
From the winding stair I crossed the Order's immense
stable, a thousand stallion ready for battle at an hour's notice
despite the truce forced on us by Satan's army. Princes back
home stabbed us in the back with intrigues and vices, and so
the Devil, taking the shape of his creature Saladin, mocked
us safe from the conquered heart of Christendom: our holy,
bleeding city of Jerusalem, which my eyes would never see
again.

"Where's the stable boys?" I whispered.

No sentries on the ramparts, only the moonlit sea. I
pushed the boy away and drew my sword. "Orders, sir,"
he whispered. "No one sees you come or go. The Master says
so."

"Why?" I kept my sword ready, and well clear of pillars
and dark doorways.

"Someone, sir. Disguised. From outside. Masked, his
cape caked with desert-dust."

"No traveller crosses the desert, it's a place of demons."

"Yes, sir," he shuddered.

It was a long, steep climb to Gondemar's quarters. No
aide-de-camp, not even a foot-soldier waiting at the stair-
top. The heavy arched door to the sanctum swung open at
my touch. The Master, shorter than I and plumper, took my
elbow without a word. The door closed softly behind. "What
of my servant?" I asked.

"Who?" Gondemar already forgot the boy. Without a
word, nervous, agitated, he led me to his private sanctum.
A few candles flickered in the great turret, casting more
shadow than illumination. The sanctum was a masonic circle
on several levels joined by stairs. Tapestries and hieroglyphs
hid the stone walls, a fortune in golden books lay stacked on

sideboards, and I was amazed by a huge Holy Bible open on a stand, the first I'd seen outside a chapel. Such knowledge is dangerous without a priest's guidance, yet thrilling; I glimpsed dense hand-written Latin, some monk's life's work, but still Gondemar pulled me forward. A candle flared in the draught from an arrow-slit, and for a moment I marvelled at a Templar world-map with Jerusalem at its centre. In a chair behind the map something moved, a shape more shadow than flesh, then a crown-circlet glinted. I gasped and threw myself to my knees. The King, but not a word was said.

Gondemar lifted me to my feet, murmuring, "Whoever you think you see here, he is not."

I nodded, for Gondemar commands me, and over him the Pope, not King Richard. Behind the English King who was not here, and a few steps below, a half-shadow moved across a lower level as though blown by the draught. I could not fix my eye on its shape; examining a book, the weave of a tapestry – I glimpsed a pale hand – moving on.

Gondemar began, "A matter of the utmost delicacy –"

I drew my sword with a clatter. "I'm your man, Master!"

There was laughter from below. A child's laughter. There was mockery in it.

"'I'm your man'," drawled the King's voice. "My dear Gondemar, is this bluff fellow really the same Sir Roger de Belcourt who famously claimed that, if it could be proven to him beyond doubt, he would deny even the existence of God?"

"Indeed, Sire." Gondemar sounded uncomfortable. "He was lucky to escape excommunication and the stake. On the other hand, as His Holiness the Pope pointed out, St Augustine proved beyond doubt that God definitely *does* exist, so the question of Him *not* doing so cannot possibly arise. Sir Roger was freed from his chains without recanting."

"An honest man, then?"

"I believe no less, Sire."

"Perhaps he is a lucky fool."

"A righteous Christian," Gondemar said. "A heart pure and true."

"Truth is dangerous," Richard murmured. "Is he ready to die horribly?"

"No man is braver." Gondemar pressed my hand, returning my half-drawn sword to its scabbard. "You won't need that tonight, Sir Roger. You're asked for by name."

I glanced at the King. "No, not by me, sir knight." Richard sounded ill, weary. "I return to England, to more troubles of my own."

Gondemar said, "By Saladin."

"Satan?" I echoed dumbly, "Satan asks for me?" A shudder ran up my back – a shudder, and a thrill.

"Your honest man's a fool!" called the child. "Time's wasting."

Gondemar ploughed on. "Your dangerous reputation spreads like a net to trap you, Sir Roger. Even Satan, it seems, hears of your, ah, controversial honesty."

"Shall I prize compliments from our enemies?"

"Is it a compliment?" laughed the child.

"Saladin wishes to meet you, Sir Roger. The moment demands an honest man."

I stared. At the Horns of Hattin the Devil-spawn captured ten thousand knights alive by a trick, and ordered them sodomised and beheaded in one afternoon. The bodies were eaten by dogs. He wished to meet me.

"My dear fellow, he's a civilized chap," Richard said. "In his way."

The King wished the meeting to happen. Gondemar tugged my arm nervously.

I said hoarsely, "Where?"

The child called up, "Jerusalem, Sir Roger. Are you tempted?"

My ears roared. I clasped the railing that saved me from falling down the steps. "Jerusalem!" I heard myself say. "I have prayed for it with all my heart."

"The holy city of Allah, al-Quds," the child mused wickedly. I realised it was no child; the voice was wrong, a devil had stolen a child's form. The shadow below me turned, gazing up. I could not see its hideous face, only its eyes flickering like candle-flames. From bending in examination of a book, suddenly it stood tall.

I cried out, "What devil are you?"

"I am no devil." It held up its hand to me, and of course I shrank back from the horrific scent of its perfume, the stink of Hell itself: a woman. "I am Leyla ad-Din Salah," she murmured, "precious and beloved daughter of the man you call Saladin, or Satan, who asks for your help."

I couldn't think. Worse than a demon. A woman.

A she-devil worse than any I could have imagined, for she would flay bare my very soul. But that was in the future; though only a short time in the future.

"A woman!" I cried out. "A woman has entered our fortress."

"Sir Roger," tsked the King, whom I suppose was quite used to the company of women, "there's no need to shout. You'll wake the horses."

"Your man's a fool after all," the woman said contemptuously. "Have I been sent on a fool's errand and risked my life for nothing?"

How could she be here? No knight would let her in. "Our fortress is impregnable," I cried. "By what magic did you enter? How did you cross the desert? How could guards protect you, a mere woman?"

"I am my father's daughter, servant and emissary. As for guards," she said coolly, turning her back to me, "I travel alone. As for the desert, it is my home. As for your silly castle, it is not impregnable to one woman, one rowboat, one rope." Examining a book with interest, not looking at me, she held a parchment over her shoulder. "The letter from my father."

I went down the steps alone, came close, and took the parchment without touching her fingers. Her perfume was stronger down here. I opened it, shaking.

Not a word made sense. Her voice mocked me. "Do you not read Arabic, Sir Roger?"

The Devil's tongue! I shook my head, contaminated by the air she breathed.

"Gondemar, your Master, does." Still she did not look round. "So many of your Order's books are in Arabic, are they not? Without our scholars you Christians would know nothing of the wisdom of the Greeks, or mathematics, or the stars."

"There's nothing wrong with knowledge, even infernal knowledge, in the right hands," Gondemar said.

The girl turned to me suddenly, squeezing a corner of the letter between her fingertips. Her eyes were wide, black-brown, deep; I saw nothing of her hair, if she had any, and her face – if she had one – was blank, concealed by a veil. Our fingers touched the same parchment. I snatched away my hands as though they burnt.

"Permit me to read aloud my father's words to you." Her voice was lighter and higher than a man's, yes, but with depths, nuance, dark smoothness: so this was how a woman's voice sounded. "'Sir Roger de Belcourt, greetings. Your name is put to me as that as an honest, rational man, a rarity among Christians.'" She gave a little giggle. "Is he not naughty, my father? Anyway, he continues. 'Such a Christian is not my enemy but, I pray, my friend. I have need of you, friend. My dear cousin Haran ad-Din, of blessed memory, is murdered most foully. The cursed murderer stole an object of great value from his body, an object of which poor Haran was the caretaker not the owner. The murderer was arrested almost at once, a Christian Jew well known to me who is now, along with his family and a steward, my house guest. His name is Belmondo; he claims you will remember him.'"

I nodded. "The richest man in Jerusalem. Rich as a Templar treasury, they said."

She raised one of her eyebrows, which were all I saw of her except her eyes, most expressively. "Rich indeed, to be so rich."

I ignored the barb. "I didn't know him well. A soldier in his youth, then a merchant. He supplied wine to the chapel, I recall. I went to his house once or twice. His son, drafted into our city guard, begged to join our Order." I groped for his name. "He was baptised William, but Belmondo practised

Jewish ritual, I believe, even as he professed Christianity to us. The boy's Jewish name was Reuben. He joined his father's business in the end, I believe."

She read, " 'There is no doubt Belmondo committed the crimes.' "

"That's difficult to believe."

She stopped, curious. "Sir Roger?"

"Why should the richest man in Jerusalem murder Satan's cousin, I mean Saladin's cousin, of all people, to steal something of value? I cannot see the reason."

"Nevertheless, that is what happened."

"Were Haran and Belmondo enemies?"

"Good friends. That night Haran was Belmondo's guest at his house."

"Can the object be of *very* great value?"

"To my father, perhaps. A jewel," she murmured, with a small sideways shrug that I would learn to recognise. "The Rose of the Nile."

"Why should Belmondo not simply purchase the bauble?"

"It would not be for sale."

I contemplated Saladin's dilemma: an Islamic leader newly ruling a fractious divided city, his dead high-born cousin whose blood must be avenged, an odd and irrational theft, and a murderer-thief who is Christian, Jewish, and rich enough for half the city to be his friend. Even great Saladin must clothe revenge with justice. Whose guilty verdict could be trusted more than that of an enemy, if he be an honest man? "So I, a trusted Christian, an incorruptible Templar knight, am to examine the crime and proclaim Belmondo damned to Saladin's satisfaction? Allowing the horrendous torment and prolonged execution of Belmondo to proceed smoothly, no doubt."

"Belmondo's guilty and the Christians and Jews will accept your verdict."

"Why hasn't your father tortured the truth out of him?"

"As I said, political considerations. Also, he genuinely seeks truth. You said yourself that the crime does not make sense unless Belmondo is mad."

"Is he?"

"He is afraid."

"That's the first thing that makes sense," I said.

Another voice spoke. "Excuse me," King Richard interposed. "I know Saladin for an honourable man. I negotiated the current truce with him in person, and his brother Saif, indeed with Haran himself. I trust Saladin as a man of his word. But we speak of Sir Roger's life. What guarantee do you offer?"

I sensed her smile. "None. He alone will see Jerusalem for one last time. Perhaps he will spy some weakness in our walls, as you and the Master plot and plan, who knows? But I don't think Sir Roger will come for that reason."

"I'd die for my eyes to behold the City of God once more," I told the King.

"You see?" she said. "It's easy."

Seventy-five years ago our Order was founded to guard pilgrims on the most dangerous way in the world, winding and twisting south-east from Jaffa to Jerusalem. No Christian dares set foot on this deadly desert track since the Holy City was lost. The hooves of my stallion, Outremer, clopped from the drawbridge at dawn. "Sir?" a voice called.

I'd forgotten him. It was too dangerous for the boy; I left him standing long-shadowed beside his palfrey. When I next looked back both boy and fortress were gone.

The woman rode a mare, of course, a black Arab of fine breeding left tied to an olive branch. She rode alongside me towards the sun even when I spurred ahead. I'd brought no water, trusting God to meet my needs. The morning grew hot. The midday heat was unbearable, my armour too hot to touch. She sipped from a spouted flagon as she rode. "Are you not thirsty?" she said at last.

I deigned to notice her. "God will provide."

Her eyes smiled. "Not here, Christian." By daylight her eyes were golden brown, with long lashes, but gave no clue to her age, young or old, comely or motherly. By night her veils and robes had been black; midday illuminated them richest, deepest purple. Her fingers were long and delicate. She rode well. I spurred ahead. She spurred beside me, her mare lithe as the wind.

She held out the flagon towards me for half a hundred hoofbeats, then laughed. "Are all Christians of the north cold like you?"

I was not exactly cold, but I knew what she meant. "Perhaps!"

"Drink, Sir Roger. The water will not poison you, neither will my hand."

I spurred ahead but the woman balanced forward, seeming to weigh nothing, her mare racing nimbly on the curves and rises. My armour jangled, rubbing, and my head baked inside my helmet. I slowed. She rode a little ahead of me, looking over her shoulder from time to time.

"Why are you silent, Sir Roger?" It was best to reply nothing to her; no man had the power to enrage me like her. No man would waste the day in irritating, cunning, time-wasting stratagems to attract my attention. She was a devil indeed. She drank the water, and I imagined her tongue beneath the veil, licking the last drops from her lips.

"Why do you stare?" she called.

Dusty waterless hills, dusty valleys under a blazing sky. At first I feared demons behind every bush and wall, ambush in every olive grove, arrows from every hillock. Nothing happened, but we were watched. She read my thoughts. "When my father gives orders, they are obeyed." We rode undisturbed all afternoon. As evening fell she swung aside from the track and I followed her to a cup between two hills, feeling for the first time that we were truly alone. A palm tree grew beside the pool. She dismounted. "You're half dead of thirst. Your cheeks are blistered. I have oil."

"Woman, don't touch me." I slid down, clanked, crouched, drank beside Outremer from the pool.

She watched. "Still you do not say my name." She left me, moving as easily as a dancer beneath her robes, and sat silent on the opposite side of the pool. She made a fire with twigs and flint as the stars came out. I realised no servant would appear with a cockerel leg and a cup of wine; hunger possessed me. She cooked pieces of meat on sticks. The scent of lamb and spice drifted on the smoke. My mouth watered.

"We aren't devils," she called. "We're Muslim. Our beliefs differ, that's all."

"You worship a false God, Allah."

"You worship a false prophet, branding a human the Son of God." She sniffed the meat and added a pinch of something.

I said firmly, "The Bible tells us Iacimus Christus is the Son of God and the Bible cannot lie."

"Iacimus Christus?" She sounded angry. "Iesous Christos to the Greeks. Yehoshua ben-Yussuf to the Jews. You cannot even say his name in your own tongue!"

That was true; I had never thought of Him in English. Latin has no J. The divine name would sound strange in English, shorn of learning and mystery, made ordinary. "Jesus," I said, my tongue clumsy as any bondman serf's. "Jesus Christ."

"There." She pricked a lump of meat on her dagger-point. "A piece of lamb for you."

But I shook my head and turned away. Somehow, she'd humiliated me.

I listened to her eating the meat. She burped and kicked out the fire. Her footsteps padded into the darkness.

"Leyla!" she called back at the top of her voice. "I'm Leyla! Even in English!"

I don't know where she slept. I hated her more than words can say. Obviously she hated me.

I awoke with the sun. My hands went at once to my cheeks. They'd been oiled and no longer pained. Had the woman dripped the oil on my flesh, or wiped it over my skin with her fingers? Had her cursed satanic fingertips actually touched my face while I slept?

I sat up, then averted my horrified gaze as I glimpsed her head bobbing in the pool. Long, long black hair hid her face and shoulders that alone broke the water. Gleaming hair; I saw the strands gleaming in my mind though my eyes remained tight shut. She could swim.

Everyone knows devils can't cross water, they sink.

When next I saw her she was dressed and veiled, breaking

her fast with yoghurt and cheese, neither of which I touch, they being female. I checked my saddlebags for food but had no Dickon to fill them.

I sat watching her, belly rumbling. She ignored me, finishing her meal. "I no longer believe you are a devil," I said. Still she ignored me. "Leyla," I said.

She smiled. I knew it even though I couldn't see the smile itself.

We saddled and rode. We were followed; once a skylined blade caught the sun, but that was all. For hours we didn't talk. "Why you?" I asked through dusty lips. "Why did your father choose someone so precious to bring me to Jerusalem?"

"Would a man survive the brutal Templars? A woman alone had the power to bring you."

"But you are his jewel."

"The Rose of the Nile is even more precious to him than I."

"More important even than finding Haran's murderer?"

"Haran, though mourned, cannot be brought back. The Rose can."

"But Belmondo –"

"Swears he does not have it. He has been searched naked, even into the orifices of his body. And his family, all of them, under my father's eye." I was starting to feel sorry for Belmondo. "He's guilty," she said. "He'll confess to you where it is."

"Perhaps your father will feed me the whole fruit, not just the pips."

"Ha!" She spurred ahead.

"Leyla," I called. She turned back. "Nothing," I said. "Just saying your name."

She slowed her mare to a walk, watching me. "He chose me," she replied, "so that he will know what sort of man you are who reaches Jerusalem."

I nodded, baking, sweat dripping from the joints of my armour. I'd have to be very stupid to be as stupid as I looked.

Three palm trees this time. I dismounted at sunset, exhausted. "You stink," Leyla said. "Swim."

"A knight bathes only for Easter."

Without warning she tugged my tabard. I recoiled, hand on sword, but her look was of wonder. "Is it true?" She nodded at the Cross of *sang réal*. "Is that truly the blood of your Jesus?"

I pulled off my tabard and hung it reverently from an olive bough.

"Is it true the founders of your Order found the sepulchre of Jesus beneath Jerusalem, and you wear your saviour's undying blood?" She knew I would not reply. Suddenly she said, "Perhaps there are wonders enough for all to be found in Jerusalem."

I knelt, bathing my face in the pond between the trees. "I shan't look," she called behind me. "See, I'm going to my prayers." Her voice became distant. I looked round and saw only the hills.

The cool waters invited me. I lay my sword close to the water's edge. As I discarded my armour and chain-mail a feeling of freedom made me laugh suddenly. My leathers and linen shift took only a moment, then I ripped the hair-shirt from my sticky flesh. My under-garb was rotted by the heat and sweat of the past six months; I peeled the soggy mess from my legs and felt evening air caress me. Sand gave way under my feet as I launched myself forward into the delicious cool waters, floundering to the middle.

But the oasis was deeper than it looked, and I cannot swim. I was sinking.

She called from the shore, "Perhaps you are the devil, Sir Roger."

I blew water from my nose and mouth, splashing. At last I felt the blessed sand catch my toes. "Turn away!"

She laughed silently. Even as she turned her back, her shaking shoulders mocked me. I crawled ashore and sat with my back to her, pulling on my clothes. "Stop," she called wonderingly. Had she looked, and seen the marks of the whip? But no, she marvelled only at my shirt. "What, woven of hair? It must feel unbearable."

"Not compared to your company."

"What can possibly justify such self-inflicted suffering?"

"Every day of my life, it reminds me that I am a fallen creature, miserable servant of the one true God."

I turned, dressed. Leyla was staring at me, her wide-open eyes dark in the dusk, gold-flecked. I had the strange impression that her veil had been off her face and she'd replaced it the moment I turned.

"No, sir knight," she said. "I do not believe you are fallen."

At the hour of Lauds I rose and prayed in the dark. Soon the hour for Prime would come, and daylight. I prayed again and heard Leyla at her prayers. Such different gods; how strange the prayers should sound the same. We rode without words, both knowing that our journey to Jerusalem was not ending but just beginning.

As we topped the rise the sun lifted over the shining domes, minarets, shield-walls and battlements of the City of God, divine oasis in the desert. Tears sprang to my eyes.

"Al-Quds is beautiful," she agreed.

The faithful were called to prayer by horns in one quarter, tolling bells in another, and everywhere chanting muezzins in their tall towers set the rooftops echoing. I rode through the great gate in the company of the woman, straight-backed, in my shining armour and white cloak and Cross of Jesus's blood, who was crucified here.

Jewish, Christian, Muslim beggars, wearing every imaginable mutilation, fell back crying and wailing as we rode up the steep rutted street. By the market we turned right, clattering up steps and along alleyways. I averted my gaze; the immense Temple built by our Order over Solomon's temple was broken down for stone, its mighty colonnades melting back into the city.

Belmondo's white house lay on a busy square, cleverly adjoining Jews on one side and Christians on another, with the new fine houses of Muslim merchants on the third side. The house was as I remembered, a cunning mixture of all three styles. Chained pails of leftover food, now empty, remained outside for the poor. The gate swung and we rode into a deep courtyard enclosed by the house on three sides. The fourth side was a high wall, topped with spikes, pierced only by the gate. Our horses drank from the fountain.

"A room is prepared," Leyla said. "My father commands that this house is yours."

I'd no time for rest. "I need your father's permission to visit Belmondo."

"He knows you are here." Someone laid out tables of sweetmeats, sherbet, turmeric eggs, water jugs, wine jugs. Leyla tossed me a sweet confection then saw my face, took it back, ate half, giggled, and did not die. It was not poisoned. She offered me the other half, but rather than risk the feminine contamination of her hand I chose another.

"I'll see the room where Haran was murdered."

She summoned a cringing servant or caretaker, the same who'd brought the sweetmeats I think, to be my guide. I stared around me, amazed: the house was a wreck inside, the tile floors broken into the soil beneath, plaster torn from the walls. I followed my guide around rubble and smashed furniture. Saladin's men had ripped the place apart.

Leyla spoke behind my shoulder. "What room was this?" I turned on her, startled, but she gave her sideways shrug. "I may not leave your side."

"Shouldn't you be reporting to your father my habits, strengths, weaknesses?"

She sounded amused. "You did not see, at the city gate, one of the beggars slip a tight-rolled paper from my sleeve?"

I hadn't. I tried to ignore her, but her light footsteps always followed me. "You!" I called to our guide. He turned, bowing, almost too old for sense. I spoke loudly to make him understand. "This was Belmondo's dining hall, I remember?"

He spoke gibberish, white beard flapping. Leyla translated. "Many people, much food. Music, dancing girls, boys." She rattled off a few questions then nodded at the old fool's replies. "He's no one, an unprofitable servant because he's lived so long. No one noticed him. He hid in the corridor listening to the music."

"Belmondo and Haran sat together at the top table?" In response the old man nodded eagerly, pointing at now-overturned tables, couches with the stuffing pulled out, broken platters. I raised my voice. "Belmondo and Haran, friends?"

"For many seasons," Leyla translated. "Good business. Much trust. You do not have to shout."

I asked quietly, "Did they drink wine together?"

Leyla said at once: "Alcohol does not pass our lips."

But the old man spoke. She hesitated. "When the other guests had gone, Belmondo and Haran stayed up drinking wine."

"Still friends?"

"Laughing, happy," she translated. The old man grinned through stained teeth, nodding. "Haran carried something on a chain around his neck. He showed it to Belmondo."

"A rose-coloured jewel?"

"It flashed."

I said, "Obviously no one has questioned this man before. Why not?"

"He's a fool," she said impatiently, getting angry. "Who wants to hear gossip that Haran of blessed memory drank wine on the night he died, and in his cups showed off something he shouldn't?"

"I."

"You're a Christian. No vice is too low for you. Your religion is cannibalism, you change wine into blood, bread into flesh —"

"Your father asked my help."

She shut her eyes, then opened them. "Of course." She listened calmly to the old servant. "He heard they parted and went upstairs, Belmondo to his bedroom on the left side of the house, Haran on the right."

The stairs were broad, leading to an equally broad and airy three-sided balcony overlooking us. "But after bed-time," I mused, "Belmondo left his wife's side, padded around that balcony in his nightshirt in plain view of anyone here below, murdered Haran and returned clutching the jewel?"

"Obviously that's what happened."

"The priceless jewel Haran looked after but didn't own. Did it belong to your father?"

Again she hesitated. "Perhaps."

"Why the strange arrangement?"

"Because." She shook her head. "I cannot answer. The matter is too sensitive."

I went upstairs, looking around the balcony, then called over the rail, "How was Haran killed? Strangled? Stabbed?"

"Belmondo stabbed him repeatedly around the heart. The knife has not been found."

I beckoned the old man. "Haran's room, you show." While he climbed the stairs one gasping step at a time I strode to the left, opening doors off the balcony. One upstairs room, grander than the rest, had been torn apart, the bed ripped by the searchers, tapestries slashed, feathers spilt from the bolsters. Belmondo's room.

I followed the old man around to the balcony's third side, to Haran's room. Here the broken couches were spattered with blood, blood on the rugs and wardrobes, blood down the walls, even the inside of the door. The attack had been frenzied, yet woke no one. Then I noticed how heavy and well-fitting the door was. The murderer had thoughtfully closed it before the deed. I slid the inside bolt closed, then opened it again to show the clean tip.

"The murderer was covered in blood."

"Do you see my father's wisdom now, Christian? Belmondo's whole family aided him in the crime, disposed of his bloodstained clothes, washed him. One, probably Reuben-William, ran out with the jewel and hid it. It could be anywhere in Jerusalem. The whole family are guilty."

I examined the wardrobes, then moved to the end wall. A door led to a small bare corridor, a gutted straw mattress. Haran's personal body-servant must have slept here, inexplicably unwoken, while his master struggled and died. A doorway opened on the room of commode. I held my nose; zealous searchers had smashed the seat and scattered the foul contents. Stepping back I noticed a second door inset discreetly in the corridor wall, used, I supposed, by household servants. I followed steep steps down to a short hall, one door to the kitchens, another to the street. I returned shaking my head.

The old man muttered a few words, grinning slyly.

"Sometimes a guest would wish to entertain a visitor . . . privately." Leyla would not meet my eyes.

"A woman?" I crossed myself.

"At least one," she said.

The old man grunted. Leyla stared firmly at the wall. "In Haran's case . . . Haran preferred . . . young men."

"The exact word?"

"A boy. Boys!" she burst out. "Sodomy! I know this is difficult for you, Christian, but it is not uncommon."

I gazed around the destroyed room. "If Haran had a boy or boys in here that night, we'll never know. He would have sent his body-servant away – intimate moments, the one time a man's apart from his servant. The servant had probably procured them from the street and knew to make himself scarce until his master had finished his pleasure."

Leyla swallowed. "That's exactly what happened. The servant swore it."

"You're sure he didn't lie?"

"A man dying a ghastly death does not lie."

"He's dead?"

"Of course. That's how we know he told the truth."

I leant on the wall. Anyone could have come upstairs from the street, anyone sneaked through the kitchens.

"The whole of Jerusalem could have killed Haran," I said. "What hour did Belmondo retire?"

The old man held up five fingers. The fifth hour of the night. Haran had been killed in the early hours, some time between the boys' departure and the body-servant's return; probably the body-servant had been taking street-pleasures of his own and the murderer, waiting his opportunity here, had struck.

"I suppose there's no hope of finding them?"

"Ah, so many boys," the old man said in English. "All will invent any story for gold, or under torture."

"I need to ask your father –" I told Leyla, and stopped, realising.

The old man chuckled. Servants scuttled around him, pulling away his matted beard and grimy turban, replacing them with clean headgear and shining gowns. The filth was washed from his face. Someone else cleaned the stains from his teeth, then the servants withdrew leaving only body-guards. A new man stood unbowed before us, about fifty years of age, of Kurdish expression, with sunstruck eyes and pockmarked face. Stood like a king.

Leyla knelt. "Father."

I looked Satan – Saladin – in the eye, and was filled with awe, horror and wonder.

Leyla kissed his hand.

"Daughter." He spoke softly, raising her to her feet. "You have done well."

"Our Christian's dangerous," she said. "Cleverer than he looks. And he learns quickly."

"Yet he remains incorruptible?" I had the terrible, de-stroying insight that I was not supposed to have come through the desert undefiled by Leyla. I was to have become Satan's creature, eliciting Belmondo's confession and the hiding-place of the jewel. The Devil indeed, to treat his own daughter so; he disgusted me.

She smiled behind her veil; I knew her so well. "He's incorruptible, Father, a pure man, a snow-white knight."

She made my heart grieve. Still I stared Satan in the eye, my hand on my sword-hilt, yet I could not move. I could not strike him down.

"Then Sir Roger is the very man I hoped for," he said simply. What should I believe? He lifted my fingers from the cold steel, taking my hand between his own hands, warm. "For-give my small deception, Sir Roger. I am indeed Salah, called Saladin in your tongue. I attended the, ah, questioning and know well what happened that night. Are you satisfied now of Belmondo's guilt?"

"I am satisfied Belmondo did not do it."

Salah made a small but ferocious gesture. "There is no other alternative."

"Let me see him."

\*      \*      \*

"Belmondo!" I called in greeting, but the bed-ridden figure was not the proud Belmondo I remembered, sleek, fat with cunning, brimming with gold-given confidence. This shadow was a broken man, but even so Belmondo would not return my greeting lying down. "Ruth," he called his wife, but she was not strong enough in her thinned state to lift him. Their son Reuben-William, standing by the arrow-slit twisting beads in his hands, did not seem to realise her plight. Finally she dragged at a bellrope, crying out, "Peter!" and the steward came from a doorway somewhere in the quiet unobtrusive way of such people, helping her lift Belmondo into a wooden chair. When I looked round he was gone, but the boy flinched as though he saw him still.

"Sir Roger, I remember you," Belmondo quavered. "Pray for me." He lifted the blanket from his legs. They were parboiled to the knee. The scalded, shiny flesh stuck to my fingertip. No doubt he had received other, more discreet, persuasions as well.

"After such torment," I marvelled, "you still claim you are innocent?"

"I am innocent!" he cried.

"Then your son must be guilty," Salah said contemptuously. "Shall we put the boy to the test now? Leyla, call them."

But instead of calling the torturers she looked to me. I shook my head.

"I know what happened that night," I said. "The father was not there. The son, too, is innocent of this crime."

There was a moment of silence while they digested my words: if I was right, that left only the women. Salah rounded on Belmondo's wife, who cowered into the corner with her two daughters, all three of them screaming and whimpering now. "Women?" he muttered, "but they're just women. They do nothing without command. Who could command them but Belmondo? He's still guilty."

"Let me question them with words, Salah, not terror." It caught at my heart to beg mercy from Satan. "God will show us the truth. I will give you the murderer and the innocent need not die."

"I require only a guilty verdict from you," Salah said, "not divine intervention." But to my great relief he drew his cloak around him and sat in a corner-chair, resting his chin thoughtfully in his hand. Leyla remained by the women, watching me with large eyes.

"Is this the only room?" I asked loudly.

Belmondo nodded.

"It's a prison not a house," Salah called irritably.

I strode at the boy Reuben-William, who flinched from me. A handsome lad. His mother and sisters screamed at me, begging me to leave him alone.

"A single room," I agreed, "but with doors nobody notices." I opened the door the steward had used. Belmondo looked blank for a moment then said, "Oh, but that's Peter's room."

"Peter?"

Belmondo shrugged. "Only my steward." I gazed at him steadily. "I don't know, he's been around the last fifteen, twenty years?"

"More," his wife said. "An ordinary servant before that."

"Is Peter a good servant?"

"I suppose so."

"That's all?"

"What more is there?" Belmondo sounded baffled. "A household falls apart without a good steward. I've never had to reprimand him. He's the perfect servant, I suppose, if there is such a thing. What's this to do with –"

I ducked past the door and closed it behind me. I leant back against the thick planks, holding it shut, for there was no bolt, and asked of the shadows: "Would you let your master die for you?"

Peter's hair was grey but he was not an old man, still strong. The room was narrow and dark, a crowded nest filled by the family's possessions stacked or fallen down, bags, clothes, shoes, all clean, a few flagons of wine, a bench for him to prepare food, a part-jointed chicken and the knife beside the carcass. Peter looked from me to the knife. The knife that had killed Haran. The knife that so obviously had an innocent purpose that it had never been noticed, just as Peter was never noticed.

His fists unclenched, then he breathed out. "My master . . ." He began again. "My master is an ignorant stupid fool."

"Rich enough to fill whole churches with silver and gold," I murmured. "That raises him very close to God."

Peter's eyes gleamed silver in the shadows. "He never saw anything important." He was close to tears. "My master supped with rulers and imams and knights and chevaliers and all the richest and most noble, and never saw what was going on in his own home, under his own nose."

"But you did."

His silver eyes blinked at the knife, then closed like darkness. "I saw. Stinking filth."

"What did you see?" A knock on the door. I kept pushing. "Peter, I think I know what you saw. Take the weight off your soul."

He groaned, then his eyes flashed open. "They were both guilty that night! Father and son, God help me, both!"

I spoke to him for a few moments while the knocking on the door grew louder. Silence fell. Leyla's voice called through, "Roger, what ails you, are you safe?"

I gripped Peter's shoulder. He nodded. He was ready.

I opened the door and pulled him through. Salah had not moved. "Who's that?" he frowned.

"No one." I held out the knife by the blade, still slippery with chicken flesh. "This is the knife that killed Haran."

Salah forgot the steward. He examined the knife curiously. "I've never seen such a thing. It's no dagger."

"It's not a weapon," I said. "It's a knife used in a kitchen. You've never been in one, I'll wager, any more than I."

He put it down with revulsion. Leyla said, "My father is distressed that Belmondo butchered Haran with a common tool."

"Your father?" I rounded on her. "Be quiet, liar."

"My father —"

"Quiet!" I shouted. I continued in a low, fast murmur, "He isn't your father. Salah wouldn't risk his real daughter –"

"I swear, I swear to you he is my father." She was a good actress.

Salah watched us with a small mocking smile.

"I don't know who you are, Leyla," I murmured, wanting her alone to hear, seeing the wide-open stricken look of denial growing in her black-brown, gold-brown eyes, but I couldn't stop. "Leyla probably isn't even your name. You're a dancing girl, a clever mimic, one of his servants, no one."

With one hand she covered her eyes and turned away from me.

Salah cleared his throat. "Please," I said harshly.

He gave the small sideways shrug. "Very well, Sir Roger," he said. "Illuminate us with your truth. Pray continue."

I gathered my thoughts. "Belmondo's guilty, but not of the crime of which he is accused. Reuben-William is innocent of murder, but guilty of a worse crime. His mother and sisters are guilty because they knew, but said nothing. They are guilty of silence." I touched Peter's shoulder. "As for this man, we shall see."

I turned to Salah. "Anyone could have killed Haran. The reason could have been simple theft: the priceless Rose of the Nile. In fact the jewel was trivial to the crime."

"Not trivial to me," Salah growled. "Yes, the jewel is mine. I am not a wealthy man, I care nothing for money. In my youth, when I ruled Egypt in all but name, the ground opened under me and my horse fell into an underground chamber, a place of ancient kings. Among the tombs shattered long ago by looters my eye found a glow in the darkness, dropped, forgotten for a thousand years. That moment is my heart. The Rose of the Nile will pay for my funeral; thus, naturally, it was in Haran's care."

"Why did you not tell me?" I asked Leyla.

She shook her head without turning, weeping. "I would not speak to you of my father's death."

I tried to ignore her weeping. "You see, I couldn't believe

the murderer walked around three sides of the balcony and back again covered in blood. Haran's door had a bolt on the inside, no doubt locked so that Haran's pleasure was undisturbed, that stayed locked while he was murdered, because the tip of the tongue was clean of blood. So the murderer didn't come that way. He came through the kitchen or from the street."

"Then we'll never know who it was!" Salah exploded.

"We know he watched and waited. He knew Haran's body-servant was out, or he'd have to have killed him too."

"The body-servant who procured the boys from the streets," Leyla nodded.

"No, he didn't. There were no boys, but only one young man." I stared Reuben-William in the face. "And he came from inside the house. Didn't you?"

Belmondo and his wife exchanged looks. "No," the mother whispered. She tried to limp to her son but Belmondo held her. His face was tragic, as though again watching events worse than his own death unfold.

"Haran, cousin of the great Salah ad-Din Yussuf," I continued. "Powerful. Well connected. Not to be resisted. A man whose word was almost literally law. Whose every whim demanded satisfaction."

"Our son could not refuse," the mother whispered. "We begged him not to go."

"I wanted to!" Reuben-William's face set. The beads dug into his hands. "You already knew. You all knew about me." He turned to me earnestly. "But, Sir Roger, I did not kill him."

"I know," I said. "If you, a young gentleman, meant to kill Haran, you'd use a proper weapon not snatch a kitchen knife. The murderer's attack was furious, with many inexpert blows around the heart, none immediately fatal. Yet I know you have military training, and your father was a soldier. The murderer was inexperienced at killing."

"The ancient Greeks had a word that we translate as *Logic*," Salah murmured. "It seems that you have studied some of the so-called infernal works on Logic seized from us by your Order, Sir Roger."

I didn't meet his eye, continuing instead: "It is well known that sodomy is the worst sin, worse even than murder, because a murdered soul flies straight to God in Heaven, whereas the souls of sodomites reek among us on the earth until their eventual certain descent to Hell –"

"Everyone knows this!" croaked Belmondo. "God save my son. What else could he do but give in to Haran? The contracts – everything I stood to lose –" He fell silent, ashamed.

"Someone observed Reuben-William sneak through the kitchens." I touched Peter's shoulder. "Whose job is it to know everything in a household? A servant. What finer servant than this, made steward for his decades of loyal service, servant above all other servants. Yet you know nothing of him but his name."

"Peter?" Belmondo said dully. "Peter killed him?"

"Stinking filth!" Peter burst out. "I remember when your sweet babe was born, master! I remember the lad running about, growing up, apple-cheeked, cheerful as a cricket. Me who never had children of my own, who knew nothing but service to you. You was my family. Your boy was like a boy of my own. I loved you all." His face crinkled. "Stinking filth!"

"Peter was in the kitchen," I said quietly. "He saw the body-servant sent away. He saw Reuben-William sneak upstairs. Peter knew what sort of man Haran was, knew what they were doing. While they were upstairs the servant struggled with his conscience, with all his years of love and service no one cared about. He hid when his master's son, whom he'd treasured like his own son, crept back through the kitchen. Peter couldn't hide his feelings any longer. He snatched the kitchen knife, ran upstairs, and stabbed Haran to death for his monstrous crime."

"And stole the jewel," Salah said dangerously.

"Stinking filth," Peter cried. "Filthy with blood. I hated its touch. I dragged it from his neck, I ran. I ran downstairs. I threw the foul thing in one of the pails, and washed myself clean."

"A pail?" Salah leapt to his feet. "You dropped the jewel

in one of the buckets of slops left over from the feast, put out for the poor?" He clutched his head, imagining the multitude that must have eaten at Belmondo's gate.

"Aye." Peter, doomed though he was, managed a smile. "Well, one of 'em's not so poor now."

The great gates of Jerusalem were thrown open at dawn. I rode away from the sun. The City of God fell into shadow behind me.

I turned one last time. In the gateway I saw Salah, hand raised in farewell, white stallion prancing. At his side, even now, I made out Leyla on her dark mare.

Her figure was veiled, motionless, fixed. I knew she still stared after me, just as she had when I rode past her without a word. Unmoving.

Justice was done. Belmondo had committed no crime that men could punish. He, his wife, his daughters, and his son returned to their house, and I supposed would pick up their old way of life. I'd seen Reuben-William standing at the window above the kitchens, his handsome face white, haunting as a ghost.

Who was Leyla? Was she Salah's daughter, his dancing-girl, his calculating emissary, his whore?

Would I ever know?

Somewhere in the dungeons beneath Salah's palace, Peter the loyal servant screamed his way to eventual, certain execution and the good God's side.

I reached under my tabard and touched the precious stone swinging there. They'd searched the family but forgot the one who really mattered: the servant. The jewel lay in Peter's pocket all along, and in the dark narrow room, in our last moments alone, he'd slipped it into my hand. Great Saladin would die without enough for a hole in the ground.

Her cloak blew in the wind. Her mare stamped one hoof and for a moment I thought she'd ride after me, galloping, and we'd ride away just as we had on the curves and rises that had led us to Jerusalem, but this time away towards the sea, the wide sea.

She too was a jewel that I found; I will never find another.

# Death in the Desert

## Jean Davidson

*From the Temple of Solomon we now travel back a further two thousand years to the time of Solomon and the legendary Queen of Sheba. The palace of Sheba was in the present country of the Yemen and is believed to be at the site now called Mahram Bilqis. She lived around the period 950 BC and is most famously associated with Solomon, to whose court she travelled. The following story is set on that amazing journey.*

*Jean Davidson is the wriring persona of literary agent and former paperback editor Dorothy Lumley, under which alias she has also written the Victorian romantic thriller* A Bitter Legacy *(1993) and the contemporary crime novel* Guilt by Association *(1997)*

They came in the night, cowards made brave by the cover of darkness. One moment Daribul was settling himself to sleep, the next he was being roughly shaken awake.

"Master, master, quickly, we are being attacked!"

All around was confusion, bodies struggling together, yells from near and afar, screaming. Someone bellowing, "Light the torches, you fools!" another, "They've got the lead camels, stop them."

More used to wielding a pen than a sword, Daribul reached for the weapons his servant Floran held out but, before he could speak, the young lad was knocked to the ground by a massive blow from behind. Daribul glimpsed wild eyes, mouth set in a savage grimace then the man was gone before he could retaliate. He knelt down and felt the boy's neck. He was alive but unconscious. "Best place for you. Keep out of trouble," he muttered, rolling the lad on his side then looking up to assess what was happening. Feet scrabbled on stony ground, boulders tripped the unwary, bodies clashed, struggled, swayed, fell, moaning, to the ground. Their camped caravan was being attacked but how was he to tell friend from foe until there was enough light?

Daribul absorbed these facts in a second, but his body was already on the move: the Queen. He must see that she was safe and protect her if needs be. He sprinted fast, crouching low, rebounding off bodies, man or beast he didn't know or care, laying about him with the hilt of his sword, all the time forcing his way towards her tent by sheer strength of will. He was only slightly built and he was not a fighting man.

With relief he saw a mass of torches approaching, but the relief was short-lived. They were carried by the soldiers of the Queen's general, Al-Hajar, who was in their midst on horseback. Daribul tried to turn away but too late as Al-Hajar jeered at him. "Hah, running the wrong way as usual – looking for the Queen's protection. Stand and fight like a man –" He was fortunately swept on by. Daribul ignored him, as he ignored all Al-Hajar's insults.

He was close to the Queen's tent now, approaching it from the side. Miraculously it seemed to stand in a pool of quietness, the men who usually stood guard at the entrance were engaged in a fierce struggle some forty paces away. Relieved, he paused for a moment to catch his breath and then by the faint light of the stars, caught sight of a movement at the rear of the tent.

It was very slight, perhaps an animal of some kind. Instinct took over and without thought he crouched low and crept towards the movement he'd seen circling around behind. Barely allowing himself to breathe he stopped and raised his head. What he saw nearly stopped his heart from beating: two figures lying flat, quietly cutting a rent in the material of the tent wall. They were swathed in dark robes that blended with the rocky desert and hard to see. Then the first rose up on all fours, preparing to move inside.

He remembered little of what happened next. It was as if a spirit entered his body flooding him with superhuman strength, perhaps the god who inhabited this dirty little oasis in the middle of nowhere. He launched himself forward, sword arm raised, crying out: what happened next was a blank. When his vision cleared one man lay dead at his feet, the other was staggering away groaning, clutching his nearly severed arm to his body. Daribul, still possessed of incredible strength, bounded after him, leapt onto his back, and forced his sword into the man's throat through the rough cloth. Gurgling blood, he collapsed.

Daribul looked down at him. He was beardless and his skin was strangely smooth. He was murmuring but no words that Daribul could recognise. Daribul stabbed him once through the heart to spare him further suffering, then went back to the other body and stabbed him again too, just to be sure. Then he ran to the front of the tent where he nearly tripped over the dead body of a guard. The others were still fighting nearby. He pushed his way inside.

There she stood, calm and unafraid, her female servants around her. She was holding her ceremonial dagger, raised ready, but lowered her arm when she saw it was Daribul. Her servants pulled her cloak around her to cover her nightwear, catching her long black hair half under it. Daribul had never seen her so informally dressed before, but she was unconcerned.

"What's happening? I wanted to go outside but my guardians here held me back," she spoke urgently but smiled at them too to soften her words.

"Desperate battles all around, but I believe we are beating them off," he said, hastily making his obeisance.

"Good – and I see my scribe's sword is red with blood too. Are you hurt?" Daribul shook his head, still filled with that strange heightened awareness, "Good, then accompany me outside so I may see for myself."

She strode towards the tent entrance. Daribul opened his

mouth to protest then closed it again. Not only was she his queen, but he also knew her too well. Her will was strong when her mind was made up – otherwise they would not be here in the wilderness, so far from home.

Outside, torches sent shadows tumbling and the smell of smoke mingled with the metallic stench of blood, and acrid human sweat. Several of the Queen's personal bodyguard now fell back to surround her, breathing heavily from their exertions. And then, a trumpet sounded and an ululating cry of victory rose across their encampment and echoed from the mountains nearby. As suddenly as the attack had started, it was over.

Reaction set in. Daribul felt all his limbs trembling and his stomach began to heave. He was glad he had been possessed and could not recall the instant when his sword – he closed his eyes. He would not think of it.

When he opened them he realised there was still much more to be done. Orders were being given for the care of the wounded, a rider despatched to Wusuf, the local warlord who had given them permission to stay at this oasis and had also been handsomely paid to guarantee their safety.

He took the opportunity to return to the men he had killed, intending to drag them round to the front of the tent. But when he reached the spot the dead bodies were gone. Blankly he stared and then, in shock, searched the ground. There was a pool of blood where he had slit the second man's throat, but no bodies. He knelt down and looked more carefully. It was difficult to tell, but regular lines in the dusty sand could have been the heels of dead men, scoring the ground as they were dragged away. All done in an instant. He looked up and all around, but could see no one. He had to return because he had left the Queen without permission. She did not ask where he had been, but asked, "Find La'ayam, bring him to me. Pray that he is alive, I think we will need his wise counsel."

"And General Al-Hajar?"

"I think he is already on his way." They exchanged looks and Daribul turned to leave but too late. He heard Al-Hajar's

voice well before he saw him, boasting of his and his men's
prowess in the battle, and then there the man was, his robes
torn, his face and beard shiny with sweat, eyes still feverish
with the fight.

"Hah, still hiding behind the women? Out of my way,
stargazer," he deliberately bumped into Daribul, making
him stagger. "Men of letters have no value when it really
counts."

Daribul gave him a furious look. How he wanted to say, if
you look behind the tent you'll see the men I killed. But
without the bodies he knew Al-Hajar would have another
excuse to let the insults fly. One day, he vowed to himself,
one day . . .

The Sheban encampment was vast. There were over two
thousand camels in the caravan as well as horses, sheep and
goats. Some men had brought their families too and tents and
sleeping places stretched far out across the wadi floor. Fortunately, as well as the many torches and campfires, the sky
was beginning to lighten, though the moon had long since
set. Daribul first made his way quickly to his own sleeping
area. Floran was sitting up.

"How are you, boy? Have you been able to drink some
water?"

Floran nodded, then winced and placed his hand on the
tender lump on his head. "I'm sorry, Master, I feel sick if I
stand up."

"Then don't. I'll seek out some herbs and ointments for
you."

"Are you hurt, Master? Your tunic needs mending."

"I may have a cut or two, but nothing serious. Wait
here."

Daribul located La'ayam soon after. His grey hair was
uncovered, and his short beard was unkempt. He was observing the treatment of several injured men while listening
to their accounts of the night.

"But what did you see," he was asking as Daribul approached. "Did you observe what type of men they were?
How did they fight? Can you tell me anything that would
help us name these people?" He frowned impatiently at the

babble of incoherent information that followed. "Queen Zar'eshta, has sent for you," Daribul said quietly.

La'ayam straightened up. "She's unhurt? Good, good, and now we must have a counsel. These brigands had the element of surprise, but it should not have happened at all. How did they creep up on us unawares? Something is amiss here."

Daribul shook his head. "I was asleep when they first attacked. My servant woke me."

La'ayam's look was grim. "They came out of nowhere and have vanished into nowhere. Al-Hajar has sent a party to follow their tracks. Let's hope they are not Red Sea pirates or we'll never see our valuables again. This way we have a chance." He glanced at Daribul. "You've been in the thick of it too?"

"I – I killed a man, two. For the first time."

"Then you have lived a charmed life."

Daribul told him briefly. "But now the bodies have disappeared. Do brigands usually take their dead with them? I don't think so."

La'ayam stopped in his tracks. "Two men trying to reach the Queen – that is unthinkable. Were they after her, or her jewels?"

Daribul shook his head. "I didn't think to find out. I simply slew them. I did look at one of them – he was quite different from the other dead men. Smooth skinned, young."

La'ayam pursed his lips. "I don't know what to make of it. Keep a lookout for them. We really need to see the bodies to find out more. Did anyone else see them?"

Daribul shook his head. "No, and you're the first person I've told – without the bodies, who will believe me, especially Al-Hajar? But the blood is still there."

"We'd better not say anything yet. We don't want to start a panic." Both men knew how devoted the whole caravan was to the Queen. Without her as their figurehead to unite them, the caravan would most likely break up, degenerate into petty squabbles. "The Queen herself should be told – leave that to me. We should double her guard too, to be on the safe side."

Daribul's blood ran chill. Whoever had taken those two bodies – he might return with more men to attack or abduct the Queen. "I will be vigilant," he said quietly. "But I have always thought this was too risky an enterprise."

La'ayam glanced at him keenly. "Since when did queens and ministers seek the opinions of scribes?" He clapped Daribul on the shoulder to take the sting from his words. "Your Queen is bold – we must protect our trade routes or King Solomon will steal them all. We must make an alliance with him. And of all the treasure and spices we carry, she is our greatest. She will dazzle this lover of woman."

They had arrived at the Queen's tent, and after despatching a doctor with ointment for Floran, Daribul was grateful to step aside and drink some water and collect his thoughts. A bold enterprise indeed. They had been travelling for six weeks now and Petra was still two or three weeks away. Plodding through scorching heat, sandstorms and across endless wastes of barren rock and sand, each day took them further from the land he had come to love. The green lands of Sheba, tall palms waving in the warm breezes, tall stately stone buildings, a land lush in fruits and vegetables and watered by the careful management of man, the control of the irrigation their Queen's most sacred duty. And where, in secret places in the hot dry rocks only fit for goats, grew the scrubby stunted trees from which came the most sacred offerings to the gods, the resins of frankincense and myrrh.

He remembered again the day she had dictated her announcement to him. As her chief scribe he had to make himself available to her whenever she asked for him, but it was her habit to call for him in the late afternoon. That day, however, she asked for him soon after sunrise. The words of her announcement had sent a shiver down his spine:

"Know this: I am your Queen, that is named Zar'eshta, and my name is known from the lands of the Indus to the islands of the Mycaenae, and I make this decree. In forty days I will leave with a mighty caravan of spices, gold and other treasures for the City of Jerusalem to meet with King Solomon, renowned for his wisdom. But your Queen is also wise and . . ."

Daribul looked up. He followed her gaze out of the window across the roofs and streets of the city of Shabwah, across the green fields to the blue-hazed rocky mountains beyond.

"Do you see?" she asked softly, "That's the source of our wealth, the water we channel and conserve from mountain flash-floods and melting snows. But everyone else would tell you our wealth is our incense and spices."

She turned back, mischief dancing in her eyes. "I think I have another riddle there, don't you? One to tease this mighty Solomon."

"You'll need plenty of riddles," he had agreed, thinking, King Solomon has enough treasure, power and women already, her wit will be the one thing to intrigue him. But it was not in his nature to flatter the Queen, and she would not have welcomed it.

Daribul had climbed a large rock that jutted out from the wadi wall where he squatted down and surveyed the camp of the Queen of Sheba under a sky flooded pink by sunrise. Thousands of camels, and beside each its burden, the boxes of gold and other metals; jewellery; oils and dried dates and other delicacies; and most precious of all, packed in sturdy baskets, the pale yellow soft tears of frankincense resin, and the darker richer resins of myrrh, as well as some seedlings of the trees of both.

As the sun rose the rocks cast darker, more intense shadows across the dusty, sandy wadi floor. The land around was soft shades of ochre, pale red, light browns. The only green was in the few palm trees by the shallow oasis. Their route over the past six weeks had brought them from southern Arabia on this trade route through land prey to pirates from the Red Sea coast, and brigands from the rocky peaks of the interior. Away along the wadi rim was the rough huddle of dwellings and the citadel of Wusuf, the local warlord. We paid him well, thought Daribul, as we've paid all whose land we've passed through, for our passage and safety. And how has he repaid us? That was no small band of brigands last night. He scuffed at the ground, flung a few pebbles in the air, followed them to gaze into the sky.

What gods lived here, high in these mountains, so close to
the brilliant blue of the sky, gods of winds and sky and high
places? Were they behind this, jealous of the incense being
carried through, taken to honour strange gods – or one God,
Daribul had heard, the Yahweh – and none for them? But
whichever god it was, all humankind desired, needed, these
scented smokes to honour them, send messages, transform
their souls and commune with them. And it was his adopted
land, Sheba, which was the richest source of these things.

A puff of dust from the direction of Wusuf's citadel caught
Daribul's attention. More like a human hand behind this
than a god's, he thought, and Wusuf was a prime candidate.
He could have given information to the brigands so that they
would know when and where to attack, and under cover of
the fighting sent in his own murderers to abduct or even kill
Queen Zar'eshta. A weak Sheba would enable this warlord to
expand his little empire, perhaps even disrupt the trade route
and hold the whole world to ransom.

Daribul closed his eyes and offered a final prayer to his
own private Ninevehen god, then hurried back down into the
camp. He was on his way to join the counsel, but he made a
detour to where he had been told the bodies of the slain were
gathered, stopping here and there on the way to greet and
talk to men he knew. One man summed up what they were all
thinking, if not saying, was their enterprise accursed? Was it
too big an undertaking and should they turn back? Perhaps
the might of this King Solomon was too great and they
should leave the trade routes to him, and return to the safety
of Sheba?

The dead Shebans were laid reverentially on one side. To
the other the bandits were flung in a tangled heap.

"You, come here," Daribul called to one of the guards.
"Who ordered this? Find some help and lay everyone out
properly. We might learn something from the dead."

The guard shrugged. His opinion of scribes was plain, so
Daribul added, "Besides, I want to see the evil faces of the
two creatures I slew last night."

The man's face brightened, and he beckoned to his friends
and after some talk, it was possible to see each dead bandit. The

heat was beginning to rise and so would the stench from the corpses. Daribul took out the tablet he always carried and counted the dead: twenty Shebans, but over fifty of their attackers. In look and build they were not dissimilar, though the attackers were smaller, their skin darker, more lined. Probably from living in the mountains or the desert, he thought. Their clothes were of serviceable rough cloth, leather, and sheepskin, and they wore their beards trimmed short.

"Are you finished?" asked the guard. "We've had enough of dead men. We need to cleanse ourselves. Which ones are your dead men, anyway?"

Daribul frowned. "That's just it. They're not here. Have all the bodies been collected?"

"Are you sure you killed someone? Perhaps it was only a nasty dream." The man and his friends laughed. "Besides, does it matter?"

Daribul laid his hand on the hilt of his sword. "Yes," he said, "It does matter. And if you love your Queen and value her life you will keep a lookout for these bodies. They are distinctive. Young, clean-shaven, swaddled in dark brown robes."

Immediately at the mention of Queen Zar'eshta the men sobered up, put their shoulders back. "We'll do that. If we find them we'll send to you immediately."

The flaps of the Queen's tent had been tied open to allow what little breeze there was to enter, and she sat on a low stool deep in its shade, her servants languidly waving fans to keep her cool. Her hair was pulled back and twisted elaborately and dressed with gold ornaments fashioned in the shape of birds and flowers. Her robe was in a rich blue accentuating the bloom on her cheek. "Sit near me," she said quietly to Daribul, "I want to keep my friends close." Though she smiled he could detect anxiety deep in her dark eyes. Had she been told about her would-be attackers?

Across the carpeted floor, smoothing his beard and moustache, sat La'ayam, and next to him was Al-Hajar, constantly sending and receiving messengers. Wusuf sat near Daribul. He had arrived brandishing knives and a long sword, with a retinue of rough-looking men, and pretended to be disappointed the fighting was over.

Light refreshments were served and talk swirled around the night's events, of the caravan, what they had seen since leaving Shabwah, exchanging gossip, sizing each other up. Daribul looked around for their high priest Qu'atabar and located him in a dark corner at the back of the tent. Attended to by two shaven-headed acolytes, he was engaged in religious rites. Daribul quickly looked away then chided himself. He thought he'd successfully espoused the Sheban gods, but it looked like his childhood learning went deeper than he thought.

"And so, Wusuf, I charge you with neglecting your duties and breaking your promise. We could ask for compensation."

La'ayam's words brought Wusuf scrambling to his feet, reaching for the sword that was not there. All their weapons lay outside.

"I did everything that was asked of me. You have churned up the dust of my land, used my water and firewood, spread yourselves like a great obstacle around my citadel."

"In return you have received plenty. But what about the safe passage across your land – Daribul, wasn't that part of your correspondence?"

"It was," Daribul answered. "I have it here. Your exact words were 'A pleasant and peaceful sojourn beside our city walls'. It hasn't exactly been either."

"How was I to know these strangers, these scavengers would attack you? I've looked at the slain – we don't know any of them. Who am I to set myself up to second guess fate?"

There was silence, and Wusuf subsided onto his cushion, until Al-Hajar said, "Perhaps these 'scavengers' were informed of our arrival by one of your people?"

"None of my people would have betrayed you," Wusuf growled. "My word here is law. Any person who disobeys –" he drew his hand across his throat in a quick gesture.

"Then it was you yourself who –" Wusuf leapt to his feet, face mottled with rage. "And I charge you, Al-Hajar, with complacency, thinking yourself still safe at home in your little kingdom of Sheba – this is the real world out here, and it's not my fault if you're not up to it."

The two men were about to throw themselves at each other when the Queen spoke.

"Please, do not add to the night's injuries with further bloodshed. Sit down." When the two men, still muttering and glowering, gave way, she continued, "We are not asking for our safe passage payments to be returned, though I have been advised we would be within our rights to do so," she nodded at La'ayam. "I want to discover whether this was just brigands, seizing an opportunity, or whether there was a more sinister purpose, so that we can plan accordingly."

Wusuf bowed his head, but Daribul saw his eyes shift craftily. "Queen Zar'eshta, your land has treasures that all the world desires, though I might venture your worth far outweighs that which you carry to King Solomon. You are the greatest prize of all."

Daribul puzzled over his choice of words. If he had sent those two men, perhaps he'd intended to hold the Queen for ransom?

"I think we should wait for King Solomon's judgment on that," she replied.

"Why no, we have evidence already. The two men who were attempting to carry you away – oh, I forgot, their dead bodies cannot be found," he stared at Daribul. "You should look into your own camp for a traitor."

Daribul opened his mouth to protest, aware of La'ayam shaking his head, but even more keenly feeling the Queen's searching gaze. He felt ashamed. He should have told her himself, not listened to La'ayam. But perhaps that had been the old man's intent? To discredit Daribul and distance him from the Queen so that he could weaken her protection. Wusuf innocent and La'ayam guilty? Who could Daribul trust?

"It's true, I killed two men last night before I came into your tent – but when I went back all that remained was their blood."

"Hah, we only have *your* word for it, where's the proof?"

Al-Hajar bellowed. "Admit it, you were trying to kill or carry off the Queen yourself."

"The Queen's servants all saw blood on my sword," Daribul protested hotly.

"You could have wiped that on any dead man. I say we should examine this Assyrian, if only to punish him for false bragging."

Daribul shuddered. He knew what Al-Hajar meant by "examining". Few survived such ordeals. "I don't need to brag, like some do. Anyway, how did you hear this, Wusuf? I only told La'ayam, and we decided to tell no-one. I saw you leave your citadel myself this morning – did one of your spies meet you on the way here and tell you your plot was foiled?"

"D'you think guards don't talk? I heard you'd been looking for missing dead men, and I told Wusuf. Satisfied?" Al-Hajar finished triumphantly.

"Then you and Wusuf have conspired together." The words tumbled out of Daribul's mouth in anger and then the insults began to fly afresh. The Queen held her hands up in despair, until the tinkling of bells halted them.

High priest Qu'atabar stood behind the Queen, flanked by his acolytes gently shaking cascades of tiny silver bells.

"The gods have answered me," his voice rang out as if conducting a ceremony. "We must now purify ourselves and this place of these violent acts and of the blood that has been spilled. And then the smoke of our funeral fires will reveal truth. The sacred incense will work its magic once more bringing us a vision of what took place. I have seen this."

Qu'atabar refused to allow anyone to help. Only he and his acolytes, amid the most obscure of rituals, were allowed to scrape a depression in the ground until they hit bedrock, beside the rock Daribul had sat on earlier that day and on which the priest set up his altar. They then heaped firewood, dead palm fronds, reeds, broken baskets, much of it brought from the nearby town, on Wusuf's orders into a pyre and then the dead bodies were brought over, to be placed on the pyre by Qu'atabar himself, friend and foe alike.

Messengers went around the camp with the news that the ceremony was to be held at sunset, and everyone was to fast, drinking only sips of water, and to spend their time in contemplation. People rested under their blanket awnings or in their tents, the rough dark brown cloth blending in with the landscape.

"He has chosen a good spot," Daribul explained to Floran who, after sleeping and more ointment, was feeling much better. "You can see far distances from up there. No one will be able to approach us without being seen."

"You – you think they'll return tonight, Master?" the boy asked nervously.

"I am worried," Daribul replied. "More so by the missing corpses. Whoever took them has unfinished business. Al-Hajar refuses to believe me, but La'ayam has insisted the Queen must be guarded every second of the day." He paused. He didn't want to voice his fear aloud, that the counsellor was putting on a show of concern, while all the time watching and waiting his chance to attack her again. Perhaps Counsellor La'ayam wanted to be King La'ayam, to lead them into Jerusalem and feast with mighty King Solomon.

"Perhaps they were just taken away by their brigand friends?" Floran suggested hopefully.

"I wish, but I had the pleasure of Al-Hajar's company earlier when his detail returned from following the trail into the mountains."

The party of ten plodded in on weary camels, but their leader leapt nimbly enough to the ground from his kneeling camel to make his report. "We followed their tracks as fast as we could – we could see them until they vanished into the rocks. After that, I was sure I could hear them once or twice up ahead, but after a while even the tracks in the sand disappeared. It was as if they had melted away. We searched various gulleys and ravines but then decided to turn back, fearing we might become lost ourselves."

Al-Hajar nodded, satisfied, then could not resist goading Daribul again. "Your friends have escaped this time, penpusher. But I will find out how much they paid you and where you've hidden it, make no mistake. Oh yes," he went on, deliberately misinterpreting Daribul's gasp of denial, "I've had your possessions searched. We haven't found anything yet, but I'll be watching you, even when you're asleep."

"You'll search in vain, then, and miss the real traitor. Unless, of course, it's you. This could be your feeble attempt to draw the scent away from yourself. Surely the Queen's safety is our biggest concern?"

The other man stiffened, and Daribul readied himself for the blow – Al-Hajar was not a tall man, but stocky solid muscle. Instead, he laughed, a grating sound. "You have more courage than I expected from a man who kills phantom intruders. I look forward to our holy leader exposing you for what you are in his holy fire! And the Queen is quite safe with me to look after her."

"I've told you the whole story, Floran, no point in hiding the truth from you. You may need to seek a new master soon."

Floran hung his head. "I, I tried to stop them from looking at your baggage but I'm not as brave as you. Surely the Queen will not believe Al-Hajar's lies. She listens to Advisor La'ayam and she's always been your friend."

Daribul shook his head. "I've not been allowed to speak to the Queen, I don't know why. Are they afraid I'm going to harm her, after all the hours we've spent together? Perhaps they think I have Assyrian friends secreted nearby. If I loved Assyra so much, I'd still be living there. Queen Zar'eshta knows that."

"No, Master. If you say you killed two men to save the Queen, I believe you. They must be somewhere. Dead men cannot walk!"

"Thank you, Floran, then I won't give up hope. I'll continue to be vigilant. Now, you had better prepare my clothes – I shall endure tonight's ordeal better if I am well-dressed."

The gathering of people around the rock waited quietly as the sun sank over the horizon and the egg-blue sky and thin strips of brown cloud were lit by the evening stars. It was still stiflingly hot on the wadi floor, but up on the rock it was cooler. Qu'atabar had spent the day purifying the rock and the altar, accompanied by his acolytes, and now continued his low chants as braziers were lit releasing the fragrant fumes of frankinsence and myrrh to waft across the expectant crowd. The priest beckoned. Al-Hajar, La-ayam and Daribul came forward to flank Queen Zar'eshta. She was already conducting her own rituals as ceremonial Queen-priestess, in white, a gauzy veil covering her head, as they did those of her female companions.

The sky darkened and the fat pale lump of the waning moon rose from behind the mountains. The murmuring of the gathered masses became hypnotic, blending with the chanting of the priest, the shaking of rattles and tinkling of bells. Now and then the Queen's voice could be heard. Daribul began to feel himself transported, his mind emptied, opened, awaiting the visions to be revealed. But he fought against it. He must remain firmly rooted in this world, every sense alert against danger to the Queen. The priest had promised a revelation, but Daribul promised himself he would die before she did.

Qu'atabar beckoned his acolytes. They came forward, lighted torches from the braziers, and began arcing them high, calling out sacred words, gradually moving forward, then raised them on high. All eyes were focussed on the funeral pyre ready for it to burst into flames – all except Daribul's. His eyes were darting everywhere – and then he saw them.

"No," he yelled, rushing forward. "Stop!" He grappled with the torchbearers and managed, such was their surprise, to pull them back.

Cries of shock and horror burst out, followed by hissing.

"You fool," Al-Hajar cried and pinned Daribul from behind, pulling his arms behind his back. La'ayam stepped forward. "Silence!" he ordered. "Continue – set the torches now, before our sacred moment passes. Quickly!"

"Why so fast," Daribul yelled. "What are you trying to conceal? Listen – our holy priest was right – Qu'atabar, listen to me, I've seen your holy truth."

But the priest, his skin pasty and sweat running into his wild eyes, was seizing the torches himself.

"He is possessed," La'ayam hissed, "We must silence him before our people are disturbed." He lunged forward, but Daribul managed to shift his balance, and the blow fell on Al-Hajar. Twisting free he shoved La'ayam aside and rushed forward to grasp Qu'atabar's arm.

"No, no," he yelled again. "I have seen them – the Queen's attackers – there in the pyre."

Heads turned in shock and in the confusion Daribul managed to grab hold of one of the torches and hold it high. Yes, he had seen them. The beardless round faces, the bodies completely hairless, no longer swathed in robes. Beside him he sensed Qu'atabar hesitate.

The Queen's voice rang out. "The gods have guided us – Qu'atabar has given us this sacred moment – we give praise – but we must continue – Al-Hajar, remove those bodies from the pyre and then we must continue."

Al-Hajar pushed forward to help Daribul. "You mean these two hairless boys?" he growled. "But I–I recognise them. They are –"

With a high-pitched scream Qu'atabar snatched the torch from Daribul and with one in each hand ran forward and leapt onto the pyre. Flames whooshed into life, roaring through the tinder dry wood and leaves, intense heat seared their skin as sparks flew into the sky. The origin of the screams did not, could not, last long in that inferno as he and all the dead bodies were consumed in the holy fire.

Daribul sank to his knees, shaking. Of course, why hadn't he thought of that before? Clean-shaven young men, part of Qu'atabar's retinue of acolytes. It was the priest's doing. If he, Daribul, had paid more attention to Sheban gods and not his own, he might have guessed sooner. The Queen was safe, but from what? What had been the priest's evil intent?

The Queen and her scribe were sitting alone together in her tent. Just outside, talking and giggling together, were her female servants. They had left the wadi two days and forty miles behind and were now camped on an open plain, the faint blue line of the Red Sea in the far distance, and no rocks or hills nearby for pirates or brigands to hide behind. A fresh wind blew and if Daribul closed his eyes he could almost imagine they were back home in Shabwah.

"Thank you, Daribul. I think that is a fair and accurate account of recent events." Zar'eshta paused. "Perhaps not accurate in one way – you don't give yourself enough credit."

"What credit should I take? Of picking up my sword like any man here to protect you?"

"That too. No, I thought – surely you'd solved the riddle already? You knew those two bodies would be in the pyre. You were looking for them."

He shook his head. "I wish I was as clever as you think I am. I was as in the dark as everyone else. No, it was my servant Floran – he convinced me to continue to believe in myself and I promised to continue to be vigilant, in your service."

The Queen sipped some of her wine, then sighed. "Qu'atabar kept his thoughts to himself, he didn't even share them with any of his acolytes, and they of course are obedient to a fault. Perhaps he only confided in those two you killed. But I remember that he was very opposed to this journey to visit King Solomon. Yet, his arguments were listened to and then, seeing it was inevitable, I thought he was resigned to the caravan. Do you think that was it, he wanted us to turn back?"

Daribul laid aside his stylus and flexed his aching hands, before reaching for his cup.

"I wonder," he said, a faraway look in his eyes. "I have travelled long distances and seen many wonders. I know that a man – or a woman – can take their soul, their strength with them. But perhaps he felt his world was cracking – he had gone beyond his limits."

"Desert madness," the Queen nodded. "Yet he must have laid his plans before we left, to make contact with the brigands, to choose the spot for the attack, and under cover of that, for his own men to attack me – it is as well that Al-Hajar acquaints himself with everyone around us and recognised them, or it might have been your ashes lying in the wadi, not Qu'atabar's."

"I suppose he's good at his work," Daribul admitted grudgingly. He did not like being in Al-Hajar's debt. "Qu'atabar must have been desperate, hiding the dead bodies all day, knowing he could not leave the camp without questions being asked, and then managing to smuggle them into the pyre. No wonder he insisted on building it himself.

"And if he was not mad then – with you no longer at the helm, who better to lead us than a priest-king?"

The Queen put down her cup. "I prefer to think the desert-devils had entered him. Thank you. Without you, he might have succeeded a second time."

Daribul thought of the past few days. His actions had been instinctive, not those of a rational man. But he kept his own counsel.

"Still," she said, her eyes dancing with mischief, "it is now one of our many adventures along this road to Jerusalem. Let's see, shall we call it one of our hundred tales of Arabia?"

Daribul smiled and they exchanged a look of understanding. Yes, eyes, he thought, that will not only captivate but enslave even the mightiest of kings.

# The Judgment of the Gods

## Robert Reginald

*Three centuries after Solomon the Assyrian Empire was entering its final phase. The following story is set towards the end of that Empire, more specifically in the year 681 BC with the death of King Sennacherib.*

*Robert Reginald is the writing alias of university librarian Michael Burgess, currently Head of Collection Development at the California State University John M. Pfau Library. He is best known for his phenomenal works of bibliography and historical research which include, amongst a list that would fill this book,* Science Fiction and Fantasy Literature *(1979) and* Lords Spiritual and Temporal *(revised, 1995). He received the Pilgrim Award in 1993 for his lifetime contribution to science fiction research. He has more recently completed two novels set in an alternate medieval Europe,* The Dark-Haired Man *(2004) and* The Exiled Prince *(2004).*

Nineveh, Capital of Assyria, Twentieth Day of Tebetu, in the Year Named for the Eponym Nabu-Sharru-Usur (January of 681 BC)

The Great King Sennacherib lay prostrate before the altar of the god, his face pressed to the cold tile floor, his arms stretched in supplication towards the huge, flickering image of the eagle-headed deity looming above him. Torches mounted in alcoves on either side of the small hall provided minimal light.

"My relatives plot against me," he murmured. "My enemies are legion. I have destroyed the city of Babylon to avenge the death of my eldest son, but those whom I let live now wish my death. Everywhere I see war and plague and famine. When shall it end? When shall the burden pass from my hands?"

A sudden breath of winter air pressed his robe against his legs. He shivered in spite of himself. A moan seemed to emanate from the mouth of the god.

"What did you say?" the Great King begged. "Tell me what to do."

A second groan echoed through the chamber. The guard captain standing just inside the door at the other end of the hall woke from his reverie at the noise, peering into the darkness.

Suddenly and quite without warning, the vast statue of the deity tipped forward and fell directly onto the king.

The guard screamed a cry of warning, echoed by the troop posted outside. But it was too late. As he could quite clearly see when he rushed to his master's aid, Sennacherib, the Great King, the Mighty King, the King of the Four Corners of the World, was quite, quite dead.

"The judgment of the gods!" the captain exclaimed, as the other soldiers rushed to his side. "The gods have spoken!"

And so they had.


Achilleus of Zmyrna in Asia Minor sends greetings to his father's father in Chios. May the son of Meles sing a thousand more songs before he rests!

In the third year of the twenty-fourth Olympiad, I accompanied the expedition of your son Telemachos to Assyria, there to establish a regular system of trade with the Great King Sennacherib and his ministers, now that their hegemony extended to the shores of the Mediterranean Sea. By your instruction I had learned the art and science of lettering from the Phoenician merchants of Akko who were wont to visit our fair harbour, and this skill, it was thought, might give our party some small edge in the bargaining yet to come.

We were three months on our journey, first by ship around the coast of Anatolia, and thence overland up the Orontes and across the great waste to Mesopotamia. When we finally arrived in the walled city of Nineveh, not long after the close of summer, we were thoroughly tired of traveling and ready to meet with the king and his officials.

This proved, however, somewhat more difficult than we had imagined.

These "Black-Haired Men", as they call themselves, are a strange folk indeed. They speak a tongue akin to Phoenician, yet etch their scratchings upon tablets of clay, like the tracks of birds upon the beach. Not even their rulers can read the inscriptions engraved upon their own monuments. They welcome the settlement of strangers within their chief citadels, so that their own people have become a minority in some of their cities, and promote such individuals to the highest levels of service in their government, but force them to bow and scrape as if they were no better than slaves. I do not understand how any man can tolerate such treatment.

We sent our embassies to various high officials, but none would receive us. We sought out the major trading companies in the city, but while all treated us courteously, none would treat with us without the approval of the government. Thus matters rested while fall advanced into winter.

I had been directed by Uncle Telemachos to acquire as much of their language as quickly as possible, and so I sought out one of the Houses of Scribes, a place where youths were regularly initiated into the mysteries of the stylus and the clay tablet. I asked the Headmaster if I could participate, even though I was older than most of these boys. A contribution to the god eased my passage immeasurably.

The study was most difficult. It was as if these men had purposely designed a system that would be impossible for the average citizen to learn, which was perhaps the whole point of the exercise. Scribes are highly valued for their services here, being among the best paid members of society.

I befriended an older lad named Asarbaniplos, which is the closest I can render his name in the Greek tongue. I understood at the time that he was related to the chief families of the city, but exactly how, I did not know. Assyrians do not talk about such matters. I never learned, for example, how old he was, for the year of one's birth is a closely held secret for these people. No one even knows the age of the Great King who rules them.

This Banu, as he was commonly known, had dark curly hair and a quick spirit which instinctively grasped that which seemed so elusive to me. We became great comrades in our battles over the meaning of the elusive stone tablets.

After four months' residence in the citadel, Uncle obtained an interview with the Second Vizier, during which he asked to see the Great King. He was laughed out of the palace. "No man may talk with the emissary of the gods," he was told.

Several days later I was studying in the House of Scribes when a commotion interrupted our lesson.

"What's happening?" I wanted to know.

"The Great King is dead," my friend replied. He shook his bushy head, unable to comprehend what he was saying. "The gods have struck him down. They have cursed Assyria." Then he ran out the door, not heeding my shouts to stop.

I returned to our apartment, but we stayed close to home the next few weeks. The streets were filled with thieves and rogues eager to steal money, food, even the clothing off one's back. Finally, order was restored by two of the old king's sons, one of whom was proclaimed his successor. Still, the evident dissatisfaction of the people was everywhere apparent.

When a month had passed, we heard of an army approaching from the west. Crown Prince Esarhaddon had gathered together his forces and was marching on the capital. The Substitute King went out to meet him, but was defeated and reportedly fled.

A few days later, a squad of guards knocked on our door, and ordered Uncle Telemachos and me to accompany them. We marched out of the Hatamti Gate, where we mounted horses and headed north-east onto the open plain. We could see our breaths blowing behind us upon the wind.

"Where are we going?" I asked.

"Speak when you are spoken to," the guard said, emphasizing the point with a wave of his spear. I dutifully obeyed.

We rode until we spied a citadel, which I later learned was called Fort Sargon. We dismounted and the guard blindfolded us.

"Do not remove these on pain of death," he ordered.

Then they took Uncle and myself by the elbow, and guided us through a series of long, echoing passageways paved with stone.

Finally, we entered a large hall, judging by the change in sound, where we were both forced to the ground, prostrate upon the cold floor. We heard the tramp, tramp, tramp of a squad of soldiers coming through a doorway and across the room. Our "gentle" companions raised us to our knees.

"What are your names?" came the harsh inquiry.

"What is he saying?" Uncle wanted to know.

"We are Telemachos and Achilleus, traders from Zmyrna," I replied.

"Te-le-ma-khu," the hidden man stuttered. "A-khu-i-lai," he added. "These are hard for the Black-Haired Men to say." He paused. "Why does your senior not speak for himself?"

"He does not understand your language," I stated. "No disrespect was intended."

"Then you may become his voice," came the response. "Tell him what I have said and what I will say, and translate his responses for me. Do you understand?"

"I do, sir," I replied, turning my head slightly so Uncle could hear, and relating what I had been told thus far.

"Who is this man? What does he want?" Telemachos asked.

I repeated these questions in Akkadian.

One of the guards struck me down with his spear.

"Enough!" came the order. "Withdraw, all of you."

"But . . ."

"Let them be seated. Then leave us."

The stools were unpadded, but they were immeasurably easier on our limbs than that tile floor had been.

"I am Ashur-Akhi-Iddina, son of Sin-Akhe-Eriba," the voice intoned, a hint of pride floating upon the air.

I sat suddenly upright.

"The Great King!" I hissed to Uncle.

"What?" he spat.

"Esarhaddon! The new king!" I said again between clenched lips.

"Yes," came the reply, "by right of succession and by conquest, but not legally until I enter the walls of Nineveh, which I must do soon, on a day and at an hour that the priests deem propitious.

"But I have a difficulty. My glorious father, contrary to popular report, was murdered. I have questioned my two rebellious brothers most vigorously (they did not escape), but they deny any complicity in the death of their sire. I believe them. Someone else in my father's court was responsible for his death, and I need to know who it was before I enter upon my patrimony.

"My son says that you Greeks have a strong sense of justice, and have been trained to discern fact from fiction. He also tells me that you desire to establish trade between your city and our empire. Therefore, we each have something to gain from the bargain.

"I give you seven days to find the culprit, no more. If you are unable to do so, you may depart in peace, but thereafter we will see no more of you within the boundaries of our kingdom, upon pain of death. If you succeed, you will have our blessing upon your enterprise."

All the while I was translating his words for Uncle Telemachos, who paused before replying with my voice.

"O great and mighty king," he intoned, "we are simple merchants, with no experience of crime beyond that of ordinary citizens, but we will do what we can to help. We will need the assistance of one of your men as intermediary, and will also require your authority to enter into any place at any time to question anyone."

I do not think that the Great King was pleased with Uncle's reply, but he finally said, "My son will accompany you." Then, "This interview is over." He clapped his hands three times to call his guards.

We were escorted from the building and back to our

horses, where we could feel the warmth of the winter sun, Great Eos, shining down upon us once again. When our blindfolds were removed, the first person I saw was my friend, Banu.

"What are you doing here?" I asked.

"I am the son," came the simple reply, and suddenly much that was murky became very clear to me.

The next day we held a council of war, and Uncle expressed reservations over what we might accomplish.

"Will not the Great King kill us if we fail this task?" he wondered.

I translated this.

"Father will not break his word," Banu replied.

"Who can help us while being discreet?" I asked Banu.

"My *Turtanu*," the lad replied. When I expressed some puzzlement over the word, he elaborated, "Erishum is my, well, you might call him my chief 'officer'. He manages my household and provides security and anything else I need."

"I was not previously aware of his presence," I indicated.

"That was deliberate," came the reply, "but he is trustworthy."

Uncle Telemachos said, "We must see the place where the crime took place."

"The temple has been sealed since my grandfather's death," Banu said. He clapped his hands once, and a short, bearded man appeared at the doorway. He was armed with a long knife or short spear. "Erishum," the prince indicated, and the man bowed. He sent the *Turtanu* to fetch the guards who would open the way for us.

We soon set out for the House of Nisroch, the god of wisdom. I had not previously heard his name, and so indicated to Banu.

"He is called Marduk in the south," the prince explained, "being reckoned there as king of the gods of Babylon."

"But not here," I emphasized.

"Here Ashur is king," he repeated. "That is why Nisroch dwells in such a small house."

The temple was a square building near the Halzi Gate,

decorated with the huge images of winged bulls pacing around the outside walls. A troop of soldiers flanked the sole entrance. They came to attention when they spied the prince approaching.

Banu presented the stone cylinder of his father's authority to the officer on duty, who identified himself as Captain Azizu. The prince had specifically asked for him to be present.

Azizu broke the clay seal linking the two massive cedar doors, and pushed them open. His guards rushed in to light the torches flanking either side of the hall.

My first impression was of the shifting images of a herd of great beasts ready to devour us if we stepped inside. Lining the inside of the structure were the images of the Assyrian gods and goddesses, culminating in the toppled stone statue at the other end.

"You were in charge that day?" the prince asked.

"I was," came the reply.

"Tell us about your procedure," Banu ordered.

"Whenever the Great King wished to talk with the god," Azizu indicated, "I or Captain Ukin-Zer would gather a squad of thirty men, whoever happened to be on duty at the time, and would proceed to the temple. There the Great King would wait outside while I and ten others searched the interior of the hall, clearing out anyone who might remain. Usually, the Great King visited during my night watch, after his appointments had been completed, when no one else was present."

"And that night?" the prince pressed.

"We found no one. After my men had cleared the changing rooms at the rear of the hall, I searched them again before allowing the Great King to enter. Then I stood duty just inside the entrance, as I always do, so that he was never left unattended."

"No one was there?" Uncle asked.

"No one," came the reply. "I swear. The temple was deserted."

"Then what happened?" Banu asked.

"The god toppled over on him without warning. I could

do nothing, although I rushed to help as soon as I saw what was happening. When I reached the Great King, he was already dead, crushed beneath the stone. We removed the body, as required, but everything else was left as you see it now."

"Did you search the hall again?" I inquired.

"Twice again we searched the rooms and the statues and the alcoves. No one was there. No one!"

This was very puzzling. Now Uncle led us into the interior, directing me to take notes of everything that we saw. Banu and Azizu and Erishum followed, the others remaining outside. We searched each of the rooms in turn before returning to the main statue.

The image of the eagle-headed god Nisroch had been partially shattered by its impact with the tile floor and the Great King's body. The face and wings of the god were separated a small distance from the rest. We saw a dark stain upon the stones where the Great King's life blood had flowed across the floor. Uncle knelt by the base of the statue and examined it closely. He took out a short knife, and probed slowly around the edges.

"Look here!" he suddenly exclaimed.

We gathered round. There were indications of tampering, both at the front and at the rear of the base, and signs that some of the alterations had been patched over with a light veneer of plaster.

"This was no accident," he stated. "This work was accomplished over a long period of time."

Someone must have known of the Great King's nocturnal habits, and planned accordingly.

"But how?" Azizu protested. "We searched the temple thoroughly, before and after. Even if someone had undermined the statue, how could it have been toppled at just the right moment to kill the Great King?"

"We must look at the underlying motives to help discover the answer to that question," Uncle said. "Who stood to gain? We should talk first with the rebel princes."

"My father will not approve," the prince stated.

"If the Great King wants us to solve the unsolvable, then

he must bear with us," Telemachos replied. "I was very proud then of your son, grandsire. He demonstrated why the sons of Meles are renowned throughout the Mediterranean for their vigour and intelligence."

Banu looked at the spot where his grandfather had perished. "I will see what I can arrange," he finally replied. "But I can promise nothing."

The next morning, however, Banu appeared at our apartment in the city with his *Turtanu* to tell us that an interview with the two rebels had been arranged. We exited the city once again, and rode for an hour until we came to a fort constructed out of mud bricks. We were led to a small, squat, windowless building in the compound.

The guards conducted us to a room empty save for a table and stools. The first prisoner was brought to us.

"This is the high and mighty Prince Arda-Mulishi," Banu stated, "he who once called himself Great King of Assyria." He spat on the ground and made a sign which I later learned was a curse, but the prisoner never reacted.

Indeed, it was clear that the man had been greatly abused. His eyes were puffy and dull, his limbs bruised, his spirit largely broken. His once fine clothes were tattered and stained with blood and dust.

Telemachos: "Did you kill the Great King?"

Prisoner, finally looking up: "Who are *you*, stranger, to question a prince of Assyria?"

Uncle: "I speak in the name of the Great King."

Banu slipped his father's seal from around his neck; it was tied to a cord threaded through a hole that pierced the green stone. He displayed it in his open palm.

Prisoner, glancing at Banu: "Spawn of that foreign bitch, Naqi'a." It was his turn to spit and laugh. The *Turtanu* struck the rebel on his back with the blunt end of his spear, sending him to his knees.

"I see you share your father's winning ways, boy," Arda-Mulishi stated. Erishum raised his weapon again, but Banu held up his hand.

"Half-uncle," the prince intoned, "you may make this day

difficult for yourself or not, as you choose. But you will answer."

Prisoner, still smirking: "What was the question?"

Telemachos: "Did you kill your father?"

Then the rebel prince turned to Uncle for the first time, looking him straight in the eye.

"No," he said. I did not need to translate.

Telemachos: "Do you know who did?"

"No."

Banu: "Why did you make yourself Great King in contravention of your father's will?"

Arda-Mulishi said nothing for a very long time, and then sighed: "When the Great King died at the hand of the god whom he had dispossessed from his rightful place in Babylon, the people of Assyria knew that the gods had turned against them.

"All of you who were there know of the turmoil of those days. The state was in danger of collapsing. Esarhaddon was far away in Armenia.

"The Great King Sennacherib told me the month before his passing that I would be restored to my rightful place in the House of Succession on New Year's Day, two months hence. I was the eldest surviving son after my senior brother, King Ashur-Nadin-Shumi, whom the Babylonians sold to the Elamites twelve years ago. My mother was First Queen to the Great King. She was Assyrian, not Phoenician. She kept her own name, and did not have to change it to something else.

"This was my birthright once, and would have been again, and so I seized what was mine. But I failed to consult with the gods, and the gods were still angry with Assyria. The real killer betrayed me, whomever that person was. I could never find out, although I tried. There was no time to continue in the midst of crisis."

Telemachos: "You investigated the death of your father? How?"

Arda-Mulishi: "I ordered the *Turtanu* who saw the murder, Captain Azizu, to interrogate those who were likely to benefit from my father's death."

Telemachos: "What did he report?"

Arda-Mulishi: "He had no time to report. Shortly thereafter, I had to join the forces being assembled to meet Esarhaddon's advancing army, and I never saw Captain Azizu again."

That was all he would say. I later learned that he had been executed not long thereafter.

We next interrogated another son of the deceased Great King, Prince Nabu-Sharru-Usur, who had supported his brother's rebellion, and for whom the present year had been named. The difference in appearance between the two men was striking. Nabu was clean and well-dressed and had not been abused. I raised an eyebrow at my young friend.

"He has to present my father to the gods when he takes his rightful place upon the throne," Banu said. "He still has a role to play."

Nabu-Sharru-Usur: "Yes, I do." His voice was high and thin, like a woman's, and I suddenly realized that this was a man who would never have to shave again.

He gathered his robes about him, and sat down on a stool with a sigh. "Get on with it," he blurted out.

Telemachos: "Did you conspire to kill the Great King?"

Nabu-Sharru-Usur: "He was my father. He made a place for me among the highest nobles of the land. You see what I am. I could never be the Great King because of that. I had a good place at court, a life of beauty and luxury and power. Why would I give that up?"

Telemachos: "For greater power?"

Nabu-Sharru-Usur: "What greater power? Already I had the Great King's confidence. Aready I lived as I pleased. There was nothing else I wanted. Because of his death, all of that is gone. I must play my little role for my half-brother, and then exit history. Isn't that true, nephew?" He looked down at Prince Banu.

Banu: "I wouldn't know."

Telemachos: "Who murdered your father?"

Nabu-Sharru-Usur: "One of those Babylonian scum. We did everything for them, and do you think they were grateful? Not a bit. Always complaining, always moaning about this and that. Yes, one of the Babylonians killed him. I have no doubt whatever. They all hated him for razing their city."

Telemachos: "Your brother said he was about to be re-named Crown Prince."

Nabu-Sharru-Usur: "Everyone knew that my father had changed his mind again about the succession. It was Nisroch, you see. The god told him that he needed to make amends for stealing the deity from his ancestral home. Mortal man may not interfere with the immortal gods. Nisroch wanted to be Marduk again. He would not be propitiated. Father refused, and the god killed him."

Telemachos: "The statue was tampered with. A man killed the Great King."

Nabu-Sharru-Usur: "The gods work through men to achieve their ends. It was the judgment of the gods."

We learned nothing else from him.

Later over dinner, we talked about our next step.

"We must locate one or more of the guards who were on duty that day," Uncle stated.

"Why?" I asked. "We've already talked to Captain Azizu."

"Yes, but having a different view of the same event might help us discover what actually occurred. Also, we should interview Queen Naqi'a."

Prince Banu did not think the latter would be possible, but agreed to inquire about the guards.

That was the end of the second day.

The next morning was cold and drizzly, but we felt we were making good progress, at least until the young prince appeared.

"They're all gone!" Banu exclaimed as he entered our apartment.

"Who?" I inquired.

"The guards who were on duty that night. They were all sent to the army shortly thereafter, and have not returned. Most are probably dead. However, I found a friend of one of the sergeants, and he may be able to tell us something."

This was Sergeant Iqisu, a rough-hewed man in his forties, waiting just outside our door. We brought him in.

The prince took the lead: "You knew Sergeant Yari?"

"I did," came the reply. "We trained together years ago, and we were assigned to the same squads throughout our careers."

"Tell us what he said about the Great King's death."

"Well, prince" – he bowed at each of us in turn – "it was all passing strange. A half-month before the, uh, incident, Cap'n Azizu brought in a bunch of new recruits, really green under the gills, if you know what I mean, and gave them to Sergeants Yari and Banba to train. Yari complained about it at the time. These novices didn't know one end of the spear from the other. They had to be taught everything. Usually, we get only the best. But they hardly understood Akkadian."

"Did the guards follow their usual procedure that evening?" I said, translating Uncle's words.

"Yes, sir," Iqisu said. "Yari said they searched the place quite thoroughly, as usual, and found no one there, before or after."

"Can you see normally inside the temple when the Great King is present?"

"No, sir. The doors are partially kept shut to give him space to talk with his god. Only the officer remains to watch over the Great King."

"What about the captain?" I posed. "Is he visible?"

"Those of us stationed near the front of the temple can often glimpse his back, but we're usually watching for danger outside, if you know what I mean. It's curious, though: Yari said he called to the cap'n once for assistance, when a drunk tried to enter the temple, and it took him a moment or two to respond."

"What happened to the squad who was on duty that night?" Uncle asked.

"Two days after the Great King's death, they were all drafted into the army. Men were being pulled from around the city to help face the threat from the north-west."

"Were any of your other guards reassigned?"

Iqisu shook his head.

Later that day, we talked about the most recent developments.

"Who *is* this Azizu?" Uncle wanted to know.

"I have no idea," the prince admitted.

Erishum thought that Azizu came from somewhere in the west, but knew little else about him. "I will ask around," he said.

"How does one become an officer of the guard?" Telemachos asked.

"Such appointments are always political," the prince said. "One must have a patron in high places."

"Then who was Azizu's sponsor?"

"I do not know," came the reply.

"One thing that I do know," Uncle stated, "is that all large enterprises keep very detailed records of such appointments. Where would such listings be found, Prince Banu?"

"In the House of Archives," he said, sitting up straight. "Yes, it would be there." He smiled. "I knew there was a reason that Father wanted me to learn the stylus."

"Then, if I may be so bold, my prince, I suggest that you and Achilleus spend tomorrow morning examining those files."

That was the third day.

The House of Archives was a nondescript structure of brick and stone near the Handuri Gate in the southern part of Nineveh. Although the prince and I had no problem entering the building, finding what we wanted proved no easy task.

"Well, yes," the librarian said, "there are filing marks on the boxes, but you would need to have one of the scribes show you the meaning of both them and the texts, and we have none available to spare for a tour."

"I can read the signs perfectly well myself," Banu noted, "and I represent the Great King's interest in this, so either cooperate or you'll find yourself copying eponym lists somewhere in Outer Armenia."

"Of course, Great Prince."

"We are looking for the record of an officer's appointment."

"When did this occur?" the librarian inquired.

"I have no idea," came the reply.

"Then how do you expect me? . . . uh, yes, I'll do everything I can," the man stated, when he saw the anger building in Banu's eyes. "Where's he stationed?"

"He's part of the Great King's personal guard," the prince noted. "His name is Azizu."

"Oh! Well, that should be relatively easy. He'll be recorded on the payroll of the Great King's own household. Let's just see," and the librarian went bustling off into the next room, looking at this box of tablets and that, reading the labels affixed in clay to each. "Yes, this may tell us something." He motioned to one of his orderlies to lift down the heavy container.

"Azizu, Aaa-ziii-zuuu. Aha! Says he was appointed in the eponymate of King Sennacherib himself, five years ago. This number" – he pointed at the leading edge – "tells me the location of his enrolment tablet."

The librarian ran into an adjoining storage area, and then into another further on. He had the orderly lift the heavy box onto a sorting table. Then he paged through the tablets, one by one.

"Yes, here it is. Azizu. Native of Qarqara in the west. Enlisted eleven years ago. Raised to officer rank by the Great King five years ago, on the recommendation of Queen Zakutu."

"Grandmama!" Banu exclaimed.

"But I thought her name was Naqi'a," I replied.

"That was her original name. Her royal name, her Akkadian name, is Zakutu, 'the lady who was freed'."

Banu suddenly noticed the librarian's interest in their conversation, and abruptly dismissed him, saying, "You will be silent, clerk, about all of these matters, or you will lose the ability to speak and write." Then he said to me, "We'll talk of this later."

But after we had returned to our apartment, the prince only brooded within himself, and finally he made his excuses and left. Only I remained to tell Uncle what had transpired.

On the fifth day we were interrupted by the appearance of Captain Azizu in our doorway.

"I hear you've been asking questions about me," he said.

"We are asking questions of many people," Uncle replied through me. "The innocent have nothing to fear."

"I just did my duty," the officer stated. "Everyone who was there will confirm my account."

"Well, that's the problem, isn't it?" Telemachos replied. "We have only your rendition of what occurred, because we cannot locate any of the other guards who were on duty that night. Where is Sergeant Yari, for example?"

"I have no idea, sir," Azizu said. "He was reassigned by order of the Substitute King, and I've not seen him since. He was in the army that the usurper took to Hani-Galbat. Many of those men have never returned."

"How convenient," Uncle noted. "What of the rest?"

"Most of them I didn't know," Azizu indicated.

"Who assigned them to you?"

"Don't know that either. I am accustomed to following my orders as presented to me, sir. I do not question orders, ever. I do my job. I do it well. No one has ever questioned my efficiency. The Great King himself has praised me."

"You were ordered by the Substitute King to conduct an investigation of the Great King's death. What conclusion did you reach?"

"War intervened before I could proceed very far, and then Arda-Mulishi was deposed, so I stopped looking. It was the judgment of the gods."

"Who recommended you for this position?" Uncle asked.

"The Great King."

"But the Great King does not usually reach down into the ranks of his soldiers to find and reward one individual, does he? So who sponsored you, Captain?"

"I cannot say," Azizu finally replied.

"Cannot, or will not."

"I cannot say."

"Then I guess we will have to continue asking our little questions, won't we?" Uncle said. "You are dismissed, Captain."

Banu did not appear at all that day, and I worried about what had happened to him. Truth be told, however, I did

not know how to reach him, and was not sure that I wanted
to.

We ate out that night, venturing down the winding back-
ways of Nineveh to one of the shops that lined Garden
Street. They had a spiced fresh lamb fixed with herbs and
late vegetables and olive oil that even at this cold time of the
year was something well worth fighting for. The place was
filled to the brim. The patrons were as raucous as black-
headed crows jostling each other for scraps, the cymbals and
drums kept warring with one another to beat a tune upon our
deaf ears, and the girls, well, the girls were simply good
enough to eat. We finally left the place satiated and satisfied,
and just a little bit drunk.

But a few blocks away we lost track of where we were, and
became uncertain of the neighbourhood, which was far less
fine than the one we had just been visiting. Suddenly I
noticed a couple of toughs trailing a half street away, and I
nudged Uncle in the ribs.

"Whaaat?" he burped.

I nodded rearward, and slowly reached under my cloak to
draw my long, curved knife, hiding the glint. When the thugs
rushed us, we were ready, and I carved my initials in one's
belly while Uncle slit the throat of the other. A third man,
hovering just beyond the rest, abruptly turned tail and ran off.

The villain whom I had sliced groaned in the mud and
offal of the open sewer.

"Who sent you?" I demanded.

When the man failed to reply, I shook him, like the rag doll
he was.

"Who?" I repeated, pressing upon his wound.

"Ohhh," he groaned, "stop, please. I don't know. Officer.
Paid me three Ishtars. Said two foreign folk would be at
Kurbanu's. One with a scar on his right cheek" – I looked
quickly at the slash on Uncle's face – "Ohhh." We would get
no more out of this one.

When we found our way home, I told Uncle what the man
had said.

"Someone does not like us making inquiries," he replied.

★     ★     ★

Wonder of wonders, Prince Banu secured for us an interview with his grandmother on the next afternoon. We were escorted to the Royal Palace of Great King Sennacherib, where once again we were blindfolded, and led through a maze of rooms and passageways, until we were deposited on comfortable couches in a small waiting area. There we abided for some time until we hear the slight rattle of a bead screen being opened.

"My grandson says you wish to ask me about the Great King my husband's passing." The words were barely audible, but I detected the faintest trace of an accent, just as I could smell the barest essence of some exotic perfume. Perhaps it was myrrh or some other frankincense that I had never before encountered. Like this woman of power, it was rare and seductive and potent.

"What can you tell us of the officer known as Captain Azizu?" Uncle wanted to know.

"Tell you? I can tell you nothing," she said.

"But you recommended him for advancement five years past."

"That may be true," she replied, "but I receive advice constantly from many different quarters, and I can scarcely remember every person whom I may have sponsored, particularly a man of low birth."

"I did not say he was of low birth."

"Perhaps I assumed it."

"You are not native to this region."

"I was born in Calneh. My father was the Governor there, head of the family that once ruled the area. The Great King visited Calneh while he was yet in the House of Succession; he was captivated, and begged my father for the favour. So I became his Second Queen."

"Who was First Queen?"

Zakutu coughed before replying, "Tashmetum-Sharrat."

"She was Assyrian?"

"Yes."

"She was the mother of Crown Prince Ashur-Nadin-Shumi, he who was made King of Babylon by his father?"

"Yes."

"Ashur-Nadin-Shumi was betrayed to the Elamites twelve years ago?"

"Yes."

"No one knows who betrayed him?"

"Yes."

"The First Queen was also the mother of Arda-Mulishi and Nabu-Sharru-Usur?"

"Yes."

"These men are accused of murdering the Great King Sennacherib, their father?"

"Yes."

"But they did not kill their father?"

A long silence, and then: "This interview is over, impertinent little man."

On the seventh day, we again met the Great King Esarhaddon at Fort Sargon, north-east of Nineveh. We went through the same routine as before.

"What have you Greeks learned?" the monarch wanted to know. "Time presses. I must enter into my capital city tomorrow, the eighth day of Adaru, at the hour chosen by my priests, or face further unrest. You see, gentlemen, how I am become even more of a prisoner of my office than my two disgraced brethren."

The three of us sat there on a bench, Uncle Telemachos in the middle, Prince Banu to his right, and I to his left. Once again I acted as intermediary.

"We have examined the circumstances surrounding the passing of Great King Sennacherib," Uncle stated. "We have interviewed the officer who was there, and we have investigated some of the events that occurred. The statue of the god Nisroch was undermined over a long period by the hand of the killer, who toppled the image onto the outstretched body of your father. This much is without question."

Then Telemachos said what he had to say to make his tale more palatable: "What I speak now is speculation, for I cannot prove any of it. The testimony indicates that the room was empty of priests, acolytes, or any visitors both before and after the Great King's murder. There is no entrance to the temple save the main door, and this was closely guarded by Captain Azizu and his thirty men. Although those soldiers are no longer available to be interviewed, we talked with one of their colleagues. What he told us largely confirms the officer's account."

"But if no one was there, then my father must have been killed by the gods, as the priests have indicated," came that disembodied voice.

"Not so," Telemachos averred. "He was murdered, and the murderer had long planned his passing, knowing of his noctural habits in visiting the god. The only man in the room, other than the Great King himself, was Captain Azizu. Therefore, only he could have committed the sacrilege. Only he had the means and the opportunity."

"Azizu?" echoed both Esarhaddon and his son.

"But how? And why?" the Great King continued. "Everyone knows him to be a loyal and faithful servant to the state."

"Consider, Great King, that we only have his word as to the sequence of events. He ushered the guards out of the temple following their usual advance inspection of the premises, and escorted the Great King Sennacherib to his place before the statue of the god Nisroch. I believe that he then struck him senseless with the end of his spear; or perhaps he waited until the Great King was lying prone upon the floor, when he was most vulnerable, and violated him then. The body would have fallen without making any sound that could have been heard by the untrained troops roaming the perimeter outside. During part of this period he was unavailable to his troops, for when Sergeant Yari called to him for help, he did not immediately respond. This was unusual enough to be remembered later.

"Then the officer returned to his usual post for a time, making certain that his back was occasionally visible to his guards. When he reckoned that enough of an interval had passed, he crept forward, pushed over the previously loosened image onto the body of the Great King, obliterating at the same time the wound upon his master's head that he himself had rendered, and then yelled as the statue shattered itself upon the floor. When the soldiers rushed in, he was already bending over the deceased body of the Great King, trying to make the dead come alive, and there was nothing anyone else could do. The subsequent search of the building turned up no one, of course, because there was no one to be found. The guards naturally believed the death to be the act of the god whom Sennacherib had offended.

"As to the why of it, this is what we know, mighty King. The Prince Arda-Mulishi was briefly heir to the throne after the unfortunate death of his full brother, King Ashur-Nadin-Shumi, who was himself betrayed by person or persons unknown to the Elamites while he was serving as subsidiary King of Babylon for his father. But Arda-Mulishi was not the charming and intelligent man that his elder had been, and so he fell out of favour with the Great King. Despite the ministrations of the First Queen, you were named to his place in the House of Succession. All of this happened eleven years ago. Queen Tashmetum-Sharrat, where is she now?"

"She dwells in the palace of the late Great King Ashur-Nasir-Apli at the Holy City of Ashur," came the rough reply. "She and my mother did not get along."

"No, they did not get along," Uncle agreed, "and that was one of the problems. Second Queen Zakutu wanted to be First Queen, but she could not assume that role, because Tashmetum-Sharrat was Assyrian, and Zakutu, whose original name was Naqi'a, was Phoenician, or, if truth be told, Calnehan. Calneh, as I know very well, is a port town not far south of the village Atalur, where we landed on our journey here. It is also the seat of governance for the entire region, is it not?"

"I believe this is so," the Great King replied.

"Does the town of Qarqara fall within its control?"

"I believe this is so."

"Captain Azizu was a native of that place, and I think that he either knew or was connected to one of the Second Queen's relations, and that that cousin recommended him to her. She made him her man, and she sponsored him five years ago for the vacant Captaincy of the Royal Household Guards.

"Your father was troubled in his mind after the death of his eldest son, and the subsequent destruction of the city of Babylon. He believed that he had committed sacrilege, but was bound to the prophecy that he had himself commissioned from the priests, that Babylon could not be rebuilt again for a period of seventy years. Once written down, the dictum ensnared him, and there was nothing he could do. But he *could* change the succession back to the next eldest son, the full brother of his much beloved Ashur-Nadim-Shumi.

"I believe that Queen Zakutu learned of his intention, and I believe she took the action she considered appropriate to preserve your inheritance. This is one explanation. You may accept or reject it, as you will."

I gasped out loud at his effrontery, and so, I think, did the prince and his father.

"You have another theory?" Esarhaddon growled. He was not a happy man.

"The Prince Arda-Mulishi plotted with his younger brother to secure the throne, knowing that his father would never give it to him, subverted Captain Azizu with promises of advancement beyond his station, and murdered the Great King Sennacherib on the twentieth day of Tebetu in the year of the eponym, Nabu-Sharru-Usur.

"That is all I have to say about the matter."

We waited then in silence for a very long time, not moving even the smallest bit, lest we be struck down by the wrath of the Great King.

"This is my pronouncement," the Great King Esarhaddon finally intoned. He clapped his hands, and when his servants entered the room, he ordered them to record his words. "We thank the Greek merchants who have visited the centre of the earth, and who have rendered us a great service. As a token of our regard, we grant unto them special trading rights with the Kingdom of Assyria, all taxes to be remitted for the first five years of the agreement. Record it!" he demanded. "Further, the stranger named

Te-le-ma-khu is to be given 100 gold pieces, and together with his party will depart our kingdom by the start of the New Year, bringing the good tidings of his new fortune to his homeland.

"However, the stranger who is named Akhu-Ilai will remain in Nineveh as chief of his station, and will be given a house of his own, with a *Turtanu* chosen by me to supervise that place, and servants and women to satisfy his every wish. He will have his own 100 lots of gold, and he will be recorded on the tablets as a man of position and power, as one who may advise the Great King on all matters relating to the west, and as friend and companion to the Great Prince in the House of Succession.

"Let this be recorded forever on the tablets of stone, let no man expunge my words or alter them in any way, lest they be condemned by the gods to unceasing torment.

"A copy of this document will be sent to you."

We heard him rise from his throne and begin to exit the room. Abruptly, he stopped and said, "Oh yes, I nearly forgot. Captain Azizu is hereby appointed as your new *Turtanu*, Akhu-Ilai."

Later that evening, Uncle took me aside and looked me in the eye. "Be careful, nephew," he warned. "You know too much, and we have made great enemies these past few days."

"And great friends too," I said.

"And great friends too," he agreed, laughing and clapping me on the back.

Not long thereafter, Uncle and the rest of our party departed for home, carrying with them this account that I have made of the strange and curious adventures that we had faced together. I shall miss him, grandsire, as I miss you now. But when you see your dear son again, when you meet Telemachos the son of Homeros, kiss him once in the exuberance of first greeting, and then let him kiss you once again on my behalf.

I do not know whether I shall see you again in this life, but so long as I have the power to ink a word upon a papyrus sheet or etch a line upon a tablet of clay, you will hear the echo of my voice within your soul, you will feel the wine-kissed wind of my breath touching your hoary brow, and you will laugh out loud once more for the pleasure of it.

This, I think, is the true judgment of the gods.

# The Oracle of Amun

## Mary Reed & Eric Mayer

*Mary Reed and Eric Mayer are best known for their series featuring John the Eunuch set at the time of the Emperor Justinian. That series started with* One for Sorrow *in 1999 and recently passed* Five for Silver (2004) *with more in the works.*

*However, in my anthology* Mammoth Book of Roman Whodunnits, *Mary and Eric introduced a new character, Herodotus, and the following is the second story in that series. Herodotus, who lived from around 490 to 425 BC, is an ideal character for an historical detective. He is known as the Father of History because for many years he travelled the Mediterranean world researching the Persian Wars and preparing his indispensable* History. *Whilst he wrote down much that he knew may not be true, he added his own opinion to it, distinguishing as much as he could between fact and fancy. This enquiring mind means that he could well have undertaken detective work into local mysteries, and for that reason when the Historical Mystery Appreciation Society initiated an award for each year's best historical mysteries in 1999 it was named the Herodotus.*

When I arrived at that point in my *History* dealing with the oracle of Amun I recalled a sequence of events during which I felt a certain kinship to the crocodile hunters of that ancient and mysterious land Egypt.

Their method is to bait a hook with a large piece of meat,

attach it to a length of strong rope, drop it into the water and then belabour a live animal on the river bank in order to attract the reptile's attention. When a leather-skinned denizen of the Nile has swallowed the hook holding what will be its last meal and thereby can be hauled ashore, having brought it to land the hunters immediately plaster its eyes with mud, for this act lessens the mighty-jawed creature's struggles so it can be the more easily dispatched.

Thus were my own eyes initially covered with mud, concealing from me the truth of the sad matter of Wosret, worshipper of Amun.

Wosret was my host during my short but eventful sojourn in Sekhet-am at the Oasis of Amun. Located some distance from the Nile and many days journey from the great river's mouth, Sekhet-am was well greened with thousands of palm trees, from which it takes its name of palm-land. The place is notable for its strange juxtaposition of sweet wells cheek by jowl with open pools so salty that fish cannot live in them.

But Sekhet-am is far more renowned for its temple to the ram-horned god Amun. The edifice, it transpired, was little different from many I saw in my travels, being a small structure built from sandstone blocks pocked with hieroglyphs and far less imposing than the priests' residences surrounding it. The god's sanctuary was of course barred from the gaze of any secular person. However, at frequent intervals a procession of priests bore Amun's image around the settlement in a flower-bedecked barque, and it was this sacred ritual I hoped to see.

After I had made a monetary offering to the god, the head priest, a man named Ti, assured me I had had the good fortune to arrive not long before one of these sacred processions.

Like most holy men in Egypt, Ti wore dazzling white linen robes and was shaved entirely bald, with even his eyebrows removed, giving to him as with other priests, I always think, a look of perpetual surprise. It was he who suggested I stay with Wosret, the most devout follower of Amun in Sekhet-am and also the largest landholder – the latter naturally proceeding from the former, according to Ti.

"He will be most pleased to offer hospitality for the name of Herodotus has travelled ahead of you," he said.

This transpired to be so.

Wosret proved an affable and informative host who spoke the passable Greek of one who needs the language to conduct business but has not studied the classics. He was big for an Egyptian, with muscles like an ox and the neck of a bull. By contrast, his wife Nodjmet was a wisp of a woman with a withered arm. Although Wosret spoke most fondly of his wife, initially I glimpsed her only from a distance, at the end of a hallway, vanishing through a doorway, or on the far side of his garden, as pale as an apparition and as silent, perhaps partly because she habitually went barefoot.

On the afternoon of my arrival, Wosret led me to a mud brick structure sitting alone in a packed dirt yard at a far corner of his estate. As we approached the building I felt a blast of heat far more intense than the glare of the Egyptian sun.

"This is my glass workshop," Wosret explained. "When Nodjmet lived in Alexandria she loved nothing better than to search the city for the finest glass. Since she can no longer travel to the sellers of such wares, I have brought the glass to her."

The air inside rippled with heat, creating an underwater effect. Most of the interior was occupied by an oven as tall as the man who stood beside it.

"My glassmaker could work for the royal court but, like me, he prefers to remain near the temple of Amun. Simut, show our esteemed visitor something of your art."

Simut replied with a slight bob of his head and grabbed a metal rod akin to a cattle prod off the floor. He was as bald as a priest. Sweat streamed down his bare chest. His eyes were blackened all around with khol, no doubt to combat the blinding glare emanating from the round aperture of the oven. I noticed his brown skin was mottled with the scars of old burns and a few newer raw patches.

"I keep a barge and several wagons busy transporting wood for this fire," Wosret remarked. "It's a very expensive enterprise as you can imagine, Herodotus."

From a table set against the workshop wall, the glassmaker selected one of several pieces of clay no longer than my thumb. After he had placed the lump on the end of the rod and worked it deftly for a short time I saw the clay had taken the graceful form of a bottle of the sort in which women store perfume.

He thrust the rod into the oven, gave a few quick twists, and pulled it out. From the glistening coat over its surface it was obvious the clay form had been dipped into a crucible of molten glass.

"Now he will roll it smooth on that stone near his feet," my host explained. "Then comes the most difficult part, the final step. I refer to chipping out the clay core without damaging the vessel itself."

Wosret looked toward the workbench against the wall and his eyes widened as if in alarm. Following his gaze, I saw only a water-filled bucket beside the bench, surely a natural precaution for such a fiery occupation.

"Simut, what have I told you?" Wosret's tone was sharp but I detected a tremble in his voice.

The glassmaker stepped hastily to the bucket and closed its lid.

As we went out into the relative cool of the sun-drenched yard I could not contain my curiosity. "I hope you will pardon me for saying so, Wosret, but although I have seen glass made before, I have never visited a house where all the buckets have lids." For this, I had already noted, was indeed the case.

Wosret appeared to be shaking slightly. "You are observant, Herodotus! There is a good reason for that, as for the fact the ornamental pond in my garden has been drained and the wells on my estate all safely surrounded by fences. You might say it is Amun's will."

When we were seated in the house, sampling the honeyed dates brought to us by his cook, a young woman as black as a Nubian, Wosret explained further.

"It might surprise you to hear this, Herodotus, but I was a traveller myself at one time. In fact, I met my wife during my last visit to Alexandria. Her family has large land holdings thereabouts." He emptied the barley beer in his cup and called for the cook, who replenished the jug, giving him what one could almost have mistaken for a scolding look.

"You haven't returned to the city?"

"No. The journey is vexatious by land, even for myself, and quite impossible for Nodjmet, frail as she is."

I took a sip of my own beer, a refreshment I have become almost inured to since it is the common drink of Egypt. "You mentioned Amun's will?"

"Yes. I have always been a follower of Amun and he has repaid me well for my loyalty. You have heard about the oracular processions, during which the god will answer simple questions, but one may also approach the oracle in the temple for advice. Though I have lived here all my life, I have but once ventured to pose the temple oracle a question of a personal nature."

He looked down into his cup as he continued. "While visiting Alexandria I contracted an illness which carried me within sight of the next world. Nodjmet and I had not been married long. When I was well, it occurred to me that had I not recovered, Nodjmet would have been left alone and unprepared. I decided it would be wise to discover when and by what means I could expect to take my final journey."

"What was the answer?" I asked with considerable interest.

"Its wording was somewhat obscure, but you know how it is with oracles. The gods do not always speak our languages readily. However, the plain meaning was that my death would come to me by water. Which is why I guard myself from being anywhere near it, and will never travel upon the Nile. It must seem strange to you!"

"Not compared to some of the things I have seen and heard," I assured him.

Because the god's procession was to be held the next day, my host held a banquet that evening. I would not be entirely truthful if I did not add the event also honoured me, although I am reticent to admit sharing honours with a god, even one of those strange deities worshipped by people not Greek.

The room was filled with local dignitaries, none of whom I recognised and all of whom addressed me by name, as if we were old friends. Even the elusive Nodjmet joined us at the table. She appeared as pale and wraithlike as she did from a distance and I saw was some years younger than her husband.

She kept her withered arm all but concealed in the folds of her robe, which was more voluminous than those usually worn in the hot Egyptian climate. However, even so, she had so little trouble doing all that was necessary with her good arm that a casual observer would never have noted her deformity. She barely spoke and politely deflected my attempts at conversation.

A description of the delicacies and entertainments which delighted our senses would be more appropriate for the *History* than for this account. The dark-skinned cook seemed to hover beside us constantly, replacing one dish with another. I believe she had been instructed to pay special attention to myself, the honoured guest, because she quite neglected Nodjmet who, more than once, had to fill her own cup from the big wine jug set on the table in front of us.

The wine was sweeter than the best, but a pleasant relief from barley beer. Wosret drank beer, as on any ordinary occasion, and plenty of it. As the banquet drew to a close, he produced from beneath his chair a small ivory box. Murmuring a few slurred words of endearment he handed the box to his wife.

She took the gift wordlessly, placed it on the table, opened the lid and drew out not one, but two, bracelets of exquisite workmanship. Their fine gold chains were strung with alternating beads of deep blue glass and garnets.

Nodjmet stood abruptly. I could see she was fighting back tears. The bracelets fell from her hand and clattered onto the plate. She fled out of the room.

Wosret sat and stared dumbly at the bracelets. A glass bead had parted from the chain and rolled off the edge of the table. I wondered why it had not occurred to him that a pair of beautiful bracelets might not be appropriate for a woman with one arm withered.

The cook, who had returned with yet another new dish, bent to pick up the stray bead.

"Take the bracelets to the workshop, Hebeney," my host ordered. "Tell Simut to repair the one needing it."

The incident had gone unnoticed, thanks mostly to the huge quantities of wine and beer the guests had consumed. The air was filled by smoke from wall torches, the scents of exotic spices and perfumes and excited words and laughter.

Wosret took another gulp of beer. "I must be honest with you, Herodotus," he finally said with the exaggerated solemnity of the truly inebriated. "My domestic situation has not been of the best this past year or so."

I murmured polite regrets at these unwanted confidences. One travels the world to write about men with eyes in their shoulders and lands ruled by warrior women. To hear tales of domestic strife one need only visit the poorer quarters of any great city.

"My rejected gift is but an outward manifestation of the troubles that beset me, my dear friend," Wosret went on, his words running together as swiftly as the tears running down his cheeks. "What can I do to please her? I have tried everything. You have seen the world, Herodotus. Tell me, what can I give Nodjmet to win back her love?"

I was spared having to give him the discouraging answer since he immediately toppled from his chair and lay on the floor in a stupor, snoring loudly with his mouth hanging open.

Shameful though it was to see a man so deep in the arms of Bacchus, his guests did not seem overly perturbed, but merely picked up the mat on which he was lying and using it as a makeshift litter carried him to his bed – all of his bearers staggering dangerously themselves – and left him there.

He was still there as the star-sprinkled night sky turned from grey to red, lying with the silence not of sleep but of death. Apart from a slight trickle of blood from the corner of his mouth there was no trace of violence.

As I arrived, Nodjmet was walking numbly down the hallway, half supported by two servants, looking more like a phantom than ever.

The room held only the bed, a carved sandalwood chest and a low table on which sat a clay lamp. Nothing had been disturbed. Wosret had seemingly died without a struggle and no outcry, for any noise would have been heard by the rest of the household.

"He died exactly as the oracle of Amun prophesied," observed the priest Ti, who had been summoned immediately.

I recalled the tale Wosret had related to me, and pointed out the absence of even a drop of water in the chamber.

Ti looked puzzled. "Wosret was killed by overindulgence," he replied. "The oracle declared that he would die by matter transparent that yet casts a shadow. This describes barley beer, just as closely as water."

I could not disagree. Wosret had joined those legions who have misinterpreted Delphic pronouncements to their detriment. He had laboured mightily to avoid water when all that had been necessary was abstinence.

Thus would the story have ended, except that as I was packing my few belongings to take my leave, not wishing to intrude upon the household's mourning, Wosret's widow appeared in my doorway, looking more angry than grief-stricken.

"Herodotus, may we speak? I need your assistance."

She led me out into the garden, to a bench surrounded on three sides by thick ornamental shrubbery.

"We can talk here without being overheard. Now, you have spoken to Ti. Do you know why he arrived with such haste?"

"I had presumed it was to make appropriate funeral arrangements since your husband was a devout follower of Amun."

"The priest was in a hurry to take possession of my husband's bequest. Wosret left half of his estate to the temple."

She made a sweeping gesture with her good arm that took in the land all around us. Nodjmet looked remarkably unwraithlike this morning, almost as if she had drawn life from her husband's death. I noticed that even in this private setting she took care to keep her withered arm hidden.

"Naturally I am challenging it," she continued. "I have already warned Ti he would be wise to abandon his claim. He is bound to lose in the end anyway."

I would never have guessed the pale creature I had glimpsed moving so furtively about the house could harbour such fury. "You weren't aware of the bequest?"

"No. Wosret said nothing of it to me."

"I can understand your dismay, but certainly it isn't unusual for a worshipper to —"

"It had nothing to do with religious devotion, Herodotus. It was Ti's reward for helping my husband take Khu's land. Among other things."

As she became agitated the cadence of her words changed. I recognized a faint accent. She was not Egyptian, but Greek! That was why she had struck me as so pale, compared to the sun-bronzed denizens of this land. I marvelled that she had been able to endure being stranded so far from civilization. "Who is Khu?" I asked.

"A landowner, or rather, he used to be one. A few years ago he and my late husband had a legal dispute. Wosret took everything from Khu. His fields, his houses, his cattle and geese, everything, right down to the poor man's cook."

She spat out the word "cook" as if it were a spoiled olive.

"Do you perchance refer to the dark-skinned girl your husband called Hebeney?"

She said this was so. Her dislike was so palpable I leapt to the obvious conclusion.

"Forgive me, Nodjmet, but I have learned that in order to uncover the truth it is sometimes necessary to ask blunt questions. It is clear you hold a strong dislike for Hebeney. Is it because you suspect her of being too familiar with your husband?"

Nodjmet laughed. "I hate her because she is a vile woman. She was Khu's mistress, but one would have thought he had married her to hear her speak. He who was high born, and she the ignorant daughter of a potter."

I was not certain whether she had answered my query or not. "You mentioned Ti was responsible for your husband's taking Khu's lands?"

"That's right. Many here at the oasis ask Amun to decide legal disputes during the sacred processions. The pronouncements of the god are accepted as binding and thus doing so is faster and less expensive than litigation. No one has ever seemed to notice that whenever Wosret was involved the decision always went his way. Disputed leases, misplaced shipments, ambiguous contracts . . . when asked whose position on the matter was correct, the oracle always chose my husband's."

"You believe he and Ti had, let us say, an arrangement?"

"Not only that, I am convinced Ti became impatient waiting for his reward and decided to fulfill Amun's prediction."

After she had broken off our conversation and left me sitting there, I considered the perplexing situation.

A philosopher might well have pondered whether a priest who carries out his god's oracle could rightly be accused of murder since the death has already been divinely ordained. Luckily, I am merely a traveller and student of history and so was content to mull over the problem of how to prove a priest guilty of such an act.

I am not so credulous as to have simply accepted Nodjmet's statement that Ti had committed the crime, although I suppose my realization that she was Greek, a lonely stranger in this desert wilderness, did commend her point of view to me.

The difficulty, as I saw it, was not that the victim had seemingly been killed by imperceptible means as that the allege murderer could simply not venture out, walk unnoticed through a house full of servants, kill someone without a sound and then leave undetected.

There had to be an accomplice involved.

Unless one was prepared to believe that Amun himself had

struck Wosret dead in order to enrich his temple, that accomplice had to be human.

Perhaps Amun had decided to take my side against his venal priest, because after I left the bench and turned down a narrow path shaded by palms, I was accosted by the young cook whose morals and conduct Nodjmet had so recently been disparaging.

"Please, sir, I must speak. I have been looking for you everywhere." Hebeney's Greek was barely intelligible, but given her position in life it was surprising she spoke it at all.

"You may tell me what you have to say while we walk back to the house. I cannot pause, I fear, for I am attending to some urgent business on behalf of your mistress."

Hebeney fell into step beside me. She was attractive in the manner of certain primitive ebony carvings I have seen which, I am told, originate beyond the Nile's upper reaches.

"My mistress? She's told you I killed Wosret, I wager! But she is the murderer, sir. I had hoped to find you before she could accuse me!"

Despite my hurry, this outburst brought me to a halt. "Nodjmet didn't accuse you of killing her husband. Why would she? And why do you say your mistress is the culprit?"

"I'm sure she put me into your mind, which is as good as saying I did it," Hebeney replied, making me wonder if she had been eavesdropping behind the shrubbery. "Nodjmet is convinced her husband was unfaithful with me, because she is such a sickly thing. I'm certain you understand what I mean by that, sir. But I must tell you, ever since I arrived here I have observed her plotting his death."

I asked what proof she had of this remarkable statement.

"The proof of my eyes and ears, sir. Nodjmet used to come out to the kitchen and peer into the pots on the brazier and ask what sauces had the strongest flavours and couldn't they conceal the bitterness of this or that noxious plant or some poison. She claimed she was afraid an enemy might try to poison Wosret since he was a powerful man. But I know she had her own reasons."

Immediately it occurred to me that given the women's

obvious mutual dislike, Hebeney might have seen her master's death as providing a way to strike back at her mistress. Especially since she was unlikely to remain employed by the wronged wife.

Remembering what Nodjmet had said concerning Khu, I asked her if she came to work for Wosret after her former master lost his lands.

She confirmed this was so. "Khu lost not only his lands but also his life, for shortly after the oracle ruled against him his body was discovered in an irrigation canal. Or at least, those parts the crocodiles had left. I for one believe he willingly embraced death, for he despaired . . ." Her voice trailed off and she lowered her eyelids for an instant.

"You must have been grateful to Wosret for taking you in."

"Not so grateful as to be used by him, sir, if that is what you are thinking."

Was she telling the truth? If she had considered herself, in her simple way, to be Khu's wife, then perhaps she felt hatred rather than gratitude towards Wosret. If so, her agreeing to serve in his household might well have been to find an opportunity to avenge Khu.

Supposing that to be true, then her only purpose in approaching me must have been to confuse matters. Did she suppose I would not suspect her merely because she had brought herself to my attention?

We had stopped where a gap in the palm trees revealed a wide canal. My eye was caught by an elongated shape floating in the water. From a distance, I wasn't certain what it was and the sturdy fence running along its bank prevented any nearer approach.

Perhaps it was just as well. This is the problem when you investigate a situation more closely.

Sometimes you discover a log, other times a crocodile.

When I returned to Wosret's house I retired to the roof, which serves Egyptians more as a living space than a shelter, there being no rain to speak of in that arid land.

From below came the noise of the household, people

moving about, talking, the sound of chests being shifted. There were preparations to be made. All around me, the palm fronds of Sekhet-am formed the green waves of a far-reaching sea.

Gazing out over it, a doubt crept into my thoughts. Did a god need an accomplice to fulfill a prophecy?

There was no hint of the cooling breeze which invariably left on the exposed skin a gritty residue, a reminder of the surrounding desert. This afternoon, the rooftop merely seemed to be palpably closer to the fiery orb of the sun.

I decided no one else would come to me with accusations about others, so I descended and went to question the glassmaker.

Simut was pulling another perfume bottle from the oven as I entered his workshop. He rolled the tiny artefact back and forth on the stone at his feet, then propped the rod holding it against the bench to allow the glass to cool. When I expressed my desire to speak with him, he remained standing by the fire, folding his arms on his chest.

"Hebeney sent you, didn't she?" His voice was little more than a dry wheezing, a sound one might expect to issue from the desiccated lips of a mummy.

He must have noted my surprise. "It is the constant, scorching wind from the oven," he explained. "It forces the breath back into the throat. We glassmakers are generally as short-lived as many of our fragile creations."

"Hebeney has spoken to you since Wosret's death?"

"Yes. But let me make it plain, sir, whatever you should hear, it was the mistress who approached me. I did not pursue her," Simut said. "Furthermore, it has been over for some time."

"You and Nodjmet were lovers?"

"Isn't that what Hebeney told you?" He could tell from my expression it wasn't. He rasped out a curse in his native tongue. "What exactly did she tell you, sir?"

"It doesn't matter, Simut. I –"

The glassmaker interrupted me. "She isn't to be believed. You can't believe either of them, sir, neither she nor Nodjmet. They hate each other. Hebeney was afraid she'd be accused of murdering Wosret. At least that's what she said."

In his tone I sensed the bitterness that can be distilled only from the most intimate of relationships. No doubt he and Hebeney had also been lovers, if they were not still. That would also explain why she had come to him.

"In my time I've heard many fabulous stories," I said. "You can be certain I don't accept as truth everything I'm told."

I decided to recount my conversation with Hebeney. "Of course, when she told me that Nodjmet had inquired about sauces and poisons, I began to suspect her tale was, well, somewhat unreliable," I concluded.

Simut released a ragged sigh. "That part at least is probably true."

I wondered why he should give credence to such a tale.

"Because Nodjmet asked me to kill her husband. I see you don't believe me, sir, nor do I blame you. I didn't believe it at first either. She suggested I strangle Wosret one night after he had lost consciousness from intoxication, which happened often with him. I was then to burn his remains in my oven, to conceal the crime. When I refused she put an end to our relationship."

He shook his head. "We used to meet here. sir. It's a lonely corner of the estate, not like the busy servants' quarter where I live. I was ill advised and stupid, sir. I thought she loved me but all the time she just had an eye on my oven."

In the ensuing silence it came to me that Simut and Hebeney were indeed still lovers, working together to incriminate Nodjmet, each having reason to harbour hate for her.

Finally I asked Simut why I should believe such a tale, given he would surely have warned his employer of the danger.

"And explained to him how I'd learned of his peril? Besides, even if I could have found a way to warn him discreetly, without endangering myself, the end of Wosret's marriage would have meant the loss of my job here, for I create nothing that is not intended to please Nodjmet."

He nodded toward the work bench, upon which were arrayed an assortment of perfume bottles, cosmetic jars and drinking vessels in colours ranging from white to deep blue. "It is vexing to spend my life making beautiful things for such a hateful creature. It is work, however, and well-paid work at that."

"But surely one with your skills could find such occupation anywhere?"

"But there is no place nearer to Amun than this estate."

He took the rod with the cooling bottle on its end, shifted it around to examine it and then scowled.

"As I thought. It is flawed, sir," he said, and without further warning swung the rod against the side of the oven sending bits of glass and clay flying. A sharp sliver hit the back of my hand, stinging like a wasp.

"Yet what is all this talk about murder, sir?" he said. "Wosret's death was Amun's will. It came exactly as his oracle had predicted. Where is the mystery in that?"

He had deftly made another clay mould and my gaze followed as he thrust it into the dazzling aperture of the oven.

As I walked away from the workshop my eyes watered as if I had stared into the sun and my head ached.

Had the priest Ti killed Wosret after they had conspired to enrich my late host, as Nodjmet believed? Why couldn't the temple wait for its inheritance? Were the servants Hebeney and Simut conspiring against Nodjmet, the widow of their late master?

Even if they hated her, why would either have killed her husband?

Well, Hebeney might have reason, since it appeared she believed he had been indirectly responsible for the death of the man she had loved, her former master, the landowner Khu.

For that matter, the man who loved her now, Simut the glassmaker, might have carried out the deed on her behalf.

Or either might have been following the priest Ti's orders.

Unless it was just as Simut had said, nothing more than Amun's will.

Because there was the troublesome matter that Wosret didn't appear to have died by any agency more palpable than Fate, helped along by habitual over-indulgence in barley beer.

I blinked. A phantom image of the glowing mouth of the glassmaker's oven kept sailing into the corner of my vision. I rubbed my eyes.

That was when the mud fell away and I saw clearly what had happened.

It took me some further reflection before I decided how I could prove my case.

It should come as no surprise that the god Amun's procession went on as scheduled and the street leading from the temple was as crowded as one might expect.

What, in this eternal land, is a man's life compared to the affairs of the gods?

Besides, there were legal disputes to be resolved.

Because it was not for profane eyes to see the sacred idol, it was therefore hidden from view in a heavily carved and gilded oblong chest carried in a flower-bedecked barque of the sort that the sun god Ra, according to his followers, daily traverses the heavens.

The sacred procession was an impressive and somewhat noisy spectacle. A large company of white-robed, shaven-headed priests clustered around those carrying the barque by means of poles fitted into metal rings on its longer sides. Flanking these holy men, acolytes held large palm fronds to shelter the boat while before and after this focal point of the procession more priests chanted and shook sistrums. I was able to pick out Ti, who as was fitting given his position as head priest, was first in the line of those grasping the gilded pole fitted to the left-hand side of the boat.

I was not too surprised to see the newly widowed Nodjmet among the crowd, for it had occurred to me she intended to challenge her husband's bequest by appealing to the oracle of Amun.

Glancing around the crowd, I noted Simut and Hebeney

stood not far away. I stationed myself a short distance from them and waited.

As I watched, a thin fellow wearing a few rags around his loins stepped out of the onlookers and the procession halted. I am not an expert in Egyptian dialects so I made out only scattered words, but enough to understood he was a farmer and a rival had claimed ownership of one of his cows. The man presented his side of the dispute. He then bowed toward the barque. "Lord Amun, is what I have spoken the truth?"

Immediately the priests stepped back in unison, almost as if drawn backwards by a movement of the barque. The man's face fell. He turned on his heel and vanished into the crowd. A few imprecations followed him. Obviously the god's answer had been no.

The procession resumed its course and as the barque drew nearer I stepped forward.

The high priest Ti looked at me with what I took to be alarm. "Herodotus? You wish to question the oracle?"

"If it is permitted of a foreigner in your land, I do."

"Before you ask, be certain you want to know the answer."

"I believe everyone in Sekhet-am wants to know the answer to my question. Not least the members of the late Wosret's household."

I glanced back to be certain those to whom I referred were listening.

Then I put my question, speaking in strong, clear tones, for although I am not an orator I am often asked to recount to audiences the many wonders I have seen in my travels.

"I have pieced together an amazing tale," I began. "This is what I believe happened. The woman Nodjmet married Wosret, an older and wealthy man. After he fell gravely ill she expected him to die. Unfortunately, he did not. They then took up residence on his estate, far from the delights of Alexandria. Not to mention a long way from her family."

Several onlookers began muttering to each other. Ignoring them, I took up my tale. "She wasn't satisfied with glass perfume bottles and bracelets or any of the gifts he lavished on her after his recovery. What she wanted was not him but his estate. And not to share it either, for as it turned out as a devout man he wished to thank his god for sparing his life by leaving the temple half of all he owned when the time came."

Ti grimaced at this remark but he said nothing and I continued. "When Nodjmet couldn't recruit her servant Simut to do as she wished, she decided to carry out the deed herself. She had seen the metal rod Simut used to dip his clay models into molten glass. It was a weapon easily concealed beneath the voluminous robes she habitually wears to hide her withered arm."

Ignoring the rising buzz of excitement in the crowd, I went on. "The guests at the banquet were all too intoxicated to have noticed the exchange she and her husband had at the table. And naturally the servants thought nothing of her coming and going from the house later that evening."

There was a stir in the crowd as I pressed on. "It was an easy matter for Nodjmet to thrust that metal rod into the unconscious Wosret's open mouth and down his throat until it pierced some vital organ. An arm made strong enough by its constant exercise to lift a heavy wine jug as easily as I had seen her lift the jug at the banquet would be more than powerful enough to accomplish such a task."

I took another step forward, bowed and addressed the barque. "That is how Nodjmet murdered her husband Wosret. Lord Amun, is what I have spoken the truth?"

The priests and the barque remained still.

I glanced back at Nodjmet. She looked away from me and toward Ti. The priest met her gaze with his own.

Then the priests, and the barque, moved forward a step.

Amun had declared me truthful.

Backed by the oracle of Amun's pronouncement, Simut and Hebeney were happy enough to reveal what they knew to the authorities.

Had Nodjmet approached me to accuse Ti, thinking that I might frighten him into giving up the temple's claim to half the estate by threatening to identify him as a murderer?

Or had she decided to start making accusations before the servants Hebeney or Simut guessed what had happened and pointed to her?

I cannot say. Nor can I be certain who spoke when the barque lurched forward, sealing Nodjmet's fate.

Was it truly Amun who propelled it? Or did Ti step out, thereby bringing the boat supported by his fellow priests forward, having seen the wisdom of settling matters for the benefit of the temple without costly legal wrangling?

That Nodjmet had murdered Wosret in the manner I deduced there can be no doubt. For it fulfilled the oracle of Amun's prophecy, as I had seen when the mud fell away from my eyes, leaving the image of the glassmaker's fiery oven.

The oracle of Amun had told Wosret his fate would be to die in a way involving something that was transparent but yet cast a shadow.

He and the priest Ti had both wrongly deduced the meaning of this statement. For does not glass fit the god's pronouncement, and did he not die by means of the rod used to form the beautiful and fragile gifts with which he hoped to win back the love of Nodjmet?

# Cupid's Arrow

## Marilyn Todd

*From ancient Egypt to ancient Rome and the unmistake-
able world of that mischievous minx, Claudia Seferius.
The young and very eligible widow, Claudia, lived during
the reign of the first Emperor, Augustus, and her adventures were first recounted in* I, Claudia *(1995). Ten
further books have followed with the latest,* Stone Cold
*(2005).*

"Let me see if I've got this right."

Claudia stopped pacing and ticked the points off on her fingers.

"In six days' time, we, as producers and merchants of fine wines, celebrate the *Vinalia*, when no lesser light than the priest of Jupiter himself will pronounce the auspices for the forthcoming vintage?"

"Correct, madam."

"Except." She turned to face her steward. "We have no grapes to lay on his altar on the Capitol as offerings?"

"Correct."

"Because some clod on my estate came down with a sniffle and the bailiff took it upon himself to quarantine the entire workforce?"

"To be fair, madam, the clod in question was the bailiff himself. He did not feel he could jeopardise the harvest by exposing –"

"Yes or no to the grapes?"

"Yes. No. I mean yes, we have no –"

"So in effect, I'm asking the King of the Immortals, God of Justice, God of Honour, God of Faith, who shakes his black goatskin cloak to marshal up the storm clouds and who controls the weather, good and bad, to very kindly *not* drop a thunderbolt over my Etruscan vineyards, even though I haven't bothered to propitiate him this year?"

The steward's adam's apple jiggled up and down as his long, thin face crumpled like a piece of used papyrus. "That does appear to pretty much sum up the current situation, madam."

"Oh, you think so, do you?" Claudia resumed her pacing of the atrium, wafting her fan so hard that a couple of the feathers sprang loose from their clip. Dear Diana, it was hot. Small wonder that half of Rome had taken itself off to the cool of the country or else to the seaside for the month of August. She thought of the refreshing coastal breezes. A dip in the warm, translucent ocean. The sound of cooling waves, crashing against rocks . . . "Well, let me tell you something, Leonides. That doesn't sum up even *half* the current situation."

According to the astrologers and soothsayers in the Forum – at least those diehards who hadn't fled this vile, stinking heat – terrible storms were in the offing, unless almighty Jupiter could be appeased. For everyone else in the Empire, storms would be a relief from this torpid, enervating swelter. Sweat soaked workmen's tunics and plastered their hair to their foreheads. Meat turned within the day and fish was best avoided unless it was flapping. Even Old Man Tiber couldn't escape. His waters ran yellow and sluggish, stinking to high heaven from refuse, sewage and the carcases of rotting sheep. But for farmers with grapes still ripening out on the vine, storms on the scale that were being predicted provoked only fear. A single hailstorm could wipe out their entire vintage.

"Prayers and libations aren't enough," Claudia said, as two more feathers flew out of the fan, "and I can hardly buy grapes from the market and palm them off to Jupiter as my own."

It was enough that that bitch Fortune happened to be

unwavering when it came to divine retribution at the moment. Claudia didn't want it spreading round Mount Olympus like a plague.

"And you're forgetting, Leonides, that I can't despatch a slave to Etruria to cut bunches until tomorrow at the earliest, because today, dammit, is the Festival of Diana – which just happens to be a holiday for slaves!"

"Oh, I hadn't forgotten," Leonides replied mournfully.

Claudia blew a feather off the end of her nose and thought at this rate the wretched fan would be bald by nightfall, and why the devil can't people make things to last any more, surely that isn't too much to ask. She stopped. Turned. Stared at her steward.

"Very well, Leonides, you may go."

He was the only one left, anyway, apart from her Gaulish bodyguard, and it would take an earthquake, followed by a tidal wave, followed by every demon charging out of Hades before Junius relinquished his post. She glanced across to where he was standing, feet apart, arms folded across his iron chest in the doorway to the vestibule, and couldn't for the life of her imagine why he wasn't out there lavishing his hard-earned sesterces on garlands, girls and gaming tables like the rest of the men in her household.

The girls, of course, had better things to do. Dating back to some archaic ritual of washing hair, presumably in the days before fresh water had been piped into the city by a network of aqueducts, the Festival of Diana was now just a wonderful excuse for slave women to gather in the precinct of the goddess's temple on the Aventine. There, continuing the theme of this ancient tradition, they would spend the day pinning one other's hair in elaborate curls and experimenting with pins and coloured ribbons. Any other time and Claudia would have been down there, too, watching dextrous fingers knotting, twisting, coiling, plaiting, because at least half a dozen innovative styles came out of this feast day on the Ides of August, and all too fast the shadows on the sun dial on the temple wall would pass.

But not today. Today she had received the news that her bailiff was covered in spots and that, rather than risk the harvest by having the workforce fall sick, he had put them in quarantine to the point where no-one was even available to pick a dozen clusters of grapes. There was a grinding sound coming from somewhere. After a while, she realised it was her teeth.

"Junius?"

Before she'd even finished calling his name, he'd crossed the hall in three long strides. Was any bodyguard more dedicated, she wondered? Sometimes, catching sight of his piercing blue gaze trained upon her, she found his devotion to duty somewhat puzzling. Any other chap and you'd think he carried a torch for her, but hell, he was only twenty-one, while she was twenty-five, a widow at that, and tell me, what young stallion goes lusting after mares, when he can have his pick of fillies?

Widow. Yes.

With all the excitement, she'd almost forgotten poor Gaius. Yet the whole point of marrying someone older, fatter and in the terminal stages of halitosis was for these vineyards, wasn't it? Well, not the vineyards exactly. She had married Gaius for what they'd been worth, although the bargain wasn't one-sided. Gaius Seferius had had what he wanted, as well – a beautiful, witty trophy wife, and one who was less than half his age at that. Both sides had been content with the arrangement, knowing that by the time he finally broke through the ribbon of life's finishing line, Gaius would be leaving his lovely widow in a very comfortable position. In practice, it worked out better than Claudia had hoped.

Maybe not for Gaius, who had been summoned across the River Styx a tad earlier than he'd expected, and certainly before he would have wished.

And maybe not for his family, either, who were written out of his will.

But for Claudia, who'd inherited everything from the spread of Etruscan vineyards to numerous investments in commercial enterprises, from this fabulous house with its wealth of marbles and mosaics, right down to the contents of his bursting treasure chests, life could not have turned out sweeter, if she'd planned it. So why, then, hadn't she simply sold up and walked away? It was how she'd envisaged her future after Gaius. No responsibilities. Draw a line. Start again. Instead, she hadn't just hung on to the wine business, she'd taken an active, some might say principal, role. And as for his grasping, two-faced family, goodness knows why she continued to support them! Something to do with not wanting them to root around in her past, she supposed, but that was not the point.

The point was, she must remember to lay some flowers beside her husband's tomb some time. And maybe she'd have his bust re-painted this year, too. After all, it couldn't exactly be improving down there in the cellar.

"Junius, I want you to run down to the Forum and hire a messenger. The ones by the basilica are usually reliable, but if there's no-one left today, and I'll be very surprised if there are, given that it's a holiday for slaves, try the place behind the Record Office."

"Me?" The Gaul was shocked. "B-but I can't possibly leave you here alone, madam."

"I promise that if a gang of murdering marauders come barging in, I'll ask them to wait until you're back to protect my honour, and that way we can both get killed. How's that?"

"With respect." His freckled face had darkened to a worried purple. "I don't consider danger a joking matter. These are the dog days of summer. Men are driven mad by the appalling heat, madam, and by the sickness and disease that grips the city. With rich folk decamped to the country, only criminals and undertakers flourish in Rome at the moment."

Claudia nodded. "Very eloquently put, Junius. You are, of course, absolutely correct and if you don't hurry, there won't be any messengers at the place behind the Record Office, either."

"But madam –"

"It's a straight choice, Junius. Either you hire a courier to gallop like the wind to my estate, pick a dozen bunches of the ripest grapes then ride straight back, where we might – just might – make it in the five days we have left and therefore save the day. Or I turn you into cash at the slave auction in the Forum in the morning."

The young Gaul drew himself up to his full height, squared his impressive shoulders and clicked his heels to- · gether. "In that case, madam." This time he didn't look at her, but stared straight ahead. "In that case, I see I have no alternative."

"Excellent. Using the full services of the post houses and changing stations, the messenger –"

"You will have to sell me in the morning."

*What?* The remaining feathers sprayed out of the fan as Claudia crushed it in her fist. "This is not a debatable issue, Junius. You will –"

"I am not leaving you alone and that's final."

Jupiter, Juno and Mars, that's all I need. The only slave left on the entire premises turns out to be as stubborn as a stable full of mules! She looked at the rigid line to his mouth, the square set to his chin and resisted the urge to punch him on it. Remind me of the position again?

A storm threatens to wipe out this year's harvest.

The offering to propitiate the god who threatens that storm isn't coming.

There's no-one available to go and fetch it.

And the only person who *could* help is throwing tantrums.

In short, if she wanted a courier, Claudia would have to trek out in this ghastly, fly-blown, disease-ridden heat and hire one herself, a role her bodyguard would be very happy for her to undertake, because at least he could be on hand when robbers, thieves and rapists set upon them.

Was there, she wondered, anything else which that bitch Fortune could throw in her path today?

The goddess's reply came almost at once.

She delivered it in the form of a bloodcurdling scream.

Which came from Claudia's very own garden.

With its stately marble statues and rearing bronze horses, Claudia's garden was a testament to her late husband's wealth and social status. A red-tiled portico provided shade and offered shelter from the rain, the water from its terracotta gutters collected in oak butts to irrigate the vast array of herbs and flowers, whose scent in turn fragranced the air throughout the year. Paved paths criss-crossed through clipped lavender and rosemary, while topiaried laurels and standard bay trees gave the garden depth and height. In the centre, a pool half-covered by the thick, white, waxy blooms of water lilies reflected sunshine, clouds or stars according to the weather. And all around, fountains splashed and chattered, making prisms as they danced, as well as an attractive proposition for birds in need of something more refreshing than a dust bath.

That such a place of beauty and tranquillity could be shattered by such a scream was nothing short of outrage.

The instant they had heard it, Claudia and her bodyguard went flying down the atrium. From then, it was as though the sequence of events had been frozen. Time slowed. She might have been watching them unfold by following their progress on a carved relief.

The screech came from a young man scrambling down the fig tree which grew against the wall. Unlike her villa in the country – indeed unlike everybody's villa in the country – this house didn't have the room to follow the traditional pattern of four single-storey wings around a central courtyard. For a start, it had two upper galleries for bedchambers and linen storage, each accessed by separate staircases, and a cellar which was accessed by steps outside the kitchens. The only possible site for a garden was behind the house and adjacent to its neighbour's. With one million people crammed into the city, space was at a premium and houses, even those of the wealthy, invariably butted up against each other. Claudia's was no exception. To the right she adjoined with the house of a Syrian glass merchant, while her garden at the rear adjoined with a general's. Paulus Salvius Volso, to be precise. Admittedly a loud-mouthed, drunken bully of a man, but all the same it was from his premises that the youth was making his rather hurried exit.

What he'd been up to in the general's house was clear from the array of golden goblets and silver platters which bulged out of the sack slung over his left shoulder. The contents nearly blinded her when the sunlight caught them. He was halfway down the fig when he let loose a second shriek.

It took a moment before Claudia realised that they were not screams of alarm, but squeals of wild abandon. The grin on his face as he jumped down was as wide as a barn.

"Hey!" Junius called out. "Hey, you! Stop right there!"

The boy spun round in surprise, but didn't falter as he belted towards the wicker gate on the far side of the garden.

"Stop!" This was a different voice. A soldier's bark. "Stop, or I'll shoot!"

Junius was already racing down the path to try and cut the thief off, so he didn't bother looking round to see who was shouting from the top of her neighbour's wall. Claudia did. It was Labeo, one of the general's henchmen and a retired captain of archers. The thief had used a ladder to make good his escape. His mistake lay in not kicking it away. Labeo had shinned up it like a monkey.

The boy shot a quick glance at the bodyguard charging down the path towards him. Halfway to the gate, he knew he could outsprint him. Claudia knew it, too, and so did Labeo. On a public holiday, the street outside would be heaving. One more thief lost in a crowd.

"Last chance," Labeo boomed. "Or I'll fire."

Claudia saw the grin drop from the boy's face. Realised that he hadn't actually seen Labeo until now. Thought it was a bluff being called by someone from inside Claudia's house, not from the top of the wall.

He turned. Saw the archer. Dropped the sack.

"All right, all right," he yelled. "Have it!"

Gold, bronze, copper and silver spilled over the pinks and the lilies. Ivory figurines knocked the heads off the roses.

What happened next would stay with Claudia for the rest of her life.

Watching the cascade of precious artefacts, she first saw its reflection in the pool. An arc of white, flying left to right.

Heard a soft hiss.

Looked up.

The arrow hit the boy in the centre of his back. She heard the splinter of bone. The soft yelp that sprang from his lips.

For three paces he didn't stop running. Then his arms splayed. His legs buckled. Red froth burst from his mouth. Still he kept going. It was only when he reached the gate and tried to unbar it, that he realised he couldn't make it. Junius had caught up by now. Was cradling the boy in his lap. Claudia could hear him whispering words of comfort as she flew to his side.

"Sssh, lad." Junius wiped the fringe from the boy's face and patted his cheek. "It's all right. There's a physician on his way now."

His expression was haunted as it met Claudia's unvoiced question.

"You d-don't understand." The boy's head rolled wildly and his breath bubbled red. "N-not s-supposed to b-be like this." Terrified eyes bored into Claudia's. She could see that they were brown. Brown as an otter. "I'm n-not going to d-die, am I?" he asked.

"Of course not," she said, only there was something wrong with her eyes, because her vision was misty. "It's just a wound, like Junius says." Her voice was cracked, too. "You'll be back on your feet in a week."

But that wasn't quite true.

The otter was already swimming the Styx.

For his part, Labeo had no sympathy for what he termed a dead piece of scum. Indeed, he would have pulled the arrow out of the boy's back to see how the head had compacted upon impact, had he not been prevented by Mistress Snooty from next door here, slapping his hand away. What a bitch, he thought. Shooting me glares which would pole-axe a lesser man. What did she expect me to do? Let the thieving toe rag go?

"The general's instructions was to shoot all intruders, whether they be on the premises or in the process of escaping," he informed her. "And it don't matter to me whether this piece of filth were carrying a dagger or not," he added coldly, when taken to task about killing an unarmed, defenceless fifteen-year-old boy. "He were guilty and the proof, if it's necessary, lies all over your flowerbeds. Ma'am."

He weren't accountable to her anyway. The bitch.

But dammit, the sulky cow just would not let it rest. On and on she went, about how young the boy was, and hadn't anyone considered what had driven the poor lad to resort to stealing, because you could see he wasn't used to it, no-one in their right mind would run off up a busy street with a sack stuffed full of golden objects and not have the army after them, and anyway what seasoned professional would go round leaving ladders against walls to make life easy for his pursuers?

Labeo let it ride. If she wanted to feel sorry for that little turd, that was her business, not his. He'd done the job he was being paid to do, and he was behind the general all the way on this. Let criminals think you're a soft touch, and every bloody thief will be climbing up the balcony! So while she ranted, he congratulated himself on being such a damn good shot. That arrow went exactly where he'd planned it.

Quite at what point Her Snootyship intended to shut up, Labeo didn't know. But he was mighty glad when he heard the general call his name from the far side of the wall. The master hadn't been expected back for ages, but wouldn't he be pleased to hear his captain had bagged a sewer rat this morning!

Except there were something different about the general's bellow. Every bit as terse. Nothing usual about that! And no less urgent, neither. (The general weren't a patient man!) But . . . Well, it just sounded different, that was all.

"I'm over here, General." He called back. "Caught a burglar stealing your gold. Shot him as he escaped."

"Is he dead?" Volso wanted to know, scaling the ladder two steps at a time. He was a tall man in maybe his forty-second summer, broad of shoulder and square of jaw, his skin weathered from years of campaigning and thickened from too many nights cradling the wine jar. But he cut a commanding enough figure on and off the field, and regular training in the gymnasium had clearly paid off. It was a lean and nimble figure that swung itself over the adjoining wall.

"Couldn't be deader," Labeo told him proudly, as his employer dropped to the ground.

"Pity," Volso snarled, wiping the dirt from his hands down his tunic. He marched over to where Junius and Claudia were conversing quietly over the body and rammed his foot hard into the corpse. "Bastard didn't deserve an easy death."

"Volso!" Horrified, Claudia stepped in front before he could land a second kick. "You are on my property, General, and I'll thank you to have some respect for it, for me, and for the dead."

"*Respect?*" Labeo feared the general's bellow would deafen the widow. "*Respect, you say?*" He pushed her roughly aside and slammed his boot into the boy's side as he had originally intended. "Save your sympathy, Claudia Seferius. If Labeo hadn't killed him, public execution certainly would."

"Stealing is a civil matter," she began.

"Stealing is," the general agreed. "Murder isn't. That boy you're so protective of didn't just rob me of my gold and silver. He robbed me of my wife." Volso turned to face his archer. "Callista's body is still sprawled across the bedroom floor," he said quietly. "Where this bastard strangled her."

Moonlight had turned the garden paths to silver. The feathery leaves of artemisia and the pale purple flowers of sweet rocket released musky perfume into heat that pulsated like a cricket, and mice rustled beneath the fan-trained peach trees, pears and apricots. Bats squeaked on the wing in search of moths. An owl hooted from the cedar three doors down, and a frog plopped gently into the pool from a water lily leaf.

The slaves were not back yet. Milking their precious holiday for all it was worth, there was none of the customary clattering of pots and skillets from the kitchens. No bickering coming out of the married quarters. The heather brooms and garden shears were silent. Everything was silent.

Seated on a white marble bench with her back against an apple tree, Claudia watched her blue-eyed, cross-eyed, dark Egyptian cat chase a mouse round the shrine in the corner of the garden and slowly sipped her wine. The wine was dark. Dark as Claudia's mood. And every bit as heavy. Cradling the green glass goblet in both hands, she stared up at the night sky without blinking. The stars would make life easy for navigation out at sea tonight, she thought. Directly overhead, the dragon roared and Hercules strode purposefully across the heavens, wielding his olivewood club. How appropriate, she mused, that it was the constellation of Sagittarius, which was starting to rise over the southern horizon. Sagittarius, the Archer . . .

The army had come, conducted its investigation in the twinkling of an eye, and departed hours ago. The young man's body had been carted away unceremoniously on a stretcher and Labeo had been lauded for a job well done, both by the army and his bereaved employer. It had been left to Claudia and her bodyguard to stack the stolen objects back inside the sack, where Junius later returned them to their owner.

Still staring at the stars, she sipped her wine.

"So then." A tall, patrician body eased itself onto the bench, leaned its back against the rough bark of the apple tree and crossed its long patrician legs at its booted ankles. "Cut and dried."

Even above the scents of the junipers and cypress, the heliotrope and the lilies, she could smell his spicy sandalwood unguent. Caught a faint whiff of the rosemary in which his trademark long linen tunic had been rinsed.

"I wondered how long it would take before Marcus Cornelius Orbilio arrived on the scene," she said without turning her head.

Up there on Olympus, Fortune must be wetting her knickers. Claudia topped up her goblet from the jar. Dammit, she couldn't make a move without the Security Police popping up in the form of their only aristocratic investigator, who seemed to view her – let's call them misdemeanours – as his fast track to the Senate. Still. What did she care? She had nothing to hide from him this time. For once, Marcus Make-Room-For-Me-In-The-Assembly Orbilio was whistling in the dark.

She couldn't see him, but knew that he was grinning. "Why?" he asked. "Were you running a book on when I'd arrive?"

"Tch, tch, tch. You should know that gambling's against the law, Orbilio."

"Which happens to be one of the reasons I've called round." A shower of bronze betting receipts scattered on the path. "Yours, I believe."

"Never seen them before in my life," she replied. Bugger. That was the best boxer in Rome she'd backed with those. Half a brickwork's worth, if she recalled.

"What about these?" he said, showering a dozen more.

And that, unless she missed her guess, was the other half, invested at five to one on a Scythian wrestler from the north coast of the Black Sea. Bugger, bugger, bugger.

"We caught the bookie touting outside the imperial palace," he said cheerfully. "You know, you really should be more careful who you have dealings with, Claudia."

She skewered him with a glare. "Damn right."

"How much of Gaius's money do you have left?" he asked.

The old adage was true, she thought ruefully. The best way to make a small fortune is to start with a large one . . .

"Jupiter alone knows what will happen to the family fortune once I'm married to you," he continued smoothly. "We'll probably be celebrating our fifth anniversary in the gutter."

She supposed it was the moon making twinkles in his eyes, but in its clear, three-quarters light she could see every curl in his thick mop of hair, the solid musculature of his chest, the crisp, dark hairs on the back of his forearm.

"I would go to the lions before I went to the altar with you, Marcus Cornelius, and if you've finished littering my garden path, perhaps you'll be kind enough to sod off. I have a pressing engagement." She patted the wine jar beside her. "With my friend Bacchus here."

"Hmm." He folded his hands behind his head and closed his eyes. "You seem to be having a lot of metal littering your garden path all of a sudden. Tell me about this morning."

"No."

Why the hell did he think she wanted to get drunk? To forget, that was why. To forget a young man with an ecstatic grin and eyes as brown as an otter. Eyes that she had watched glaze in death . . .

"Oh, no. There's more to it than that," he said, clicking his tongue. "I know you inside out." He re-crossed his ankles, but did not open his eyes. "Tell me."

"If I did, you wouldn't believe me."

"I don't believe you've never seen these betting receipts. I don't believe you've never defrauded your customers, or that you've never smuggled your wine out of Rome to avoid paying taxes, and that's why I love you, my darling, and that's why I know that when you marry me, life will never be dull –"

"See a physician, you have a fever."

"– and I know, equally, that I'll never be able to trust you with money or business, but I do trust your judgment, Claudia Seferius. What is it about this morning that bothers you?"

"You really want to know?" Claudia drew a deep breath. Stared up at the celestial Archer. Let her breath out slowly to a count of five. "What bothers me, Orbilio, is that a woman was murdered today and the wrong man took the blame. A young man who, conveniently, is not around to tell his side of the story."

"You think Labeo –"

Claudia snorted. "That arrogant oaf?" In her mind, she heard again the sickening thud as the general's boot thudded into the dead boy's ribs. Heard the youth's exuberant yell as he scrambled down the fig tree on the wall.

"No, Marcus," she said wearily, 'Labeo did not kill Callista." She thought of her tiny, fair-haired neighbour laid out on her funeral bier in the atrium next door, cypress at the door, torches burned at her feet. "The thing is, Volso is a domineering drunk and a bully." She sighed. "Who liked to beat his wife and his children."

Juno in heaven, how often had she heard them. The muffled screams. The pleading. Racking sobs that lasted well into the night . . . Many times she would rush round there, only for the door to be slammed in her face, and the next day Callista's story would be the same. The children had fallen downstairs, she'd say, or she had walked into a pillar. Sweet Janus, how often had Claudia begged her to leave the vicious brute? One day, she'd told Callista, he will end up killing one of the children.

"Think of them, if not yourself," she'd advised.

Months passed and nothing changed, until, miracle of miracles, last week Callista called round to confide that she was leaving. Enough was enough, she'd said. Claudia was right. One of these days she feared Volso *would* go too far and as soon as she'd found suitable accommodation for herself and the children, she would pack her bags and leave.

"So you think Volso killed his wife?" Marcus said.

"No," Claudia replied sadly, "I killed her."

She could easily have taken Callista and the children in, but she had not. She'd been too busy trotting round placing bets on boxers and wrestlers, ordering new gowns for the *Vinalia* in six days' time, planning parties, organising dinners, garlanding the hall with floral tributes. A battered wife with moping children would have got in the way. Put a dampener on everybody's spirits.

As surely as Paulus Salvius Volso throttled the life out of poor Callista, so Claudia Seferius had provided him with the ammunition.

Orbilio was forced to admit that, when Claudia told him he wouldn't believe what she was going to tell him, he was wrong. He'd said he was convinced that he'd believe her. But. Wrong he was.

That Volso killed his wife he could accept. The minute he'd heard that Callista had been found strangled in the course of a burglary, his suspicions were aroused. Having listened to the report of the centurion sent to investigate the killing of the thief, he'd not been at all satisfied with the army's neat conclusion. Volso's reputation preceded him and Marcus knew him as the type who vehemently believed that his wife and children were his property, that he would say who came and who went, and that nobody, but nobody, left him unless *he* threw them out. That was why he'd called on Claudia this evening. To hear her view on the matter.

But that she was in any way morally responsible was bullshit.

In time, of course, she would come to see this for herself, and surely the best way of helping her to reach this point was for her to help him clap the cold-blooded bastard in irons.

"The killing required a lot of planning," he said.

And together, as the Archer rose and the level in the wine jug sank, they gradually pieced together the sequence of events.

First, Callista, having made her decision, must have somehow given the game away. Perhaps she had started to put things together in a chest. Maybe she'd confided to one of the older children. Who knows? Hell, she might even have lodged her claim in a divorce court, where Volso was just powerful enough to have the scribe report the matter back. Either way, he knew about her plan but did not let on.

Instead, he went out and hired himself a thief. A military man, he'd know exactly where to look and, as a commander of long standing, he would know what type of character to choose. Someone gullible, for a start. Someone who would believe the story he had spun them about having fallen on hard times and how the debt collectors would be knocking at his door any day now to seize his assets. But if he could beat them at their own game? Stage a burglary, whereby the thief was paid handsomely to steal the goods, which he would hand over to the general's henchman outside in the street to be converted into liquid assets, which the debt collectors would not know about.

"How do you know he'd told the boy there would be an accomplice?" Orbilio asked.

"The yells," she explained. "The yells were to alert the person he believed would be loitering in the street to move up to my back gate in readiness to relieve him of the sack and pay him whatever price Volso had agreed." She shrugged. "As I said, it had to be somebody gullible."

Older boys would not have swallowed the bait. This boy had to be new at the game. No-one else would have been told to leave the ladder up against the wall and actually left it!

"Except his yells alerted Labeo instead," Marcus said.

"Who had been primed beforehand by his master that, on a slaves' holiday, the house might well be a target for thieves and that he was to shoot on sight."

Perhaps it wasn't Labeo's fault, after all, Claudia mused. He'd been as much a pawn in the game as the boy, the one lured by greed, the other by pride. The only difference, Labeo was alive.

"So." Orbilio steepled his fingers. "The house is empty, because all the slaves are out celebrating. It's just Labeo in there on his own, and Callista, who Volso had undoubtedly drugged. The boy sneaks in, probably through your garden, shins up the fig tree and over the wall. He then places the ladder so he can make his escape. Inside, he fills the sack with the items he's been instructed to pick and then, when he's finished, he screams like a banshee, because it's vital the accomplice is outside for a quick handover."

"Unfortunately, the yell alerts Labeo, who finds no trouble chasing him, thanks to the ladder Volso thought to set in place." Claudia could see why he'd made general. In military tactics, timing is crucial. "Because while we're all nicely diverted by the robbery and the killing, the master of the house is free to walk in through his own front door and throttle his wife at his leisure."

"Ah." Orbilio plucked a blade of grass and chewed it. "That's where it starts to get tricky. You see, Volso refused point blank to give his porter the day off today, and the porter is adamant his master left the house shortly after dawn and did not come back until *after* the boy had been shot. He knows this, because, when Volso came home, the porter told him about the robbery and he was actually with him when he found Callista's body."

He paused. Cracked his knuckles. Spiked his hands through his hair in frustration.

"Therefore, Volso could not have killed his wife."

Dawn was painting the sky a dusky heather pink when Claudia finally stood up. The first blackbird had started to sing from the cherry tree, mice made last-minute searches for beetles and frogs began to croak from the margins of the lily pond. She shook the creases from her pale blue linen gown, smoothed pleats which had wilted in the heat and forced half a dozen wayward ringlets back into their ivory comb.

The first of the slaves had begun to trickle home three hours ago. Gradually, the rest had staggered in, singing, belching, giggling under their breath, their footsteps and their voices restoring order to the silent house. Without their presence, it was as though the bricks and mortar had been in hibernation. Now it was a home again, for them as well as Claudia, the rafters resonating with their drunken squabbles and their laughter, the clang of a kicked pan here, the spluttered expletive from a banged shin there, the bawling of too many over-tired children.

For most of the night, she and Orbilio had sat in silence in the moonlight, trying to figure out how Volso could have done it. Twice Marcus got up to fill the wine jar and fetch cheese, dates and small cakes made from candied fruit, spices and honey to help mop it up but now, as dawn poked her head above the covers of the eastern horizon, the Security Policeman admitted defeat.

"He's got away with it, hasn't he?" he said, yawning. There was a shadow of stubble around his chin, she noticed. And lines round his eyes which didn't come from lack of sleep. "The cold, conniving bastard is going to walk."

Claudia stretched. Massaged the back of her neck. And smiled.

"You fetch the army and arrest him," she said. "I'll give you the proof."

She glanced across at the garden wall, then back at her own house. *Gotcha, you son-of-a-bitch.*

It started in the garden, it was fitting that it should end there, she supposed. By the time half a dozen legionaries came clunking in, their greaves and breastplates shining in the sun, Claudia had changed into a gown of the palest turquoise blue and was seated in the shade of the portico beside the fountain, taking breakfast. In her hand was a letter from her bailiff and the news was good. The spots were not contagious, he had written. According to the estate's horse doctor, they were the result of eating tunnyfish. The grapes for Jupiter were on their way.

She should bloody well hope so, too. Caught up in the tragedy of yesterday, she had quite forgotten about sending a courier to fetch them and maybe she might call in at Fortune's temple in the Cattle Market later to drop off a trinket or two. Fickle bitch, but not so bad when you boiled it down.

"You'll pay for this!" Volso thundered, as the soldiers dragged him down the path. "By Hades, I'll have you in court for slander, Claudia Seferius, and I'll take every penny that you own in damages. This house. The vineyards. I'll have the bloody lot, you'll be so poor, you won't be able to afford the sewage from my gutter."

"Save it for the lions, Volso." She bit into a peach, and the juice dribbled down her chin. "You planned Callista's murder like a military campaign and thought you'd get away with it." She mopped the juice up with a cloth. "Only there were three people you underestimated."

"Come on," he taunted, his square face dark with rage. "Let's hear this crackpot theory, you bitch, because believe me, it will make for interesting evidence at your slander trial."

Behind the group, she watched Marcus Cornelius let the bronze statue of a horse absorb his weight. He hadn't had time to change his tunic, yet she swore that, above the smell of soldiers' sweat, the leathery scent emanating from Volso and the pungent perfumes of the herbs in the flowerbeds – basil, thyme and marjoram – she could detect a hint of sandalwood. An expression had settled on his face as he watched her, which with anyone else, she would have interpreted as pride.

"Firstly, Volso, you underestimated the boy. He was young, keen, gullible, vulnerable, in fact, all the things you'd wanted him to be, and that was the problem. He was *too* young, *too* keen, *too* gullible."

He ought to have picked someone who was greedy, not needy. The screams gave it away. Yes, he'd yelled as he'd been instructed. But the shrieks he'd let out were wild and exuberant. Whoops of pure joy. *I've done it*, they'd said. *I've got away with the stash, the accomplice is outside, I am going to be RICH!* She remembered the grin as wide as a barn. The dancing light of triumph in his eyes. That was not the expression of a thief who'd just strangled a woman in a burglary that had gone horribly wrong.

"Secondly, you underestimated my steward."

Volso might run a tight ship next door, checking up for specks of dust and fingerprints on statues, taking the whip to his wife and his slaves if he found so much as one thing out of order. What he'd overlooked is that not everyone gets off on that level of control. It might work on the battlefield, but Claudia's slaves wouldn't know what a whip looked like, for gods' sake, and Leonides wasn't the type of steward to have his crew running around doing unnecessary tasks. The cellar was cleaned thoroughly, but only twice a year, and that was twice as often as any public temple.

She turned to Orbilio. "Did you find any of the substances I listed?"

"Oh, yes. We found traces of them on his boots and tunic from where he'd bumbled around your cellar in the dark while he counted out the timing. Flour from the grinding wheel, cinnamon where it had spilled out from the sack, a vinegar stain, a smear of pitch, the corporal has the full list."

"You planted that, you bastard," Volso snarled.

"We didn't plant your bootprints in the dust," Marcus retorted. "The impression from a shoe is almost non-existent unless there's a body inside to make tracks."

But the general wasn't going down without a fight. "The fact that I was in the cellar proves nothing. In fact, I remember now. Two or three days ago, I called round to borrow some charcoals, ours had run out."

Even the legionaries couldn't stop sniggering. Paulus Salvius Volso running next door to borrow some coals? Jupiter would turn celibate first!

Volso turned back to Claudia. "And the third person I'm supposed to have underestimated? That's you, I imagine?"

"Good heavens, no." Claudia shot him a radiant smile. "My dear Volso, that was your wife."

Apart from the fact that frogs would grow wings before Volso came back early to check on his wife who had not been feeling well, had he not left Callista's body sprawled on the bedroom floor, he might still have talked his way out of it. But what devoted husband wouldn't have lifted the remains of his beloved on to the bed? Only a callous bastard of the highest order could think of leaving her in an ignominious and distorted heap for people to gawp at.

In death, Callista had had the last word after all.

The legionaries were gone, their prisoner with them. The tranquillity of the garden had returned, and there was no indication among the rose arbours and herbiaries of the tragedy that had taken place here. Not just one death, either, but three. Callista's. The boy's. And Volso's to come in the arena.

He had planned the two murders like a military campaign. Coldly and ruthlessly, he chose the day when slaves everywhere, not just his own, would be out. No doubt he'd expected his neighbour to be out, too, as she usually was on the Festival of Diana, but it wouldn't matter unduly.

He would climb into Claudia's garden using the ladder, then kick it away after him. He would hide in the cellar, biding his time until he heard screams and then whoever *might* have been in the house would certainly rush outside. He would give it a count of twenty before leaving the cellar, but then comes the daring part. He actually walks across the garden while everyone is clustered round the thief's body! If challenged, of course, he can bluff it out by claiming he'd heard a scream as he was returning home and came to help. Then he would just nip over the garden wall to "check on his wife", only to report back that she was dead.

As it happened, no-one saw him. Up and over, throttle the missus, up and back again in no time – before calmly letting himself out of Claudia's house and sauntering up to his own, whistling without a care in the world as the porter had testified.

And now they were gone. All of them. Volso. Callista. The otter.

"Do you think we'll ever know his name?" she asked Marcus.

In reply, he pursed his lips and shrugged. "I doubt it," he said. Urchins like him disappeared by the dozen every day. It was the unseen tragedy of the big city and so-called civilisation.

Across the garden, a chink of gold reflected from beneath the mint. A small child's goblet with a double handle. And so the tragedy goes on, she thought . . .

She looked up into his eyes. Resisted the urge to brush that stupid fringe from where it had fallen down over his face and trace her finger down the worry lines round his eyes.

"I was here," she said, "when I saw the reflection of the arrow in the pool."

There was a pause. "*Here?*" he echoed, frowning.

"Right here." She pointed to the spot with a determined finger. Sweet Jupiter in heaven, she would never forget it. "White as snow, I actually watched it are through the air."

Orbilio scratched his ear. "Not from here you didn't," he replied. "If Labeo was standing on the ladder and the boy was near the gate, and if he kept on running like you said after he'd been hit, then the arrow travelled like so."

He indicated the trajectory of the missile with his hand.

"As you can see, the path doesn't curve as you describe it. Also, the arrow wasn't white, it's almost black, and Labeo's is far longer than the one you saw reflected in the water. What's more, if it was travelling at the speed, angle and direction that you say, it would be you who was lying dead, not your little otter. Oh, and by the way, did I ever tell you that you're stunning when you're angry and you're stunning when you're not, and that you're even more stunning when you're breaking generals' balls? I think a spring wedding would be rather fun, don't you?"

"I'd marry an arena-full of Volso's before I married you," she said, "but what I don't understand is this. If it wasn't Labeo's arrow that I saw reflected in the pool, what was it?"

Orbilio thought of the suffocating heat that played strange tricks by bending light. He thought of the emotion of the moment, the reflection of a white dove overhead, in fact, he could think of any number of rational explanations. But then . . . But then . . . There was also the matter of a certain mischievous little cherub by the name of Cupid. So he said nothing.

He just pulled Claudia Seferius into his arms and kissed her.

# The Spiteful Shadow

## Peter Tremayne

*From the world of ancient Rome we pass to Celtic Ireland. This is the home of Sister Fidelma, an Irish religieuse who is the creation of Peter Tremayne. She has appeared in fifteen books to date, starting with* Absolution by Murder *(1994) plus many short stories, including the past two* Mammoth Books of Historical Whodunnits *where she first appeared in "The High King's Sword" in 1993. There is even talk of a television series. You can find all the up-to-date information you need on the Sister Fidelma website at* www.sisterfidelma.com

*Peter Tremayne is the alias used in his fiction by Celtic scholar Peter Berresford Ellis. His many reference books include* The Celtic Empire *(1990),* The Druids *(1994) and* Erin's Blood Royal *(revised 2002). Peter is also one of the few people who is fluent in the Cornish language.*

"It is so obvious who killed poor Brother Síoda that it worries me."

Sister Fidelma stared in bewilderment at the woe-be-gone expression of the usually smiling, cherubic features of Abbot Laisran.

"I do not understand you, Laisran," she told her old mentor, pausing in the act of sipping her mulled wine. She was sitting in front of a blazing fire in the hearth of the abbot's chamber in the great Abbey of Durrow. On the adjacent side of the fireplace, Abbot Laisran slumped in his chair, his wine left abandoned on the carved oak table by his side. He was staring moodily into the leaping flames.

"Something worries me about the simplicity of this matter. There are things in life that appear so simple that you get a strange feeling about them. You question whether things can be so simple and, sure enough, you often find that they are so simple because they have been made to appear simple. In this case, everything fits together so flawlessly that I question it."

Fidelma drew a heavy sigh. She had only just arrived at Durrow to bring a Psalter, a book of Latin psalms written by her brother, Colgú, King of Cashel, as a gift for the abbot. But she had found her old friend Abbot Laisran in a preoccupied frame of mind. A member of his community had been murdered and the culprit had been easily identified as another member. Yet it was unusual to see Laisran so worried. Fidelma had known him since she was a little girl and it was he who had persuaded her to take up the study of law. Further, when she had reached the qualification of *Anruth*, one degree below that of *Ollamh*, the highest rank of learning, it had been Laisran who had advised her to join a religious community on being accepted as a *dálaigh*, an advocate of the Brehon Court. He had felt that this would give her more opportunities in life.

Usually, Abbot Laisran was full of jollity and good humour. Anxiety did not sit well on his features for he was a short, rotund, red-faced man. He had been born with that rare gift of humour and a sense that the world was there to provide enjoyment to those who inhabited it. Now he appeared like a man on whose shoulders the entire troubles of the world rested.

"Perhaps you had better tell me all about it," Fidelma invited. "I might be able to give some advice."

Laisran raised his head and there was a new expression of hope in his eyes.

"Any help you can give, Fidelma . . . truly, the facts are, as I say, lucid enough. But there is just something about them . . ." He paused and then shrugged. "I'd be more than grateful to have your opinion."

Fidelma smiled reassuringly.

"Then let us begin to hear some of these lucid facts."

"Two days ago, Brother Síoda was found stabbed to death in his cell. He had been stabbed several times in the heart."

"Who found him and when?"

"He had not appeared at morning prayers. So my steward, Brother Cruinn, went along to his cell to find out whether he was ill. Brother Síoda lay murdered on his bloodstained bed."

Fidelma waited while the abbot paused, as if to gather his thoughts.

"We have, in the abbey, a young woman called Sister Scáthach. She is very young. She joined us as a child because, so her parents told us, she heard things. Sounds in her head. Whispers. About a month ago, our physician became anxious about her state of health. She had become . . ." He paused as if trying to think of the right word. "She believed she was hearing voices instructing her."

Fidelma raised her eyes slightly in surprise.

Abbot Laisran saw the movement and grimaced.

'She has always been what one might call eccentric but the eccentricity has grown so that her behaviour has become bizarre. A month ago I placed her in a cell and asked one of the apothecary's assistants, Sister Sláine, to watch over her. Soon after Brother Síoda was found, the steward and I went to Sister Scáthach's cell. The door was always locked. It was a precaution that we had recently adopted. Usually the key is hanging on a hook outside the door. But the key was on the inside and the door was locked. A bloodstained robe was found in her cell and a knife. The knife, too, was blood-stained. It was obvious that Sister Scáthach was guilty of this crime."

Abbot Laisran stood up and went to a chest. He removed a knife whose blade was discoloured with dried blood. Then he drew forth a robe. It was clear that it had been stained in blood.

"Poor Brother Síoda," murmured Laisran. "His penetrated heart must have poured blood over the girl's clothing."

Fidelma barely glanced at the robes.

"The first question I have to ask is why would you and the steward go straight from the murdered man's cell to that of Sister Scáthach?" she demanded.

Abbot Laisran compressed his lips for a moment.

"Because only the day before the murder Sister Scáthach had prophesied his death and the manner of it.

"She made the pronouncement only twelve hours before his body was discovered, saying that he would die by having his heart ripped out."

Fidelma folded her hands before her, gazing thoughtfully into the fire.

"She was violent then? You say you had her placed in a locked cell with a Sister to look after her?"

"But she was never violent before the murder," affirmed the abbot.

"Yet she was confined to her cell?"

"A precaution, as I say. During these last four weeks she began to make violent prophecies. Saying voices instructed her to do so."

"Violent prophecies but you say that she was not violent?" Fidelma's tone was sceptical.

"It is difficult to explain," confessed Abbot Laisran. "The words were violent but she was not. She was a gentle girl but she claimed that the shadows from the Otherworld gave her instructions; they told her to foretell the doom of the world, its destruction by fire and flood when mountains would be hurled into the sea and the seas rise up and engulf the land."

Fidelma pursed her lips cynically.

"Such prophecies have been common since the dawn of time," she observed.

"Such prophecies have alarmed the community here, Fidelma," admonished Abbot Laisran. "It was as much for her sake that I suggested Sister Sláine make sure that Sister Scáthach was secured in her cell each night and kept an eye upon each day."

"Do you mean that you feared members of the community would harm Sister Scáthach rather than she harm members of the community?" queried Fidelma.

The abbot inclined his head.

"Some of these predictions were violent in the extreme, aimed at one or two particular members of the community, foretelling their doom, casting them into the everlasting hellfire."

"You say that during the month she has been so confined, the pronouncements grew more violent."

"The more she was constrained the more extreme the pronouncements became," confessed the abbot.

"And she made just such a pronouncement against Brother Síoda? That is why you and your steward made the immediate link to Sister Scáthach?"

"It was."

'Why did she attack Brother Síoda?" she asked. "How well did she know him?"

"As far as I am aware, she did not know him at all. Yet when she made her prophecy, Brother Síoda told me that she seemed to know secrets about him that he thought no other person knew. He was greatly alarmed and said he would lock himself in that night so that no one could enter."

"So his cell door was locked when your steward went there after he had failed to attend morning prayers?"

Abbot Laisran shook his head.

"When Brother Cruinn went to Síoda's cell, he found that the door was shut but not locked. The key was on the floor inside his cell . . . this is the frightening thing . . . there were bloodstains on the key."

"And you tell me that you found a bloodstained robe and the murder weapon in Sister Scáthach's cell?"

"We did," agreed the abbot. "Brother Cruinn and I."

"What did Sister Scáthach have to say to the charge?"

"This is just it, Fidelma. She was bewildered. I know when people are lying or pretending. She was just bewildered. But then she accepted the charge meekly."

Fidelma frowned.

"I don't understand."

"Sister Scáthach simply replied that she was a conduit for the voices from the Otherworld. The shadows themselves must have punished Brother Síoda as they had told her they would. She said that they must have entered her corporeal form and used it as an instrument to kill him but she had no knowledge of the fact, no memory of being disturbed that night."

Fidelma shook her head.

"She sounds a very sick person."

"Then you don't believe in shadows from the Otherworld?"

"I believe in the Otherworld and our transition from this one to that but . . . I think that those who repose in the Otherworld have more to do than to try to return to this one to murder people. I have investigated several similar matters where shadows of the Otherworld have been blamed for crimes. Never have I found such claims to be true. There is always a human agency at work."

Abbot Laisran shrugged.

"So we must accept that the girl is guilty?"

"Let me hear more. Who was this Brother Síoda?"

"A young man. He worked in the abbey fields. A strong man. A farmer, not really one fitted in mind for the religious life." Abbot Laisran paused and smiled. "I'm told that he was a bit of a rascal before he joined us. A seducer of women."

"How long had he been with you?"

"A year perhaps a little more."

"And he was well behaved during this time? Or did his tendency as a rascal, as you describe it, continue?"

Abbot Laisran shrugged.

"No complaints were brought to me and yet I had reason to think that he had not fully departed from his old ways. There was nothing specific but I noticed the way some of the younger religieuse behaved when they were near him. Smiling, nudging each other . . . you know the sort of thing?"

"How was this prophecy of Brother Síoda's death delivered?" she replied, ignoring his rhetorical question.

"It was at the mid-day mealtime. Sister Scáthach had been quiet for some days and so, instead of eating alone in her cell, Sister Sláine brought her to the refectory. Brother Síoda was sitting nearby and hardly had Sister Scáthach been brought into the hall than she pointed a finger at Brother Síoda and proclaimed her threat so that everyone in the refectory could hear it."

"Do you know what words she used?"

"I had my steward note them down. She cried out: 'Beware, vile fornicator for the day of reckoning is at hand. You, who have seduced and betrayed, will now face the settlement. Your heart will be torn out. Gormflaith and her baby will be avenged. Prepare yourself. For the shadows of the Otherworld have spoken. They await you.' That was what she said before she was taken back to her cell."

Fidelma nodded thoughtfully.

"You said something about her having to know facts about Brother Síoda's life that he thought no one else knew?"

"Indeed. Brother Síoda came to me in a fearful state and said that Scáthach could not have known about Gormflaith and her child."

"Gormflaith and her child? Who were they?"

"Apparently, so Brother Síoda told me, Gormflaith was the first girl he had ever seduced when he was a youth. She was fourteen and became pregnant with his child but died giving birth. The baby, too, died."

"Ah!" Fidelma leant forward with sudden interest. "And you say that Brother Síoda and Sister Scáthach did not know one another? How then did she recognise him in the refectory?"

Abbot Laisran paused a moment.

"Brother Síoda told me that he had never spoken to her but of course he had seen her in the refectory and she must have seen him."

"But if no words ever passed between them who told her about his past life?"

Abbot Laisran's expression was grim.

"Brother Síoda told me that there was no way that she could have known. Maybe the voices that she heard were genuine?"

Fidelma looked amused.

"I think I would rather check out whether Brother Síoda

had told someone else or whether there was someone from his village here who knew about his past life."

"Brother Síoda was from Mag Luirg, one of the Uí Ailello. No one here would know from whence he came or have any connection with the kingdom of Connacht. I can vouch for that."

"My theory is that when you subtract the impossible, you will find your answers in the possible. Clearly, Brother Síoda passed on this information somehow. I do not believe that wraiths whispered this information."

Abbot Laisran was silent.

"Let us hear about Sister Sláine," she continued. "What made you choose her to look after the girl?"

"Because she worked in the apothecary and had some understanding of those who were of bizarre humours."

"How long had she been looking after Sister Scáthach?"

"About a full month."

"And how had the girl's behaviour been during that time?"

"For the first week it seemed better. Then it became worse. More violent, more assertive. Then it became quiet again. That was when we allowed Sister Scáthach to go to the refectory."

"The day before the murder?"

"The day before the murder," he confirmed.

"And Sister Sláine slept in the next cell to the girl?"

"She did."

"And did she always lock the door of Sister Scáthach's cell at night?"

"She did."

"And on that night?"

"Especially on that night of her threat to Síoda."

"And the key was always hung on a hook outside the cell so that there was no way Sister Scáthach could have reached it?"

When Abbot Laisran confirmed this, Fidelma sighed deeply.

"I think that I'd better have a word with Sister Scáthach and also with Sister Sláine."

Fidelma chose to see Sister Scáthach first. She was surprised by her appearance as she entered the gloomy cell, which the girl inhabited. The girl was no more than sixteen or seventeen years old, thin with pale skin. She looked as though she had not slept for days, large dark areas of skin showed under her eyes that were black, wide and staring. The features were almost cadaverous, as if the skin was tightly drawn over the bones.

She did not look up as Fidelma and Laisran entered. She sat on the edge of her bed, hands clasped between her knees, gazing intently on the floor. She appeared more like a lost waif than a killer.

"Well, Scáthach," Fidelma began gently, sitting next to the girl, much to the surprise of Laisran who remained standing at the door, "I hear that you are possessed of exceptional powers."

The girl started at the sound of her voice and then shook her head.

"Powers? It is not a power but a curse that attends me."

"You have a gift of prophecy."

"A gift that I would willingly return to whoever cursed me with it."

"Tell me about it."

"They say that I killed Brother Síoda. I did not know the man. But if they tell me that it was so then it must be so."

"You remember nothing of the event?"

"Nothing at all. So far as I am aware, I went to bed, fell asleep and was only awoken when the steward and the abbot came into my cell to confront me."

"Do you remember prophesying his death in the refectory?"

The girl nodded quickly.

"That I do remember. But I simply repeated what the voice told me to say."

"The voice?"

"The voice of the shadow from the Otherworld. It attends me at night and wakes me if I slumber. It tells me what I should say and when. Then the next morning I repeat the message as the shadows instruct me."

"You hear this voice . . . or voices . . . at night?"

The girl nodded.

"It comes to you here in your cell?" pressed Fidelma. "No where else?"

"The whispering is at night when I am in my cell," confirmed the girl.

"And it was this voice that instructed you to prophesy Brother Síoda's death? It told you to speak directly to him? Did it also tell you to mention Gormflaith and her baby?"

The girl nodded in answer to all her questions.

"How long have you heard such voices?"

"I am told that it has been so since I was a little girl."

"What sort of voices?

"Well, at first the sounds were more like the whispering of the sea. We lived by the sea and so I was not troubled at first for the sounds of the sea have always been a constant companion. The sounds were disturbing but gentle, kind sounds. They came to me more in my head, soft and sighing. Then they increased. Sometimes I could not stand it. My parents said they were voices from the Otherworld. A sign from God. They brought me here. The abbey treated me well but the sounds increased. I was placed here to be looked after by Sister Sláine."

"I hear that these voices have become very strident of late."

"They became more articulate. I am not responsible for what they tell me to say or how they tell me to say it," the girl added as if on the defensive.

"Of course not," Fidelma agreed. "But it seems there was a change. The voice became stronger. When did this change occur?"

"When I came here to this cell. The voice became distinct. It spoke in words that I could understand."

"You mention voices in the plural and singular. How many voices spoke to you?"

The girl thought carefully.

"Well, I can only identify one."

"Male or female."

"Impossible to tell. It was all one whispering sound."

"How did it became so manifest?"

"It was as if I woke up and they were whispering in a corner of the room." The girl smiled. "The first and second time it happened, I lit a candle and peered round the cell but there was no one there. Eventually I realised that as strong as the voices were they must be in my head. I resigned myself to being the messenger on their behalf."

"And the voice instructed you to do what?"

"It told me to stand in the refectory and pronounce their messages of doom."

Abbot Laisran learnt forward in a confiding fashion.

"Sometimes these messages were of violence against the whole community and at other times violence against individuals. But it was the one against Brother Síoda that was the most specific and named events."

Fidelma nodded. She had not taken her eyes from the girl's face.

"Why do you believe this voice came from the Otherworld?"

The girl regarded her with a puzzled frown.

"Where else would it be from? I am a good Christian and say my prayers at night. But still the voice haunts me."

"Have you heard it since the warning you were to deliver to Brother Síoda?"

The girl shook her head.

"Not in the same specific way."

"Then in what way?"

"It has gone back to the same whispering inconsistency, the sound of the sea."

Fidelma glanced around the cell.

"Is this the place where you usually have your bed?"

The girl looked surprised for a moment.

"This is where I normally sleep."

Fidelma was examining the walls of the cell with keen eyes.

"Who occupied the cells on either side?"

"On that side is Sister Sláine who looks after this poor girl. To the other side is the chamber occupied by Brother Cruinn, my steward."

"But there is a floor above this one?"

"The chamber immediately above this is occupied by Brother Torchán, our gardener."

Fidelma turned to the lock on the door of the cell.

Abbot Laisran saw her peering at the keyhole.

"Her cell was locked and the key on the inside when Brother Cruinn and I came to this cell after Brother Síoda had been found."

Fidelma nodded absently.

"That is the one puzzling aspect," she admitted.

Abbot Laisran looked puzzled.

"I would have thought it tied everything together. It is the proof that only Scáthach could have brought the weapon and robe into her cell and therefore she is the culprit."

Fidelma did not answer.

"How far is Brother Síoda's cell from here?"

"At the far end of this corridor."

"From the condition of the robe that you showed me, there must have been a trail of blood from Brother Síoda's cell to this one?"

"Perhaps the corridor had been cleaned," he suggested. "One of the duties of our community is to clean the corridors each morning."

"And they cleaned it without reporting traces of the blood to you?" Fidelma was clearly unimpressed by the attempted explanation. Fidelma rose and glanced at the girl with a smile.

"Don't worry, Sister Scáthach. I think that you are innocent of Brother Síoda's death." She turned from the cell, followed by a deeply bewildered Abbot Laisran.

"Let us see Sister Sláine now."

At the next cell, Sister Sláine greeted them with a nervous bob of her head.

Fidelma entered and glanced along the stone wall that separated the cell from that of Sister Scáthach's. Then she turned to Sister Sláine who was about twenty-one or two, an attractive looking girl.

"Brother Síoda was a handsome man, wasn't he?" she asked without preamble.

The girl started in surprise. A blush tinged her cheeks.

"I suppose he was."

"He had an eye for the ladies. I presumed that you were in love with him, weren't you?"

The girl's chin came up defiantly.

"Who told you?"

"It was a guess," Fidelma admitted with a soft smile. "But since you have admitted it, let us proceed. Do you believe in these voices that Sister Scáthach hears?"

"Of course not. She's mad and has now proved her madness."

"Do you not find it strange that this madness has only manifested itself since she was moved into this cell next to you?"

The girl's cheeks suddenly suffused with crimson.

"Are you implying that . . .?"

"Answer my question," snapped Fidelma, cutting her short.

The girl blinked at her cold voice. Then, seeing that Abbot Laisran was not interfering, she said, "Madness can alter, it can grow worse . . . it is a coincidence that she became worse after Abbot Laisran asked me to look after her. Just a coincidence."

"I am told that you work for the apothecary and look after sick people? In your experience, have you ever heard of a condition among people where they have a permanent hissing, or whistling in the ears?"

Sister Sláine nodded slowly.

"Of course. Many people have such a condition. Sometimes they hardly notice it while others are plagued by it and almost driven to madness. That is what we thought was wrong with Sister Scáthach when she first came to our notice."

"Only at first?" queried Fidelma.

"Until she started to claim that she heard words being articulated, words that formed distinct messages which, she also claimed, were from the shadows of the Otherworld."

"Did Brother Síoda ever tell you about his affair with Gormflaith and his child?" Fidelma changed the subject so abruptly that the girl blinked. It was clear from her reaction that Fidelma had hit on the truth.

"Better speak the truth now for it will become harder later," Fidelma advised.

Sister Sláine was silent for a moment, her eyes narrowed as she tried to penetrate behind Fidelma's inquisitive scrutiny.

"If you must know, I was in love with Síoda. We planned to leave here soon to find a farmstead where we could begin a new life together. We had no secrets from one another."

Fidelma smiled softly and nodded.

"So he did tell you?"

"Of course. He wanted to tell me all about his past life. He told me of this unfortunate girl and her baby. He was very young and foolish at the time. He was a penitent and sought forgiveness. That's why he came here."

"So when you heard Sister Scáthach denounce him in the refectory, naming Gormflaith and relating her death and that of her child, what exactly did you think?"

"Do you mean, about how she came upon that knowledge?"

"Exactly. Where did you think Sister Scáthach obtained such knowledge if not from her messages from the Otherworld?"

Sister Sláine pursed her lips.

"As soon as I had taken Sister Scáthach back to her cell and locked her in, I went to find Brother Síoda. He was scared. I thought at first that he had told her or someone else apart from me. He swore that he had not. He was so scared that he went to see Abbot Laisran . . ."

"Did you question Sister Scáthach?"

The girl laughed.

"Little good that did. She simply said it was the voices. She had most people believing her."

"But you did not?"

"Not even in the madness she is suffering can one make up such specific information. I can only believe that Síoda lied to me . . ."

Her eyes suddenly glazed and she fell silent as if in some deep thought.

"Cloistered in this abbey, and a *conhospitae*, a mixed

house, there must be many opportunities for relationships to develop between the sexes?" Fidelma observed.

"There is no rule against it," returned the girl. "Those advocating celibacy and abstinence have not yet taken over this abbey. We still live a natural life here. But Síoda never mixed with the mad one, never with Scáthach."

"But you have had more than one affair here?" Fidelma asked innocently.

"Brother Síoda was my first and only love," snapped the girl in anger.

Fidelma raised her eyebrows.

"No others?"

The girl's expression was pugnacious.

"None."

"You had no close friends among the other members of the community?"

"I do not get on with the women, if that is what you mean."

"It isn't. But it is useful to know. How about male friends?"

"I've told you, I don't . . ."

Abbot Laisran coughed in embarrassment.

"I had always thought that you and Brother Torchán were friends."

Sister Sláine blushed.

"I get on well with Brother Torchán," she admitted defensively.

Fidelma suddenly rose and glanced along the wall once more, before turning with a smile to the girl.

"You've been most helpful," she said abruptly, turning for the door.

Outside in the corridor, Abbot Laisran was regarding her with a puzzled expression.

"What now?" he demanded. "I would have thought that you wanted to develop the question of her relationships?"

"We shall go to see Brother Torchán," she said firmly.

Brother Torchán was out in the garden and had to be sent for so Fidelma could interview him in his cell. He was a thickset, muscular young man whose whole being spoke of a life spent in the open.

"Well, Brother, what do you think of Sister Scáthach?"

The burly gardener shook his head sadly.

"I grieve for her as I grieve for Brother Síoda. I knew Brother Síoda slightly but the girl not at all. I doubt if I have seen her more than half a dozen times and never spoken to her but once. By all accounts, she was clearly demented."

"What do you think about her being driven to murder by voices from the Otherworld?"

"It is clear that she must be placed in the care of a combination of priests and physicians to drive away the evilness that has compelled her."

"So you think that she is guilty of the murder?"

"Can there be any other explanation?" asked the gardener in surprise.

"You know Sister Sláine, of course. I am told she is a special friend of yours."

"Special? I would like to think so. We often talk together. We came from the same village."

"Has she ever discussed Sister Scáthach with you?"

Brother Torchán shifted uneasily. He looked suspiciously at Fidelma.

"Once or twice. When the abbot first asked her to look after Sister Scáthach, it was thought that it was simply a case of what the apothecaries call tinnitus. She heard sounds in her ears. But then Sláine said that the girl had become clearly demented saying that she was being woken up by the sound of voices giving her messages and urging her to do things."

"Did you know that Sláine was having an affair with Síoda?" Fidelma suddenly said sharply.

Torchán coloured and, after a brief hesitation, nodded.

"It was deeper than an affair. She told me that they planned to leave the abbey and set up home together. It is not forbidden by rule, you know."

"How did you feel about that?"

Brother Torchán shrugged.

"So long as Síoda treated her right, it had little to do with me."

"But you were her friend."

"I was a friend and advised her when she wanted advice.

She is the kind of girl who attracts men. Sometimes the wrong men. She attracted Brother Síoda."

"Was Brother Síoda the wrong man?"

"I thought so."

"Did she ever repeat to you anything Brother Síoda told her?"

Torchán lowered his eyes.

"You mean about Gormflaith and the child? Sister Sláine is not gifted with the wisdom of silence. She told me various pieces of gossip. Oh . . ." he hesitated. "I have never spoken to Scáthach, if that is what you mean."

"But, if Sláine told you, then she might well have told others?"

"I do not mean to imply that she gossiped to anyone. There was only Brother Cruinn and myself whom she normally confided in."

"Brother Cruinn, the steward, was also her friend?"

"I think that he would have liked to have been something more until Brother Síoda took her fancy."

Fidelma smiled tightly.

"That will be all, Torchán."

There was a silence as Abbot Laisran followed Fidelma down the stone steps to the floor below. Fidelma led the way back to Sister Scáthach's cell, paused and then pointed to the next door.

"And this is Brother Cruinn's cell?"

Abbot Laisran nodded.

Brother Cruinn, the steward of the abbey, was a thin, sallow man in his mid-twenties. He greeted Fidelma with a polite smile of welcome.

"A sad business, a sad business," he said. "The matter of Sister Scáthach. I presume that is the reason for your wishing to see me?"

"It is," agreed Fidelma easily.

"Of course, of course; a poor, demented girl. I have suggested to the abbot here that he should send to Ferna to summon the bishop. I believe that there is some exorcism ritual with which he is acquainted. That may help. We have lost a good man in Brother Síoda."

Fidelma sat down unbidden in the single chair that occupied the cell.

"You were going to lose Brother Síoda anyway," she said dryly.

Brother Cruinn's face was an example of perfect self-control.

"I do not believe I follow you, Sister," he said softly.

"You were also losing Sister Sláine. How did you feel about that?"

Brother Cruinn's eyes narrowed but he said nothing.

"You loved her. You hated it when she and Brother Síoda became lovers."

Brother Cruinn was looking appalled at Abbot Laisran as if appealing for help.

Abbot Laisran wisely made no comment. He had witnessed too many of Fidelma's interrogations to know when not to interfere.

"It must have been tearing you apart," went on Fidelma calmly. "But instead you hid your feelings. You pretended to remain a friend, simply a friend to Sister Sláine. You listened carefully while she gossiped about her lover and especially when she confided what he had told her about his first affair and the baby."

"This is ridiculous!" snapped Brother Cruinn.

"Is it?" replied Fidelma as if pondering the question. "What a godsend it was when poor Sister Scáthach was put into the next cell to you. Sister Scáthach was an unfortunate girl who was suffering, not from imagined whispering voices from the Otherworld, but from an advanced cause of the sensation of noises in the ears. It is not an uncommon affliction but some cases are worse than others. As a little child, when it developed, silly folk – her parents – told her that the whistling and hissing sounds were the voice of lost souls in the Otherworld trying to communicate with her and thus she was blessed.

"Her parents brought her here. She probably noticed the affliction more in these conditions than she had when living by the sea where the whispering was not so intrusive. Worried by the worsening affects, on the advice of the apothecary, Abbot Laisran placed her in the cell with Sister Sláine, who knew something of the condition, to look after her."

Fidelma paused, eyes suddenly hardening on him.

"That was your opportunity, eh, Brother Cruinn? A chance to be rid of Brother Síoda and with no questions asked. A strangely demented young woman who was compelled by voices from another world to do so would murder him."

"You are mad," muttered Brother Cruinn.

Fidelma smiled.

"Madness can only be used as an excuse once. This is all logical. It was your voice that kept awakening poor Sister Scáthach and giving her these messages which made her behave so. At first you told her to proclaim some general messages. That would cause people to accept her madness, as they saw it. Then, having had her generally accepted as mad, you gave her the message to prepare for Síoda's death."

She walked to the head of his bed, her eye having observed what she had been seeking. She reached forward and withdrew from the wall a piece of loose stone. It revealed a small aperture, no more than a few fingers wide and high.

"Abbot Laisran, go into the corridor and unlock Sister Scáthach's door but do not open it nor enter. Wait outside."

Puzzled, the abbot obeyed her.

Fidelma waited and then bent down to the hole.

"Scáthach! Scáthach! Can you hear me, Scáthach? All is now well. You will hear the voices no more. Go to the door and open it. Outside you will find Abbot Laisran. Tell him that all is now well. The voices are gone."

She rose up and faced Brother Cruinn, whose dark eyes were narrowed and angry.

A moment later they heard the door of the next door open and a girl's voice speaking with Abbot Laisran.

The abbot returned moments later.

"She came to the door and told me that the voices were gone and all was well."

Fidelma smiled thinly.

"Even as I told her to do so. Just as that poor influenced

girl did what you told her to, Brother Cruinn. This hole goes through the wall into her cell and acts like a conduit for the voice."

"I did not tell her to stab Brother Síoda in the heart," he said defensively.

"Of course not. She did not stab anyone. You did that."

"Ridiculous! The bloodstained robes and weapon were in her cell . . ."

"Placed there by you."

"The door was locked and the key was inside. That shows that only she could have committed the murder."

Abbot Laisran sighed.

"It's true, Fidelma. I went with Brother Cruinn myself to Sister Scáthach's cell door. I told you, the key was not on the hook outside the door but inside her cell and the door locked. I said before, only she could have taken the knife and robe inside and locked herself in."

"When you saw that the key was not hanging on the hook outside the door, Laisran, then did you try to open the door?" Fidelma asked innocently.

"We did."

"No, did *you* try to open the door?" snapped Fidelma with emphasis.

Abbot Laisran looked blank for a moment.

"Brother Cruinn tried the door and pronounced it locked. He then took his master keys, which he held as steward, and unlocked the door. He had to wiggle the key around in the lock. When the door was open the key was on the floor on the inside. We found it there."

Fidelma grinned.

"Where Brother Cruinn had placed it. Have Cruinn secured and I will tell you how he did it later."

After Brother Cruinn was taken away by attendants summoned by Abbot Laisran, Fidelma returned to his chamber to finish her interrupted mulled wine and to stretch herself before the fire.

"I'm not sure how you resolved this matter," Abbot Laisran finally said, as he stacked another log on the fire.

"It was the matter of the key that made me realise that

Brother Cruinn had done this. Exactly how and, more importantly, why, I did not know at first. I realised as soon as Sister Scáthach told me how she was awoken by the whispering voice at night that it must have come from one of three sources. The voice must have come from one of the three neighbouring cells. When she showed me where she slept, I realised from where the voice had come. Brother Cruinn was the whispering in the night. No one else could physically have done it. He also had easy access to Brother Síoda's locked cell because only he held the master keys. The problem was what had he to gain from Brother Síoda's death? Well, now we know the answer – it was an act of jealousy, hoping to eliminate Brother Síoda so that he could pursue his desire for Sister Sláine. That he was able to convince you that the cell door was locked and that he was actually opening it, was child's play. An illusion in which you thought that Sister Scáthach had locked herself in her cell. Brother Cruinn had placed the key on the floor when he planted the incriminating evidence of the blood-stained weapon and robe.

"In fact, the door was not locked at all. Brother Cruinn had taken the robe to protect his clothing from the blood when he killed Sioda. He therefore allowed no blood to fall when he came along the corridor with robe and knife to where Sister Scáthach lay in her exhausted sleep. Remember that she was exhausted by the continuous times he had woken her with his whispering voice. He left the incriminating evidence, left the key on the floor and closed the door. In the morning, he could go through the pantomime of opening the door, claiming it had been locked from the inside. Wickedness coupled with cleverness but our friend Brother Cruinn was a little too clever."

"But to fathom this mystery, you first had to come to the conclusion that Sister Scáthach was innocent," pointed out the abbot.

"Poor Scáthach! It is her parents who should be on trial for filling her susceptible mind with this myth about Other-world voices when she is suffering from a physical disability. The fact was Scáthach could not have known about Gormflaith. She was told. If one discounts voices from the Otherworld, then it was by a human agency. The question was who was that agency and what was the motive for this evil charade."

Abbot Laisran gazed at her in amazement.

"I never ceased to be astonished at your astute mind, Fidelma. Without you, poor Sister Scáthach might have stood condemned."

Fidelma smiled and shook her head at her old mentor.

"On the contrary, Abbot Laisran, without you and your suspicion that things were a little too cut and dried, we should never even have questioned the guilt or innocence of the poor girl at all."

# Catherine and the Sybil

## Sharan Newman

*We now enter the Middle Ages and who better to introduce us to that period than Sharan Newman, medieval scholar and author of the recent* The Real History Behind the da Vinci Code *(2005). Newman became well known for her trilogy about Queen Guinevere, but starting with the award-winning* Death Comes as Epiphany *(1993), she has developed a fascinating series set in twelfth-century France. This features Catherine LeVendeur, a young novice who comes to study at the Convent of the Paraclete, run by the abbess Héloïse, famous for her love affair with Peter Abelard. The series now runs to ten books. The following story brings together Catherine with another of the great women of the period, the visionary Hildegarde of Bingen.*

The day was clear and cloudless, a rare gift in late autumn. Albrecht was eager to get back to work on the church for the new convent. Unlike many of the other workers, he had no fear of climbing on the skeletal scaffolds set up along the walls. He loved looking out across the river Nahe to the valley beyond. He imagined sometimes that he could see his village, where his wife and children waited for him to return in the spring.

He climbed the scaffolding with confidence. He had faith in his skill at carpentry and that of the master builder. Even more, he had faith in the visions of the prioress. Many, including the pope, admitted that God spoke to her directly. If she said they should erect the buildings at this site, so close to the river, then it was certain that it was according to a heavenly plan.

Albrecht swung across the beams of the roof, landing on the platform suspended from the far wall.

There was a loud crack as the narrow board split, sending Albrecht tumbling to the stone floor.

His last emotion was astonishment. God's plan should not have included someone working by night with a saw.

In his palace in the city of Troyes, Thibault, Count of Champagne, glared at his granddaughter. He was trying to be patient but his bad hip was sending knives down his leg and she was being extremely trying.

Margaret opened her eyes wide in an effort to keep tears from spilling over. She fought a nervous urge to chew the end of her red braid.

"You are eighteen years old, girl," Thibault barked. "I've offered to find you a suitable husband or dower you enough to enter any convent you wished. Why can't you make up your mind?"

From a corner in the shadows, Catherine watched this trial of her husband's sister. She longed to interrupt but knew this was not the time or place. And what could she say? Tolerant though he usually was, Thibault would not be pleased to learn that his Margaret had long ago decided upon the impossible. She had fallen in love with a Jew.

Catherine sighed. She had thought this folly merely a child's fondness but as she grew older, Margaret's attachment to Solomon had only deepened and now Catherine feared Solomon returned the feeling. Keeping them apart had no effect. Something irrevocable had to be done.

Margaret knew that to admit her feelings could mean death for Solomon and shame for herself. She had stalled as long as she could. She closed her eyes and let the tears flow where they would. But when she spoke, her voice was steady.

"My lord," she bowed her head and quickly wiped her cheeks with her sleeve. "You have been more than indulgent with my indecision. I beg your forgiveness. I have thought long upon this for I seem to have neither a vocation for monasticism or marriage."

"Well, those are your choices, Margaret," Thibault said. "You can hardly set up as a seller of trinkets in the market square."

Since that was close to what she did want, Margaret bit her tongue before she spoke again.

"Therefore, rather than inflict myself upon a man who deserves a devoted wife, I shall become a bride of Christ and pray that He send me the grace to be worthy of Him."

Thibault nearly cheered. "Splendid! I'll have Countess Mahaut make arrangements for you to enter the Paraclete. Don't weep, child. It's close enough that your family can visit you often."

"No!" Margaret took a step closer to him. "I love the Paraclete, but I cannot stay there. I must go somewhere else, somewhere far away."

"What?" Catherine leapt to her feet, knocking over the stool she had been sitting on. "You can't do that! Please, my lord Count, don't let her leave us."

The count gave her a look that reminded her she was only in the room on sufferance. Margaret's choice was not in her power to change.

Thibault rose from his chair and put his arms around Margaret.

"I had thought to make the break a gentler one by letting you stay nearby," he said. "But I agree that it might be easier for you to start your new life in new surroundings. Now, have you considered where you wish to go?"

Margaret avoided looking at Catherine as she answered.

"Yes, I want to join the sisters at the new convent at Rupertsberg."

Thibault released her quickly. "The one that the visionary woman is building? I don't know. The pope and Abbot Bernard seem to think well of her, but I understand she can be very difficult."

Margaret didn't answer. Thibault thought another minute.

"Still, she only accepts women from the best families," he considered. "It might be even better than a marriage alliance. And, of course," he added hastily, "Hildegarde has a great reputation for wisdom and piety as well. Yes, it might be the best place for you. I'll see to it."

"Thank you, Grandfather," Margaret whispered.

She left the room.

Catherine looked at the count in stupefaction. He shrugged.

"You heard for yourself," he told her. "Margaret made her choice. Can you and your husband accompany her there?"

Numbly, Catherine nodded.

At Rupertsberg, Albrecht was buried quietly. Prioress Hildegarde promised his widow that she and the children would be cared for and saw to it that his name was added to the book of the dead for whom the nuns prayed.

"A terrible accident," she said to Ludwig, the master builder. "I thought the men always went up in pairs."

She looked at him with an intensity that seemed to stake him to the ground.

"They should," the Master answered. "Albrecht always was one for climbing on his own, though. He used to laugh at the men who didn't like being up so high."

The prioress shook her head. "He should not have had to pay such a price for his hubris."

"No, my lady," Ludwig wasn't sure what hubris was, but could agree it was not a sin worth dying for. He hoped he would soon be dismissed. There were things that worried him about Albrecht's "accident" and he would rather the Lady Hildegarde didn't find out about them. He bowed. Perhaps she would take the hint and let him leave.

"Ludwig?"

He looked up. Hildegarde was gazing over his head at the church. With a heart full of dread, Ludwig turned around.

He saw nothing amiss. The walls of an earlier church were being cannibalized to build the one for the nuns. Chunks of old stone blocks stuck with cement lay in a pile next to the rising nave of the new building. The men were working. Embrich was dutifully walking the treadmill that helped the scaffolding to rise. Ludwig hoped he wouldn't take a swig from his beerskin while the prioress was watching. The man was the worst worker he had ever hired. The treadmill was the only task he could be trusted to do properly.

He turned back to Hildegarde, still wary. Everyone knew she was a prophet, the only one in the modern world. Perhaps she saw disaster in their future.

"Yes, my lady," he quavered.

"This isn't the first accident we have had," she said, still looking, for all Ludwig knew, into the soul of the earth, demanding answers from Nature herself.

"No, my lady," he admitted. "There was the problem with the cracked windlass and some rope has gone missing, but these things happen in all projects."

"Do they?" The prioress' expression told him that he had better see to it that nothing more happened here.

Margaret's brother Edgar had not been pleased with her decision to enter Hildegarde's convent. But there was little he could do in the face of the count's approval.

"They've only been building it for a year or so," he grumbled. "How do we even know she'll have a roof over her head?"

"If you're not certain about the place, we could stop at Trier for a few days on the way there, to visit my sister," Catherine suggested to him. "If there is anything irregular about the convent, Agnes will know."

"Do you think we could leave the children with her while we go on to Rupertsberg?" Edgar asked hopefully.

"It would be good for her to have them," Catherine agreed.

The promise of time alone with his wife eased somewhat the prospect of leaving his much loved little sister with foreign nuns.

But not completely.

"I don't see why she has to marry or enter a convent," he grumbled. "I can provide for her here."

"You and Solomon are partners," Catherine reminded him. "You would both provide for her."

Edgar gave her a sharp glance. Solomon was his best friend but . . .

"If we're to reach Germany before winter," he decided, "we'll have to leave at once. I doubt Solomon will be back from Rome before we go. Margaret will have to leave him a letter."

Sadly, Catherine agreed. It bothered her greatly that Margaret was entering the religious life because she couldn't marry the man she loved. But better to find a haven as the bride of Christ than suffer the danger and shame of abandoning her faith for a Jew, no matter how good a man he might be.

Catherine's sister Agnes had married into a good German family near the city of Trier. Her husband was the uncle of the present lord, Peter, a young man of twenty. Until he married, Agnes was happy to run the household. Peter suspected that she would continue to do so even after that happened. He hoped his unknown wife wouldn't mind.

"Of course I know about Hildegarde," she told Catherine, Edgar and Margaret over dinner on the night they arrived. "You must remember how they read the account of her visions at that council here in Trier. Since Bernard of Clairvaux and the pope agreed that they were genuine, almost everyone has been asking her to tell their future. And she writes to those who haven't asked to warn them to mend their wicked ways."

"Her convent doesn't sound exactly like a calm haven," Catherine said with a worried glance at Margaret.

"Hardly," Agnes signalled the servants to clear the cloth and bring in the fruit and sugared almonds. "She's usually in a middle of a whirlwind. At the moment she's decided to move her convent to Rupertsberg. Several of the nuns have rebelled at being dragged from the comfort of St Disibod and the monks there are furious that she wants to leave their protection, taking her fame and property with her."

"I know these things," Margaret assured them. "I would

like to be a part of a new religious foundation. And it would be interesting to have a prophet for an abbess."

"Prioress," Agnes corrected. "She can't get the monks of St Disibod to free her entirely from their control."

"At least in principle," her husband, Meinhard, added. "She has her ways. When she had a vision telling her to move to Rupertsberg, they refused to let her go. Remember?"

"Oh, yes," Agnes said. "Then Hildegarde was struck down with a paralysing illness. The abbot thought she was feigning until he tried to lift her from her bed."

"He said it was as if she were being held in place by a powerful force," Meinhard concluded. "He couldn't move her. Not until he agreed to let her leave."

"You see?" Margaret said. "She is under divine protection. I shall be quite safe there."

Her brother wasn't so sure. "God has a way of protecting his chosen ones right up to the point of martyrdom," he said. "It sounds to me as if you are entering a maelstrom rather than a convent."

"Perhaps I should accompany you there," Peter spoke up. "In case there are problems."

Everyone stared at him. Peter rarely gave an opinion and he had never shown an interest in leaving his own lands.

"You are foreigners and your German, while good, isn't perfect," he explained. "It would be terrible if the kin of my Aunt Agnes came to grief because I wasn't there to speak for them."

Meinhard and Edgar exchanged a long look, then they both turned to consider Margaret, animated with wine. She did not look at all like a nun.

"I believe Peter is right," Edgar said. "We would be pleased to have your company."

Ludwig stood once more before Prioress Hildegarde, twisting his knit cap in his hands.

"The stand for the pitch cauldron was steady," he insisted. "I checked it myself. There was no reason for it to tip over."

Hildegarde nodded. "No natural reason," she agreed.

"My lady!" Ludwig dropped his hat in astonishment. "You don't think there are demons at work in this holy place?"

"The holier the place, the more likely the Evil One is to send his minions to destroy it," Hildegarde said calmly. "Demons are unnecessary, though, when there are enough weak human souls to consent to his desires."

Ludwig gave a deep sigh of relief. He was used to evil in human form. It was monsters from the depths of Hell that frightened him.

"Someone is trying to keep us from finishing the church?" he guessed. "Who would be so foolhardy? You would know them at once, wouldn't you?"

The prioress smiled gently. "I am but the servant of the Living Light," she explained. "I do not ask for revelation, but accept it when it comes to me. We shall have to find the miscreant ourselves. Of course, it's possible that a vision may be sent while we are endeavoring to do so."

She seemed so confident that Ludwig felt ashamed of the worry still gnawing at his gut. He bowed and backed to the door.

"Ludwig!"

He froze to the spot. Had God spoken to the lady while he was still in the room?

"Ludwig," she repeated. "You forgot your hat."

That afternoon, Hildegarde called one of the nuns into her chamber.

"Richardis," she greeted the woman with a tender smile. "How are my daughters doing in their new home?"

"Most are offering up the increased discomforts as a sacrifice to Our Lord," Richardis told her. "A few still looked pained. Trauchte's father, Lord Gerlac, is in Bingen, ready to take her to a less austere convent the moment she sends word. She thinks no one knows, but he's been seen lurking outside the dorter walls."

"Has he, now?" Hildegarde did not seem surprised by the knowledge. "I shall remember him in my prayers. Now, I have received a message that the granddaughter of the Count of Champagne has requested a visit with the intention of joining our sisterhood. She has apparently been raised at the Paraclete."

Richardis' eyebrows rose. "And she wishes to join us? If it isn't to flee some offence committed there, then she would be a most welcome addition. Heloise's nuns are renowned for their learning."

"I would rather she were renowned for her piety," Hildegarde remarked. "However, both can be ascertained when she and her family arrive. I have had a message from a relative of theirs in Trier. They should be here within a day or so. I only wish that I could find out who has been creating these 'accidents' among the workers before then."

Richardis hesitated. "Relatives in Trier? Mother Hildegarde, I believe I have heard of this Margaret and her family. If you permit it, they might be able to assist us."

Hildegarde was doubtful at first, but as Richardis related what she knew, the prioress began to form a plan.

Catherine had resigned herself to being assigned a bed in the women's section of the guest house. Marital relations were unseemly when one was the guest of celibates. She wasn't prepared, though, for how primitive the accommodations were.

"I had heard that *Magistra* Hildegarde encouraged moderation in the renunciation of the flesh," she moaned as she inspected the bare room. "Perhaps her opinion has changed. It's good that we brought our own mattresses. I didn't know we'd need to bring bed frames too."

"I wonder what the conditions are in the nuns' quarters," Margaret said.

"You and I will inspect them thoroughly before I agree to leave you here," Catherine assured her.

"It doesn't matter," Margaret answered. "I am prepared to subjugate my body to the needs of my soul."

Catherine bit her tongue to keep from arguing. Her mind said that Margaret was right, but her heart believed otherwise. Like Edgar, she wished there were a way to keep his sister with them forever.

      ★      ★      ★

Edgar hadn't noticed the state of the guest rooms. He had taken one look at the construction work, thrown his pack on the ground and gone to survey the building.

Lugwig growled as he saw Edgar.

"Look sharp, if you can, Embrich," he said to the worker. "We're about to have another visit from some noble know-it-all who wants to give us advice on how to do our jobs, even if he can't tell his axe from his adze."

He turned around to see if Embrich were looking halfway competent and discovered that, wisely, the man had made himself scarce. Ludwig forced a smile.

"Greetings, my lord," he bowed. "Come to see where your daughter will be saying her prayers?"

"Hmm?" Edgar was gazing up at the tower with a worried frown. "Oh, yes. My sister. Building rather close to the edge, aren't you? A few bad winters and the river could eat away your foundations."

This was what Ludwig had thought when the Lady Hildgarde had told him the site, but he'd never admit it to a stranger.

"The rock is solid under the church," he insisted. "We had a hell of a time digging into it."

"That's good," Edgar squinted at something hanging halfway up the tower. "What is that rope attached to?"

Ludwig turned. "It's wrapped around the crank for pulling the baskets of *rubbez* to fill in the space between the walls."

"I see," Edgar smiled. "Why is it hanging from a wooden tower?"

"Trade secret," Ludwig smiled back. "If you'll excuse me, my lord."

He turned and hurried away without waiting for leave. Edgar studied the building for a minute more. A movement by the pile of stones caught his eye. Curious, he wandered over to find a young man dozing against the rubble. As he approached, the man woke with a start. Seeing Edgar, he crossed himself in relief.

"Thank the virgin!" he exclaimed. "I thought you were Ludwig!"

Edgar smiled at him, noting the bruised hands and dusty clothes.

"Not been at the craft long?" he asked.

A look of fear crossed the man's face. "I'm a journeyman! Don't believe what Master Ludwig says! He has some grudge against me, I don't know why. I didn't slit the canvas on the tents or spill the lime, but I'm the first one he shouts at. Don't tell him, my lord, that you found me asleep. I beg you."

Edgar reassured the man. The tolling of a bell reminded him that Catherine and Margaret were waiting for him.

Catherine met him at the door of the guest house.

"Margaret and I have been speaking with one of the nuns here," she told him. "Prioress Hildegarde has made a very odd request. It seems that there have been a number of odd happenings in the construction of the convent buildings. She thinks she has discovered who is responsible, but needs help in proving it."

Edgar listened.

"What do you think?" Catherine asked when she had finished.

"I think that, whether or not her visions come from Heaven, *Magistra* Hildegarde is a very wise woman," he answered. "Tell her that we will do as she requests."

The next morning Catherine suggested that Peter might like to take Margaret on a short walk around the convent walls.

He agreed with delight.

"Margaret," Catherine whispered as they left. "Remember what I told you."

"I won't do anything foolish," she promised.

As soon as they left, Catherine shook out her skirts and checked the soles of her shoes. "Ready?" she asked Edgar.

"Yes, just don't be too convincing," Edgar kissed her cheek. "I wonder who told Hildegarde that you were inclined to be clumsy."

The clapper was sounding for Sext as Edgar and Catherine headed over to the church. They could hear the chanting of the nuns in their private chapel.

As they drew near, Edgar pointed up at the men working on the scaffolding. Embrich had been promoted to hod carrier. He was carefully climbing a ladder, balancing the box of bricks against his shoulder.

"You see," he told her loudly. "That hod is way over-loaded. No wonder they have so many accidents here. You there! Come down before you lose your grip and fall!"

Startled, Embrich swayed on the ladder, the bricks teetering wildly. Every eye was on him. Suddenly, Catherine gave a cry and tumbled into a pile of hide-covered tools. They clattered to the ground.

"Oh, Oh, *Ow!*" she cried, rocking back and forth. "My ankle!"

"What idiot stacked that?" Edger shouted. "You've broken my wife's ankle! Dearest, can you hobble? Who's responsible for this?"

His ranting grew louder until the portress came running from the chapel to see what the problem was.

"I'm not leaving my sister in a place so obviously badly maintained!" Edgar shouted. "My wife may be crippled because of the slovenly behaviour of your workmen! What does Lady Hildegarde intend to do about it?"

"My lord, I . . . I have no idea!" the portress stepped away from him. "I shall report this as soon as they are finished saying the Office."

"I want this addressed immediately!" Edgar thundered. "You!" He jabbed his finger at a group of men gaping at him. "Can you be trusted to carry my wife back to the guest house without breaking anything else?"

Catherine had been moaning under his diatribe, rather like a crumhorn accompanying a minstrel's tale. She rocked back and forth in pain but managed to smile weakly as the two men made a cradle of their arms to lift her.

Soon after, the still bewildered workmen were lined up before the church facing Edgar and, even worse, the Lady Hildegarde.

She spoke quietly but even those in the back heard every word.

"I see the dark wind of the North bringing the seeds of

evil, destroying our green sanctuary," Hildegarde looked at them sadly, then closed her eyes. "I see the Wicked One, like a burrowing vole, finding the weakness in someone's heart and driving him to heed the advice of the serpent."

She opened her eyes and regarded the group of gaping workers.

'I have long been concerned by the number of mishaps involved in the work on my church. The death of Albrecht was not by chance, but design. You all know that one of the boards was tampered with. I tried to convince myself that it was only a jest gone horribly wrong, but too much else has occurred since then. Now this poor woman has also been harmed by the malice at work here. I cannot tolerate it any longer."

Ludwig stepped forward. "I understand, my lady," he said. "I, too, have had my suspicions. I never should have taken on a man known to none of the others. He told me the monks of St Disibod sent him, but I wonder. If so, it was to destroy the work of God. Embrich! Hold him, fellows! Don't let him run!"

"Get your hands off me!" Embrich protested as the men nearest dragged him forward. "I haven't done anything!"

"You are the worst mason I ever saw in my life," Ludwig said. "An apprentice on his first day would make fewer mistakes."

There was a murmur of agreement from the men.

Hildegarde faced the man.

"Your brother workers condemn you," she said. "Have you nothing to say for yourself? You know that, if it is proven that you caused Albrecht's death, you will hang."

"I did nothing!" Embrich drew himself up. "It's true that I lied to be hired on here, but not to stop the building, at least, not like that."

"Yes, I know," the prioress sat on the folding chair one of the servants had brought. "You are here because of my daughter, Trauchte."

Embrich's jaw dropped. Hildegarde continued.

"You will not win her, no matter how unhappy she is here," she informed him. "She is a professed nun. Your soul would be forfeit if you stole her away. Does her father know about your disguise?"

"No, my lady," Embrich's shoulder's drooped. "I overheard him telling a friend that Trauchte hated Rupertsberg and he was going to get her. I thought that might mean that she would consider me again."

"Foolish man!" Hildegarde shook her head. "She is pledged to a Heavenly Bridegroom who will care for her in this world and the next. What have you to offer her to compare with that?"

As Embrich was hunting for a response, Sister Richardis came from the guest house. She leaned over and said something softly to the prioress.

"Good," Hildegarde told her. "Bring him here."

A few moments later Peter and Margaret arrived, escorting a man who looked as if he would rather be anywhere else. Embrich took one look at him and blanched.

Hildegarde gave him a withering look. "Lord Gerlac," she said. "If you wished to visit Trauchte you could have applied at the gate."

"She feared that you wouldn't let me see her," Gerlac answered. "My lady," he fell to his knees before her. "I only wish the best for her. She is not meant for conditions such as these."

Hildgarde regarded him with loathing. "Good fruit comes only from good seed. Your seed is full of tares. By appealing to you, Trauchte has shown herself unfit to associate with my daughters here. Her soul, and yours, may only be saved by deep penitence.

"Take your daughter," she ordered. "Trauchte is mine no longer."

Lord Gerlac stood. "It is not God but Satan who speaks through you, Woman! I'll make sure no girl is ever entrusted to you again."

He turned to go.

"Lord Gerlac!" Hildegarde called after him. "Take your servant, as well."

He turned around slowly.

"What are you talking about?" he asked.

"Ludwig." The prioress beckoned to him.

The master mason looked in terror from Gerlac to Hildegarde and back.

"What madness is this?" he asked. "My lady, I am a master mason!"

"That you are," she said. "And your last assignment was the chapel at Lord Gerlac's family monastery."

She turned back to Gerlac.

"You hired him to see to it that I abandoned God's plan to establish a house here," she accused him. "You are equally guilty of his crimes. I shall be writing to the archbishop to inform him of your deeds. I've no doubt that he will feel obliged to report them to the emperor."

"This is nonsense," Gerlac sputtered. "I know nothing of this man or his crimes."

"I've done nothing!" Ludwig insisted. "It was Embrich; you know it was. He wanted the convent to fail so he could rescue his beloved."

Hildegarde shook her head. "As you have often said, Embrich doesn't have the skill to hammer a nail. He wouldn't know how to create such perfect ruin. Lord Edgar?"

"My lady," Edgar bowed. "As you bid me, I examined the materials that had been damaged. The work was skillfully done to cause the most disruption. The only exception was the board that broke under the worker, Albrecht. I think it was intended only to crack but he must have landed on it harder than anticipated."

Ludwig started to protest once more. Edgar held up his hand.

"I couldn't be certain that you were doing it," he said. "But, when my wife fell, I watched you. Others came to help her. You ran to retrieve the hide she slipped on. You had greased it, hadn't you?"

"Of course not!" he shouted. "You can't lay this on me. My lord!" He appealed to Gerlac.

"I don't know this man," Gerlac put on his gloves. "What ever he has done is of his own design."

"You bastard!" Ludwig screamed.

Lord Gerlac eye's dared Hildegarde to try to detain him. She considered him a moment, then waved him away. "Heaven will see to your punishment," she stated confidently. "Go."

When Lord Gerlac and his weeping daughter had left and a still sputtering Ludwig been locked in the gatehouse to await the judgment of the bishop, Hildegarde summoned Catherine, Edgar, Margaret and Peter to the gatehouse.

"I am grateful for your aid," she told them. "I had suspected Ludwig for some time, but needed someone from the outside to create a situation that would allow me to accuse him. Lord Gerlac may have hired him, but the abbot of St Disibod recommended him. If I had dismissed him it would have been an insult and relations between us are difficult already."

"It was little enough to do, *Magistra*," Edgar said. "A bit of play-acting."

"I thought I fell quite realistically," Catherine added. "I've had practice."

Edgar took Margaret's hand. "I am ready to give you my treasured sister. I know she will blossom here."

Margaret was trembling, but nodded agreement.

Hildegarde shook her head.

"She is not meant for the convent," she said. "I have seen her standing in the breath of the north wind, struggling to overcome its force. I have seen the warm wind of the south wrap itself around her in protection. I have not seen her reciting the Divine Office."

"But, but . . ." Catherine was totally taken aback. "Do you think her unworthy?"

"No, my child," Hildegarde sighed and held out her hand to Margaret. "You are bright and pious and obedient, all I could wish. I fear that your life would be easier if I took you in, but the Living Light has another path for you. I am sorry."

Margaret couldn't believe it. "But I must marry," she said. "If not Christ, then whom?"

Behind her, Peter's face shone with hope.

Hildegarde kissed Margaret's cheek. "Have faith, my child," she said. "An answer will present itself. You have done me a great service. When the north wind beats against you, send word and I shall pray for the south wind to find you. This I promise."

And with that, Margaret had to be content.

# The Jester and the Mathematician

## Alan R. Gordon

*By day, Alan Gordon is a veteran attorney with the New York Legal Aid Society, with a hundred criminal trials to his credit. By night, though, he is the author of the Fools' Guild series, featuring the characters in Shakespeare's* Twelfth Night, *which began with* Thirteenth Night *(1999), and now runs to five books and several short stories. Gordon has also joined the Lehman Engel/BMI Musical Theatre Workshop as a lyricist, and has adapted Roald Dahl's "A Lamb to the Slaughter" as a fourteen-minute musical.*

*The following story introduces us to the great Italian mathematician Leonardo Fibonacci, who lived in Pisa, but who was acquainted with the studies of the Arab world. This story is in fact set only a few years after the events described in Philip Boast's story and shows again the impact between the Arab and Catholic worlds. We have Fibonacci to thank for the fact that we now use Arabic numerals rather than Roman. But it could all have been so different had it not been for the Fools' Guild.*

My wife returned from the town with a new sheaf of paper for me, which means that I no longer have any excuses for putting off writing. I had no idea that I would live long enough to qualify as a historian, but nowadays, long life seems to be the only qualification.

My wife, bless her, is quite the pitiless taskmistress. She

came to Folly later in life than I, but, as a convert, embraced it with a fanaticism rivalling that of our good friends of the Inquisition. She is adamant about having me record everything.

"While you still can," she usually adds acerbically. "Lord knows you're too old to do anything else around here. And the Guild has been asking whether or not you're still alive. What should I tell them?"

"I haven't made up my mind yet, dearest." What a blessing it is to have such a helpmate late in life!

The Fools' Guild relocates periodically. As they have no need of my services as a jester anymore, they generally don't bother letting me know where they are. Nor can I rely on the old troubadour routes, not since so many troubadours were wiped out for suspected heretical sympathies during the horrors of the Albigensian Crusades.

So, we sit in this pleasant little hostel funded from the usual mysterious sources and wait upon passing pilgrims. Once in a blue moon, a familiar Irish lilt will greet my ears, and we will clandestinely meet our contact and turn over my latest jottings. It was on the latest such occasion that he brought me some sad news.

"Fazio died last month," he said. "Peacefully on his farm. I thought you might want to know."

"Poor Fazio," I said. "He'd been with the Guild even longer than I had. I must be nearly the oldest now."

"You're up there," he jibed. "You certainly look older than anyone I've ever seen. I only keep coming back hoping for a chance with your widow."

"Really?" my future widow exclaimed, perking up.

"Shall I call you out at dawn?" I huffed.

"You're up at that hour anyway, old man," he retorted. "Why not?"

"Now, now," she chided him. "Don't let him waste his energy. He has more of the Guild's history to complete. Let him be."

He grinned and retired to his room.

"I'm sorry about Fazio," she said, kissing me gently. "Was he a close friend?"

"Not close. An acquaintance and a respected colleague. At least he can stop worrying now."

"What did he have to worry about?"

"It's a long story. I might as well write it down and let you read it. No point in doing things twice at my age."

She kissed me again and placed my quill and ink within reach. "I'll leave you to it, then. Good night, my love."

She lit a single candle and placed it by my writing stand. Father Gerald used to say that any story that cannot be told by the time a single candle has burned down is too damn long, and I have lived by that advice ever since. I thought back some thirty-odd years.

It was the spring of 1198, and I had finally made it back to the Guildhall from Apulia after an unexpected delay in Assisi. I was hoping for a little rest and recuperation from my journey, but no such luck. Father Gerald was actually standing in the courtyard glaring in all directions at once. I espied some of the younger novitiates hiding in the doorway of the stables, fearfully peering at our peerless leader. I assumed, having hid in that same doorway looking at that same man with that same look when I was their age, that some practical joke had gone painfully awry, but my assumption was quickly proved wrong.

"Theophilos," he barked.

"Hail, Father," I intoned. "I have returned in triumph. Prepare the feast, slaughter the fatted calf, and throw in the skinny one, too. I have walked for leagues and have a powerful hunger."

"We expected you a week ago," he said, ignoring my speech.

"You haven't been standing here waiting all that time, have you?" I asked, concerned. I heard some suppressed giggling from the stables.

"Well, there's no help for it," he said. "You're off to Pisa."

My feet screamed in horror.

"Um, exactly why am I doing that?"

"Because I need to get a message to Fazio as soon as possible. Things are heating up with the Genoese, and we have to get the Pisans talking to them again. Which means we have to first get the Pisans talking to each other again."

"But isn't that on a troubadour route?" Back then, jesters generally stayed in one place while the troubadours travelled a regular circuit, collecting information and passing on the Guild's directives.

"It is," snapped Father Gerald. "And the preening oaf who rides it is lying in an upper room with his leg in a splint. Tantalo got drunk last night and decided to demonstrate his balancing skills on the local rooftops."

"Oh, dear. We used to tell him that if he had any talent for tumbling, he would have made a fine fool."

"His timing isn't worth a damn, either. I've just sent out all my available people. The only ones I have left are the novitiates, and they can't go to Pisa. They couldn't even find their way out of town if I was kicking their sweet behinds every step of the way . . . which I may very well do!" This last was directed at the top of his lungs in the direction of the stables. There were some muffled shrieks inside. He turned back to me and winked.

"I'm truly sorry, Theo," he continued. "The fatted calf will keep until you get back. We'll fatten it up a little more."

"Could I at least have something to ride this time?" I asked.

"Brother Dennis!" he shouted.

Our hostler emerged from the stables.

"An ass for my gallant fool, if you please. Are those children still hiding there?"

"What children?" replied Brother Dennis innocently.

"Yes. Tell them that if they're late for class, they're on kitchen duty for a month, and that class begins the moment I get back to the hall, but that I'm old and I walk slowly."

"Certainly, Father. Come on, Theo. I'll give you Tantalo's ass. He knows the route better than his master, and drinks less."

And so I was off to Pisa.

The trip was uneventful. The ass was a good-natured beast who knew not only the route but all of the spots with the most succulent grasses. Nevertheless, we made good time and a few days later found ourselves just north of the town.

We were passing by a farm when the ass greeted a patch of clover with a bray of joy, as if he had been reunited with a long-lost friend. It was as good a place to stop as any, so I rummaged through my pouch for some bread and cheese.

My wineskin was empty, which was not surprising. There was not a wineskin made that would last me through a journey, at least not one that could fit on an ass. Sadly, I was forced to seek water.

There was a brook running beside a low stone wall that marked a pasture. The water was cold and clean. I took a long drink, then reapplied my make-up to make my entrance into the town. I looked up to see a young man seated cross-legged on the wall, gazing dreamily into the field. He was wearing a bright green and yellow cloak with the hood down. The breeze kept blowing his hair into his eyes, and he would sweep it back without any real success.

Curious, I walked up to him to ascertain the target of his gaze, but all I saw was empty pasture. He started upon my approach, then did a very creditable double take, for an amateur, upon seeing my make-up and motley.

"Forgive me, Signore," I said, bowing. "I did not intend to cause you alarm. I was intrigued by the object of your perusal."

He smiled. "Nothing to warrant any interest. I was merely counting rabbits."

I looked out upon the pasture again. "Let me assist you. There aren't any rabbits."

"Not now."

"Were there rabbits before?"

"No."

"Are you expecting rabbits shortly?"

"Not really."

I pulled my cap and bells off my head and held them out to him. "I think, Signore, that perhaps these truly belong to you."

He laughed. "Well met, fellow fool. My name is Leonardo, son of Gulielmus Fibonacci."

"I am Forzo, the Fool." It was a name. I've had many.

"I was thinking about rabbits," he continued. "What would happen if you placed a pair in a field such as this, and in a month they produced another pair, then that pair reaches maturity in another month while the original pair produces another, and so on?"

"I myself enjoy counting sheep, but only when I am stretched out on a pallet somewhere. Why on earth do you wonder about this?"

"The sequence of numbers interests me."

"Ah. You're a mathematician, then."

"Would that I were. No, merely a merchant's son, plying his father's trade. I came in on business from Bugia, but now that the business is completed, I await the changing of the winds to travel back across the sea. Having nothing better to do, I came out here to count invisible rabbits."

"A worthwhile hobby, and an inexpensive one as well. Tell me. Signore, what if the first pair produces a litter of three?"

"Then the third doesn't get to join the party. Who will it breed with?"

"Poor little runt. Still, the problem with your conjecture is that the stock will weaken unless you breed them with some outsiders. Otherwise, your series of rabbits will peter out in the long run."

"You're being far too practical for a fool."

I offered him my cap again. "Perhaps we should trade lives."

He sighed. "Sometimes I wish I could. It would make my life simpler. I've been thinking about writing a book of mathematics, but who would read it?" He hopped off the wall. "Are you heading into town?"

"I am, and would be glad of your company. I seek an old colleague of mine."

"That would be the Great Frenetto?"

"The very one indeed."

"I know where he lives. Come, good fool."

So, my ass having had his fill, we ambled amiably on-wards, and soon the towers of the city rose before us. It had been several years since I last set foot there, and I was eager to see how it had changed. Since the routing of the Saracens from Sicily, the trade had poured in, and the town had grown fat and prosperous. They had been working on a baptistery and a campanile to join the cathedral. I inquired as to their progress.

He gave me an amused look. "The baptistery is a fine building. All they need to finish is the dome. The campanile – well, I'll tell you about it when we get there."

We soon arrived at the great plaza. I liked the baptistery, despite my usual aversion to ecclesiastical profligacy. Like the cathedral, it was covered with pirated marble, white with dark green ornamentation. The campanile was beyond them, surrounded by scaffolding and cranes. It was about three stories to the good now, and the design was becoming apparent, the arcades echoing those of the cathedral opposite. Quite nice, yet there was something off about it.

"What is wrong with it?" I asked my companion. "I keep wanting to tilt my head slightly."

He shook his head. "Our greatest folly. They planned to build a tower to rival Babel, but they only dug the foundation ten feet. Everyone knows the ground is soft around here. It couldn't possibly support the weight. It's starting to go off the vertical. They've stopped construction temporarily and are trying to figure out what they are going to do next. I keep telling them that they should tear it down and start over, but they are talking about building it higher on one side to compensate. Ridiculous. One of the architects was from Innsbruck, but the other, Bonanno, is from here. He should have known better. So instead of increasing the glory of Pisa, we'll become the laughing stock of the Mediterranean."

"There's still ample competition for that title."

He shrugged. "In any case, your colleague lives on the Via Roma. Take this road, then turn right when you reach the Arno. It's an inn across from the third wharf that you see."

"Thank you, Signore. I hope that you have favourable winds for your voyage home."

It didn't take me long to find Fazio. He was out the back near the stables, practising his rope-walking while juggling four knives. He caught sight of me, somehow managed to wave in the middle of all of that activity, then did a back-flip off the rope, catching all of the knives in midair before landing.

"Not bad," I said. "*Stultorum numerus . . .*"

"*Infinitus est,*" he replied, completing the password. "Theo, riding Tantalo's ass. That can't be good. What happened?"

"He got drunk and thought he was you," I replied. "A broken leg."

"Oh, dear. Well, it's good to see you again. It must be three years."

"Five."

"Really? Yes, I remember now. You were coming back from beyond the sea with some minor royal personage or other. I take it you bring instructions from our childless father?"

I handed him the scroll from my pouch. He slit the seal, read it briefly, then snorted.

"Reconcile the Pisans with the Genoese by midsummer. Is that all? Maybe he would like me to resolve the Ghibelline-Guelph matter while I'm at it?"

"If you have the time. I'd help, but he wants me to unify the Latin and Eastern Churches."

"By King David, if I didn't know better, I'd say we were undertaking fools' errands."

"Did you make that up yourself?"

"Hmph. Theo, I can't even get the Pisans talking to each other. Everyone here is so rich that they can't be happy unless they have more than their friends and neighbours. The only thing that ever unites them is their hatred of the Genoese. And the only thing that ever unites them with the Genoese is their mutual fear of the Saracens. Tell Father Gerald that this place is getting too big for just one fool. There must be ten thousand people here year-round, plus whatever the tradewinds bring."

"I'll tell him."

"Well, please stay a few days. It's been too long since I've done any two-man work. We could do the Mirror, and the Puppeteer, and throw knives and clubs at each other."

"Sounds like old times. I'd be delighted."

"But please, for goodness' sake, don't be funnier than me. I have to keep working here after you leave. What instruments did you bring?"

"Lute, flute, and tabor."

"You always were good on the tabor. Excellent. Here, watch this." He whirled and flung the knives with both hands in rapid succession. They plunged into the post supporting the stable roof, one above the other.

"Nicely done," I said, inspecting the alignment. "Only they're slightly off the vertical."

"Of course," he said, grinning broadly. "We're in Pisa."

We rehearsed through noon, then gathered our gear.

"There's a party at the Gherardesca palace," Fazio informed me. "No particular occasion, just the usual ostentatious display. The Podestà will be there, along with the Viscontis, the Gualandis, the Albizzonis, and so forth."

"Any topics I should play with? Or avoid?"

"I completely forgot!" he cried, stopping short. "You don't know about the Great Conundrum."

"What Great Conundrum?"

"Oh, it's the main topic of gossip here," he said. "About two weeks ago, one of our more patriotic ladies of pleasure informed the Guard about a Saracen spy. They broke through the door, but the fellow leaped out the window and unfortunately impaled himself on the spears of the soldiers outside."

"Ouch."

"Indeed. So, they seized his things and found a letter written in Arabic script, only the words are complete nonsense."

"Some form of code."

"Of course, but it's a very good one. And that leads to the Great Conundrum: What does it mean, and more importantly, who is it for? The spy was coming here, which means that somewhere in Pisa, a Saracen agent is in place. Now, the Podestà has the letter in safekeeping. He can't show it around because he may end up showing it to the spy as a result."

"A pretty puzzle. How do they propose to solve it?"

"I planted an idea in their heads which may help. Send for an outsider who is a scholar of such things. That way, his loyalties won't be questioned. They're thinking about it. So, that's the Great Conundrum."

The palace in question was decked with pink marble. A giant pair of ebony doors led to the great hall. Above them were a series of balconies overlooking the family wharf where even now dozens of men were scurrying about unloading barges from further inland.

We, of course, did not use the ebony doors, but skulked around to the rear and came in through the kitchen. The household staff greeted Fazio, or Frenetto, with a great deal of warmth that they also extended to his friend and colleague Forzo once I had been introduced as such.

We worked our way through the crowd of guests, dropping a deft pun here, a pratfall there. The Mirror went well, the Puppeteer delighted the children. Yet we were not the principal entertainment, as it turned out.

While we were rigging Fazio's ropes from one balcony to another, a debate broke out in the group feasting below us. To my surprise, I saw the young man I had met in the morning at the centre of it, his dreaminess replaced by a fierce passion.

"I am telling you that the Islamic world has surpassed us in almost every way," he shouted. "They have preserved all that is good from antiquity and are building upon it. We just continue to close our minds and refuse to change anything because change frightens us."

"These are strong words, Signor Fibonacci," said the lord of this particular house. "Are you prepared to back them up?"

"Bring on your champion," challenged the youth. "The best man you have."

I was fully expecting armed combat at this point, but the man they brought in was of slight build and some fifty years. He was neither armed nor armoured, and carried only a flat wooden case tucked under his left arm. Neither was Fibonacci prepared for instant battle. I saw not a trace of steel upon his person. I beckoned to Fazio, and we sat on the rope above the group and watched.

The challenger reached into the case and produced . . . an abacus!

"What on earth are they going to do?" wondered Fazio. "That's Biolani, the chief abacist for the Gherardescas. Fastest beader in the city, according to those who care about such things. The young man . . ."

"His name's Leonardo Fibonacci. I met him on the way in. Says he's a merchant's son."

"He's being modest. His father now holds some diplomatic post in Bugia. The son's been all over the Mediterranean, knows the Arabs inside and out. So well, in fact, that many wonder if he's the Saracen spy the message was meant for."

A crowd gathered around the two, many actually betting on the outcome before they even knew the nature of the contest.

"Ten librae on your man," said Signor Albizzoni. "I don't see how this fellow could possibly do it short of conjuration."

"Ten on Fibonacci," cried Bernardo, a lesser Gualandi. "I have no idea what you're doing, Leonardo, but I knew your father well. You have smart blood in you, lad."

Leonardo bowed in his direction and settled on a chair, crossing one leg over the other. Biolani glared at him and set his abacus on the table before him.

Signor Gherardesca stood at the head of the table. "Forty-seven plus one hundred and ninety-three," he called out.

"Two hundred and forty," said Fibonacci as Biolani clicked away. "Too easy."

"Three hundred and twenty-seven less two hundred and sixty-three."

"Sixty-four," said Fibonacci. There were shouts of astonishment from the assemblage. "Try multiplication."

Gherardesca glanced around the room as money changed hands furiously. He cleared his throat. "Four hundred and fifty-three times ninety-eight."

Fibonacci leaned back in his chair with his eyes closed, his fingers twitching slightly. Apart from the chattering beads of Biolani's abacus, there was not a sound in the room.

"Forty-four thousand, three hundred and ninety-four," said Fibonacci, smiling.

"No!" cried Biolani, hands flying. "It isn't possible. He can't be right." He worked for another minute, then slumped in his seat, his hands falling by his sides.

"What magic is this, Leonardo?" asked Signor Gherardesca.

"No magic," replied Fibonacci. "Just superior mathematics. The Roman system is ridiculously designed for advanced calculations, but this Hindu-Arabic system is near miraculous. And I can teach anyone in this room how to use it, even Signor Biolani." All laughed, excepting the abacist, who flushed angrily.

"He's made an enemy there," whispered Fazio. "Biolani and the rest of the abacists virtually control the finances around here, thanks to the ignorance of the rest of us."

"Fibonacci's right, though," I said. "I learned the Arabic numbers when I was in Alexandria, although I would still need paper and ink to work them out. He seems to have mastered doing it with his mind alone."

"All right, check those knots again. I have work to do."

The Great Frenetto soon had the crowd enraptured, and I took the opportunity to observe them. I noticed a particularly stunning young woman in a crimson gown talking to Bernardo, the Gualandi brother who had won his bet on Fibonacci. She was gazing at the prodigy with an intensity bordering on ravin. The Gualandi said something. She laughed, never taking her eyes off Fibonacci. He turned, caught sight of her, and turned nearly the colour of her gown.

A little while later, Fazio came up to me. "Yon genius has conquered more than an abacist tonight," he said. "The widow Lanfranchi seems desirous of private instruction."

"Would that be the lady in crimson?"

"I see you've spotted her. She married young and old. That is to say, she was young, her husband old. And rich, of course. One day, his ship came in with silks and spices in the hold and the husband in a coffin. Ever since then, she's galloped from one young swain to the next."

"She does tend to attract the eye."

"And other parts, apparently. I hope Signor Fibonacci is

well fortified. He at least had the good taste to hire me for a serenade to start things off right."

"Good. Do you need me for a second voice?"

"No, thank you. Wait a second." He glanced around the room and laughed. "Would you be up for a bit of amusement?"

"It is only my reason to exist."

"See that unintelligent-looking fellow sulking by the fire?" I followed his gaze to see a somewhat horse-faced man staring at his feet. He looked up only to moon after the widow Lanfranchi.

"Luigi Tedesco, a merchant from Lombardy," Fazio informed me. "Her most recent former lover. I think he's just figured that out. Wouldn't it be funny if he hired you to serenade her tonight. A duel by proxy, with fools as their weapons of choice."

"I take it that the widow has wronged you sometime in the past."

"An unpaid serenade."

"A capital offense. All right, let me work my magic on the longing, long-faced Lombard."

I sidled over to Tedesco and leaned against the wall in an exact replica of his posture. "You seem distraught, Signore," I commented. "Perhaps I can be of assistance."

He sighed. "What could you possibly do to help me, Fool?"

"Sir, my mission in life is to fortify the forlorn, to rescue those in the fearsome clutches of boredom, and to bring parted lovers together again."

He looked up. "How do you manage the last one?"

"Signore, I am a practitioner of the craft of wooing through song. I have learned at the knees of the greatest masters of the art of courtly love. Retain me for a serenade tonight, and I assure you that you will want me for an aubade in the morning."

He brightened. "That sounds promising. What's an aubade?"

"The song sung to alert illicit lovers that dawn approaches, and that they must part to preserve appearances."

"I like the sound of that. All right, do you see that lady yonder?"

"By whose side Venus herself would blush with envy?"

"That's good!" he exclaimed. "Could you work that into the song?"

"Consider it done."

"And something with my name. It's Luigi."

"Meet me under her balcony at sunset," I said, wondering what on earth rhymed with "Luigi".

The party began to break up. Fazio and I collected our gear and some silver and returned to his room to plan the evening's entertainment.

"We should arrive by different routes," he said. "When we get close enough, I'll go ahead and seek out Fibonacci. You go around the other way and find Tedesco. This will be one well-serenaded widow."

As the sun began to set, we set forth for the lady's villa on the south part of the city. Fazio stopped me short of our destination and gave me directions to the side where her balcony was situated. I walked, tuning my lute and rewording a ballad by de Bornelh that I thought would suit the occasion. I was still puzzling over how to insert the merchant's name when I heard a woman scream. I peeked around the corner to see Fazio running in my direction. Someone was shouting for the guard. Dogs barked in the distance, followed by the clanking of armour.

"Come on," cried Fazio, and we took to our heels. He stopped abruptly and pulled me into an alleyway. We hid behind a pile of refuse just as several guards came running by.

"What's happening?" I whispered.

"Looks like neither of us is getting our fee tonight," replied Fazio. "My mathematician has slain your merchant."

"What?"

"As I was approaching, I heard the widow scream. Then I came upon Fibonacci standing over the body of Tedesco. He must have stabbed the poor fellow when he found out they were after the same thing." He struck himself on the side of his head. "Stupid, stupid Fazio. Have a little joke, and a man dies."

"Something's wrong there."

"Murder is rarely a righteous action, fellow fool."

We hid as the guards returned, dragging Fibonacci in chains. Four more carried the body of the late merchant on a plank.

"But he was dead when I arrived," the mathematician protested. "I never even saw him before."

"Save it," said the captain. "Plenty of time to confess in the morning."

We waited until it was quiet, then emerged from the alley.

"Poor mathematician. I fear his days are numbered," said Fazio. "It's all my fault."

"Did you see a knife?" I asked.

"What?"

"Did you see a knife? In his hand or in the body?"

"I don't think so," he said, considering. "I turned tail pretty quickly."

"Fibonacci was dressed in the same clothes he wore at the party this afternoon. Did he say he would come straight from the Gherardescas to meet you here?"

"Yes. There were going to be some games after we left."

"Then he couldn't have stabbed him. He was completely unarmed when we saw him earlier."

He stared at me. "Someone else killed Tedesco."

"Yes."

"But now Fibonacci's going to lose his head for it."

"Unless we do something about it."

He sighed. "I guess we have to, don't we? All right, let's go and take a look at the widow's balcony."

We strolled and strummed together, looking the way two fools ought to look in early evening. There were still several guards scurrying beneath the balcony when we went by. There was a crowd of onlookers watching from a distance, kept back by the sight of several spearpoints glinting in the light of the ascending moon.

"What do you think they're looking for?" wondered Fazio.

"Maybe the missing knife. Look, up there."

The widow was momentarily at the window, watching the activity below.

"Would you say that she is smiling?" I murmured.

"I would. Strange. One might think that the terror of such an experience, coupled with the simultaneous loss of past and future lovers, would have more of a heartrending effect on such a tender soul."

"Yet it has not. Let's go back to your place. I don't think we can get anything accomplished tonight."

He lit a candle while I unrolled my bedroll and stretched out.

"Who else would have a motive for killing Tedesco?" I asked.

"If we're talking about rivals for the widow's favors, then half the eligible bachelors in town, not to mention quite a few married men."

"Any other reasons? Enemies of Lombardy? Commercial competitors?"

"He's never struck me as the sort to make enemies. He's an unassuming fellow, competent but not exceptional at his work. Pays his debts on time, doesn't drink to excess, and is not possessed of sufficient wit to insult anyone to that extreme."

"Then why was he killed? Unless . . ." I sat up. "What if he was not the intended victim?"

"There's a thought. Someone wanted to kill Fibonacci, and waited in the shadows for a lusty swain to arrive. Only he got the wrong lusty swain."

"And fled, leaving Fibonacci to be caught with the body. Now, the Podestà may finish the task for him."

"Which leads us to the question of why kill Fibonacci?"

I fluttered my fingers across a row of imaginary beads. He nodded.

"It's a good place to start," he said. "We'll seek out Biolani in the morning."

The abacist was in the counting house, counting someone else's money. We barged in and sprawled across his table.

"Get out, fools," he growled. "Unlike you, I have to work for a living."

"As do we," protested Fazio. "Harder than you, in fact,

with far less in return. Oh, that these fingers could have acquired your skill with beads rather than the useless plucking of lutestrings."

Biolani sat back and glared. "I have no need of entertainment. Leave before I call the guard."

"It is those who say they have no need of entertainment who oft need it the most," I observed. "But call the guards if you must. We have no objection. We would welcome their presence in your office."

He looked at us suspiciously. "What would you here?"

"We just dropped by to congratulate you on your good fortune," cried Fazio. "A recent rival of yours has been most discomfited."

"Rival? Who, the Albizzonis' abacist?"

"A rival to all of your profession," I said. "And one who publicly humiliated you yesterday."

He snorted. "That pup, Fibonacci. So, what happened? Did he fall into the Arno?"

"Haven't you heard?" asked Fazio. "He was on his way to an assignation, only to find an assassination."

"Is he dead then?" asked Biolani.

"Would that grieve you?" I asked.

"I'm sorry for any man's loss," he replied carefully. "Actually, I was quite impressed by the lad. If he knows a faster way of doing this, I would be happy to learn it."

Fazio and I looked at each other. "But wouldn't that deprive you of your domain?" I asked.

Biolani chuckled. "My lords and masters are wealthy, stupid men who need poor, smart people like me to do their work for them. Whether by beads or by this Arabic system, it will still be Biolani who is trusted to count their money."

"So, you aren't worried about Fibonacci's fate?"

"Hasn't it been decided already?"

"It is in the Podestà's hands."

He looked puzzled. "But I thought you said he was murdered."

"Oh, dear," said Fazio. "I've muddled it again. No, Luigi Tedesco was killed, and they are saying Fibonacci did it to gain the widow's favours."

Biolani shrugged. "Foolishness. A pity that the young don't see the futility of lust until it's too late."

"Or greed," I said. "Consider sharing a coin with those who share such priceless news."

"Gossip is always free. Get out."

We got out.

"Not much reaction there," I commented.

"He even sounded sincere about wanting to learn the new system," said Fazio. "Maybe we should go back to the idea of another suitor for our widow."

"You know the gossip of this town. Who is a possibility?"

He pondered the question for some time as we walked along the river. "She's been dallying with Tedesco quite happily for the last two months. I was a little surprised that she would drop him so readily."

"Even given the impressive performance at the party? It may have piqued her interest when she saw what Fibonacci could do."

He shook his head. "That puzzles me as well. She's not a creature susceptible to the attractions of the mind. Her desires are decidedly more physical in their expression. And Fibonacci, although a pleasant enough fellow, is not exactly what I would consider meat for her table."

"Then maybe it was her intention to kill him," I said. "She lured him into a trap."

"But what would she have against him?" he protested. "What would anyone have against him? He's just a merchant. And he's been here all winter. Why now?"

"Something had to happen recently to make someone see him as a threat. Maybe something at the party." I stopped.

"Why are you striking yourself on the head?" asked Fazio with concern. "That's one of my moves."

"Chastising my brain for working so slowly," I said. "It's your Great Conundrum. What if the code requires not only knowledge of Arabic, but of the Arabic numbers?"

"And Fibonacci revealed that he had the ability to break it when he gave his demonstration last night! Excellent. You've narrowed the suspect list down to the hundred people at the party. Tell you what, let me buffet you a few times about the noggin and see if anything else falls out."

I waved my hands over my head like a cheap magician, tapped it once, and pretended to pull something out of my mouth which I then mimed reading.

"Tell me what you know about Bernardo Gualandi," I said.

"Why him?"

"Because he was talking to our widow right before she sought out Fibonacci."

"Interesting. Let's see. He's the third brother, so not in line for the lion's share of the business. Probably has the most talent in the family, but gets shipped around looking after their interests overseas. Speaks Arabic, which qualifies him. As far as the widow – I remember now, he came back on the same ship that carried her husband's body home for burial. He was unusually solicitous towards the poor grieving waif. Tongues were wagging briefly about it, but nobody knew for certain what they were up to."

"Maybe he knows something he could blackmail her with. Sounds like an excellent candidate."

"Even so, how do we go about proving it?"

"I have one idea."

Later that morning, we unfortunately got into an argument in the street.

"It couldn't have been that many," he protested.

"It was," I said. "How would you know? You weren't the one who went with them, you coward."

"Me? A coward?" he shrieked. "How dare you! Look, you've always stretched the truth, but this time I have you."

"Tell you what, we'll settle this fairly," I said. "You, sirrah. A favour, if you please." I grabbed a man passing by. It just so happened that it was Bernardo Gualandi. He stopped and looked at us in exasperation.

"What do you want?" he asked.

"Just to settle a wager between my brother fool and myself," said Fazio. "My colleague Forzo believes that since he trailed after the last Crusade begging their crumbs in exchange for his piteous attempts at amusement that he is now an expert on military matters."

"We've been having a dispute over how many soldiers passed through this town en route to the Holy Land," I said. "Now, I remember that there were fifteen boats leaving from Venice, and they each carried a hundred and thirty Crusaders. I say that makes two thousand men."

"And I say it makes eighteen hundred," said Fazio.

Gualandi looked at us wearily. "You're both wrong. It's nineteen hundred and fifty. Now, settle your differences and leave me alone."

"A thousand pardons," I said, bowing low.

"Nineteen hundred and fifty pardons," said Fazio, bowing even lower.

Gualandi walked away.

We turned into a narrow alleyway. The Podestà was standing there, watching Gualandi disappear.

"Very interesting," he said. "Come with me."

Fibonacci was being held in, what else, a tower, guarded heavily from below and inaccessible by any other means. The Podestà produced a set of keys from his robes and opened the entryway. The guards looked at us with mild curiosity, but made no comment. We climbed a long, spiral staircase until we came to the highest landing in the building. Another door gave way to the Podestà's keys to reveal Fibonacci sitting disconsolately by the window of his cell. He leapt to his feet upon our entry.

"Signore, you must believe me," he said urgently. "I am innocent of this foul deed."

The Podestà looked at him for a moment, then reached into a pouch at his waist and pulled out a sheaf of papers which he tossed onto a small table.

"These papers contain a message to someone in this town," he said. "I want you to decipher it, and tell me what it is you are doing as you do it. I will then take it to someone else to see if you are correct."

Fibonacci looked back and forth at us and the papers, then sat by the table and scanned them. "The characters are Arabic," he said. "But they make no sense. There are no words here. However . . ." He stopped. "Look how the letters of the words line up vertically. If you read them that way, they spell out the names of the Hindu-Arabic numbers. And if you were to take the numbers and apply them to the corresponding Arabic letters as they occur in their alphabet, they start to spell out, 'Bernardo Gualandi. Your information regarding the Pisan shipping routes proved accurate. Return by messenger the Gherardesca shipments and the boats carrying them.' It goes on."

"No need," said the Podestà. "I shall return later. Take hope, Leonardo." He motioned to us, and we followed him back down the stairs.

"I would prefer it if you kept quiet about your roles in this," he said.

"Suits us fine," said Fazio. "And we would request that you keep quiet about our roles in this as well. It's hard enough work being a fool without being called upon to solve murder cases all the time."

"I wouldn't worry about that," said the Podestà. "How often do people get murdered around here?"

There would be one more, as it turned out.

Fibonacci's solution to the Great Conundrum was confirmed, and he and Gualandi soon traded places. Shortly thereafter, Fazio received a message that we found greatly disturbing.

"Gualandi wants to speak with us," he informed me.

"What on earth for?"

"Let's go and find out."

We received permission to entertain the prisoners and eventually climbed to the top cell in the tower which Gualandi now called home.

"What shall it be?" asked Fazio. "A song? Some juggling?"

"I was thinking more along the lines of an escape act," said Gualandi.

"Really?" I replied. "Why would we do that?"

"Because I know about the Fools' Guild," he said.

"Everyone knows about the Fools' Guild," said Fazio. "All the best fools get their training there. So what?"

"Not everyone knows about the Guild's underlying mission," he said. "I know that you are spies and manipulators of kings, popes, and everyone underneath."

"Given that we regard kings and popes as the lowest of the low, that doesn't leave many others," commented Fazio. "But you speak of vague fancies, Signore. What proof have you?"

"It just so happens that I got drunk with a troubadour of your acquaintance," he replied. "One Tantalo. He got even drunker than I, and told me quite a few interesting stories."

"Oh, dear," Fazio and I said simultaneously.

"I know that you are working with your counterpart in Genoa to bring peace between the two cities. Not a bad idea on its face, but there are many here who might resent the effort. Such knowledge of your activities could be kept secret for a small price."

"Your freedom," I stated.

"There you have it. There's little time. A decision concerning my fate will be made by tomorrow."

"But we can't just walk you down the stairs past the guards," protested Fazio.

I glanced out the window. It was a good sixty feet to the flag-stones below. Another tower faced us from across the street.

"There's a way," I said.

Around midnight, Fazio and I perched on the top of the tower facing the jail. A candle was lit in the uppermost cell, and I drew my bowstring back past my ear and sent an arrow arcing across the street into Gualandi's cell. The string tied to the end uncoiled rapidly. Gualandi pulled the arrow from his door and held the string taut. I slipped the bow over the string and sent it spinning across. He took it, threaded the arrow and string around the leg of his cot, and shot it back in our direction. It landed on the tower roof beside us.

We tied a sturdy rope to our end of the string and began to coil up the end by the arrow. The rope travelled the string's route to the cell, then around the cot leg and back to our perch, giving us a two-rope bridge high over the guards below. So far, nothing we had done had made enough noise to attract their attention.

I tied both ends of the rope tight around the iron loop of

the door leading to the steps. Then, the Great Frenetto, another rope secured around his waist, walked lightly across the street into Gualandi's cell.

He held the second rope about four feet over the first. I held it tight at my end, and Gualandi carefully made his way from one tower to another, clinging to the upper rope for security. Once he had made it over, Fazio practically danced his way back, carrying the bow. We untied the rope ends, then pulled carefully back until the end repassed the anchoring cot leg. Then I gave it a good, hard tug, and it sailed safely back into our waiting arms, leaving another Great Conundrum for the Pisans: How did Gualandi escape the highest cell of the jail without leaving a trace of his flight?

We sneaked him down the stairs and through a back alley, then scampered northwards.

"Nicely done," he whispered as we approached the holy trinity of cathedral, baptistery, and campanile. "I'll definitely be able to make good use of you fellows."

"What do you mean?" I asked. "We've done our part." Fazio drifted behind us, looking back to make sure no one was following.

Gualandi smiled. It wasn't a pleasant sight. "If my knowledge of the Guild will make you do this, then it will make you perform other tasks I have in mind. I'm taking the two of you with me."

"Maybe we should leave you here," I said. "As it happens, I heard that the Podestà was thinking of using you to Pisa's advantage. He was planning to keep you alive."

"Unlike us," said Fazio, and his hands fluttered in the darkness.

Gualandi pitched forward, four knives in a perfect vertical formation in his back.

"Nice placement," I commented.

Fazio shrugged. "Just wanted to show you I can do it if I want to." He turned suddenly. "There's a patrol coming! What are we going to do?"

"Run?"

"We can't leave him," he said in panic. "The Podestà is sure to suspect us. We have to get rid of his body. But how?"

And then . . .

"And then what?" asked my wife, shaking me awake.

"What?" I mumbled.

"You fell asleep before you finished," she said accusingly. "What did you do with Gualandi's body? And why was Fazio still worrying afterwards?"

"There was a construction pit nearby," I said. "We dragged him to it, pulled our cloaks over it, and buried him with our hands."

"Oh, is that all?" she said, disappointed. Then she frowned. "Wait a minute. The only construction site would have been . . . You mean to say you buried him at the campanile?"

"As Fibonacci said, the ground was soft there," I said, grinning. "The scandal died down eventually, but the tower of Pisa leaned more and more, and Fazio lived in constant terror that they would dig up the foundation and find a corpse with a characteristic set of knife wounds in its back.

"We saw Fibonacci later that day . . ."

"I understand that I have the two of you to thank for my freedom," said the mathematician, blushing slightly.

"Us?" said Fazio, puzzled. "It was the Podestà who freed you, and you who led him to the true murderer. We were just passing through."

"If you say so," said Fibonacci.

"We do," I said. "This will all be forgotten soon enough, and we will be forgotten even sooner."

"Not by me," he said firmly, and he clasped our hands in a friendly farewell. "By the way," he added. "Did you hear that Gualandi escaped?"

"He won't get far," Fazio assured him.

"Not horizontally, anyway," I added.

Fibonacci looked at us, puzzled. "Your meaning, Fool?"

"It is my belief that he's going straight to Hell. Good day, Signore."

"I remember him!" my wife said excitedly. "When we were at the court of Frederick the Second, we visited Pisa. The emperor challenged this mathematician to solve some incomprehensible problems, and we all gathered and watched while he did it. That was your Fibonacci!"

"It was, my dove. Look at this." I pulled down a copy of the *Liber abaci* from a shelf and handed it to her.

"From him?" she asked. I nodded. She opened it to where I had placed a bookmark. "There it is! 'A certain man put a pair of rabbits in a place surrounded by a wall . . .'" she read. "Let's see. One, two, three, five, eight, thirteen, twenty-one . . . Well, it's a pretty series, but of what use could it possibly be?"

"None that I know of, but I'm just an ancient fool."

"There's an inscription here."

"Read it."

She smiled at me as she did, which was all the reward I needed in life. " 'To my many-named friend: The number of fools is finite, but of the counting of many rabbits there is no end. Yours, Fibonacci.' "

AUTHOR'S NOTE: The Fibonacci sequence has tantalized mathematicians and scientists for centuries. Related to the so-called Golden Mean, its numbers have been found to describe the patterns of seeds in sunflowers, scales on pine cones, and possibly even atomic nuclei and business cycles.

After decades of skirmishing, Genoa defeated Pisa in the Naval Battle of Meloria in 1284. The campanile, as of this writing, is still leaning.

# The Duke's Tale

## Cherith Baldry

*We all remember Geoffrey Chaucer as the author of the* Canterbury Tales, *composed during the 1380s, but it's easily forgotten that in his youth he was an agent for the King, some might say spy, and served throughout Europe, in particular France, Flanders and Italy. He is thus an ideal candidate for a genuine historical sleuth and Cherith Baldry first put this to good use in "The Friar's Tale" in* Royal Whodunnits *and again in "The Pilgrim's Tale" in the previous* Mammoth Book of Historical Whodunnits. *This is Chaucer's third outing.*

*Cherith Baldry is a former teacher and librarian who has turned to writing children's books and other fantasies. Her most recent offerings include a series of historical mysteries for young adults set in twelfth-century Glastonbury, which starts with* The Buried Cross *(2004).*

Jean Froissart rubbed his temples, trying to banish a pounding headache, and let the mild airs of the castle garden flow over him. He felt as if he had been sitting for a lifetime in the ante-chamber, while priests and physicians came and went on soft feet, and the last drops of Duke Lionel's life trickled away. Froissart could not hope any longer that his lord would recover.

He stood by the open door of Duke Lionel's apartments, screened from the rest of the garden by a rose trellis. The flowers were withering now that summer was over; a few dark crimson petals scattered the grass like gouts of blood. Laughter came from somewhere beyond, and instinctively Froissart drew back. He had no stomach just now for these Milanese, who could laugh while a man was dying. He wished there was something he could do, save write the letter he had been struggling with all morning, to tell King Edward in England that his son was no more.

He started at the sound of a brisk step coming from the passage that led to the main castle courtyard, and stared incredulously at the man who paused under the archway.

"Master Chaucer!" His voice was hoarse; he cleared his throat and tried again, hurrying forward the few steps that brought him to the newcomer's side. "Master Chaucer, I thought you were in England."

"Master Froissart, well met." Geoffrey Chaucer gripped his hand. His neat blue cottae and the brown cloak over it were dusty from the road, and he looked tired, but his eyes were as bright and his look as alert as when Froissart had known him in the English court. "My lord Edward sent me with letters for the duke. I travelled to Milan first, then to the court at Pavia, and they directed me here to Alba." He let out a faint puff of relief. "But now I see I've caught Duke Lionel at last."

Froissart shook his head. "No. Nor will you. He goes out on that last long road where none can follow."

Chaucer stared at him, his expression changed to consternation. "Dying?"

"Yes, he –"

Froissart broke off, turning towards the renewed sound of laughter. From this vantage point he could see past the rose trellis to the open space beyond. Autumn sunlight gilded the hair of the young man who sat with negligent grace on a marble bench beneath a tree. His companion, dark as he was fair, had just plucked a rose from the trellis beside them, a late bud, half-opened, as deeply crimson as a gout of heart's blood. The same colour smouldered in a ruby on the hand that held the flower, glinting in the warm light. Both men wore velvet doublets, tight-fitting in the latest fashion, with chains of gold and pearl that spoke of their nobility, or at least of their wealth.

Unable to restrain a soft sound of contempt, Froissart stiffened as both faces turned towards him. Their scrutiny was not hostile, but curious, he thought, the look of a cat before her paw flashes out to pin the mouse.

Chaucer bowed; reluctantly Froissart did the same, murmuring, "The fair sprig is Gian Visconti, son of Duke Galeazzo. The other is Ottone, Marquis of Montferrat, lord here at Alba." His private opinion of the pair of them he left unspoken.

"Duke Galeazzo?" Chaucer's voice was soft as his own. "That is the father of Duke Lionel's bride? The Duke of Milan?"

Froissart nodded. "With his brother Bernabo. The story is that they rule jointly – though Bernabo is keen enough to thrust his brother out of Milan to the lesser court in Pavia."

Gian had inclined his head in response to their marks of respect, but except for that single glance, half amused and half contemptuous, the young Marquis ignored them entirely. Speaking a few words in his own tongue to his friend, with a derisive tone that needed no translation, he turned and lounged away, sniffing delicately at the rose as he went.

Gian waved a hand in dismissal; Froissart took Chaucer along the path and through the door which led to a stair and then a tapestried ante-chamber. It lay empty as when he had left it, but he could hear the murmur of voices from deeper within the suite of apartments. Quietly pushing open the far door, he entered a larger room where a knot of courtiers were muttering together in a corner. At his entry with Chaucer they fell instantly silent, their gazes swivelling round to take in the new arrivals, then fell to their urgent muttering again. The door of Duke Lionel's bedchamber was still shut.

"Tell me what is happening," Chaucer asked, worriedly fingering the leather wallet he carried. "Is Duke Lionel truly not well enough to read these letters – or have them read to him? News from his father might cheer him."

"He'll never be well again in this world." Froissart lowered his voice, casting a glance at the group of courtiers. "He has lain in a fever for days now, and he grows ever weaker. These Milanese doctors are fools." He indicated another

closed door. "Duke Bernabo's personal physician has been in
the bedchamber with Duke Lionel these last three hours –
for all the good it will do."

"The duke is so close to death?" Chaucer's voice was
shaking.

Froissart nodded grimly. "I fear only God can save him
now."

"I must consult the physician," said Chaucer. "King
Edward will want to know – but I don't speak their tongue,"
he finished, sounding exasperated with himself.

"Nor I," said Froissart. "But they are not quite barbarians.
You will find they speak quite adequate French. They –"

He was interrupted by a shivering wail from the bedchamber, a woman's voice raised in a paroxysm of grief.
"*Morto! È morto!*"

Froissart and Chaucer stared at each other; Froissart felt
the breath catch in his throat. In any language there was no
mistaking what that cry meant.

The bedroom door was flung open; a young girl stood on
the threshold. Her cloud of dark hair was wildly dishevelled,
and as Froissart watched in consternation she tore at the
heavy pearl collar she wore, snapping the threads and sending pearls bouncing to every corner of the room. "*È morto!*"
she repeated.

An older woman came up behind her, dressed in the
russet gown and white wimple of a servant, and put an arm
around the girl's shoulders, murmuring words of comfort.
The girl began to pull away, then suddenly clung to her,
burying her face in the old woman's shoulder and breaking
into noisy sobs. The woman led her away, still hushing
her gently, and the group of courtiers, stark dismay in
their faces, hurried out after them, ignoring Froissart
and Chaucer.

Froissart felt as if the floor beneath his feet was about to
give way, as if the world itself was skidding out of control,
like one of the scattered pearls. All his memories of Lionel
showed the duke in motion: on horseback, or wrestling a
practice bout, or leading a lady into the dance. Impossible to
imagine him in the stillness of death. "Why did we come to

this accursed land?" He drove one fist into the other palm. "Are there no women left in England, that he must cross the sea to wed?"

"That was his lady – Violante?" Chaucer nodded towards the door where the distraught girl had left.

Froissart muttered assent. "No wonder she grieves," he added. "To wed a son of the King of England, and a decent, clean-living man at that – and handsome, as women reckon these things – and then to lose him, after no more than four months. I pity her." He spoke abruptly, half-ashamed to admit it. Running his hands through his hair, he went back to his work table in the window alcove and stood frowning down at the blank piece of parchment he had been staring at all day. "And now what am I to write to his father?"

Chaucer did not answer. Stooping, he began to gather up the pearls, collecting them in one cupped hand. "You still have not told me how it happened that the duke fell ill," he said after a moment.

Froissart sighed, not wanting to remember. "We stayed in Milan after the wedding," he began. "These Milanese . . . no extravagance is too much. Duke Bernabo poured out gold like water. Then we moved to Duke Galeazzo's court at Pavia – more feasting and ostentation. I thought it would never end, but at last Duke Lionel decided to take his leave and turn for home."

Chaucer trapped a large and lustrous pearl that was almost hidden by the edge of the tapestry. "This town isn't on the most direct route," he said.

"No." Froissart sniffed disdainfully. "Lord Ottone, the Marquis of Montferrat, invited Duke Lionel to be his guest. God, but he's a vicious young rogue! I'd hopes Lionel would refuse, but no, he thanked the wretched little viper for his courtesy, and everyone – Bernabo and Galeazzo and all their retinue – came here to Alba."

"And when did Duke Lionel fall ill?" Chaucer asked.

"Almost as soon as we arrived. There was a feast to welcome him on the first night. On the following morning he complained of feeling heavy and feverish –" Froissart clenched his hands at the memory "– but he rose and went riding with the dukes and the marquis. They brought him back on a litter made of green boughs, and he never rose from his bed again." For all his efforts, he could not stop his voice from breaking, and he stood with his back to Chaucer, a hand shading his eyes.

He heard the rattle of pearls as Chaucer deposited his collection tidily on the work table, then felt a hand rest on his shoulder. Froissart whipped round to face his friend. "There was treachery here," he whispered. "These Milanese are serpents all. Duke Lionel was poisoned!"

Chaucer swung round as he spoke, staring at the outer door. Froissart felt his stomach lurch with apprehension as he saw young Gian Visconti standing in the doorway, with two other men behind him. One of them was his father Galeazzo, tall and slender like his son, with the same red-gold hair and sleepy eyes. The other, a shorter, burly man with close-cropped dark hair and beard, was Galeazzo's brother Bernabo.

As Gian turned to his father to pour out an agitated stream of words, Duke Bernabo pushed past him and strode across to Froissart, grabbing him by the shoulders and giving him a rough shake. "Poison?" Rage made his voice so thick that his words were scarcely intelligible. "You dare say poison? *Falsità! Spergiuro!*" He lapsed into his own language, his face suffused with anger.

Froissart struggled vainly to free himself, visions flitting through his mind of his body broken and cast aside, or strangled under the furious duke's blunt hands. Chaucer stepped forward with a word of protest; at the same moment Duke Galeazzo snapped out a few words to his brother in his own tongue. Bernabo let out a roar of rage, but he released Froissart and pushed him contemptuously into a chair.

Shocked out of his usual languid affectation, Gian crossed the room to Chaucer and Froissart, and spoke quietly. "You have made an accusation. Our honour is tainted. My uncle says that if there was poison it was an English hand that gave it to your duke. There must be a traitor in his retinue, and here we have punishments for traitors – the *strappado*, the rack, the gouging of eyes –"

"Stop!" Chaucer exclaimed, looking sickened. "Until just recently, I was myself in Duke Lionel's household. He was a good lord to all of us."

The young man's lips twisted cynically. "And so powerful a man has no enemies? Truly the English must all be angels!"

Meanwhile the brother dukes confronted each other in the centre of the chamber. Though Froissart could not understand a word they said, their hostility was palpable, Duke Bernabo growling like a hound, his head thrust forward aggressively, while Duke Galeazzo spoke sharply but kept his temper under control. Eventually he grasped his brother by the arm and thrust him into Duke Lionel's bedchamber, tossing a few words over his shoulder to Gian as he went.

"My father is angry," Gian said unnecessarily.

Froissart could understand why. Duke Galeazzo had gone to much trouble, and spent a mountain of gold, to ally the Visconti family with the Crown of England, and with Lionel's death both effort and gold were wasted. If any man might be accused of poisoning Duke Lionel, it was surely not Galeazzo Visconti.

"My uncle wishes to have the whole of Duke Lionel's entourage put to the rack until one of you confesses," Gian went on. "For the moment my father restrains him, but if my uncle should prevail . . ." He shrugged, hesitated for a moment with an anxious look, and followed the two dukes.

"These Visconti!" Froissart exclaimed when he had gone, quivering with a mixture of fear and anger. "Tyrants!"

Chaucer signed to him for silence, his brow ridged in thought. Froissart realised that his unguarded accusation had brought this trouble on them; if he had known that their hosts could hear him he would have kept silence.

"We must ride for England," he said edgily, cursing himself for the indiscretion. Lionel's household could find themselves tortured or put to death for an imagined crime. He had no confidence that the milder Duke Galeazzo would prevail for long over his bloodthirsty brother.

His spine pricked with apprehension as Chaucer shook his head. "No, my friend. Duke Lionel's whole retinue could not pack up and leave without alerting the Visconti. That would be an admission of guilt. Our best hope is to stay for Duke Lionel's funeral ceremonies and take our leave in the usual way."

"And wait to be dragged into the dungeons?" Froissart made a wordless sound of contempt.

"Or," Chaucer added thoughtfully, "we could discover ourselves who did this deed."

Before Froissart could reply, the bedchamber door opened again and all three of the Viscontis emerged. They had not taken long to pay their respects to the dead man; probably they had only wished to make sure that he was truly dead. They did not speak as they crossed the ante-room, though Duke Bernabo fixed a glare on Froissart and Chaucer that promised retribution.

Chaucer followed them to the door and waited until their footsteps receded. Then he turned back to Froissart. "Perhaps we should see whether Duke Lionel's body can tell us anything."

He went into the bedchamber; Froissart stared after him, immobile for a moment, then with an effort flung off his paralysis and followed. Here the shutters were closed, the air heavy with the smell of herbs, blood and sweat. Chairs and benches were strewn with robes of silk and velvet, heavily embroidered with gold. A surcoat bearing Lionel's arms was wadded up on the floor. A plumed, gilded helmet stood on the table beside a gold cup encrusted with rubies that winked in the dim light.

A priest was kneeling at a prie-dieu by the door, muttering his prayers. In the shadows of the bedcurtains, a tall, greying man bent over the body of Duke Lionel, as if he had just finished composing it. Chaucer drew nearer to look down at the man whose servant he had been; Froissart stood at his shoulder, half afraid of what he would see. Lionel's handsome face looked pale and waxy. His jaw had dropped; his springing golden hair was dull as straw and dark with the sweat that had soaked it. Froissart shook his head. His lord had departed, leaving only this shell.

If Chaucer felt the same sense of loss, he showed it only in an increase of gravity as he faced the man by the bed. "My name is Chaucer; I have come from the duke's father in England," he said. "You are the physician?"

The man bowed his head in assent. "I am Master Jacopo, physician to Duke Bernabo. I assure you that nothing more could have been done." He took from the chest beside the bed a jar with a giant leech clinging to the inside, clicking his tongue in vexation as if it was somehow responsible for the death of his patient. "All the aspects were evil," he added with a sigh of resignation. "His death was written in the stars."

"And what was the cause of it?" Chaucer asked.

"A fever struck him down. He overtaxed his body and unbalanced the humours," Master Jacopo explained disapprovingly.

Froissart was not sure how far they could trust this man. He reflected that Duke Bernabo's personal physician would hardly talk of poison, especially if Duke Bernabo had any hand in administering it. Brought up short by the thought, he wondered whether Bernabo might really have murdered Duke Lionel; he was violent enough. Yet like Duke Galeazzo, Bernabo would have valued the alliance between Milan and England, and would have done nothing to destroy it.

Master Jacopo had turned away to fiddle with the electuaries in his chest. Chaucer gave Froissart a thoughtful glance, and spoke in a voice too low for the physician to hear. "Is he an honest man? Could he have given poison in the place of physic?"

Froissart shrugged. "Honest but incompetent," he replied bitterly. "Duke Lionel fell ill almost as soon as he arrived in Alba. The doctor had no reason to attend him before that."

"Then we must acquit Master Jacopo," Chaucer murmured.

Froissart let out a faint sigh. When the king had sent him with Duke Lionel on this mission to Milan, he had looked forward to the fabled splendour of the court, to the music and especially the poetry that poured from this land. The great Petrarch himself had attended Duke Lionel's wedding, though he had not deigned to speak to an obscure clerk. Chaucer must have felt the same, Froissart realised, remembering his friend's scribbled verses. Now he was faced with his lord dead, and the shadow of treason over all the English retinue.

Murmuring thanks to Master Jacopo, Chaucer returned to the ante-chamber, closing the bedroom door softly behind him. "Nothing there to tell us who wrought the duke's death. Tell me, Master Froissart, you said that he felt ill at first on the morning after he arrived. If he was poisoned, most likely it was at the feast the night before."

"True, yet . . ." Froissart shook his head thoughtfully. "The wine was poured from ewers to all the guests equally. And each of the dukes' dishes was tasted before they ate. A murderer could not have poisoned Duke Lionel without poisoning half the court as well."

"Who sat next to the duke at table?"

Froissart's gaze grew unfocused as he made himself remember. "Duke Galeazzo on one side," he said at last. "And the Marquis of Montferrat on the other." He snorted. "The Marquis would poison his own grandmother for a jest."

"Would he now . . ." Chaucer's gaze sharpened, and Froissart guessed he was remembering the dark young man in the garden, his derisive look and the rose smouldering in his hand. "Then I must find occasion to speak with *Messire* Ottone."

Before supper that night the whole court was summoned into the chapel to attend a Mass for the repose of Duke Lionel's soul. Duke Lionel lay there in state, on a bier covered with a silken pall that bore his coat of arms.

Chaucer made sure he and Froissart arrived early, and stood unobtrusively near the doors to observe the greater folk as they came in.

Duke Galeazzo was one of the first, leading his wife, the Duchess Blanche, and their daughter, the widowed Violante. She had recovered self-control since Froissart had seen her fleeing from Duke Lionel's bedchamber, and followed a pace behind her mother, her face pale, her huge dark eyes fixed modestly on the ground. She was gowned all in black, with no jewels, no ornament at all except for a darkly crimson rose fastened in her bosom.

Her uncle Bernabo strode in after her and halted, glaring round as if he expected to confront an enemy. Seeing none, he stalked forward and planted himself in front of the altar with a commanding expression as if he was about to issue an order to God.

More knights and ladies followed, some unknown to Froissart, and a few of Duke Lionel's own people, their worried looks showing that the rumour of poison had already reached them. Last of all, when the candles were lit and the priest appeared to begin the Mass, came Gian and Ottone, their heads together, a murmuring conversation between them that only ceased when Duke Galeazzo turned and fixed a severe look on his son.

Throughout the familiar ritual of the Mass, Froissart saw Chaucer narrowly observing Lord Ottone, and wondered if his friend was coming to any conclusion. The Marquis was making no attempt to disguise his boredom, fidgeting and yawning elaborately, and leaning across now and then to whisper something to Gian, who kept his gaze fixed dutifully on the altar.

When the service was at an end and the priest had dismissed the congregation, Chaucer stepped into the Marquis's path as he made to leave the chapel. "With your leave, *Messire*, a word with you."

Lord Ottone's look darkened; he spat out something that sounded like a curse. To Froissart's relief, Gian appeared beside him.

"My lord," Chaucer said hastily, "it is vital that I speak to my lord Ottone in this matter of Duke Lionel's death."

Gian nodded. "They are right," he said persuasively to his friend. "This dishonour will taint all of us if we cannot come to the truth. Do you wish men to say that murder was committed under your roof?"

The Marquis still frowned, but he allowed Gian to lead him out of the chapel as far as an alcove in the passage beyond, where a window of tiny panes of leaded glass blurred and distorted the image of the darkening garden. Froissart followed them, everything in him alive with suspicion.

"My lord Ottone, why did you invite Duke Lionel and his followers to Alba?" Chaucer began.

Ottone's brows went up. "It was for hospitality, to do honour to the English duke. Why else?"

Froissart considered that. The gesture was no more than might have been expected of a friend of the Viscontis, yet he could not help reflecting that the invitation would have drained Lord Ottone's coffers, and wondering what he hoped to gain in return for his generosity.

"You were seated beside Duke Lionel at the welcome feast?" Chaucer went on.

Lord Ottone's look was bland as he answered. "Of course. He had the place of honour."

"You saw no one place poison in Duke Lionel's food or wine?"

"Of course not." Now the Marquis sounded bored. "Would I have kept silence if I had?"

"Perhaps not." Chaucer took the deep breath of a man who prepares to dive into icy water. His hand shot out and gripped Lord Ottone by the wrist. Froissart could not restrain a gasp of shock. What was Chaucer about? A lowly esquire did not lay hands on the Marquis of Montferrat and hope to escape with those hands intact.

"And this?" Chaucer said evenly.

Before the Marquis, with a hiss of outrage, could pull away, Chaucer flicked at the great ruby he wore. Froissart felt almost limp with relief to see the stone hinged back to reveal a cavity between it and the setting. A few specks of white powder still clung there.

"A poison ring!" he breathed.

Lord Ottone freed himself, covering the ring defensively with his other hand. His face contorted with fury, he spat out a long stream of words in his own tongue, then stopped himself with a snarled curse and continued again in French.

"The ring is a curiosity – I wear it for a jest. I do not use it. I did not use it that night."

Chaucer was looking sceptical; Froissart shared his doubts. He was certain that Lord Ottone would find many uses for his poison ring in the convoluted courts of the Milanese. Had he really used it to murder Duke Lionel?

"Why should I kill your English duke?" the Marquis added contemptuously. "What was he to me? Why should I wish to break the alliance with England? It advantages me nothing."

"True, you care nothing for the alliance." Apprehension flickered over Chaucer's face and Froissart tensed as he wondered what his friend would say next. "But you care a great deal for Duke Lionel's wife."

Fury flared again in Lord Ottone's eyes. "*Scellerato!*" he hissed, and flung away down the passage.

Gian watched him go. His face was white and his voice trembling. "My sister was to have wed Ottone, until my father made this marriage with the English duke. Do you truly think. . . ?"

"What do you think, my lord?" Chaucer countered.

Gian could find no answer. He cast one more desperate look at Chaucer and then fled down the passage in pursuit of his friend.

"Are you mad?" Froissart demanded. "Accusing the Marquis of murder in his own castle! You're lucky not to be strung up by the thumbs in his dungeon – and me with you," he added.

"It was you who first spoke of poison, my friend," Chaucer reminded him tranquilly.

"And how did you know – that Lord Ottone had cast his eyes on Violante?"

Chaucer smiled; he looked almost smug, Froissart thought, trying to hide his annoyance.

"I saw the rose she wore," Chaucer explained. "Surely the same rose that the Marquis plucked from the trellis. Winter draws near, and there are so few flowers left. That he gave it to her, and she wore it, even in her grief . . . it's not hard to understand."

"If she truly grieves," Froissart said, a cloud of suspicion swirling in his mind.

It was Chaucer who gave voice to it. "Indeed. She would have spent the night with Duke Lionel. Perhaps he was not poisoned at the feast at all."

"But she's a child!" In the end, Froissart could not bring himself to believe it. "Scarce fourteen . . . surely she would not? It must have been Lord Ottone!"

Chaucer sighed and let himself slip down onto the bench in the window alcove, running his hands through his hair. He looked exhausted; Froissart remembered that he had already travelled far before he arrived at the court.

"If Duke Lionel was poisoned at the feast," he began slowly, "only Lord Ottone had the chance to do it. Or Duke Galeazzo, but he had the best reason of all for keeping our duke alive. So perhaps we must consider whether the poison was given to him in some other way. Violante had the best chance to do that."

"I'll never believe it!" Froissart argued. "Besides, there are many ways to kill a man. Poisoned tapers in his bedchamber . . ."

"But that would have killed Violante too," Chaucer reminded him. His fingers tapped an impatient rhythm on the bench where he sat. "If we discover how Lionel was poisoned, then we will surely know who poisoned him. Did he eat or drink nothing except at the feast? You were close to him, you would have seen. No boxes of tainted sweetmeats?"

Froissart shook his head. "Only the wine when he first arrived."

"What?" Chaucer sprang to his feet again, fatigue wiped from his face. "What wine?"

"We dismounted in the courtyard." Froissart closed his eyes in an effort to picture exactly what happened among so many milling men and horses. "Lord Ottone came out to welcome us."

"And gave wine to the duke?" Chaucer asked eagerly.

"Yes . . . no! It was Duke Bernabo who gave him the wine."

Chaucer let out a long sigh. His eyes were blazing and his lips moved into a small, feral smile. Froissart felt chilled; for a moment his friend looked quite unlike the quiet, unobtrusive esquire of the king's household.

"No – no," he protested. "Duke Bernabo himself drank

from the cup before he gave it to Duke Lionel. The wine couldn't have been poisoned."

Chaucer's triumphant look gave way to frustration. "Yet *Bernabo* gave it to him. Why Bernabo? Duke Lionel was the Marquis' guest."

Froissart shrugged. "Duke Bernabo thrusts himself forward everywhere."

"Yes, true." Chaucer's eyes lit again and he gripped Froissart by the shoulders. "True! And yet he did not demand for himself the place of honour at the feast that night. Duke Lionel sat between the Marquis and Duke Galeazzo. Where was Bernabo?"

Once again Froissart closed his eyes and caught at memory. "Violante was beside the Marquis, and the Duchess Blanche beside Duke Galeazzo . . . Bernabo was further down the table."

"Such humility! Why so – unless to distance himself so that no one could suspect him of poisoning Duke Lionel at the feast?"

"But why should he kill our duke?" Froissart protested. "Why, when he went to so much trouble to make the alliance?"

"A good question." Chaucer released his clasp on Froissart's shoulders, paced a little way down the passage and turned back. "But the wrong question, for all that. Duke *Galeazzo* made the alliance, wedding his daughter to the son of the King of England. You said yourself that though the dukes are supposed to rule equally in Milan, Bernabo was eager to thrust Galeazzo out into the lesser court at Pavia. But with Violante married to Lionel, the balance of power shifted. Perhaps Bernabo would have found himself thrust out, when his brother had so powerful an ally as England."

"But he shared the wine with Lionel!"

Chaucer let out a puff of strained laughter. "Of course . . . once again to prove his innocence." Frowning, he thought briefly and then asked, "Where did the cup come from?"

"I'm not sure." Froissart remembered the chaos in the courtyard, with the retinues of all three dukes, men and horses, getting under each other's feet. "I saw Bernabo standing beside Duke Lionel's horse, with the cup in his hand. He took a mouthful of the wine, then handed the cup up to Lionel. It was one of these massive things with two handles, gold, covered in jewels. Lionel drained the cup and made to give it back, but Bernabo said it was a gift."

Chaucer's eyes narrowed. "And where is the cup now?"

"In Duke Lionel's bedchamber. You must have seen it there yourself."

Froissart started as Chaucer gripped his arm and towed him down the passage, back to Duke Lionel's apartments. The bedchamber was empty now, the priest and physician long gone, the body removed to lie in the chapel, but Lionel's possessions lay where they had been scattered. The jewelled cup stood on the table beside the gilded helmet, the rubies glittering in the light of the taper Chaucer held.

Froissart reached out for it, but Chaucer held him back. "Have a care, my friend. Here, hold this close so we can see."

Handing Froissart the taper, he picked up a heavy hawking glove that lay on the floor at his feet and put it on. Only then did he dare to touch the cup, turning it towards the light.

Froissart drew in a harsh breath, hardly sure of what he was looking for in the uncertain, dancing flame. Then as Chaucer gripped the handle a thin needle shot out of the elaborate gold ornamentation, missing his forefinger by a hairsbreadth. It flicked back again, like the tongue of a snake, but not before Froissart had seen the discolouration on the tip. In his mind he could recall a bright picture of Duke Bernabo in the castle courtyard, holding the cup by the base and reaching up to the mounted Duke Lionel, who bent to take it by the handles.

"Not the wine," Chaucer said, with a drawn-out sigh of satisfaction. "The cup."

Servants thronged the passageways as the hour of supper drew near. Froissart waited anxiously as Chaucer intercepted a man with a golden ewer just outside the door to Duke Galeazzo's apartments. "Tell Duke Galeazzo that I need to speak to him in private."

The servant gave him a contemptuous look. "*Insolenza!*

Duke Galeazzo has better things to do. Wait with the other petitioners when he holds court tomorrow."

He tried to push past, but Chaucer stood his ground. "Tell your duke," he said levelly, "that he had better speak with me unless he wants war with England."

The servant's superior expression abruptly vanished. He hurried into the apartment and reappeared a few moments later to beckon Chaucer and Froissart inside. Duke Galeazzo received them in a small side chamber, heavily tapestried, with few furnishings except the chair where he sat. The door closed behind them, cutting off the sound of chattering and laughter from the courtiers in the next room. Froissart glanced back to see Gian Visconti standing with his back to the door, his languid posture not masking the fact that his hand rested on a small, jewelled dagger. Froissart swallowed. He realised that there was a good chance he and Chaucer would never leave the room alive.

"Well?" Duke Galeazzo said. "What do you want?"

"To show you this, my lord." Chaucer was still holding the poisoned cup, with the hand that wore the hawking glove. "Observe, but do not touch." He gripped the handle again and the poisoned dart flickered out and vanished once more.

The duke's brows snapped together in a frown. He examined the cup carefully, then raised his gaze to meet Chaucer's. Froissart breathed a little more easily to see that his impatience had vanished; he seemed to show no more than honest concern.

"Where did you get this?"

It was Froissart who replied. "This is the cup that Duke Bernabo gave to Duke Lionel when he came here to Alba."

There was a harsh gasp from Gian, who had drawn closer so that he too could examine the cup. His father glanced at him, but addressed Chaucer. "I could have the two of you killed, and the cup melted down."

Fear thrilled through Froissart, but if Chaucer felt the same he did not show it. "I do not think you are such a man, my lord."

Duke Galeazzo shook his head. "Then what am I to do?"

Froissart noticed that he made no attempt to defend his brother or argue that he could not be guilty. Clearly he knew Bernabo too well.

"Arrest my uncle!" Gian leant urgently over his father's chair. "Put him to death for murder – then you can rule alone in Milan."

Froissart would not have thought there was such a fire in the young man. It smouldered in his eyes as his father waved him away.

"I cannot do that," he said. "Milan would split into factions, his followers and mine. There could be war."

"There could be war with England," Chaucer reminded him.

The duke looked trapped. Froissart could see his dilemma. He could imprison them or order their deaths, but that would only raise more questions, among the rest of Lionel's retinue and back in England.

"A bargain," Chaucer continued, when the silence had dragged out for a century. "Keep the cup. Allow us and the rest of our duke's people to take our leave unharmed. In return, we will keep silence. We will tell King Edward that Duke Lionel died of over-exertion, as Duke Bernabo's physician told us."

Struggling with the injustice that Bernabo would not pay for his crime, Froissart could not help an inarticulate protest, but Chaucer cut it off with a glance.

"You would trust me?" Duke Galeazzo asked indecisively.

"We must trust each other," Chaucer pointed out. "I think none of us here wants war."

After another long silence Duke Galeazzo nodded, and at once Gian broke in eagerly. "Ottone and I mean to hunt tomorrow. We will invite my uncle to go with us. If the chase takes us far enough – and it will – we can spend the night at Ottone's lodge in the mountains. By the time we return, Duke Lionel's retinue can be long gone."

Froissart looked at the young man with a sudden, startled respect. The plan was a good one. He had been wrong, he could see, to dismiss Gian as an empty-headed peacock. Perhaps he had the makings of a finer ruler than his father.

"Very well." Duke Galeazzo rose to his feet. "And now I must go to supper, or Bernabo will begin to wonder what we speak of, closeted alone like this. Gian, attend me."

He went out, but for a moment his son did not follow him. He drew closer, and rested a hand lightly on Chaucer's arm.

"My father is weaker than his brother," Gian said, "and he loves peace. My uncle despises him. He despises me, too." A small smile curved his lips, but did not touch his eyes. "One day he will discover how foolish that is. Do not fear, my friends. Your English duke will not go unavenged." His voice dropped; Froissart shivered at the look in his eyes. "Do they not say that revenge is a dish best eaten cold?"

# Sea of Darkness

## Sarah A. Hoyt

*One of the great forgotten European heroes is Prince
Henry of Portugal, known as Henry the Navigator. He
was the son of King João of Portugal and, through his
mother, was a grandson of the English John of Gaunt. He
lived from 1394 to 1460 and much of his life was as a result
of the wars between the Portuguese and the Muslims –
again we are back to the continuing spectre of the Crusades. Henry, or Henrique as we should call him, established a school for navigators and erected an observatory.
It was thanks to Henry's efforts, education and finances
that the islands of Madeira were discovered in 1418, the
Cape Verde Islands in 1446 and the Azores in 1448. Most
of Henry's efforts were put into exploring the west coast of
Africa, but it's possible that some of his navigators ventured further west and could have reached America before
Columbus. Henry was driven not just by the desire for
discovery but for the determination to spread the Christian
faith against the growth of the Muslims.*

*Though now resident in America, Sarah Hoyt was born
in Portugal and is of Portuguese descent. Local legend has
it that her mother's family is descended from Goncalo
Mendes da Maia, the Portuguese kingmaker. She has
published three Shakespearean fantasy novels, starting
with* Ill Met By Moonlight *(2001), which was short-
listed for the Mythopoeic Award, and has an historical
mystery novel in the pipeline.*

"The body will smell, Your Highness," the priest said.

Father Alexandre was new in the village, a young man of gangly build. He went lurching down the uneven path over the cliffs to the beach, his black habit flapping like wings with his every movement – a crow of a man in the bright sunlight.

Prince Henry, Infante of Portugal, his master and mine, followed behind, managing to walk smoothly and calmly over the same path looking cool and collected in the same black the priest wore.

"We should have buried it, already," the priest said. "Why Your Highness wants to pollute himself by going near a suicide's body, I don't understand."

Following behind, more reluctantly, I didn't understand either. But then I was a 21-year old secretary of plebeian origin. In Prince Henry's village, at Sagres, at the edge of the world, surrounded by learned men and cunning ones, I was used to not understanding most of what happened. And my prince's mind was a mystery to me, as it was to most.

Prince Henry – or as the local parlance went Infante Anrique – the third son of the late king of Portugal and brother of the current one, rarely explained his ideas or his motives to anyone.

A large man, or at least large for the Portuguese mold, he wore black tunic and hose and – outside – a broad-brimmed black hat. Between tunic and hat an average face appeared: high bridged nose and square chin, generous lips and eyes narrowed against the glare of the same sun that had tanned the skin a reddish gold.

His paternal grandmother had been a farmer's daughter, impregnated by Don Pedro, king of Portugal.

But my prince's mother was Philippa of Lancaster, from the islands of Britain. Though I knew little of the history of those distant lands, it was said that Queen Philippa's father had been a prince named John of Gaunt, whose ambition and intelligence made him eclipse even the kings he ostensibly served. And my prince was his mother's son.

His being the third son of a king, it would have been easy for Prince Henry to lead a life of leisure. Dispensations could be sought for his vows as Master of The Order of Christ. He could have had any pleasure he craved, carnal or otherwise.

But Prince Henry moved upon a different tide. In him the craving for power and dominance had turned to a longing to master the unknown ocean – those lands that learned men marked as terra incognita, those oceans they charted as Sea of Darkness.

The prince said he wanted to take the light of Christ to those lands. He said he wanted to claim them for Portugal.

But I thought his ambition was more than faith or love of country. I'd been his secretary for five years, I'd seen him peruse maps and send ships off, then wait with anxious hope for their return and I thought I understood him. He wanted to uncover the world with trembling hand and to possess it naked and whole in his mind's eye. What mortal flesh could compare to that? What earthly pleasure could compete?

This thirst had led him to build this village – Vila do Infante – the scattering of white houses behind us. His ambition had ran his purse bare to populate those plain, square houses with learned men – Christian and Jew and Arab, cartographer and ship builder and inventor of nautical instrument.

His anxiety for his village had brought him here, running to the beach, at the report of a drowned man found upon the sand, wearing clothes fine enough to belong to one of the apprentice discoverers at the school.

The priest complained and the prince remained silent past the road and onto the rocky ground, then past that, to where the dunes rose that hid the flat, white-sand beach beyond. Between the dunes I caught a glimpse of the emerald sea and was filled with a sense of eternity.

The ancients believed this land, Sagres – which they called the Sacred Promontory – was at the edge of the world and the beginning of never-ending ocean. My prince believed differently. If he was right –. If he . . .

"I will go no further," the priest said and stopped, where rock met sand. He turned to look at us. He had pale skin and curiously hard features, the features of a spoiled noble youth who'd been hemmed – possibly against his will – into the discipline of the Church and God's service. He crossed his arms on his chest. The sensuous mouth gone hard opened to pronounce unforgiving words. "It is just a suicide, Milord. We're not commanded to give him charity nor Christian burial. He is but refuse and should be disposed of as such."

Silently, the prince walked around the priest, onto the soft, white sand and removed his fine-suede court slippers. Flinching at the heat of the sand on his feet, he walked gingerly into the whiteness of the dunes.

I took my slippers off and followed. For a moment it looked as if the priest would put out a hand to stop me, but his half-started movement stopped and I ran past, catching up with the prince.

"Ah, Tiago," he said, as I caught up. "Do you know who the unfortunate is?"

I shook my head. I thought of Luis who hadn't been seen in the village – nor even in the tavern outside it – for a week but I shook my head. There were three or four young men who'd disappeared over the last month, in just such a way.

Young men aged anywhere from fourteen to twenty-one – and older men too – came here to learn the skills they hoped would make their names as great discovers of new lands. And just as many left, dismayed that such heroic deeds required that they learn to read, to interpret maps, to calculate a course. Luis could not be dead. He'd been too afraid to meet me, that was all. Afraid of what I might truly know. Doubtless, he'd left in the night without even taking his effects and was now somewhere in Spain. Conferring with his masters . . . I bit my inner cheek, wondering what he was telling them and if any of it – anything he'd learned about maps or navigation – would be of use to them. I hoped not. I'd given him warning. A chance to escape. And a chance for me to get fair Leanor's attention in Luis's absence.

The prince stared at me, and the silence weighed heavy between us.

"No. Some fishermen found him and brought the alarm to the village. They said men from the school were keeping watch," I said. "And that he was dressed as one from the school."

Prince Henry inclined his head sideways. "And yet Father Alexandre is so sure he is a suicide."

I bit my lower lip. Indeed. How else could a young man from the school drown? After all, most were all from families from the extreme North and extreme South of Portugal, families that of necessity survived by fishing and probably smuggling and piracy. They all could swim like fishes. And they never went to sea from the school itself, save in training boats with a large crew. No loss from those boats had been reported. So, what other way could one of them have drowned, but self murder, jumping from one of the precipitous cliffs around the village into the sea below?

But I was not about to correct the prince. I held my silence.

Descending the dune, on the other side, my feet sliding on the loose sand, I caught a whiff of rotted meat laced with that peculiar sweetness that marks human cadavers – that stench that our body recognizes as a smell of our own mortality.

I hesitated, but Prince Henry went on, adjusting his stride to climbing down the hill, slippers in hand. I could only follow.

It was low tide. The sea had deposited the corpse on the sand, then retreated, as though appalled at its daring. Before us, the beach opened as a wide expanse of sand, most of it wet. Near the sea, two young men stood by a dark bundle sprawled on the sand.

As we neared the stench grew worse and the bundle resolved itself into a human body. It lay sprawled on the sand, arms wide like Christ on His cross. The hair was reddish, the body large. It wore a fine dark tunic and stockings.

At first I thought the corpse had belonged to an enormously fat man, but then I realized it was merely swollen with gases. Likewise, up close, I could see the hair was not red; something had made red highlights gleam on the dark strands. Long green tendrils of seaweed wrapped the head like a macabre headdress.

The young men beside the body were my age or just about.

They were Pedro and Miguel Aguila. I knew them well. Oh, not from our normal duties or interaction in the course of our chores. No. But a few of us had taken to frequenting the tavern outside the village, after our round of daily work was done. Brothers from the far North and looking like it, Pedro and Miguel were dark-haired young men with ruddy cheeks and dark eyes who looked much like the Castillians on the other side of the ill-defined northern border with Spain. Miguel, the older one, was good at dice, a power to be reckoned with at the gaming tables and, as such, always flush with money. And Pedro was good with an improvised rhyme and had a strong, melodious voice that turned many a head in the tavern. Including Leanor's. The innkeeper's fair daughter had been paying Pedro a lot of attention since Luis had left. I thought of the blonde beauty leaning on his broad shoulder and sighed. My plan had not worked as I'd hoped.

Prince Henry walked right up to the corpse, looked down at the pale, bloated face, and grunted as if he'd found something of interest. Setting his slippers down beside him, on the wet sand, he started examining the corpse. He ran his large, reddish hands along the corpse's clothes, felt the spongy skin and pulled aside the curtains of crimson-stained hair.

Prince Henry's hands were tanned and callused, and this was how he always used them, like an extra pair of eyes, picking up instruments, and tracing outlines on maps with his finger. It was as though the blood of his working-man ancestors running in his veins made him incapable of understanding anything he could not feel and touch.

I approached hesitantly. The stench was worse. It was a taste in the mouth, a sense of salty, rotting dampness to the flesh, a knot at the throat. I suspected it would stay with me long after I left the corpse behind. Not all the perfumed oil in the world would rid me of it.

The prince felt around the greyish, swollen neck, and brought forth a silver chain. The chain held a locket. The prince's blunt fingers – skilled at manipulating small objects as very large hands sometimes were – opened the catch, revealing a lock of blond hair.

Prince Henry looked interested, but I flinched, because the hair was the colour of a walnut shell. Like Leanor's. The prince probed further. From within the sleeve, pressed close by the swollen flesh, he brought forth a small satchel of oil cloth, of the type all of us had and all of us used, to keep letters or tokens we didn't want wet in the course of our daily duties – since our daily duties, even mine, often took us to the shipyard at Lagos where the prince was building his new type of ship, his caravel.

Delicately, the prince pulled at the pouch and extracted from it a single sheet of paper. I recognized the handwriting and the paper – a small piece of a sheet I'd plundered from the prince's scriptorium – from the edge of one of his own letters.

I knew the line the prince was reading: *I know all. Meet me at the church well before the afternoon mass.*

I looked closer at the corpse's face trying to see beneath swollen flesh and loose grey skin, past the empty eye sockets and the teeth that showed in a rictus. And thought it was Luis, after all. Luis Vilalonga, whatever his real name was.

"You know him?" the prince asked, turning towards me. "You know him, Tiago?"

The sound of a surprised gasp hung in the air between us. I realized it had come from me. My tongue felt thick and dry as cork in my mouth. I swallowed hard.

I knew Luis. I knew more about him than anyone else here did. If what I knew about him became known . . . If it became known that I had told him to meet me in a secret location. If it were known he'd never appeared . . . Oh, I would be lost. They would think I had killed him. And yet the prince had the note and he knew my handwriting. Lying would not save me.

My voice sounding, to my own ears, as if it came from a great distance, I said, "Yes. His name is Luis Vilalonga. He came from the North . . ." And there I faltered and stopped, unable to tell the truth and unwilling to tell a lie.

The prince's gaze remained trained on me, as though looking into my soul. "Do you know any reason why he'd kill himself?" he asked.

Thoughts came to my head in tumult. *Because I'd found his secret. Because he knew I was willing and able to use his secret against him.*

Some sense of self-preservation kept me from saying it. But neither could I manage to utter what I would normally have said, under the circumstances. That he might have been bested at love. That he might have lost a great sum at dice. Instead, I bit my lip and shook my head.

And the prince smiled, a pleased smile as if I'd performed a very clever trick. "That is good," he said, approvingly. He turned back to the corpse and pulled at the black, blood-stained hair. He spread the hair showing a wound beneath – a smooth indentation in the skull and broken skin from where vast quantities of blood must have flooded to stain the hair.

"That is good," he said. "Because this man didn't kill himself, you see. See the blood that stained the hair? There had to be a lot of it, for it not to be completely washed away in the water. That means he was not dead yet when he received this wound. Any man who's been to war knows dead men do not bleed freely."

"But," Pedro said. "Perhaps he hit his head on a rock when he fell?"

"No. The wound is too smooth. A rock would have left a jagged wound. Whatever caused this wound was smooth and rounded, probably a man-made instrument. Which means Luis Vilalonga was murdered."

I expected the call. After the prince had ordered the corpse taken to the church, for proper funeral mass and Christian burial, after we'd returned to the prince's house, I expected the call. And the call came. Diogo, the prince's elderly servant, came for me in my room and said, "Tiago, the prince wishes to speak to you."

Thus I found myself in the scriptorium, where my master sat at his desk which was strewn high with parchment, paper, and strange instruments, some quite new and some looking brittle and frail.

The room was dim and cool, because this house was built as the natives built in sun-drenched Algarve, with mosaic floors, tall ceilings and narrow, high windows which allowed ventilation but kept heat and light out. The prince had a lit oil lamp hanging beside his desk.

He'd removed his hat and the light of the lamp shone yellowish-pale on his dark, thinning hair.

"Sit down, Tiago," he said, softly.

I looked around for a place to sit, amid the broad wooden trunks piled with manuscripts, the narrow writing tables piled with manuscripts and the piles of manuscripts on the floor. Many a time I'd seen my master pluck a single fragment of vellum, a single sheet of paper from the middle of this seeming confusion. But to the rest of us it was nothing but unnavigable chaos.

"I believe there's a stool there, in the corner, under those Moorish maps from Ceuta," the Prince said.

I walked to the corner like a man in a dream and started pulling the paper – Moors used paper more than we did – from atop the stool.

"Please keep them in the same order if you can," the prince said.

Something of his calm, slightly amused voice, finally penetrated my skittering thoughts and steadied my trembling hands. The prince didn't think I'd committed murder. I'd seen Prince Henry in high dudgeon, filled with righteous rage over lying or self-aggrandizing of one's knowledge. Over drunken revelry. Over wastefulness.

Did he but even suspect I'd killed Luis, his voice would have been such as to flay my skin from my bones. Or make me wish it did.

Breathing deep, I brought the three-legged stool, stood it in front of the prince's desk, and sat.

Prince Henry was still looking at me with the same deep calm. And perhaps I just imagined the glimmer of amusement in his dark eyes. "Tiago, what do you know about Luis? That you didn't tell on the beach out there?"

"I – Milord, I –" I said, trying to piece a lie that wouldn't discredit me.

The prince's eyebrows arched. "Tiago, cease. I know you're not guilty of murder. I knew it out there on the beach. Had you killed the man you would have told me there was some reason for him to commit suicide. Having stooped to take human life, you'd not have hesitated to cover your crime with a lie."

"Milord, there might have been," I blurted, "a reason for him to commit self-murder. Look, I knew Luis no better than I knew most of these men," I said. "All the young men who come here to learn, most of whom give up after some months."

"Because they're swaggering little fools, with minds un-used to learning," the prince said.

I swallowed and made a gesture, not quite a nod. Most of the young men who came here didn't even know how to read and write and were neither prepared for nor tolerant of the prince's demand that they learn. "Well, normally I only see them when they come to you with their recommendation letters from family or friends, and then when I cross their path in the street or in the yards, and, unless one of them distinguishes himself in some way, not again until the young man leaves. If he takes leave of you."

"In disgrace," the prince said.

I nodded. "I knew Luis from when he came and intro-duced himself as being the second son of a noble family from the neighbourhood of Caminha . . ."

"Which is a town on our border with Spain, now on this side, now on that through the centuries. But now on ours."

I opened my mouth. "If you know . . ." I said.

"I do not know *exactly*," he said, his voice gone even softer and acquiring the distant tones of a storyteller. "Luis Vila-longa always seemed different to me. He spoke with too careful a diction for a youth from that area. You, yourself, being from Porto, carry the accent of the region, but not all your words are precisely as I would expect them to be. Your mother is Castillian, is she not, Tiago?"

"My loyalties are all on your highness' side," I began, defending myself. "I am all Portuguese. My grandfather arranged my father's marriage through his contacts as a cattle merchant. It does not mean . . ."

"I told you to cease, Tiago. I do not suspect you. And I

know your father very well. One of my most ardent backers."
He smiled, a controlled smile. "I only mention it because
your mother is Castillian and gave your name after an
answered prayer to the Saint in Compostela. I don't suspect
you of feeling any loyalty to Castille as such, but would you,
perhaps, have felt some loyalty to a young man of the same
background? Was that what your note was about? Seeking to
warn him that he might go without punishment?"

"Luis did not have my background," I said, my voice
rising, injured. "He was all Castillian. Probably noble.
Certainly educated. He sometimes slipped and mentioned
names of villages and people, names I've heard my mother
mention, but which wouldn't come naturally to a Portuguese
nobleman."

The prince nodded. "I'd noticed so too. I pay more attention to those young men than you think, Tiago. After that
incident with the Gran Canary that both Portugal and Spain
claimed, a case which is still before the Holy Father's tribunal,
I could do no less. It is quite possible the Spaniards are seeking
to hinder us and I know they would like to beat us at our game.
Find lands to enlarge their already large country. We must not
allow that, else they'll swallow Portugal. But what did you
discover that solidified your suspicions?"

I shrugged. "My father went to Caminha. On business. I
told him of Luis, and asked him to find out about his family.
My father wrote me a letter back. There are Vilalongas on
the outskirts of Caminha but no one such as Luis is known
thereabouts. So I knew he had to be a spy. I could allow him
to be arrested, and maybe ransomed for surely he was of
noble family . . . Or I could warn him."

"Granted that you were probably right, still I'd like to
know what about Luis so interested you that you went
through the trouble of even asking your father. And why
you'd warn him."

I took a deep breath. Here was frailty in a form my celibate
master would never understand. "There was a girl," I said.

"There usually is."

I felt colour rise to my cheeks and started. "She's not . . .
She's not . . ."

"Anyone your parents would allow you to marry?" He shook his head. "They usually aren't."

"Your Highness, I want you to understand –"

"Tiago. I am human and have lived in the world. I will grant you my own interests, my passion for the sea and for the lands beyond to which I hope we can take the light of our Lord have allowed me little time for lusts of another order. Still I know the power of all-consuming lust and youthful love." He waved my objections away before I could voice them. "Though no one dare mention it now, I think you're as aware as I am that my father was a bastard and not the only bastard son of his father." He frowned at me. "So, who is this girl and in what way was she involved with Luis?"

She was younger than I. Probably all of seventeen. Blonde, as some women are, without resort to artifice. Exotic, particularly in these southern lands where all the beauties were dark haired and dark skinned.

Mid-afternoon, outside, she looked even better than she did by torchlight while helping serve at tables in her father's tavern. Her hair was somewhere between a walnut shell and clear starlight. But her eyes were dark and hard. "He was just a boy," she told the prince, and wagged her hips a little, as if she had hopes of seducing Prince Henry, too. "Well dressed and probably wealthy, but just a boy."

The prince removed the tarnished silver locket from his pocket, opened it. Confronted her with her own lock of hair.

She smiled, pleased, like a cat with cream. "Well," she said. "What does that mean?" and laughed. "It was just a little bit of hair. It did not hurt me. And he set such a stock by it."

"You were not *his* then?" I asked. The words were out of my lips before I thought. The prince shot me a withering look, but she – Leanor-a-bela, *Leanor the beautiful*, as we called her, looked at me and shaped her lips to a very little smile.

"I am no one's," she said and tossed her curtain of fair hair.

But she wasn't offended and had made no protest of her maidenhood. That meant . . . I felt suddenly nauseous.

Luis had bragged that he'd done it all with her, and I'd still wanted her. I knew how life could be for the poor. Doubtless, being the mistress of a rich man was better than being a poor man's wife. I understood. It was all I, myself, could offer her. But her brazen acceptance of it, with no hint of regret for a more honourable condition, shocked me. "Luis said," I said. "Luis said –" I could go no further.

But the prince understood. "Would your father have killed Luis to avenge your honour?"

Leanor's eyes grew very large, startled. Then she threw her head back and laughed, the unbridled laughter of a mad woman. "My father doesn't give this," she showed a small, clenched fist, "for my honour. As long as he can sell me to a wealthy man, and as he's well on his way to managing that, what Luis might brag of did not bother him."

"I don't know whether to condemn her or pity her," the prince said.

We were walking back to his house under the blazing midday sun when the whole village was quiet and everyone asleep inside, escaping the heat.

He shook his head. "Am I to understand you talked to Luis about her, in church? And about what you'd found out about him? And you thought he'd left? As you wanted him to leave?"

"I wanted him to leave because I was afraid if he were arrested his family would ransom him. I thought his family . . . I thought he might then have taken Leanor with him to Spain and I'd never see her again." I hesitated here, feeling foolish. "I did not talk to him in the church. I only wanted to tell him where to meet me later. The church was not a place to discuss something that . . . People might think what I was doing . . ."

"Was treason?" the prince supplied, but his voice was amused.

I sighed. "They might think it more serious than it was. I

didn't think Luis had learned anything that justified arresting him. Not yet."

I saw the prince raise his hand.

"He'd been too busy with Leanor to do much spying," I said in a rush. "So I told him I knew something about him and asked him to rent a boat from a fisherman and come and meet me in the cave of the magi, which is offshore and well known to all. People go there to pray or think, or for less licit purposes with local girls. I wanted to go there late at night, when it would be empty. It's a good place because the splashing sounds of any other boat coming into it alert you to someone else's presence. I wanted to convince Luis to leave or I would denounce him. I thought if he left, Leanor might consider me." I felt myself blush at these words. "But Luis never came. I thought he'd just run."

The prince nodded. "And now we're to assume he was waylaid on his way to meet you. Perhaps by one of the many suitors of your fair lady. Don't you know the name of at least one of them?"

"Pedro Aguila. The one who found the body. Leanor has been very close to him since Luis left."

"It is probably for naught," the prince said. "But we'll see Pedro."

We found Pedro outside, tuning his lute under an olive tree. He looked up as we approached. "I thought you'd come to see me," he said, as his fingers played with the chords, seemingly of their own accord. "I know you've talked to Leanor."

"You're close to her, then," the prince said. "And she warned you we found out about your murdering Luis?"

Pedro looked surprised, then frowned and shook his head. "I didn't murder Luis. I wouldn't murder for Leanor, anyway. One like her in every village. Only the foolish and the innocent fall for her." He gave me a malicious look. "Besides, she says her father is setting her up to be the mistress of an older man. He already has the gentleman bespoken and Luis told me it had all been decided a while ago. She's a fine instrument, but I knew I'd not get to play her."

"You talked to Luis. When?"

"The night he disappeared," Pedro said. "We drank and sang in the tavern. I walked him to the boats. He said he was renting one, and going out on a fishing expedition. Don't know what he meant, but I guess he died of it." He looked at us, his face serene and self-satisfied. "Perhaps it was another woman."

"Somehow I don't think so," the prince said. We were back on the road and walking towards the house of the fisherman who rented his two rowboats privately – to students who wanted to talk, or think – or seduce a wench – away from the boiling anthill that was the village. "Pedro walked him to the boats. So Luis intended to meet you. Something must have happened on the boat."

The fisherman's home was little more than a hut, set on the beach proper. The brightly painted boats sat beside it, where their owner had pulled them out of the reach of high tide.

The owner heard us approach and scrambled from inside the home. Somewhat overwhelmed by the prince's presence, he gladly allowed us to look at the boats. And he gladly confirmed they'd both been rented a week ago. "First one to this gentleman," he said, gesturing towards me. "Second to a taller, darker one. The other one must have returned it during the night but this gentleman only brought his in after matins had rung. I was awake then."

The prince examined the two long, narrow vessels – one called My Loves and the other Good Hope. I'd rented My Loves, but they were identical. Both had enough space for two rowers to sit, facing each other, and then a good space between them.

Under each of the benches was a roomy storage space, filled with nets and dark blankets.

The prince tugged at blankets and nets with impatient hands. On the bottom of the Good Hope, he stooped to look at a stain, then called me over. The stain was dark and glossy and a bit of it was smeared up the side of the boat and over the edge to the outside. Blood. Dried blood.

The prince dug under a bench and came out with the nets. The nets had circular weights made of some heavy metal. Just large enough to fit a man's hand, just large enough to take a man's life. One of the weights had the same stain as the boat.

"Someone hid in that boat, that night, under one of the rowing benches," the prince told me. "Someone who knew Luis was going to rent it. And, in the dark of night, a person, pressed under there, would look like no more than a bunched sail, a net, a bit of cloth. Who could have heard you talk to Luis, at the church?"

"No one," I said. "We were alone. Just the two of us, in the silent church and a breeze whistling in, blowing the altar cloth."

"Were you quiet?"

"I was quiet," I said. "Luis was not quiet for long. He shouted and tried to tell me I had nothing on him and he had no reason to go to some blessed cave. But in the end he agreed to meet me."

"Someone must have heard you. Let's see if we can find anything in the church."

The church was cool and silent. Luis' plain pine coffin, mercifully closed, stood before the altar. The altar cloth was still.

Just then the outer door of the sacristy opened. The sacristy was part of the church and yet set apart by a strong iron gate. And it had its own entrance from the outside, which permitted the priest to come in without walking amid the assembled congregation. Both the outer door and the gate were kept locked to prevent the theft of communion plate.

The altar cloth fluttered briefly. Then the door was shut gently and the fluttering stopped.

The priest appeared behind the gate, unlocking it with the key from the ring at his waist.

He bowed perfunctorily to the prince. "The burial mass will be this evening, Your Highness," he said, assuming we'd come to enquire about Luis. "Frankly, the sooner he's buried the better. I'm still not sure why you think he didn't kill himself. He was such a low boy, always boasting of seducing women." He spoke with withering disdain but his mouth closed hard, in anger, and his eyes flashed with aggrieved ire.

The prince took a deep breath. "Which is why you killed him," he said, firmly.

The priest opened his mouth, but said nothing.

"You killed him because he seduced the tavern keeper's daughter, after whom you'd lusted for a while. You meant to make her your mistress, but you were not willing to share her." The prince lifted his hand, silencing the priest before he could speak again. "You were in the sacristy, just closing the back door or just opening it, I don't know, and you overheard Tiago and Luis talking. You hid and stayed quiet. Only the fluttering altar cloth betrayed that the door was open. That night you followed Tiago and, after he took one boat out, you hid in the remaining boat. With your dark habit, in the night, you'd look like an old blanket, like the fishermen keep under there. When the boy was far enough from shore, you hit him hard, with the weight from a net. And then you dropped him overboard, but not so fast that the bottom of the boat escaped being covered in blood. You were not smart enough to put weights on the corpse. You never thought anyone would think of anything but suicide."

The priest took a deep breath, like a drowning man. He went so pale his lips looked grey. "Sorcery," he said at last. "Only sorcery could have revealed all that to you. You've consorted with infidels too much. I did only what was good and holy. I could not let him go around bragging of what he did to her. She was too good for him. Too innocent. Too gullible. She was –"

Only then did he realize he'd given himself away. He made an attempt at running. But the prince was faster and stronger.

"You see," Prince Henry said, sitting behind his desk, while I perched on the three-legged stool in his paper-choked scriptorium, "I realized that the church has only one narrow front door and no windows that open. The windows are solid panels of glass and none of the squares are broken. The only way the cloth could have fluttered was if the sacristy door had opened. And only the priest had the key."

"But –" I opened my mouth in shock, took a moment to find the words. "The priest!"

"Priests are human too," Prince Henry said. "And many of them do not choose the church of their own free will but are sent into the church by parents who do not wish to divide their land or their small fortune. And that young lady was clearly available for . . . other than marriage. The young man, Luis, was bragging of what he'd done with her. It was too much for Father Alexandre's mind. He might never have done anything, but he heard you plan your rendezvous and he knew he could take his enemy alone, in the dark of night. I doubt his mind had much time to weigh on it. It was a crime of passion."

The prince glanced over his shoulder at the narrow, high slit of a window beside him, and through it at the distant glimmer of the sea. "Ah, Tiago, one day we'll navigate all the corners of the ocean and bring the light of reason to them all. In our maps, there will no longer be a space marked 'Sea Of Darkness'. But I'm afraid that in the heart of man, the darkness shall always remain."

# The Stone-Worker's Tale

## Margaret Frazer

*The following is the latest story to feature Dame Frevisse of St Frideswide's Priory in fifteenth-century Oxfordshire. The character was originally created by the writing duo Mary Monica Pulver and Gail Frazer with* The Novice's Tale *(1992), but the series has been continued by Gail alone since* The Prioress's Tale *(1997). The series has now reached thirteen books. Gail has written other non-series stories of which "Neither Pity, Love nor Fear" from* Royal Whodunnits *won her the Herodotus Award in 2000.*

When Dame Frevisse had last been in St Mary's church at Ewelme, it had been a quiet place, its brief nave divided from its side aisles by graceful stone pillars, the chancel and high altar remote beyond a richly painted wooden screen topped by a gilded crucifix and saintly statues. Now, its quiet, ordered peace was gone. Near the high altar the south aisle was given over to scaffolding, stone dust, and workmen. The summer morning's heavy sunlight poured through the hole in the wall that would someday be a stone-mullioned window of richly stained glass. The crane, with its ropes and pulleys, still straddled Lady Alice's stone tomb from yesterday, when it lowered into place the tomb's slab top, complete with a full-length carving of Lady Alice lying in prayerful repose, gazing serenely up to heaven.

Presently, though, Lady Alice was anything but reposed,

serene, or prayerful. She was angry and not bothering to hide it as she demanded at her master mason, "He's gone? Simon Maye is gone? Just gone? He was here yesterday and now, like that, he's gone?"

Master Wyndford, in open distress, holding one arthritic-twisted hand against his chest, rubbing at the back of it with the fingertips of his other hand in an agitated, uneven way, not seeming to know he was doing it, betraying how over-set he was by her anger, said, "Yes, my lady. In the night sometime it must have been."

Lady Alice looked past him to his workmen clustered in and outside the someday-window that opened now to the stoneyard where they should have been busy at their tasks. "You," she said at them all. "Do any of you know aught of this? Where he might be off to?"

One and all, they shook their head, a few of them taking courage to say, "No, my lady," one of them even making bold to add, "He was here at suppertime. Then he wasn't. We've none of us seen him since."

She looked behind her, past Frevisse standing at her shoulder to the three ladies-in-waiting as far off as they dared, the two younger ones rather huddled together and looking as if they wished they could hide behind the nearest pillar. Lady Alice's anger had already washed over them this morning and her displeasure was by no means lessened now as she demanded, "You still don't know anything else either?"

"No, my lady. No," they hurriedly assured her. "Elyn never said anything."

Frevisse was sorry for them but that was no help, she knew. She had no place here except as Lady Alice's cousin, come on a bishop-granted visit to Ewelme three days ago from her cloistered life as a nun in St Frideswide's nunnery the other end of the shire. She had worried that Alice's summons meant there was trouble of some sort and her help was needed. She had soon realized, though, that all Alice wanted was her companionship – and maybe someone new to show off her tomb to. Frevisse had hardly brushed off the dust of travel before Alice had brought her here, to show her the work on both church and tomb and tell at length how it all would be when it was finished, the church beautiful with many-coloured light through the stained glass of the new window, the tomb made in the latest of fashions.

The tomb was well toward being done. Only the stone-carved canopy remained to be finished, now that the alabaster image of Lady Alice in beautiful robes had been settled into place atop the tomb chest. The chest itself, carved around with standing angels bearing shields to be painted with the heraldic arms of her ancestors, was raised above the floor on an open-worked, stone-carved screen behind which, directly under the chest, could be seen a second full-length effigy, this one of a semi-shrouded corpse in the latter stages of its decay, meant to remind those that lived of the fate that came to all, no matter what their earthly glory.

"Not that that's kept me from giving myself a glorious tomb," Alice had said, laughing at herself for it as they walked back to the manor house afterward. "Given the expense of it, I thought I'd have it to enjoy while I was alive, rather than leave money for it in my will and never see it. Besides, on the chance I may live for a long while yet, I thought it best to have my image done now, before I go any older and more wrinkled."

"Ah, vanity even unto death," Frevisse had teased her.

Alice had said back, "It's not much use after death, is it?" and they had laughed together, their friendship firm despite how differently they had gone about their lives – Frevisse gladly into a nunnery and a life of prayer, Alice into worldly wealth and power by way of three marriages. Now in her third widowhood, she was using that wealth and power to have made for her a tomb fine enough to comfort her against the time when death would make worldly wealth and power of no more use to her. Frevisse, as a Benedictine nun vowed to poverty as well as chastity and obedience, knew her own grave would lie nameless under a stretch of grass-grown turf in the nunnery orchard, and she found that a quiet, pleasing thought.

Alice's choice, though, was Alice's choice, between her and God, and Frevisse had no quarrel with it. The trouble this morning was that others had made choices of their own that did not suit with Alice's, and Alice was very angry and had been growing angrier about it ever since one too few of her ladies-in-waiting had come to her bedchamber at dawn to ready her for the day. To Alice's question, "Where's Elyn?" Lady Sybille, senior among her ladies-in-waiting, had looked at Beth and Cathryn, youngest of her ladies – girls whose well-born families had set them to serve and learn in Lady Alice's household until they were old enough for the marriages made for them. That was usual enough, but there should have been three of them there this morning, and Lady Sybille had said sternly, "Tell my lady."

Beth and Cathryn had traded guilty looks before Beth answered with a rather desperate boldness meant to show her innocence in the matter, "We don't know, my lady. She went out last night and never came back to bed."

The three girls shared a bed in the small chamber off the chamber where Alice's older ladies and some of the waiting women slept. They were particularly Lady Sybille's charge and she said, not needing to hear Alice's next question, "We saw you and Dame Frevisse to bed. Then I saw them to theirs as always. So far as I knew, Elyn settled properly to bed, and these two did not see fit to say she did not."

"She said she would be back!" Beth protested. "Then we fell asleep and didn't know she didn't come!"

"Not until we woke up this morning," Cathryn added.

"Has she ever done this before?" Alice demanded.

"She most assuredly has not!" Lady Sybille said indignantly.

But Frevisse saw yet another guilty look pass between Beth and Cathryn and quietly asked, insisting, "Has she?"

Cathryn began hesitantly, "She's . . ." and stopped.

Beth, with the impatience of someone wronged by another's foolishness, said, "A few times, yes."

"Why?" Alice had demanded, with growing anger.

"To see Simon Maye," Beth whispered, as if in the confessional.

Lady Sybille drew a sharp breath. "At that hour? Surely not."

"We think so," Cathryn said hurriedly. "She didn't say."

"And she's done it before this?" Alice said. "It's gone that far between them?"

"But she's always come back!" Cathryn wailed, "She's never not come back!"

"Because she knew what trouble we'd be in if she didn't," Beth had said with a grimness that told Alice she would not be alone in having something to say to the erring Elyn when the time came.

Cathryn, with sudden enterprise and some desperation, added, "She maybe did come back and we were asleep and didn't know it, and she woke up before we did and is only gone out for an early walk."

"That's more likely," one of the other women had offered. "She'll be back for breakfast, surely,"

"That's somewhat too late," Alice had snapped. Already in her undergown of cream-coloured linen, she had pointed at her green outer gown and ordered, "Finish dressing me." And to Lady Sybille beginning a protest over the tray waiting with bread and cold meats for her to break her fast, "No, I'll eat when I come back."

"Come back?" Lady Sybille had faltered.

"From seeing what Simon Maye has to say about this," Lady Alice had said grimly.

And there was where Elyn's other fault – as deep as the first – lay: if what Beth and Cathryn said was true, she had brought Simon Maye into a disgrace that Alice could not ignore. Frevisse had taken no particular note of this Elyn in her few days here, but she remembered Simon Maye well enough . . . He was the journeyman carving the angels for the canopy above Alice's tomb, and when she had first gone with Alice to the church, he had been so intent on his work that Master Wyndford had had to draw his heed, saying beside him, "Simon, my lady has come to see your work again." Then Simon had hurriedly laid down his tools and turned and bowed, a young man with stone-dust greying his brown hair and not particularly different from uncounted other young men.

Until Frevisse had looked past him to the angel he was carving.

Half-length, its hands raised as if in praise, it was rising from the waist out of the stone. Framed by the curves of its wings behind its shoulders, there was an other-worldness to its face, a fineness to the stone-made folds of its gown, an aliveness to every delicately detailed feather of the wings that went far beyond an ordinary journeyman's skill to the something else that came to only some few, God-touched craftsmen.

But now he was not here. Alice's sharp questions at Master Wyndford had determined that, and Elyn had become a lesser matter because, "Who's going to finish my angels then?" Alice demanded at the master mason. "If Simon Maye is gone, who is going to finish them?"

There were to be eighteen of them along the tomb's canopy, set in groups of three. The panels so far finished were set on the church's aisle floor a safe distance away from where the building still went on, leaned partly upright against the wall, the angels gazing upward rather than downward as they would when in place above the tomb. Some were crowned and some were not. Some had their hands folded on their breast; others held them palm to palm in prayer; still others had them raised in praise, like the one that Frevisse had first seen. Besides that, each face was its own rather than simply the same again, and all in all they were as masterful a work as Frevisse had ever found herself smiling at for the plain pleasure they gave. But as yet there were only twelve, not eighteen there were meant to be, and Master Wyndford said, looking aside from Alice's anger to a heavy-shouldered youth standing a little aside from the other workers, "My son Nicol. He's as skilled a carver of stone as Simon Maye. He'll finish the angels, my lady."

Lady Alice turned her critical look on Nicol Wyndford as he bowed to her. Dressed like any workman in a plain tunic and hosen, he had pale, flat hair and a pale, flat face that just now was heavy with sullenness. "Are you?" she demanded at him. "Are you as good as Simon Maye?"

Nicol Wyndford looked from her to his father and back again, hunched his shoulders in not quite a shrug, and said toward the floor, "Nearly, my lady."

"Nearly," Lady Alice said with raw displeasure. "Master Wyndford, I am not paying for 'nearly'."

At that moment Frevisse was more sorry for Master Wyndford's discomfiture than for Alice's disappointment. Sorry, too, that he could not offer himself for the work, as master of the lesser workmen here. He might well have been, in his day, a master carver of stone in his own right – that often went together with being a mason – but he had no hope of being one now, misshapen as both his hands were by arthritis, the fingers swollen and crooked and bent sideways at the knuckles, past hope of ever doing fine work again. They pained him, too. The other times she had come with Alice, Frevisse had noted him gently rubbing one hand's thumb in slow circles on the palm of the other, first one, then the other, as if to ease a constant aching, if not outright pain, that today was shifted to the back of the hand still clutched to his chest. Frevisse suspected that the bitterness of his lost skill accounted, even more than his years did, for the deep lines down his face and the sour look he seemed always to wear; but his voice was strong now with respect and certainty as he insisted, "I promise you, my lady, the work will not suffer if you charge Nicol with it."

"Nicol doesn't think so," Alice pointed out sharply.

Master Wyndford sent his son a hard look. "Simon Maye is his friend. He speaks from that rather than honestly about his own skill."

And his father would take him to task for it later, Frevisse thought.

Alice, unsatisfied, looked from father to son to father again, and said impatiently, "I'll think on it and tell you later."

She swung away from him in a swirl of long skirts and fine veiling. It was to her back that he bowed, saying, "My lady," Nicol and all the workmen bowing, too, as she swept away across the church toward the outer door in even worse humour than she had come, Frevisse and her ladies following her.

The day was still so young the dew was not yet off the grass, but though the day promised to be warm and fair,

Alice plainly did not mean to enjoy it, and probably no one around her would either. Instead of to the house and her morning duties, she went aside toward her gardens. "To pace off my anger at both Elyn and at Simon Maye," she said, and at the garden gateway ordered at her ladies, "Go to your duties. I'll walk with only my cousin. Beth and Cathryn, to you I'll talk later."

The threat in that was not veiled. Her women and both girls made hurried curtsies and more than willingly hastened away as she went into the garden, Frevisse still following her until Alice waited for her and when they were walking side by side between the herb-bordered beds of late summer flowers, said, "It's Sir Reginald Barre. That's who's talked Simon Maye away from me. Sir Reginald's a jealous cur and always has been. He and his wife both. I should never have talked about my tomb where they could hear. They've bribed Simon Maye away, and Elyn has gone with him. How could they both be so foolish at once?"

"Love?" Frevisse suggested.

"Love is all very well," Alice said with sharp disapproval. "But there's no good reason to let it take the place of common sense."

Frevisse had rarely seen love and reason keep company together. It was more usual that when love came in, reason went out; and if the matter were lust instead of love, then reason only went out the faster. Having barely seen and never spoken to either Elyn or Simon, Frevisse had no way of knowing whether it was lust or love between them, but whichever way it was, reason seemed to have gone completely out. This running away together would likely gain them more trouble, both now and to come, than good.

"What I don't see," Alice said, snatching a spire of flowers from a lavender plant as she walked past, "is why Elyn would do something this headlong. She's always showed sensible before this. Even in her dalliance with Simon Maye she hasn't been foolish until now. I've already told her, when she asked me, that I'd speak favourably to her parents about him."

"She asked you? You said you would?" Frevisse echoed in

surprise. "They'd countenance such a thing? Marriage between her and a journeyman stone-worker?"

"Oh, they're none so fine as all that," Alice said easily. She held the lavender to her nose and breathed deeply. "Elyn's grandfather on the father's side was a merchant out of Gloucester who bought himself into land and his son into marriage with a squire's daughter. He was a friend of my father. That's how I know the family. Elyn isn't even their eldest or heir, just a younger daughter, here to be given some graces. If she had caught the eye of a young lord while in my household, they'd not have minded." Alice's small laughter at that was her first lightness of the morning. "But they'll not mind a master stone-worker for her, which is what this Simon Maye will shortly be."

"And Elyn knows that?"

"Oh, yes." Alice's humour darkened again. "She only had to wait. What are they thinking of? It's Sir Reginald. He's behind this in some way. I swear I'll tell everyone he can't find good workmen of his own but has to steal mine. I'll making a laughing-stock of him. He found some way to turn Simon Maye's head . . ."

"How would he have gone about that?" Frevisse asked. "Wouldn't anyone he sent be noted here?" Ewelme being a small place and most of it centred on Lady Alice's household. "Wouldn't any stranger whose only business was with one of the workmen be talked about?" And talk of it would almost surely be brought to Alice by way of any of her household officers whose duties included knowing such things as went on around her. Alice's frown acknowledged as much as Frevisse went on, "Besides that, is Simon Maye such a fool?"

"I wouldn't have thought so," Alice snapped. "But I'd not have thought it of Elyn either. Oh, how could either of them have been so foolish? And no matter what Master Wyndford avers about his son, I won't have the drunken lout touching my angels."

Surprised, Frevisse said, "Was he drunk?"

"What else would you call how he looked this morning? Or if he wasn't outright drunk, he was at least ale-addled. Did you see when he bowed? He swayed near to falling over."

"I thought him a little unsteady, yes, but thought he was simply unnerved at your talking to him."

Alice made an impatient sound, dismissing that. "He's not touching my angels," she said again and threw the sprig of lavender away. The scent of lavender was supposed to soothe. Perhaps it had; with a little more resignation, she said, "Ah well. All this doesn't mean the rest of us should waste our day. My chamberlain will be waiting, and then my steward."

Being lady of a large household and of lands spread over a goodly number of counties did not mean she lived a life of plain leisure. She was responsible for a great many people, must deal for hours at a time with her officers over a great many matters. Frevisse, of no use to her with any of that, went her own way after they returned to the house, seeking out Beth and Cathryn. They were at their morning work of tidying Alice's bedchamber and did not mind stopping when Frevisse said, "Tell me, what did Elyn take with her?"

"Take with her, my lady?" Cathryn echoed a little blankly.

Beth was quicker. "When she went out last night, you mean? She didn't take anything that I saw. Unless she had it ready, waiting for her somewhere else."

"But you haven't looked to see for certain," Frevisse said.

"No, my lady." Cathryn was openly surprised at the thought. People living constantly together in a household learned the courtesy of leaving each other's possessions alone. Cathryn looked as if the thought were beyond her, but again Beth quickly understood and said, "Her chest is in our room."

Elyn's chest sat along one wall, with Beth's and Cathryn's, and as soon as Beth put up the lid, Frevisse could see that nothing was gone from it. Small, it was meant to hold only a few clothes, a few personal things. Everything was carefully folded, carefully placed, with no space from which something might be missing.

"Is this the way it always is?" Frevisse asked.

"Oh, yes," said Beth.

"That's how Elyn is about everything," Cathryn added, sounding faintly aggrieved, as if at some affront or fault.

Frevisse was more taken with the thought of how unlikely it was that this very careful Elyn had run off into the night so foolishly and unprepared, taking nothing with her. Still, women thinking themselves in love had done far more foolish things than that, and Frevisse supposed the next question had to be: How foolish was Simon Maye?

Beth was slowly, perhaps thoughtfully, closing the chest while Cathryn, gazing wistfully into the air at nothing, sighed, "They must be wonderfully in love to run away like this." Turning her smile to Frevisse, she said a little dreamily, "We'd go with her sometimes when she was going to meet him. Sometimes Nicol Wyndford would be there because he's Simon's friend. We'd talk with him while Elyn and Simon talked together." She gave a sly, teasing, sideways look at Beth. "Beth favours him. Nicol. But he favours Elyn."

"He doesn't!" Beth protested. "I don't!"

"You do, too. You've even said you wished he'd look at you like he looks at her."

"I never did!"

"You did!"

"None of which makes any difference to Dame Frevisse," Lady Sybille said, crisp and disapproving from the room's doorway. "I doubt, too, there'll be any meeting with anyone after this for you two, or Elyn when we get her back. Have you finished with my lady's bedchamber?" Probably knowing full well they had not.

The girls made swift curtsies and scurried away, while Frevisse made apology to Lady Sybille, taking blame for their delay on herself before leaving, too, out of the house and back to the church.

It was empty of workmen, but by the sound of men's voices mixed with the chink of chisels on stones outside the window-hole in the wall she guessed they were at work in the stone-yard there, and there she would likely find Master Wyndford and his son. She meant to ask them more questions, but she paused in the aisle beside the panels of Simon Maye's angels; stood looking at their proud, serene faces, and found it harder by the moment to think a man with the skill of hand and eye and mind to create such beauty would desert his work for a lesser love.

Except, of course, he probably did not think his Elyn was a lesser love.

Master Wyndford came into the aisle through the gap in the wall. Not seeing her where she stood aside, he stopped and stood staring at Alice's tomb for a long moment, with one crippled hand still held against his chest, still rubbing at it with the other. His face was set with both sadness and worry. Sadness for the trouble Simon Maye had brought on them all; worry for the work and Alice's displeasure, Frevisse supposed.

He turned and saw her. The hard set of his mouth did not change and his bow was curt, but she took no offence, simply said, "Master Wyndford," as he came toward her.

"My lady," he returned and nodded at the angels along the wall. "Nicol will finish those well enough. My lady need have no worry that way. That carving there is Nicol's. You can see he's skilled."

Master Wyndford moved one hand in a small gesture at the stone corpse lying below the tomb chest. Frevisse had already seen it clearly enough to want no further look at it. In its ghastly way the decayed thing was as much a masterwork as the angels. Every detail of a rotting body – the arch of the barely fleshed ribs, the gaunt thrust of the hipbones past the sunken belly – all were done with exacting care, and if there was no pleasure in looking at it, well then, there was not meant to be, reminder as it was of where all worldly pride and riches came at last. But death and decay were certain and reminding of them was not something of which Frevisse felt in need. The thing ever in doubt until the last was the soul's salvation, and so she preferred the angels' promise of hope beyond death, of love stronger than decay.

And so, she thought, did Master Wyndford, who had waited for no answer from her but stared past her, down broodingly at the angels, and said, "They were his masterwork, those angels. When they were done, he would have been his own man, no journeyman anymore but a master in his own right."

"And now?" Frevisse asked. "Now that he's broken his contract and gone off?"

Master Wyndford pulled his shoulders a little straighter – the broad shoulders of a man who had worked with stone all of his life – and said, as if trying to straighten his thoughts along with his shoulders, "Eh, well, he may come back. There's no saying. If he's any sense, once the lust has gone out of him he'll come craving pardon then and to have his work back."

"Will you give it to him?"

Master Wyndford held silent a long moment before finally saying with a nod toward the angels. "There's little I'd not forgive a man who does that kind of work." His sadness and worry went into bitterness, and he said with open anger and frustration, "I warned him. When he came talking to me about this girl, I warned him well no good would come of wanting a woman instead of his work. I told him that letting her turn his head would only bring him to grief. I warned him marriage would be his ruin."

"You're married," Frevisse said. "Or you were. You have a son. Surely you . . ."

"Oh, aye, I was married. I was warned against it, the way I warned young Simon, but I was set on her, just like him on this Elyn, and I married her. The young don't listen. They don't hear. No matter what's said to them, they think it'll go differently for them. It never does but they think it will."

"I listened, Father." Just come through the wall's gap from the stoneyard, Nicol Wyndford bent his head respectfully to Frevisse but as he came forward, it was still at his father he said, "I've listened to you every time and done as you bid. I left Elyn to Simon. Now he has her and I don't. Can't that be enough to satisfy you?"

"Satisfy me?" Master Wyndford said bitterly. "No. I'm to be satisfied to watch him ruin his life with a marriage he didn't need? Watch him lose everything he could have been and go dark with disappointment and failure? Watch him never do all he could have if he hadn't thought he needed this girl, this . . ."

"It wasn't marriage to Mother that ruined your hands," Nicol said sharply at him.

His angry flow of words broken, Master Wyndford started to pull his hands away from him as if to look at them, saying as if suddenly bewildered, "My hands?" Then he clutched them to him again and said, his anger flooding back, "No. They weren't her fault. What she did was done years before they finished me. She kept me from what I could have done. That's what she did. All those years when she needed this and she wanted that. Everything had to be the way she wanted it to be. She had to have everything she wanted to have. She wouldn't let me go where the best work was to be had and she never give me peace enough to give my mind to what work there was. She clung and she nagged through every unblessed hour I was married to her. She wore me out and made me nothing. Then she died and the arthritics finished what she'd started."

"That isn't Elyn, though," Nicol protested. "There's sweetness in her. She . . ."

Master Wyndford pounded his fisted hands against his chest. Disgusted and dismissing, with old, embedded anger, he snapped, "You think your mother didn't show sweet when she was wooing me? It's after they have you, that's when you find out what they are."

"No," Nicol said, stiff with useless rebellion. "Father . . ."

But Master Wyndford swept onward with growing rage and bitterness. "Years of misery when he could have years of making. That's what a man gets when he marries." He nodded harshly at the line of angels. "I did work like that once. ONCE. You'd ruin yourself if I let you, but I won't. Do you think I could stand to watch it happen again?" He held his twisted hands a little out from his chest, then clutched them back against him. "They're gone. Simon and this Elyn. They're gone and there's all the proof you need of what a fool she's made of him!" Dropping the quarrel that was all his own as suddenly as he'd taken it up, Master Wyndford demanded instead, "You left your work to come in here for other than to pick a quarrel with me. What did you want?"

Nicol had begun rubbing his forehead while his father was still talking and now said, "I don't remember," and began to turn away.

"Remember your courtesy to the lady," his father snapped.

Nicol dropped his hand, turned back, bowed to Frevisse without looking at her, and made to turn away again, his hand returning to his head as if it hurt.

Frevisse, sorry for his father's harsh set-down and wanting to show what sympathy she could, asked, "Are you ill?"

Still turning away, Nicol said, "The weather is in my head, is all. The heat, I think. There's maybe a storm coming."

"You drank too much last night," Master Wyndford snapped. "That's all. You always drink too much."

"I don't," Nicol said in the flat voice of someone who's said the same too many times to care much anymore.

But he stopped in his turning away, held unmoving a moment, frowning at the floor as if tracking a fugitive thought across the paving stones, then lowered his hand, turned back toward his father, and said slowly, "Last night. I've remembered something. I woke up from some bad dream. I don't know what time it was, but I wanted a drink. I was thirsty. I went down to the kitchen."

"You went downstairs?" Master Wyndford said, sharp with surprise. Then sharp with disgust, "You didn't. I never heard you. You dreamed it."

"No. I was awake. I don't know where you were . . ."

"In bed. Asleep and not drunk, which you surely were."

Following his thought more than his father's words, Nicol went on, "The shutter was open. You'd left the shutter open. There was moonlight in the room."

"It was a warm night. I forgot to close it," Master Wyndford said impatiently at him. "That happens. Best you give up ale altogether if it sets you to muttering through the next day like this. Get back to work."

Nicol lifted and twisted his shoulders, shaking his father's words away, intent on his memory and the unease of it. "There was the moonlight and I could see . . ." He stopped, then said slowly, as if only beginning to be sure of it, "There were three cups on the table." More firmly, sure of the thought now, he said more strongly, "There were three cups there. Why were there three cups?"

"There weren't any three cups," said Master Wyndford. "You were drunk and dreamed it."

"I wasn't drunk. I wasn't dreaming. You and I, we sat there at the table after supper and drank together. I filled my cup twice and no more, and it would take stronger ale than that was to get me drunk on two cups. Then I put my cup back on its shelf and went to bed. 'Put away now and you'll not need do it later.' That's what Mother beat into me when I was little, and I still do it. Sober or half-drunk, I always 'put away', and last night I wasn't even half-drunk. I was . . ." He gripped his fingers into the side of his forehead. "I was something, but I wasn't drunk."

"You were drunk," Master Wyndford said flatly. "And I'd not say you were sober now. Best you . . ."

Nicol lowered his hand. Stared at his father. "Three cups and none of them mine. They were there last night, weren't they? They . . ."

"There was nobody there," Master Wyndford said, angry and uneasy together. "You went to bed drunk. You dreamed things. You . . ."

"I wasn't drunk!" Nicol shouted. He took a step toward his father, his uncertainty gone suddenly to anger of his own. "You put something in my ale, didn't you? You have that potion you take when the pain is too bad. The draught that lets you sleep when you can't otherwise. You put that in my ale!"

"You're a fool. I never . . ."

"So I'd be asleep when Simon and Elyn came to see you. They were there. Simon and Elyn were there, weren't they? That's why there were the three cups on the table. Because Simon and Elyn . . ."

"You're off your head!" his father shouted back at him. "I haven't enough I'd waste any of my draught on your thick head for anything and they weren't there last night!"

"It was to have me out of the way. You knew they were coming! You wanted me out of the way! You . . ."

"I pray your pardon," said Alice, cold and precise on every word. "Is this about my tomb? Because otherwise I can see no reason for such shouting in a church."

Frevisse was as taken by surprise as both the Wyndfords. Come in by the far door, Alice had crossed the nave at an angle that had kept her hidden beyond the pillar nearest where they stood. She had not done it by design, surely. She was lady here, with no need not to be seen. But it made her appearance sudden, and both men spun to face her, bending in hurried bows as Frevisse turned, too, and curtsied and said with very false calm as she straightened from it, "It seems Elyn and Simon talked with Master Wyndford last night. Now he's going to tell us why."

Not so willing to accuse a nun of lying as he was his son of drunkenness, Master Wyndford stared, speechless, from her to Lady Alice, past Lady Alice to her three ladies who had come with her, and back to Frevisse again, as Alice said, impatient at his failure to answer, "Well, Master Wyndford? I came to say I was willing to let your son work on my angels. Now I won't say it until I've heard more about this. Did you talk with Elyn and Simon last night?"

Stiffly, now looking at the nearest pillar rather than at anyone, Master Wyndford said, "Yes, my lady."

"And yet did not see fit to say so when I was here before."

"No, my lady." Still to the pillar.

Still feigning a calm she no longer felt, Frevisse said, "What did they come to see you about, Master Wyndford?"

He gave her a look as black as any he had had for his son before answering sullenly, "About being married."

"And to tell you they were running off," Alice said.

"No." Master Wyndford heaved a breath far too heavy to be called a sigh. "They didn't say anything about running off. They wanted to talk about marrying. How soon I thought they could do it and all. I told them not to be fools. They went away. That was all."

"They said nothing about leaving?" Alice pressed.

"Nothing," Master Wyndford said bitterly. "We talked and then they went away." His face and voice darkened with deep-set grief and long-nurtured rage. "I told Simon marriage would rob him of everything he might be and do. I told her that if she loved him, she'd let him go. They didn't listen.

It wasn't what they wanted to hear. They'd never have listened."

"And so you poisoned them," Frevisse said quietly.

Master Wyndford jerked his head around to stare at her, along with everyone else.

"While they sat there, trusting you," Frevisse said, still quietly, "you poisoned them. And while you were ridding yourself of their bodies, Nicol came downstairs and saw the cups on the table."

"No!"

Master Wyndford's protest was fierce, but Nicol, his stare gone from Frevisse to his father, said wonderingly, "You dosed me enough to make me sleep. So I wouldn't know they'd been there. Then you gave them enough to kill them." The thought took hold on him, going past guess into belief, and with an on-rush of anger he yelled, "You killed them! How could you? How could you kill them!"

"I couldn't!" Master Wyndford cried back at him. "I didn't! I . . ." But his eyes were going from Nicol to Frevisse to Alice to Nicol again, and he must have seen their growing certainty and anger arrayed against him, and the same weakness that had betrayed him to ruin by a vile-humoured wife betrayed him now. Defiance and denial went out of him, turned only into weak assertion and a pleading that they understand with, "I didn't kill them. Death . . . I couldn't see Simon dead. The dead are so . . . empty. There's nothing there when someone is dead. I couldn't bear to see Simon that way. I gave them sleep, that's all. With my syrup of poppies. I gave them sleep. That's all I did."

"Where are they?" Frevisse demanded.

Master Wyndford shook his head, refusing that. "They're sleeping. Leave them. They'll never know. They'll sleep away and never find out all the ugliness that comes afterward. Never have to live through all the years after this 'love' they think they're in is gone. They'll just sleep. They'll just . . ." He was a man who had worked more with his hands than with words through his life. He gestured outward now, groping for words, needing to make someone, anyone, understand. "They'll sleep," he pleaded. "They'll sleep and go free and never know . . ."

Frevisse grabbed him by one wrist and wrenched his hand over to see what she had glimpsed as he gestured. There, red and raw across his palm, was a fresh wound of . . .

Master Wyndford jerked loose from her but Nicol grabbed him by his other wrist, dragged his arm out, fighting him for it, forcing his hand palm-upward to show the same fresh wound there; and Nicol said as if only half-believing it, "Rope-burn!"

Together, in the same rush of understanding, he and Frevisse looked toward the crane with its ropes and pulleys still straddling Lady Alice's tomb; and Frevisse with the horror of certainty, said "No" as Nicol flung his father's hand away from him and made for the gap in the wall to the stone-yard, yelling, "I need men here! All of you! Hurry!"

For Master Wyndford, alone and in the dark last night, the lifting of the stone slab with its alabaster figure from its place atop the tomb chest must have been brutal work, and later lowering it into place again would have hardly been easier. The pulley-ropes had left raw testament of that on his hands.

The workmen who came at Nicol's call made quicker business of it; and when the slab was lifted and swung aside, Simon and Elyn were there, still sleeping. A little longer and they would have slept away to death, smothered in the sealed darkness without ever – if God were merciful – rousing. That was the end to which they would have come if the summer night had been longer, so that Master Wyndford could have set to his work at the tomb sooner; or if Frevisse had been less willing to question the twists in what had at first seemed straight; or Nicol refused his uncertain, half-dreamed memory of something that seemed to make no sense. Instead, they were lifted out of the stone darkness and carried from the church, into sunlight and wide air and life again. Master Wyndford stood in the church's stone-pillared shadows, tears sliding down his face. Nicol went to him, leaving Simon and Elyn to the exclaims and care of Alice's women, and put an arm around his shoulders and stood with him, waiting for what would come next; and Alice, once she had given all the necessary orders, came to Frevisse, still standing beside the angels, and said softly, "They likely wouldn't have been found until the time came to bury me there. Thank you."

And Frevisse, her eyes on the stone-carved angels smiling as they gazed into eternity, said, "You're very welcome." And smiled, too, and said, "You'll have your eighteen angels now, anyway."

"And thank you for that, too," said Alice.

*Lady Alice's tomb still stands in Ewelme Church, Oxfordshire, with her stone-carved angels above, below, and all around it, still smiling as they gaze into eternity.*

# The Witching Hour

## Martin Edwards

*Martin Edwards is a solicitor in Liverpool, just like the
main character in his noted series of books starring Harry
Devlin which began with* All the Lonely People *(1991).
Edwards is constantly busy. When not writing new novels,
he is producing many reference works or editing anthologies, let alone being a partner in his firm of solicitors. In the
following story Edwards looks back at what might have
been the judicial or prejudicial process in a witch trial in
the 1600s.*

### Tomorrow she dies

Richard Norley laid down his pen. For hour after long hour,
its scratching had been the only sound in this musty attic at
the top of the Judges' Lodgings. He had wanted to write,
needed to write. Anything to distract his thoughts from the
image haunting his brain. The tallow candle still burned, but
it was past midnight. His writing arm was weary, the old
wooden chair was uncomfortable, and he ought to be asleep.
But no man could sleep when his heart was full of dread. He
feared the approach of daybreak. For it would be Martha
Beeston's last dawn.

Had he dreamed the beseeching look when her gaze fell
upon him, as she was taken so roughly out of the courtroom?
She had looked over her shoulder and their eyes had met.
No, there was no mistaking it: for all her terror, she was a

young woman of spirit. For all her poverty and degradation, her eyes – so strange and lustrous! – shone with a challenge.

*You believe me and I have no-one else to turn to. I am innocent, and I see from your face that you know this is so. So why do you sit there, mute and head bowed? Will you not try to save me from an agonising death?*

The night was cool, but Richard's skin was clammy, as though he had become feverish with apprehension. Better than most, he understood that often it is no straightforward matter to determine whether a person's testimony is true or perjured. Experience had taught him that even the most apparently decent folk may spin a web of lies, even a cruel malefactor is capable of intermittent honesty. Yet he counted himself a student of his fellow man and flattered himself that he could interpret Martha's character from her demeanour when on trial for her life. She had undergone so many indignities that it would surely have been tempting for her to yield to Fate and make a confession – but she had remained defiant. Notwithstanding his long apprenticeship in the discipline of logic, Richard was certain that Martha Beeston was innocent.

An absurd notion, of course. How bitterly he reproached himself! He was Clerk of Assize, a most responsible office for one so young, behaving as foolishly as a mawkish old maid. Evidence is all that matters, any man steeped in the ways of the law knows that. Without evidence, there is nothing, and the declaration of evidence in these proceedings under King James's Witchcraft Act was as compelling as any Richard had ever heard. A courtroom is no place for idle fancies, far less for unsuitable attractions. The young woman, poorly dressed with black hair that descended to her shoulders, impenitent and sardonic, was scarcely a proper match for an ambitious fellow who pursued his calling with a single-minded zeal. And yet he could not help himself. Hot with self-disgust, he told himself that she must indeed be a witch, so effectively had she entranced him.

In law, Martha had no cause to complain. Justice had been seen to be done. First, the case had come before one of his Majesty's justices, John Hankelow, a local squire with a good name for vigilance. The Magistrate, a deeply religious man, was aghast when he learned about the hellish practices of Annie Beeston and Martha, her granddaughter. The women came from a remote corner of rural Cheshire, close to the border with Salop. Richard, born and bred within Chester's Roman walls, had never had cause to travel to Clough, the lonely hamlet where they dwelt. The place was not so many miles away from the old city, but the baneful happenings in Clough might have taken place in a different world.

John Hankelow took lengthy depositions and committed the two prisoners for trial at the next Assizes. Annie, a withered, worn and decrepit old crone, was confused in her speech but so contrite and repentant that but for the damnable nature of her crimes an onlooker might have been moved to pity. Martha, in contrast, remained aloof and steadfast in her denial of guilt. Annie's husband, Mungo, was four score years and seven. For years he had been ailing and his mind was even more of a muddle than his wife's. He was not even aware that Annie and their granddaughter had been imprisoned in poky cells at Chester Castle, far less that Annie had died from a seizure of the brain a week before the trial was due to commence.

Thus it was Martha alone who came before Baron Elbourne's court and a jury of gentlemen of understanding. The indictment cited the felonious practice of divers wicked and devilish arts called witchcraft and enchantments upon one William Stubbings, farmer in the parish of Clough, and by force of the same witchcraft, the killing of him *contra pacem*. For the trial of her life, Martha insisted upon her innocence and put herself upon God and her Country, but the facts left no room for uncertainty as to the verdict. Annie's deposition was read out to a hushed courtroom and the prosecution adduced consistent evidence. The witnesses included persons of standing, two landowners and a distinguished antiquary. Martha's wickedness had been proven beyond a reasonable doubt and the judge's solemn task was to condemn her to death.

In the aftermath of the trial, Baron Elbourne concluded that it would be necessary and profitable to publish to the world the proceedings of the court and he deputed Richard to the sober task. Decent God-fearing folk need to know, His Lordship pronounced, the means whereby witches work their mischief, their wicked charms and sorceries, the better to prevent and avoid the dangers that may ensue if their evil acts remain unchecked. For Richard, this was an opportunity to serve the most distinguished judge on the Northern Circuit and to earn a small place in history by chronicling the workings of justice in an extraordinary case. He had dreamed of receiving such a commission. Yet upon his wish being granted, he was more deeply troubled than at any time before in his twenty-nine years. No matter how he fought his sinister infatuation, he could not bring himself to believe that Martha Beeston was a witch.

Or was it simply, he asked himself as he sat alone in the flickering candlelight, that he could not accept the consequences of the verdict? His head told him that this was closer to the mark. He trembled at the thought of the agonising fate that awaited the young woman and therefore had persuaded himself that she was pure and not a creature of the Devil.

He had believed he was mature enough to conquer the uncertainties that had beset him in youth. Absurd as it might seem today, there had been times when he had questioned whether witchcraft should be a crime. Some pamphleteers argued that witches were no more than poor and foolish creatures who preyed upon the superstitious by way of elementary conjuring tricks, but His Royal Highness had no doubts and the Scriptures supported him. Sensible men recognised that it was unwise to quarrel with the King, whatever private reservations they might entertain, and Richard was nothing if not sensible. Besides, His Majesty's arguments were sound. Lewd priests exploited witches in the most sinister fashion to incline the ignorant towards blind Papistry. Women claiming to be possessed with unclean spirits would concoct strange illusions to draw people together and extract promises of loyalty and devotion. Their misdeeds must be punished and the Act was fair. Those who cast a spell to find a love-potion or to damage property were punished merely by the pillory and a year in gaol. The penalty of death was reserved only for those who conjured up evil spirits or used spells to harm a fellow human being.

Richard wiped his brow. The proof of Martha Beeston's sins reached beyond her ailing grandmother's confession that the two of them practised witchcraft, far beyond the testimony of a simple thirteen-year-old girl. The pinched face of Dorothy Losh swam into his mind. The daughter of a labourer who worked in William Stubbings' fields, she had dirty red hair and wore a frayed cotton dress. Richard could hear her whining voice now, see the pretty little bracelet shining on her wrist as she stabbed a grubby finger towards the dock.

"I heard the two of them whilst I was walking in the wood. The old woman has always frightened me and so I hid behind an elm tree. I listened to them talking, I was afraid that they might be plotting against my poor widowed mother. Mungo Beeston's family has always hated mine, for as long as they have been our neighbours. I believe they are jealous of our land. And so I know that they would be glad to do me an injury, for it would cause my mother such distress. I could hear the old woman telling Martha that she might have and do what she would, if only she would give herself to the Devil. If she surrendered her soul to him, she would want for nothing. Martha refused, saying she feared God, and I could hear her crying, but the old woman said she soon would change her opinion."

The judge was stern, but not inhuman. He questioned the child with patience. To Richard, her expression seemed shifty, but she swallowed hard and held her head up high. For all her tender years and malicious smirks at the prisoner, she impressed Baron Elbourne as a credible witness. Her account scarcely differed from the contents of her original deposition to the Magistrate.

"After that, I kept watch on Martha whenever I could. Our cottage was only a furlong distant from hers. The old woman was a witch, of that I was sure. But she was infirm and seldom left home. Her powers were failing, but Martha was different. She was seventeen years old and ever since her mother's death, she did whatever she liked. Her grandmother was feeble, but I knew that Martha might inflict upon us terrible harm if she agreed to serve the Evil One."

In the still of the courtroom, Dorothy's story cast its own spell upon those present. Even Baron Elbourne seemed to hold his breath as the girl continued.

"One evening, I was going home after a visit to my aunt. It was late, but there was a full moon to guide me. I was hurrying back, lest my mother worry about what might have happened to me, although I had been too fearful to tell her what old Mad Annie Beeston had said to her granddaughter. As I passed along our little lane, close to where the Beestons lived, I heard a strange and mournful barking and shrank into the shadows. Through the hedge I saw a huge black dog with fierce yellow eyes, bounding towards the cottage."

At this point, the girl's whole body began to shake, but the judge allowed her time to compose herself.

"As the dog howled outside the front door, I saw Martha open her window. She listened to the creature for what seemed to be an eternity. I had a painful cramp in my legs, but I dared not move. At last she disappeared from sight, but a few moments later, I saw the door open. Martha was there. She was wearing a loose white shift, as though the dog had roused her from sleep. She seemed to hesitate and then she stepped over the threshold. The dog did not move as she went toward it. Then, with a single movement, she lifted the shift over her head and stood before the creature as it slavered for her. I could see everything clearly in the moonlight. I wanted to weep for her shame, but I knew that if I made a noise, my fate would be sealed. Then she bent forward and – and I saw the black dog sucking greedily at her breast."

The judge leaned forward. His face was a mask, his voice as cold as the draught in the courtroom.

"At the pap?"

"Yes, my Lord. After a few moments, Martha – Martha let out a cry. It was a most horrid sound.

"What sort of cry?"

"My Lord, it was a cry of joy."

"No! No! She lies!"

Martha was crying out again, but now she was protesting against the girl's evidence. Her face was ashen and she trembled with emotion beyond her power to control. In his sternest tone, the judge insisted that she should not interrupt the witness. If such intolerable conduct were to be repeated, he would have no hesitation in having her punished severely for contempt of court. His wrath was all the more menacing for being articulated in such a chill tone. Martha shrank back, and it seemed to Richard that if her slight figure became any smaller, it might disappear. There was no hatred in her expression, merely horror at the girl's relentless accusations.

"I could bear it no longer, and so I fled. But a week later, I was walking down the lane again, watching out for them, so that I might run away if either of them were about and saw me. Through a gap in the hedge I could see the pair of them. The old hag and the young, next to the ditch that runs close to their cottage. They had a mound of marl and Annie Beeston was telling her granddaughter what to do. She was describing the way that William Stubbings's face and body were shaped while Martha made something out of the clay."

Tears were running down Martha Beeston's cheeks, but she dried them with the back of her hand, brushed a stray hair off her face and made not another sound. Her coltish frame was stiff with fear, but she did not lack pride. She would not give in. At that instant, Martha resembled not a witch, but a girl much younger than her years, a girl less wise in the ways of the world even than her child-accuser. She could not, Richard told himself, ever have contemplated selling her soul to Satan.

Unable to sit still any longer, Richard strode across the room and threw himself upon the bed. The floorboards creaked in protest under his feet, but he was sure that Baron Elbourne, slumbering in his chamber below, would not stir. The judge always slept the sleep of the just. If one walked past his door, one could hear his thunderous snoring. Richard closed his eyes, praying to the Lord that the mercy of sleep might be granted to him as well, but it was no good.

The attic room was furnished simply, for a Clerk of Assize was expected to have plainer tastes than a justice. But near the door stood a long case clock made of yew and already it was chiming one o'clock. Dawn was creeping nearer all the time.

*Tomorrow she dies.*

Richard clambered off the bed and returned to his desk. He wanted to check his record of the trial and refresh his memory of the evidence given by Hugo Frandley. Other than William Stubbings deceased, Frandley was the principal landowner in Clough. He was bald and fat, with dark little eyes sunk deep into the fleshy, sweat-caked recesses of his face. A widower aged fifty, he wheezed unpleasantly whenever he spoke. It seemed to Richard that the man's pompous speech was in keeping with his self-regard. As if bestowing a kindness, he had proposed marriage to Martha not three months before. The girl swiftly declined his offer, offering the excuse (as it seemed to Richard) that she was too young. Fiddling with the jewelled ring that adorned his chubby forefinger, Frandley damned her with his jealous words.

"She seemed angry with me, though I could not understand it. Had she accepted my hand, she would have bettered herself. I count myself a man of some consequence in the neighbourhood and for such a slip of a girl to refuse my hand caused me no little dismay and embarrassment. Having only wished to assist her, I asked for her assurance that she would not mention the matter to a soul. She gave her assent, but it was as if I had offended her and she made me pay a price. As I walked home that very night, my Lord, a hare spat fire at me. Within a fortnight, one of my cows went mad. Within six weeks, five of them were dead. I know they were not afflicted by any disease. She bewitched them, I have no doubt of it."

A spiteful child and a rejected suitor. Neither of them troubled to conceal their hostility towards Martha. One might contend that they were partial witnesses, and that no human being, far less a young woman, should be put to death by reason of their unsubstantiated allegations. But the same could not be said of Joshua Carrington and George Stubbings, far less Martha's own grandmother. Annie Beeston was an infirm old woman, hunch-backed and disfigured by many warts. Her deposition to John Hankelow was rambling to the point of incoherence, but there was no uncertainty concerning the one fact that mattered to the Magistrate and he ensured that the record of it was clear as crystal. Speaking, as it seemed to Richard, with a wild and reckless determination to air the truth, Annie Beeston was quite prepared to admit indulgence in witchcraft.

"An evil spirit came for me, in the shape of a boy. He wore a coat, half black, half brown. He told me that if I wanted to be revenged of anything, I should call on him and he would be ready. All he asked was for my soul."

Crimson-faced, she confessed that the Devil had made her kiss his buttocks and swear eternal allegiance. In return for this act of infamy, he granted her uncanny powers. She could bewitch ale and turn milk into butter and cast spells upon those who misused her. She and her sick husband were in the twilight of their days and she seldom had occasion to utilise her extraordinary gifts, but Martha's whole life was ahead of her. That was why she implored Martha to become a witch. Annie's only wish was for her grand-daughter to have everything she desired.

"Revenge is sweet, I told her. I have been wronged many times in my life and I did not wish Martha to suffer as I have done. If any man mistreated her, there is a speedy way to make him ill or take his life. I taught her that all she needed was to make a picture of clay. The art is to make it like unto the shape of the person you mean to kill."

The picture should be dried thoroughly, she explained to the grim Magistrate. When a witch intended to do any man harm, she would take a thorn or pin and prick it in that part of the picture where she would have him be sick. If she wanted any part of the body consumed away, she should take away that part of the picture. If she wanted the whole body consumed away, she should take the remnant of the picture and burn it. By that means, the body should die.

The dead man was Annie Beeston's cousin, William Stubbings. A formidable and God-fearing man, he was a notoriously hot-tempered fellow. William owned an extensive tract of farmland in Clough and had quarrelled with the old woman over the precise location of the boundaries between his property and hers. Later, a mare belonging to him had died. His younger brother George stated that William accused Annie and her granddaughter of sorcery. George had, as he asseverated, a strong belief in family obligation, and he and William were the Beestons' closest living relatives. Even though the Beestons had always kept themselves to themselves, George maintained his refusal to accept there was any truth in William's charge that the animal was bewitched. Moreover, the Beestons' smallholding was poor in yield compared to William's acres, and George had for the past twelvemonth assisted the women with heavy work in the fields, insisting that he would accept no reward for his pains. Although he had little property of his own, he had a passion for agriculture and had become something of a herbalist. Before the court, however, he testified in halting terms that he would take his regrets to the grave. Scepticism, coupled with a natural fondness for the Beeston women, had caused him to do nothing to save his brother from the witch's fearsome vengeance. His kindnesses betrayed, he could not now help but nurse a natural hatred for them. Yet he did not neglect his duty, as he saw it, toward Mungo Beeston, and arranged for the old man to be cared for by a local woman from the village while his wife and granddaughter languished in gaol.

The grim task of describing his brother's death to the judge and jury brought tears to his eyes.

"One evening William and I were together and he clutched his chest. 'My heart is bursting!' he cried. Within a few moments he was dead in my arms."

William had always been a fit and healthy man, George confirmed. Voice trembling, he recalled the dreadful night of his brother's sudden death. It was a shocking blow, yet George did not at once associate William's demise with a spell cast by Annie and Martha. Not until a week later, after discussion with an acquaintance by the name of Joshua

Carrington and his neighbour Hugo Frandley, was he driven to the opinion that William had fallen victim to foul play.

Carrington was well known in Chester. Richard himself had encountered the fellow more than once. Elderly and eccentric with a mass of wild grey hair, he was a man of remarkable knowledge, the grandson of an alderman who had devoted his inheritance to the study of antiquities. Dwelling in a black and white house within a stone's throw of Eastgate, he possessed a noted collection of artefacts from the old legionary fortress. Over the years, he had published a number of learned papers and spoken about his researches at meetings that Richard, himself an enthusiast for uncovering traces of the past, had been eager to attend in rare moments of escape from legal duties. Importantly, he lacked both Frandley's wounded pride and George's grief-stricken rage and accordingly the story that he had to tell carried even more weight than theirs.

While in George's company, Carrington had met and befriended the Beestons. He had talked at length with Annie and even purchased an old beaker from her. He found the old woman amiable if foolish, while her daughter was a comely lass for whom he conceived a strong affection, albeit entirely paternal in character. She was headstrong yet intelligent, whereas her grandmother was ill-educated and lacked a disciplined mind. He was startled, therefore, to call at the Beestons' home seven days after William's sudden death and overhear *both* women finishing a prayer in Latin as he stood on the threshold. He caught only a few words, but they seemed to be giving thanks for a blessing. When he knocked loudly, silence fell in the little cottage.

"Martha opened the door. She seemed ill-at-ease, which I found unaccountable, since we were on cordial terms. The price I had paid for the beaker was handsome, for it was an interesting item although of little historic consequence. I believe she recognised that, although I am very far from being a rich man, I nourished a considerable sympathy for her, of an entirely platonic nature. Her parents and older brother had died when she was still young and there was little money. In the days following William's tragic passing, therefore, I urged George to offer them some assistance by purchasing Mungo Beeston's plot of land and amalgamating it with his and William's. I reasoned that this would allow the women to remain in their home without needing to cope with the burdens of tillage. William would not have entertained such a notion, but George is a kind-hearted man and was easily persuaded that this was a proper means of discharging the obligation he considered that the blood-tie imposed upon him. He shared my wish for Marie to have enough to live on, even if her grandparents died soon, until – if she was wise enough to reconsider – she accepted Frandley's proposal or in time found herself another husband. All in all, this seemed to me to be a most equitable way of proceeding, and George responded with characteristic goodwill, telling me that to assist his cousin he would be willing to offer a little more than the land was truly worth, to overcome any reservations that the women might have. Gratified, I went to the cottage to ascertain whether the suggestion met with their favour."

It did not. Annie was incoherent, but Martha would not countenance the idea and denounced Frandley in particular. He made her flesh creep, she said, and she would sooner die than be his bride. Determined not to accept charity, however kindly the proposal was meant, she said she would never be beholden to any man. This was Beeston land, she said, and so it would remain. Shocked by her vehemence, Carrington pointed out that, since George had inherited his brother's farm, he would be a busy man and unlikely to have the time to continue to help the women as he had done in the past. As for his own motives, they were entirely disinterested and honourable. Martha remained adamant and chided her visitor for daring to hint that she was incapable of looking after her grandmother and their own property.

"There was nothing more that I could do. The girl has the stubbornness of her sex and I could see nothing to be gained by pressing upon her the obvious advantages of the arrangement. The effect would only have been to increase her intransigence."

After he took his farewell, however, a disturbing incident occurred. As he walked along the lane towards where George

Stubbings lived, he heard a commotion coming from the Beestons' cottage.

"It was not quite like anything I had heard before. I can only liken it to the yowling of a multitude of cats. This bewildered me, for to my knowledge, neither Annie nor Martha had ever kept even a kitten."

Increasing his pace, he soon reached the Stubbings farmhouse. George was saddened that the girl had spurned his offer, but her lack of gratitude was of little consequence to a man who had so recently lost his brother. He confirmed that the Beestons kept no cats. While they talked, another visitor arrived, whom he recognised as Frandley. The farmer was in a state of great agitation. He said he had been talking to Joseph Losh, Dorothy's father, and he had recounted Dorothy's claim that Martha had surrendered her soul to the Devil. Shocked, Carrington protested that the girl would never do such a thing. The old woman's mind was fuddled and Martha had a fierce temper, but that did not mean that they put spells upon their enemies.

Carrington explained to the court that over the years, he had learned much about witches and their heinous deeds. He had studied *Malleus Maleficarum*, a text composed by two Dominican friars, which provided guidance on the denunciation and arraignment of suspected sorcerers. Nor was this merely a matter of intellectual fascination. As a loyal subject of His Majesty, he believed that the King's fiercest opponent was the Devil. All respectable men knew that it was through the work of witches that the Evil One sought to establish his supremacy on Earth. This Carrington readily acknowledged, and yet he insisted that Martha was an unlikely witch. In the end, however, he had perforce to concede that she and her grandmother had a case to answer. Frandley insisted that he should report the matter to John Hankelow. The following day he told George Stubbings that he had spoken personally with Dorothy Losh. Her tale was indeed damning of the Beeston women.

A slight, lone figure beset by a roaring tide of hideous allegations, Martha was to the witnesses a creature of the darkness. To John Hankelow, she was stripped of humanity and even her name. In the depositions she was referred to merely as "the examinate". To Richard, listening to her in court, she cried out with the frantic insistence of one who is unjustly accused.

"My grandmother was a sick woman long before she died, afflicted in mind as well as in body. When the Magistrate questioned her, she did not know what she was saying. For years I strove to protect her, since she was incapable of taking care of herself. In all that time I have been very busy, but never have I cast a single spell, far less bartered my soul with the Devil!"

Even when fighting for her life, she could not keep a sardonic edge out of her replies to Baron Elbourne, but spirit served her ill. She insisted that Dorothy Losh and Hugo Frandley were jealous of her and had conspired to perjure themselves, yet was constrained to acknowledge that George Stubbings and Joshua Carrington had treated her kindly. When asked why they should lie, she had no answer.

"They – they must be in error."

"Both are sensible men, are they not?"

"Yes, my Lord."

"Mr Carrington, in particular, gave his evidence even-handedly, and with every appearance of regret?"

"Yes, my Lord."

"Why then should the jury conclude that he and Mr Stubbings were mistaken?"

Silence.

"Do you have an answer?"

"I cannot say, my Lord."

Overcome by anguish and frustration, Richard smacked his fist down on the wooden table. Added to Annie's confession, the evidence from each of Dorothy, Hugo Frandley, George Stubbings and the troubled Carrington was powerful. Taken together, it was overwhelming. The case against Martha was watertight. Yet it could not be sound.

Impossible to rid his mind of the picture he had conjured up in his mind, the picture of what would happen to Martha within a few short hours. For this would not be an ordinary death, not a quiet death in the presence of a grieving family, such as any man or woman might anticipate at the ending of their days.

Women prisoners were burned, not drawn and quartered. It was a small mercy, a distinction made out of consideration for their sex. It would be indelicate to subject a female to the fate of men, who were half-strangled and had their privy members cut off and their bowels extracted while they were still alive, before being decapitated and having their bodies quartered. Richard's gorge rose when he remembered the last burning he had seen, up at Lancaster. A foul-mouthed termagant, convicted of petty treason, had her clothes, limbs and bonnet smeared thickly with tar. He could still hear the crowd's jeers as she was dragged, barefoot, on a hurdle to the site of execution. The chaplain said prayers and then she was manhandled on to a barrel of tar beside the stake. Chains were used to tie her and her neck placed in a noose at the end of a rope which ran through a pulley attached to the stake. As the wood was lighted, the executioner tried to pull the rope, but the flames roared up and scorched his hands and he had to retreat. The woman struggled in vain and men threw faggots on the fire to hasten her end. Her face turned black and her tongue swelled and as the flames consumed her nether parts, she ceased to move.

No! He could not watch Martha suffer such indignities, even in his imagination. Breathing hard and noisily, he cursed her out loud. Certainly, the woman had bewitched him too. It was the simplest explanation for his tormented bewilderment that a woman convicted on clear evidence, probed in the most painstaking manner, could yet persuade him that she had never given herself to the Devil or sworn to carry out his wicked work.

*Tomorrow she dies.*

The clock was inexorable, ticking away the minutes of her life. As he listened, a thought struck him. An anomaly so obvious that it shamed him not to have noticed it before.

A moment later, candle in hand, he was clattering down the wooden stairs, on his way to the library. The Judges' Lodging was well-stocked with dusty tomes and learned papers. In idle moments he often leafed through them. From memory, he thought that he might find what he was looking for.

He spent the next hour poring over the texts he had sought and when he was confident that he had unravelled the conundrum, he made his way to Baron Elbourne's chamber. Tonight the judge's snoring was louder than ever. Tomorrow the woman he had sentenced would die, but that consideration would not interrupt his slumber. Even Richard hesitated to do so. Yet he had no choice, if Martha was to be saved.

"What is the meaning of this?"

Baron Elbourne's face was ruddy with anger at the disturbance. Clad in his nightshirt, he yet conveyed the majesty of the law through narrowed eyes and lips. Richard knew well that if he failed to persuade the judge of the merit of his speculations, not only Martha's life but also his own reputation and standing would be set at naught. But this was no time to hesitate, and he did not. He spoke rapidly and with a passion that might have been envied by an advocate of distinction. The judge was strict and unforgiving of error, but Richard knew that his mind was acute. There were *prima facie* grounds for an objective mind to conclude that Martha was not a culprit, but rather a victim. If only Baron Elbourne were willing to consider the matter afresh!

At first, the judge scorned what Richard had to say. Yet as he listened, his brow began to furrow in thought. When Richard thrust the pamphlet into his hand, he studied it in silence for several minutes.

The author of the pamphlet was Joshua Carrington. He recorded therein divers researches he had conducted into the activities of the Roman cavalry in Cheshire, and in particular, those of the First Pannonian Regiment. The paper outlined his theory that senior officers who had received their discharge on conclusion of their active service had settled in the county to farm or produce salt. They would, he reasoned, be men much wealthier than the native inhabitants and thus any settlement that they might have established was likely to reflect their riches, if only it could be found. Richard had attended a lecture some years ago at which Carrington had described his speculations. It was pleasing to think that the retired Roman officers might have lived cheek by jowl with the local populace, but Carrington lacked proof to substantiate the notion. All he had been able to do was to chart the site of the principal Roman forts and the line of the arteries linking them. They included Watling Street, which ran from London to Wroxeter, where it met the military road running between Chester and Caerleon. In turn that road connected with a route which, on entering Cheshire, passed through Malpas and Tilston as it skirted the marshes of the Dee estuary on its way towards the city. This last road, as Richard pointed out to the judge, also ran close to Clough.

"Suppose Carrington encouraged his friend George Stubbings to dig in the environs of the hamlet in search of evidence of Roman occupation. Suppose George did more than that. Suppose he uncovered evidence of treasure that the Romans had buried underground."

"Supposition is not evidence!" the judge muttered. "In a Clerk of Assize, that is not necessarily a quality to be desired. In this case, so overwhelming was the weight of . . ."

"Hear me out, my Lord!" Richard could hardly believe that he dared to interrupt Baron Elbourne and the judge's face suggested that he could not believe it either. "Did we not see a different kind of evidence before our very eyes? What of Frandley's jewelled ring or, to my mind more significant, Dorothy Losh's bracelet? I swear that it was made of silver. How could a young peasant girl come by such a thing honestly? And there is more. What of the beaker that Carrington bought from Annie Beeston? Might it not have been a trophy implying a Roman presence on the Beeston land? No wonder George Stubbings was willing to assist with their ploughing. He was Carrington's envoy, scouring the land for Roman remnants."

"Mr Norley, have a care. You are suggesting that persons of repute have embarked upon a wicked conspiracy. Carrington and Stubbings are . . ."

"Do not forget Frandley!" Richard cried. "I believe they plotted together. How it must have hurt those men, that the stretch of land where the valuables were to be found belonged to a sick man married to a mad old crone. The first strategem was for Frandley to marry the girl and take possession of her property. When Martha spurned his overtures, they became desperate. Mungo Beeston was sick and likely to die soon. If his wife and grand-daughter predeceased him, his property would pass to his cousin. But what if Martha lived and were to marry a young, healthy fellow who discovered the hoard beneath their fields? This consideration, I am sure, drove Carrington and his friends to hatch their plan. But Annie and Martha Beeston were not their only victims. William Stubbings, who owned the land adjoining the Beestons' property, had to die. Harsh and devout he might have been, but he would not have been a party to a fraudulent attempt to convict his cousin and her granddaughter of witchcraft for financial gain."

Richard thrust into the judge's hand another yellowing document that he had found in the library. "Consider this treatise upon poisons, my Lord, and remember that George was a herbalist. The foxglove is a pretty plant, growing in profusion in the county, but he would be familiar with the fact that there is a substance capable of being extracted from its leaves that, ingested, stops the heart from beating. To outward appearances, the death in such a case is natural. In actuality, it is feloniously contrived."

The judge stared at him. For the first time in Richard's recollection, his voice carried a note of uncertainty.

"Your inferences have a certain superficial plausibility, Mr Norley . . ."

"There is more," Richard said eagerly. Sensing that he had won an advantage, he must not to let it slip. "Can it really be credited that the foolish old woman would have mastered the Latin in which she supposedly thanked Satan for enabling her to kill William? Can we . . ."

"A witch may have many strange talents," the judge

insisted. "Let me repeat what should be obvious. None of this is *evidence*."

"I recognise the difficulties, my Lord, but . . ."

"How can you expect me to halt the execution in such circumstances? So many of the points you draw upon in support of your argument bear more than a single interpretation. Is this a proper basis upon which to interfere with the punishment duly prescribed by law?"

"I need time!" Richard hissed. "With time, there will be proof in abundance, of that my conviction is firm. But there is one other fact that supports my case for Martha's defence. It derives from simple observation of the testimony in court and yet seems to me to be incontrovertible."

"Tell me," the judge said softly. And in that instant, Richard knew that he had won.


"So when my grandfather dies, I am unlikely to be rich."

Martha spoke in bewildered tones. So much had happened to her in so short a time that her bafflement was understandable. Initial digging on her land had yielded an extraordinary variety of finds: gold, coins, brooches and other jewellery. Yet there remained a question as to whether the goods constituted "treasure trove" and would in any event belong to the Crown rather than the owner of the land. This conundrum had taxed Carrington and his cronies; in their eyes, it underscored the need for secrecy about what the antiquary had discovered. Richard was in the course of preparing a legal case for title to the goods that might ultimately achieve an equitable division of the spoils. But much would depend upon the judgment of the coroner and Richard had ceased to believe that the law always delivered a verdict that was true and fair.

He tightened the grip of his arm around Martha's slender waist. They were lying together before the fire in the little cottage. From upstairs came the sound of Mungo Beeston's stertorous breathing. A physician from Chester whom the lovers had engaged to care for the old man had advised them that Mungo's life would draw at last to a close within the next few days. He was rarely conscious and remained ignorant of his granddaughter's narrow escape from death by judicial decree.

"Who knows? In any event, I can claim that I loved you when most certainly you had nothing."

She laughed. "Alone in my cell, I used to pray that you might use your good offices on my behalf. But as the fateful hour drew near, I lost all hope. When the gaoler told me that the judge had granted a stay of execution, I dropped at his feet in a faint. Even without being told, I knew you were the man who had saved me."

"Not just myself. His Lordship risked his reputation by asking the Magistrate to look into the matters I had raised. How fortunate that the girl Dorothy crumbled when he challenged her. For the sake of a bribe, she was willing to sacrifice your life. Once she confessed that Stubbings and Carrington had given her the bracelet and trained her in her testimony, the plot was laid bare for the world to see."

Martha shuddered. "So you were vindicated, my darling. But what made you certain of the truth?"

"You will recall my telling you that I believe that a person cannot conceal his natural disposition if questioned with sufficient subtlety? Well, then, the answer is simple. When Carrington made the supposedly generous suggestion that your land should be sold to George, he revealed that he knew that Hugo Frandley had asked for your hand in marriage."

"Indeed."

"As Frandley gave his evidence, I studied him with care and formed the view that he was as vain as any man that I have ever met."

She nodded. "Your judgment is correct."

"In that event, I found it impossible to believe that he would have disclosed to his friends that a slip of a girl had rejected his proposal of marriage. Unless he had good reason for candour, that is. I believe that once he became aware of the existence of the Clough hoard, he was willing to suffer any indignity if he thought it guaranteed him both revenge for your slight and a share in Carrington's booty."

Martha stared into the leaping flames. "How strange that all of them must now confront a far, far greater indignity."

Richard said nothing. Much as they deserved their fate, he could not help flinching as he contemplated what lay in store for the scoundrels who had so nearly murdered his beloved.

*Tomorrow they die.*

# The Dutchman and the Wrongful Heir

## Maan Meyers

*One of those delightful moments, when you stumble across a book you did not hitherto know and discover it is a box of delights, happened when I found a copy of* The Dutchman *(1992) by Maan Meyers. It's set in New Amsterdam in 1664 and features the investigations of the Dutch "schout" or sheriff, Pieter Tonneman, at the time of the British invasion. The book was the first of a series which traced the descendants of Tonneman in New Amsterdam/New-York through to the 1890s. I wanted to know more about Pieter Tonneman and so was delighted when the authors produced the new story set in New-York as it was then spelled, very soon after the British had taken control.*

*Maan Meyers is the combined alias of husband-and-wife team Annette and Martin Meyers. Both have written books separately including the Olivia Brown stories by Annette set in 1920s Greenwich Village, one of which will be found in my* Mammoth Book of Roaring Twenties Whodunnits.

### Tuesday, 30 November. Dawn

Even before dawn, the screech of the red-tailed hawks echoed through the village as the scavengers swooped low over the thick woods that covered the hills beyond the Wall. The noise was the sort that could raise the dead.

It did not raise the dead, but it did set every four-footer

barking, including the small, black and tan spaniel of Colonel Richard Nicholls, the Governor of His Majesty King Charles's new English colony of New-York, who slept only fitfully when he was not on board his flagship, the thirty-six gun *Guinea* idling in the harbour.

The hideous screeching came from beyond the Wall, and though the Governor used his glass, the sun was not yet high enough for him to see. He called for his aide to fetch the Dutchman, his Sheriff, Pieter Tonneman.

On this sharply cold morning, it seemed almost as if the sun was loath to present herself, though the village, by habit and necessity, was beginning to stir.

Pieter Tonneman had heard the screeching of the red-tailed hawks well before Nicholls's aide thumped on his door. Now he could see them swooping low over the thick woods that covered the hills beyond the Wall.

He reined in Venus as he approached the Broad Way Gate, one of the two official openings in the Wall, noting logs missing again from the top of the Wall. Stolen, he had no doubt, by Indians for firewood as winter approached.

Sam Dolittle, the rheumy-eyed English soldier on sentry duty, was alone at the Gate. No sign of Pos. The Sheriff found his pipe, filled it, but made no attempt to light it even though Dolittle's fire was close by. Pos, the old rascal, after a night of carousing, had failed to remember their morning appointment to inspect the woodland beyond the Wall for signs of hostile Indians.

Tonneman, former Schout of New Amsterdam and current Sheriff of New-York, pointed his mare in the direction of the circling hawks. Thanks to the harsh wind from the north, he could smell the poisonous fumes from Keyser's tannery – all tanneries having been banished from the town proper – wafting toward him.

As he passed the van Cortlandt estate, which spread from the Broad Way all the way to the North River, he thought, van Cortlandt might be rich, but for all his riches he couldn't escape the stench.

The irony was van Cortlandt had built outside the Wall to get away from the stink and noise of the village.

Tonneman called back to Dolittle. "Captain Pos was to meet me . . ."

"Who?"

The Sheriff didn't know if Dolittle was deaf or simple or simply English. "Lodowyk Pos, my Deputy, was to meet me at the Gate. Tell him I've gone ahead. Tell him I said to follow."

The Broad Way travelled along the upward rise of the Island, from the Fort to the mostly uncharted wilderness – which remained so despite the Indian trails – continuing all the way to the high cliffs on the north end of the Island. Except for Shellpoint, the lake-sized freshwater pond that served as a basin collecting the waters flowing from the surrounding hills, these hills were steep, rock-covered, and densely wooded.

Even so, the Island was full of sweetness, if one looked in the right places. The beautiful widow Racqel Mendoza was never far from Tonneman's thoughts. He had found the bones of her missing husband not three months past. Nine more months till her mourning period was finished. She'd promised him.

After they were married he would buy a patch of land, perhaps near the East River. That Racqel was a Jewess and he a Christian, was no trouble at all to Tonneman, but he knew it was for her.

He pocketed his unlit pipe as he approached the forest. The eerie screeching of the hawks grew intense, bringing his mind back to practical matters. Venus let out a fearful whinny and pawed the ground, steam streaming from her nostrils. The hairs on the back of Tonneman's neck bristled. At the edge of the wood, he dismounted and tethered the dun mare to a slender hickory.

Brush crunching under his boots, the Sheriff made his way into the forest following the old Indian trail.

Stands of ancient trees, hickory, oak, tulip, so thick that even leafless as now, full sunlight could not pass, soon surrounded him. No sign of the Indian war party. The screeching gained in intensity as he left the path and with the aid of his sturdy cudgel, pushed through the undergrowth.

Christ's bloody fingers, if he couldn't still smell the tannery stink. No, it was something worse. As he stood in the hollow of a rocky rise, the sense that he was not alone was so strong he caught himself glancing over his shoulder.

Plash. A fat chunk of reeking offal spattered on his boot. Sweet Jesus, that's what he'd been smelling. The second disgusting glob fell on his upturned face. "God's blood," he shouted, using his nose cloth to wipe the filth from his face.

He could hardly see for the hawks pestering something in the thick old oak under which he stood. Raising his cudgel, he gave the trunk a mighty wallop and shouted again. The hawks screeched and departed, albeit reluctantly.

Draped over the branch of the old oak was a scarecrow, a hat clamped on its head. But scarecrows don't drop pieces of human flesh.

His eyes darted left and right for tracks but there was no sign – but for the body – that anyone had been here.

All woods have their own melody; on Manhattan Island the patterns went from frogs to wolves and all manner of birds and beasts. Now, except for the hawks and their ilk, that never moved south in winter as the songbirds did, the woods were oddly silent.

The Dutchman moved out from under the body and hollered again to drive away the hawks, as they had begun stealing back to the child-small body draped over the limb.

Children climbed trees, and though his daughter Anna and husband Johan Bikker, farming in New Haarlem, had produced a son not a month past, he knew little of children. Anna had been his and poor dead Maria's only child who'd lived past infancy.

Indians were tree climbers as well . . . Bears?

Someone had climbed this tree, or had been put there – for whatever reason – and been taken for an enemy, or dinner.

More slop dropped to the ground near him. Tonneman listened. Hearing nothing but the hawks, he leaned his cudgel against the trunk and climbed up the backside of the oak until he neared the carcass, which was about fifteen hands off the ground. He grabbed hold of another branch just above and pulled himself into a prone position so he could look down on the small body. The stink was ferocious.

Again he went, listening, watching, noting that he was arse end to Shellpoint.

The hawks circling overhead screeched at him. He'd come between them and their prey. The more aggressive swooped down trying to dislodge Tonneman, but he thrashed on his branch and yelled them off. They kept their distance for the while but continued circling.

Extending his arm to grasp the hat of the creature beneath, he managed instead to knock it to the ground, revealing long, tangled yellow hair and confirming what instinct had told him: the body was a woman. Sacred heaven! He knew her. No breath-clouds came from her nose or mouth. Dead as a doornail, as the Johnnies liked to say.

He tried to get ahold of her dangling arm and lost his balance, ended up swinging like a clown from the branch. There came a mighty creak. The branch cracked and bent downward. Seemingly, the tree cast him out, and he and the woman came down together.

He was too old for climbing trees like a fool. That went through his mind as he fell, hoping he wasn't going to land on the sharp rocks and break his bones and hers as well, though Gretchen Goderis no longer had need of hers.

Instead, flailing, he landed flat bellied into the frigid pond with a splash the like of a water spout.

When he came up for air, the Sheriff thought he heard eerie, harsh laughter. He dragged his sodden self onto the bank, shaking, wringing icy water from his clothing as best he could.

The sun was bright in the wintry sky, but it gave no warmth, at least none that Tonneman could feel. A sharp wind ruffled the branches, chilling him to the bone. The laughter came again, mocking him, floating in the frigid air, around and above him, moving farther and farther away until the silence and the screeching took charge again. Shivering, he sniffed the air. There'd be snow by evening, and unless he got into dry clothes he'd become a human icicle.

Tonneman found what the hawks had left of Gretchen Goderis not far from the oak, lying on her back as if sleeping in her own bed. The stiffness was just setting in on her, but he could see what he had to see, what he hadn't seen when she was draped over the limb.

Protruding from her chest was an arrow. Iroquois from the look of it. Man Who Walks Like A Fox, whom the settlers called Foxman, was a Mohawk-Iroquois. Tonneman thought of the eerie laughter. Indians didn't laugh like white men. The arrogant Man Who Walks Like A Fox would consider Tonneman falling out of a tree into the pond a big joke. It could be Foxman's arrow.

Tonneman bent closer to the body. Her garment, though worse for the wear and ill fitting, had been one of the late Widow van Lundt's best. Her eyes were gone, of course, and parts of her face.

"Jesus save us," Tonneman muttered. So much for a goodly inheritance.

Not even a fortnight past Gretchen Goderis, a maidservant, had been left the entire van Lundt estate by the widow van Lundt herself, having no blood heirs.

In addition to Margarieta van Lundt's trunk of gold guilders, which Tonneman had seen with his own eyes, there was the extensive property cheek by jowl to Stuyvesant's *Bouwerie* and comparable to the former Dutch Governor's estate.

The Sheriff bent over the body. The arrow was missing a fletch.

Perhaps it had been displaced when she fell from the tree, but he saw no sign of it. The hawks would not trouble the feathers, and the other feathers were unmarked. Without the missing feather to help guide it, the arrow would not have gone far. And certainly not steady to its mark. Foxman was too much of a warrior to fly a poorly made or even damaged arrow.

Gretchen Goderis may have been felled by the arrow, but it was possible that no bow had dispatched it. Had the arrow,

then, been used as a dagger? In that case she had been
stabbed. And then, God help her, quick or dead, the killer
had propped her in the tree, carrion for the hawks.

Willem Stael, carrying the post from New-York through
to New Haven in Connecticut, had brought warning from a
courier that an Indian war party, or the Frenchies or re-
negade Dutch in Indian war garb, were harrying the settlers
and burning farms in the countryside around New-York.
Colonel Nicholls had alerted the settlers in the outlying
farms and estates. All citizens were ordered into town until
the area outside the Wall was deemed safe from incursion by
Indians. The populace, never without complaint, was not
pleased with this state of affairs, a virtual imprisonment. Just
the day before Tonneman had warned Nicholls that the
citizens were growing fractious.

Nicholls had agreed to lift the curfew but only after
Tonneman inspected the perimeter to be certain that no
enemy lurked in the woods beyond the Wall. Tonneman
could have told him there wouldn't be. The Dutch settlers
believed in live and let live, and the Frenchies had gone north
with the Iroquois.

Then the screeching of the red-tailed hawks had hastened
Tonneman's rounds. Another day and little would have been
left of Gretchen Goderis.

"Halloo, Tonneman!" The voice was unmistakable.

"Here. The rise. Follow the hawks."

Pos, a short, muscular man with a fine black beard,
crashed through the brush. His lope came to a halt when
he spied the body on the ground. "Horse piss!" He called to
Tonneman's back, "Where are you going?"

"Keep the hawks away," Tonneman said. "And when we
get back to town send someone to replace the missing logs on
the Wall." Cudgel in hand, he walked back to where he'd
tethered Venus and rode the anxious mare to the Broad Way
Gate.

Dolittle was dozing, his wheel-lock at his feet.

"Sentinel Dolittle!"

"What? Sir?" Half asleep Dolittle leaped to attention,
presenting his weapon backwards with the barrel facing him.

Tonneman groaned. A lot of good this one did, but he had to admit, no worse than the Dutch. "Did you hear anything unusual before I arrived?"

"Everything in this goddamn country is unusual. Tell me whose arse I have to kiss to get back to Bow Bells."

The Sheriff laughed. "I need a blanket or canvas."

Dolittle shuffled into the guard hut and came out with a mangy blanket roll. "What do you need it for?"

With the laugh in his voice Tonneman said, "To wrap a bloody body in, of course." He unrolled the rag of a blanket and threw it over his own coat, now, thanks to the chill wind, covered with a fine surface of ice that soon would be stiff as a board from his dunking.

Already, the townspeople were coming from their homes and shops, moving toward the Gate, calling out to him. Beyond the Wall, the cries of the red tails reached a fevered pitch as, ignoring Pos, they swooped into the wood. All this and Tonneman caught a movement on the Broad Way Road from the direction of Keyser's tannery.

"Blimey, Sheriff, it's me own sleeping blanket," Dolittle said, taking Tonneman's attention from the speck in the distance.

Tonneman dug a stuiver from his sodden wallet and tossed it to the old soldier, who caught it expertly.

Dolittle's face brightened, "I got me another blanket in the hut. You want to buy that one, too?"

Tonneman waved a dismissive hand at the soldier and paced to keep his blood flowing. He would have been on his way back to Pos and the dead woman, but the speck on the Broad Way Road turned into a young man with shiny black hair, a Johnnie by the look of him, swatting his black steed on the flank with his wide-brimmed, abundantly red-plumed, black hat to goad it on. A man in a hurry. He galloped at full tilt, his black velvet cloak flying behind him. At the Gate he reined in his horse.

"Good day, sir." The-man-in-a-hurry swung his hat first left and then right and bowed from the waist sliding danger-ously in his saddle in the process.

"And who might you be?" Tonneman said, trying to keep

his teeth from chattering. "We are under curfew due to an Indian war party seen in Johnnie Land." The traveller was ruddy complected, high of cheekbone, narrow-eyed.

"I am John Lundt from New Haven way. I have just passed the night in Greenwich and there was no sign of any war party."

"What business have you here?"

"Who is asking?"

"The Sheriff of New-York."

"There's a blessing. Would you be so kind as to direct me to the home of my Aunt Margarieta van Lundt?" With another grand gesture, the stranger replaced his hat and slid off his horse, landing splat in the road.

## Tuesday, 30 November. Early morning

"There the fool was lying on the ground like Gretchen Goderis, as if he, too, was sleeping in his own bed. Only while poor Gretchen was dead, this buffoon was drunk. I left him with Dolittle to sleep it off. We have more important fish to fry." Tonneman was standing backside to the Governor's fire, so close he'd begun to steam, giving off putrid odours as the frost melted from his wet clothing. His boots were caked with mud.

The Governor's nostrils twitched; he took a lacy cloth reeking of lavender from his sleeve and held it to his nose. "You mean the death of a charwoman?"

Nicholls's response was so like that of his former boss, Pieter Stuyvesant, Tonneman had to repress a laugh. "It was murder, sir."

The Governor picked up his dog and laughed when the animal licked his lips. The spaniel, satin eyes shining, stared at Tonneman as if to say, see how grand I am.

"What would you have me do?" The Governor was irritated. He'd just received another missive from Connecticut Governor Winthrop, instructing him on how to govern New-York. Nicholls knew that he had thwarted John Winthrop's ambition, which was to extend his own domination into New-York.

James, Duke of York and His Majesty King Charles's brother, had directed that Nicholls take possession of the Island of Manhattan as it was crucial for trading routes. James had no intention of letting New England become supreme in the colonies. Nicholls gave the brocade band a firm tug and somewhere in the house came the faint sound of a bell.

"The Director-General always liked to know what was going on," Tonneman said, thinking that Governor Nicholls seemed very much at home in Stuyvesant's Great White House in town, having banished Stuyvesant to the *Bouwerie* until he was ready to return to The Netherlands. On the other hand, Nicholls was of the sea.

Tonneman, who'd been a sailor as a young man, after his father had lost everything when the bottom had dropped out of the tulip market, knew the call of the sea. But for their guns, he'd actually enjoyed watching the English vessels sweeping through the water with their beautiful milky sails puffed and billowing.

Nicholls's aide, Captain Geoffrey Hughes, entered with a steaming cup of tea and a platter of biscuits, along with a stack of documents. Tonneman, inhaling the fragrant steam of the strong tea halfway across the chamber, longed for his own hot dark brew and a change of his filthy garments, from which a noxious vapour was rising as the ice melted.

Hughes set his burden down on the fine Dutch desk, then retreated.

"The death of a charwoman is of no importance to me," Nicholls said, biting into a biscuit.

"A very wealthy charwoman." Tonneman's innards growled. He was reminded he had left his house without so much as a bite of bread and cheese, it having been too early for Katrina Root to lay out his breakfast. What he wouldn't give for a bowl of hot soup. Perhaps he could get some at the jail in the basement of City Hall where Vrouw Root also provided meals for prisoners housed there.

"What say you?" Nicholls demanded.

"This charwoman inherited the van Lundt estate. Former poor charwoman or not, she owned a large estate on the East

River and a trunk full of gold guilders. She was out of duffel and into silk to fit her new station before her benefactor was cold in her grave. I'll wager the suitors, both English and Dutch, were lining up at her door."

"Balderdash," the Governor exploded, his face going dark, words flying from his mouth like pieces of shot. "Lord deliver me from Dutch nonsense. Under English law women inherit neither property nor lands. New-York is an English colony. English law will prevail."

"Our citizens will not be pleased." English law struck Tonneman as grossly unfair. Every child should have the same share of a legacy.

Nicholls moved on. "And who will now inherit the estate and the gold guilders?"

Ah, Tonneman thought, I have finally got through to him. "I'll have a little talk with the drunken lout sleeping it off in Dolittle's shack. He claims to be kin to the late widow van Lundt. I'll have to break the news to him that she's dead."

Nicholls stroked his dog's sleek head and looked down at the documents on his desk. If there was legitimate kin, the vast estate and the gold guilders would not go into the coffers of the colony's namesake, the Duke of York.

"Be off and do your duty, Sheriff, and let me do mine, but make well certain this lout is the legitimate heir." After a pause the Governor added, "If he's not, there might be a recovery fee in it for you."

Tonneman kept a bland expression. He knew what Nicholls was offering. "And the curfew?"

"Any sign of this raiding party?"

"Not a one." Who, come to think of it, had started the ridiculous rumour about an Indian raiding party? A courier? What courier? He had never seen any courier. Was the point to keep anyone from stumbling on the murder and finding the body before the red tails had picked it clean? Or had Stael lied about the courier?

A man stood waiting in the outer room when Tonneman left Nicholls. "Good day, Tonneman."

"Van Brugge." Tonneman noted that the miller wore

clean clothing befitting an English gentleman and fine leather boots. There was not a flake of mill dust on him.

"Bridge."

"So you've turned back into a Johnnie, have you?" Tonneman wasn't surprised. Years before, when he'd come to New Amsterdam and opened his mill, Charles Bridge had taken the Dutch equivalent of his name, Carel van Brugge.

"We are an English colony now, Tonneman."

"We are indeed."

"What is driving the hawks?"

"Gretchen Goderis is dead."

"Ah, the illegitimate heir."

"Legitimate by our laws. There was a will, after all."

"Our laws." Bridge practically spat the words. "Our law is English now. Women have no right to property of their own."

"And a good day to you, too, Bridge," Tonneman said, with a touch of irony as he stepped outside.

No sooner had Tonneman opened the front door of the Great White House into the bitter wind, than he was besieged by the grumbling populace crowding the Broad Way.

"I have an announcement," he shouted over the noise.

"Is the curfew lifted?" Sybout Huygens ran the Indian trading post just outside the Wall. With the curfew, he was losing money.

Tonneman waved Huygens off. "Gretchen Goderis has been murdered. In the wood beyond the Wall."

The crowd oohed and aahed. A woman cried out. Babies were hushed.

"By Indians?" someone yelled.

"Perhaps, perhaps not."

This piece of news gave everyone pause. Tonneman knew that most were thinking more about the van Lundt fortune than the danger of Indians. No one could ever say that his village was not interested in commerce. And money.

"Did anyone see her come into town for the curfew?"

Many glances were exchanged, but no response came.

"Did you see any Indians?" Keyser called out, eager to return to his tannery.

"Not a one," Tonneman said.

"Then lift the curfew!"

"Yes, yes," a chorus began. "Lift the curfew."

"Consider it lifted."

"You might have told us sooner."

"Go back to work," Tonneman growled, tensing his body against the wind. "Except you, Keyser. I have a job for you."

Keyser, small and wiry, a hard drinker, more belligerent than most, was immediately suspicious. "What kind of job? I'm a busy man."

"Horse thieves! Horse thieves!"

The citizens, who'd begun to drift off to their various labours, stopped to watch the blacksmith, Dirk Baalde, running toward them, hollering like a wild man. Baalde, who maintained a forge inside the Fort, had arms and legs like tree trunks; his red beard was stained with oily soot. Tonneman didn't like Dirk Baalde. He was a cruel man, to horses and to people.

"They've taken my Gretchen."

Tonneman was shocked and surprised. He had no idea that Gretchen Goderis had anything to do with Baalde. "I don't know how to tell you . . ."

"That damn mare is always slipping her reins however I tie her. Someone has stolen her, for sure. And the cart she was hitched to as well. I told Pos last night. She's a bay. What have you done about it, Sheriff?"

"Nothing," Tonneman admitted. "But you can be assured we intend to scour the village and beyond for her." And, he thought, perhaps when we find Gretchen the mare and her cart, we'll find they were used to carry Gretchen the former maidservant to her death.

He told Keyser to fetch Gretchen Goderis's remains to the churchyard for burial. "And tell Pos to meet me at City Hall."

"I want to be paid in shillings."

"Which I do not have in my purse right now. A stuiver will have to do."

"I want shillings."

"One shilling. Submit your reckoning and I'll see it's paid."

As the crowd dispersed, Tonneman hurried toward City Hall. Who was it had brought news of the band of Indians? He had to get things done before he could go home for clean, dry clothes and bread and cheese.

Instead of going to City Hall, he headed for the King Charles, the tavern formerly known as the Pear Tree.

The Sheriff had seen Willem Stael there often enough, and it was where he would start looking for the post rider, who carried the post among the Dutch settlements as far north as Beaverwyk. Since September and the English take-over of New Amsterdam, Stael was doing the same from New-York to New Haven, where he met the post from Boston and exchanged letters.

Stael was the one who had told of a courier warning about the Indian threat. Had he lied? If, so, why?

It had gotten colder, but the weather mattered not to the children, who screamed as they played their hoop games along the shore, nor to the old woman, her skirts grazing the incoming tide, who was digging for clams with a long shovel.

Tonneman breathed in the fragrant beer and gin aroma of the King Charles, which he still thought of as the Pear Tree. He remembered when he and Hendrik Jansen Smitt and Joost Zoelan would drink and talk through soulful nights until they became ghosts of themselves with the dawn.

He shook off the memories, good and bad, for the business at hand: Willem Stael himself. With a few well-placed thumps, he ejected Stael's outraged companions; it was obvious from the coins scattered about that Stael was paying the fare. The drunken sot didn't even chase after the vagrant English penny that fell from his leather purse and rolled off the plank table to the floor, where a fellow drinker artfully hid it under a wet boot.

Tonneman seized Stael by the collar, lifting the little man out of the tavern and onto Pearl Street. The yellow dog, sleeping near the back door roused itself and began to bark.

"Good day to you, Sheriff." The post rider was slobbering drunk. "Just getting my throat wet before my next ride to New Haven."

"Any wetter you'll drown." Tonneman set the little man

on his feet, but Stael's feet wouldn't support him and he collapsed on the ground, a clump of wet rags. Almost immediately, such a great snore arose from the clump, that the yellow dog showed his teeth. Tonneman nudged the drunken post rider with the toe of his boot. Dead to the world, for a time at least.

Hearing Tonneman's roar of frustration, Arent Evertsen, the owner of the King Charles, came running to the door. "What's ailing you, Tonneman?"

"When did Stael get here?" The Sheriff bent over the sleeping post rider and detached his leather purse. All English money. A considerable amount that the fool hadn't yet drunk away.

"Well . . . I didn't notice. Not long since I opened." Evertsen was wary, his eyes on the money. He'd obviously kept open after hours.

"Nonsense! Stael couldn't have gotten this drunk this fast."

Evertsen looked bemused.

"Where did Willie get all the money?"

"How would I know?"

"I'm not concerned right now that you were serving after hours."

"Come in and we'll have a pipe," Evertsen said, suddenly full of goodwill.

"I'd rather have something hot," Tonneman said, heading directly to the fire.

"Rum."

"Food."

"Rabbit stew."

"Good." His backside nearly normal, Tonneman turned to warm his front.

"And a beer?"

"How would you like my knife up your arse? You know I gave up the drink. Fetch my rabbit stew."

"As you say."

When the tavern keeper didn't move, Tonneman shouted, "Now."

They sat on two empty brandywine barrels near the fire.

Evertsen filled his pipe while Tonneman shovelled in the stew. It was terrible but it was hot. The yellow dog lay at their feet, his tongue occasionally darting out for any drops of gravy Tonneman let fall.

Sated, Tonneman filled his pipe. "Well?"

"Someone else went to New Haven, not Stael," Evertsen said.

"Another post rider took his place?"

"I suppose."

"Who?"

Silent, Evertsen made a show of lighting their pipes. They breathed in the rich tobacco.

"Then why does Stael have all this money?" The Sheriff patted Stael's purse.

Shouts rang out for Evertsen to fill empty tankards. The tavern owner stood. "Maybe someone paid him for the privilege of taking his place."

And why would someone do that, a warmer, dryer, less hungry Tonneman thought, as he walked through the noisy tavern to the street. He'd have to wait till Stael was sober to get his answer.

The sun glared in his eyes as he stepped outside. For a moment he could see nothing. When his vision cleared, he saw that the bundle of rags called Willem Stael was gone.

"It's a bloody conspiracy," he shouted. He was alone on the street, the only sound the lap, lap of the water, driven by the icy wind, hitting the beach.

He led Venus into her stall, gave her water and oats, and removed her saddle. His hurried brushing of her damp coat was far less than the dependable beast deserved.

Only then did he enter his house. No warmth greeted him. The fire Vrouw Root had left hours earlier was barely smoldering. He added a good sized log and it came to life. Under a cloth were a slab of cheese, a fragrant loaf of bread, and a mug of buttermilk. As always, the good Vrouw had filled a pitcher with fresh water, which he held now to the fire to melt the ice crystals, then poured into a basin. After a wash-up and a change of clothing he chipped the icy veil on the buttermilk, and eased his wolfish hunger, banishing the vile taste of Evertsen's stew. Pos arrived as he was finishing.

"No beer?" The Deputy set his knapsack on the floor.

"No beer, what is worse, no post rider."

"Stael?"

"He was slobbering drunk in the King Charles treating everyone in sight to brandywine."

"Ah," Pos said, cutting himself a wedge of cheese.

"Yes, and he had a purse full of English money."

"Where –?"

"Don't ask me. I left him sleeping under the pear tree, hoping the cold would sober him up."

"Or kill him."

"That, too," said Tonneman. "Evertsen said Stael was talking about someone paying him not to take the post to New Haven. That someone may have taken Stael's place."

"Let's go to the jail and beat the truth out of him."

Tonneman slammed the table. "Your fool of a Sheriff didn't watch close enough and the scoundrel had a chance to walk away."

"Horse piss." Pos lifted his hat and scratched his head. "Dirk Baalde claims someone stole his bay mare and a small cart."

"The better to carry a dead woman unseen to the wood?"

"Practical." Another head scratch from Pos. "Maybe not dead? Alive and even talking. But why would she go? Did she go willingly?"

Tonneman agreed. "No problem with Keyser?"

"Always a problem with Keyser. He wants to be paid a bounty because I took something from the body and what was left of poor Gretchen's clothing wouldn't make a nose rag." Pos reached for his knapsack and brought out the mismade arrow.

"Good man." Tonneman studied the murder weapon, turning it over and over in his hand.

"I tried the same thing," Pos said, "but it's not talking. Maybe a little beer would help."

"Have a look in the taverns for Stael." Tonneman was grave. "But if you drink more than one beer . . ."

Pos winked at him. "I'm as good as my word. Where will you be?"

"It's time I talked to the other sot, John Lundt, who's sleeping himself sober in Dolittle's guard post. Unless he too has crawled off."

### Tuesday, 30 November. Noon

"Sorry, old girl." Venus swung her head around and nipped at his shoulder as Tonneman re-saddled the weary mare.

The winds had calmed but Tonneman still sniffed snow in the air. Even with his belly full, his clothing clean and dry, he was not content, what with a murder so soon after the English took the town. He whistled through his teeth as he rode back to the Broad Way Gate and the sentinel hut. His mood changed quickly when he found Dolittle and the man who called himself John Lundt, breeches down, throwing dice over who would enjoy the charms of Honore, Sweet Lips' newest whore, who was dancing half naked around the gamblers, egging them on.

Swinging his cudgel, Tonneman ended the game like Samson in the unholy temple, very nearly breaking the heads of the gamblers as they scrambled to escape the club. He sent Honore on her way with orders to tell Sweet Lips that she and her girls were banned from New-York for a week because of Honore's transgression. "But she'll be angry with me," Honore said, draping herself over Tonneman, her red, unbound hair lashing his face.

Tonneman pushed the whore away. "I'm depending on it. I don't judge you for your trade, but I will not have it interfering with me, my work, or my town."

Honore dressed quickly. As she left she stuck her tongue out at the Sheriff. He laughed, kicked Lundt and told him to get dressed. He didn't even bother to talk to Dolittle; mercifully the soldier was Nicholls's problem, not his.

Pos stumbled out of the Rocking Horse. He could hardly see straight. In every tavern he'd set foot – and there were more than a dozen just on Pearl Street and the Broad Way – no one would tell him anything unless he put down a stuiver for a beer. Pos wouldn't have had it any other way. And stuiver for stuiver, tankard for tankard, no one had seen Stael since the previous day.

The Broad Way was teeming with riders, carts, commercial activity. It was giving him a headache. He was leaning on the hitching post when with a bleary eye he caught sight of a slightly built boy in black garments across the road staring at him intently.

He beckoned to the boy, who had taken on the aspect of a deer, with its soft eyes and shy manner. Horse piss. A deer in a black suit. Pos shook his head, wiped his eyes. The boy was not a deer, but in fact, one of the Jews, and he was opening his mouth to speak.

Pos stood up as straight as he could while holding tight to the hitching post.

"The Sheriff," the boy said. His beard was like fine moss.

"Not me. Tonneman."

"Heer Levy told me to find the Sheriff or his Deputy."

"You have found his Deputy. Captain Pos, at Heer Levy's service."

"You must come at once to his tavern. It is very important."

Levy's tavern, where Pos had not thought to go, was at the Water Gate. Pos's spirits brightened. "Lead on, boy. Let's see how good Jewish beer is this month."

Tonneman and a subdued Lundt rode through the Broad Way Gate and into the countryside beyond the Wall. Snow, soft as meal, began to fall, seeming to hesitate for a brief moment in the heavy clouds before spilling to earth.

"Tell me again," Tonneman said. "In what way are you related to the Widow van Lundt?"

The young man leaned sideways and vomited. He wiped his mouth with his sleeve and edged his horse even with Tonneman. Tonneman repeated the question, but he was distracted by Lundt's eyes. For the first time he noticed that they were two different colours. One blue as Delft tile, the other green.

"My dear departed father was her brother . . . ?" Lundt's voice drifted into a question.

They were riding again when Tonneman remarked, "The Widow van Lundt was born a Dircksen."

The young man looked momentarily puzzled, then brightened. "You didn't let me finish. I mean, my dear departed father was her brother-in-law."

Tonneman grunted. He turned Venus onto a curved road. They'd reached the van Lundt estate. The manor house looked deserted. No smoke from the chimney, no light in the windows. There was light, however, and chimney smoke coming from the much smaller house a distance beyond the manor, where Jacobus Oopdyk, the estate manager, lived with his old mother.

A horse and cart stood in front of that house while Jacobus Oopdyk and his mother unloaded provisions they had obviously purchased while they were quarantined in town. As Tonneman and Lundt dismounted, Oopdyk left the labours to his mother and walked toward them with that rolling gait that proclaimed him a former sailor.

"Halloo, Tonneman. What brings you here?" Though he wasn't known as a drinking man, Oopdyk's knobby red nose and his face, a collection of damaged veins, belied the fact. Oopdyk with his broken teeth was no souse. But he was a fighting man ready to take the smallest word or the slightest remark as an insult.

"Ah, you've come about my late mistress, the heiress," he said with a vulgar laugh. "And who'd be this dandy Johnnie giving me the evil eye?" He stared at young Lundt as if challenging him to combat.

"You didn't like poor Gretchen?"

"Poor?" Oopdyk sneered and spat. "Poor? Nothing poor about her. She saw to that, didn't she? Made herself an heiress, then told me to get out. She had plans, she said, and they didn't include me and my poor old mother."

"You don't say?" Tonneman glanced beyond Oopdyk to where his mother was carrying a heavy bag of meal into their house. No sign that they were in the process of moving out.

"Can we get on with this? I demand to know where my kinswoman is."

"It distresses me to break the sad news, but your kinswoman van Lundt died well over a month ago," Tonneman said.

"Good heavens! What a terrible shock! Dear Auntie van Lundt." Lundt swayed against his horse, fumbling for his nose cloth and then made a show of dabbing non-existent tears from his eyes.

The performance stopped even Oopdyk from speaking. Tonneman rolled his eyes heavenward. God save him.

"It's very cold standing out here." Lundt whining, tucked his lace-trimmed nose cloth away. "I'd like to sit by a warm fire and think about this sad occasion."

"Your dear auntie left her property to her maidservant, Gretchen Goderis. If you are the proper heir, why did she not leave it to you?"

"We had not seen each other for years," Lundt said, retrieving his nose cloth once more and sobbing into it. "Besides, didn't you say that this maidservant is dead?"

"Oh, yes," Tonneman said. "Very dead."

"Has any other heir stepped forward?"

"None. Unless we consider yourself."

"Ipso facto." Lundt gathered himself together and strode to the front door of the house. "I am the rightful heir." With a self-satisfied smirk he ended with, "I will not trouble you further, Sheriff." He turned to Oopdyk, who had followed him to the door. "Consider yourself rehired. I'll have a fire and some victuals. I'm tired and hungry."

Oopdyk's face lit up. "Thank you, sir, fine sir," he said, bowing and scraping.

"Not just yet, I'm afraid," Tonneman said. "This problem must be adjudicated by your aunt's attorney-at-law. There was a will."

A crafty expression appeared on Oopdyk's gnarled face. "Now that you mention it, I do remember the Widow van Lundt speaking about her long lost nephew."

"Get out of here, Oopdyk."

"I'll have the house made ready for you, sir, don't you

worry." The knobby-nosed man ran off, loudly calling the good news to his mother.

When Tonneman turned back to Lundt, he saw Lundt entering the house. The Sheriff hurried after and found Lundt, playing the Burgher, inspecting the great room with its heavy Old Country furniture and Eastern rugs.

"Very nice," Lundt murmured, pleased.

"We'll have to ride back to town," Tonneman said, but he too was impressed by the opulence, by the portrait paintings on the walls. Everything seemed to be in place, no sign of disturbance. "We have to talk to the lawyer for the estate."

"It's not right," Lundt said, petulantly. "You heard the man. He knows I'm the legitimate heir."

"Oopdyk knows what's in his purse and his belly, nothing more." Tonneman paused in front of a portrait of a youthful woman and a child, a boy of perhaps two years with a moon-shaped face, hooded eyes, and a vacant smile. He recognized the woman as a much younger Margarieta van Lundt, but the child? To his knowledge, the van Lundts had been childless.

"Do you recognize these people?" Tonneman asked Lundt, who was holding an ornate silver candelabrum close to his breast.

"No." Lundt resumed inspecting his inheritance.

"Well, your dear auntie van Lundt is the lady."

Lundt opened a large kas, then closed it. The women's dresses inside didn't interest him. But the bottles and glasses in the low cabinet opposite did.

Foregoing a glass, he drank from the bottle. The perfume of brandy filled the air as Lundt wandered back to the painting. "I wouldn't have known her that youthful."

As good an answer as Tonneman expected. He tried again. "Who might the child be? You, perhaps?"

"I hardly think so," Lundt said, his words slurred. "That is obviously an idiot child."

It was Tonneman's own thought.

They headed back to town with the wind swirling the snow around them.

"Halloo, halloo," Dolittle called as they approached the

Broad Way Gate. They could barely see him for the snow, nor hear him over the wind. "Tonneman, you are to go at once to the Jew's tavern."

## Tuesday, 30 November. Early Afternoon

Sitting on pilings above the water line of the East River, was Asser Levy's slaughterhouse, the stink almost as foul as Keyser's tannery. Levy's slaughterhouse, butcher shop, and tavern were positioned immediately inside the Wall.

Pos had tipped over the horse trough in front of Levy's tavern while Levy and four other Jews formed a human barrier to keep the curious away. As Tonneman came close, he saw the missing post rider Willem Stael, lying like a dead fish in the icy water from Levy's horse trough.

Tonneman sighed. For a former drinking man the Sheriff was usually tolerant of drunkards. But, by Christ, today had been too much. While Lundt gaped, Tonneman dismounted.

"Dead?"

"What else?" Pos said. "A drowned or frozen drunk is what it looks like. Should we be suspicious?"

Tonneman turned Stael's sodden body and rolled back the collar of his coat. "What do you think, Deputy?"

"Marks on the back of his neck."

"As if someone held him down till he drowned."

From behind them, came a distinctive moan. They turned to see fear on Lundt's face. He was gripping the reins, hands trembling. Tonneman cocked an eyebrow at Pos. Without comment, the Sheriff and his Deputy turned back to the corpse.

"Come, lad." Pos motioned to a young Jew. "Help me get this fool out of there."

The youth backed away, holding his palms up in front of him.

Tonneman shook his head at his Deputy. "You're asking the boy to commit a sin."

Asser Levy's black eyes burned. He nodded. "The Sheriff is correct." The butcher was one of the original twenty-three Jews who had settled in New Amsterdam after leaving Recife in Brazil in '53. A respected man of the Book, he spoke for the Jewish Community.

"Will you send one of these men for Keyser?" Tonneman asked Levy.

"I will. But you must remove the dead man yourself. The dead are unclean and corrupt. No one of my people can touch the water trough. This trough will be burned and I will have a new trough built."

"Have you found my horse and cart?" Baalde shouted, ploughing through the onlookers.

"Not yet, Baalde, can't you see we have a dead man here?"

"So, he's dead. The dead must wait on the living. I am a citizen and I demand you —"

"Let the Sheriff do his job," came another voice. Bridge pushed people aside and looked down at the drowned man.

"Another country heard from," Pos muttered to Tonneman.

"The Governor would like to know what you're doing about . . ." He tilted his head at Lundt, who was slumped low in the saddle, face hidden.

"I'll let the Governor know as soon as —"

"You may let me know and I'll tell the Governor."

Tonneman avoided looking at Pos, who had made a rude noise. "As soon as I have investigated, you can be sure the Governor will get my report." He raised his voice. "It is now time for everyone to go about his business."

The crowd slowly dispersed. Though snow still drifted lazily downward, the sky was beginning to reveal fragments of clouds. "Pos, get yourself to New Haven. If you drink too much and fail to come back in one week, you'll get no wages till St Nicholas comes around."

Pos sniffed. "One week will be a miracle in this weather." He meandered to his horse. After a turn that was not a hundred yards down the road, Pos gleefully pulled out his flask for a quick nip, not so much out of thirst but for the mere joy of having his own way. Having slaked his mirth and his thirst, he spurred his steed into a steady gallop for the post road.

★　　★　　★

Tonneman waited until Bridge was no longer in sight. The man was an irritation, his nose up Nicholls's arse. More interested in feathering his own nest than anything else. "As for you, my lad," Tonneman told Lundt, whose colour, though decidedly green, was no match for his peculiar eye. "We're going to pay a visit to your dear late auntie's lawyer."

Lubbertus van Dincklagen, one-time Vice-Director-General under Stuyvesant, was an old comrade of Tonneman's. They'd been schoolmates at the university in Leiden in '37.

As usual, the corpulent lawyer was dining. "Tonneman, my friend. How good to see you. Come out of the weather. Bring your friend, too. Would you care for some roasted lamb?"

Without waiting for an answer the lawyer called, "Helga." Immediately a plump, young maidservant appeared. Tonneman wondered if the old reprobate was tupping the girl. Old and gross as he was, he was also rich. Who could blame a poor maid for ambition? On the other hand, in spite of his girth women had always been attracted to Lubbertus.

"Two more plates and two goblets for my friend Tonneman and his friend. I didn't get your name, sir."

"Lundt, he claims," Tonneman said, before Lundt could respond.

Lundt looked wounded. "That is my name, sirs. For truth."

The girl served the Sheriff and Lundt sizeable portions of meat and potatoes. Lundt attacked the food and drink with gusto.

"Young Lundt has an appetite," was van Dincklagen's only comment.

"For more than food, I reckon."

"Lundt, you say?" van Dincklagen said, as he filled his pipe. "Now there's a familiar name."

"This young fellow claims that his dead father was the Widow van Lundt's brother-in-law."

"Very interesting," Lubbertus said. "With Gretchen Goderis so soon demised, how serendipitous your arrival, young man."

"I most certainly do not know any Gretchen Goderis," Lundt said.

"When I drew up Margarieta van Lundt's last will and testament, she informed me that she had no living blood heirs and instructed me to designate her loyal maidservant Gretchen Goderis as sole heiress of the entire van Lundt estate. There was no mention of a nephew."

"I am betrayed," Lundt said. He broke into a sweat and swayed in his chair. "It will not go well for me."

"What do you mean, 'it will not go well for you'?" Tonneman demanded. What was Lundt afraid of?

The young man rose in his chair, then fell back, his head in his hands.

"There, there, young man," Lubbertus said. "All is not lost. We will need some verification of your story."

"I have sent Pos to New Haven for that very thing," Tonneman said.

"I am a lawful citizen of New Haven," Lundt said, sitting up. "I'm sure there's been some dreadful mistake."

"Well, let us suppose there has been," Lubbertus said mildly. "While we wait to hear from New Haven, you shall be a guest in my house."

"One can only hope you will not regret your hospitality," Tonneman told Lubbertus as he took his leave.

## Tuesday, 30 November. Mid-Afternoon

The snow had stopped and the sky was clear. Only a small amount had settled on the ground. Tonneman hoped Pos would have an easy ride to New Haven and that he would return with Lundt's true history.

Tonneman was perplexed by the painting he'd seen on the wall in the widow van Lundt's house. Who was that child and what had become of him? Tonneman was walking toward home, leading Venus, when he was hailed by young Conraet Ten Eyck, the nine-year-old son of Tonneman's good friends, Antje and Conraet, whose home was on Coenties Slip.

"Hallo, young man, and what is the news?"

"You're to come home with me at once, Tonneman," the boy said. "No questions asked."

"May I ask but one question?"

"No."

"Ah, you're sounding more and more like your mother every day," Tonneman said.

The Ten Eyck house was warm, the air filled with smells of sugar and spice. Antje was taking cookies from the oven while Racqel Mendoza in mourning cloth sat near the fire, her dark eyes and olive skin making a lovely contrast with the fair infant Pieter Ten Eyck, Tonneman's godchild, gurgling in her arms.

"Don't stand there letting the cold air in," Antje said. "Close the door." She smiled to see how Racqel and Tonneman could not take their eyes from each other. "Sit awhile and talk to my guest." She took the infant from Racqel and put him in his cradle.

Tonneman set his cudgel outside and closed the door. He hung his hat and coat on a hook, and sat on a low oak bench beside Racqel. How he wanted to put his head in her lap and let her stroke his hair. She'd asked him to respect her year of mourning, and he'd promised, but it was not easy. If only he could take her in his arms and —

"What is the news?" Racqel said, as if she knew what he was thinking.

Antje placed steaming mugs of tea in front of them. "Yes, tell us. What a bad end for that little schemer."

"Schemer? You mean Gretchen Goderis?"

"Yes, of course. Everyone knew she wanted Margarieta's money and poor Margarieta was such a sad and lonely woman. But I don't think Gretchen was alone in this."

"Everyone knew? I didn't know. How could I not know? And you think she had partners?"

Racqel laughed. Her hand rested on Tonneman's, almost as an afterthought, then as if too close to the fire, she pulled away. "I did not know. Perhaps she was taken in by other schemers."

"You are a nice woman, Racqel," Antje said. She piled cookies on a platter and set them on the table.

"If you know so much, Antje Ten Eyck, who then is the strange child in the portrait with Margarieta I saw in the van Lundt house?"

That puzzled Antje. She stood there, floury hands on her round hips. "Strange child?"

"Moon faced, perhaps two or three years."

"There were no children that anyone knew of, as long as we've been here."

"Well, maybe it was before you arrived. Who would remember such a thing?"

Antje and Racqel exchanged knowing looks. "Tonneman, you booby," Antje said. "Who would recall family histories going back years?"

"I don't know. You'd better tell me before I lose my temper and blow the house down." He grinned at Racqel.

"Reverend Megapolensis."

"He's younger than we are. How would he know?"

"Not that one, the old man, his father. He knows everyone's history."

"The old man? I thought he went back to Amsterdam."

"No. He's been very ill. I hear he's still living on his farm up past Maiden Lane."

## Wednesday, 1 December. Early Afternoon

It was the odd bit of warmth that made Pos open his eyes. He shut them immediately against the glare of light. His head hurt like the Devil himself was pounding on it, and he groaned.

"He's alive, father, thank the Blessed Lord." A woman's voice, sweet enough for Pos to open his eyes again.

"Where am I?" His lips were so stiff he could hardly speak. His words were Dutch.

A young woman in grey was looking down at him with concern. Her white ruffled cap covered most of her hair, except for a lock or two, brick in colour that had broken loose around her ears.

Pos sat up. Melted snow streamed from his clothing. The

man she called Father wore black and had a white beard. Quakers, or that like.

"I am Abraham Fallows," the old man said in English, "This is my daughter, Ruth." He was a lean man, of unusual height. "Your horse took a fall and you lay buried in a snow bank. Were it not for my daughter on her way to the milking, you might have frozen to death. Your horse, no worse for the fall, came to our barn in search of food. We have rubbed him down and fed him."

"Well, I thank you, sir," Pos said, in English. He was sitting on a blanket in front of the hearth. His stomach growled. He smelled fresh bread and hot food. "Now I must be on my way."

"You have travelled all the way from New-York?"

"I have. I am Deputy Sheriff in the city, Lodowyk Pos. I have business in New Haven."

The woman smiled. Near as tall as her father, she had a face as sweet as her voice, and her eyes were a greyish blue and filled with humour. She took a kettle from the fire. "You will have time for tea and stew."

While his daughter prepared the meal, Fallows helped Pos to his feet. "The Devil came for you with his evil intoxicants and would have had you, were it not for my daughter."

Late that evening, more sober than he cared to be, Pos stopped at the tavern opposite the New Haven city hall and with the aid of a little trick he knew with three playing cards, managed to buy drinks all round at no cost. And along the way he gained an impressive bit of knowledge.

He had a long, restful sleep in a stable he shared with his horse before riding back to New-York, fairly certain that he had the answer Tonneman required.

## Thursday, 2 December. Afternoon

Old Reverend Johannes Megapolensis had retired after the peace treaty with the English two months previously. He lived with his son Samuel and daughter-in-law Elsbetta and their five children on his small farm off the Bouwerie Road.

His parcel of land was closer to the village than that of the much larger estate of his old friend Pieter Stuyvesant. Services in the old Stone Church were now conducted by Johannes's son Samuel.

The farmhouse had been added on to significantly, as Elsbetta, a large, agreeable woman, produced additional children.

It was Tonneman's second attempt in two days to speak with the old minister, who was feeling too poorly to have visitors.

"Papa, see who's come to visit." Johannes was snoozing in a chair in front of the fire, breathing asthmatically. Elsbetta brought another chair for Tonneman and spoke gently, but with raised voice, to her father-in-law. "Sheriff Tonneman."

The old man opened cataract milky eyes and blinked rapidly. "Tonneman." He coughed and sat up in his chair and thought for a moment. "I am retired. I cannot give you religious advice, except you must attend church, which I assume is still a rare practice for you."

Tonneman smiled. "I am a lost cause." The Sheriff paused. "I have come to ask you to search your memory."

Elsbetta appeared with mugs of tea and bread and butter. She buttered the bread for her father-in-law and put the mug in his palsied hand.

"My memory? I may be good for that, if for nothing else. What is this village coming to these days, with the English in charge? Has this to do with the wretched Gretchen Goderis?"

"Wretched, you say? I thought she was a poor, innocent servant girl."

"Poor perhaps. Innocent? That I would never say. Is this why you're here?"

"No. Let her lie in peace. I came to ask you about Margarieta and Claes van Lundt, after they arrived from the Old Country. You were here then."

The old man frowned, coughed, spat into a nose cloth. "I was here, yes. We were all so young. It was our beginning."

"Was there a child? There is a painting in the manor showing a child with Margarieta."

"A child?" He closed his eyes. "I do not remember . . ."

"An odd child, moon faced –"

"No. Wait. There was a child. A boy, yes, moon faced, yes. A strange afflicted child."

"Strange?"

"In the head. Touched by God – or the Devil."

"And afflicted you say?"

"The eyes. Most peculiar. Unnatural. How she doted on the hapless lad." The old man shifted in his chair and drank from the mug of hot tea. "Yes. I remember now. A tragedy. We must trust God. It is His will. Minuit went back on his word and the Indians raided the farms. Innocent people were slaughtered, burned alive in their houses. The van Lundts had come into town and left the child with a maidservant. The house was burned to the ground with everyone in it."

## Friday, 3 December. Afternoon

Though he had not yet wet his throat with a tankard of beer, Lodowyk Pos sang as joyfully as if he'd quaffed his fill. "There was an Indian maid, tra la, who lay in the glade with a brave, tra la, of a paler shade, tra la. La-la-la-la-la-la-la-la-la." Over and over the Captain sang his silly ditty. And when he wasn't singing he was laughing.

At the first inn he came to he added drinking. Singing, laughing and drinking. And thus Pos spent a delightful afternoon going into one inn after another until he finally left the last one, mounted his steed and made his way to New-York where Tonneman awaited his report. Pos was certain he'd taken care of his duty. And quite well at that.

"An Indian maid lay in the glade, tra la-la-la-la-la-la-la-la-la-la."

Pos had a head full of happy songs and thoughts and laughter. It wasn't often that he came out a step ahead of Pieter Tonneman, and he was anticipating the moment when he told his friend the Sheriff his news.

What neither Pos nor the man who called himself John Lundt realized was that each was travelling the same road. Albeit in opposite directions.

★      ★      ★

Lundt rode van Dincklagen's horse past the sleeping sentry and out of the village with a sackful of the fat old lawyer's money and several silver vessels that he was sure would fetch him a fine price in Fort Orange.

His future in New-York, he well knew, was in doubt, given his poor performance. It wasn't his fault. He had been told the barest essentials. And he saw no reason to linger in hopes of the compensation he'd been promised, for he had no wish to end his miserable life like that unfortunate wretch, drowned like a rat in a Jew's trough. The man who had paid his debts and gotten him released from debtors prison in New Haven on the condition that he pretend to be the old lady's heir was not one to anger. He'd been warned sure enough at the trough.

Lundt was so intent on seeing that his sacks of plunder did not take flight as he rode that he didn't notice the rider coming toward him until it was too late.

"Hoy, you!" Pos shouted. "Where do you think you're going?"

Van Dincklagen's horse shied and Lundt flew off, crashing into a snow-covered bramble along with all the silver loot clanking and banging like so many dissonant church bells.

## Friday, 3 December. Afternoon

It was coming on to late afternoon when Tonneman, impatiently awaiting Pos's return, thought to stop by van Dincklagen's house and check on young Lundt. As he tied Venus to the hitching post in front of van Dincklagen's house, the door burst open.

"Help! Help! Thief!" Helga, van Dincklagen's servant girl, stood on the stoop wailing. Her cap was askew and her yellow hair streamed from under. "Oh, sir, oh sir, thank the good Lord you're here."

"What's happened?" Tonneman moved the distraught girl aside and there was Lubbertus, in as much disarray as his servant girl.

Hangdog, Lubbertus said, "While I was tending to my

accounts, young Lundt managed to drink my brandy and make off with everything that wasn't pegged down."

"Not everyone is as kind and trusting as you, my friend," Tonneman said. "He can't have gotten far. I'll find him and a few nights in our jail will teach him manners."

Tonneman gave Venus a reassuring pat on her flank and mounting, rode off after the rascal Lundt, thinking he was no nearer in solving the murders of Gretchen Goderis and Willem Stael.

As Tonneman arrived at the Broad Way Gate, Dolittle emerged from behind the guard shed. "So many travellers today," the Londoner said, edging toward the waning embers of his small fire. "Carts and wagons and walkers and even one man running as if the Devil himself was biting his arse. You'd think it was a parade before the King."

Tonneman suppressed a smile at the stain on the front of the soldier's breeches. In this weather the man's pissy breeches would likely freeze.

"Did young Lundt pass this way?"

"Not long. Made enough noise to –"

"Wake you?"

"Pshaw, Sheriff. I do my duty, but the hours are long and the cold gets into me bones. And with nobody to talk to –"

Tonneman would have moved off, but what had Dolittle said? A parade? "Who else has come through the Gate since Lundt?"

"The blacksmith, Baalde."

"Baalde?"

Dolittle shrugged. He pointed beyond the Gate. "You can probably still see him with his horse and cart though he's such a rude fellow, I don't know why anyone would want to talk with him. I asked him where he was off to and he told me he was hunting meat and I would do as well if he didn't find what he was looking for."

Tonneman saw no sign of Baalde, not even cartwheel tracks in the crusty snow, but the man could have gone off the road anywhere in search of game. No matter. It was not Baalde he was seeking.

At the third bend on the road to New Haarlem, Tonneman

heard shouting and laughter echoing through the snow-covered hills. It was always so when he came upon the Red Rooster, hardly more than a hut under a stand of pines, but a thriving, noisy tavern owned by the Spaniard, One-Eye Vega. Vega always had a crowd when word came that he'd received a shipment of sack, the strong, light-coloured Spanish wine.

Among the horses tied to the hitching post were Pos's and next to Pos's was van Dincklagen's stolen steed. Side by side.

"A fine thing," Tonneman said aloud. He dismounted and tied Venus to the rail. "We won't be long," he told her, noticing where wheel tracks in the snow trailed off the road and around to the back of the Red Rooster. Dirk Baalde?

In spite of the shoulder-to-shoulder drinkers and the thick haze of pipe smoke, Tonneman spied Pos and Lundt side by side, unsteady on their pins, singing and slobbering, clinging to each other. They would have been lying on the dirt floor were it not for the crowd of drinkers giving them no room to fall. But Pos had not forgotten his duty completely. Hooked on his left arm – the one he wasn't using for drinking – were the sacks of stolen goods.

"Greetings, Sheriff," One-Eye Vega yelled above the noise, and there came a sudden hush. "Have a drink, on me."

"I thank you, but I'm here on business," Tonneman said, signalling Pos outside with his thumb. When Pos and Lundt stared back at Tonneman with bleary eyes, he strode toward them, slapped the drinks from their hands and seized Lundt by the seat of his breeches and the scruff of his neck. To Pos he said, "We have a lot to talk about. And it's jail for this thief."

"Wait," Pos shouted, suddenly more sober than he'd appeared. "Don't take the lad back yet." He followed Tonneman outside.

"And why the bloody hell not?" Tonneman demanded.

"Because," and here the not-so-drunk Pos beamed, "I've solved our bloody mystery."

"Bah," Tonneman said, dropping Lundt. "Don't you move, Lundt, you're naught but a thief and a thankless wretch."

"My name is not Lundt, Sheriff. I am John Tatlock." The young man struggled to his knees. "I –" His eyes rolled up and with a small groan he fell over backward.

The arrow had come out of nowhere.

## Friday, 3 December. Late afternoon

Dolittle blinked his eyes rapidly. He was weary and his replacement, Merriweather, the lazy sot, was late. But what was this? A procession was coming toward him. The Sheriff first, holding the reins of blacksmith Baalde's bay mare, which was pulling Baalde's cart. Then Captain Pos followed on his horse, leading a trussed-up Dirk Baalde, afoot, snarling like a beast, and still another horse brought up the rear.

Lying in the cart Dolittle saw the newly arrived young Lundt, half dead he appeared, a red fletched arrow piercing his right shoulder.

Word travelled quickly, probably because Dolittle's replacement had arrived and Tonneman had told Dolittle to have physician Ditmar Wolters meet them at City Hall. Now the streets were filled with townspeople who became yet another procession as Tonneman's made its way down the Broad Way to City Hall and the jail.

"Put him in irons," Tonneman told Pos. "You can be sure Baalde wasn't working alone."

"You'll never get away with this, Tonneman," Baalde yelled. "I have friends."

"Friends?" Tonneman gave a coarse laugh. "Friends in Hades, for all the good it will do you."

By the time Tonneman had the villain Baalde in irons, the physician had arrived and removed the arrow from Tatlock's shoulder.

"What did you need me for?" the physician complained. "The arrow hit bone and went no further. You could just as well have plucked it out yourself and not bothered me."

Wolters was nothing but a barber and a drunkard, at that, Tonneman thought, and decided to ask Racqel, whose father had been a physician, to look at the wound and prepare a poultice of the medicinal herbs she collected and stored.

"What is the meaning of this, Tonneman?" Bridge said, shoving his way through the crowd. "Governor Nicholls –"

"I'm on my way to White Hall to give my report to the Governor."

"You can tell me, Tonneman, and save yourself the bother."

"Now, Bridge, old friend, what kind of Sheriff would I be if I didn't report to our esteemed Governor myself?"

"Hoy, Tonneman!" Lubbertus, moving like a heavy old horse down Pearl Street, hailed Tonneman. "The news is good, they tell me."

"Everything lost is found," Tonneman said.

"Very good, but I hear young Lundt has been woefully wounded."

"Baalde shot him with an arrow. And his name is not Lundt. It's Tatlock."

Lubbertus looked askance.

"It's a long story, and we'll have to wait until our young and doltish thief has recovered to get the whole of it, but what I can tell you is that Pos has come from New Haven and knows more of the story than I do."

"Well," Lubbertus said. "I have a good feeling about young Lu – Tatlock, you say? I will have my servants bring a pallet and he will stay with me until he's recovered."

"Lubbertus, you are a good Christian."

And this is how John Tatlock came to be transported to Maiden Lane to the home of Lubbertus van Dincklagen, where his wound was treated with a poultice containing various herbs by a mysterious woman clothed entirely in black, even to the veil that concealed her face, and where, with the additional care and attention of Lubbertus, he soon recovered.

## Wednesday, 8 December. Evening

Lubbertus van Dincklagen's great chamber was richly furn-ished with ample pieces of furniture to accommodate his girth, beautiful carpets and draperies, all of which he'd either brought with him from the Old Country or bought from traders passing through. He'd had his servants arrange a grand chair set behind a banquet table in the centre of the room. Helga had put out mugs of hot cider and the room was lit by two massive candelabra and the blazing logs in the hearth on the back wall.

To the side, a second chair had been set out for van Dincklagen, but he was not present. John Tatlock, his arm in a sling and intent on not being observed, sat a distance away perspiring profusely.

Tonneman, brushing snow from his coat, looked about the room. Except for Tatlock and Pos, none of the others who had been invited to attend were present. He sat in the grand chair at the banquet table, then rose.

"Go round them all up," he told Pos.

A short time later, Pos ushered Old Lady Oopdyk and her son Jacobus to their seats. Oopdyk wore an obsequious smile, had a cut on his forehead, a bloody lip, and a blackened eye. His mother's shawl was torn and filthy. She was taking in the opulent surroundings as if putting a price on every item.

Van Dincklagen followed, a huge entity who by himself took up most of the space in the room. He seemed oblivious to the long rent in the sleeve of his coat. He set the large bundle he carried on the banquet table and unwrapped it, revealing a giant wheel of cheese. Old Lady Oopdyk jabbed her son with her sharp elbow. Immediately Oopdyk cut a healthy wedge of cheese for his mother, which she chewed much like a furtive rat.

Bridge was the last to arrive. He was breathing hard. His hat was askew. "What is this about, Tonneman? I thought you talked with the Governor."

"I have the Governor's approval. Be seated, Bridge."

Bridge, fuming, took the bench Pos brought over for him.

"Are we all here?" Tonneman asked.

"Everyone but Baalde," Pos said.

"Invite him to join us," Tonneman said.

"Murderers should be hanged," Bridge said, smugly.

"What are we here for?" Old Lady Oopdyk demanded.

"Consider this an inquest into the fraud conducted by

persons I will soon name that led to the deaths of Gretchen Goderis and Willem Stael."

"My son and I had nothing to do with any of that," the old woman said, tucking a dank grey strand of hair under her cap. She rose to her feet and motioned for her son, who was cutting yet another wedge from the wheel of cheese.

"Sit down. Deputy Pos will be back shortly with our last guest, and we will begin."

"And while we wait, we'll have cider and cheese," van Dincklagen said. "Helga will serve."

Tonneman stepped outside to wait for Pos, who was conveying the prisoner, Baalde. Snow came down like fine grains of sand, almost obliterating sight. He heard Pos before he saw him. The Deputy was on the run and alone. Something had gone wrong with Tonneman's plan.

"Hanged," Pos yelled. "In his cell."

"Suicide?"

"I think not. He had a knob on his head the size of a duck egg. But it would have taken strength to get that fat neck in a noose. What will we do now?"

"Christ's blood!" Tonneman said. "I thought you posted a guard."

"I did, but I didn't account for Evertsen suddenly offering free drinks from the King Charles."

"Did he now? Surely not a coincidence."

"Whatever it was, my two guards were gulping down the free drinks without a thought to their duty."

"All right. We'll make it up as we go along. Tatlock will help us."

"I'm glad you're so sanguine," Pos replied.

They returned to the great room and found everyone standing, eating and drinking, as if it were a social occasion.

"Everybody sit, please." Tonneman seated himself behind the banquet table. Pos remained near the doorway.

"Let's get this over with quickly," Bridge said, officiously. "I have the Governor's business to attend."

"The Governor has charged me with investigating the death of Gretchen Goderis, who inherited the van Lundt estate as specified in the Widow van Lundt's last will. Am I right, Lubbertus?"

"Correct," van Dincklagen said. "There being no legitimate heirs."

"No sooner was Gretchen dead, than a so-called legitimate heir appeared, calling himself John Lundt. You will see the young man sitting over there, who called himself John Lundt and claimed to be the nephew and heir. His real name is John Tatlock."

Everyone turned to stare at Tatlock, who grew pale and shrank into his chair.

"How did you come to present yourself, sir, as John Lundt?"

Tatlock opened his mouth to speak but nothing came out. He tried again. "I was hired to do so, in New Haven," he said, shamefaced. "I was down on my luck."

"Pos?" Tonneman said.

"The Sheriff sent me to New Haven to learn what I could about young Lundt."

"And what did you find?"

"That young Lundt's real name is John Tatlock, that he was in debtors prison in New Haven, and that his debts were paid by the man who hired him to represent himself as the heir to the van Lundt estate."

"This is taking too long, Tonneman," Bridge said getting to his feet. "Just put this fraud into jail along with Baalde."

"Not so fast, Bridge. We're just beginning."

Pos came and stood behind Bridge and Bridge sat down.

"Tatlock, what do you have to say for yourself?"

"I am deeply sorry for my part in this, sir."

"Yes," Tonneman said. "Did you have anything to do with Gretchen Goderis's murder?"

"No, sir. I didn't even know about her."

"What about the murder of the post rider, Willem Stael?"

"I didn't know him either, sir. And I was with you when we came upon him."

"This is true," Tonneman said. "Stael was murdered because he was paid not to ride his assigned route. He was also paid to report hostile Indians in the vicinity. In

English money. The Governor would then summon everyone into town for safety and Gretchen Goderis could be
murdered in the forest with no one to know. Were it not for
the noise of the hawks that I was sent to investigate, there
would have been nothing left of her by the time the curfew
ended."

"So the murderer is not one of us," Oopdyk said. "We
have nothing to do with this." He reached out a hand to his
mother, but she pushed it away and stood up solidly.

"Sit down, Oopdyk."

Jacobus Oopdyk sat. His mother did not. "I'm weary,"
she said.

Pos put her bench behind her knees and, surprised, she
sat. "No, no," she protested.

"Baalde reported his horse and cart stolen, but it was a
ruse. It was his arrow that killed Gretchen. He transported
her to the woods in the cart he later reported stolen."

"And who, if you know so much, killed Stael?" Bridge
said.

"Jacobus Oopdyk and his mother," Tonneman said, signalling van Dincklagen to guard them.

"That's it, then," Bridge said.

"No. There's more. I'm sure you'll want to hear it."

"This is not all our doing," Old Lady Oopdyk cried.

"Yes, you are right, Vrouw Oopdyk. I'm coming to that.
But first, I want to tell a little story, which Pos will complete.
In the van Lundt house, I saw a painting of a young
Margarieta van Lundt and in the painting was a moon-faced
child. To my knowledge, the van Lundts were childless.
After I sent Pos off to New Haven, I went to see old
Reverend Megapolensis, who told me there was a child, a
strange child, who died with a maidservant when Indians
raided the outlying farms and slaughtered settlers. The van
Lundts had been in the village at the time and were spared."

"So there is no true heir," Bridge said.

"Pos, will you continue," Tonneman said, ignoring
Bridge.

Pos picked up the story. "John Tatlock?"

"Sir?"

"Were the Tatlocks your real parents?"

"They took me in when I was but a babe."

"Took you in?"

"I was found in a church in New Haven."

"A white infant," Pos said, "wrapped in Indian swaddling, was delivered by an ancient woman in Indian dress. The minister was told that the infant's father, now dead, had been stolen by the Iroquois from a farm near New Amsterdam when he was very young."

John Tatlock looked surprised. "I didn't know this. I was told only that I was given to the Tatlocks who had no children. They brought me up as their own boy. But I brought them no joy before they died. I was a drunkard and a gambler. I ended up in debtors prison. But I am no murderer." He wiped a tear from his eye.

Blue eye and green eye, Tonneman thought. What had old Reverend Megapolensis said? Eyes peculiar, unnatural. Was it possible? Had the Indians taken the strange van Lundt child? He looked over at Pos, who was nodding.

"The infant was white, you say?" Bridge said. "This Tatlock has a ruddy complexion."

Pos said, "It was the child's eyes. One blue, one green. No Indian child would have such."

"The van Lundts's child was thought to have died when the Iroquois raided and burned their farm. That child had peculiar, unnatural eyes, old Reverend Megapolensis told me."

A gasp came from Tatlock.

"I think, sir," Tonneman said, "that you are the rightful heir, that your name is John van Lundt."

"Then why are we here?" Bridge said, rising again. "The wrongful heir is the rightful heir. Baalde and Oopdyk are the murderers —"

"Ah, but we haven't found the greedy culprit who set everything in motion."

"Well, you won't find him here."

"Oh, but we will." The Sheriff jerked his chin at Pos. "Bridge, I am arresting you for contriving the plot and the murders of Gretchen Goderis and Willem Stael, and for the murder of your accomplice, Dirk Baalde, who was ready to give it all up, and for scheming to get your hands on the riches of the van Lundts by hiring a fraudulent heir."

"Outrageous!" Bridge cried. "You can't arrest me. I am English."

Tonneman laughed. "Well, we all are now, aren't we?"

# *If Serpents Envious*

## Clayton Emery

*Clayton Emery describes himself as "an umpteen-genera-
tions Yankee, Navy brat, and aging hippie". He's probably best known for his stories in* Ellery Queen's Mystery
Magazine *featuring Robin Hood and Maid Marian,
which began with "Dowsing the Demon" in 1994. His
hard-boiled detective story "Totaled", featuring Susan
"Tyger" Blake, was short-listed for an Edgar Award as
one of the best short stories of 2002. He has also written a
series set in Colonial America featuring Joseph Fisher
which began with the following powerful tale.*

Seagulls flapped and pecked around an iron cage hanging
from a post. The grey-white birds were frustrated by something black that fouled their beaks. Joseph Fisher stopped
and the birds flapped away. The cage was a gibbet. Propped
inside was a dead man, neck elongated by hanging, body
coated with tar. Joseph reached with a bony finger, touched a
black foot. Tar pulled loose in a string.

"'Hurl'd headlong . . . to bottomless perdition, there to
dwell in adamantine chains and penal fire, who durst defy th'
Omnipotent to arms,'" murmured the student. Wiping his
finger, he trudged into Newport. What the Narragansett
Indians had called Aquidneck, "Isle of Peace".

The road was dusty and deeply rutted, almost impassible
even dry, and wandered between stone walls and pastures
and maple trees that nodded great green heads uneasily.

Seeking food and escape from the blistering sun, Joseph aimed for the first store.

On a narrow porch of warped unpainted boards blackened by salt hunched an Indian, face slack and cracked from drinking, in a filthy shirt with breechclout and leggins. At the feel of footsteps he extended a shaking hand, begging for anything but mostly rum. The stuporous Indian blinked when the young white man addressed him in Algonquin tangy as pine sap. "Seek you the woods, brother, and drink the water that flows from the headlands."

The shop had two ends. The front, anchored to the road, bore farm implements – singletrees, harness, grain buckets, feedbags, horse liniments. The rear hung over the harbour on pilings with a dock below, contained chandler's supplies: boathooks, cordage, buckets of tar and oakum, fishhooks, oars. The store was hot, any loafers dispersed. The lonely proprietor in a cocked hat and flour-dusty apron of green baize braided something from rope and codline. From a back pantry came the squawling of a baby.

The storekeeper ran his eye over Joseph, peered into his pockets. The student was short and thin, shabby in a brown waistcoat and breeches with small pewter buttons, tattered hose and broken shoes. A blanket roll and and chunky satchel marked him as a traveller, yet he wore no hat and let his long brown hair fall free. His complexion was fish-belly white with deep-sunk burning eyes. A man not long for the world, who sought day-old bread and green cheese that wept in the heat.

With pennies in the till, the shopkeeper talked as he knotted. Where was Joseph from, where bound, what the news? Boston, just travelling, new blue laws heaped on sinful heads by the Massachusetts Legislature. Out loud, the Scottish Presbyterian thanked God he lived in godless Rhode Island.

Joseph munched bread and sipped cider. The baby screamed on and on, and he wondered idly where its mother had gone. Instead he asked what the storekeeper braided.

"Nigger whip." Codline wrapped a rope handle that split into seven thick strands ending in overhand knots. The owner slapped the scarred counter like pistol shots. "Had three in stock and sold 'em this morning. The old sailor who made 'em took to selling 'em on the street, damn his eyes, so I must fashion my own. But t'ain't hard. Not fancy like a horse whip: you shouldn't never hit a horse. Just stiff enough to smart but not break the skin. Say, you wouldn't care to buy a baby?"

"A baby?" Joseph choked on crumbs, racking and hacking, so badly the shopkeeper splashed rum into his cider from a jug under the counter.

"No charge. Here, I'll show you."

The shopkeeper fetched the shrilling infant, toting it by the ankles. He spread a bloodstained butcher's sheet and laid out the child like a smoked ham. Naked and dusky, the boy had black hair flat and straight above a purple face. It clenched its fists and screamed.

"He's mostly nigger. Got some Indian in him, but that'll help him tolerate the winters. Good lungs, good grip, good size. Stick it on a wetnurse and in three, four years, it could help around the house and dooryard. Raise it right, don't spare the rod, and it'll suit better than any scrawny bound boy off the ship from London."

Numbly Joseph regarded the screaming infant. It kicked and thrashed, too young to even roll off the counter. "Where is its mother?"

The shopkeeper prevaricated, finally sighed. "In jail. She's to be burned at the stake tomorrow. That's her mate ripening out there." He nodded towards the distant gibbet. "That's why I'm stuck with this brat. Their goods was forfeit, and the mistress bade me take them all, including this'n. No one wants it, reckon it's bad luck. But I don't hold with that."

Joseph nodded absently. Only Negroes were burned at the stake, and he could guess the couple's crime. "They killed their master?"

"Aye. You must'a heard. They fed him a snake in his sleep. A timber rattler. Bit his insides and poisoned him. He screamed from dawn till dusk. But it's an ill wind. Lots of folks've never seen a burning, so they'll flock in from all over the colony. And everyone's beating their niggers for fear of an uprising, so I'm clean out of whips."

He had to speak over the baby's squawling. He tried slapping the child's face lightly, then harder to stun it, but the infant only howled louder. Finally he pulled the jug from under the counter, soaked a bar rag to squeeze rum into the baby's mouth. "Some Mother's Mercy might –"

His hand was arrested by Joseph's, slim and cold but surprisingly strong. "I'll buy the child."

"Well, now, that's mighty fine." A broad smile. "I'd say it's worth –"

"Two shillings."

"Oh no, I don't think so. A bonny bairn like this –"

"Two and six, and a swaddling cloth."

The shopkeeper shrugged in largesse and fetched a rag crusted with pine pitch and shavings. "You won't be sorry. Raise 'em right and they're loyal as puppies. I'm glad you took him. I'd'a strangled it for the dogs or pitched it off the wharf for the crabs." The shopkeeper wrapped the baby neatly and handed it to Joseph. "There, enjoy it. You're a good Christian, son."

"'Christ, conceived by the Holy Ghost, born of the Virgin Mary: suffered under Pontius Pilate, was crucified, dead, and buried.'" But Joseph quoted in Aramaic, and the shopkeeper only looked puzzled.

Shouldering his blanket roll and book satchel, hugging the screaming baby to his chest, the student stepped into the hammer of summer sun. The wasted Indian by the door stuck out his palsied hand. Angry with the world, Joseph snapped, "Fly to the wilderness, far from this Gehenna, where backsliders sacrifice children to Moloch and Baal!"

Aware only that he got nothing, the Indian slouched against the wall. Joseph stalked into Newport. The child's crying brought seagulls keening overhead as if in sympathy, but in fact seeking a meal at the source of distress.

At the first stream that cut the road, Joseph squatted and dipped his finger. Immediately the child stopped bawling to suck. Spooning more, Joseph traced a cross on the child's forehead. "I never completed my studies, child, and am more French than English regarding baptism, but I reckon you need succour, spiritual and corporeal."

Thirst slaked, the child's hunger set it crying loud as before. The student tucked the baby close and steered down the widest street. Newport jammed a narrow spit jutting into Narragansett Bay, which itself was hemmed by bluffs of purple and red-grey granite before reaching the ocean in the south. Some hundred white gambrels with barns made up the town. Warehouses encroached on the water, and half a hundred wharves pointed to a forest of masts in the harbour: sailing ships returned from Europe and the Caribbean and Africa, fishing smacks no bigger than a wagon. Heat made people veer for shade. Joseph hailed a black girl in a head scarf and patched apron who carried a basket of blue crabs. She told of a Negro wetnurse named Maroca who lived along Butcher's Brook.

Blanket and satchel chafed his sweaty shoulders and the baby cried in his ear as he trailed the Sakonnet River. He found a rocky defile split by the brook, then a shack made from tarred and barnacled lumber salvaged from shipwrecks. A large black woman washed clothes in the stream while a brood of dark children worked in the shade or splashed in the brook.

The infant's crying made the woman abandon her washing. Her face stayed blank as a slate, but her yellow eyes quickened as she took the baby and tugged open her bodice. Joseph glimpsed a pink Y branded on her right breast as she cradled the child to nurse.

"You know this child?" asked Joseph.

"Yea, mon. He be the boy-child of Cuffy and Hazel, and an orphan both ways soon." Her voice dripped with molasses from the Sugar Islands. She wore a claret-coloured skirt and bodice like any English woman, but a yellow turban covered her head above big gold hoop earrings. "How'd'joo get him?"

"I bought him for two shillings and sixpence."

"Bought him? You be a bad bargainer, white man. Black babies dey give away like puppies. Storeman should'a paid you to take him." Irony rang bitter. "Poor unfortunate, but not as unfortunate as his parents be."

"These parents who murdered their master by making him swallow a snake?"

"Yea, mon." The large woman swung towards her shack, the baby gurgling at her breast. "They 'ministered a snake to Marsa' Pearson, or snake poison. Caught red-handed. 'Course, she had good reason, de way she was used so ill. But she'll return to Ah-frica soon, lay her burden down."

Joseph trailed her across the river-rounded rocks of the defile. "When she dies, you mean."

"Yea, mon. Cuffy, don't know where he'll end up, but it be to glory somewhere. He was a gen'le man and no two ways 'bout it. 'Course, no one knows de human heart. I can't keeps dis child, you knows."

"Eh?" Shuffling ideas in his head, Joseph found himself surrounded by children with brown-white features and kinky red-brown hair. "No, I expect you can't."

The shack had no windows. Summer glare through the doorway showed a room fitted like a ship's forecastle with bunks along the walls and a table that hinged down. The floor was dirt strewn with cattails. Nursing with one arm, Maroca shooed children hither and thither to wash their hands, sweep the table, lay out wooden bowls and spoons.

"I'se a freewoman. My husband's white. He sails on de slavers. He fancied me and bought me. My chillun was born free, and we'll stay that way, long's as we stay close to home where ever'body knows us. We journeys elsewhere, we likely collect a chain on our laig." Introduced, she fixed Joseph with bulging yellow eyes.

"Um, I am called Joseph Fisher. I was captured young in the late war,[*] raised by Penobscots, trained by Jesuits in Quebec. Peace returned me to the English sphere, and they sent me to Harvard to be a missionary to Indians. Lately I . . . wander."

"I'm not surprised," Maroca snorted. "You been blown 'bout so much, you almost a black white man. 'Stead's you

---

[*] The first French & Indian war, King William's War of 1689–97

red and white. You ever think dem Penobscots what raised you might'a killed your folks?"

A boy fished in Joseph's pockets, caught a rap on the skull from his mother. "I have meditated upon that. But I was young and they were kind. They called me Monminowis, Silver Cat."

"I call you to supper. You care for one of ours, you share our food." Maroca nodded to the table. The children hopped to their places, packed as herring, hands clasped, eager to see Grace done. "And since you comes from Hahvard, you say de blessing."

There was only fishhead chowder, pickled sorrel, and ship's biscuit. As the children devoured their portions, Joseph settled for a biscuit and spring water. Maroca nursed the child, which wouldn't get a proper name until its first birthday: it was just "the baby". Supper was quiet, the children shy before a stranger. Joseph absently gazed about the room. A fat-bellied grotesque on a shelf was adorned with chicken feathers: a voodoo fetish.

Abruptly Joseph said, "Do you believe a man could be forced to swallow a snake?"

Maroca's thoughts and emotions were sealed like brandy in a dark brown bottle, but she shrugged. "De man died. He was all swoll up, dey said, like when you gets bit. And he screamed 'bout snakes, and tried to claw his own belly open till they had to tie his han's. Dere's timber rattlers here'bouts. Men'll dig a cellar, come back de next day, de hole swarmin' wid 'em, have to kill dem with shovels. You should have a snake charm you'self. Hang four buttons around your neck, ward off de consumption."

Joseph nodded, half-hearing. "Did anyone actually *see* the snake? Did anyone think to – open him?"

Even Maroca, who'd seen everything, blinked at the idea of dissection. But she nodded. "Dere was a snake. De mistress seen Cuffy wid it in his own han'." Sweat ran off her round face in the evening heat, the droplets splashing the baby's flat black hair.

" 'Faith is the substance of things hoped for, the evidence of things not seen,' " Joseph murmured. "Do you know aught of the murdered man?"

Another shrug of round black shoulders. "Marsa' Pearson was a merchant-man. Dey's the richest in Newpoht. Owns a fine house and warehouse and ships and docks and six slaves – four now. His ships travel all over de world, dey say. Includin' Gambia." In the six years since the British Parliament had legalized the slave trade, Newport had boomed. Gambia on the Ivory Coast was its chief port of call.

"So a man who lived by slavery died by it, eh?"

"Mebbe so. But Cuffy, he was a gen'le man, good in the heart. He plied cures on all de coloured folk here'bouts. Learned dem from his mother. But I don't wants to be talkin' about de dead. Nor 'bout Hazel, neither, poh thing. And poh thing you." She bobbed the near-orphan at her breast.

"Hazel . . ." Joseph pictured a slave woman alone in an oven-hot cell, fearing the flames that would lick her thighs the next day. "Has a minister attended her?"

"No minister for coloured folk. We stand at the back of the church, behind a curtain, is all."

Suddenly animated, Joseph reached for his clumsy satchel, extracted a King James Bible, its black leather cover worn white. "'There is no salvation outside the church.' Will someone show me the jail, please?"

Maroca ducked her head to peer out the door. "Evenin' comin' on."

Slaves were not allowed out after dark, Joseph knew. "But I thought you were freemen."

"Freedom's for white folk, and not all of dem."

"I'll show you. I can help." The eldest, a womanly girl, Quamino spoke with only a trace of brown sugar. Her mother opened her mouth to object, then sighed and nodded.

Toting his heavy bible, Joseph stroked the baby's head for luck. Black girl and white man passed into the gathering gloom.

At the last corner, Quamino hung back in the shadows, so Joseph went on alone. Newport's jail was near the waterfront, handy for rowdy sailors or captive pirates. The old wooden building tilted alarmingly over the street. A torch-lit crowd watched the oak-barred windows of the second floor for a glimpse of the murderess. All were white, many drunk, faces sweat-shiny under tricorn hats and mob caps. "We'll burn your hide blacker tomorrow, witch!" "Fat's gonna be in the fire!" "Stuff an apple in your mouth before the pigroast!"

Disdaining the crowd, Bible in hand, Joseph glided nose-high towards the jail like a Harvard don. Not recognizing him, the crowd nudged one another. Ducking inside the cockeyed doorway, the student almost collided with a jail-keeper and two lackeys who crowded a small stifling hall. The keeper of the keys perched on a three-legged stool with a noggin of ale. Obviously they guarded against the villainess being seized and lynched before her appointed time – and a proper crowd.

The jailkeeper barked blearily. "What the hell are you about? Get out!"

The two lackeys unfolded arms and iron-tipped batons, but Joseph stood firm with the Bible in his hands. "I would see the slave woman Hazel. Despite her heinous crime, she has yet a chance to enter into a personal covenant with God, to grasp at the keys to the kingdom of Heaven. To save her soul."

The lackeys looked to their boss, who stared at Joseph. "Uh . . . She ain't allowed any visitors. Besides, nigger ain't got no souls. They're animals, like."

Pompously, Joseph snapped open the Bible where his finger marked. "*You* would block God's work? You would *contradict* the Bible, breathed by God, therefore infallible and stamped with God's own authority? Consider the parable of the sheep and the goats. 'I was in *prison*, and ye came unto me. And the King shall answer, inasmuch as ye have done it unto the least of my brethren, ye have done it unto *me*.' Else, 'Depart from me, ye cursed, into everlasting fire, prepared for the devil and his angels. *Everlasting* punishment!'"

Threats of doom made the tipsy jailkeeper squirm. "All right. T'ain't no harm, I suppose. Take him up, John, but watch him. Don't let 'im slip her a knife to end it early." Joseph fought down a grin as he marched up the lopsided stairs.

The second floor had four cells with stout oak doors broken by thick slats. In the last cell huddled a black figure wrapped in a bodice and gown so faded they had no colour at all. African-black, the woman's skin glistened like an oiled whetstone in the heat, yet she shivered uncontrollably as she rocked on her knees. Bloodshot eyes, stark white in her black face, stared at the corner.

Joseph leaned on the oaken bars. "Hazel. Child." He called her name repeatedly without result. "Hazel, please listen. Your baby is safe. He's with Maroca. She'll care for him."

The white eyes flickered, and Joseph pressed. "Hazel, for the sake of your child, can you tell me why – your husband – had the snake? What did he intend with it? He was a gentle man, we know, and wouldn't kill Master Pearson. But what was the snake for?"

Hazel whispered, a shuddery hiss like a teakettle come to a boil. "Cuffy, he – he had a dream. 'Bout a snake. A snake read his – heart. Snake tole him, someone'd kill him. *Did* kill him . . ." Choking on sobs, she curled into a black ball of misery.

"Dreamt of a snake?" Joseph was electrified. He called, "Bear up, Hazel. God is many things, but above all, love, patience, and mercy."

He barely heard the turnkey's order to leave, or the crowd's questions. He walked into the hot night in a daze, muttering, "– The baby has straight hair. *Straight* hair."

Quamino hissed and he slipped into an alley beside her. "Why didn't you tell me Cuffy had Indian blood?" In his excitement, he named the dead man.

He felt the girl shrug. "He didn't look it, hardly. His mama was a red woman."

"It shows in his child. One-quarter Indian, it has lank hair, not kinked like an African's. I couldn't see the dead man's features for the tar, yet the storekeeper mentioned it. Can you show me Master Pearson's house, please?"

The girl squeaked. "That's a hoodoo place! Mama said Mars'er Pearson's death'll fetch all his slaves with him. Like the cannibal kings in Dahomey what files their teeth and takes a thousand slaves to their graves. What d'you want there?"

"I want to rifle a king's midden."

It felt strange to Joseph, a child of two cultures, to see through the eyes of a third, the African slaves of New England who remained unseen until summoned. For instead of walking the thoroughfare, Quamino led a torturous path through dooryards and gardens that reeked of garbage and privies and apple trees that gave off a winey perfume in the summer night. The third time Joseph tripped over a sleeping pig, he opined, "I dislike this. Pigs have a passion for snakes." Quamino said nothing, though her white eyes were large and luminous.

Threading apple trees and gardens and outbuildings, she approached the back of a tall square mansion, pressed her ear to a window, rapped an erratic tattoo.

A bar slid aside, and a young black in a shirt and bony knees stuck his head out. He'd obviously been sleeping on a pallet in the corner. "Quammy! What'choo doing here? You wanna – eh?" He froze upon spotting Joseph's wan face, skeletal in the summer night.

"Hush up, Prosper! This here Indian gots a order for you! So you do it or he'll tomahawk that wooly poll a'yours and hang it for the crows to peck! Fetch the spade you uses to turn the midden! Gittup!"

Agitated, Prosper blundered down the stairs, remembered he wore only a shirt, stumbled back and grabbed his shabby breeches and ancient shoes, fumbled into the barn where horses nickered. Fetching a punched-tin lantern and a spade, he threaded a small orchard. Silky leaves rustled at either hand.

Prosper moaned, "I din't wish you'd make me work the night long too, Quammy. I works enough durin' the day. At night, I'd a thought you'd come for somethin' else."

"Day I needs what you gimme is the day I die," snapped the girl. "Hush up."

The back of the property was screened by a woven-wicker fence. Prosper stopped at a baulk of half-rotten timber and thumped his shovel on it. Quamino slapped his shoulder for silence. The girl struck the candle alight, then lifted her skirt and set the lantern between her ankles to obscure the glow. The silhouette of her legs and hips distracted the men, but Joseph tipped up the flat cover of wood. A sour reek fermented by summer sun gushed up in a wave.

Gasping, Joseph asked, "Why this baulk?"

"Mistress don't like pigs in the garbage, not hers nor nobody else's. Say if she's eat pork, she'll know what the pig's et first. Our pigs stays in the crib. Eat better'n me, most days."

"Serves you right for wasting your substance with riotous living, and devouring thy living with harlots," quipped Joseph. Prosper just stared at the cadaverous white man who came in the dark to pick at rubbish. "Tell me. Have you seen a dead snake in the past days?"

"T'was a snake killed Master Pearson," whispered the boy.

"If so, and I doubt it, *that* snake was interred with Master Pearson." Since ashes went into a hopper for potash, vegetable and table scraps to the pigs, and bones to the dogs, the trash was mostly dried stalks and fish bones and lobster shells. And fragments of glass, expensively cut. "What is this crystal?"

"Master Pearson took sick at the table. He fell out of his chair, kicking and yelling and clawing his belly. He pulled down the tablecloth and broke some goblets. I would'a got whupped for it, 'cause I sets the table, but Mistress Pearson was so upset I din't. I's always getting whupped for no reason a'tall."

"You hush up or I'll flatten your thick head with that spade," spat Quamino. "I never saw such a whiney –"

"Eureka!" Joseph's hand stabbed down, plucked up a snake. Scarcely a foot long, dark green with long yellow stripes, lacking a head, it resembled a thick bracelet. "Cuffy discarded this, didn't he?"

Prosper shook. "I dunno, I dunno. He catched it in the garden, under the hubbard squash –"

"After your master took sick, no?" Excited, Joseph's

French intruded. "He plied this snake on Master Pearson –"

"No sir! Beg pardon, but he plied it to *hisself*! T'was *t'other* snake he voodooed on Mas'er Pearson!"

"What? What other snake?" Joseph's deepsunk eyes glittered like a skull on a spike. "No, there couldn't be another snake."

"There was! I seen it! Cuffy took sick, and he catched that snake and drank the blood!"

Now everyone was confused. Joseph persisted, "No, he gave the blood to Master Pearson!"

"No, he drunk it himself! He was crazy! I stayed clear'a him!"

"Oh!" Quamino blinked. "He's right! Cuffy came to see my mama! He had the stomach cramps, and she dosed him with hellebore. He puked the night long, kep' all the chillun awake!"

"*Cuffy* took sick? When was this?"

Quamino didn't hesitate. Reared in oral tradition, Africans had phenomenal memories. "Monday last, day after meetin'."

Joseph rolled the flaccid snake in his fingers as if hunting a hidden message. "But this is fresh, a day or two. So there *must* be two snakes . . . Hazel could attest, but . . . Oh, Lord, I see! Cuffy was seen bleeding a snake, and someone assumed he poisoned the master *with* the snake!"

"Tha's what happened, master, 'xactly!" breathed Prosper. "Mistress seen the snake in Cuffy's hand and screamed to wake the dead! She were screaming, crying Cuffy had to get out, then she flung herself out the door with the chillun afore her! Us niggers was huddling close, trying not to get whipped! Sheriff's men came and they beat Cuffy so bad he couldn't stand, and when he tried to talk they smashed his mouth with clubs! And Hazel they kicked in the stummick, and tooken her babe away and her shriekin' –" The boy stopped, his voice shuddery.

"Fie on people with short sight!" rasped Joseph. "But if Cuffy . . . How?"

Unknowingly, Joseph stroked his chin with the dead

garter snake. He hunkered, silent, so long that Quamino gave an experimental push to his shoulder. Roused, he shielded his eyes from the lantern light and looked east. "Dawn not two hours off, and Hazel to be burned at noon." Coiling the dead snake in his coat pocket, he took the lantern.

Prosper tipped the baulk over the midden. "Please don't tell no one I was out here, sir. The mistress she'd have the bulls take off my hide a strip at a time –"

Quamino chopped the air, imitating a tomahawk. Prosper peeked at Joseph's back and felt his head. "Scalped, whipped, an' all. Be lucky if'n I don't go to the stake 'longside poor Hazel too."

Trinity Church perched on a hill that it might overlook Newport. Behind it stood the parsonage, a solid, fresh-painted, proud building connoting the congregation had money to spend. Joseph found the church empty, the front door of the parsonage unresponsive, the kitchen open to the morning heat. In the back yard a black woman plied a long-handled paddle to turn baking bread in a beehive oven. Joseph waited patiently by the picket fence. There was no seawind this morning, and heat lay like a wool blanket higher than his head. Still, rather than clog his lungs with consumption, as was thought hereabouts, the warm salt air seemed to bake his lungs and clear the phlegm, as water is baked from a clay jug by a kiln. Yet Joseph had been up all night, pacing and thinking, and felt tired both inside and out.

His reverie was interrupted by a brusque, "What do you want?"

The slave flung the picket gate open as if to bat Joseph away. Her dark eyes ranged over his shabby clothes and shoes, marked him for a mechanic or beggar, and a diseased one at that.

But Joseph introduced himself as a divinity student to see the parson. "Please. Maroca thought I should pay him a visit."

"You know Maroca?" No trace of African or Caribbean accent here: a blind man would think her an English house-wife born in Sussex.

"Yes. I'm a guest in her house."

That raised an eyebrow. "How's her son faring?"

"You mean Zingo, with the cast in one eye? He's been croupey all week, but dosings of sweet-fern tea have tamed it."

"That's good." Warming, the woman started over. "Reverend and Mistress Treat attend a gentleman who only takes callers in the morning." From four to eight. "They'll return soon. You're welcome to await them. I can feed you."

"That's most gracious of you." Ten minutes later Joseph was seated at the kitchen table, and heaped before him was ham, hasty pudding with maple syrup, pickled cabbage, baked beans, cranberry tarts. Identified as an upright member of the lowest class, the slave gossiped as if they were old friends. Her name was Jin, "like an old she-mule". Inevitably she came to the morbid death of Master Francis Pearson from swallowing a snake. Although her talk circled around blame, Joseph understood Master Pearson had been a cruel and callous man, and it was high time someone murdered him. But to see poor Cuffy, the kindest coloured man in Newport, hanging as crowbait, and to think of "poor suffering Hazel" going into flames at midday was a shame. Even as she talked, the woman packed a basket: a picnic for a burning.

Time slipping away made Joseph fidgety. He interjected, "I've heard it said time and again that poor Hazel was misused, but –"

A voice carolled from the front of the house. Wiping his mouth, Jin hustled Joseph through a closed door into a house smelling of book leather and ink. It gave him a flutter of nostalgia, and a wish to be somewhere else, if only he knew where.

The parson was a dark-browed, thick-haired man not much older than Joseph, his wife a plain thing in a gown and bodice of burgundy and a sunbonnet with a matching ribbon: clothes considered scandalous in Boston were demure in free-and-easy Newport. Both frowned at the shabby guest.

"A divinity student, eh? Belike." The young parson still

aped the pedantic speech of his teachers. In Latin he quoted, "'Of making many books there is no end: much study is a weariness of the flesh.'"

Joseph completed the passage in the same language. "'Let us hear the conclusion of the whole matter: Fear God, and keep his commandments: for this is the whole duty of man.'"

The young man's face lit up, banishing his feigned dotage as if throwing off a heavy cloak. Plunking his fellow scholar in his study, Reverend Treat called for wine and water. As Jin delivered and left, the reverend said, "I don't hold with slavery, myself, but, uh, Jin came with the house." Out in the hall, the slave woman snorted.

The reverend poured Joseph madeira, red wine from Portugal, then offered well water after local custom. Joseph took more water than wine: he needed a clear head. Coming out of the heat and a dusty road, the minister gulped his portion and poured more. "So, Joseph, what brings you to 'Rogue's Island'? Have you lost your faith? Reverend Doctor Mather tells us, 'If a man were to lose his religion, he'd be sure to find it in Newport.'" He chuckled.

Joseph did not. Time flew. "Reverend, I've come about this burning."

The man's enthusiasm slipped. "Ah, yes, a dolorous business. I'm opposed to burning, myself. An invention of Catholics and Episcopalians. Hanging is quicker and less messy. But the gentry are set on a gruesome punishment to deter other slaves from considering assassination. There's no way I can intervene. It wouldn't be, uh, prudent." Not for an upstart paid by the congregation.

"But suppose she's innocent, and Cuffy were too? You could intercede then, surely."

"Well, uh, surely there's no way to prove her innocence. Cuffy was found, uh, administering a snake to the, uh, deceased."

To the reverend's amazement, Joseph pulled a headless snake from his pocket. "I found this. A garter snake, entirely harmless. They don't even have teeth, but crunch crickets and spiders. Cuffy was half-Indian, I've learned. Half Wampanoag. He spoke the words of Passaconaway, an Indian powahee, a prophet of the last century, who made snow burn and trees dance. Passaconaway said that a snake can read your heart, and see the future, and know if an enemy conspires to kill you."

"God cursed the snake," interrupted the parson. "Genesis 3:14."

"Nonetheless, Indians revere snakes. Mohawks consider At-o-sis the mother of their race. Snake blood is a nostrum for women in childbirth: even a spoonful will deliver a healthy baby in a trice. Cuffy learned the cure from his mother, and tried to administer the potion to Master Pearson. He'd tried to cure himself of a stomach ailment just the week before. But the woman of the house saw the snake and concluded Pearson died of snake poisoning, or ingesting a snake even."

"He died in agony, screaming. The venom –"

Joseph shook his head, made his brown hair ripple. "Only pit vipers have venom, only timber rattlers around here. Garter snakes have none."

"Then what killed him?"

"Some other poison, I suspect. I don't know which. There are so many."

"An Indian root? One Cuffy might know?"

Joseph shrugged like a Frenchmen. "There are roots will sicken a man, but few that kill. Snakeroot from the Carolinas is so potent that should a cow even eat it, children can die drinking her milk. But Master Pearson might have had a crab in his stomach, too. Whatever the cause, a physician should have found it. And given that Cuffy tried to *cure* his master, we must err with mercy."

"Negroes are notorious poisoners," Treat insisted. "Everyone here in Newport is careful. They make the slaves eat from the pot first. Masters hold the cellar keys and open their own bottles."

For answer, Joseph held up his goblet. Treat reached to pour more wine, then got the message. "Oh. Yes, I see . . . But Jin has served this parsonage since she was a girl, and . . ." He set down his goblet carefully. "I suppose we better talk to the sheriff. He oversees the execution, but the Pearsons pay the piper, so they call the tune. Yes, I suppose we best see the Pearsons." He sighed at the prospect of disrupting his parishioners – and employers.

The Pearson family, friends, and parlour were draped in black for mourning. Joseph thought they looked more like Quakers than the normally-gay citizens of sinful Newport, yet an incongruous festive air permeated the crowd, for outside Negroes waited with carriages to ferry them to the field where Hazel would be burned.

Reverend Treat was welcomed quietly, shaking hands all around. People peered at moth-eaten Joseph, "a travelling divinity student". The white Indian glimpsed a black face at the kitchen door: Prosper, wide-eyed and appalled that someone who associated with servants should be received cordially in the parlour.

Joseph accepted more madeira with water while the Pearsons took theirs straight from deep goblets. Mistress Pearson – so far not "Widow" – bore finery and a plumpness that bespoke a rich merchant's wife. Pearson brothers George and Chad matched a black-draped portrait of the late Francis: a curly head, lips like a mink trap. John Williams was Pearson's business partner. Despite open windows and high ceilings, the room was roasting.

The Reverend Treat, having again donned his elderly persona, made consoling noises. "Gone to God . . . In the bosom of the Lord . . ." Joseph fidgeted. In an hour Hazel would be tied to a stake and committed to flames while all of Newport bore witness. The student had come to beg a stay of execution, but was unsure how to begin – especially since he'd need to accuse someone else of murder.

Wine-sodden talk buzzed angrily. All present were slave owners. "Burning's the best thing we can do! Put the fear of God into 'em!" "We've been too sparin' of the whip hand and now Francis's paid for it!" "Too familiar, that's what they're getting!"

"But what if Hazel's not guilty?"

Joseph's mild outburst stunned the room. Wine sloshed in goblets as all eyes turned. Reverend Treat sidled away as if from contagion.

"Why," blistered Mistress Pearson, "would you think her innocent? She's a slut! A filthy lying trollop who deserves to die!"

"You must be mad to come here and insult us so!" chorused a brother. "Treat, who is this dimwit?"

"Negroes are notorious poisoners!" added another brother. "There's none we trust with our lives!"

"Even if she were innocent, it's time we burned a nigger to teach the others a lesson!"

Amidst a hail of angry remarks, a heavy hand clamped around Joseph's elbow. The sheriff hoicked the student from the room as if gigging a frog, towed him across the kitchen, and pitched him down the back stairs. Joseph clambered up, shedding dirt and clam shell crumbs, only to receive a jab in the belly from an iron-shod baton that doubled him over, set him coughing.

"I'm warning you out, rascal! Hie back to Massachusetts and your tight-arse Puritans! Now get!" A rap on Joseph's elbow sent electric pain rippling up and down his arm. Joseph was dragged to the street, obviously to be frog-marched clear to the town limits and flung over the line.

Yet rounding the corner, they almost collided with Reverend Treat, who stumbled down the front steps, apologies spilling from his lips. Prosper slammed the front doors. The stunned Treat whirled as Joseph gasped, "I'm a guest – of the reverend."

The sheriff halted at Joseph's rapid rise in status. "Is 'at true, sir?"

"No!" snapped Treat. "Oh, dash it all, yes. I brought him. I'll be responsible." The sheriff reluctantly ceded control of the miscreant, but added his orders still applied.

Joseph stumbled after Treat, who flipped his hand as if to banish the Devil. "Why, why, *why* did you say that? Why intimate that Cuffy and Hazel don't deserve to die? You can't imagine the ruckus you've stirred up! You dandisprat! You hog-rubber! Those people trusted me, and there you jabber like a Barbary ape! How *dare* you –"

"I *dare*," Joseph rubbed his stomach, "because Cuffy was innocent of any crime and Hazel is *still*! Yet these mugwumps will see her burned to death, shrieking to Almighty God, because it's *convenient* to punish her! 'The judge is condemned when the criminal is absolved!'" The last in Latin.

"*There's* your downfall!" retorted the reverend. "Steeping your mind in classics, clouding your judgment with pagan passions when you should study Holy Writ instead!"

"'Out of thine own mouth will I judge thee' then!' 'They sold the righteous for silver, and the poor for a pair of shoes!' 'The faces of all of them gather blackness!' '*Thou* art slave to fate, chance, kings, and desperate men!'" He had to stop, out of breath.

"'Judge not according to appearance!'" Then a sneer. "'Behold the Lamb of God, which taketh away the sin of the world!'"

"'For I desired mercy, and not sacrifice; *and the knowledge of God more than burnt offerings*!'"

Treat merely stamped harder down the dusty road. Joseph stumped alongside, alternately rubbing his stomach and elbow. After they'd gone a hundred yards, the student asked quietly, "'Can two walk together, except they are agreed?'"

"I don't know what you expect of me!" rapped the preacher. "Or God either! You should be gone hence! You're not wanted!"

"I'll go an hour after midday. I'll go then as did Lot. Nor shall I look back."

Treat stopped dead in the middle of the road and glared at Joseph. But the student's pale, hollow-eyed stare was like something dead, and the parson looked away. In the silence came a foot-slapping, a man half-trotting to catch up. Chad Pearson, the dead man's brother. "Hold up! Reverend, you!"

The two clergymen waited in the hot dusty street while Chad Pearson clopped to a stop. Yet having caught up, the man only hemmed and loosened his stock. "I, uh, wanted to say. This, uh, whole affair. It's deuced bad."

Joseph waited, staring, as did Treat.

Reddening, and not from heat, Pearson went on. "Um, I'm sorry you were ejected that way. We don't, uh, usually have the sheriff in –"

"Why does Mistress Pearson hate Hazel so?" shot Joseph.

"Oh, uh. You can't believe everything she says. You know how women are . . ."

"*Why?*"

Treat cleared his throat. "There's no need to be rude."

Chad Pearson looked up and down the street. "It's damned difficult to explain. It's easier if you're drunk. It's just that, well, Sister didn't like having Hazel around – Hey!"

Joseph grabbed the man by the lapels, and only Treat's imploring hands kept Chad Pearson from being rattled like a dice cup. The student rapped, "Tell me and be quick!"

"All right!" Chad backstepped, smoothed his coat. "Francis would – we'd be drinking and he'd – spice up the betting. George and I don't have any nigger women, you see. No good-looking ones, anyway. So he'd, uh, bet her –"

Joseph chopped off his maundering. "You'd hand her around the table. Whoever trumped slept with her."

Chad turned redder. Joseph whirled to Reverend Treat. "Why didn't you tell me this?"

"I didn't know! That's not the sort of thing they'd tell a minister! Sometimes I don't know anything my parishioners are doing!"

"'Haste thee, escape thither,'" quoted Joseph. "Sodom and Gomorrah are rebuilt in the new Israel, and not even Lot's family shall escape this time . . . This news wounds our cause. What could Cuffy think seeing his wife steered to bed at the behest of his master? It's enough to kill for. How know his child is even of his blood?"

"He couldn't complain much," insisted Chad Pearson. "Francis gave Hazel to him for a wife, bought her special. Cuffy should have been grateful . . ." His voice trailed off at Joseph's black look.

Growling, the student went on. "Worse yet. Hazel herself might have poisoned her master. But so could any of you Pearsons be guilty."

"What?"

"All of you stand to inherit, and anyone could have poisoned his food or spirits! And his partner too! Wait.

You import slaves from the Sugar Islands, yes? And own ships, and warehouses? Ships in tropical waters suffer from toredo worms, do they not? The warehouse, have you the keys? Good!"

Bedazzled by this babble, Pearson and Treat were taken in tow as Joseph plowed like a frigate under full sail for the docks.

Chad Pearson fumbled to unlock the side door of the warehouse. Seagulls banked and keened, hungry for scraps, but the wharfs were oddly deserted, for most everyone had trekked to the burning field. As Joseph waited, he noticed tucked behind a narrow two-storey building of stone with iron-barred windows: the slave hut into which "black gold" was herded by midnight moons. He shook his head, tried to ignore the sun striking his shoulders, the ache in his skull.

It was no relief to step into the stifling warehouse. Among crates and bolts of cloth stood pyramids of small casks, called butts, branded in Portugese. The hot air reeked of wine and spices and tar and cedar and turpentine.

Joseph stopped short. "Wine. The best way to introduce the stuff. Yes . . . We know the wine was adulterated because Cuffy fell victim also."

"We do?" asked Pearson and Treat. "He did?"

"Yes. A week before Francis Pearson died, Cuffy suffered a stomach ailment that he tried to treat with his own snake potion, then Maroca's potions. Nothing worked – a potion can't undo poison – but he recovered. From this we infer that one of those times when Master Pearson had been dosed, Cuffy, in clearing the table, drained Pearson's glass: all servants will when they can. He got the poison intended for Pearson: the stuff is heavy and it sinks."

"But Francis didn't drink that much madeira because of his gout," insisted Chad. "He took it with water always."

"Wait. What stuff?" asked Reverend Treat.

"I'll show you. Where is your paint locker?"

The paint locker jutted under the eaves of an addition, with a boarded wall and door that could shut and lock, though no lock was in sight. Joseph stepped into the sharp stink of turpentine. By the light of a tiny window he hunted, under a table found a small cask with a wooden cover. Lifting the cover showed a grey-white powder and a wooden scoop.

"This stuff. Arsenic." Joseph took down a dry paint pot and scooped. "It's used to kill pigs and rats, but is also mixed into red-lead bottom paint to kill toredo worms that riddle hulls so fiercely in the Caribbean, even white oak. There's enough arsenic here to kill half of Newport."

"What?" Brushed by death, Chad Pearson touched his breast.

Treat shook his dark head. "It makes no sense. Only Master Pearson was poisoned, but everyone drank madeira and other wines. You haven't been troubled by stomach cramps, have you, Chad?"

"What? No, never!" The man felt his throat now.

"Perhaps it was meant the whole family to succumb, and something went wrong. Perhaps everyone else was immune." Joseph mused, not believing it himself.

Abruptly he turned to a pyramid of casks, grabbed up a cracked one that had leaked its contents. Joseph rapped a knuckle on the oak bung, peered inside at the wider end. "These bungs are hammered from the inside, then the casks are filled and sealed in the Canary Islands. When broached, the bung falls inside the cask. I see no way a man could remove a bung, poison the wine, then replace it. It would be impossible to tamper with these casks and not have someone notice."

"Of course not," snapped Chad Pearson. Fright was giving way to anger. "But someone did poison my brother, you say. Who? How?"

Joseph paced, passing the pot of arsenic from hand to hand, juggling possibilities in his head until he was dizzy. The oven-heat of the warehouse made him dizzy too, and he stepped outside. The sun was like a hammer, so he moved against the building. The shady strip was a popular place this blistering summer, and posted along the wooden wall were notices announcing auctions or the sale of pirated goods.

Unintentionally, the student read the broadsides, as he read everything that came before his eyes. One poster announced a forthcoming auction conducted by Pearson and Co. "Prime Likely Negroes, both Male and Female, from Ten years of age to Twenty, imported the Last Week from Nevis, and were Brought from Guinea. Seasoned against Smallpox. Also a House Servant, able to Read, trained to Table, raised from a Boy –" The rest was obliterated by the black word CANCELLED. The holder's sudden death had thrown his estate into limbo.

Chad Pearson's jaw and fists were knotted. He looked ready to smite the wall, or Joseph. "You haven't told me yet! Who killed my brother? Who?"

Joseph shrugged his shoulders like some Quebecois. "I don't know! Too many could want him dead! The puzzle needs sorting, wheat from chaff! It's best, I don't know . . . It's best to ask, which single person would most prosper from his death?"

Pearson growled, Treat sighed, while Joseph rubbed his temple. Something nagged him, buzzed in his brain like a rattlesnake's warning. Stock still, he waited for the idea to settle and take root.

Yet Chad Pearson, furious, grabbed Joseph's shoulder and spun him around. "I demand –"

Joseph gazed over the man's shoulder at the auction broadside. Slowly he breathed in Latin, "'I do not distinguish by the eye, but by the mind, which is the proper judge of a man.'"

"Eh?" asked the parson and merchant.

Joseph pointed at the poster, turned without a word and ran up the street, careful not to spill the arsenic. "We must make the field! We must stop the burning!"

"What?" called Pearson. "Come back here!"

"What can you say?" objected Treat. "They won't like it!"

But Joseph was gone, running flat out.

All of Newport filled a pasture near where the tarred Cuffy hung in his "iron suit". Children grabbed the bottom of the cage and squealed to be swung. Adults jammed the shade along the stone walls or else sat on horse blankets under parasols. In the full glare of the sun, a stake was surrounded by pine shavings from a mill and branches culled from nearby orchards: applewood burned so hot it would melt andirons in winter. Against the stake was propped a four-legged stool with a cracked seat. In the seat sat Hazel, feet amidst the fagots, chains on her wrists and ankles. A noose around her neck bound her to the stake, half-throttling so she sat bolt upright. At four corners of the pyre, men with batons keep gawkers at bay. The sheriff talked to a large man sweating in a purple coat, gesturing to the pyre with a birchbark torch. Foremost on blankets the Pearsons sipped madeira proferred by the house servant Prosper. Far back in the sun stood the colony's few free Negroes, including Maroca's brood. The onlookers droned like cicadas.

The buzz deepened when Joseph hopped the stone wall, Chad Pearson and Reverend Treat trotting behind. The sheriff cursed Joseph in round tones, Reverend Treat and Chad Pearson shouted him down. Joseph held his chest, breath rattling and sobbing. He held up the tin, but the sheriff slapped it out of his hand so white powder dusted everyone. "What the hell's that?"

"Your 'snake'!" gulped the student. "Arsenic! It kills by stomach cramps, making a man swell up and suffer terrible thirst, so he drinks more and poisons himself further! But it *wasn't* stirred into the madeira, because no one else fell sick. Pearson suffered from gout. Straight madeira was too rich for his blood, so he took his wine *watered*, the only family member to do so. And who fetched him the water? It *wasn't* poor Cuffy yonder! He fell sick with stomach cramps himself, rest his soul, and a man would hardly drink wine he'd poisoned. But there was *another* in the household who might *prosper* by Pearson's death!"

Joseph's rasping was quiet, but everyone heard. "At the bottom of a broadside for a slave auction, Master Pearson advertised for sale a house servant raised from a boy, trained to table, able to read. A young servant who ran errands to the docks, where he could read an auction notice, and lay hand to arsenic. Rather than be sold, this young slave poisoned his master's water. Pearson's sudden death froze his assets and stalled the slave's own sale."

The stunned crowd swivelled to stare where the Pearsons sat in the place of honour. The family members drew back, open-mouthed, until the house slave Prosper stood alone. His dark face went grey as smoke.

A muttering, then a howl rose. Men broke from the crowd, shoved the Pearsons aside, grabbed the terrified slave. At the stake, the sheriff's men loosed the rope throttling Hazel and hurled her off the stool to make room for Prosper, who shrieked and blubbered as a score of hard hands banged him in the seat. A chant rose. "Burn him! Burn him! Burn him!"

Joseph caught Hazel's chains and led her into the sturdy arms of Maroca. Hazel was more dead than alive with fright and shock, shambling like a statue of ebony wood, chains clinking. Yet she enfolded her son, kissed the head of flat black hair. Prosper screamed, prayed, begged as he was lashed with rope, swaddled like a mummy. Men slapped his head, kicked fagots under his feet. Cries went up for a torch.

Keeping his back to the morbid scene, Joseph pushed amidst the Pearsons to fix the mistress with a deep burning stare. "Hazel has suffered much in her innocence, being damned and incarcerated and near-burned after losing her husband. She'd have precious worth in your household now. Will you give her to me? As a fee for uncovering the true murderer?"

The merchant's wife ran a rapid calculation in her head, then discarded it. "Yes, yes, you may have her. She wasn't good for much anyway. Only to my husband and brothers-in-law," she flared.

"You are all witnesses, eh?" Excited, Joseph's French mannerisms surfaced. "She belongs to me. Then witness, too, I set her free and charge her to the care of Maroca, a freewoman."

He turned to go, but Chad Pearson caught his sleeve. "Wait. Prosper poisoned Francis to stay in our household? That makes no sense! What difference the master?"

The student shrugged. "What does a slave own? Nothing, not even himself. Only his station, the only life he knew. Think on Cuffy, who despite seeing his wife abused, fought to save his beloved master with a snake panacea. 'The slave loves the whip.' And remember this: 'Master, be good to your slaves, for know that you have a master in Heaven.'"

A sheriff's man had unlocked Hazel's manacles. Sweeping his arms wide, Joseph gathered in Maroca and her children and Hazel and her baby, urged them, pushed them, hurried them down the dusty road towards Newport and home. He had to drag Quamino, who stood stricken. Tears spilled down her cheeks, the first tears he'd seen on any black. "Quickly, apace!"

They weren't fast enough. Prosper screamed as flames licked his legs. To cover the noise, Joseph thought to recite. But all he could quote was, " 'If poisonous minerals, and if that tree, whose fruit threw death on else-immortal us, if lecherous goats, if serpents envious cannot be damn'd; why should I be?'"

# The Uninvited Guest

## Edward D. Hoch

*Edward Hoch continues to be a literary phenomenon as the world's most prolific living writer of crime and mystery short stories, having just passed the 900 mark. He is also approaching his fiftieth anniversary as a writer. In all that immense output Hoch has written quite a number of historical mysteries. Probably his most celebrated series are the narratives of Doctor Samuel Hawthorne who looks back over his remarkable career in the twenties and thirties when almost every month there seemed to be a new impossible crime to solve. Some of the early ones have been collected as* Diagnosis: Impossible *(1996). Then there's his western gunslinger turned sleuth, Ben Snow, believed to be a reincarnation of Billy the Kid, some of whose stories are included in* The Ripper of Storyville *(1997). A more recent series is set at the time of the American War of Independence and features Alexander Swift, aide to George Washington.*

The spring of 1779 was an unusually quiet time for the American colonies in the midst of their war of revolution. Perhaps it was a result of the imperceptible merging of the seasons that year. Neither side in the struggle found it necessary to break camp and move out with the coming of spring because in truth there had been hardly a snow or frost since mid January.

General Washington and his wife Martha were with the

troops at their winter quarters in Morristown, New Jersey; when Alexander Swift arrived there on April first in the company of Molly McVey. The camp itself consisted of sturdy huts and cabins, a far cry from the conditions at Valley Forge two winters earlier. And spring had indeed come early to the region, with buds already visible on the fruit trees.

"All is quiet," Washington said, greeting Swift with a firm handshake. The general was a tall man with big hands and feet. At age forty-seven his hair was still reddish-brown, and his large grey-blue eyes looked out from a pale face slightly marked by smallpox. "It is as if the war had gone away."

"The support of the French has been a great help," Alexander Swift replied. Indeed, since France had signed a treaty of aid with the revolting colonies and sent its fleet briefly into American waters the British had evacuated Philadelphia the previous year, leaving it to General Benedict Arnold to enter the city with a corps of Massachusetts troops. Arnold, wounded at Saratoga and unable to walk without support, had been made military commander of the capital. It was a post suitable for a wounded hero who was also an old friend of General Washington.

"And this would be Miss McVey?" Washington asked, extending his hand to the slender, dark-haired young woman at Swift's side.

"Excuse my rudeness. General Washington, may I present Miss Molly McVey, who was of great help to me at Camp West Point."

"A pleasure," the general said. "I have heard much about you, Miss McVey. Will you be living in this area?"

She blushed nicely. "I am travelling with Mr Swift at the present time. I may be returning north soon."

"So might I," Washington responded, walking back to take a seat behind his desk. "In a month's time I plan to move north along the Hudson. I may set up headquarters at New Windsor, beyond West Point on the eastern bank."

"A wise move," Alexander Swift said. "It will bring you closer to the enemy activity."

"Meanwhile, I have a particular assignment of a social nature for you – for both of you, as a matter of fact."

"A social nature?" Swift could not imagine what the general had in mind. Until now his special assignments as a civilian had involved informal action against the British, sometimes as a spy.

"Two old friends, General Benedict Arnold and Miss Peggy Shippen, are to be married in one week's time. I cannot attend personally, but I would like you to represent me and take a gift from Martha and me."

"So Arnold is marrying again!" Swift knew the wounded hero only slightly, but was interested in the news. Benedict Arnold was a widower with three half-grown sons. "He must be nearly forty."

"Thirty-eight, I believe," Washington said. "Peggy is much younger, of course, not quite nineteen. She is the daughter of Judge Edward Shippen, a prominent Quaker and something of a Loyalist, I do believe. I've known her since she was a child."

"They remained in Philadelphia during the British occupation?"

The general nodded. "And I daresay Peggy waltzed with British officers. Young women her age can be terrible flirts. I visited the city this past winter and saw them all, including Arnold. These are difficult times for him. He harbours some bitterness at others being promoted ahead of him. When our rebel troops re-entered the city, Arnold placed Philadelphia under martial law. Shopkeepers resented that. As you know, Arnold has since resigned his post. But a faithless friend of mine, Joseph Reed, now president of the state's Supreme Executive Council, has actually brought charges of malfeasance against him, and Congress is considering the matter." He lowered his voice slightly. "I must admit, Alexander, that when I visited Philadelphia this past winter I found the general living in a grand style of which I could not approve."

"How is his leg?"

"Not good. He needs help standing upright, and four men must assist him in and out of his coach. Still, he claims to be improving. Certainly young Peggy sees some improvement, but then love is blind."

"Where will next week's wedding be held?"

"At the Shippen home in Philadelphia. It will be a quiet ceremony, and I am sorry I cannot be there. Will you go? You can both attend as my representatives."

Alexander Swift glanced at Molly. He could see that the suggestion intrigued her. The social world of a Philadelphia wedding was a long way from the tavern at West Point where she was employed. "Certainly," he told General Washington. "We would consider it a great honour."

Washington had sent a message ahead to inform the family that Swift and a guest would be attending in his place. Arrangements were made for Alexander and Molly to arrive the evening preceding the wedding and spend two nights with Major Cutler, an aide to Benedict Arnold.

Cutler proved to be a slender, taciturn man in his early thirties, about Swift's age, who also would be attending the following day's ceremony. His wife Louisa was more talkative. She was a plain but lively woman a few years younger than her husband. Molly liked her at once, and the two fell into a lengthy conversation following dinner.

Swift and Major Cutler stepped outside for a cigar, but the major still said very little. "How is Arnold's leg mending?"

"Better."

"Does he still need support for standing and walking?"

Cutler drew on his cigar. "Sometimes he tries hopping about. He'll probably use his cane at the wedding."

"Do you think the British are gone from this city for good?"

"I think so."

"It was a great victory for our side."

The slender officer shrugged. "They pulled out, we came in."

Later, when they were beneath the covers of the great feather bed in Cutler's guest room, Molly spoke quietly to Alexander Swift. "Louisa Cutler told me some interesting things about Benedict Arnold while you and the major were enjoying your cigars."

"I'm sure it was more interesting than our conversation."

"She said Peggy Shippen's brother was arrested as a Tory sympathizer, and most of their rich friends are not really loyal to America. Peggy herself was courted by Major John Andre, a British officer, and wore a lock of his hair in a locket on her necklace. More than that, Louisa hinted at Arnold's extravagant living and illegal business partnerships."

Swift wasn't surprised at the latter. "Washington mentioned something about charges of malfeasance being brought against him." He considered the situation as he drifted into sleep. Washington was an old friend of General Arnold. Perhaps he'd had more than one reason for sending a representative to the wedding in his place, especially a representative like Swift who'd handled special assignments in the past.

Washington's gift to the bride and groom was a silver sugar bowl and creamer fashioned by Paul Revere. It seemed a fitting wedding present, linking these patriots who had fought the British from the beginning. If Arnold was marrying into a family of Tory sympathizers, Swift felt sure he could hold his own against them.

They left their horses at the Cutler house the following morning and the two couples travelled by carriage to the Shippen family home, the box containing Washington's gift on the floor at their feet. It was Thursday, the eighth of April, four days after Easter, and the Philadelphia streets were bright with springtime. In the front yard of the Shippen home the apple trees were blossoming weeks ahead of schedule.

It was to be a quiet ceremony, with only the family and a few friends and neighbours in attendance. The minister was a solemn Church of England gentleman who stood apart with Mr Shippen. Swift introduced himself and Molly, expressing General Washington's regrets and presenting the gift he had sent. Judge Shippen, in turn, introduced Peggy's mother, brother, and two older sisters, as well as Arnold's boys. The guests milled around the large parlour speaking with family members, and Swift counted about two dozen people in all. He walked over to where a broad-shouldered

General Arnold sat in full dress uniform, awaiting the appearance of his bride.

"I'm Alexander Swift. You probably don't remember me, sir."

Arnold's stern hawkish features turned toward him, the blue eyes seeming out of place in such a swarthy face. When he stood with the help of a thick walking stick he was shorter than Swift remembered. "You're General Washington's man."

"That's correct. He is sorry he could not be here in person. Both he and Martha send their regrets and promise they will visit you both at their earliest opportunity."

A man in formal clothes had begun to play a harpsichord, and all conversation ceased. Suddenly the bride appeared on her father's arm. Peggy Shippen, twenty years younger than Arnold, had the blossoming freshness of a young girl in springtime, a slim blue-eyed beauty who seemed totally in control of the moment. Her hair was piled high on her head in an elaborate European style and she wore a flowing white wedding gown. As the minister stood by, Judge Shippen delivered her to Benedict Arnold. For a moment Swift was reminded of his own marriage, which ended with the coming of the revolution when he left New York while his wife Amanda stayed on with a British officer.

Arnold stood with some difficulty at Peggy's side, supported by his cane, while the minister read the vows, concluding with, "I now pronounce you man and wife." The happy couple kissed while the small audience applauded.

Some bottles of French champagne were produced and servants filled glasses for the guests to toast the new husband and wife. Following the toast, Swift noticed for the first time a tall, angular man whose clothes seemed a bit loose. He sipped the champagne as he moved about the parlour, stopping first at one group and then another. No one seemed to acknowledge his presence until he finally reached the Cutlers and Molly. Major Cutler and his wife said a few words to him and he set his champagne glass on a table momentarily to take something from his pocket to show them. Swift turned as General Arnold approached with his bride. Across the room he spotted Molly conversing with a woman guest.

"Mr Swift, I have the pleasure of introducing my bride, Peggy."

Seeing her close up, Swift was struck again by her youthful beauty. "I wish you both every happiness," he said. "General Washington was quite disappointed that he was unable to attend."

"Tell him we missed him," Peggy Arnold said, her voice soft and melodious.

When they'd finished making their rounds of the guests, Arnold signalled for quiet. He thanked everyone for coming and then announced that as a wedding gift to his bride he had purchased Mount Pleasant, a large Philadelphia estate on the banks of the Schuylkill River. It had a hundred acres of gardens and orchards, and Peggy seemed to glow with pleasure at the news.

"How can he afford such a place?" Swift wondered, speaking to the Cutlers a few minutes later.

As usual Major Cutler said little, but Louisa lowered her voice and told them, "I hear that he is deeply in debt with loans from moneylenders. He has borrowed on his house in New Haven and pledged the back salary and commissions he hopes to obtain from the Congress."

Swift was troubled by the news. He knew Washington would not be pleased.

Others were proposing toasts now, and the lanky man in the ill-fitting suit stepped forward to raise his glass. "To the Sons of Liberty!" he announced, speaking the name of a patriotic society, originally secret but now disbanded. "To Sam Adams and Paul Revere!"

He took a long drink from his glass as someone else started to propose a toast. Then, barely a moment later, he uttered a sharp cry and doubled over, clutching his stomach. Swift stared at him, frozen to the spot like everyone else. The man seemed to fold in half, then topple slowly to the floor.

A doctor emerged from among the guests, a neighbour of the Shippens named Caleb Wade. He was a big man with long white hair, though his face was not especially old. He quickly knelt by the body, feeling for a pulse.

"This man is very sick," he announced after a moment's examination. "Can we get him to a bed?" Several of the men came forward to help carry the stricken man upstairs. By now he seemed almost unconscious, struggling to breathe.

"Who is he?" Swift asked Major Cutler. "I saw you speaking with him earlier."

For a moment Cutler looked blank. "Did you?"

"Of course, dear," his wife reminded him. "He was the odd man who came up to us and started talking. Remember? We were wondering if he was a friend of the bride or the groom."

"What was he talking about?"

"Just the wedding," Louisa Cutler replied. "He took out a little drawing of an animal to show us. I thought it very odd."

"It was a deer," Molly McVey verified. "A female deer. I said it was nice and he gave it to me."

General Arnold came up to them then, much distressed. "Do any of you know that man? I've spoken to the judge and his wife and he wasn't on their guest list. They assumed he was a friend of mine."

"We spoke to him," Cutler replied, "but we don't know who he is."

"I had better see to him," Swift decided. "Is it all right if I go upstairs?"

"Of course," Arnold said. "Dr Wade is still with him."

He found the doctor in the bedroom of one of Peggy's sisters, at the top of the stairs. He was bending over his patient but he straightened up as Swift entered. "Can he speak, Doctor?"

"I'm afraid he's passed away, just a moment ago."

Alexander Swift stared down at the body, suddenly smaller in its ill-fitting garments. "Did he say anything before he died?"

"Just one word. It sounded like *dough*, or perhaps *do*, as in music."

Swift remembered the drawing the man had shown to Molly and the Cutlers. "Could it have been *doe*, a female deer?"

"I suppose so."

"We'd better go tell Judge Shippen and General Arnold that he's dead."

The death of the uninvited guest cast a pall over the wedding party. While arrangements were made for the removal of the body, Alexander Swift again separated Benedict Arnold from his bride. "I think we should talk about what happened, General. Washington will want a full report when I return."

They were in the judge's library at the rear of the house, looking out on a sloping yard with more apple trees in bloom. "I never saw the man before," Arnold insisted. "I have found no one who invited him." As he spoke his hand went to his injured leg, massaging it as if to drive away the pain.

"Could he have been someone to whom you owed money?"

"Certainly not!" The question seemed to offend him. He stood up, leaning heavily on his walking stick. "If you will excuse me, I must rejoin my bride. We have nothing more to discuss."

Swift helped him out the door but did not follow immediately. The body was being removed under the supervision of Dr Wade. The rest of the wedding party had gone outside while the grisly task was performed. Swift caught the doctor's eye and motioned him into the library.

"Would you care to speculate as to the cause of death, Doctor? Could it have been a heart attack?"

"Certainly not that. The stomach cramps, together with his death within such a short time, suggest a poison of some sort."

"Do you mean the man took his own life?"

"Either that or someone took it for him."

The festivities had been dampened by the death of the unknown man, but once the body was removed the family seemed determined to make the best of it. Before long there were more toasts to the bride and groom, and with a final round of goodbyes the happy couple went off in a carriage for a bit of privacy. "He's a real American," Judge Shippen remarked. "My daughter is lucky to have him for a husband. That's a beautiful estate he's bought for her."

Later, as the party was breaking up, Swift asked Major Cutler about his brief conversation with the dead man. "He showed you a drawing of a female deer, and Dr Wade thinks his final word might have been *doe*. Would that have any meaning to you?"

"None at all."

Swift and Molly walked to the carriage with the Cutlers and the major instructed the driver to take them home. On the way the conversation was mainly about the wedding, with only a passing reference to the dead stranger. It wasn't until they were alone in their bedroom at the Cutler house that Swift reminded Molly of the drawing she'd said the unknown man gave her.

"I have it here, but it is hardly a work of art."

He took the small sheet of stiff paper which she'd rolled into a tube and slid up the sleeve of her dress. It was not an original pencil sketch, he saw at once, but a printed copy. The deer seemed to be prancing through some underbrush. On the back a name was written, very small: *John Slate*. It was followed by the words *Penn House Inn*.

"Do you think that's the artist or our uninvited guest?" Molly wondered.

"I don't know," he admitted. "But it gives me something to work on."

"To work on? General Washington sent us to attend a wedding, nothing more!"

"He told me Judge Shippen has Loyalist sympathies. If that's the case, a killing at his home – on the very day of his daughter's wedding to an American general – could be important."

Molly thought it over. "Most likely he was simply an old beau of Peggy's and she didn't want to admit it."

"Wouldn't her father know him if that was the case? Certainly he'd be a familiar figure at the balls she attended." He looked again at the back of the picture. "Where is Penn House Inn?"

"It's here in the city, down near the waterfront. Did you

see me speak to that girl at the wedding? We worked together briefly in Albany. She told me she's a waitress at Penn House."

"Strange that she was invited to such a small wedding." He tapped a finger thoughtfully on the drawing. "Of course there's another possibility."

"What's that?"

"She might have come with the man who was killed. Did you notice her after his collapse?"

"No," she admitted, "but I wasn't really looking for her."

"What's her name?"

"She calls herself Persia Tolliver."

"Suppose we pay a visit to Penn House Inn."

Alexander and Molly excused themselves, telling the Cutlers they wanted to see a bit of the city before they headed home the following day. Molly had changed into a riding costume and they set out in early afternoon, heading their horses toward the Delaware River. "I never expected to be in Philadelphia," she confessed. "A few days away from the tavern at West Point seemed a good enough idea. I should have known nothing is ever simple with you, Alex."

"If this man Slate, or whatever his name was, is a murder victim, Washington will want the details. Philadelphia is full of Loyalists, and they seem to be getting closer to Benedict Arnold all the time."

"I don't like your getting involved in these things. You could have been shot as a spy when the British captured you in New York last year."

"Washington needed me there," he said simply. It was something they'd talked little about.

"You saw your wife in New York."

"*And* her British lover," he emphasized. "There is no love lost between us."

Molly rode silently for a time, until at last they came to a large three-storey building that displayed the sign *Penn House Inn*. They dismounted and went inside.

"You have rooms for the night?" Swift asked the inn-keeper, a bearded man with sly eyes.

"That we have! Our rates are posted on the wall."

"I'm looking for John Slate. Is he staying with you?"

"Slate? We may have had someone by that name, but he is no longer with us."

"What did he look like? Lanky, with ill-fitting clothes?"

"Perhaps."

Molly could see his mounting frustration and she asked a question of her own. "Is Persia Tolliver working today?"

The sly eyes shifted. "You know Persia?"

"An old friend. I saw her this morning at a wedding and she told me she was working here."

He nodded. "I expect her soon. She's due in at two o'clock."

They waited at a table in the bar and presently the young woman Swift had glimpsed at the wedding came through the door from the kitchen. She had changed out of the dress she'd worn to the wedding and she carried a bar rag, ready for work. Molly stood up and addressed her. "Hello, Persia. My friend wanted to meet you. This is Alexander Swift."

She shook her head, a look of fear shooting across her face. "I don't know anything about what happened."

Swift tried to keep his voice low and non-threatening. "Were you invited to the wedding, Persia?"

"I know the family. Peggy's brother comes in here sometimes." Up close she was older than he'd thought, easily into her thirties. Her pale blond hair was already showing some grey.

"So you decided to attend the wedding and take John Slate with you."

"Who?" she asked.

"Don't play games. The tall thin man who had to borrow a wedding garment that was a poor fit. The man who was poisoned, Persia."

"Yes," she agreed. "It was a bit loose, wasn't it? He got it from the cook here, just before we left for the wedding. But what's this about poison?"

"You know he's dead, don't you?"

Her eyes widened a bit. "I slipped out after he fell down. I thought he was drunk and they'd find out we weren't invited. I didn't know he'd been poisoned."

"Who was he?" Molly asked.

Persia Tolliver sighed and made a sour face. "You had it right. His name was John Slate, or at least he told me it was. He'd been here at the inn for three or four days. He told me a lady friend had information that would make him rich. When I mentioned knowing Peggy Shippen's brother he insisted we must attend the wedding."

"Her brother didn't recognize you?"

She blushed a bit. "I didn't really know him. I only waited on him once. His father approached us before the ceremony and I said we were friends of General Arnold."

"He showed us a drawing of a female deer," Molly said. She took it from her pocket. "What does it mean?"

"I have no idea."

"His name was written on the back, along with the name of this inn," Swift told her. "It was meant as a message, an address where he could be reached."

"I know nothing about it," she insisted.

"This city was under martial law," he reminded her, "and the army retains a great deal of power here. You could be imprisoned as a spy."

She snorted. "For what? For spying on a wedding?"

"Are John Slate's belongings still here at Penn House?"

"I suppose so. They'd be up in his room."

"The innkeeper said he'd left."

"Morris? He probably heard of Slate's death and hopes to keep his possessions for himself."

"Could you get a key to his room?"

Persia frowned at the question. "Are you trying to get me in trouble?"

"John Slate was murdered. We're trying to keep you out of trouble."

She thought about that, wiping the table with her rag. "I've got a key," she said finally. "I'll take you up there."

She disappeared into the kitchen and returned after a moment, nodding for them to follow her. They went up the stairs quickly while the innkeeper was busy with his ledgers. She stopped at the third door on the left and inserted a long slender key into the lock. The room was somewhat drab, with a big brass bed as its major feature. Persia went immediately to a closet and opened the door. A jacket, pants, and shirt hung there.

"These are uniform pants," Swift said at once, examining them closely. "Was he in the Continental Army?"

"I know next to nothing about John Slate. He appeared at Penn House on Easter Sunday morning and took a room for several nights. I had some drinks with him after my work was done, and came up here a few times because he was lonely. I guess he was in the army for a while."

"What did he talk about?" Molly asked.

"Not about himself. Nothing about himself. He asked about Benedict Arnold and his officers. When he found out I knew Peggy's brother he insisted we go to the wedding, even though we weren't invited. I was crazy to agree to it, but he said he had to see somebody to get his money."

While they continued talking, Swift went quickly through the few clothes in the closet. He found nothing, nor was there anything of interest in the leather saddlebags on the closet floor, other than a paper confirming that John Slate had indeed served in Washington's Continental Army as a private. He was about to abandon his search when he noticed a small sheet of paper on a writing desk near the window. It was a duplicate of the printed drawing of the deer Slate had produced at the wedding.

There was a small cast-iron stove in the room for heating purposes, and Swift noticed a few scraps of paper waiting to be burnt. He picked them up and saw at once that it was a letter, or the draft of one. The date and salutation were missing, but after piecing the rest together he was able to read it: *This is your second warning. I know your secret. Leave one thousand pounds at Penn House* –

Something after that had been crossed out, and then he'd torn it up and probably started over. There could be no doubt it was the beginning of a blackmail letter, threatening someone with exposure. Probably it had been written that very morning, before the wedding, since the stove would have been lit the previous night to take away the chill. Even with the early spring that year, the Philadelphia nights could be cool in early April.

John Slate had written that note in the morning, knowing he was to attend Arnold's wedding with Persia Tolliver. It seemed likely that the blackmail message was meant for someone who would also be attending the wedding. Had he delivered it, and had that caused his death?

Molly paused in her examination of the room to peer over his shoulder at the assembled pieces of torn paper. "It is certainly not a suicide note," she observed.

"No," he readily agreed. "If John Slate was contemplating suicide he would hardly be hatching a blackmail scheme. It seems likely that the person being blackmailed acted quickly to remove the threat."

"That quickly, Alex? Who would carry a vial of poison with them, especially to a wedding?"

It was a logical question and he had no immediate answer for it. Something was stirring in his memory, though. Something –

"Didn't General Arnold own a pharmacy and bookstore in New Haven before the war?"

"I don't know, Alex. I know nothing about his early days."

"A pharmacist, even a former one, might be a source for poisons."

"But he must have sold the store long ago."

Swift shook his head. "I believe he left it in the care of his sister."

"Certainly you can't imagine he might have poisoned a guest at his own wedding."

"Anything is possible."

"But what was the meaning of the drawing? How would Arnold be linked to a female deer?"

He'd forgotten about the picture of the doe. "Tell me exactly what happened when John Slate approached your group with that illustration."

"As I remember it, he said something about the wedding and then took some papers from an inside pocket. He showed us the drawing of the doe and asked if any of us had ever seen it before. Louisa said she had not, and passed it to her husband. When it was my turn I admired it and he said I could have it, that he possessed more copies."

Swift turned to Persia Tolliver, hovering near the door as if waiting a chance to escape. "Thank you for your help here. We'll be on our way."

"You won't tell them I was at the wedding, will you? I had nothing to do with his death."

"You will be kept out of it if at all possible," Swift assured her.

John Slate's body had been taken to an undertaker frequently used by the Continental Army in Philadelphia. Swift and Molly rode there from Penn House Inn, arriving around four o'clock. After a brief conversation the undertaker took them into his office and showed them the contents of the dead man's pockets. "Nothing unusual here, as you can see. A money purse with a few sovereigns, a handkerchief, a key."

Alexander Swift picked it up. "That's to his room at the inn. You found no letter or message of any sort?"

"Nothing like that."

He thanked the man and they returned to their horses. "What do you think, Alex?" Molly asked.

"Assuming he wrote a final version of that letter, it seems that he managed to deliver it to someone at the wedding. He and Persia went nowhere else."

"How would Slate even know who would be at the wedding? It was a small, private affair."

"Exactly! Think about it, Molly. Who would he know with certainty would be attending? The bride and groom, and the bride's family. I think we can rule out Arnold's children by his previous marriage. They're hardly old enough to have a secret of interest to a blackmailer. And his sister is still in New England. But there is one other person who would certainly be at the wedding – Major Cutler, Arnold's personal aide."

"Cutler!"

"I'm sure I'm right, Molly, and I want to confront him with it. Can you get his wife out of the house on some pretext this evening?"

"I'll try, but I can't believe that Cutler –"

"That's who Slate spoke with. That's who he showed the drawing to."

"True enough," she agreed.

"All I have to do is trace the poison to him."

"Do you think General Arnold got it for him?"

"There's one other possibility. The Shippens' neighbour, Dr Wade."

After a light supper Molly suggested a walk by the river, and Louisa Cutler agreed, though it was already growing dark outside. When they were alone, Swift lit one of Major Cutler's cigars and said, "This has been a full day. At least Arnold and his bride will be relaxing now."

"And most enjoyably so," Cutler agreed with a little chuckle. "Peggy is a lovely young woman." He opened a bottle of French brandy and filled their glasses.

Swift put down the cigar after a few puffs and cleared his throat. "I've spent a few hours this afternoon looking into the death of that strange fellow at the wedding."

"Oh? Have you learned anything?"

"Quite a bit. The man's name was indeed John Slate and he had a room at the Penn House Inn. He came to the wedding uninvited, in the company of a waitress at the inn named Persia Tolliver. She exited quickly after his collapse."

"What was his purpose in attending?"

"The man was a blackmailer," Swift told him. "He came to deliver a second blackmail note to someone he knew would be present. Because of his ill-fitting clothes, he attracted my attention from the outset. Though he approached several groups, yours was the first party he spoke to, and the first he showed the drawing of the deer. I believe, Major Cutler, that you were the object of the blackmail, and that you eliminated the threat immediately by poisoning the man's drink when he set it on the table next to you."

"You're very observant." The major smiled slightly. "Where did I obtain this poison, and how did I happen to bring it with me to General Arnold's wedding?"

"You obtained it from the Shippens' neighbor, Dr Wade,

with the excuse that you needed to kill some rats in the house."

"I see you have spoken to him. We do have rats and Wade gave me some poison for them. But I never killed this man Slate or anyone else, except in battle!"

Alexander Swift smiled slightly as there came a knocking on the front door. "I asked Dr Wade to come over here after supper. That should be him now."

The portly physician was shown in by a servant. He shook hands with Swift and Cutler and took a seat. "Now how can I be of service, gentlemen?"

It was Major Cutler who took up the conversation. "Mr Swift believes that I poisoned that man today with the dosage you provided for the killing of our house rats."

"Well –" The doctor seemed suddenly embarrassed. "He asked if I had ever provided you with poison and I remembered that instance last month. I certainly cast no suspicion in your direction, Major."

Swift took from his waistcoat pocket the pieces of the note he'd found in John Slate's room, plus the folded picture of the deer. "This is my proof of a blackmail plot, gentlemen. It was the motive for the crime."

"What motive is this?" Major Cutler demanded. "This picture of a doe means nothing."

But it was Dr Wade who spoke again. "*Doe* was the dying man's last word. I didn't see this picture until now so I didn't connect the two. This is the symbol of D.O.E., a Loyalist secret society that is the antithesis of the Sons of Liberty."

"D.O.E.?"

The doctor nodded. "The Daughters of England."

And in a flash Swift realized his terrible mistake. He had sent Molly off in the darkness with a murderess.

It was almost dark by the time Molly and Louisa Cutler reached the river, which was swollen with spring rains. Louisa was as talkative as ever, chattering on about life in Philadelphia since the British withdrawal. "It's certainly nice to taste French brandy and champagne again," she enthused. "And that Lafayette! Why, he's little more than a boy!"

"He is three years older than General Arnold's new bride," Molly pointed out.

"Well, she's just a child too! I do hope she doesn't ruin the general with her extravagant ways."

"The man who was poisoned at the wedding – John Slate – apparently came there to blackmail someone. Do you think it could have been Peggy?"

"I doubt it. We never saw her until she entered on the judge's arm, and following the ceremony she was clinging to General Arnold the whole time. When could he have slipped her his note?"

Molly felt an instant chill down her spine and stopped walking. "Louisa," she said carefully, "how did you know about the blackmail note? I never mentioned a note."

"Isn't that what blackmailers usually send? The word itself implies mail."

Everything was falling into place for Molly. "When Slate approached us at the wedding it wasn't to give a message to your husband. You were the one he was after. He handed the drawing of the doe to you first, and the folded note would have been underneath. It was you who dropped the poison into his glass, not your husband."

"Oh, I don't think anyone would believe that," Louisa said. She reached out to grab Molly's arm. "Come on, let me help you. It's treacherous along the river in the dark."

Molly shook her off. "You'd had a prior threat and prepared yourself with a vial of poison. You saw your chance and you took it. What is your secret, Louisa? Does your husband know it?"

Now the woman grabbed both her arms, dragging her toward the water. "My secret is that I am loyal to the mother country, loyal to England. If that is a crime for which I can be blackmailed, so be it! There are plenty of others like me, including Arnold's wife. What you win on the battlefield may be lost in the bedroom."

The earth went out from under Molly's feet and she grabbed at the woman's sleeve, pulling her down too. Then she felt a strong arm grip her waist just as her feet hit the water, pulling her up and free. It was Alex, come from somewhere in the dark like a charging animal.

Louisa Cutler screamed once from the darkened water, and then she was swept away.

"She killed that man," Molly gasped, trying to catch her breath.

"I know," Swift said. "I figured it out just too late."

"It was soon enough for me."

"She belonged to a secret society called the Daughters of England. Slate found out from one of his lady friends and tried to blackmail her. She obtained some poison her husband was using to kill rats, and when Slate appeared at the wedding with a second warning she slipped it into his drink when he set it down to take out the picture."

"That's when he passed her the note. After the first message she was expecting him at any time."

"We'd better get back and tell Cutler what's happened. An accidental drowning, perhaps."

"Alex, right at the end she said Arnold's wife was involved too. Can we believe that?"

He breathed a sigh. "Perhaps General Washington should not be told of this until we are certain. The war is not yet won. There are dangerous days ahead."

# Benjamin's Trap

## Richard Moquist

*Minnesota-born Richard Moquist graduated from North Dakota State University with a degree in pharmacy, a fact that may become obvious in the following story. It comes from his first book,* The Franklin Mysteries *(1994) in which Benjamin Franklin provides a ready hand and mind to help his nephew, Constable Wendell Franklin, solve crimes in eighteenth-century Philadelphia. Franklin is, of course, a major figure in American history and it's not surprising he's been selected as a literary sleuth. Robert Lee Hall has also written a series of novels with him as the detective starting with* Benjamin Franklin Takes the Case *(1988), though he chose Franklin's years in London. For his next book Moquist moved forward a century.* Eye of the Agency *(1997) features Chicago newspaper reporter Sadie Greenstreet and her husband, a Pinkerton detective, involved in a murder on a Mississippi riverboat. Moquist's third novel,* The Concord Street Irregular, *is in the pipeline and has moved forward another century to the 1950s.*

"You have arrived at precisely the critical moment," said Uncle Benjamin in a more than jovial tone.

He was at his workbench, connecting a shiny cylindrical apparatus to his electrical storage device. Above the cylinder, a piece of cheese hung by a thin metal wire. Another wire was attached to the metal cylinder below, which, in turn, was connected to a small ramp leading to the cheese. With wooden tongs, Benjamin reached in a covered bucket, producing a rather large grey mouse. He set the mouse on the metal cylinder with its front legs touching the metal wire where the cheese hung. The mouse stiffened momentarily, then Benjamin loosened his grip and the mouse dropped into the cylinder.

"Ha, ha! Wendell. The apex of science! The pinnacle of physical philosophy! The perfectly useless device using the limits of man's knowledge! This, my dear nephew, is the world's first and only electrical mousetrap." He raised his forefinger exuberantly toward the ceiling. "Perhaps I shall send one to the Marquis de Lafayette. It may become all the rage in European society."

A southern gale blew a continuous sheet of rain against the study window and Benjamin looked out with a frown, as if only now noticing the inclement weather. "And what brings you out calling on a night like this?"

I shook my soggy constable's hat and waistcoat, placing them on the rocking chair that faced the fireplace. It was indeed a shame to disturb his buoyant mood with morbid news from beyond those friendly study walls, so it was with some reluctance, and a sigh that I began.

"It is one of the most diabolical crimes in the history of Philadelphia," I said, warming my hands by the fire.

Benjamin set down his wooden tongs on a side table while taking his customary chair. His jovial smile was now replaced by an earnest, questioning look.

"It was early morning when I was called to the Salisbury Inn. The place was quiet as a mouse when I arrived – the guests and innkeeper's wife, along with a few bystanders, were all huddled in the lobby room. No one spoke a word; they just pointed up the stairs to the lodging rooms.

"It was in the first room on the right that I found Dr Shippen laying a blanket over a man in a bed as Mr Salisbury, the innkeeper, looked on.

" 'It's poison,' the doctor said. 'There's no denying it. But just what kind of poison is beyond my knowledge.'

"The dead man was in his bed with something close to a

smile on his face. Yet his eyes fairly bulged out of their sockets in a manner so frightful and unnatural it set my hair stiff on my neck. I asked if a poison would cause that unnatural expression of terror in his eyes while the rest of his face remained tranquil, and Dr Shippen replied, 'No, but this would certainly explain that ghastly look in his eyes.' And then he pulled back the blanket.''

I cleared my throat, turning to face my companion. "Uncle Benjamin, the man's right hand was cut clean to the bone and was lying limp at his side. It was as if someone had tried to cut it off.''

I paused, gazing at Uncle Benjamin's awed expression as he sat motionless in his chair. The rain beat on the window and I threw a birch log onto the fire grate. Benjamin's forefinger rested on the side of his temple and at length he said in a coarse whisper, "Go on.''

I took the chair opposite his. "The doctor was of an opinion that the dead man had witnessed the cutting of his hand. And this seemed likely, for it had bled profusely, more than would be expected had he died first and the wound inflicted later. His position on the bed indicated that no struggle had taken place, nor had the man even moved before or after that gruesome deed.''

Benjamin shifted uneasily in his chair. "A poison that renders a person so paralysed he cannot move, yet can be alert enough to watch his hand being nearly cut off. That is altogether more than gruesome. Who was this unfortunate man?''

"His name was Edward Huggins,'' I continued. "A British sales merchant of exotics – Oriental spices and teas along with liquors and tobaccos. He came to Philadelphia with two fellow merchants to seek buyers for their goods. The two remaining merchants were understandably in quite a state over the affair. Their papers confirmed they worked for Chesterton's of London, a large trading company. I also found that these Englishmen had queer habits for merchants. You see, according to the innkeeper, they stayed in their rooms by day and left only for an hour or two at night. The three were secretive to the point that their meals were left outside their doors and eaten in their rooms.''

"Each had his own room then?" Benjamin inquired.

"Yes. And when questioned about their actions, they just shrugged and said it is often the custom to be confidential in business dealings, as one must be wary and not arouse the competition.

"Now," I continued, "the inn has few guests this time of year, the one other boarder being a man named Pascales, a broker who also sells tobacco, though of the South American variety. This man left the inn early this morning before the alarm went up. He has not been seen since."

"He sells tobacco too, you say? That is of interest," said Benjamin as he rose from his chair, then walked toward the fireplace and pulled on the thick bell rope which hung by the mantel. "Anything further?" he asked, returning to his former position in his horsehair chair.

"The innkeeper is Charles Salisbury, a young man who works the inn with his wife, Elizabeth. I have heard the Salisburys have come on hard times of late and employ only the skeleton of a staff. A chambermaid is the only permanent worker, but, due to illness, she was not on duty last night."

"Yes," said Benjamin, nodding. "As I recall, the inn was once called the King's Inn and was owned by Elizabeth Salisbury's father. He was a Loyalist who helped the Tory cause during the war. He died about 1778, I believe, leaving the inn to his daughter, who soon married Mr Salisbury."

"Mr Salisbury was quite adamant that we find the murderer – bad for business, you know. But here is something you may find of interest," I said, and showed Benjamin an old piece of parchment that had been deeply folded into quarters. "I found this curious note in the dead man's pocket."

"Carpenters' Hall, West Wing, Northwest Corner, Nine," Benjamin read with a pondering exactness. "Possibly a meeting place. What was the time of his death?"

"He was served his dinner very late – it was nearly ten – and did not leave his room after. Dr Shippen estimates he died between that time and midnight."

Benjamin drew the paper nearer his bifocals. "This paper, despite its good condition, is of an old English parchment type no longer in use. And the deep lines indicate it was kept under something heavy, or possibly in the pages of a book."

A knock on the study door was followed by the ample figure of Benjamin's yellow-aproned maid, carrying a silver tea tray piled high with cakes and honey. A rolled and tied piece of paper was on the tea tray and she handed it to me.

"A note from Constable O'Boyle at the station house," I said after the maid had curtseyed and closed the door behind her. "It states that the lost tobacco broker has returned – claiming to have been out all day selling to the tobacconists in town. He was questioned, but says he never met Edward Huggins. Further, Dr Shippen reports that the dead man's food was most definitely poisoned. The doctor gave the remainder of Huggins's supper to a sickly cat, who experienced several seconds of complete paralysis before being put out of her misery."

"Confirming the presence of poison was, of course, an essential point in our investigating," said Benjamin as he took his cup of tea. "But since the two associates of the deceased deal in spices, I should have liked to examine the poisoned dish for traces of spices. Remember that most poisons are quite unpalatable and would need to be masked by spices or some other means."

"That is true," I said, shaking my head but trying to mask the bitter taste in my mouth for having overlooked such a simple point, "though if the dish was left outside his door, the food could have been tainted by any of the guests or even by someone with access to the inn's kitchen."

"Who was it that cooked the meal?"

"It was Mrs Salisbury."

"And did she deliver it to the room, as well?"

"No, it was brought up by Mr Salisbury himself."

With squinted eyes, Benjamin stared into the air as if trying to see an idea more clearly. "Well, well," he said finally. "This case certainly has its peculiarities. The attempted cutting off of a man's right hand is a very suggestive act, but, as for now, I believe we can do no better than speculate on the motivation. Tomorrow, if you wish, I should be happy to assist you in your inquiries."

The tea, honey and cakes soon diverted Benjamin's mind to other matters – from an account of the tea party in Boston to a prolonged discussion on the industry and sociability of bees. But at length, I retrieved my hat and waistcoat, now dry and warm from the fire, replaced the Diderot that Benjamin had pulled down from his book shelf and, promising an early return, headed for Mrs Marshall's Boarding House.

The hard rain had ceased when I reached the street, taking with it the impurities of beasts and humanity, leaving the stone streets of Philadelphia clean and glistening. I washed my mind of unpleasant thoughts as well and decided a detour in the direction of the Blue Anchor was in order.


A bright early morning sun hung low over the Delaware and shone through the windows of Benjamin's coach as we rode down Fourth Street towards the Salisbury Inn. We first passed a line of solemn Quakers piously filing into the Friend's Meeting House, and listened to the mirthful sound of children chanting their morning lessons in the adjacent open-windowed school house. But as we reached the Salisbury Inn, we found that scene to be anything but mirthful. Mr Salisbury and his wife sat at a table by the stairs, comforting a chambermaid, whose face was as white as the apron she wore. Mr Salisbury rushed toward us, arms swinging wildly in half circles.

"Constable!" he cried. "It's murder, just like before." He pointed in the direction of the upstairs rooms. His young but well-lined face grimaced in a woeful expression as he grabbed my arm. "It will be my ruin. Who will stay at an inn where two men have died? And in such a manner!"

I mounted the steps and was soon standing before an open door. And the sight that met my eyes I shall not soon forget. A bearded man in his mid-thirties sat erect in a wooden arm chair. His lifeless face was ashen and showed no emotion. Yet on the floor lay a dark pool of blood and above it hung the man's nearly severed right wrist.

Soon Benjamin arrived at the door and we were joined by two other men, Mr Kenneth Becker, a black-bearded fellow of some forty years, tall, handsome, with a commanding air, and Mr Rafael Pascales, a bespectacled Spaniard of some fifty years with a face that showed the effects of a bout with smallpox. The former rushed to the dead man's side, crying "Albert!" He cringed at the horrific sight, then turned to me. "Is there no law in this town? First Edward and now Albert. I demand satisfaction."

"You are not in a position to demand anything, sir. I suggest you return to your room where we will have an interview directly. And I suggest you do the same," I said to the other.

Pascales took my orders well and retreated across the hall, but the bearded compatriot of the dead man stood defiantly for a moment at the door, then turned on his heels abruptly.

"I have sent for Dr Shippen," Mr Salisbury reported, somewhat out of breath. "Do you wish me to leave also?"

"No, there is a question or two first. Who was it that served his dinner?" I pointed to a half-eaten plate of mutton on a side table.

Mr Salisbury was startled by the question, as if suddenly realizing he had more to lose than guests at his inn. "I served it myself, Constable Franklin. My wife cooked the meal and we ate of it ourselves. I assured our guests the food was not tainted and, in accordance with their custom, I left each of the gentlemen a plate at his door. Later, Mr Pascales came by and after being questioned by a night constable, he took his dinner at a table downstairs. As you can see, none but this unfortunate man showed any ill effects."

As I spoke to the young innkeeper, Benjamin browsed about the room, stopping finally at the bay window overlooking Chestnut Street and Carpenters' Hall. "Carpenters' Hall, west wing, northwest corner, nine," he murmured, then spoke aloud. "Did the three British brokers request rooms on this particular side of the inn?"

"They did," Salisbury replied eagerly. "Some three weeks past, I received notice announcing their future arrival and requesting rooms facing south. They said that due to their business dealings they would require extraordinary privacy and quiet."

At this, Benjamin dismissed the innkeeper and I proceeded to search the room minutely for clues while Benjamin continued to stare out the window. The room was simple: a wood bed, high boy drawers, and a soft-cushioned wing chair with a small table by its side. A black cape coat hung on the back of the chair and in its pocket was a metal talisman. I passed it to Benjamin, who studied it with critical interest. It was the size of a dollar, white, and had a red cross on either side.

"It is the cross of St George, the patron saint of British soldiers," explained Benjamin. "This man was either a soldier or, considering his age, a former soldier." He stared at me as if this muddled mess was slowly beginning to take a clearer shape in his mind.

"You see a solution?" I asked, eagerly.

"Perhaps. There are some indications, though this matter is far from clear in my mind."

Presently, our heads were turned by hurried voices on the staircase. Dr Shippen appeared first and hastened to the dead man's side, then Constable O'Boyle arrived and hastened to mine. Though we knew what verdict would come, we waited for the pronouncement of the doctor.

"It's poison, just like before," he reported, "though this one's last moments were not as horrible as the other. There is considerably less blood here than in the case of the other – this one died before the hand was cut."

Constable O'Boyle looked first at Benjamin and then at me with an almost apologetic countenance. "Chief Constable Duncey has placed me in a most awkward position. He has heard of Dr Franklin's interest in the case and, owing to the unofficial nature of several previous investigations, has put me in full charge." O'Boyle faced Benjamin again, this time with a hopeful expression. "For my part, however, I would be honoured, Dr Franklin, if you would continue to assist us."

"You are a good man, Constable O'Boyle. Success often breeds jealousy but a truly successful man avoids it. Let us all three then put our heads together." Benjamin tossed him the talisman. "This may be significant or it may not. It was found in the dead man's coat pocket. Wendell and I are about to interview the remaining English businessman. I suggest you do likewise with the other guest – Mr Pascales I believe is his name – after which we shall turn our inquiries to the innkeeper, his wife and the chambermaid."

We left O'Boyle to his task and proceeded to the room of Mr Becker. The door was open and we watched the tall figure of the man with black britches tucked neatly in his half boots. He paced the room with that peculiar gait and pomp common to his countrymen. When he reached the far wall, he turned with precision, revealing a troubled face. Then, upon seeing us, he stood erect.

"I see by your walk that, like your unfortunate companions, you also served in King George's army," Benjamin said. "Did you all serve together?"

The man was speechless for a moment as he considered Benjamin's observation and his question. At length, he spoke with a precision that matched his walk. "I was a lieutenant in His Majesty's army and did, as you say, serve over my companions. But our careers were short-lived. General Cornwallis unfortunately surrendered a week before we were to be shipped abroad."

"Yes, unfortunately," Benjamin muttered ironically. "You have never been to our city before?"

"No."

"Then I must apologize for the totally unacceptable welcome you and your unfortunate associates have been given. Be assured we will not rest until justice is served."

Becker gave us a slight bow.

"And I must apologize," I interjected, "that certain questions must be asked of you and that a search of your room must be conducted."

"I understand completely."

As I searched the boarding room, Benjamin began his questioning of Lieutenant Becker. "Do you have any idea who would commit such crimes?"

"No. We have had few contacts since our arrival. I cannot imagine who would have cause to kill them."

My search of the closet soon proved well spent, as it

yielded a short military hilt sabre. After a minute examination of its formidable blade, I placed the sabre on the table. Benjamin raised his brows upon seeing it, and we both rested our eyes squarely on the Lieutenant.

Becker stiffened his frame to an even more rigid posture than before. "It is a preposterous notion you are thinking," he said with an imperious wave of the hand. "Why would I travel to Philadelphia to do such a thing when the deed could have been just as easily committed in England? And they were my men, sirs. There is a bond between a commander and his men that would not allow such an act." He spoke those last words with a seemingly heart-felt conviction.

"You must admit," said Benjamin, "your actions have been out of the ordinary to say the least. You claim to be a broker of spices and tea. Yet where are your goods? And how can you expect to make sales for your company when you rarely leave your room?"

"We are here only to acquaint ourselves of the market and report to our firm. You have already seen our papers from Chesterton's of London," he said defensively.

While the two were conversing, I was continuing my examination of the room when I came upon another article of interest. "I can understand an old soldier travelling with his military hilt sabre," I said, lifting an iron lever bar from a drawer and holding it in outstretched arms for both to see. "But why do you travel with this?"

I set on the table a three-foot bar with one chisel end and one end bent for leverage. Becker paled a bit but recovered quickly. "I am at a loss to say what possessed me to bring it along, but I cannot see how that relates to this affair."

Our interview was interrupted by a general clamour of men's voices coming from down the hall. Over this I heard my name being called. Rushing to the room occupied by Mr Pascales, I found Constable O'Boyle standing by the door, a pistol in one hand and a small amber bottle in the other. "We have our man," he said with a proud voice. Pascales slumped into a chair and pulled at his dark hair with a groan. O'Boyle passed around the small bottle on which was written the word "MARAKU" and below that, "POISON".

"He acted overly alarmed when I told him I'd have to search the room," O'Boyle began. "So I thought I'd make a proper top-to-bottom job of it. Under his pillow I found three bottles, all with the word poison on them. This one, as you can see, is only half full."

Constable O'Boyle stepped past the accused, opening a travel chest with his free hand. The trunk revealed an assortment of Indian beads and jewelry, smoking pipes and tobacco pouches and several bags filled with tobacco. Pushing a large tobacco bag to the side, the constable pulled out two decorative knives with Indian-carved handles.

"Scoundrel!" cried Lieutenant Becker from the doorway, as O'Boyle lifted them high into the air.

"Let us not pronounce judgment before we have even heard the man's story," Benjamin advised, as he set his rather bulky frame on the bedside and his hook cane on his lap.

A tense and unnatural silence fell over the room as the man of Spanish descent sat in his chair, preparing to speak. Pascales' shoulders sagged, as if under the weight of our accusing stares. Then his chest heaved as he took three heavy breaths and with wide, earnest eyes he began to tell his tale.

He claimed to be an adventurer of sorts, commissioned by South American plantation owners to travel up the Orinoco and its side rivers in search of new lands to grow their tobaccos. When the crops came in, he was likewise commissioned to find markets for that tobacco in other countries. During one expedition up an uncharted river, he came upon a tribe of Indians who used a very peculiar arrow poison which, unlike the arrow poisons of other tribes, could be taken by mouth. The poison was so powerful a few drops could produce a total paralysis of the body.

"The natives called it maraku," he continued after wiping his brow with a sleeve, "an extract taken from the seed of a particular shrub that grows wild along the river bank. I thought it might have some value as a medicine, so I traded a few trinkets for the three bottles you see here. I knew there would be physicians in Europe who would surely think it a curious, perhaps even a useful substance and I anticipated a handsome reward someday when my travels took me there."

The bottles had been placed on the bed table and Pascales gave them a rueful glance. "When the first of the English gentlemen was murdered, I did not even think of my bottles of arrow poison. But when the second died, I checked on them and you can imagine my horror when I found one of the bottles was only half full. I considered telling of my loss – but how would it look? No one would believe a foreigner. There was no time to rid myself of the poison, so I placed the bottle beneath my pillow and hoped against hope no one would make a search."

"And what of the knives?" asked O'Boyle. "They are small, but in the right hand could easily have performed those grisly deeds we have all witnessed."

With eyes raised to the heavens, Pascales uttered what seemed to be an oath in Spanish. "Can you not see?" he pleaded. "The knives and jewelry are merely artifacts from my Indian trade."

As the man spoke, I observed Benjamin's eyes had left Pascales and were now engaged in a one-by-one study of the faces of those in the room. He gazed fixedly for some time in turn on the pallid chambermaid, the impassive Mrs Salisbury, and the stern-faced Mr Salisbury, before finally coming to rest on Lieutenant Becker. Benjamin rubbed his cane against his face in an almost feline manner, his features showing a concentration as if he were weighing some thought in his mind. Then he returned, with a vague smile, to the narrative of the accused.

"I swear," continued Pascales in a tremulous voice, "I had nothing to do with the deaths of these men and have no idea what happened to the missing poison."

Rising from the bedside, Benjamin stood before the Spaniard. "Did you always keep your doors locked when you left the room?"

"I did."

"And there was no sign of forced entry?"

"Not that I am aware."

"That is unfortunate. Well, I believe the matter is quite

clear," said Benjamin, now facing the others. "And the evidence appears overwhelming. Despite his protests of innocence I cannot help but think we have our man. His motivations are as yet somewhat unclear, but perhaps he shall be more inclined to reveal them after some time at the station house.

"At any rate," Benjamin proceeded, turning toward the Englishman, "the case appears to be at an end. As for you, Lieutenant Becker, there will be some ill talk in town when it is found you were British soldiers and I should not like an incident. I suggest it would be best for all concerned if you leave town. There is an American packet shipping out for Amsterdam tomorrow morning. I will make arrangements for your passage."

The Englishman was taken aback for a brief moment, then with a military bow, assented. "As you wish, Dr Franklin."

I thought this action unwise, but when I began to voice such an opinion, Benjamin's stiff sideward glance made me hold my tongue.

We soon made our way down to Chestnut Street, where Constable Woodford arrived with the prisoner wagon. Benjamin whispered a few words in the prisoner's ear before the wagon departed, leaving Benjamin, Constable O'Boyle and me alone in the street.

"Now," Benjamin said, taking my arm. "We all have a long night before us. I suggest we meet in the library wing of Carpenters' Hall at half past eight. We have not yet witnessed the final scene in this affair, Mr O'Boyle," he told the young constable. "Your actions have been a credit to the service and I trust you will wish to see this matter to its conclusion."

O'Boyle gave me a look first of surprise, then of resignation, then gave the old philosopher a tip of the hat. "I would be honoured to help you in any way."

Benjamin turned toward his waiting coach, walking with an uncharacteristically youthful step. "Ha, ha! gentlemen. The drama awaits!" were his parting words, as he left two open-mouthed constables scratching their heads in the street.

\*    \*    \*

At eight-thirty sharp, we gathered in Carpenters' Hall library. Benjamin studied the view from a side window, then pushed a chair in front of it. "I trust you have brought your pistols?"

I nodded and O'Boyle pulled his weapon from his belt.

"Splendid! You are on a dangerous mission, gentlemen, and you must promise to keep your wits about you at all times." He gave us each a compelling stare. "Then all is ready, and now we must wait. That," he said, pointing his cane at a row of high bushes, "shall be your waiting place. As I am too old for such occupation, I will be with you at least in spirit and will watch through this window as the events unfold."

"And just what events do you expect will unfold?" asked my fellow constable.

"That, even I am unsure of. But let me again warn, you may have a long wait. Do not for a moment let your guards down!"

We took our places as darkness fell and patiently stood sentry as the night passed by. When the bells tolled nine, a yellow-haired young girl appeared from the brown house across the way. She carried a water bucket in one hand and a candlestick in the other. Sitting on the wooden steps in front of the house, she washed her feet by candlelight. Her movements were of a steady but dreamy kind, and when she finished, she leaned back on her elbows, gazing steadfastly at the vast expanse of stars and sky. Occasionally, a passerby would exchange a "Good evening Miss Hannah" for a "Good evening to you Mrs Walker" or "a fine evening to you too, Mr Springfield," but then the girl would soon return to whatever world she saw in those starry skies.

I felt a bit uneasy – an intruder into that world – but, at length a voice from within the house called her name. Pegging the towel about her shoulders, she carefully poured the bucket of water on a wild rosebush that climbed a treillage in front of her house, then gently closed the door on the quiet half hour she had unknowingly shared with two onlookers.

At ten, it was the dogs that took a turn with our thoughts. A distant howl began a procession of barking that seemed to blanket all of Philadelphia. Just when all became still, another dog would begin and the process would start anew. It took some forty minutes for the game to lose its appeal and once again all was quiet.

At eleven, the nightwatch made his way down Chestnut Street. With his oil lantern swinging in hand, he travelled back and forth on the stone street, checking windows and doors and making sure all was well. The light of his lamp disappeared as he turned up Fifth, and I thought of my own time on the night watch. I wondered if ever some unseen eyes had once followed my movements just as we followed the watchman tonight.

And so from our little lookout, the night passed, nine to ten, ten to eleven, and finally a far-off bell tolled twelve times. The lights of the Crow on the Shoulder Tavern were the last to be extinguished and the street before us lay in hushed quietude.

Presently, the grilled iron-gate that stood before Carpenters' Hall creaked, then swung open by some unseen hand. A shadowy figure of a man, tall though barely visible under the pale moon, tread softly down the stone path, then onto the grassy lawn. His footfalls nearly inaudible, he crept steadily forward with what appeared to be a musket in his right hand.

The mysterious apparition stopped for a moment, alerted by the approaching footsteps of another man making his way down Chestnut. The first ducked behind an elm, settling into a crouch. Constable O'Boyle and I took the same posture. We all looked on for five minutes as the stranger strolled leisurely down the street before disappearing into a house on Fifth.

The night prowler continued toward us, passing at one point within arm's length from our secret vantage. He halted at the north-west corner of the west wing and seemed to be counting planks on the wall. I glanced at the library window where Uncle Benjamin waited in darkness, but I saw nothing save the reflection of a half moon on the glass.

The musket in the man's hands proved not to be a musket

at all, but rather a lever bar with which the man set to work, removing a board from the corner of the building. When there was a sufficient space between board and building, he pushed the bar into the groove and gave it a jerk, whereupon the board groaned, then snapped. The man eagerly reached his right hand in and groped for some unseen object in the open space where the board had been.

The events that transpired next came in such rapid succession I cannot say what thoughts passed through my mind. It was, to be sure, one of those occasions when one's body is set into motion before the mind has had sufficient time to decide on a proper course. It was our raptured watch of these strange activities that caused us not to hear and see the approach of another figure whose presence, beneath a dark, hooded cape coat, was only revealed when the glint of steel was seen shining through the darkness. The metal object landed with a thud on the board directly above the first man's hand.

Springing through tangled branches I landed full-force on the back of the mysterious hooded figure who fought and thrashed like a trapped animal. But the struggle was short-lived and I soon slipped my manacles around a pair of wrists. O'Boyle likewise had the first man in check, though the constable used only the reason of his pistol.

A light was lit in the library window and we were soon joined by our out-of-breath companion. Benjamin stepped toward us and lifted his lantern high. Its light reflected on a metal kitchen cleaver stuck tightly into the wood, just above a missing wall plank. He reached into the empty space and, with some effort, his hand emerged with a rather large cloth sack. But the sack must have been old, rotted by time and weather. When Benjamin drew his light close to it, the bottom gave way, and pieces of eight, paper notes, and silver plate spilled onto the lawn of Carpenters' Hall.

"Ah ha!" he exclaimed. "So that is what you were after, Lieutenant Becker." Benjamin turned to the two prisoners, now both under the guard of O'Boyle's pistol. "Now, let us see what face lies hidden behind this hooded cape coat." Benjamin stepped forward and pulled back the hood. The lantern was raised, and its light fell on the piercing, vengeful eyes of Elizabeth Salisbury.

When I arrived at Market Street the next morning, Benjamin was again at his workbench, making some adjustments on his curious trap. His monotone whistling sounded like the plucking of a single out-of-pitch lute string and gave no clue to the identity of the tune. Upon seeing my face, he dropped everything and ushered me to our waiting chairs in the drawing area. His eyes showed the readiness of a man eager to reveal his astute line of reasoning.

"Now, where should I begin, Wendell? Oh yes, the parchment. You see, the parchment paper found on the first dead man contained a message which was unclear, though it seemed to indicate a meeting at Carpenters' Hall. But the paper itself was the most telling detail, for it was, as I mentioned, an English parchment of a kind not used in some five to ten years. This bit of information I stored away for a time." He tapped the side of his head with a forefinger.

"The next morning when we found a second man dead, I discovered two more very telling facts. The first was that the three English spice merchants were once soldiers. This, of course, I induced from the cross of St George and the military airs of Mr Becker. And as things turned, Becker freely admitted they were once in the service of the King, though he claimed they had not served in America. But I knew this was not so, and I further knew that they were once in General Howe's army, which occupied Philadelphia during our war for independence."

"How could you have possibly come to that conclusion?" I asked, with astonishment.

"Ah! Wendell. You are becoming more and more adept at uncovering a case's relevant details, but oft times those details are more subtle than footprints or poisons – they are merely words. Mr Becker claimed he and the two other Englishmen had never visited Philadelphia. Yet recall the words of the innkeeper, who reported that arrangements were made weeks in advance for their quarters. And those arrangements included the requesting of rooms with windows facing Carpenters' Hall. How was it that men who had never visited our city could give such a specific request?"

Benjamin paused, offering a liquorice drop from a bowl on the side table and, after taking one for himself, continued. "During the war, the British soldiers were housed at the various inns and in Carpenters' Hall itself. As you know, Deborah and the rest of my household were forced to leave Philadelphia at this time and my own house became home to the notorious villain and thief, Captain John Andre of the British Army.

"In those days, Elizabeth Salisbury's father was a wealthy man, but he died penniless soon after the English occupation. How could this be? It is my theory that during the war, the old innkeeper, being a Loyalist, gladly quartered the British soldiers. He was, to be sure, a very wealthy man but, it is said, he hoarded his fortune. The two young recruits must have found his hiding place one day and planned to keep the fortune for themselves. But then the French navy sailed up the Delaware and was joined by the brave men of the Continental Army." Benjamin paused and gave me an acknowledging nod. "It appeared Philadelphia would soon be liberated. And so, the two soldiers must have enlisted the aid of their lieutenant and told him of the innkeeper's fortune. However, since they could not retreat with gold coins and silver plate in their pockets, they would have to leave it and return later, at war's end. It so happened that one wing of Carpenters' Hall was under repairs at that time and so they hid the old innkeeper's loot behind the ninth board in the north-west corner of the west wing.

"Soon after the British were forced to leave, the innkeeper became deathly ill and told his daughter of the soldiers and how they had stolen from him. It must have been quite a horrible shock to the young woman. Through the years, their faces become etched in her memory. Despite the beards that they all wore to disguise their faces, she recognized them at once."

"It all holds well," I said in some amazement. "But how did Pascales fit in?"

"Pascales was a victim of fortune, Wendell. Elizabeth Salisbury knew the men stole from her father. But how would she exact her revenge? Fate stepped in and offered an opportunity. The chambermaid was ill, you will recall, and so Mrs Salisbury would have been required to perform the maid's duties. When she cleaned the room of the South American tobacco broker, she found several bottles of poison. She then merely took a small amount and, one by one, began to poison the three. When the young woman checked on the poison's progress, it must have been quite a shock to find her victim completely immobile, yet very much alive. She retrieved a cleaver from the kitchen with plans to perform before their very eyes the ancient punishment for thieves.

"Well, how does my reasoning hold up?" Benjamin asked with some satisfaction as he sat back in his armchair.

"It holds well. But how did you know of the hiding place and that the lieutenant would try to make an attempt last night?"

"Ah, yes, the iron lever bar found in Captain Becker's room was the final clue. Why would a seller of spices and sundries carry one with him? To get at some object seemed a likely answer. But the criminal is a wily creature and, like a clever mouse, not so easily trapped. So I decided to give him a little incentive and he took the bait very nicely. I informed Lieutenant Becker that many Philadelphians still harbour ill feeling toward British soldiers. To avoid further incident, he would be required to leave town immediately.

"Then all that remained was to wait to see if the trap was set properly. I thought it certain that Becker would make an attempt on whatever he was after, and that his steps would, in all probability, be followed by the murderer. Who that murderer was came as a shock, however, for I did not think it likely Mrs Salisbury capable of such crimes. I was inclined to think Mr Salisbury was the guilty party."

"It all fits very well, Uncle Benjamin," I said. "Very well, indeed."

Benjamin took another liquorice drop from the bowl on the table. "And now the story is complete," he said, then sat back comfortably in his chair with the contented look of a fat Tom cat.

# The Serpent's Back

## Ian Rankin

*Ian Rankin is undoubtedly Britain's best-selling male writer of detective fiction, best known for his novels featuring Inspector John Rebus of the Lothian and Borders police. The series began with* Knots and Crosses *(1987) and from the start has portrayed a psychologically dark and violent world. In the later novels in the series Rankin became fascinated with how echoes of the past haunt the present, the novels almost taking on an extra dimension of time against the existing harsh dimensions of place. Rankin's fascination with the past led him to write several short radio plays set in Edinburgh at the end of the eighteenth century, the first of which was adapted into the following short story. It features Cullender, a "caddy", or personal escort who looks after the safety of visitors, but who knows only too well the perils of the city.*

This was, mind you, back in 1793 or '94. Edinburgh was a better place then. Nothing ever happens here now, but back then . . . back then *everything* was happening.

Back then a caddie was indispensible if you happened to be visiting the town. If you wanted someone found, if a message needed delivering, if you wanted a bed for the night, fresh oysters, a shirt-maker, or the local hoor, you came to a caddie. And if the claret got the better of you, a caddie would see you safely home.

See, the town wasn't safe, Lord no. The streets were mean.

The hifalutin' were leaving the old town and crossing the Nor' Loch to the New. They lived in Princes Street and George Street, or did until they could no longer stand the stench. The old loch was an open sewer by that time, and the old town not much better.

I was called Cullender, Cully to my friends. No one knew my first name. They need only say "Cullender" and they'd be pointed in my direction. That's how it was with young Master Gisborne. He had newly arrived by coach from London, and feared he'd never sit down again . . .

"Are you Cullender? My good friend Mr Wilks told me to ask for you."

"Wilks?"

"He was here for some weeks. A medical student."

I nodded. "I recall the young gentleman particularly," I lied.

"I shall require a clean room, nothing too fancy. My pockets aren't bottomless."

"How long will you be staying, Master?"

He looked around. "I'm not sure. I'm considering a career in medicine. If I like the faculty, I may enroll."

And he fingered the edges of his coat. It was a pale blue coat with bright silver buttons. Like Master Gisborne, it was overdone and didn't quite fit together. His face was fat like a whelp's, but his physique was lean and his eyes shone. His skin had suffered neither disease nor malnourishment. He was, I suppose, a fine enough specimen, but I'd seen fine specimens before. Many of them stayed, seduced by Edinburgh. I saw them daily in the pungent howffs, or slouching through the narrow closes, heads bowed. None of them looked so fresh these days. Had they been eels, the fishwives would have tossed them in a bucket and sold them to only the most gullible.

The most gullible, of course, being those newly arrived in the city.

Master Gisborne would need looking after. He was haughty on the surface, cocksure, but I knew he was troubled, wondering how long he could sustain the act of worldliness. He had money but not in limitless supply. His parents would be professional folk, not gentry. Some denizens would gull him before supper. Me? I was undecided.

I picked up his trunk. "Shall I call a chair?" He frowned. "The streets here are too narrow and steep for coaches. Haven't you noticed? Know why they're narrow?" I sidled up to him. "There's a serpent buried beneath." He looked ill at ease so I laughed. "Just a story, Master. We use chairmen instead of horses. Good strong Highland stock."

I knew he had already walked a good way in search of me, hauling his trunk with him. He was tired, but counting his money too.

"Let's walk," he decided, "and you can acquaint me with the town."

"The town, Master," I said, "will acquaint you with itself."

We got him settled in at Lucky Seaton's. Lucky had been a hoor herself at one time, then had been turned to the Moderate movement and now ran a Christian rooming house.

"We know all about medical students, don't we, Cully?" she said, while Gisborne took the measure of his room. "The worst sinners in Christendom."

She patted Master Gisborne on his plump cheek, and I led him back down the treacherous stairwell.

"What did she mean?" he asked me.

"Visit a few howffs and you'll find out," I told him. "The medical students are the most notorious group of topers in the city, if you discount the lawyers, judges, poets, boatmen, and Lords this-and-that."

"What's a howff?"

I led him directly into one.

There was a general fug in what passed for the air. Pipes were being smoked furiously, and there were no windows to open, so the stale fumes lay heavy at eye level. I could hear laughter and swearing and the shrieks of women, but it was like peering through a haar. I saw one-legged Jack, balancing a wench on his good knee. Two lawyers sat at the next table along, heads close together. A poet of minor repute scribbled away as he sat slumped on the floor. And all around there was wine, wine in jugs and bumpers and bottles, its sour smell vying with that of tobacco.

But the most noise came from a big round table in the furthest corner, where beneath flickering lamplight a meeting of the Monthly Club was underway. I led Gisborne to the table, having promised him that Edinburgh would acquaint itself with him. Five gentlemen sat round the table. One recognised me immediately.

"Dear old Cully! What news from the world above?"

"No news, sir."

"None better than that!"

"What's the meeting this month, sirs?"

"The Hot Air Club, Cully." The speaker made a toast of the words. "We are celebrating the tenth anniversary of Mr Tytler's flight by montgolfier over this very city."

This had to be toasted again, while I explained to Master Gisborne that the Monthly Club changed its name regularly in order to have something to celebrate.

"I see you've brought fresh blood, Cully."

"Mr Gisborne," I said, "is newly arrived from London and hopes to study medicine."

"I hope he will, too, if he intends to practise."

There was laughter and replenishing of glasses.

"This gentleman," I informed my master, "is Mr Walter Scott. Mr Scott is an advocate."

"Not today," said another of the group. "Today he's Colonel Grogg!"

More laughter. Gisborne was asked what he would drink.

"A glass of port," my hapless charge replied.

The table went quiet. Scott was smiling with half his mouth only.

"Port is not much drunk in these parts. It reminds some people of the Union. Some people would rather drink *whisky* and toast their Jacobite 'King O'er the Water.'" Someone at the table actually did this, not heeding the tone of Scott's voice. "But we're one nation now," Scott continued. That man did like to make a speech. "And if you'll drink some claret with us, we may yet be reconciled."

The drinker toasted Bonnie Prince Charlie; another lawyer, whose name was Urquhart, now turned to Gisborne with his usual complaint to Englishmen. " 'Rule Britannia,' " he said, "was written by a Scot. John Bull was *invented* by a Scot!"

He slumped back, having to his mind made his point. Master Gisborne looked like he had tumbled into Bedlam.

"Now, now," Scott calmed. "We're here to celebrate montgolfiers." He handed Gisborne a stemless glass filled to the brim. "And new arrivals. But you've come to a dangerous place, sir."

"How so?" my master enquired.

"Sedition is rife." Scott paused. "As is murder. How many is it now, Cully?"

"Three this past fortnight." I recited the names. "Dr Benson, MacStay the coffin maker, and a wretch called Howison."

"All stabbed," Scott informed Gisborne. "Imagine, murdering a coffin maker! It's like trying to murder Death himself."

As was wont to happen, the Monthly Club shifted to another howff to partake of a *prix fixe* dinner, and thence to another, where Scott would drink champagne and lead a discussion of "the chest".

The chest in question had been found when the Castle's crown room was opened during a search for some documents. The crown room had been opened, according to the advocate, by special warrant under the royal sign manual. No one had authority to break open the chest. The crown room was locked again, and the chest still inside. At the time of the union with England, the royal regalia of Scotland had disappeared. It was Scott's contention that this regalia – crown, sceptre, and sword – lay in the chest.

Gisborne listened in fascination. Somewhere along the route he had misplaced his sense of economy. He would pay for the champagne. He would pay for dinner. A brothel was being discussed as the next destination . . . Luckily, Scott was taking an interest in him, so that

Gisborne's pockets were still fairly full, though his wits be empty.

I sat apart, conversing with the exiled Comte d'Artois, who had fled France at the outset of revolution. He retained the habit of stroking his neck for luck, his good fortune being that it still connected his head to his trunk. He had reason to feel nervous. Prompted by events in France, sedition was in the air. There had been riots, and now the ringleaders were being tried.

We were discussing Deacon Brodie, hanged six years before for a series of housebreakings. Brodie, a cabinetmaker and locksmith, had robbed the very premises to which he'd fitted locks. Respectable by day, he'd been nefarious by night. To the Comte (who knew about such matters), this was merely "the human condition".

I noticed suddenly that I was seated in shadow. A man stood over me. He had full thick lips, a meaty stew of a nose, and eyebrows which met at the central divide the way warring forces sometimes will.

"Cullender?"

I shook my head and turned away.

"You're Cullender," he said. "This is for you." He slapped his paw onto the table, then turned and pushed back through the throng. A piece of paper, neatly folded, sat on the wood where his hand had been. I unfolded it and read:

"Outside the Tolbooth, quarter before midnight."

The note was unsigned. I handed it to the Comte.

"You will go?"

It was already past eleven. "I'll let one more drink decide."

The Tolbooth was the city jail where Brodie himself had spent his final days, singing airs from *The Beggar's Opera*. The night was like pitch, nobody having bothered to light their lamps, and a haar rolled through from the direction of Leith.

In the darkness, I had trodden in something I did not care to study and was scraping my shoe clean on the Tolbooth's corner-stone when I heard a voice close by.

"Cullender?"

A woman's voice. Even held to a whisper, I knew it for that. The lady herself was dressed top to toe in black, her face deep inside the hood of a cloak.

"I'm Cullender."

"I'm told you perform services."

"I'm no minister, lady."

Maybe she smiled. A small bag appeared and I took it, weighing the coins inside.

"There's a book circulating in the town," said my new mistress. "I am keen to obtain it."

"We have several fine booksellers in the Luckenbooths . . ."

"You are glib, sir."

"And you are mysterious."

"Then I'll be plain. I know of only one copy of this book, a private printing. It is called *Ranger's Second Impartial List* . . ."

". . . *of the Ladies of Pleasure in Edinburgh*."

"You know it. Have you seen it?"

"It's not meant for the likes of me."

"I would like to see this book."

"You want me to find it?"

"It's said you know everyone in the city."

"Everyone that matters."

"Then you can locate it."

"It's possible." I examined my shoes. "But first I'd need to know a little more . . ."

When I looked up again, she was gone.

At The Cross, the caddies were speaking quietly with the chairmen. We caddies had organised ourselves into a company, boasting written standards and a Magistrate of Caddies in charge of all. We regarded ourselves superior to the chairmen, mere brawny Highland migrants.

But my best friend and most trusted ally, Mr Mack, was a chairman. He was not, however, at The Cross. Work was nearly over for the night. The last taverns were throwing out the last soused customers. Only the brothels and cockpits were still active. Not able to locate Mr Mack, I turned instead to a fellow caddie, an old hand called Dryden.

"Mr Dryden?" I said, all businesslike, "I require your services, the fee to be agreed between us."

Dryden, as ever, was willing. I knew he would work through the night. He was known to the various brothel-keepers and could ask his questions discreetly, as I might have done myself had the lady's fee not been sufficient to turn me employer.

Me, I headed home, climbing the lonely stairs to my attic quarters and a cold mattress. I found sleep the way a pickpocket finds his gull.

Which is to say easily.


Next morning, Dryden was dead.

A young caddie called Colin came to tell me. We repaired to the Nor' Loch, where the body still lay, face down in the slime. The Town Guard – "Town Rats" behind their backs – fingered their Lochaber axes, straightened their tall cocked hats, and tried to look important. One of their number, a red-faced individual named Fairlie, asked if we knew the victim.

"Dryden," I said. "He was a caddie."

"He's been run through with a dagger," Fairlie delighted in telling me. "Just like those other three."

But I wasn't so sure about that . . .

I went to a quiet howff, a drink steadying my humour. Dryden, I surmised, had been killed in such a way as to make him appear another victim of the city's stabber. I knew, though, that in all likelihood he had been killed because of the questions he'd been asking . . . questions *I'd* sent him to ask. Was I safe myself? Had Dryden revealed anything to his killer? And what was it about my mistress's mission that made it so deadly dangerous?

As I was thus musing, young Gisborne entered the bar on fragile legs.

"Did I have anything to drink last evening?" he asked, holding his head.

"Master, you drank as if it were our last day alive."

Our hostess was already replenishing my wine jug. "Kill or cure," I said, pouring two glasses.

Gisborne could see I was worried and asked the nature of the problem. I was grateful to tell him. Any listener would have sufficed. Mind, I held back some. This knowledge was proving dangerous, so I made no mention of the lady and her book. I jumped from the messenger to my words with Dryden.

"The thing to do, then," my young master said, "is to track backwards. Locate the messenger."

I thought back to the previous evening. About the time the messenger had been arriving, the lawyer Urquhart had been taking his leave of the Monthly Club.

"We'll talk to Urquhart," I said. "At this hour he'll be in his chambers. Follow me."

Gisborne followed me out of the howff and across the street directly into another. There, in a booth, papers before him and a bottle of wine beside them, sat Urquhart.

"I'm pleased to see you," the lawyer announced. His eyes were bloodshot, his nose like a stoned cherry. His breath I avoided altogether. Aged somewhere in his thirties, Urquhart was a seasoned dissolute. He would have us take a bumper with him.

"Sir," I began, "do you recall leaving the company last night?"

"Of course. I'm only sorry I'd to leave so early. An assignation, you understand." We shared a smile at this. "Tell me, Gisborne, to which house of ill fame did the gang repair?"

"I don't recollect," Gisborne admitted.

Urquhart enjoyed this. "Then tell me, did you awake in a bed or the gutter?"

"In neither, Mr Urquhart. I awoke on the kitchen floor of a house I did not know."

While Urquhart relished this, I asked if he'd taken a chair from the tavern last night.

"Of course. A friend of yours was front-runner."

"Mr Mack?" Urquhart nodded. "You didn't happen to see a grotesque, sir?" I described the messenger to him. Urquhart shook his head.

"I hear a caddie was murdered last night," Urquhart said. "We all know the Town Rats can't be expected to bring anyone to justice." He leaned toward me confidentially. "Are you looking for justice, Cully?"

"I don't know what I'm looking for, sir."

Which was a lie. For now, I was looking for Mr Mack.

I left Gisborne with Urquhart, and found Mack at The Cross.

"Yes," he said, "I saw that fellow going in. A big fat-lipped sort with eyebrows that met in the middle."

"Had you seen him before?"

Mack nodded. "But not here, over the loch."

"The new town." Mack nodded. "Then show me where."

Mack and his fellow chairman carried me down the steep slope towards the building site. Yes, building site. For though Princes Street and George Street were finished, yet more streets were being artfully constructed. Just now, the builders were busy on what would be called Charlotte Square. We took the simpler route, down past Trinity Hospital and the College Kirk, then along Princes Street itself. There were plans to turn the Nor' Loch into either a canal or formal gardens, but for the moment it was a dumping ground. I avoided looking at it and tried not to think of poor Dryden. Joining the loch to the old town sat The Mound, an apt name for a treacherous heap of new-town rubble.

"All change, eh, Cully?" Mr Mack called to me. "Soon there'll be no business in the old town for the likes of you and me."

He had a point. The nobility had already deserted the old town. Their grand lands now housed wheelwrights and hosiers and schoolmasters. They all lived in the new town now, at a general distance from the milling rabble. So here the foundations were being laid not for the new town alone but for the death of the old.

We passed into George Street and the sedan chair was brought to rest. "It was here I saw him," Mr Mack said. "He was marching up the street like he owned the place."

I got out of the chair and rubbed my bruised posterior. Mr Mack's companion had already spotted another likely fare. I waved them off. I must needs talk to my mistress, and that meant finding her servant. So I sat on a step and watched the work carts grinding past overloaded with rocks and rubble. The day passed pleasantly enough.

Perhaps two hours had passed when I saw him. I couldn't be sure which house he emerged from; he was some way along the street. I tucked myself behind some railings and watched him head down towards Princes Street. I followed at a canny distance.

He was clumsy, his gait gangling, and I followed him with ease. He climbed back up to the old town and made for the Lucken-booths. Here he entered a bookshop, causing me to pause.

The shop belonged to a Mr Whitewood, who fancied himself not only bookseller but poet and author also. I entered the premises quietly and could hear Whitewood's raised voice. He was towards the back of his shop, reciting to a fawning audience of other *soi-disant* writers and people to whom books were mere fashion.

The servant was pushing his way to the front of the small gathering. Whitewood stood on a low unsteady podium, and read with a white handkerchief in one hand, which he waved for dramatic effect. He needed all the help he could get. I dealt daily with the "improvers", the self-termed "literati". I'll tell you now what an improver is, he's an imp who roves. I'd seen them dragging their carcasses through the gutter and waylaying hoors and scrapping with the tourists.

The servant had reached the podium, and the bookseller had seen him. Without pausing mid-stanza, Whitewood passed the wretch a note. It was done in an instant and the servant headed back towards the door. I slipped outside and hid myself, watching the servant head as if towards the courts.

I followed him into the courthouse. I followed him into one particular court . . . and there was brought up short.

Lord Braxfield, the Hanging Judge, was deciding a case. He sat in his wig at his muckle bench and dipped oatcakes into his claret, sucking loudly on the biscuits as he glared at the accused. There were three of them, and I knew they were charged with sedition, being leaders of a popular convention for parliamentary reform. At this time, only thirty or so people in Edinburgh had the right to vote for the member of parliament. These three sad creatures had wanted to change that and a lot more besides.

I glanced at the jury – doubtless hand picked by Braxfield himself. The accused would be whipped and sent to Botany Bay. The public gallery was restless. There were guards between the populace and the bench. The servant was nodded through by one of the guards and handed Whitewood's note to Braxfield. Then he turned quickly and left by another door. I was set to follow when the Hanging Judge noticed me.

"Cullender, approach the bench!"

I bit my lip, but knew better than to defy Braxfield, even if it meant losing my quarry. The guards let me through. I forbore to look at the accused as I passed them.

"Yes, my Lord?"

Braxfield nibbled another of his infernal biscuits. He looked like he'd drunk well, too. "Cullender," he said, "you're one of the least honest and civil men in this town, am I correct?"

"I have competitors, my Lord."

He guffawed, spitting crumbs from his wet lips. "But tell me this, would you have a man live who committed treason?"

I swallowed, aware of three pairs of eyes behind me. "I might ask myself about his motives, my Lord."

Braxfield leaned over the bench. He was unquestionably ugly, eyes black as night. In his seventies, he grew increasingly eccentric. He was what passed for the law in this city. "Then it's as well *I'm* wearing this wig and not you!" he screeched. He wagged a finger, the nail of which was sore in need of a trim. "You'll see Australia one day, my friend, if you're not careful. Now be gone, I've some justice to dispense."

It had been a long time since Braxfield and "justice" had been even loosely acquainted.

Outside, the servant was long gone. Cursing my luck and the law courts both, I headed down to the Canongate.

I engaged Mr Mack's services regarding my lady's book, warning him to be extra vigilant and telling him of Dryden's demise. He suggested going to the authorities, then realised what he was saying. The law was as effectual as a scented handkerchief against the pox, and we both knew it.

I sat in a howff and ate a dish of oysters. Having been to look at the university, Master Gisborne joined me.

"It'll be fine when it's finished," was his opinion.

I supped the last of the juice and put down the platter. "Remember I told you about the serpent, Master?"

His eyes were red-rimmed, face puffy with excess. He nodded.

"Well," I continued thoughtfully, "perhaps it's not so far beneath the surface as I thought. You need only scratch and you'll see it. Remember that, even in your cups."

He looked puzzled, but nodded again. Then he seemed to remember something, and reached into his leather bag. He handed me a wrapped parcel.

"Cully, can you keep this somewhere safe?"

"What is it?"

"Just hold it for me for a day or so. Will you do that?"

I nodded and placed the parcel at my feet. Gisborne looked mightily relieved. Then the howff door swung inwards and Urquhart and others appeared, taking Gisborne off with them. I finished my wine and made my way back to my room.

Halfway there, I met the tailor whose family lived two floors below me.

"Cully," he said, "men are looking for you."

"What sort of men?"

"The sort you wouldn't have find you. They're standing guard on the stairwell and won't shift."

"Thanks for the warning."

He held my arm. "Cully, business is slow. If you could persuade some of your clients of the quality of my cloth . . . ?"

"Depend on it." I went back up the brae to The Cross and found Mr Mack.

"Here," I said, handing him the parcel. "Keep this for me."

"What's wrong?"

"I'm not sure. I think I may have stepped in something even less savoury than I thought. Any news of the *List?*"

Mack shook his head. He looked worried when I left him; not for himself, but for me.

I kept heading uphill, towards the Castle itself. Beneath Castle Hill lay the catacombs where the town's denizens used to hide when the place was being sacked. And here the lowest of Edinburgh's wretches still dwelt. I would be safe there, so I made my way into the tunnels and out of the light, averting my face where possible from each interested, unfriendly gaze.

The man I sought sat slouched against one of the curving walls, hands on his knees. He could sit like that for hours, brooding. He was a giant, and there were stories to equal his size. It was said he'd been a seditionary, a rabble-rouser, both pirate and smuggler. He had most certainly killed men, but these days he lay low. His name was Ormond.

He watched me sit opposite him, his gaze unblinking.

"You're in trouble," he said at last.

"Would I be here otherwise? I need somewhere to sleep for tonight."

He nodded slowly. "That's all any of us needs. You'll be safe here, Cullender."

And I was.

But next morning I was roused early by Ormond shaking me.

"Men outside," he hissed. "Looking for you."

I rubbed my eyes. "Is there another exit?"

Ormond shook his head. "If you went any deeper into this maze, you could lose yourself forever. These burrows run as far as the Canongate."

"How many men?" I was standing up now, fully awake.

"Four."

I held out my hand. "Give me a dagger; I'll deal with

them." I meant it too. I was aching and irritable and tired of running. But Ormond shook his head.

"I've a better plan," he said.

He led me back through the tunnel towards its entrance. The tunnel grew more populous as we neared the outside world. I could hear my pursuers ahead, examining faces, snarling as each one proved false. Then Ormond filled his lungs.

"The price of corn's to be raised!" he bellowed. "New taxes! New laws! Everyone to The Cross!"

Voices were raised in anger, and people clambered to their feet. Ormond was raising a mob. The Edinburgh mob was a wondrous thing. It could run riot through the streets and then melt back into the shadows. There'd been the Porteous riots, anti-Catholic riots, price-rise riots, and pro-revolution riots. Each time, the vast majority escaped arrest. A mob could be raised in a minute and could disperse in another. Even Braxfield feared the mob.

Ormond was bellowing in front of me. As for me, I was merely another of the wretches. I passed the men who'd been seeking me. They stood dumbfounded in the midst of the spectacle. As soon as the crowd reached the Lawnmarket, I peeled off with a wave of thanks to Ormond, slipped into an alley, and was alone again.

But not for long. Down past the Luckenbooths I saw the servant again, and this time he would not evade me. Down towards Princes Street he went, down Geordie Boyd's footpath, a footpath that would soon be wide enough for carriages. He crossed Princes Street and headed up to George Street. There at last I saw him descend some steps and enter a house by its servants' door. I stopped a sedan chair. Both chairmen knew me through Mr Mack.

"That house there?" one of them said in answer to my question. "It used to belong to Lord Thorpe before he left for London. A bookseller bought it from him."

"A Mr Whitewood?" I asked blithely. The chairmen nodded. "I admit I don't know that gentleman well. Is he married?"

"Married, aye, but you wouldn't know it. She's seldom seen, is she, Donald?"

"Rarely, very rarely," the second chairman agreed.

"Why's that? Has she the pox or something?"

They laughed at the imputation. "How would we know a thing like that?"

I laughed too, and bid them thanks and farewell. Then I approached the front door of the house and knocked a good solid knock.

The servant, when he opened the door, was liveried. He looked at me in astonishment.

"Tell your mistress I wish to speak with her," I said sharply.

He appeared in two minds at least, but I sidestepped him and found myself in a fine entrance hall.

"Wait in here," the servant growled, closing the front door and opening another. "I'll ask my Lady if she'll deign to see you."

I toured the drawing room. It was like walking around an exhibition, though in truth the only exhibition I'd ever toured was of Bedlam on a Sunday afternoon, and then only to look for a friend of mine.

The door opened and the Lady of the house swept in. She had powdered her cheeks heavily to disguise the redness there – either embarrassment or anger. Her eyes avoided mine, which gave me opportunity to study her. She was in her mid twenties, not short, and with a pleasing figure. Her lips were full and red, her eyes hard but to my mind seductive. She was a catch. But when she spoke her voice was rough-hewn, and I wondered at her history.

"What do you want?"

"What do you think I want?"

She picked up a pretty statuette. "Are we acquainted?"

"I believe so. We met outside the Tolbooth."

She attempted a disbelieving laugh. "Indeed? It's a place I've never been."

"You would not care to see its innards, Lady, yet you may if you continue in this manner."

No amount of powder could have hidden her colouring. "How dare you come here!"

"My life is in danger, Lady."

This quieted her. "Why? What have you done?"

"Nothing save what you asked of me."

"Have you found the book?"

"Not yet, and I've a mind to hand you back your money."

She saw what I was getting at, and looked aghast. "But if you're in danger . . . I swear it cannot be to do with me!"

"No? A man has died already."

"Mr Cullender, it's only a book! It's nothing anyone would kill for."

I almost believed her. "Why do you want it?"

She turned away. "That is not your concern."

"My chief concern is my neck, Lady. I'll save it at any cost."

"I repeat, you are in no danger from seeking that book. If you think your life in peril, there must needs be some other cause." She stared at me as she spoke, and the damnation of it was that I believed her. I believed that Dryden's death, Braxfield's threat, the men chasing me, that none of it had anything to do with her. She saw the change in me and smiled a radiant smile, a smile that took me with it.

"Now get out," she said. And with that she left the room and began to climb the stairs. Her servant was waiting for me by the front door, holding it open in readiness.

My head was full of puzzles. All I knew with certainty was that I was sick of hiding. I headed back to the old town with a plan in my mind as half-baked as the scrapings the baker tossed out to the homeless.

I toured the town gossips, starting with the fishwives. Then I headed to The Cross and whispered in the ears of selected caddies and chairmen. Then it was into the howffs and dining establishments, and I was glad to wash my hard work down with a glass or two of wine.

My story broadcast, I repaired to my lodgings and lay on the straw mattress. There were no men waiting for me on the stairwell. I believe I even slept a little. It was dark when I next looked out of the skylight. The story I'd spread was that I knew who'd killed Dryden and was merely biding my time before alerting the Town Rats. Would anyone fall for the ploy? I wasn't sure. I fell to a doze again but opened my eyes on hearing noises on the stair.

The steps to my attic were rotten and had to be managed adroitly. My visitor – a lone man, I surmised – was doing his best. I sat up on the mattress and watched the door begin to open. In deep shadow, a figure entered my room, closing the door after it with some finality.

"Good evening, Cully."

I swallowed drily. "So the stories were true then, Deacon Brodie?"

"True enough," he said, coming closer. His face was almost unrecognisable, much older, more careworn, and he wore no wig, no marks of a gentleman. He carried a slender dagger in his right hand.

"I cheated the gibbet, Cully," he said with his old pride.

"But I was there, I saw you drop."

"And you saw my men cut me down and haul me away." He grinned with what teeth were left in his head. "A wooden collar saved my throat, Cully. I devised it myself."

I recalled the red silk he'd worn ostentatiously around his throat. A scarf from a female admirer, the story went. It would have hidden just such a device.

"You've been in hiding a long time," I said. The dagger was inches from me.

"I fled Edinburgh, Cully. I've been away these past five and a half years."

"What brought you back?" I couldn't take my eyes off the dagger.

"Aye," Brodie said, seeing what was in my mind. "The doctor who pronounced me dead and the coffin maker who was supposed to have buried me. I couldn't have witnesses alive . . . not now."

"And the others, Dryden and the wretch Howison?"

"Both recognised me, curse them. Then *you* started to snoop around and couldn't be found."

"But why? Why are you back?"

The dagger was touching my throat now. I'd backed myself into a corner of the bed. There was nowhere to go.

"I was *tempted* back, Cully. A temptation I could not resist. The crown jewels."

"What?"

His voice was a feverish whisper. "The chest in the crown room. I will have its contents, my last and greatest theft."

"Alone? Impossible."

"But I'm not alone. I have powerful allies." He smiled. "Braxfield, for one. He believes the theft of the jewels will spark a Scots revolution. But you know this already, Cully. You were seen watching Braxfield. You were seen in White-wood's shop."

"Whitewood's part of it, too?"

"You know he is, romantic fool that he is." The point of the dagger broke my skin. I could feel blood trickle down my throat. If I spoke again, they would be my last words. I felt like laughing. Brodie was so wrong in his surmisings. Every-thing was wrong. A sudden noise on the stair turned Brodie's head. My own dagger was hidden beneath my thigh. I grabbed it with one hand, my other hand wrestling with Brodie's blade.

When Gisborne opened the door, what he saw sobered him immediately.

Brodie freed himself and turned to confront the young Englishman, dagger ready, but not ready enough. Gisborne had no hesitation in running him through. Brodie stood there frozen, then keeled over, his head hitting the boards with a dull dead sound.

Gisborne was the statue now. He stared at the spreading blood.

I got to my feet quickly. "Where did you get the blade?" I asked, amazed.

Gisborne swallowed. "I bought it new today, heeding your advice."

"You saved my life, young Master." I stared down at Brodie's corpse. "But why are you here?"

Gisborne came to his senses. "I heard you were looking for a book."

"I was. What of it?" We were both staring at Brodie.

"Only to tell you that I am in possession of it. Or I was.

The lawyer Urquhart gave it to me. He said I would doubt-less find it useful . . . Who was this man?"

I ignored the question and glared at him. "*You* have the book?"

He shook his head. "I daren't keep it in my room for fear my landlady might find it."

I blinked. "That parcel?" Gisborne nodded. I felt a fool, a dumb fool. But there was Brodie's corpse to dispose of. I could see little advantage in reporting this, his second de-mise, to the authorities. Questions would be asked of Master Gisborne, and a young Englishman might not always receive a fair hearing, especially with Braxfield at the bench. God no, the body must be disposed of quietly.

And I knew just the spot.

Mr Mack helped us lug the guts down to the new town, propping Brodie in the sedan chair. The slumped corpse resembled nothing so much as a sleeping drunk.

In Charlotte Square we found some fresh foundations and buried the remains of Deacon Brodie within. We were all three in a sweat by the time we'd finished. I sat myself down on a large stone and wiped my brow.

"Well, friends," I said, "it is only right and proper."

"What is?" Gisborne asked, breathing heavily.

"The old town has its serpent, and now the new town does too." I watched Gisborne put his jacket back on. It was the blue coat with silver buttons. There was blood on it, and dirt besides.

"I know a tailor," I began, "might make something fresh for an excellent price . . ."

Next morning, washed and crisply dressed, I returned to my Lady's house. I waved the parcel under the servant's nose and he hurried upstairs.

My Lady was down promptly, but gave me no heed. She had eyes only for the book. Book? It was little more than a ragged pamphlet; its pages were thumbed, scribbled margin-alia commenting on this or that entry or adding a fresh one. I handed her the tome.

"The entry you seek is towards the back," I told her. She looked startled. "You are, I suppose, the Masked Lady referred to therein? A lady for daylight assignations only, and always masked, speaking in a whisper?"

Her cheeks were crimson as she tore at the book, scattering its shreddings.

"Better have the floor swept," I told her. "You wouldn't want Mr Whitewood to find any trace. That was your reason all along, was it not? He is a known philanderer. It was only a matter of time before he got to read of the Masked Lady and became intrigued to meet her."

Her head was held high, as if she were examining the room's cornices.

"I'm not ashamed," she said.

"Nor should you be."

She saw I was not mocking her. "I am a prisoner here, with no more life than a doll."

"So you take revenge in your own particular manner? I understand, Lady, but you must understand this. Two men died because of you. Not directly, but that matters not to them. Only one deserved to die. For the other . . ." I jangled the bag of money she'd given me that first night. "These coins will buy him a burial."

Then I bid her good day and left the whole shining new town behind me, with its noises of construction and busyness. Let them build all the mighty edifices they would; they could not erase the stain. They could not erase the real town, the old town, the town I knew so intimately. I returned to the howff where Gisborne and Mack awaited me.

"I've decided," the young master said, "to study law rather than medicine, Cully." He poured me a drink. "Edinburgh needs another lawyer, don't you think?"

The image of Braxfield came unmasked into my mind. "Like it needs another plague, Master."

But I raised my glass to him anyway.

# *Botanist at Bay*

## Edward Marston

*The time span of the last five stories, from Emery's to this one, is just under fifty years, yet they have covered a remarkable range of events and circumstances. This one takes us to Britain's penal colony in Australia, the renowned Botany Bay, and explores honour, or the lack of it, amongst thieves.*

*Edward Marston is perhaps the best known alias of author Keith Miles who, over the last sixteen years, has established a strong reputation for the diversity and authenticity of his historical mysteries. They range from the Nicholas Bracewell series, set in the world of the Elizabethan theatre, through the Domesday series, set after the Norman Conquest, to the Merlin Richards series (written under his own name) set in the architectural world of Frank Lloyd Wright in the 1920s.*

"How long are ye lagged for?"

"Only seven years."

"Where is one-eyed Luke of St Giles?"

"Oh, he's aboard for a seven yearser."

"Did you see Ned Paget in Newgate?"

"He stood his patter last assizes and got a bellowser."

I tried to bury my own crime deep in the past. Like most of the others on the convict ships to Botany Bay, I was charged with minor theft and transported for seven years. At the time, it seemed like an eternity but at least I escaped a bellowser, a dreaded life sentence. Ned Paget, who sailed on the *Charlotte* with me, had stolen enough silver to warrant the noose and he was duly given an appointment with Jack Ketch, only to have his death sentence commuted at the last moment. He could never decide if his reprieve was a stroke of good fortune or yet another instance of the bad luck that had always dogged him.

Compared to Ned's crime, my own was ridiculously petty. I'd just finished serving my apprenticeship as a cabinet-maker and wanted to celebrate with a proposal of marriage to my beloved Hannah. Since I also had a small additional income as an auctioneer's clerk, I felt that I'd soon be in a position to support a wife and who better to fill that role than Hannah Richardson? To increase my chances of acceptance, I decided to accompany the proposal with the gift of some flowers but – having no ready money on me and flushed with youthful exuberance – I borrowed some roses from a garden that I passed on my way to Hannah's house.

Nobody told me that the garden in question belonged to a judge of the King's Bench, or that his dog could bite so hard, or that his servant could run like the wind. I was gnawed, chased and apprehended. What began as a romantic gesture ended up as the height of folly. I never set eyes on Hannah Richardson again. After spending four months in a rotting prison hulk, I joined the First Fleet and set off on a nautical nightmare that lasted thirty-six excruciating weeks. When you pass most of the voyage below deck, surrounded by the dregs of humanity, you lose all sense of refinement. You become one of them.

I suppose that I did better than most. Some of the convicts died on the way, others were flogged into oblivion, and others again, like Ned Paget, spent the whole time in fetters that weighed 28 pounds. Every time he moved in that foul, crowded, rat-infested hold, the iron clanked like a death knell. I even enjoyed a few privileges. Because I taught him to read and write, one-eyed Luke Fillimore gave me a portion of his meagre rations. Because I passed on the food to Davy Warren, he paid me with coin that he'd somehow smuggled aboard. With that money, I was able to lose my virginity to Annie Creed, one of the thirty or so women convicts who travelled on our ship. In her ragged clothes and with her noisome smell, Annie was nothing at all like the fragrant Hannah Richardson but, for the two minutes that it lasted, I pretended that she was.

Imagination is truly a blessing.

Annie Creed, a buxom farm girl, got seven years for feloniously stealing a live hen to the value of 2d and a dead hen worth the same amount. One-eyed Luke Fillimore was found guilty of making off with a wooden box that, to his chagrin, contained nothing apart from a piece of linen and five books, the last thing an illiterate criminal needed. It was that experience which had given him the burning desire to learn to read that I was able to satisfy on the *Charlotte*. Davy Warren was a fencing cull, a receiver of stolen goods and a dabbler in the art of forgery. Such were my companions on this journey into the unknown.

It was in January, 1788, that the miracle finally happened. We reached our destination and dropped anchor with the other vessels. When the marines had seen their fill, they opened the hatches and brought us up on deck to take a first look at Botany Bay. It was absolutely stunning, a glimpse of paradise, a Garden of Eden that lay unspoiled in the bright sunshine. But, then, of course, almost anywhere would have seemed wonderful to emaciated, desperate, disease-ridden convicts who had spent over eight months in a storm-tossed purgatory. My two awe-struck eyes were deceived just as easily as the single one belonging to the now literate Luke Fillimore.

We'd been led to expect grassland with deep black soil and well-spaced trees, where crops could be planted without clearing. Instead, we were gazing at a flat heath of paperbark scrub and grey-green eucalyptus trees, stretching far into the distance. There was no obvious source of building stone and no protected anchorage. Botany Bay was at the mercy of the violent Pacific rollers. The water was shallow, the holding ground poor. This was no place for a permanent settlement. Disappointment swept through the whole fleet like an icy wind yet I didn't shiver in its blast. Alone of that ragged band of watchers, I saw my future in those massive eucalypts and in the cabbage-trees and lush vegetation that sheltered beneath them. I was filled with an elation I had not felt since my two minutes of joy between the ample thighs of Annie Creed, the hapless chicken thief. A whole new life beckoned.

I would one day be a botanist.

"What shall we do today, Mr Beresford?" he asked, deferentially.

"Work in the top field," I said, "lifting those carrots. You can take Ned with you but tell him not to eat too many of them."

"Yes, sir."

"And the same goes for you, Davy."

Fifteen years had made a new man of me. Long before I'd served my allotted seven, I stopped feeling like a criminal. I earned the trust of the administration and was given responsibility as a result. Ned Paget called me a catchfart but I was no sycophant. I simply learned the rules and bent them to my advantage. Ned, by contrast, kept getting into trouble and feeling the lash upon his back. He was even deported to Norfolk Island at one point. One-eyed Luke Fillimore was also his own worst enemy. Persistent theft and disobedience meant that his sentence was increased indefinitely. The repeated attempts at escape by little Davy Warren kept him in the convict barracks for years beyond his release date. It was almost as if he wanted to remain in custody.

As I became respectable, they remained what they'd always been and the gap between us widened. Out of a misguided nostalgia, however, I asked for my old friends to work on my farm. Ned Paget and Davy Warren were employed as labourers with Luke Fillimore, keeping his one eye on them as overseer. Luke also made sure that Ned didn't pick another fight with Cicero, my Jamaican gardener, an ebony giant of a man who'd been convicted of robbery with violence at the turn of the century so had only been in Sydney Cove for three years. Cicero was a friendly, placid, easygoing character who'd been driven to crime by hunger. The burly Ned Paget resented the fact that he had to toil in the fields while Cicero had real status and a softer time of it as my gardener. It rankled with Ned.

"Why can't *I* dig your garden, Tom?" he whined.

"The name is Mr Beresford," I corrected, reminding him that we were on different sides of the law now. "And I need you to lift the carrots, potatoes and turnips."

"So you prefer that big, black scabbado to me, do you?"

"He's no scabbado. You're the one who caught syphilis."

"Cicero is a cooler-kisser."

"Stop calling him names."

"He's a satchel-arsed son of a whore."

"Cicero has a proper respect for plants and flowers. In return, they grow for him," I said, indicating the dazzling colour and richness of the garden. "You respect nothing and nobody under the sun, Ned. What do you know of mosses, ferns, roses, carnations, orchids, gymea lilies and waratah? How many species of camellia can you identify? You couldn't tell me the difference between a wollemi pine and a mint bush. If I put you in charge, this garden would turn into a wilderness."

"And I thought we was mates," he said, spitting with disgust.

"Perhaps you should remember who had you brought back from Norfolk Island. I had to use my influence with the governor to do that. Would you like to be sent back there?"

Ned Paget glowered at me but said nothing. He knew that I had power over him. After shooting a murderous glance at Cicero, he went off to join Davy Warren in the field. Luke Fillimore went with him. They were not the only convicts that I employed but they were the sole survivors of the voyage of the First Fleet. Others who'd served their time had gained release and become part of the growing community of Sydney, a town with a magnificent harbour, lying some seven miles to the north of Botany Bay. It was the latter place that remained synonymous with transportation but the convict prison of slab timber was actually sited in Sydney, named after that callous bastard of a Home Secretary who decided to send us all here – Viscount Sydney.

After the early years of struggle and starvation, the colony had slowly begun to prosper and I prospered with it. While I was still a convict, my skill as a cabinetmaker was recognised both by Arthur Phillip, our first governor, and by our second, John Hunter, who, like his predecessor, was a tough old sea dog. They each commissioned pieces of furniture and helped me to build a reputation for quality work that stood me in good stead on my release. Settlers came from England and looked upon my craftsmanship as a reassuring sign of civilisation. Their wives were soon seeking items of furniture that would turn their huts into something akin to a home.

As my success grew, I earned enough money to buy a farm in Parramatta, where the rich black soil allowed me to indulge my passion for botany and to do a favour for those who had sailed with me in the *Charlotte* all those years earlier. My crime had now been buried forever but theirs still hung around their necks like halters. I tried to offer a modicum of relief. Davy Warren was obsequiously grateful, one-eyed Luke Fillimore was proud of his rank as overseer and Ned Paget, exiled for life, hated me because I'd bettered myself.

It was only Cicero who appreciated what I was trying to do.

"The garden is beautiful now, sir," he said, approvingly.

"You must take some credit for that, Cicero."

"I only do what I'm told, sir."

"But you do it without complaint," I observed, "and that's more than I can say for Ned Paget and some of the others. The first thing I noticed when I came here was the diversity of vegetation. Sydney is built on sandstone so its plants offer little sustenance. There were no tasty fruits, roots and berries growing here until I imported some from Africa and South America."

"You have acres of them now, sir."

"I wanted to vary our diet. Unlike the Aborigines, we could never learn to suck those honey-filled flowers. There were countless species of plants growing within a small radius of Sydney but none that we could eat. I've tried to remedy that."

"It's good to help you, sir."

"You worked on the land in Jamaica. You have a feel for it."

"Thank you, Mr Beresford."

"My fruit and vegetables now bring in a tidy income," I said. "One of these fine days, I may be able to stop being a cabinetmaker altogether and devote my efforts to this garden."

"Will you keep your promise, sir?" he asked, seriously.

"I always keep my promises, Cicero."

"You'll teach me to read?"

"Not directly, perhaps, but I'll find someone to act as your tutor."

"Luke told me that you taught *him* to read and write."

"Yes," I recalled, "and I did it with the help of a Bible. Luke may have learned to read the words but he certainly didn't mark any of them. He's still the same crooked, one-eyed, God-forsaken thief he was when we sailed from England."

Cicero burst out laughing. It was a braying, uninhibited, full-throated expression of mirth that made his muscles flex involuntarily and his whole body ripple with sheer joy. Laughter was freedom for him. He savoured it for minutes. When he stopped, Cicero became penitent.

"I'm sorry, sir," he said.

"No apology is needed."

"So I *will* be able to read?"

"If you study hard enough."

"I want to know the names of all these plants," he said, gesturing towards the botanical profusion that was my garden. "The real names, sir, in that strange language you sometimes speak."

"It's called Latin."

"I know, sir. And even Luke Fillimore never learned any Latin. I want to be able to read your book, Mr Beresford."

It was another reason that I liked Cicero. He was slow, uneducated and ponderous in his movements but he was a man with whom I felt able to share things. Everyone knew that I was writing a book but only Cicero had been shown the illustrations that accompanied it. Having read everything on botany that I could import, I'd become something of an expert and had started to write a column for amateur naturalists in the *Sydney Gazette*. I'd also corresponded with botanists in England and astounded them with drawings and descriptions of the remarkable fauna that abounded on this eastern strip of the Australian coast. The next logical step was to write a definitive work on the subject.

I intended to dedicate it to my bride.

The pilfering began early on. Since it was intermittent and on a small scale, I tolerated it. When you employ convict labour, you have to allow for occasional irregularities. I knew full well that people like Ned Paget ate some of the fruit and vegetables they were employed to pick, and, having lived off their mean diet myself, I didn't begrudge them their pickings. When a few things were stolen from my house, however, I had to draw the line.

"I'll not stand it, Luke," I warned.

"No, sir."

"Tell the others. If this goes on, there'll be repercussions."

"Yes," said Luke Fillimore. "I will, sir."

"You're the overseer – see over them, man!"

Smarting from my rebuke, he slunk away to pass on my comments to the others. It's axiomatic that you should set a thief to catch a thief but a mangy, one-eyed lag like my overseer was not an ideal choice. Also, of course, Luke Fillimore had divided loyalties. He owed gratitude to me for employing him and friendship to those who shared his convict life. Though he tried to be more vigilant, the thefts continued. What upset me was that the crimes slowly became more personal. It's one thing to have a tiny amount of your farm produce stolen from time to time but quite another to have an item of great sentimental value taken from your workshop. It was an exquisite little table that I'd made as a wedding present for my bride-to-be. Its disappearance proved that someone was deliberately getting at me.

It was galling. When I called at her house in Sydney that afternoon, Margaret saw the distress in my face immediately.

"Why, Tom," she said with concern. "What's the matter?"

"Nothing – nothing, my love."

"You look so anxious. Are you not pleased to see me?"

"I'm always pleased to see you, Margaret," I promised her, trying to hide my worries behind a warm smile. "I can't wait for the time when I'll be able to see you every day."

"The wedding is exactly six weeks away now."

"It couldn't come soon enough for me, my love."

Margaret Lentle was the best thing that had happened to me since I left England. She was the daughter of Silas Lentle, a farmer from Devon with a sense of adventure that impelled him to take his wife and family on the perilous voyage to Australia. There were three children in all. Margaret, at twenty-one, was the oldest, bright, buoyant and questing, a charming creature with the kind of hidden beauty that only reveals itself when you get to know her properly. While making some furniture for her parents, I was lucky enough to be in a position where my acquaintance with her could mature gently into friendship before blossoming into love.

"Are you sure there's nothing wrong, Tom?" she asked.

"Quite sure."

"You would tell me, wouldn't you?"

"Of course."

"If we're going to be man and wife, there should be no secrets between us. You must tell me if there is something amiss."

"I will, Margaret."

"And is there?"

"Well . . ." I admitted with a deep sigh.

"Go on."

"As a matter of fact, there is."

"I knew it!" She clasped my hands between hers. "Oh, my poor darling! Share your troubles with me. That's what I'm here for, after all. Why that worried look in your eye?"

"Because," I replied, pretending to be more melancholy

than ever before giving her a sly grin, "because I can't marry you this very day!"

Margaret giggled and I stole a kiss before her mother came in.

I'd been a model suitor. Everything was done with the consent of her parents. Knowing how I came to be in Australia, her father was so impressed with the way that I'd survived imprisonment and put it triumphantly behind me, that he was ready to welcome me into the family. Rose Lentle, his wife, was more cautious at first though she later confessed that she found the notion of my criminal past faintly exciting. Yet I never saw myself as a real lag. Stealing a few flowers didn't make me a thief. It was a highly prophetic act. Thanks to that brief moment in the garden belonging to a judge of the King's Bench, I was guided towards my destiny as a botanist.

Of necessity, there were several things that I concealed from Margaret and her family. I never talked to them in the criminal cant that I'd had to master, and I certainly made no mention of my initiation into manhood on board the *Charlotte*. There'd been many other women since, all of them wondrously compliant but none remotely respectable. They'd merely satisfied an immediate need. Margaret, by contrast, would give me the lifelong love and devotion of a wife. Her wholesomeness would obliterate the memory of Annie Creed and her kind.

Marriage would complete my redemption.

Luke Fillimore was waiting for me at the farm. The other convicts had all been marched back to the prison but the overseer had stayed behind for a private word about the thefts. His one eye glinting, he sidled up to me. His voice was a hoarse, conspiratorial whisper.

"I think I know who it is," he said.

"Ned Paget, taking his revenge on me?"

"No, Mr Beresford."

"Davy Warren, then?" I asked. "Prompted by envy."

"Davy wouldn't do anything like that to you."

"Then who would?"

"Cicero."

"Never! I put full trust in Cicero."

"Then you're a fool, Tom."

"Mr Beresford to you," I snapped, "and you're wrong to tell tales about my gardener. He respects me too much. Don't point at him, Luke."

"I have to, Mr Beresford," he said, introducing a slight snarl into my name. "I saw that black horse-leech, looking through your window this afternoon and he's not allowed anywhere near the house. I know what he was staring at – it was them leaves you showed me."

I was jolted. Cicero was a good man but I confined him exclusively to the garden. He had the use of a shed where he kept his tools but it was well away from the house. He knew about the display case because he had seen me working on it, and he'd even helped me to collect some of the specimens. It was another wedding present for Margaret, a hundred leaves, each from a different species of tree (many of them from the huge range of eucalypts), mounted artistically inside a display case with a glass front. It was a botanical calling card. It was also a symbol that, in getting married, I was turning over a new leaf.

I'd shown the case to Cicero – and to Luke Fillimore – before I moved it to the house. From that point on, it was kept under lock and key. My gardener had no reason to peer at it through the window. If, of course, that was what he'd actually done. I only had Luke's word for it and honesty wasn't something with which he'd ever been closely associated in the slums of St Giles. He sensed my doubts at once.

"Then there was that little table, sir," he said.

"What about it?"

"Cicero knew where it was. His shed is close to your workshop. He'd have been able to slip in there when your back was turned."

"He only goes in there at my invitation," I insisted. "Besides, why would Cicero steal the table? It's no use to him. He could hardly take it back to the convict barracks with him. No, Luke," I decided, "you're making this up because you're jealous of Cicero. My gardener has too much to lose. He's the one person I don't suspect."

"We found the table," he said, bluntly. "What's left of it, anyway."

"*Where?*"

"In your garden, sir."

I was shaken. I made him take me to the spot straight away. In a far corner, hidden behind an explosion of foliage, was a vast pile of mown grass and rotting vegetation that would in time be used as fertiliser. It was Cicero's domain, the place where he'd wheeled his wooden barrow a thousand times since he'd worked for me. Sticking out of the mound were the remains of my table. It had been smashed to pieces and concealed in the one part of the garden where I wouldn't go. I felt sick.

"Who found this?" I demanded.

"Davy Warren, sir."

"What the devil was he doing here?"

"Ask him."

As soon as the convicts arrived next morning, I confronted Davy Warren. Of the three of them, he was the one I liked most because of his impish sense of humour and his determination not to be quashed by authority. I never forgot that it was Davy's money that earned me my first, succulent taste of Annie Creed and, even though the coins later turned out to have been minted out of pewter by Davy himself, I didn't hold it against him. Annie – poor girl – never got to see a penny of it because the money was paid as rental to the naval officer enjoying her favours on a regular basis. When he discovered that I'd hired his mistress by means of forgery, he rewarded me with fifty lashes but I didn't even blame that on Davy. Those two magical minutes with Hannah Richardson (in the person of Annie Creed) had filled me with the spirit of forgiveness. Besides, the scars on my back eventually faded.

"I'm told that you found that table of mine, Davy," I said.

"Yes, sir."

"You're not supposed to be in my garden."

"I was taking a short cut to the woods," he explained.
"It's where we go for a shit. I did no harm in the garden,
sir."

"Someone did. They destroyed my table."

"I know. I saw a piece of it, poking out of that mound."

"What did you do?" I asked.

"I told Luke about it so he could report it to you."

"And you think Cicero put the table there?"

"Who else, sir? He's the only one of us who could have
done it."

"Why?"

"He knew where the table was kept and knew where to
hide it."

"But he had no *reason* to take it," I argued. Davy turned
his weasel face away as if wanting to contradict me but
unwilling to do so. I grabbed him by the shoulders. "You
believe he did, don't you?"

"Yes, sir."

"All right, what was his motive?"

"It's not my place to say, Tom – Mr Beresford, that is."

"Tell me, damn you!" I ordered, waving a fist.

Davy shrugged. "It's this marriage of yours, sir. Cicero is
afraid that it will change things."

"Change things?"

"He likes it how it is – you and him, tending this lovely
garden together. Mrs Beresford would change all that. Cicero is afraid that he'll lose you, sir. You're everything he's
got."

I was chastened. I'd never seen it from my gardener's
point of view. As a Negro, he'd always been an outsider
among the convicts, resented, baited, mocked and abused.
Working for me had given him back a small degree of
dignity. My garden was his escape. My readiness to confide
in him was the only sign of affection he'd been given since his
arrest. Davy Warren may have seen something that eluded
me. Cicero didn't want me to take a wife because – in a sense
– I was already married to him. We were botanical spouses.

"It's what it stood for, sir," said Davy, hammering home
his point. "That table was a wedding present and Cicero

doesn't want the wedding to take place. If it did, you'd have someone else."

My gardener was usually the first to arrive and the first to get started on the work that he loved so much. Because he was late that day, I began to wonder if he was trying to keep out of my way. When an hour had passed, I had doubts about his turning up at all. Eventually, however, he ambled into sight and gave his accustomed salute before moving towards the garden with his head down. I called him over and soon understood why he was avoiding me. It's difficult to see two black eyes on a black man but the swollen lip, the flattened nose and the gashes on his temple could not be missed. My anger flared up.

"You've been fighting with Ned Paget again," I accused.

"He attacked me, sir."

"I told you to keep clear of him."

"Ned was saying terrible things about me, sir."

"What sort of things?"

"He said that I was a thief," replied Cicero, "and that I took things from your house. I'd never do that, Mr Beresford. I swear it."

"But you did look into my house, didn't you?"

"Is that what Ned Paget told you?"

"No," I said, "it was Luke Fillimore and I believe him." Cicero was shamefaced. "Well," I pressed, "did you or didn't you go up to the house?"

"I only peeped through the window, sir."

"You trespassed, Cicero. You know my rules. No convict is permitted within twenty yards of the house. Why did you do it?"

"I wanted to see those leaves again, sir."

"Then you should have asked me."

"You weren't here, sir."

"No, Cicero. I rode over to Sydney to see my betrothed. How do you think that she'd feel if she's sitting in our house – and it will be *our* house when we marry – and she sees you staring at her through the window? That's enough to scare any woman."

"It'll never happen again, sir."

"The best way to ensure that is to find myself another gardener."

"No!" he cried. "I like it here. I work hard for you, Mr Beresford. You've been kind to me. You've been my only friend."

"I'm wondering if I've been too kind and too friendly," I said, watching him carefully. "I'll not let anyone take liberties with me, Cicero, and I won't brook any dishonesty. Do you hear me?" He nodded. "Now – did you steal that little table I made?"

"No, sir!" he attested.

"Did you take anything else of mine?"

"No, sir!"

"How did that table end where it did?"

"I don't know, sir."

There was an edge of defiance in his voice that worried me. He'd been truthful with me in the past but I was less convinced that he was being wholly honest with me this time. I remembered what Davy Warren had told me about a possible motive for the thefts.

"Are you happy about me getting married?" I asked.

"It's nothing to do with me, sir."

"But it is, Cicero. My future wife is very fond of gardening so you'll have to take your orders from two people. How will you cope with that?"

His eyes flashed for a second. I had my answer.

Ned Paget wasn't working with the others in the field. Instead, he was sleeping against a monstrous eucalyptus tree with a girth of over twenty feet. It was a most appropriate place for him. Eucalypts break all the rules of botany by shedding leaves throughout the year. Out of a similar perversity in his nature, Ned Paget also broke all the rules. I kicked him unceremoniously awake.

"Get up, you lazy dog!" I yelled.

He swore, he spat and he hauled himself awkwardly to his feet. It was clear that he'd come off worse in the fight. His face was heavily bruised, his lips twice their normal size and his eyes blackened. Cuts and grazes abounded. But it was the way that he held himself that told me how much punishment he'd taken. He was hunched over, pressing one arm gently against some damaged ribs. Ned Paget couldn't stand properly on both legs. Long periods of time in fetters had left him with a limp but there was a more serious disability now. I had no sympathy.

"It looks as if Cicero gave you the hiding you deserve," I said.

"I'll kill that cunt-faced nigger!"

"Not in a fair fight. He's got the measure of you, Ned."

"Black bastard!"

"In any case," I went on, sternly, "you were warned not to brawl with him. Left to himself, Cicero is a peaceable man. I told you that you'd lose your job here if you set on him again – yet you did."

"Only because of you, Tom," he claimed.

"Mr Beresford, please!"

"You'll always be Tom to me, no matter how high and mighty you think yourself. And because we went through that hell of a voyage together," he said, shifting his feet to ease the pain, "I still got loyalties, see? I won't let any man – white, black or yellow – steal from Tom Beresford. I was hitting Cicero for *you*."

"No, Ned. You were disobeying my orders."

"I couldn't let him get away with it."

"If he's guilty," I assured him, "then Cicero won't get away with it, believe me, but I'm not convinced of his guilt yet. I've suspended him from his duties until I've found the real culprit."

"*He's* the real culprit!"

"Is he – or did you steal that table so that suspicion fell on him?" He glowed with indignation. "And it's no good giving me that look of injured innocence," I said. "You want Cicero's job and the only way you could get that was by having him dismissed."

"Kangaroo shit!"

"Go back to the barracks, Ned. One of the guards will take you."

"But I've work to do here."

"Not in that state. Besides, I won't have you on my property until this crime has been solved. And if you turn out to be responsible," I added, wagging a finger, "I'll recommend to the governor that you're sent to Van Diemen's Land."

It was a threat that struck him like a blow. Muttering a string of expletives under his breath, Ned Paget hobbled off gingerly. Judging by his movements, he'd not be able to fight with Cicero for some time.

Days of calm ensued. Since there were no more thefts, I was persuaded that either Cicero or Ned Paget had been responsible for the earlier crimes. When they were absent, everything settled down. And then, the unthinkable happened. I came downstairs one morning to find that my other wedding present, my display cabinet of a hundred leaves, had gone. Instinct made me run to the place where the little table had been found. Sure enough, my botanical bounty was also there, smashed beyond recall, the century of leaves scattered to the winds. I felt a rage deeper than I'd ever experienced before. I didn't just want to catch the thief. I lusted for blood.

"I'll be away for a couple of days, Luke," I told him, "staying with friends in town. I expect you to take responsibility here."

"Yes, sir."

"You know what's to be done. Make sure that they do it."

"You can rely on me," said Luke Filimore, glad to be put in charge. "I'll crack the whip over them."

"Do that. And keep everyone away from the house."

I gave him no indication that I knew about the theft the previous night. What I wanted Luke to do was to pass on the information to the others. It would then work its way back to my two main suspects. Convicts had to be in the prison before curfew each night but there were ways of making nocturnal excursions. Locks could be picked, guards bribed. Cicero was my chief suspect because he knew where the display case was and just how much it meant to me. Ned

Paget, on the other hand, had greater malevolence. Also, he was a practised thief. Even in his wounded condition, he could have sneaked out at night and made his way to Parramatta.

I did some gardening of my own that evening. Instead of quitting the property, as I had told Luke Fillimore, I simply stayed in my house. I knew that the man I wanted would come again. Having me out of the way was too great a temptation. I also knew what the target would be – the manuscript on which I'd worked for over two years and which was almost complete. *Botanical Observations in New South Wales* by Thomas Beresford would make my name and establish me once and for all as the botanist I yearned to be.

Because of its importance, I kept the manuscript locked in a solid wooden box under my bed. It was the reason that the thief who stole my display case of leaves had been unable to get at it. Coming into my bedroom while I was there was too big a risk to take. With the house empty and unguarded, he'd be able to search every part of it. All that I had to do was to wait. It was hours past midnight when he finally came. I heard the crackle of vegetation under his feet. It was my cue to hide in the cupboard in my bedroom. I had a loaded pistol in my hand. I wasn't there to take a prisoner.

He let himself into the house by forcing open the back door. I listened intently for sounds of movement. Would it be Cicero's shambling walk or Ned Paget's exaggerated limp? Davy Warren's patter, perhaps? Or was my visitor one-eyed Luke Fillimore, a common thief who had – albeit unwittingly – stolen books once before? It might even be someone else altogether. The search of the downstairs was thorough. When I heard footsteps on the staircase, I tensed myself for action.

The door of my bedroom squeaked open. The footsteps got closer. Another search began. It was not long before the box was dragged out from beneath my bed and the lock smashed open. I could hold back no more. Somebody was trying to destroy me, to stop me from turning myself into a happily married man with a reputation as a botanist. With cold fury, I flung open the door, saw, to my horror, that he was about to set my precious manuscript alight with the flame of a candle, and fired the gun. The bullet split his skull wide open.

When I'd calmed down, I wrapped him in a blanket and dragged him downstairs. I'd already dug the grave. It was tucked away in a quiet corner of the garden. Using the wheelbarrow, I took the corpse to the deep slit in the ground and tipped it in as if it were so much rubbish. Then I grabbed the spade and covered that treacherous employee of mine with six feet of earth. I was saved at last and my botanical masterpiece was saved with me. It could still be dedicated with love to Margaret.

I was congratulating myself on my success when a figure suddenly stepped out of the gloom to tower over me. Cicero gave a macabre laugh.

"I knew it was Davy Warren," he said, "because I followed him when he climbed out of prison. I was going to kill him for you, sir. But you took care of him yourself. I could have you hanged for that."

"I could have you flogged for escaping from custody."

"You wouldn't do that, sir, or the truth would come out."

"Shut up!" I yelled, "or I'll kill you as well."

It was an absurd threat. Cicero was much bigger and stronger than me. Besides, I was exhausted from filling in the grave. My only hope lay in retrieving the gun from the house. He'd anticipated that.

"I heard the shot," he explained, calmly. "When you dragged Davy out, I went into the house to get your gun and hide it in the garden. It belongs to me now, Mr Beresford. And so do you."

"Don't tell on me, Cicero," I begged. "I'll pay you anything."

"Money is no use to me, sir."

"You can't betray me – we're *friends*, aren't we?"

"Yes," he said, "we're good friends. That's why you have to think again about this wedding. You can't ask a wife to live in a house with a body buried in the garden. It's not right. It's not Christian. You don't need to get married, Mr

Beresford," he went on, stating the terms of his contract with quiet menace. "Your wife would only come between us. We're accomplices in murder, you see. That means I save you from the hangman – and you teach me how to read your book." He looked down at the grave. "We can plant some bushes there to hide our little secret. Nobody else will ever know, Mr Beresford, will they?"

Cicero grinned in the darkness. It was his garden now.

# The Living and the Dead

## Judith Cutler

*Judith Cutler is probably best known for her series of novels featuring Sophie Powers who, like Cutler, was a lecturer at an inner-city college in Birmingham. That series began with* Dying Fall *(1995). More recently in* Power on Her Own *(1998), Cutler started a new series featuring Kate Power, a former Metropolitan Detective transferred to Birmingham following a personal tragedy. These hard-edged contemporary series might not prepare you for the fact that Judith Cutler has also written several short stories in which cricketer W. G. Grace is the sleuth, plus the following story, set during the period of the Regency.*

After the ungodly wickedness that took place in Stelling St Anthony, some might wonder why I should choose to stay.

The living, deep in the heart of the Midlands, was bestowed on me by a distant cousin on my mother's side. It did little more than provide me with hearth and home, but for a young man fresh from Cambridge with no family to support that was enough. My wants were more generously provided for than those of my parishioners, who never seemed to begrudge me the tithe that was my due. They took me, a stranger, into their homes, and treated me with the simple courtesy that is the very heart of hospitality. If their meals were little more than the herbs of which the Book of Proverbs speaks, they were nonetheless more enjoyable than the stalled ox provided on occasion by the family at Elmstead House. Here the dowager Lady Elmstead still ruled, her husband and his brother having ended their lives in violent hunting accidents. Her son, Lord Elmstead, as weak-willed as he was weak-chinned, had yet to find a wife that met his mother's stringent requirements.

The Elmsteads could, as her ladyship never tired of reminding me, trace their ancestry back to the Norman Invasion. As a student of history, I could have pointed out that William tended to bestow largesse on the most vicious of his henchmen; as a student of human nature, I knew better than to bite the hand that provided me with my after supper cup of tea in an exquisite china cup. It would succeed an admirably cooked repast, her ladyship's chef sending up a succession of elegant courses.

Her ladyship abhorring anything lacking style, there was never any doubt that I was there simply to make up the numbers at table when we took our places in the lofty dining room, complete with huge Tudor fireplace. Sometimes I was there to partner a tongue-tied maiden recently out but yet to gain town bronze; at other times I was to squire an elderly farmer's wife, intent on eating her way through every dish, be it Davenport fowls, salsify fried in butter or Rhenish cream. Most of my partners, aware of my status, preferred to converse with the man to their other side. I was left to contemplate the linenfold panelling and set of family portraits; my favourite was an enchanting Lely redhead.

The ladies having withdrawn, I was never expected to do more than sip and circulate the port. I might listen to the latest masculine *on dits*, but not contribute to them. Not, it has to be said, that Lord Elmstead provided much in the way of conversation. His less than robust health was the excuse for his having been tutored at home. Others said it was because he was beyond control. Whatever the reason, he lacked the social skills and ease with one's peers that a spell at school imposes. Much as one strives to love all one's fellow men, I confess to having found it hard to be attracted to this ginger-haired, loose-lipped, ungainly young man, whose ease in ferreting out his interlocutors' weaknesses was matched only by his enjoyment of exploiting them. An aristocrat he might be by birth, but a gentleman in behaviour he was not.

All too often in my walks from one part of my parish to another, I would find evidence of what my parishioners insisted was his favourite pastime: killing innocent creatures. Living in the country, one cannot be squeamish. If the Almighty provides for our sustenance the birds of the air and the animals that creep on the earth, then we know that we must kill them first. A pig-sticking is a village event: it means plenty in the midst of lack. Moles that destroy crops will contribute to a warm winter waistcoat. No villager would simply kill an animal or bird – one of God's creatures – and leave it a bloody mess attracting vermin, as young Matthew, the head gamekeeper's son, pointed out.

He scuffed a shallow grave next to the path and kicked in the stinking rabbit, first its body and then its head, torn off, apparently, by the killer. "Confound his lordship! Would have filled someone's pot, that," he said. "Letting good food go to waste!"

I forbore to tell him of the food left lying untasted at the end of one of the Elmstead dinner parties – and at the rest of their meals as far as I knew. Matthew, quite unlike his sober and modest father, was inclined to be a hothead, questioning the natural order. I had reasoned with him countless times when I had prepared him for confirmation. "Even our Lord told us that the poor were always with us," I urged.

"He hadn't seen the way those up at the House, our *betters* –" he almost spat out the word "– disport themselves!"

"Such revolutionary words do you no credit at all," I told him.

He nodded ruefully, but not entirely in agreement. "Aye, getting rid of their rightful king didn't do them Froggies much good, did it? We don't want no Boney setting himself up as an Emperor over here."

Indeed we didn't. It was bad enough that he should be rampaging over Europe, and that any able-bodied young man was likely to be recruited, or worse, press-ganged into fighting him. Of course, there was great honour to be won, and the prize money was a tempting bait, but even in the most just of wars, there was pain and suffering, and not just for the young men seeking the glory.

Would young Matthew sign up? Had he not been walking out with the most beautiful girl in the village, I'm sure he would have been tempted. But the knowledge that some half a dozen young men, more eligible than he, were more than half in love with Lizzie Woodman, must have inhibited him. Her swains were not just village lads or farmers' sons, either. Employed as she was in the kitchen at Elmstead House, she was the honey pot around which all the menservants buzzed, yes, and their masters too. Low born though she was, she could have had her pick – many a gentleman had been pleased to pluck a woman from her place and embrace her as his duchess, or, I fear, his *inamorata*.

And who could wonder? She was tall for a woman, but neither willowy not Junoesque. Indeed, her figure was perfection itself: the plain clothes of her household uniform could not deny it. Her complexion was pale, as you often find with hair the shade Titian would have been proud of, her eyes the blue-green of the far-distant sea and her voice as sweet and low as the Bard himself would have liked.

Lizzie was one of my parishioners, of course, and a more humble and devout churchgoer there could not have been. When I preached my sermon or chanted a psalm, there were all too many moments when I wished that I could approach her not as a man of the cloth but as a lover might. My head insisted that with her skill with the cooking pot and with the needle she would have made a wonderful parson's wife. My heart confessed that I cared not the least for such accomplishments, only for her.

Had she not already made her preference clear for Matthew – but I must not let my thoughts run that way. I must turn them to something else.

Many of my fellow clergymen took advantage of their regular perambulations about their parishes to study what they saw about them. I was in regular correspondence with a friend from Cambridge who had become a keen astronomer as a result of long rides back from night-time deathbeds. Another was a meteorologist of note, while a third was credited with important geological observations. What could my humble brain espouse as an interest? I mildly enjoyed flowers and birdsong: could I develop a passion for either?

From time to time I would sit on a fallen log or a convenient stile and look around me, hoping to be inspired by the sublimity of nature, but in truth merely reflecting on my own unhappiness.

In one moment, however, my unhappiness was to become the deepest anxiety, and soon true anguish.

My servants were all too used to the clangour of my doorbell and the beat of the knocker at any time of night or day. Both death and the onset of new life had no regard to the clock and I was as accustomed to the summons of those in need as my good friend the doctor: indeed, Dr Edmund Hansard, a sage old man still sporting a wig, and I often rode side by side. But this time it was no young husband or grieving son who burst into my study, but Matthew, his face distorted with panic

"She's gone!" he cried. "She's gone, no one knows where! Lizzie, Mr Campion. My Lizzie!"

Pressing into his hand a glass of wine, I begged him to elucidate. What I heard was almost enough to unman me, too.

He had waited and waited for her on her monthly afternoon off, ready to walk her home to her parents' cottage and then back to Elmstead House before the night-time curfew. That was the sum of their courtship, except for the fortnight at home grudgingly permitted to domestic staff and changed at will by such as Lady Elmstead. Thinking that some whim of her ladyship had prevailed that afternoon, he made his way up to the servants' entrance and asked when she might be free.

I could see the young man standing there, wringing his hat between his hands, and trying not to jiggle from one foot to the other like a guilty child. I could almost feel his pain as the housekeeper declared implacably that Lizzie Woodman had never returned to the house after divine service the previous Sunday.

The pain now recollected made him forget his manners.

"What have you done with her?" he thundered, grabbing me by the shoulders and shaking me.

I shook my head. I had done nothing except look upon her sweet head deeply bowed in prayer. I had shaken hands with her as she left, bestowing a silent blessing on her, retaining in my heart the gentler and respectful pressure of her fingers against mine. Perhaps – yes, her hands were shaking. Certainly her eyes were awash with tears. In my selfish concern for my own feelings, why had I never asked dear Lizzie the cause of her distress?

Such reflections were useless, however. What was needed was immediate action. Seizing my hat, I almost dragged Matthew to the Woodmans' cottage. I had a suspicion that despite her deep curtsey and respectful offer of refreshment, Mrs Woodman was not pleased to see us, and that while she appeared duly shocked when we explained our mission, and denied all knowledge that anything might be wrong, there was something she was concealing. Perhaps I would pay a further visit without Matthew.

My persistence was rewarded. With much circumlocution and many tears, Mrs Woodman confessed a terrible truth, one I was glad Matthew did not have to hear. Lizzie was with child. She had absolutely declined to name the father, but had insisted to her mother that Matthew was innocent, that she herself was innocent – that the child was the product of a quite undesired union. In short, she had been raped by one she had believed a gentleman. It was clear, however, that in some obscure way Mrs Woodman thought Lizzie to blame. Terrible words penetrated the inarticulate sobs: 'No daughter of mine,'' I distinguished.

It was clearly my painful duty to confront Lady Elmstead, whose very presence in the house should have prevented such a terrible violation. I believe it was divine fury that enabled me to overcome my natural reticence and confront her with the facts as I knew them. Never had her ladyship looked more regal, so intimidating, staring down that beak of a nose.

"The wench has been taken care of," she declared, the rouge standing out on her otherwise ashen cheeks.

"Some workhouse –!"

"Indeed no. And," she added, with a thin smile, "I can guarantee that the babe will not be abandoned in some foundling hospital. We Elmsteads know better than that. There is one proviso, Mr Campion, to my generosity. Neither you nor any others of her suitors will attempt to find her. Or my protection will be at an end."

At last the long icy winter of our grief turned to spring. The whole of nature declared itself a time of rebirth. Where there had been cold earth, now there were snowdrops and crocuses; there were early buds; birds scurried forth building their nests. Charmed by their energy, their ability to build from nothing, I resolved to make ornithology my study. But I was slow to learn, despite my eagerness to find something to assuage my grief. Though I knew the little bird I was watching, flitting two and fro through the woodland to what must be his as yet unseen nesting place, to be one of the genus *Sylviidae*, the warblers, I could not tell in the dim light whether he was a sedge warbler or a whitethroat. I resolved to tread softly in the hope of seeing him more closely – perhaps even finding his nest.

A rank, sweetish smell permeated the otherwise perfect sylvan scene – no doubt one of Lord Elmstead's illicit kills left to rot. A badger, perhaps. If I saw it, I would send Matthew to bury it.

There! I was almost upon the little bird! A whitethroat, surely, with the building material of its nest in its beak – soft, delicate tissue, blowing in the breeze as it darted purposefully into a rowan tree. The tissue was red.

It was red hair.

It was Lizzie's hair.

Cursing my morbid imaginings for such a fancy, I stumbled blindly away, only to find the source of that sweet nest-lining – a wash of hair tumbling from a sinister mound. A cloud of flies confirmed what I knew – that this was the source of the evil, pungent, sickly smell. I fell in what I hoped would be eternal oblivion.

*  *  *

"It is she, my good friend," Dr Hansard whispered, pressing a draft of something bitter between my lips. I had swooned again when I had returned with him to this terrible place. "The poor child. I will see that she is prepared for a decent burial. Will you wish to see her again before you read the service?" He regarded me from beneath his thick brows: clearly he had penetrated what I had hoped was a secret, and resumed his gentle brushing of the earth away from the shallow grave.

"Of course," I whispered, steeling myself for the ordeal. "And what better place than in this vernal setting?"

The church has constantly reminded us that we must return to earth. The Bard makes Hamlet joke about worms. This was the first time I had seen either process for myself. Waves and waves of nausea reduced me to the weakness of a child, but I forced myself to observe what the good doctor indicated – the long slice that had almost severed poor Lizzie's head. There was another gash.

"They plucked out her womb," Hansard breathed, ashen as myself.

As Justice of the Peace, Hansard had another function: he had to determine the identity of the killer. The poor body decently stowed in the cool of his cellar, he pressed me to join him for dinner to assist him, as he kindly put it, in his cogitations. The meal was a homely affair, his housekeeper sensing that quality rather than quantity was needed. We drank deeply first of sherry, then of claret, or I swear no morsel of the excellent pheasant could have passed my lips. But when he offered port and brandy, I waved the decanters away. We needed our wits, I said, to be unfuddled.

"You are sure, my young friend, that young Matthew is innocent?"

"I take my oath that when he came to see me that day which seems so very long ago he did not know where she was. Indeed, he believed me in some way responsible for poor Lizzie's disappearance."

He leant across and patted my arm. "I know, Tobias, I

know. You are a good man never to have pressed your case. And even better not to accuse your successful rival."

"Not so successful that he was responsible . . . that he would have fathered a child upon her."

"Indeed no, God rest her soul. So what Lady Elmstead says may be true – that someone at the House betrayed her."

"Violated her," I corrected him with a shudder.

He nodded. "We both know Lord Elmstead's proclivities – the decapitation of squirrels, disembowelment of rabbits. Would he be capable of committing such atrocities on a woman?"

I leapt to my feet, ready to go and challenge him directly. "The villain who did that to her is capable of anything!"

"Sit down, Tobias. That is not the question I asked."

I subsided.

"Fortunately as Justice of the Peace I am in a position to ascertain whether he was in residence at the House when the crime may be presumed to have occurred." He lifted a finger in admonition. "You must leave that to me, my friend. You have another role to play. You are to play a parson grieving for a parishioner he found in quite normal circumstances – as if the poor child was caught on her journey by inclement weather and simply collapsed with exhaustion seeking the shelter of a hedgerow."

"A stout countrywoman? Never!" In any case, all feelings would be offended by such an insinuation.

"In my experience, a criminal can best be unmasked if he believes that he has not been found out. Trust me, Tobias. We both have our parts to play." He helped himself to a thimbleful of brandy – with the War in Europe this was indeed a precious commodity – as if to end the conversation.

"Have you ever known of a case where the perpetrator was a woman?" I pursued.

"Why do you ask?"

"Because her ladyship told me that she had taken poor Lizzie under her protection! That neither she nor her babe would ever be forced on to the parish! Could it be that it was she who –?" I was on my feet, ready to make the accusation to her face there and then.

"Can you imagine, my dear young friend, the scandal if we confront her without a shred of proof? We need," he said, raising a strong finger to mark each point, "a motive, an opportunity and evidence."

"A confession? The Church of England neither insists nor denies confession – it permits it."

"And if her ladyship were unwise enough to make one, would it not have the same confidentiality as a similar one in the Roman Catholic Church? You are using your passions, not your powers of deduction. I have instructed my housekeeper to make up a bed for you; I myself have prepared a draught to help you sleep. Lead my little household in our evening prayers, Tobias, and then allow yourself to rest. We have much to do over the next few days."

I found Matthew waiting for me when I returned to the rectory, taller and broader than ever, in the bright spring sunshine.

"They say in the village that you've found her, Rector. May I say one last goodbye?"

I led him round to the back garden, to my favourite bench in the pretty wilderness where I sometimes blow an evening cloud. Although he withdrew his tobacco pouch, he made no effort to fill a pipe.

"Why do you want to bid her farewell, Matthew?"

His face worked, but at last he straightened and spoke like a man. "Because I wish to walk out with another young maid, Mr Campion. And I want to do the decent thing by everyone."

What better philosophy could that be? I was torn between two desires: to show him the poor corpse, and revolt him into a confession, and to let him think of the girl as she once was, so that he might take his new sweetheart without care. Patting him gently on the shoulder, I left him there while I repaired for a moment's silent prayer.

I returned with my smaller Bible in my hand.

"I want you to swear on this, with as much solemnity as if you were in a court of law, that you had nothing to do with her death."

Without hesitation he laid his rough hand on the Book. "I take God as my witness that I loved sweet Lizzie Woodman and harmed not a hair on her head. Nor did her any other harm neither," he added, as if wishing to cover all points. "And I swear that had I had her by my side now, my thoughts would never have strayed to any other maiden, be she never so beautiful."

It seemed to me a good oath. Would it satisfy Doctor Hansard?

"Why did you not walk with her back to the Big House after morning worship?"

"Because her ladyship had decreed that walking out was no longer permitted. The House servants must walk two by two on their way there and back." He had removed his hands from the Bible.

I recalled the tears shimmering on her lashes. "Or had you had a lovers' tiff?" I asked suddenly. "She was plainly unhappy."

He flushed deeply. "No! No!"

"Had she told you she was carrying your child? Did you wish to dispose of her so you could walk out with this young woman of yours?"

"With child?" I had shocked him on to his feet. "But she was as pure as the day she was born! With child!" He turned to me, his eyes awash. "Had it been my babe, Mr Campion – here, give me the Good Book again – I swear I would have run straight down here with all my heart and soul to ask you to read the banns!"

I nodded. It was the way of things down here. Long courtships often led to the young anticipating their marriage vows. Indeed, some coarser souls said the young men liked to test their sweetheart's fertility before they took her on.

"Off you go now, Matthew," I said. "As for saying your farewells to Lizzie, let me think on it a little longer."

I found Dr Hansard in his potting shed, selecting hyacinths for his study. Blinking at me over his spectacles, he greeted me with the news that Lord Elmstead was no longer at home.

The steward had informed him that his lordship had embarked on the Grand Tour.

"The Grand Tour? It was one thing for young men of his father's generation doing it – indeed, I remember the late Lord undertaking it some eighteen or twenty years ago – but today, with Europe in uproar? What is the man thinking of?"

"What," the good doctor asked slyly, "does Lord Elmstead ever think of? Do you see him, my young friend, enjoying what the continent has to offer? Good wine, good food, the glories of music and the arts? Is he, in short, capable of appreciating the Birthplace of Civilisation? I think not. If he did not go voluntarily, might he have been sent?"

"You imply that Lady Elmstead might have sent him there to escape punishment?"

"If he has indeed embarked on such a journey, that might well be the implication. But consider, my friend: a tour like that is never undertaken lightly. There must be preparations made, items purchased. I am not aware of any concomitant upheaval at Elmstead House. Leave me to make further inquiries. We are not alone in this, you know. Justices such as I have colleagues upon whom we may make demands."

My head reeled, whether with the news or with the heady perfume of his bulbs I could not say. I staggered into the open, filling my lungs as deeply as I could. Before I took my leave, however, I must raise young Matthew's request.

"What has filled your nose, your eyes, your mind since your sad discovery?" Hansard asked, holding my gaze. "Can you, with such knowledge, imagine courting a fresh young maid? Let the young man be a pall-bearer. Let him – if he can – read a lesson at her obsequies. But, unless we have the strongest of grounds to suspect him to be such a villain, let us not sully his innocence."

My path took me next to the Woodmans' cottage. Mrs Woodman must have heard the news by now, and needed divine comfort.

I read to her the most inspiring words I could, and we bowed our heads for many moments in prayer. At last, I took it upon myself to refer to the harsh words she spoke about Lizzie when she first disappeared.

"You said she was no daughter of yours, Mrs Woodman. Can you not find it in your heart to recant now you know her cruel fate?"

She raised tear-filled eyes to mine. "But Rector, they were the honest truth! True, I should not have uttered them, since I vowed by all I held sacred that I would never reveal the secret. I was Lizzie's wet nurse. No more. I never knew her true parents, but I suspected. I suspected. But a woman like me can't make accusations, especially when my mouth is stopped with a golden guinea every quarter, regular as the moon. I was to bring her up like my own, they said –"

"Who said?" My pulses were racing.

"The legal men who brought her to me. I made my mark on their paper, Rector, and as God is my witness I've spoken of it to no one till now."

"He will surely forgive you." I got to my feet, uttering my kindest platitudes. Dr Hansard must hear this news, and immediately. As I bent my head to quit the cottage, I asked, "I suppose the men of law left you no papers?"

"Nothing," came the sad reply. "But," she added with the incurable optimism of her sort, "my guinea still comes each quarter, so belike they don't know she's gone."

If I had committed murder, the last person I should wish to suspect the crime would be a man with a legal bent. So I gave one final blessing and went on my way. Over our supper at his house, the good doctor and I exchanged news of our activities. I grew more and more drowsy, the scent of his hyacinths almost overwhelming me.

"Blue again," he sighed, as I touched the tight, crisp head.

"Again?"

"Indeed. I have it in mind to breed a pink flower, but whenever I get close, the blue returns to dominate. Good God, man, what ails you?"

I had leapt to my feet, knocking over the port glass.

"The hyacinths keep returning to blue," I said slowly. "The blue dominates. Does not the same happen in human beings, Edmund? Does not a trait run from father to son, or even from grandfather to son – blue eyes or large hands?"

He comprehended in a flash. "You are saying that our dear

Lizzie – a by-blow of the Elmstead family – by heavens, Tobias, I believe you may be right!"

"That Lely portrait; Lord Elmstead's paler orange; Lizzie's Titian glory – they must be connected!"

"Not to mention Lady Elmstead's nose," he added dryly. "You were ever too much in love to notice your Lizzie's only defect." Then he clamped his hand over his mouth. "But why should Lizzie resemble her ladyship? Though one cannot condone it, one must expect a man of means to have an occasional by-blow. But a lady – every feeling is revolted!"

"Did you not say that his late lordship travelled some years ago? Soon after the birth of the present lord?"

Edmund nodded. "Indeed. And I wondered at it at the time. The Tour is usually made between university and marriage, to introduce a young man to . . . to the pleasures of the flesh, Tobias."

"One would imagine that in his case he had already experienced them," I objected.

"So why should he go abroad? Don't worry, my young guest. Lead us in our prayers, I beg you, and in time the truth will emerge."

I had spent many hours in prayer since that evening, and was even now before the altar on my knees. Recognising Dr Hansard's nimble footfall, I breathed "Amen" out loud and turned to face him. It was clear even in the dim light that he had news. We stepped into the churchyard together, the early evening calm hardly broken by the sounds of lads practising on the green for the summer's cricket.

"What would you say if I were to tell you that a closed conveyance was seen leaving Elmstead House late one night at the very time his lordship was supposed to be speeding for the Continent? That it made its way to the self-same asylum where his father spent a year after the birth of his son, grief at seeing such a puny specimen having apparently turned his brain? In vain did his doctors tell him that all babes are red-faced and bald at birth! He had expected the sort of infant depicted by our Great Masters! My suspicion is this, Tobias, that her ladyship, believing as many women foolishly do, that having given birth will prevent another conception, took a lover – Elmstead's brother. The result would be Lizzie, immediately farmed out and provided for."

"Suspicion! Your mind races apace, Edmund. Can people behave like this?"

His glance was cynical. "Your innocence does you credit. But believe me, some aristocratic households comprise not just legitimate children but the by-blows of both man and wife. Once an heir is provided, preferably two, then eyes are permitted to stray. These are not love matches, remember, but alliances between great houses, the young participants consenting, merely. There are rumours of such a deed in the Duke of Devonshire's household even now!"

My mind reeled, but I managed to say, with a fair assumption of calm, "Even if it were so, how could we persuade her ladyship to confess? And how would we persuade a jury of her peers to convict her?"

Perhaps the same problems had already occurred to him. He paced between the graves, pausing to tweak a weed here and there. "I suppose," he said at length, "that we could demand that whoever delivers Mrs Woodman her bounty reveal its source?"

"And deprive the old lady of valuable income? In any case, they are almost certainly ignorant of the principal in this case. God grant inspiration will visit us as we sup together."

My servant was wide-eyed as she brought in the cold meat and cheese that were to be our repast. "They do say, sirs, that there's great doings at the big house. It seems her ladyship's taken it into her head to join his lordship on his travels. Such a hurrying and scurrying you never did see!"

"Thank God for the nosiness of villagers!" cried Edmund, as she left us. "My good friend, there's no time for that now! We must be on our way! Up to Elmstead House, of course. Have your horse saddled this instant!"

We rode too hard to speak, grateful for the brightness of the spring evening.

"Her ladyship is not At Home," the butler declared.

"She will see us," Dr Hansard announced grimly, veritably pushing his way into the marble entrance hall. "Where is she? Her boudoir? Don't worry: I know my way well enough."

Even Hansard tapped on the door before pushing it open. Although shocked by our entrance, her ladyship tutted with irritation at something left lying on the carpet. To my surprise, instead of ringing for a servant, she picked it up herself.

"Some refreshment, gentlemen? No? Forgive me if I take some of my drops, Dr Hansard – I feel my palpitations coming on." Her back to us, she measured a quantity of laudanum into a glass, and turned to us, raising it as if in a toast. She swallowed convulsively, gasping a little. "And why are you here? You can see it is not convenient."

"I am here not as your physician, but as a Justice of the Peace," Hansard said portentously. "And I believe you know all too well why I am here, My Lady. Lizzie's death. Murder, I would say. And worse than murder, evisceration."

It seemed to me that she paled. Certainly her breath came in ugly gasps.

"She was with child, My Lady. And it seems to me someone wanted to ensure that she bore no more babes."

"Do not repine over the unborn child's death," she whispered. "It would have been a halfwit. Inbreeding, Doctor Hansard – surely a man of your calibre knows the problems it brings! Every great family has members confined to attics or elsewhere. What hope could there be for any child of my son's, especially one begotten of his sister?" Her eyes focussed on me, with some difficulty, I thought.

Urging her to a seat, I took her hand and knelt beside her. "There is still time to make your peace with the Almighty," I urged.

"No time. No time at all."

Hansard did all he could as a man of medicine, but it was clear I was superfluous. I busied myself looking round the room. What could it have been that she wished so much to pick up. Where had she put it? There was nothing untoward on the little silver tray that held her drops and the jug of water. I followed the line of the wainscoting.

"If only we knew what poison she has taken," Hansard groaned. "Then I might try an antidote."

I proffered a pellet I had just picked up.

"Rat poison?"

"She must have told her staff that there were mice here, thus ensuring a ready means of escape. Good God, Hansard, how long will she be like this?" I looked on her ghastly features and prayed for a rapid end to her suffering. Then I remembered poor Lizzie's death, and changed my prayer, that the Almighty might in His infinite wisdom suit the punishment to the appalling crime.

It took her ladyship till noon the next day to die.

Matthew's first child, a lusty and handsome baby, arrived in the world seven months to the day after his wedding. Lucy has since presented him with two more tokens of her affection. Hansard was so delighted by the pink strain of hyacinth he managed to produce he swept away in matrimony the housekeeper up at Elmstead Hall, now administered by a board of trustees, Lord Elmstead being deemed of unsound mind, having torn apart his physician's cat. As for myself, I did think of leaving this parish, but I am about to publish a monograph on the nesting habits of the genus *Sylviidae*. It may be that I shall be invited to present it at the Royal Society. As it is, I have ample reason to visit the spot where I discovered poor Lizzie, and I can visit her grave every day.

# *Footprints*

## Jeffery Farnol

*When I compiled the first* Mammoth Book of Historical
Whodunnits *in 1993 I included an Appendix which listed
the major historical mystery novels up to that time. It was
only after I had completed that, that I became aware of
another pioneer of the historical whodunnit, Jeffery Farnol. Farnol (1878–1952) was Birmingham born and bred
and might have spent his life in a brass foundry had he not
been fired for hitting the foreman. He then trained as an
artist and for a while worked as a painter of stage scenery
in America before having success with his first novel* The
Broad Highway *(1910), a Regency swashbuckler. He
soon found that this was a profitable vein to mine and
the Regency period provided a setting for many of his later
works. He was an influence on the young Georgette Heyer.
His second novel,* An Amateur Gentleman *(1913), in the
same setting as* Broad Highway, *included a Bow Street
detective Jasper Shrig, who became a regular feature in
many later novels. Over time he took centre stage and
Farnol wrote several atmospheric Regency whodunnits
including* The Loring Mystery *(1925),* The Way Beyond *(1933),* The Happy Harvest *(1939),* Murder by
Nail *(1942),* Valley of Night *(1942) and* The Ninth
Earl *(1950). Fortunately Farnol also wrote the following
short story featuring Mr Shrig, which admirably portrays
his idiosyncratic style.*

Mr Jasper Shrig of Bow Street, leaning back on the great, cushioned settle, stretched sturdy legs to the cheery fire and, having lighted his pipe, sipped his glass of the famous "One and Only" with a relish that brought a smile to his companion's comely visage.

"Pretty cosy, Jarsper, I think?"

"There ain't," sighed Mr Shrig, glancing round about the trim, comfortable kitchen, "a cosier place in London, say England, say the universe, than this here old 'Gun' – thanks to you, Corporal Dick. You've only got an 'ook for an 'and but you're so 'andy wi' that 'ook, so oncommon 'andy that there ain't no word fur it, so, Dick – your werry good 'ealth, pal!"

Corporal Richard Roe, late of the Grenadiers, flushed and, being a man somewhat slow of speech, muttered:

"Thankee, comrade," and thereafter sat gazing at the bright fire and caressing his neatly-trimmed right whisker with the gleaming steel hook that did duty for the hand lost at Waterloo.

"On such con-wiwial occasions as this here," murmured Mr Shrig, also gazing at the fire, "when I'm as you might say luxooriating in a pipe, a glass, and the best o' pals and comrades, my mind nat'rally runs to corpses, Dick."

"Lord!" exclaimed the corporal, somewhat surprised. "Why so, Jarsper?"

"Because, Dick, in spite o' windictiveness in the shape o' bludgeons, knives, bullets, flat-irons, and an occasional chimbley-pot, I'm werry far from being a corpse – yet. Fur vitch I'm dooly thankful. Now talkin' o' corpses, Dick."

"But, Jarsper – I ain't."

"No, but you will, for I am, d'ye see. Now folks as have been 'took off' by wiolence or as you might say The Act, wictims o' Murder, Dick – with a capital M – said parties don't generally make pretty corpses, not as a rule – no."

"Which," said the corporal, shaking his comely head, "can't 'ardly be expected, Jarsper."

"But," continued Mr Shrig, sucking at his pipe with very evident enjoyment, "contrairywise I 'ave never seen an 'andsomer, cleaner, nater ca-darver than Sir W. Glendale made – so smiling, so peaceful – and mind ye, Dick, with a knife, an ordinary butcher's knife, druv clean into 'is buzzum, up to the werry grip, or as you might say 'andle. Smiling he was, Dick, as if 'e 'ad been 'took off' in the werry middle of a bee-ootiful dream . . .

" 'Twas the face of a man . . . as died . . . in his sleep . . . fast asleep!" mused Mr Shrig. "Now why should a man sleep . . . so werry sound . . . ? You'll mind the case, I think – eh, Dick?"

"For sure, Jarsper, the misfortunate gentleman was murdered about a year ago –"

"A year?" mused Mr Shrig, pausing with toddy glass at his grim, clean-shaven lips. "Say nine months, say ten – stop a bit till I take a peep at my little reader."

Setting down his glass he drew from the bosom of his neat, brass-buttoned coat a small, much-worn notebook whose close-written pages he thumbed slowly over, murmuring hoarsely:

"D. E. F. G. . . . Griggs . . . Goreham, Grant – and 'ere we are – Glendale . . . Sir William . . . Baronet . . . Murdered . . . June 1 . . . sitting at desk . . . Murderer – wanting!"

"Ay," nodded the corporal, leaning forward to touch the cheery fire with a caressing poker, " 'tis one 'o them crimes as was never found out."

"And, Dick, your memory sarved you true – for the Act was commit – eggsackly a year ago this here werry night!"

"And I suppose it never will be found out now – eh, Jarsper?"

"Why, since you axes me so p'inted, Dick, I answers you, ready and prompt – oo knows? Hows'ever I'm a-vaiting werry patient."

"Ay, but wot for?"

"Another chance p'raps . . . dewelopments!"

"Jarsper, I don't quite twig you."

"Dick, I didn't expect as you would. Lookee now – there's murderers vich, if not took and 'topped' or, as you might say, scragged – as gets that owdacious, well, murder grows quite an 'abit wi' 'em and – wot's that?"

"Eh?" said the corporal, starting. "I didn't hear anything."

"Sounded like a dog whining somewheres," murmured Mr Shrig, glancing vaguely about. "There 'tis again!"

"That's no dog, Jarsper!" muttered the corporal. "Somebody's ill or hurt – that's a child's voice or a woman's."

"No, Dick, that's the voice o' fear . . . terror, Dick – lad. Now, stand by, pal."

Then soundlessly the corporal unbarred the door, drew it suddenly wide, and with a slithering rustle, a vague shape swayed in and lay motionless at his feet.

"A woman, Jarsper!" said he in a hushed voice, stooping above this vague shape.

"Oh, dead, Dick?"

"Looks that way, Jarsper."

"Then in wi' her – so! Now shut the door – quick! Lock it, pal, and likewise bar it and shoot the bolts!"

"Lord love us, Jarsper!" whispered the corporal, ruffling his short curly hair with a glittering hook, and staring at the lovely form outstretched upon the wide settle. "Anyway, she ain't dead, thank God!"

"No, Dick, she's only swounding."

"But what's to do now, Jarsper? What's the correct evolution? How to bring the lady round, comrade?"

"Cold vater applied outwardly is reckoned pretty good, Dick, but sperrits took innardly is better, I fancy. So get the rum, pal, or brandy – vich ever comes 'andiest – stop a bit, this'll do!"

And reaching his own glass of the "One and Only", Mr Shrig knelt beside the swooning girl whose face showed so pale beneath its heavy braids and coquettish ringlets of glossy, black hair, and tenderly raising this lovely head, he set the toddy to her lips – but, even then, she shuddered violently and, opening great, fearful eyes, recoiled so suddenly that the toddy-glass went flying.

"Dead!" she cried in awful, gasping voice, then checking the outcry on her lips with visible effort, she stared from Mr

Shrig upon his knees, to the towering, soldierly figure of Corporal Richard Roe, and wringing her slim, gloveless hands, spoke in quick, breathless fashion:

"I want . . . who . . . which is Jasper Shrig, the Bow Street officer? I . . . I want Mr Shrig of Bow Street –"

"Ma'am," answered Mr Shrig gently, "that werry identical same is now a-speaking."

"Yes," she cried, leaning toward him with a strange eagerness. "Yes . . . I see you are, now! You . . . oh, you surely must remember me?"

"Ay . . . by Goles . . . I surely . . . do!" nodded Mr Shrig.

"I am Adele Glendale . . . a year ago I was suspected of . . . of –"

"Not by me, lady, never by me, ma'am."

"No, no, you believed in me then, thank God! You were my good friend – then! But to-night . . . Oh, Mr Shrig – dear Jasper Shrig . . ." she cried, and reaching out she clutched at him with both trembling hands in frantic appeal.

"You believed in me then, you were kind to me then, you stood between me and shameful horror a year ago . . . Oh, be kind to me now, believe in me now . . . for to-night . . . it has happened again . . . horrible! Oh, God help me, it has happened again!"

"Eh? . . . Murder?" questioned Mr Shrig in a hoarse whisper.

"Yes – yes . . . and the house full of guests! But he's dead . . . Uncle Gregory is dead – horrible! See – look at me!"

And with swift, wild gesture she threw open the long mantle that shrouded her loveliness and showed her white satin gown – its bosom and shoulder blotched with a hideous stain.

"Look! Look!" she gasped, staring down at these dreadful evidences in horror, "his blood . . . I'm foul of it . . . dear Uncle Gregory!"

Mr Shrig surveyed these ghastly smears with eyes very bright and keen, his lips pursed as if about to whistle, though no sound came; then he drew the cloak about her.

\*     \*     \*

"And now," said he, when their visitor seemed more composed, "now, Miss Adele, ma'am, s'pose you tell us all as you know."

"But what – what can I tell you?" she answered, with a gesture of helplessness. "I only know that Uncle Gregory . . . dear Uncle Gregory is . . . horribly dead. Oh, Mr Shrig, I shall never forget the awful –"

"There, there, my dear!" said Mr Shrig, patting the quivering hand that clasped his so eagerly. "But you mentioned summat about guests."

"Yes, there were people to dinner, five or six . . . But –"

"Oo invited them?"

"My half-cousin, Roger . . . but oh, when I think of how Uncle –"

"Any strangers among 'em – these guests, Miss Adele?"

"No, they were family friends . . . But Uncle Gregory had not been very well to-day, and so soon as dinner was over he excused himself and went to his room."

"Upstairs to bed, ma'am?"

"Not upstairs. He sleeps on the ground floor at the back of the house, looking on to the garden."

"And 'e vas ill to-day, you tell me? Sick, eh?"

"Oh, no, no, it was only a touch of gout."

"Gout, eh? Now did 'e say anything to you afore 'e went to his room?"

"Yes, he told me he felt very drowsy and could hardly keep his eyes open."

"But gout, ma'am, don't make a man drowsy. Had Sir Gregory drank much wine at dinner?"

"Very little."

"And yet," murmured Mr Shrig, staring down at the slender hand he was still patting gently, "and yet – so werry sleepy! Did he say anything more as you can call to mind now?"

"He ordered the butler to take his coffee to the bedroom, and told me he would come back later if the drowsiness passed off . . . And those were his last words, Mr Shrig, the very last words I shall ever hear him speak –"

"And now, ma'am, tell me o' poor Mr Roger, your cousin."

"Half-cousin, Mr Shrig!" she corrected hastily. "Roger was poor Uncle William's stepson –"

"Bit of an inwalid, ain't 'e?"

"Roger is a paralytic, he can't walk and uses a wheeled chair, but surely you remember this, Mr Shrig, you seemed to fancy his society very much a year ago . . . when –"

"A year ago this werry night, Miss Adele, ma'am!" said Mr Shrig with ponderous nod. "And a parrylitick . . . to . . . be . . . sure! Instead o' legs – veels, and at his age too, poor, unfort'nate young gentleman!"

"Roger is older than you think, older than he looks . . . sometimes I think he never was young, and sometimes –" here she shuddered violently again and clasped the strong hand she held fast between her own. "Oh, Mr Shrig," she gasped, "what . . . what can I do . . . Uncle Gregory . . . I left him . . . sitting there in his great elbow-chair beside the fire . . . so still and dreadful! Oh, tell me . . . what . . . what . . . what must I do?"

"First," answered Mr Shrig gently, "tell me just 'ow you found him?"

"As soon as I could leave the company I stole away . . . I knocked softly on his door . . . I went in . . . the room was dark except for the fire, but I . . . could see him . . . sitting in his great chair. I thought him dozing so I crept up to settle him more cosily and . . . to kiss him. I slipped my arm about him, I . . . I kissed his white head . . . so lightly, and . . . Oh, God, he slipped . . . sideways and . . . I saw –!"

"Dick," murmured Mr Shrig, clasping a ready arm about that horror-shaken form, "the brandy!"

"No, no!" she gasped, "I'm not going to . . . swoon. Only help me, Mr Shrig, be my friend for I . . . I'm afraid . . . terribly afraid! I was the last to speak with him, the last to see him alive –"

"No, Miss Adele, ma'am, the last to see 'im alive was the man as killed him."

"Oh . . . friend!" she murmured. "My good, kind Jasper Shrig," and, viewing him through tears of gratitude, bowed her head against the shoulder of the neat, brass-buttoned coat and, with face thus hidden, spoke again, her voice ineffably tender: "But I'm afraid for – another also, Mr Shrig."

"Ay, to be sure!" nodded Mr Shrig, "Oo is 'e, Miss Adele, ma'am?"

"John!" she murmured. "Mr Winton – you remember him? He was Uncle Gregory's secretary. But, oh, Mr Shrig, three days ago they quarrelled! That is, Uncle was very angry with poor John and – discharged him because – John had dared to fall in love with me."

"Humph! And do you love said Mr John, ma'am?"

"With all my poor heart. So you see if you're my friend and believe in me, you must be his friend too, for the danger threatening me threatens him also . . . there is a dreadful shadow over us –"

"But then, ma'am, a shadder's only a shadder – even if it do go on veels –"

"Oh, Mr Shrig –"

"And 'ave you seen Mr John since day of discharge?"

Here she was silent, staring down great-eyed at her fingers that twined and clasped each other so nervously, until at last Mr Shrig laid his large, firm hand upon them and questioned her again:

"Miss Adele, ma'am, if Shrig o' Bow Street, bap-tismal name, Jarsper, is to aid you and said Mr John you must say eggsackly 'ow and also vereabouts you seen 'im this night."

"I . . . I thought I saw him . . . in the garden," she whispered.

"Didn't speak to 'im, then?"

"No, I was too distraught . . . sick with horror, I could only think of –" the faltering voice stopped suddenly as there came a loud, imperious knocking on the outer door.

"Now oo in the vide universe –"

"That must be John, now!" she cried, looking up with eyes bright and joyous. "I hope, I pray it is –"

"But 'ow should he come to the 'Gun' if you didn't tell 'im as you –?"

"Oh, I bade Mary, my old nurse, tell him I'd run off to

you . . . and, oh, please see if it is indeed John." So, at a nod
from Mr Shrig, away strode the corporal forthwith.

Voices in the passage, a hurry of footsteps, and in came a
tall young man who, with no eyes and never a thought for
anything on earth but the lovely creature who rose in such
eager welcome, dropping his hat, was across the kitchen, and
had her in his arms, all in as many moments.

"My dear," he murmured, "oh, my dear, why did you run
away? What new horror is this –?"

"John, tell me, tell me – why were you in the garden tonight?"

"Dear heart, for word with you. Roger wrote me he'd
contrive us a meeting, like the good, generous friend I'm sure
he is –"

"Oh, John," she wailed, clasping him as if to protect,
"how blind, how blind you are!"

"And, Mr Vinton, sir," murmured Mr Shrig, pointing
sinewy finger, "your fob as was – ain't!" the young gentleman started, turned, clapped hand to fob-pocket, and
glanced from the speaker to Adele with an expression of
sudden dismay.

"Gone!" he exclaimed. "The seal you gave me, dear
heart."

"Ay, 'tis gone sure enough, sir," nodded Mr Shrig. "The
question is: how? and likewise where? And now, seeing as
none of us ain't likely to tell, vot I says is – Corporal Dick,
send out for a coach."

Pallid faces, voices that whispered awfully and became as
awfully hushed when Mr Shrig, opening the door of the fatal
room, passed in, beckoning Corporal Dick to follow.

"Dick," said he softly, "shut the door and lock it."

A stately chamber whose luxurious comfort was rendered
cosier by the bright fire that flickered on the hearth with soft,
cheery murmur; and before this fire a great, cushioned chair
from which was thrust a limp arm that dangled helplessly
with a drooping hand whose long, curving fingers seemed to
grope at the deep carpet.

"So, there it is, pal!" quoth Mr Shrig briskly. "Let's see

vot it's got to tell us," and crossing to the chair he stooped to peer down at that which sprawled so grotesquely among its cushions.

The big corporal, who had faced unmoved the horrors of Waterloo, blenched at the thing in the chair which death had smitten in such gruesome fashion amid the comfort of this luxurious room.

"Oh – ecod, Jarsper!" he whispered.

"Ay," nodded Mr Shrig, bending yet closer, " 'e's pretty considerable dead, I never see a deader, no! And yet, in spite o' the gore, 'e looks werry surprisin' peaceful . . . werry remarkably so! . . . Killed by a downward stab above the collar-bone, lookee, in the properest place for it . . . A knife or, say a dagger, and same wanished . . . eh, where are ye, Dick?"

"Comrade," exclaimed the corporal in sudden excitement, "will ye step over here to the winder?"

"Eh . . . the vinder?" murmured Mr Shrig, his keen gaze roving from the figure in the chair to the gleaming moisture beneath it, to those helpless fingers and the shining object they seemed to grasp at, to the small table nearby with open book, the box of cigars, the delicate Sevres cup and saucer. "Eh . . . the vinder? Why so, Dick?"

"It's . . . open, Jarsper!"

"Oh?" murmured Mr Shrig, his roving gaze fixed at last. "Is it? Look thereabouts and y'may see summat of a dagger, pal, or say, a knife –"

"Why, Jarsper . . . Lord love me, here it is!"

"Werry good, bring it over and let's take a peep at it . . . Ah, a ordinary butcher's knife, eh, Dick? Vally about a bob – say, eighteen pence. Has it been viped?"

"No, comrade, it's blooded to the grip –"

"That cup and saucer now?" mused Mr Shrig. "Half full o' coffee . . . vot's that got to tell us?" Saying which, he took up the dainty cup, sniffed at it, tasted its contents, and stood beaming down at the fire, his rosy face more benevolent than usual. Then from one of his many pockets he drew a small phial into which he decanted a little of the coffee very carefully, whistling softly beneath his breath the while.

"What now, Jarsper?"

"Why, Dick, I'll tell ye, pat and plain. There's coffee in this vorld of all sorts, this, that, and t'other and this is that. And, Dick, old pal, the only thing as flummoxes me now is veels."

"Wheels?" repeated the corporal, "Jarsper, I don't twig."

"Vell, no, Dick; no, it aren't to be expected. But you've noticed so werry much already, come and take another peep at our cadaver. Now, vot d'ye see, pal?"

"Very remarkable bloody, Jarsper."

"True! And vot more?"

"The pore old gentleman 'ad begun to smoke a cigar – there it lays now, again' the fender."

"Eh, cigar?" exclaimed Mr Shrig, starting. "Now dog bite me if I 'adn't missed that. There 'tis sure enough and there . . . by Goles . . . there's the ash – look, Dicky lad, look – vot d'ye make o' that, now?"

"Why, Jarsper, I makes it no more than – ash."

"Ay, so it is, Dick, and werry good ash too! Blow my dicky if I don't think it's the best bit of ash as ever I see!"

Here, indeed, Mr Shrig became so extremely attracted by this small pile of fallen cigar ash that he plumped down upon his knees before it, much as if in adoration thereof and was still lost in contemplation of it when the corporal uttered a sharp exclamation and grasping his companion by the shoulder turned him about and pointed with gleaming hook.

"Lord, comrade – oh, Jarsper!" said he in groaning voice. "See – yonder! There's evidence to hang any man, look there!" And he pointed to a small, shining object that twinkled just beneath the grasping fingers of that dangling, dead hand. "Mr John's . . . Mr Winton's seal!" he whispered.

"Oh, ar!" murmured Mr Shrig, his gaze roving back to the cigar ash. "I've been a-vonderin' 'ow it got there, ever since I see it, Dick, so eggsackly under corpse's daddle."

"Why, Jarsper, he must ha' snatched it, accidental-like, in his struggle for life and, being dead, dropped it."

"Lord love ye, Dick!" exclaimed Mr Shrig, beaming up

affectionately into the corporal's troubled face. "Now I never thought o'that. You're gettin' as 'andy with your 'ead as your 'ook! Deceased being alive, snatched it and, being dead, naturally drops it. Good! So now s'pose you pick it up and we takes a peep at it."

"It's his'n, Jarsper, and no mistake," sighed the corporal. "See, here's a J. and a W. and here, round the edge: 'To John from Adele.' So, God help the poor sweet creetur, I says!"

"Amen, Dick, vith all my heart. So the case is pretty clear, eh?"

"A precious sight too clear, comrade."

"Couldn't be plainer, eh, pal?"

"No how, comrade."

"Then, Dick lad, the vord is – march! No – stop a bit – the window. Open? Yes. And werry easy to climb. But this here bolt now . . . this latch . . . pretty solid – von't do! But that 'ook o' yourn's solider, I reckon, and you're precious strong, so – wrench it off."

"Eh? Break it, Jarsper?"

"Ar! Off with it, pal. Ha – so, and off she comes! By Goles, you're stronger than I thought."

"Ay, but Jarsper, why break the winder lock?"

"Hist – mum's the vord, Dick – so march it is and lively, pal."


In the hall they were stayed by one who goggled at Mr Shrig from pale, plump face, bowed, rubbed nervous hands, and spoke in quavering voice:

"A dreadful business, sirs, oh, a terrible –"

"Werry true!" nodded Mr Shrig. "You're the butler, ain't you? Is your master about, I mean your noo master?"

"Mr Roger is . . . is in the library, sir. He desires a word with you. This way, if you please."

For a long moment after the door had closed, Mr Roger Glendale sat behind his desk utterly still, viewing Mr Shrig with his dreamy yet watchful eyes.

"So, Shrig, we meet again?" he said at length. "Our last meeting was –"

"A year ago this werry night, sir!"

"A strange coincidence, Shrig, and a very terrible one. By heaven, there seems to be some curse upon this house, some horrible fate that dogs us Glendales!"

"Werry much so indeed, sir!" nodded Mr Shrig, and his voice sounded so hearty as to be almost jovial.

"And 'ow do you find yourself these days, Mr Roger, pretty bobbish I 'opes sir?"

Mr Roger blenched, throwing up a white, well-cared-for hand:

"An odious, a detestable word, Shrig!" he expostulated.

"Vich, sir?"

"'Bobbish'! A hideous word and most inappropriate as regards myself for –" the sleepy eyes glared suddenly, the pale cheek flushed, the delicate fingers became a knotted fist. "I am the same breathing Impotence! The same useless, helpless Thing, Shrig!"

"I shouldn't eggsackly call ye 'useless', sir, nor go so fur as to name ye ''elpless', not me – no!"

"Then you'd be a fool, for I'm a log! I'm Death-in-Life, a living corpse, live brain in dead body – look at me!"

"And yet," demurred Mr Shrig, "you're astonishin' spry with your fambles, sir, your 'ands, Mr Roger, or as you might say, your daddles, sir!"

Mr Roger glanced at the white, shapely hands in question and flickered their fingers delicately.

"Well, Shrig, my cousin, Miss Adele, forestalled me in summoning you, it seems, but you have seen . . . you have looked into this new horror that has smitten us Glendales?"

"Vith both peepers, sir!"

"Well, speak out, man! Have you discovered any trace of the assassin? Formed any conclusions?"

"Oceans, sir!" nodded Mr Shrig. "The ass-assin is as good as took! Ye see the fax is all too plain, sir! First, the open vinder. Second, by said vinder, the fatal veppin – 'ere it is!" and from a capacious pocket he drew an ugly bundle and, unwinding its stained folds, laid the knife before his questioner.

"Very horrid!" said Mr Roger in hushed accents, viewing the dreadful thing with a very evident disgust. "Anything more, Shrig?"

"Sir, me and my comrade, Corporal Richard Roe, found all as was to be found – this! Number three! A clincher!"

And beside that murderous knife he laid the gold seal, beholding which Mr Roger started in sudden agitation, took it up, stared at it and, dropping it upon the desk, covered his eyes with his two hands.

"Aha, you reckernise it, eh, sir?" asked Mr Shrig, thrusting it back into his pocket, and wrapping up the knife again. "Yes, I see as you know it, eh, Mr Roger?"

"Beyond all doubt . . . to my sorrow! And you found it . . . near . . . the body?"

"Beneath its werry fingers, sir, looked as if it had fell out of its dyin' grasp. Pretty conclusive, I think. And now, sir, 'aving dooly noted and brought along everything in the natur' of evidence, I'll be toddling – no, stop a bit – the cup!"

"Cup, Shrig? Pray, what cup?"

"The coffee cup used by deceased."

"Why trouble to take that?"

"Well," answered Mr Shrig dubiously, "I don't 'ardly know except for the fact as 'twere used by deceased aforesaid and might come in as evidence."

"How so, Shrig? Evidence of what?"

"Well," answered Mr Shrig, more dubiously than ever, "I don't 'ardly know that either, but I'd better take it along. Ye see, sir, there's some coffee in it as they might like to examine."

"But my poor uncle was stabbed, not poisoned."

"No more 'e wasn't!" nodded Mr Shrig. "And I ought to get my report in sharp. And then again if the said cup should be wanted I can fetch it tomorrow."

"You locked the door, Shrig?"

"Seein' as the key was a-missin', I did not, sir, but I've took all as is needful and vot I've left ain't a-goin' to run away, no, 'twill stay nice an' quiet till the undertaker –"

"Good night!" said Mr Roger, ringing the bell at his elbow.

"Sir, good night!" answered Mr Shrig, and, turning at the opening of the door, he and Corporal Dick followed the pallid butler, who presently led them out into a pitch-black night.

Whereupon Mr Shrig became imbued with a sudden fierce energy.

"Now Dick – at the double!"

"Eh, but Jarsper what . . . where –"

"Run!" hissed Mr Shrig, and seizing his companion's arm, he broke into a heavy, though silent trot . . . In among shadowy trees, across smooth, dim lawns, along winding paths to a terrace whence a row of windows glinted down at them; which he counted in breathless whisper:

"Number five should be it . . . At Number five she is! After me, pal!" And, speaking, he opened this fifth window and clambered through with surprising agility. "Eh – back again?" whispered the corporal, glancing at the great chair before the dying fire. "What now, comrade?"

"The bed, Dick it's big enough to hide us both, and – sharp's the vord!" The heavy curtains of the huge sombre four-poster rustled and were still, a cinder fell tinkling to the hearth, and then came the corporal's hoarse whisper:

"What are we waiting for, Jarsper?"

"The murderer."

"Lord!" . . . A distant clock chimed the hour.

Silence, for the great house was very still; the clock chimed the quarter, the dying fire chinked, this room of death grew slowly darker; the clock chimed the half-hour . . . A faint, faint rattle at the door and into the room crept a sound of soft movement with another sound very strange to hear – a crunching rustle that stole across the carpet towards the hearth; a moving, shapeless blot against the feeble fire-glow, a faint tinkle of china, and then a voice sudden and harsh and loud:

"In the King's name!" A leap of quick feet, a whirl of sudden movement, a flurry of desperate strife, an inhuman laugh of chuckling triumph, and then Mr Shrig's gasping voice:

"Ecod, Dick, he's done us! Catch that arm . . . no good! I'm diddled again, by Goles, I am! Get the candles a-goin' – sharp!"

"Lord love us!" gasped Corporal Dick, the lighted candle wavering in his grasp, "Mr Roger!"

"Ay – but look – look at 'im!"

Roger Glendale lolled in his wheeled chair, his eyes fixed upon the speaker in awful glare, his lips upcurling from white teeth . . . and from these writhen lips issued a wheezing chuckle.

"Right, Shrig . . . you were right . . . I'm not . . . not so helpless . . . as I seemed. I was Master of Life . . . and Death. I'm . . . master still! I'm . . . away, Shrig, away . . . And so . . . Good night!" The proud head swayed aslant, drooped forward – the shapely hands fluttered and were still, and Corporal Dick, setting down the candle, wiped moist brow, staring with horrified eyes.

"Love us all!" he whispered. "Dead – eh?"

"As any nail, Dick! Pizen, d'ye see?"

"Comrade, how . . . how did ye know him for the killer?"

" 'Twas very simple, Dick – in that bit 'o cigar ash as you p'inted out to me, I see the track of a veel, his foot-prints, so to speak, and – there ye are, pal!"

"Why then . . . what now, comrade?"

"Now, Dick, get back to them as is a-vaitin' so werry patient in the coach and tell 'em as Jarsper says the shadder, being only a shadder, is vanished out o' their lives and the sun is rose and a-shinin' for 'em and so – let all be revelry and j'y!"

# The Tenth Commandment

## Melville Davisson Post

*Melville Davisson Post (1869–1930) was both a lawyer and one of the most successful writers of magazine fiction of his day. He grew up in West Virginia, the setting for his best-known series of stories featuring Uncle Abner, which take place in the early years of the nineteenth century. Abner is one of those God-fearing upright citizens who believes that justice should prevail, even over man-made laws. He's often a one-man detective, judge and jury, dispensing his own form of justice based on God's laws. The stories were first collected in* Uncle Abner: Master of Mysteries *(1918) whilst some later ones remained uncollected until* The Methods of Uncle Abner *(1974). The best-known Uncle Abner story is "The Doomdorf Mystery", which I included in the first* Mammoth Book of Historical Whodunnits. *Francis M. Nevins, attorney and Professor of Law as well as a writer and biographer, has called the following story, which considers the whole basis of justice, "one of the finest of all the tales of Uncle Abner".*

The afternoon sun was hot, and when the drove began to descend the long wooded hill we could hardly keep them out of the timber. We were bringing in our stock cattle. We had been on the road since daybreak and the cattle were tired. Abner was behind the drove and I was riding the line of the wood. The mare under me knew as much about driving cattle as I did, and between us we managed to keep the steers in the road; but finally a bullock broke away and plunged down into the deep wood. Abner called to me to turn all the cattle into the grove on the upper side of the road and let them rest in the shade while we got the runaway steer out of the underbrush. I turned the drove in among the open oak trees, left my mare to watch them and went on foot down through the underbrush. The long hill descending to the river was unfenced wood grown up with thickets. I was perhaps three hundred yards below the road when I lost sight of the steer, and got up on a stump to look.

I did not see the steer, but in a thicket beyond me I saw a thing that caught my eye. The bushes had been cut out, the leaves trampled, and there was a dogwood fork driven into the ground. About fifty feet away there was a steep bank and below it a horse path ran through the wood.

The thing savoured of mystery. All round was a dense tangle of thicket, and here, hidden at a point commanding the horse path, was this cleared spot with the leaves trampled and the forked limb of a dogwood driven into the ground. I was so absorbed that I did not know that Abner had ridden down the hill behind me until I turned and saw him sitting there on his great chestnut gelding looking over the dense bushes into the thicket.

He got down out of his saddle, parted the bushes carefully and entered the thicket. There was a hollow log lying beyond the dogwood fork. Abner put his hand into the log and drew out a gun. It was a bright, new, one-barrelled fowling-piece – a muzzle-loader, for there were no breech-loaders in that country then. Abner turned the gun about and looked it over carefully. The gun was evidently loaded, because I could see the cap shining under the hammer. Abner opened the brass plate on the stock, but it contained only a bit of new tow and the implement, like a corkscrew, which fitted to the ramrod and held the tow when one wished to clean the gun. It was at this moment that I caught sight of the steer moving in the bushes and I leaped down and ran to head him off, leaving Abner standing with the gun in his hands.

When I got the steer out and across the road into the drove

Abner had come up out of the wood. He was in the saddle, his clenched hand lay on the pommel.

I was afraid to ask Abner questions when he looked like that, but my curiosity overcame me.

"What did you do with the gun, Uncle Abner?"

"I put it back where it was," he said.

"Do you know who the owner is?"

"I do not know who he is," replied Abner without looking in my direction, "but I know what he is – he is a coward!"

The afternoon drew on. The sun moved towards the far-off chain of mountains. Silence lay on the world. Only the tiny creatures of the air moved with the hum of a distant spinner, and the companies of yellow butterflies swarmed on the road. The cattle rested in the shade of the oak trees and we waited. Abner's chestnut stood like a horse of bronze and I dozed in the saddle.

Shadows were entering the world through the gaps and passes of the mountains when I heard a horse. I stood up in my stirrups and looked.

The horse was travelling the path running through the wood below us. I could see the rider through the trees. He was a grazer whose lands lay westward beyond the wood. In the deep, utter silence I could hear the creak of his saddle-leather. Then suddenly as he rode there was the roar of a gun, and a cloud of powder smoke blotted him out of sight.

In that portentous instant of time I realized the meaning of the things that I had seen there in the thicket. It was an ambush to kill this man! The fork in the ground was to hold the gun-barrel so the assassin could not miss his mark.

And with this understanding came an appalling sense of my Uncle Abner's negligence. He must have known all this when he stood there in the thicket, and when he knew it, why had he left that gun there? Why had he put it back into its hiding-place? Why had he gone his way thus unconcernedly and left this assassin to accomplish his murder? Moreover, this man riding there through the wood was a man whom Abner knew. His house was the very house at which Abner expected to stop this night. We were on our way there!

It was in one of those vast spaces of time that a second

sometimes stretches over that I put these things together and jerked my head toward Abner, but he sat there without the tremor of a muscle.

The next second I saw the frightened horse plunging in the path and I looked to see its saddle empty, or the rider reeling with the blood creeping through his coat, or some ghastly thing that clutched and swayed. But I did not see it. The rider sat firmly in his saddle, pulled up the horse, and, looking idly about him, rode on. He believed the gun had been fired by some hunter shooting squirrels.

"Oh," I cried, "he missed!"

But Abner did not reply. He was standing in his stirrups searching the wood.

"How could he miss, Uncle Abner," I said, "when he was so near to the path and had that fork to rest his gun-barrel in? Did you see him?"

It was some time before Abner answered, and then his reply was to my final query.

"I did not see him," he said deliberately. "He must have slipped away somehow through the thicket."

That was all he said, and for a good while he was silent, drumming with his fingers on the pommel of his saddle and looking out over the distant treetops.

The sun was touching the mountains before Abner began to move the drove. We got the cattle out of the wood and started the line down the long hill. The road forked at the bottom of the hill – one branch of it, the main road, went on to the house of the grazer with whom we had expected to spend the night and the other turned off through the wood.

I was astonished when Abner turned the drove into this other road, but I said nothing, for I presently understood the reason for this change of plans. One could hardly accept the hospitality of a man when he had negligently stood by to see him murdered.

In half a mile the road came out into the open. There was a big new house on a bit of rising land and, below, fields and meadows. I did not know the crossroad, but I knew this place. The man, Dillworth, who lived here had been some-time the clerk of the county court. He had got this land, it was said, by taking advantage of a defective record, and he had now a suit in chancery against the neighbouring grazers for the land about him. He had built this great new house, in pride boasting that it would sit in the centre of the estate that he would gain. I had heard this talked about – this boasting, and how one of the grazers had sworn before the courthouse that he would kill Dillworth on the day that the decree was entered. I knew in what esteem Abner held this man and I wondered that he should choose him to stay the night with.

When we first entered the house and while we ate our supper Abner had very little to say, but after that, when we had gone with the man out on to the great porch that overlooked the country, Abner changed – I think it was when he picked up the county newspaper from the table. Something in this paper seized on his attention and he examined it with care. It was a court notice of the sale of lands for delinquent taxes, but the paper had been torn and only half of the article was there. Abner called our host's attention to it.

"Dillworth," he said, "what lands are included in this notice?"

"Are they not there?" replied the man.

"No," said Abner, "a portion of the newspaper is gone. It is torn off at a description of the Jenkins's tract –" and he put his finger on the line and showed the paper to the man "– what lands follow after that?"

"I do not remember the several tracts," Dillworth answered, "but you can easily get another copy of the newspaper. Are you interested in these lands?"

"No," said Abner, "but I am interested in this notice."

Then he laid the newspaper on the table and sat down in a chair. And then it was that his silence left him and he began to talk.

Abner looked out over the country.

"This is fine pasture land," he said.

Dillworth moved forward in his chair. He was a big man with a bushy chestnut beard, little glimmering eyes and a huge body.

"Why, Abner," he said, "it is the very best land that a beef steer ever cropped the grass on."

"It is a corner of the lands that Daniel Davisson got in a grant from George the Third," Abner continued. "I don't know what service he rendered the crown, but the pay was princely – a man would do king's work for an estate like this."

"King's work he would do," said Dillworth, "or hell's work. Why, Abner, the earth is rich for a yard down. I saw old Hezekiah Davisson buried in it, and the shovels full of earth that the Negroes threw on him were as black as their faces, and the sod over that land is as clean as a woman's hair. I was a lad then, but I promised myself that I would one day possess these lands."

"It is a dangerous thing to covet the possession of another," said Abner. "King David tried it and he had to do – what did you call it, Dillworth? – 'hell's work'."

"And why not," replied Dillworth, "if you get the things you want by it?"

"There are several reasons," said Abner, "and one is that it requires a certain courage. Hell's work is heavy work, Dillworth, and the weakling who goes about it is apt to fail."

Dillworth laughed. "King David didn't fail, did he?"

"He did not," replied Abner; "but David, the son of Jesse, was not a coward."

"Well," said Dillworth, "I shall not fail either. My hands are not trained to war like this, but they are trained to lawsuits."

"You got this wedge of land on which your house is built by a lawsuit, did you not?" said Abner.

"I did," replied Dillworth; "but if men do not exercise ordinary care they must suffer for that negligence."

"Well," said Abner, "the little farmer who lived here on this wedge suffered enough for his. When you dispossessed him he hanged himself in his stable with a halter."

"Abner," cried Dillworth, "I have heard enough about that. I did not take the man's life. I took what the law gave me. If a man will buy land and not look up the title it is his own fault."

"He bought at a judicial sale," said Abner, "and he believed the court would not sell him a defective title. He was an honest man, and he thought the world was honest."

"He thought wrong," said Dillworth.

"He did," said Abner.

"Well," cried Dillworth, "am I to blame because there is a fool the less? Will the people never learn that the court does not warrant the title to the lands that it sells in a suit in chancery? The man who buys before the courthouse door buys a pig in a poke, and it is not the court's fault if the poke is empty. The judge could not look up the title to every tract of land that comes into his court, nor could the title to every tract be judicially determined in every suit that involves it. To do that, every suit over land would have to be a suit to determine title and every claimant would have to be a party."

"What you say may be the truth," said Abner, "but the people do not always know it."

"They could know it if they would inquire," answered Dillworth; "why did not this man go before the judge?"

"Well," replied Abner, "he has gone before a greater Judge." Abner leaned back in his chair and his fingers rapped on the table.

"The law is not always justice," he said. "Is it not the law that a man may buy a tract of land and pay down the price in gold and enter into the possession of it, and yet, if by inadvertence, the justice of the peace omits to write certain words into the acknowledgment of the deed, the purchaser takes no title and may be dispossessed of his lands?"

"That is the law," said Dillworth emphatically; "it is the very point in my suit against these grazers. Squire Randolph could not find his copy of Mayo's Guide on the day that the deeds were drawn and so he wrote from memory."

Abner was silent for a moment.

"It is the law," he said, "but is it justice, Dillworth?"

"Abner," replied Dillworth, "how shall we know what justice is unless the law defines it?"

"I think every man knows what it is," said Abner.

"And shall every man set up a standard of his own," said Dillworth, "and disregard the standard that the law sets up? That would be the end of justice."

"It would be the beginning of justice," said Abner, "if every man followed the standard that God gives him."

"But, Abner," replied Dillworth, "is there a court that could administer justice if there were no arbitrary standard and every man followed his own?"

"I think there is such a court," said Abner.

Dillworth laughed.

"If there is such a court it does not sit in Virginia."

Then he settled his huge body in his chair and spoke like a lawyer who sums up his case.

"I know what you have in mind, Abner, but it is a fantastic notion. You would saddle every man with the thing you call a conscience, and let that ride him. Well, I would unsaddle him from that. What is right? What is wrong? These are vexed questions. I would leave them to the law. Look what a burden is on every man if he must decide the justice of every act as it comes up. Now the law would lift that burden from his shoulders, and I would let the law bear it."

"But under the law," replied Abner, "the weak and the ignorant suffer for their weakness and for this ignorance, and the shrewd and the cunning profit by their shrewdness and by their cunning. How would you help that?"

"Now, Abner," said Dillworth, "to help that you would have to make the world over."

Again Abner was silent for a while.

"Well," he said, "perhaps it could be done if every man put his shoulder to the wheel."

"But why should it be done?" replied Dillworth. "Does Nature do it? Look with what indifference she kills off the weakling. Is there any pity in her or any of your little soft concerns? I tell you these things are not to be found anywhere in Nature – they are man-made."

"Or God-made," said Abner.

"Call it what you like," replied Dillworth, "it will be equally fantastic, and the law would be fantastic to follow after it. As for myself, Abner, I would avoid these troublesome refinements. Since the law will undertake to say what is right and what is wrong I shall leave her to say it and let myself go free. What she requires me to give I shall give, and what she permits me to take I shall take, and there shall be an end of it."

"It is an easy standard," replied Abner, "and it simplifies a thing that I have come to see you about."

"And what have you come to see me about?" said Dillworth. "I knew that it was for something you came."

And he laughed a little, dry, nervous laugh.

I had observed this laugh breaking now and then into his talk and I had observed his uneasy manner ever since we came. There was something below the surface in this man that made him nervous and it was from that under thing that this laugh broke out.

"It is about your lawsuit," said Abner.

"And what about it?"

"This," said Abner. "That your suit has reached the point where you are not the man to have charge of it."

"Abner," cried Dillworth, "what do you mean?"

"I will tell you," said Abner. "I have followed the progress of this suit, and you have won it. On any day that you call it up the judge will enter a decree, and yet for a year it has stood there on the docket and you have not called it up. Why?"

Dillworth did not reply, but again that dry, nervous laugh broke out.

"I will answer for you, Dillworth," said Abner. "You are afraid!"

Abner extended his arm and pointed out over the pasture lands, growing dimmer in the gathering twilight, across the river, across the wood to where lights moved and twinkled.

"Yonder," said Abner, "lives Lemuel Arnold; he is the only man who is a defendant in your suit, the others are women and children. I know Lemuel Arnold. I intended to stop this night with him until I thought of you. I know the stock he comes from. When Hamilton was buying scalps on the Ohio, and haggling with the Indians over the price to be paid for those of the women and the children, old Hiram Arnold walked into the conference. 'Scalp-buyer,' he said, 'buy my scalps; there are no little ones among them,' and he emptied out on to the table a bagful of scalps of the king's soldiers. That man was Lemuel Arnold's grandfather and that is the blood he has. You would call him violent and dangerous, Dillworth, and you would be right. He is violent and he is dangerous. I know what he told you before the courthouse door. And, Dillworth, you are afraid of that. And so you sit here looking out over these rich lands and coveting them in your heart – and are afraid to take them."

The night was descending, and I sat on a step of the great porch, in the shadow, forgotten by these two men. Dillworth did not move, and Abner went on.

"That is bad for you, Dillworth, to sit here and brood over a thing like this. Plans will come to you that include 'hell's work'; this is no thing for you to handle. Put it into my hands."

The man cleared his throat with that bit of nervous laugh.

"How do you mean – into your hands?" he said.

"Sell me the lawsuit," replied Abner.

Dillworth sat back in his chair at that and covered his jaw with his hand, and for a good while he was silent.

"But it is these lands I want, Abner, not the money for them."

"I know what you want," said Abner, "and I will agree to give you a proportion of all the lands that I recover in the suit."

"It ought to be a large proportion, then, for the suit is won."

"As large as you like," said Abner.

Dillworth got up at that and walked about the porch. One could tell the two things that were moving in his mind: that Abner was, in truth, the man to carry the thing through – he stood well before the courts and he was not afraid; and the other thing – How great a proportion of the lands could he demand? Finally he came back and stood before the table.

"Seven-eighths then. Is it a bargain?"

"It is," said Abner. "Write out the contract."

A Negro brought foolscap paper, ink, pens, and a candle and set them on the table. Dillworth wrote, and when he had finished he signed the paper and made his seal with a flourish of the pen after his signature. Then he handed the contract to Abner across the table.

Abner read it aloud, weighing each legal term and every lawyer's phrase in it. Dillworth had knowledge of such things and he wrote with skill. Abner folded the contract carefully and put it into his pocket, then he got a silver dollar out of his leather wallet and flung it on to the table, for the paper read: "In consideration of one dollar cash in hand paid, the receipt of which is hereby acknowledged." The coin struck hard and spun on the oak board. "There," he said, "is your silver. It is the money that Judas was paid in and, like that first payment to Judas, it is all you'll get."

Dillworth got on his feet. "Abner," he said, "what do you drive at now?"

"This," replied Abner. "I have bought your lawsuit; I have paid you for it, and it belongs to me. The terms of that sale are written down and signed. You are to receive a portion of what I recover; but if I recover nothing you can receive nothing."

"Nothing?" Dillworth echoed.

"Nothing!" replied Abner.

Dillworth put his big hands on the table and rested his body on them; his head drooped below his shoulders, and he looked at Abner across the table.

"You mean – you mean –"

"Yes," said Abner, "that is what I mean. I shall dismiss this suit."

"Abner," the other wailed, "this is ruin – these lands – these rich lands!" And he put out his arms, as toward something that one loves. "I have been a fool. Give me back my paper." Abner arose.

"Dillworth," he said, "you have a short memory. You said that a man ought to suffer for his lack of care, and you shall suffer for yours. You said that pity was fantastic, and I find it fantastic now. You said that you would take what the law gives you; well, so shall I."

The snivelling creature rocked his big body grotesquely in his chair.

"Abner," he whined, "why did you come here to ruin me?"

"I did not come to ruin you," said Abner. "I came to save you. But for me you would have done a murder."

"Abner," the man cried, "you are mad. Why should I do a murder?"

"Dillworth," replied Abner, "there is a certain commandment prohibited, not because of the evil in it, but because of the thing it leads to – because there follows it – I use your own name, Dillworth, 'hell's work'. This afternoon you tried to kill Lemuel Arnold from an ambush."

Terror was on the man. He ceased to rock his body. He leaned forward, staring at Abner, the muscles of his face flabby.

"Did you see me?"

"No," replied Abner, "I did not."

The man's body seemed, at that, to escape from some hideous pressure. He cried out in relief, and his voice was like air wheezing from the bellows.

"It's a lie! a lie! a lie!"

I saw Abner look hard at the man, but he could not strike a thing like that.

"It's the truth," he said, "you are the man; but when I stood in the thicket with your weapon in my hand I did not know it, and when I came here I did not know it. But I knew that this ambush was the work of a coward, and you were the only coward that I could think of. No," he said, "do not delude yourself – that was no proof. But it was enough to bring me here. And the proof? I found it in this house. I will show it to you. But before I do that, Dillworth, I will return to you something that is yours."

He put his hand into his pocket, took out a score of buckshot and dropped them on the table. They clattered off and rolled away on the floor.

"And that is how I saved you from murder, Dillworth. Before I put your gun back into the hollow log I drew all the charge in it except the powder."

He advanced a step nearer to the table.

"Dillworth," he said, "a little while ago I asked you a question that you could not answer. I asked you what lands were included in the notice of sale for delinquent taxes printed in that county newspaper. Half of the newspaper had been torn off, and with it the other half of that notice. And you could not answer. Do you remember that question, Dillworth? Well, when I asked it of you I had the answer in my pocket. The missing part of that notice was the wadding over the buckshot!"

He took a crumpled piece of newspaper out of his pocket and joined it to the other half lying before Dillworth on the table.

"Look," he said, "how the edges fit!"

# Murder in Old Manhattan

## Frank Bonham

*Frank Bonham (1914–88) may all too simply be remem-
bered as a writer of cowboy stories but, as he himself
remarked, he tried to avoid the conventional cowboy story
and preferred to write about the Old West, recreating the
hardship and perils of the pioneers. A good sample will be
found in* Best Western Stories of Frank Bonham *(1989),
compiled by Bill Pronzini. Bonham's career stretched for
over fifty years and when the pulp magazines died in the
mid 1950s Bonham turned to writing for children and for
television, including scripting several episodes of* Wells
Fargo. *But Bonham wrote a lot more than western stories.
His feel for the period and for the people made him an ideal
candidate for writing period detective stories. Here is a
long-forgotten historical whodunnit written in 1945 and
set in the New York of 1857.*

In Ludlow Street a fine rain was falling. Tom Church kept
his shawl wrapped about the lower part of his face as the
shrewish wind drove the fine drops against his skin like
birdshot. There was no sidewalk; he and his companion kept
their eyes out for the deeper puddles among the cobbles.
They stopped across the street from a two-storey frame
building.

"It's Number Twenty-five," Church said. "That's it."

There was no crowd. Death was no novelty in the Sixth
Ward, even violent death. The landlady, a Mrs Garrity, took

them to a room down a musty dark hall. With the key in the lock, she turned a resentful eye on them.

"I suppose you'll be telling this to the *Sun*, won't you, to help them sell a few papers and drive my renters away?"

"That's as it may be," said Detective-Sergeant Church. "Have you taken anything out of the room since you found her?"

Mrs Garrity sniffed. She was a slatternly creature, like her apartment-house, antiquated and ugly. "I aint been past the door," she declared. "That is, only when I went in to see why she hadn't been out today. Nor will I, while *she's* in there!"

Dr Lucas, the district surgeon, went in as emotionlessly as though it were a patient he was going to see. But Church entered with sombre eyes. Say what you would, Death left a bit of himself in a room when he passed through. He greyed the light; he made the atmosphere musty.

He had done nothing for Jenny Thomas, the girl on the bed, either. He had blackened her features and drawn her eyes half out of her head. He had twisted her body under the blanket. She might have been pretty; it was hard to tell. The hair on the pillow was a rich brown. The arm slanting toward the floor was plump. She had been about twenty-five.

Dr Lucas had to cut the cord about her throat to loosen it. He had a way of muttering aloud everything he discovered: "Cyanosis, marked. Dead several hours. Scratches on face –"

Church stood by the bed, studying the carpetless flooring. He was a large man, growing slightly grey on the temples and more than a bit stout. His eyes, for all the grief they had witnessed, were still cheerful. He had developed leg-muscles and self-confidence in the Fourth Ward, in the days when a patrolman hadn't even a uniform, only a badge and a club and a prayer; and now he was back again in civilian clothes as a detective. For this work he received a small raise in salary and his share of snickers.

Under a table at the head of the bed he found a pair of scissors. There was blood on one blade, though the only marks on Jenny's body were the shallow scratches on her face. Near the bed he discovered a little rubble of cigar ash. It was scattered, as if the smoker had let the cigar drop here.

"Somebody," he grunted, "knows where the good cigars are. That ash is as white as bone." He hadn't seen an ash like that in six months. Crop failures in the South, and a shortage of Havanas, had brought cigar-smokers to dark days.

He asked the landlady when she had seen the girl last.

"Two or three days ago," Mrs Garrity told him. "But I heard her going in and out every day. And I'd hear her and her friends in here at night, laughing and carrying on like fools."

"Gentlemen?"

Mrs Garrity crossed her skinny arms. "Well, detective, she worked in a millinery shop. Girls that work in millinery shops don't live in up-to-date rooms like this one. I dare say some gentleman knows who paid the rent."

She probably was telling the truth, Church knew. Even a dingy, airless room in Ludlow Street was above most shop-girls, with their fifty-cents-a-day earnings. He asked: "Do you know any of her friends by name?"

"No sir. She had only one or two lately. Except there was a new one that came this morning. A ship's captain. I let *him* know this was no Sailor's Snug Harbour! Asking for *Missus* Thomas! He went in, but I dare say he didn't stay two minutes. Even Jenny drew the line."

"Did she have any visitors last night?"

"Well, yes – I heard a doctor leave her room just after the eleven-o'clock watch. 'That will fix you up, young woman,' he said. 'But don't be drinking swan gin on an empty stomach any more!' "

Church began to inventory the dead girl's possessions. When he glanced over the list, one thing surprised him. Poor, Jenny Thomas may have been; but she had possessed luxuries far above the Sixth Ward. There were a small mother-of-pearl box, a picture worked in peacock's feathers, five bottles of French perfume, a packet of China tea. On several of the articles he found an embossed gilt seal which read: "*South Seas House. New York.*"

\*      \*      \*

There was, in addition to these, a small sheaf of letters addressed to Mrs Evan Thomas, in Bloomingdale. They were all from a Captain Evan Thomas, aboard the brig *Philadelphia*, at sea. In a bottom drawer, under some clothing, he found a fold of currency. He counted it; he counted it again.

"Look here!" he said to Dr Lucas. "Two hundred and thirty-seven dollars!"

Dr Lucas had looked long on the sordid side of life. He smiled cynically at Mrs Garrity. "You say she had gentlemen friends?"

"Enough, apparently! I dare say she couldn't have made that much in a year."

Tom Church put the letters, the money, and the trinkets in a pillowslip. He made a last tour of the room. "Whenever you're ready, Doctor," he said finally.

Dr Lucas was wrapping the girl's body in a blanket. "Call a hack," he said.

They laid the bundle across the floor of the hackney-cab and started uptown.

"Funny about the tea," Church said, after a moment.

"What tea?"

"There was a package of China tea on the table. Now, where would a girl like Jenny Thomas –"

The district surgeon stared at him. "Deliver me!" he said sardonically, and turned his face to the window.

After that, Church stared out his own window and kept his own thoughts. Even a police surgeon like Lucas was inclined to sniff at scientific crime-detection. People forgot that this was 1857, that the whole nation was in an upsurge of science; man's brain had liberated his back from a thousand enslaving tasks. But when it came to law-enforcement, they were still back in the old days of watch-and-ward. If the thief was not caught with his hand in the till, the tendency was to forget about it.

But Tom Church knew that if you assembled enough molehills, you had a mountain. What about the tea and the mother-of-pearl box, for instance? What about the two hundred and thirty-seven dollars? Jenny Thomas had not been a street-walker – she had held a job; and anyway, street-walkers did not make that kind of money.

But then, he recalled, there was her husband, and yet none of the letters had mentioned enclosing any money. They were all stilted and self-conscious, the letters of a sea-captain who had no thought beyond the caprices of the weather and of his ship, and who signed himself, "*Your husb., Evan Thomas.*" The envelopes bore the dogged rubric: "Evan Thomas, Master, Brig *Philadelphia.*"

Well, this was a starting point. In the spiteful drizzle, Church left Sixth Ward station. A clerk in the harbourmaster's office opened the Arrivals ledger for him. His finger stopped at the top of the third to the last page.

"'Brig *Philadelphia*, May 7,'" he read. "'Master, Evan Thomas.' But I wouldn't wait dinner on him," he added with a grin. "She's flying the yellow flag, suspected of cholera. The last ship in from San Juan was rotten with it."

"You mean," Church said, "that no one has been ashore?"

"And won't be for forty days!"

There was no other Captain Thomas on the books. This left Church the unpleasant task of learning whether or not Thomas was still aboard ship.

He took the Staten Island ferry, and debarked at Castleton in mid-afternoon. Behind the town were the new brick pest-houses about which the citizenry was raising such a cry. Offshore stood the *Philadelphia*, sea-worn and wet, a yellow quarantine flag hanging limp from a forestay.

A grizzled lobsterman agreed to row the detective to within speaking-distance for a dollar. In a snub-nosed dory they thrust across the grey water of the bay. They approached another rowboat in their path whose owner was casting for junk. He let them pass, and then the dragnet splashed again just astern of them.

The lobsterman rested on his oars. "Far as we go, mate."

It was the distance of a long shout, but Church cupped his hands and succeeded in bringing to the rail a square-set figure in black jacket and trousers. "Sergeant Church, Metropolitan Police," he announced. "Would you be good enough to call the captain?"

"You're talking to him," the other man shouted; "but if you're from the police, the only favour you'll find here is a bucket of slops amidships. I'll talk to you when this damned yellow flag comes down!"

Church thought, *For a sea-captain, he talks like a fool.* But he said patiently: "You must understand, Captain, that the quarantine laws are for the good of the city."

The master leaned on the rail. "For the good of someone, yes," he agreed, "and I could tell you who. But there's no more cholera aboard this brig than there is in your back yard. We haven't been within two hundred miles of San Juan!"

Church had the quick warm tingle a hunting dog must experience when he flushes game. To the lobsterman, he said: "Another dollar if you'll row me closer."

The lobsterman pocketed the money. He brought the dory alongside. Close up, the master appeared to be in his forties, his face as brown and hard-looking as the leather visor of his cap. His beard was crisp and blond, and followed the line of his jaws.

"Perhaps," said Church, "we can make a trade. If your log bears you out, I'll see what's to be done toward putting you ashore. But in return I want a plain answer to a plain question."

Thomas stared down at him. "That's a fair bargain." He disappeared. The junkman, drifting close, made a great clatter by pulling in a rusty contraption resembling an old ship's-lantern.

Then the captain came back to lower, by a line, a fat volume which Church laid on the thwart.

"Now, then," he said, "why would anyone want to keep you from going ashore?"

"A little matter of supply and demand," returned the other. "If you're a cigar man, you'll know that New York hasn't a cigar worth setting fire to. I had the news in Havana, so I loaded up with all the good tobacco I could buy. But a certain gentleman has cornered what decent smoking is left in the city, and he can't afford to let me unload until he's made his profit. So it's cheaper for him to cross the proper palms with silver. For your information, his name's Hawes, of South Seas House."

"Is this guesswork?"

"No sir! I had it in a letter from my wife. His warehouse is supposed to be full of Havanas that he's selling as dear as diamonds."

Tom Church asked carefully: "Your wife lives in the city?"

Thomas nodded. "In Bloomingdale, up-island."

"If it's as you say," Church declared, "I'll speak to the Health Commission. And now, maybe you'll tell me this: how long were you ashore this morning?"

Captain Thomas did not stir. "I've been telling you I haven't been ashore since I left Cuba."

"Then how was it that a man answering to your description was asking for a Mrs Thomas in Ludlow Street?"

Thomas began to look grave. "There's something wrong, here," he said.

It put Church in a corner, but he said what he had to. "I'm sorry if I'm the first to bring you this news, Captain; but there is indeed something wrong. Your wife has been murdered. From the landlady's testimoney, it seems that you might have visited her about the time she died."

Thomas' hand passed over his face. He said falteringly: "This is – I don't quite understand, sir –"

Church repeated it. "It's very sad, Captain, and I wouldn't trouble you, except for –"

Thomas was still staring down at the dory, but he wasn't seeing him. "Will you do what you can," he asked, "about clearing my ship? I'll talk to you later. I – I don't think I can – You understand?" He vanished from the rail.

When they pulled away, the junkman was standing in the stern of his boat, trying to raise the dragnet.

It was dusk when Tom Church reached Manhattan again. The rain had cleared off, but a grey ceiling pressed down on the island, and the cobbles glistened in early gaslight. He bought hot-buttered corn from a girl, and ate as he walked.

He felt sorry for the Captain; he seemed an honest and

sincere man. But unless Jenny Thomas had had other sailor friends, he had been lying about not having been ashore.

There was time for one more small excursion tonight. In about an hour the shops of Manhattan would release their underfed pigeon-chested army of clerks and shopgirls. He might, before then, sift the place Jenny Thomas had worked, for a lead or two.

He found the Gotham Hat Works in an old frame building near South Street. A bay window infringed on the sidewalk: behind it he saw work-tables and shelves, and three women bent over half-finished work.

Mrs Emma Flynn, who operated the shop, was a bony woman with a long nose and a smudge of dark hairs on her upper lip. She was treadling a sewing-machine when the bell over the door tinkled. Two girls sat at tables, stitching breakfast-caps, and on the tilted shelves along the left wall was displayed a variety of millinery.

Tom Church held his high-crowned derby against his stomach. He introduced himself. He said: "I suppose the unfortunate news –"

Mrs Flynn said: "Yes." She continued to hold a ruffle of ribbon under the foot of the machine. "What do you want?"

"Just a bit of information," Church told her. "It may possibly save both of us some trouble. Strange as it may seem, the law requires you to answer correctly anything I may ask you relative to the death of Jenny Thomas."

Mrs Flynn laid the work aside. "Does it, now?" Her smile said he would get nothing here worth carrying away.

Church walked past the bonnets on the shelves. He picked one up and abstractedly inspected it. "What was Jenny's work, Mrs Flynn?"

"Capmaker."

"Did you know any of her friends? The men she knew?"

Mrs Flynn hesitated. "Well – I dare say she had a many, but they came and went. Right now it's Harry Burritt, from Mr Hawes'. There'll be a long face for you! He'll have to find somebody else to walk home and spend his money on!"

Church put the bonnet down again. "Hawes – would that be Hawes, of South Seas House?"

Mrs Flynn selected a spool of green ribbon, and threaded a needle. "He's the only Hawes *I* know, and he's enough! He charges for his silk as though the Emperor's own silkworms had spun it!"

"I don't suppose," Church said, "that you would have known Jenny's husband?"

The way the girls at their tables looked up told Church he had cracked a nut with meat in it. "In a way," Emma Flynn said. "He's a ship-captain. He was in this morning, looking for Jenny. I think," she added, "that he left a paper of some kind."

She found it under a pile of scraps, a wrinkled envelope addressed to Captain Thomas, with a return address in Bloomingdale. "Seems as though he couldn't find her at the old address," she said. "She was still using it for mail, though, and picking letters up there. It's almost like she was hiding from him! I gave him the new address, and he copied it down, and forgot this when he left."

Church kept the envelope. He turned, as the bell over the door jingled. A man in a brown linsey-woolsey suit and a heavy jacket came in. He carried a gunnysack over his shoulder. He was about forty-five, with a swarthy handsomeness that gin was eradicating; his hair was curly, and his eyes were dark, but bloodshot.

Looking at him, remembering him, Church knew he had his hand in a tangle of threads like a spider-web. Somewhere there was a radial point; somewhere there was a connection between them all – Hawes and Jenny Thomas and this grubby hat-shop; for the man in the door was the scavenger who had been casting his net beside the brig two hours ago, while Church talked to Captain Thomas.

"Well, Flynn!" Mrs Flynn said, "has it taken you all day to bring home such a handful as that?"

Flynn grunted, passed her and opened a door in the rear to throw the sack through. It landed on a dirt floor several steps below shop-level. He sat down, rubbed his hands together, and stared at Church.

"This gentleman," Emma Flynn told him, "is a detective, come about Jenny."

"What about Jenny?" Flynn's face did not admit that he had ever seen Tom Church before.

"Dead," Mrs Flynn said. "Murdered!"

Flynn slowly sat up. "Murdered! *Jenny?*"

"A terrible thing," said Mrs Flynn, but her eyes were wickedly bright. "She was such a pretty little chit. We shall miss her, sha'n't-we?"

There was one thing about women, thought Church: their emotions tricked them into saying things they would not have put into writing. He had a whole history, now, of jealousy and suspicion, of kisses stolen behind doors, or merely imagined by a woman who was not young and not pretty any more.

Flynn sat with his elbows on his knees, thumbnail digging at a callus; and just then the front door opened again, and a young man in a claw-hammer coat, with an unbrushed silk hat, poked his head in to say: "Pardon, ma'am. Mr Hawes says, will there be any hats tonight?"

Mrs Flynn's cheeks burned, but she kept the treadle rocking. She said: "No. Not tonight."

"But he said you promised –"

"Tell him I'm sorry! This thing of Jenny put me behind. And then there are the police to entertain – detectives, and all."

"Detectives –" The young man's eyes found Church. "Yes, I suppose there would be. Well, good evening, Mrs Flynn. I'll tell Mr Hawes."

He closed the door briskly, and his tall form passed the shop-window.

Mrs Flynn remarked dryly: "That was Burritt, Jenny's young man."

"So I judged," Church said. Presently he too started toward the door. "I'm sorry to have troubled you," he told Mrs Flynn. "But I have to bother a lot of wrong people to find the right." Then he picked up one of the bonnets from the display shelf. "Forgive my masculine ignorance, ma'am. All I truly know of millinery is what Mrs Church's bonnets cost me. But I wasn't aware that mull had been used for several years."

"When you're as busy as we are," snapped Mrs Flynn, "you can't always keep your display shelves up to the minute. All our hats are sold wholesale, anyway."

"Of course!" Church said goodnight, nodded to Mr Flynn, and went out. He was smiling to himself as he started home. *Yes ma'am*, he thought, *you doubtless keep very busy indeed. But I suspect it isn't with hats!*

In the morning he took a four-cent omnibus to 106th Street. Here commerce defiled the pure air of Harlem with the odours of Indian rubber factories, breweries and tanneries. Hawes's place appeared no grimier nor less grimy than the rest, a two-storey brick structure with a gateway at the left by which drays might enter and leave the warehouse.

Clerks were already busy, their fingers scuttling over accounts and copy-books. Behind a railing, a little army of women was packaging and labelling merchandise. Farther back was a corner walled off by waist-high wainscoting topped by windows. Church was not surprised to see, working just outside the door of this cubicle, the young man in the claw-hammer coat who had come to Flynn's about the bonnets for Mr Hawes. But he passed by him to knock at the door.

Mr Hawes was a precociously stout gentleman who left his desk to greet the visitor. He put much of his weight on a stout snakewood cane; Church could sympathize with a lame man of his avoirdupois. Mr Hawes wore a frock coat with a cream-colored waistcoat; his face was pink and pouched. When Church mentioned Captain Thomas, he slapped his thigh and went into wheezy laughter.

"Ah, poor old Thomas!" he chuckled. "Yes, I might have had something to do with the cholera story. But it's quite all right, now; I have sold my stock well. You may release him, with my best wishes!"

He balanced his cane against the desk as he sat down; Church saw it falling, and reached forward to catch it. He said, holding it an instant: "Of course you realize that charges can be pressed —"

Back of the merry little eyes was shrewdness. "I don't believe Captain Thomas will make me any trouble. You see, there is the matter of a ton of sugar he sold me one time which was so weevilly I had to let it go to a candy-maker, at a loss . . . We're old friends, Thomas and I."

He reached to open a cabinet on the desk and offer cigars. "Take several, detective. You won't find these on the market, I'll vow. A gentleman's cigar, from the Vuelta Abaja."

Church brazenly took six. He lighted one and let his taste-buds revel in the benediction of the warm smoke. Then he said: "Oh, yes – I thought these might mean something to you –" He began to take a number of articles out of his pocket which he laid before the importer.

Hawes picked up the packet of China tea. "Where did you get these?"

"In the room of Jenny Thomas, who was murdered yesterday morning."

Hawes grunted. "I heard about Jenny. A shame; such a pretty girl. You know," he said, "it's very curious about these. Generally, a retailer would have substituted his stamp for mine, or at least have added his. We never sell tea, by the way, in amounts this small. Someone packaged this from the bulk, and closed it with my seal. I am wondering if one of my clerks hasn't been making her gifts, at my expense."

Through the open door, Church watched Burritt's neck redden. "It seems possible," he remarked. "Did you know the girl?"

"She used to bring an order, occasionally, from Flynn's hat-shop."

"But you don't deal in hats yourself?"

Hawes looked at him, steadily. "I have. There's no profit in them. I don't handle any at present."

Church stood. "I think that's all, then. No, don't get up," he said. "I may visit you again, sir. Good day."

He stopped at Burritt's desk and appropriated a sheet of foolscap. He dipped a steel pen and wrote slantwise across the page: "*The Hen and Chickens, at twelve.*" He said, "Thank you," and departed, leaving the foolscap on the desk.

The Hen and Chickens was a chophouse in lower Harlem, where a man with Church's appetite could lunch well for thirteen cents, beer included. Burritt arrived a little after the hour. He took the other seat in the booth.

His skin was moist; a little colony of pimples on his chin stood out. "I don't understand this at all, sir," he declared.

Church picked up his cutlet. "Shall we be hanged for a thief or a murderer?" he asked.

Burritt gripped the edge of the table. "Sir, I would appreciate –"

Church laid down the cutlet and wiped his fingers. "Of course," he said. "My reasoning is somewhat in this direction: that, according to Mrs Flynn's testimony, you were Jenny Thomas's current lover. That many of the more valuable objects in her room came from South Seas House. It is my guess that you stole them."

Harry Burritt's amber-coloured eyes closed. His narrow chest took a shallow breath. Resolution and defiance were deserting him; when he opened his eyes again, they looked down at his clenched hands, resting on the table.

"A thief, yes," he said. "But not a murderer. Believe me!"

"Is there," Church asked him, "such a difference? A man steals to please a girl; he trades his honesty and peace of mind for her kisses. And then he finds she is already married, that he had played the fawning poodle for nothing, and for a moment the poodle becomes a mastiff, biting, snarling, killing –"

Burritt looked as though he were strangling. "I swear –"

"You needn't. I can't prove a word I'm saying. But when I take a trail, young man, I don't easily lose it."

Burritt hesitated a moment and then declared fervently: "I'll tell you all I know about her. I was in love with Jenny, yes. I met her at Mr Hawes's about six months ago. She loved to get presents, and I – I got to stealing. If I didn't bring something one week she would pout; she'd talk about the other men who wanted to marry her."

"She had others?"

"I used to see Flynn walking her home when she had

worked late. Maybe it didn't mean anything; she said it
didn't. But I've caught her in lies before. The last time I
saw her was the night before she was killed. I'd walked her
home, but she wouldn't let me come in. Tired, she said. And
then the next day I heard about it."

Church drank deeply of his beer and wiped his mouth.
"Did it ever strike you as strange," he asked, "that Mr
Hawes should handle ladies' bonnets?"

Burritt shrugged. "We handle almost anything."

Church signified, by wiping his mouth and pushing away
his plate, that the dinner and the questioning were over.
"Just remember," he said, "that I shall regard it as eminently suspicious if you change lodgings or leave the city. If
you try to run away, I'll have you in Tombs before you reach
Stryker's Bay."

Burritt was too emotionally wrung out to do more than
swallow. "All right," he said. "All right."

Tom Church was on the South Street wharf when the brig
*Philadelphia* was brought to the dock. As soon as the plank
was run out, he boarded her, to find Captain Thomas putting
a gang to work in the holds.

Thomas had a hard handshake for him. But Church said
regretfully: "It's hard lines, Captain, to have to lay by
another week. But there is some difficulty. Mr Hawes has
been properly reprimanded; but the Health Commission
thinks you should wait seven days before unloading. Saving
face, I suppose."

The Captain swore. "And a copper-bound crew eating the
profits of the trip as fast as their jaws'll wag! They should
have been paid off a week ago."

"You and the crew," said Church, "are at liberty to go
ashore when you like. You can pay the men off today." Then
he added, with a sidewise smile, "Any sugar this trip,
Captain?"

Thomas chuckled. "Ay, he told you that, did he? Well, he
was of age; and in this business a merchant wants a sharp eye
in his head."

"*Caveat emptor*," said the detective. "Well, good luck,

Captain. Oh, yes – there was this, that you left at Mrs Flynn's. You might want to keep it."

Captain Thomas was still staring at the wrinkled envelope when Church went down the gangplank.

His trade, Tom Church thought, was not unlike lobstering. You baited your trap with care, set it down on the sand as nicely as possible, but after that, you could do nothing but wait with as much patience as possible.

He did not leave the harbour district until he saw the crew of the *Philadelphia* swing down South Street to their long-awaited pleasures, to the whisky and soft arms waiting to solace and fleece them. He wandered the dusk-softened streets until night, hearing the cries of shad- and clam-vendors, the clattering progress of a tinker with his pack.

Over a glass of spruce beer he tested, in his mind, the cords he was holding. He thought of Mrs Flynn, with her out-of-date bonnets and the backward air of her shop. And her husband, with his dragnet and his dory, quietly working the waters where the big ships lay, watching and listening. And poor Harry Burritt, with the soul of a rabbit but the desires and passions of a man. And Mr Horace Hawes, with his mysterious dealings with the Flynn family.

By midnight Harlem had turned out the lights of its shops, thrown its slops into the streets and gone to bed. But in South Seas House someone still worked, the small light of a lamp just touching the windows. Church stood in a doorway across the street.

He had had five beers on the way uptown, and it was making him sleepy. He roused groggily when the church clock at Dominie Hook sounded two. It was not long after this that a solitary dray came up the street. Church made out a man on the driver's seat, and someone else who stood in back among a load of boxes.

The dray stopped before South Seas House. The one in back went to open the warehouse gate. He watched the dray move into the dark interior, and then quickly walked to the business entrance of the building and rapped. Through a window he could see Mr Hawes leave his office and limp to the front. Then he saw the big revolving pistol in his hand. Hawes was taking no chances this time of night.

The door opened a crack. Hawes squinted out.

"Who is it?" he asked.

"Detective Church. Do you realize you are being robbed?"

Hawes gasped: "What?"

"I've been watching your warehouse for two hours. Just now a dray pulled in to it. What's the matter with your watchman?"

"We'll soon see!" Hawes admitted Church and started off down the room, stopping to secure the lamp. Church had taken a locust-wood club from under his coat. They descended a short flight of stairs and followed a long gloomy hallway. They came to a turn, beyond which light gleamed under the crack of a door.

Hawes snuffed out the lamp, grunting as he stooped to place it on the floor.

After an instant the door flew open, giving Church a view of a big cluttered store-room. The dray was halted directly in front of the door. At the tail-gate, Flynn and his wife were handling a load of battered wicker boxes.

Hawes had his pistol in his hand. He was going through the door as fast as a lame man could move, and he was crying out: "You damned thieves! I'll teach you to come robbing and pilfering!"

Flynn stood befuddled in the back of the dray. Mrs Flynn's hands were upraised to receive a crate. Church had not expected quite so much speed from a fat man. He had to step out, the club swinging, to reach Hawes before the gun went off. Even so, the pistol filled the whole room with its thunder just as he cracked down on Hawes' forearm. The bullet struck the stone floor and went wailing off to finish against a wall.

Flynn jumped down from the dray. Church reached the door an instant ahead of him. He stood with his back to it. Flynn's hand went to his belt, and a knife came out. When

his arm went back, Church knew he was going to have to go
back to his Fourth Ward tactics.

The club shot out like a sword, punching Flynn in the
belly. Flynn grunted, making him throw quickly and wildly.
Church came into range, measuring the force he put into the
club-swing. A little too hard, and you had a corpse on your
hands. Not hard enough was worse. He thought, from the
sound of it, that this was just about right.

Flynn took a step forward, reached out as though to
grapple him, and collapsed.

Mrs Flynn, burly, mustached, terrified, started blindly for
the door; and with fine sagacity Church stepped aside. Let
the wagon handle the ladies, he liked to say. When he turned
back, Hawes was on his knees, groping for the gun, but Tom
Church hurried to recover it from under the dray and tuck it
in his belt. Hawes pulled himself up. In the lamplight, his
pink face was wild.

"Why did you stop me?" he demanded. "If a few of these
sneak-thieves were killed, we might have fewer robberies. A
man scrimps and saves, and then –"

"And then," said Church, "a little chit like Jenny Thomas
comes along and threatens to expose him for buying stolen
goods. I don't wonder she ended as she did!"

Hawes' face became less hysterical. His pudgy lips pressed
together. "Do I understand, sir –"

"Sit down, Mr Hawes," Church said. "That leg must
bother you considerably. A pair of scissors makes an ugly
wound."

"This is beyond me!" Hawes declared. "My leg – it's
something chronic. Are you implying that I – that Jenny –"

"I'm implying," Church said, "that you killed her, Mr
Hawes. That she knew the Flynns sold only enough hats to
keep the police from knowing that their real business was
harbour piracy. They stole from the ships and sold the cream
to you. Jenny didn't come here with orders. She came to ask
for money to keep her from going to the police. She wasn't a
nice girl, but clever, and even courageous, in a way. That last
night, when you went to her room, she realized that what you

had brought this time was really a noose, rather than money. But the best she could do was to stab you in the leg with the scissors. And then you went out, letting the landlady think you were a doctor."

Hawes desperately held his eyes. He said: "I've bought from the Flynns, yes. Tonight it was Captain Thomas's tobacco. Flynn was so sure there was no risk, with the crew all discharged. But I didn't kill the girl! Perhaps Flynn, or even his wife . . . I suppose you knew Flynn and Jenny were lovers?"

"I assumed; I didn't know. Just as I assumed that because of your limp you were the one whose blood was on the scissors, back in Jenny's room. I added to this the fact that you were clumsy with your cane, even dropping it once. And then your boot – A chronically lame man, one who walks with his foot splayed out as you do, doesn't wear his boots evenly. Yours should be badly worn on the outside: but it is worn as evenly as mine."

For a moment Hawes was silent, and then he began to nod. "I see. I see." He was perspiring, but the tension had gone out of him. This was the moment, Church well knew, when a man either broke, pleading, cajoling, or accepted what was inevitable. He watched closely as Hawes picked up one of the wicker cases and broke the wrappings.

But Hawes was merely taking a mahogany cabinet of cigars out of the package. He was saying thoughtfully:

"I – I'm sorry about Jenny, detective. But after it was started, I knew how it must end. She never intended to protect me. She meant to have all she could out of me before she told the police. It's the old story: when it comes to business, a woman seldom behaves like a gentleman."

He offered the cigars. "Havanas! It's on Captain Thomas, this time." And he smiled.

Well, it might be stolen goods, but the gesture was just as generous. Church bit the end off one and lighted it. He filled his mouth with the smoke and blew it gently at the lamp. It was as sweet as hickory; it was smooth and rich.

"Mr Hawes," he said, "you may be a poor judge of blackmailers, but you never go wrong on a cigar." But just the same, remembering Jenny Thomas, Tom Church did not dally long about producing the manacles.

# The Abolitionist

## Lynda S. Robinson

*Lynda S. Robinson is best known for her mysteries set in ancient Egypt, featuring Lord Meren, the series starting with* Murder in the Palace of Anubis *in 1994. But for the following story she brings us to events on the eve of the American Civil War. We have already encountered one story involving slaves, Clayton Emery's "If Serpents Envious", and this story reminds us again of the theme of prejudice.*

### Richmond, Virginia, June 1860

He was outnumbered.

Temple Forbes paused on the threshold of the drawing room in the Jessops' grand Federal townhouse and surveyed the family gathered for afternoon tea. Uncle Henley, Aunt Laurietta, his cousin Oram and his wife, and the spinster sister, Clemency – secessionists all. He would keep his blamed mouth shut during this visit. Nothing worse than a guest who argued with his hosts, even if they were wrong. He was only staying here to satisfy Pa, who wasn't up to travelling all the way from Texas to visit his sister.

Henley Jessop turned and saw Temple. "There he is. Temple, come meet our new daughter, Odette Moreau, now Mrs Oram Jessop."

Plastering a smile on his face, Temple bowed over the hand of cousin Oram's new wife and uttered the usual wishes for a happy future. Oram stood beside Odette, grinning proudly. Odette stood out among the black-haired Jessops, the only blond except for the stately Laurietta. She had a doll-like face, round with plump cheeks and small, red mouth, and she promptly thwarted Temple's resolution to avoid divisive conversation.

"Papa Jessop tells me you were quite a while in New York, Mr Forbes. It must have been uncomfortable being so deep in the land of abolition." The family exchanged uncomfortable looks.

"No, ma'am," Temple replied. "I was tending to matters of business and didn't have a powerful lot of time for politics and such."

He was lying. He'd talked to a lot of his friends about the recent Democratic Convention. William Lowndes Yancey and his fire-eaters had sabotaged all efforts at unity, and the party split. Now Stephen Douglas headed the northern Democrats while the southern pro-slavery faction backed John C. Breckenridge and the border states had thrown their support to John Bell of Tennessee. As the fire-eaters intended, the self-destruction of the Democrats meant victory for the Republicans and Lincoln, which would prod the southern states to leave the union. Temple wondered if anyone in the Jessop drawing room understood how a minority of fanatics had engineered the desperate political showdown that was coming. Yancey and those of his persuasion were keeping the south whipped up to a fury with their dire forecasts of the forced end of slavery.

"But surely you championed the cause of states' rights while you were there," Odette was saying.

"Well, ma'am, I don't think I would have changed any opinions, no matter how eloquently I phrased my arguments. Folks up there are real fond of the Union, and they just don't take kindly to the idea of slavery. Everybody knows that."

Oram cleared his throat. "Odette, my dear, Cousin Temple doesn't favour slavery either. Remember, he has a ranch down in Texas, and there's not much call for it there."

Eyeing him as if he'd sprouted a forked tongue and tail,

Odette murmured, "Oh, I see. Good heavens. The wilds of Texas."

"Cattle, ma'am. Lots of cattle in the hill country. The cotton plantations are farther east."

"But don't let old Temple fool you," Hezekiah said, joining them. "His folks sent him to Harvard to get educated. That's where he learned all those odd notions of his."

"What, like reading?" Temple asked with a grin. If they didn't abandon this subject, there was going to be arguing.

Aunt Laurietta saved him when she spoke from her place of honour on the settee. "Tea, everyone." She looked pointedly at the tall Negro butler, Augustus, who entered bearing a silver tea tray and the footman who followed with another bearing cake and sandwiches. Politics and abolition weren't discussed in front of Negroes.

Temple scuttled away from Odette before the lady could ask him another flammable question. Laurietta beckoned to him, and he sat beside her to help serve the tea. Augustus, a stately man in black and starched linen, glanced at him as he set his tray before his mistress. Temple winked at him. Augustus frowned, but Temple saw the cynical amusement in the butler's eyes. Laurietta, like many ladies of the southern aristocracy, could ignore most anything if it didn't fit with her notions of gentility. To Laurietta, Odette and Cousin Clemency, slaves were "servants", gentlemen never consorted with "serving women", and only disobedient or dishonest Negroes suffered the whip.

Temple was holding a cup and saucer for his aunt when he heard a door slam and footsteps pound through the reception hall. Cousin Hezekiah, the oldest Jessop son, rushed into the room, breath coming in gasps, and stumbled to a halt.

"Zachariah is speechifying again!"

The china teapot rattled, and Laurietta put it down quickly. Henley jumped to his feet, as did Oram.

"Where?" Henley asked.

"At the markets on Wall Street."

"Oh, no!" Laurietta cried.

Oram had turned red with agitation. "Not again."

"What's wrong?" Temple asked as he rose to join his uncle.

"I was going to talk to you about it," Henley said. "Zachariah came home two weeks ago. Just suddenly appeared and started preaching on the streets."

"Preaching? Zack? I thought he was reading law in Baltimore." Temple found it hard to imagine his cousin as a Bible preacher.

"Not any more," Henley replied while drawing a hand through his white hair. "Seems he met that fool William Lloyd Garrison and a bunch of other damned abolitionists. They've turned him into a madman."

Hezekiah was hovering in the doorway. "Are you coming? He's going to get himself killed for sure this time!"

"Serve him right," Oram said from his place beside Odette. "He won't listen to us any more than he did last time. I'm staying here."

"We could use your help," Henley said with a scowl at Oram. He turned back to Temple. "Zachariah has got it in his head to preach his message to 'the worst sinners', as he calls them. He won't listen to reason. Nearly got himself killed a couple of times. Been arrested and warned and threatened, and I don't know what all. He promised me he'd stop the last time I got him out of jail, and now he's stirring up trouble at the slave markets."

"Damnation," Temple muttered. Cousin Zack was the youngest Jessop, the smartest, and the most arrogant, his brothers would say. He and Temple had been at Harvard together, but they'd lost touch since Temple went back to Texas. If Zack was confronting people at the slave markets, there would be a hell of a fight. Slave owners didn't take kindly to being preached at and reminded of the essential injustice of slavery. "You go ahead, Uncle Henley. I'll meet you there."

He wasn't far behind the Jessops when he reached the Wall Street slave markets mounted on Henley's big bay stallion. The markets were low, mostly whitewashed buildings where slaves were auctioned. Holding cells lurked in the back, out of sight.

Temple found himself stuck behind a bakery wagon and had to work his way around it. Ordinarily the street was busy with traffic, but the flow carriages, pedestrians and wagons had been staunched by the cart that had been drawn sideways across the road. Zack Jessop was standing in the cart, hair wild in the southern breeze. Although he was a block away, Temple could hear his cousin clearly as he harangued his offended audience. At the same time Henley and Hezekiah were fighting their way through bystanders toward the speaker.

Zack was waving a Bible as he shouted, " 'And he that stealeth a man, and selleth him, or if he be found in his hand, he shall surely be put to death!' That is Exodus chapter 21, verse 16, gentlemen." Zack pointed at several men in the crowd. "Sinners! Evil are your deeds. You, Nathaniel Stiles, and you, Langdon Shaw, and you, Joshua Pendleton, dealers in flesh, heed the words of the Lord. 'If a man be found stealing any of his brethren of the children of Israel and maketh merchandise of him, or selleth him; then that thief shall die!' Deuteronomy 24: 7."

By now the men whom Zack had singled out had heard enough and were shouldering their way toward their tormentor. Temple heard the grumbling of the crowd increase in volume. Its mood had turned from astonishment to fury. Henley and Hezekiah were still a few yards away from the cart when Langdon Shaw and his fellow slave traders jumped into the cart. Shaw was an ox of a man in a grey frock coat and tall hat who loomed over the slight abolitionist.

"You hush up, Zack Jessop," Shaw bellowed. "Reverend Percy preaches how the Bible supports slavery in Leviticus."

Zack shook his Bible at Shaw. "Flesh peddler! 'Stand fast therefore in the liberty wherewith Christ has made us free, and be not entangled again with the yoke of bondage!' Galatians 5:1. So much for your false reverend. You can't have freedom and slavery in the same country, Shaw."

"Shut him up!" someone yelled from the listeners on the ground.

At this Temple kicked his horse, and the big stallion began

a relentless walk through the onlookers. Men jumped or stumbled out of the way. The Jessops had reached the cart and were trying to convince the slave traders to leave, when suddenly Zack jumped on the driver's seat.

"Citizens of Richmond, take a lesson from our founders! Washington hated slavery, as did Franklin and Madison and Adams! They knew slavery is a sin. They left its destruction to us. Think! We cannot speak of the rights of man, of freedom under God, while slavery exists. It is an abomination!"

"Get him!" Joshua Pendleton shouted. He lunged at Zack along with Shaw and Nathaniel Stiles.

Zack went down under their fists. The Jessops hopped onto the cart and started trying to pull the slave traders off their victim, but Stiles landed a punch on Hezekiah's jaw. Henley stumbled over someone's foot and went down beside his son. Zack cried out under the barrage of fists. Both Stiles and Pendleton started kicking. The crowd surged toward the cart, and other men jumped into the fray. Temple had seen enough. He reined in the bay and drew the Colt revolver from the holster he'd donned before he set out. Aiming at a giant oak, he fired one shot into a thick limb. The shot sent wood splinters spewing from the branch. The brawlers turned toward him, and Temple cocked the gun, aiming over the head of Langdon Shaw.

"Gentlemen, I insist that this unseemly conduct cease at once."

Those on the ground scuttled away from Temple while the slave traders gawked at him for a moment. He didn't give them time to recover from their surprise.

"Uncle Henley, Cousin Hezekiah, would you be so kind as to help Zack? I'm of a mind to take him home. He has no further business in Wall Street, I reckon."

Henley grabbed Zack by the collar and lifted him to his feet. Hezekiah hauled his brother off the cart. Zack's nose was bleeding, and he had a cut on his forehead. He could hardly walk, and he protected his ribs with one arm. Hezekiah half carried his brother to the bay. Temple holstered his revolver and helped Hezekiah push Zack into the saddle.

Retrieving his weapon, he held it so that the barrel pointed at the sky. Temple turned his horse and moved him back through the crowd. One bystander, braver or more foolhardy than the rest, snarled at them.

"We shoulda strung that troublemaker up right here."

Raising an eyebrow, Temple paused to consider the man. "Don't hold with murder. Sure glad you didn't try. I would have hated to put a bullet in anybody today. Haven't had to shoot anyone since I left San Antonio." Temple nudged his horse into a trot, leaving Wall Street behind. He felt Zack's head drop to his shoulder.

"Idiot."

"Hello, Temple." Zack slurred his words.

"Hold on. I'm taking you home. Idiot."

Zack groaned. "Slavery's evil."

"Look, Zack. Did you convince anyone back there? No. Did you do those poor Negroes who were being sold any good? No. All you did was rile up the slave traders and their customers, who will likely take out their tempers on the black folk."

"Someone has to stick up for them," Zack muttered behind Temple's back.

"Yeah, they do. But listen to me, my friend. We got to try to free the slaves peacefully."

"Never happen."

Temple turned the bay down the street on which the Jessops lived. "But we got to try, because the alternative is bloody and tragic. Isn't it enough that the planters think the North is going to destroy the South's whole way of living? Do you have to come down here and make it worse?" He pulled up at the townhouse and dismounted. Handing the reins to the Jessop groom, Temple helped Zack off the horse. The moment his feet touched the ground, his knees buckled. Temple hauled his cousin's arm over his shoulder and helped him into the house. "Blamed fool. You haven't got a subtle bone in your scrawny body."

"All true Christians know slavery's a sin," Zack mumbled.

"Really? You think so? 'Cause I wasn't sure."

"No need for sarcasm, old man. God, my head hurts."

Laurietta Jessop was waiting in the entry hall with her daughter. "Zachariah! What happened to you?" She hovered over her son, touching his bruised face. Zack gazed at his mother blearily.

"He's fine, Aunt," Temple said. "Just had a little accident."

Clemency gave a ladylike snort and pointed up the sweeping, curved staircase. "Please take him to his room. We'll attend to him directly."

"I'll send for Dr Benson," Laurietta said as she examined her son. "Zachariah's head looks like it may need stitching. I declare I don't understand you, child. I really don't."

Shaking their heads, the ladies proceeded to the pantry and warming kitchen at the back of the house where Aunt Matilda, the housekeeper, kept medical supplies. Temple learned from Augustus that Oram and his wife had gone home in disgust. Henley and Hezekiah arrived soon afterward and were swept along to be doctored. After the injured ones had been tended to, Hezekiah went home. Temple retreated to his room to clean his gun and wonder where the police had been in all the ruckus at the slave markets. Dr Benson came and went, also shaking his head.

An hour later, the mayor of Richmond and a gaggle of police officials arrived and closeted themselves with Henley. Temple kept out of it, knowing that it would take all of his uncle's powers of persuasion to keep his son out of jail. Over an hour later, Henley emerged from his study and escorted his guests out of the house. Temple was in the library off the front hall buried in a Dickens novel he'd found there. Through the library doorway he saw the mayor and his party leave. Sighing, he tried to return to his reading. He was a lover of peace and tranquillity in the home, and the ructions in the Jessop house had irritated him into a foul mood. Back home he'd built his house south of Austin on a small hill among ancient live oaks, as far away from town as he could get without being too troubled by the distance. And there wasn't anybody to cause trouble there either, for he hadn't yet succumbed to his parents' pleas to get married.

The front door opened again, and Temple saw Henley

shoot into the hall dogged by a red-faced, stocky man in a tight, cheap suit. Henley scurried around a marble-topped table, putting it between him and his pursuer.

"I'm terribly sorry for your loss, Mr Coutts." Henley hovered nervously behind the table as Coutts charged toward the table.

"Look, Mr Jessop, that boy of yours has absconded with my Nigra," Coutts growled over the marble at Henley, "and I want to know what you're going to do about it."

"Do?"

"Seems to me like you and Zachariah owe me the price of the Nigra!"

At the mention of money, Henley drew himself up to his full height and stared at his persecutor. "Are you mad? I owe you nothing. Your man could have run off by himself, and in any case, you've no proof my son has done anything wrong."

"Now see here!" Coutts' face turned a darker shade of red. "It's the middle of harvest, and I done lost my only field hand. I seen – saw Zachariah hanging around the cabins last week a preachin' and carrying on. I chased him off my land and told him not to come back or I'd take my shotgun to him. Next thing I know, my Nigra up and disappears. I can't afford to get another field hand, and half my crop is going to ruin if I don't get more help. It's all 'cause of your boy, and I mean to have satisfaction."

"I know the law, Coutts, and you must have proof that my son aided in the escape. You don't have it, or you'd have said so."

Coutts pounded his fist on the table, his face now almost purple with rage. "By God, Jessop, Zachariah is responsible, and one way or another, he's going to pay!"

Jamming his hat on his head, Coutts stomped out of the house. Temple watched Henley wipe his forehead with his handkerchief and retire to his study. The Dickens story forgotten in his lap, Temple wondered how many more people Zack had riled near to violence. Coutts appeared to be one of those men of modest origins who burned to rise to the rank of planter. He'd bought a field hand much too expensive for his means, even dressed in a suit that seemed to be his idea of a refined gentleman's outfit. Zack had riled a lot of folks who didn't take kindly to being riled. Whatever the case, this visit was turning out to be an even worse experience that he'd feared. He was going to make his excuses and leave in the morning.

Dinner was a quiet, solemn event with only the immediate family. It was a stifling evening, the air full of moisture and insects. The windows throughout the house were open to take advantage of any breeze, and a small Negro lad plied the overhead fan as the Jessops and Temple dined. Earlier Hezekiah and Oram had returned to give Henley the benefit of their opinions about what to do with Zack. Then they left again to try to placate their scandalized wives.

"He's got to leave," Hezekiah had pronounced. "You can't protect him any longer. The mayor is going to arrest and charge him again, and this time you won't be able to stop them from trying him. He's already disgraced the family, Father. Get rid of Zack before it's too late."

When Henley demurred, his eldest son lost his temper. "Damnation! You've pampered that boy since he was born. Let him have his way, let him become an irresponsible rascal while Oram and I had to conduct ourselves like perfect gentlemen. And look at the result!" Under his breath Hezekiah muttered, "And we know you love him above us all." He had stomped out of the house, but Oram was ready to take his place.

"Listen here, Father. It's not just the disgrace. Old Tobias Coutts is just a small farmer, and if he doesn't get his man back, he'll be ruined. There's no telling how many Negroes Zack has talked into absconding. And once the authorities find out, there will be no saving your favourite son. He'll be lucky if they don't hang him! And think of the scandal. Everyone will say our family has offended against propriety and decency."

The arrival of the mayor had cut short Oram's diatribe, and now Henley was morosely silent. Everyone was pre-occupied, and no one brought up the subject of the family scandal. Augustus served coffee and liquor in the drawing room after dinner, then left the Jessops and Temple to sit in silence around the dark, cold fireplace. Finally Clemency sighed and set down her cup.

"Papa, what did the mayor say? Is he going to arrest Zachariah?"

Henley, whose lower lip was swollen, hunched his shoulders and refused to look at his daughter.

Clemency pressed her thin lips together. "Hez and Oram are right. We are talked about in the most disgusting manner because of Zack. I receive horrible looks on the streets, and soon we'll be dropped from everyone's invitation list. Today's outrage is beyond endurance. If you don't separate yourself from Zack, we're ruined." When her father remained silent, Clemency jumped to her feet. "Can you say nothing? What are we to do? Zack will ruin any prospect I have of marriage. If you let him do that, I'll never forgive you!"

"Clem." Laurietta's steely voice cut through the shocked silence. "You're overwrought. Please retire to your room at once. I'm sure your cousin Temple will forgive your rudeness."

"But Mama, you know –"

"At once, Clemency."

Laurietta didn't have to raise her voice. She was one of those women whose relentless calm and assurance achieved more than many women could with their vapours and hysterics. Clemency gave her father a fulminating glance before rushing out of the room.

Feeling distinctly uncomfortable, Temple said, "I shall retire, Aunt, and give you both some privacy."

"Please stay," Laurietta replied. "Your uncle and I would like to discuss Zachariah's situation with you, my dear. You've known him for a long time, and you're not so caught up in this tangle as we are. Cool advice is what we want, and Mr Jessop respects you. Don't you, Mr Jessop."

Rousing from his stupor, Henley said, "Yes, Mrs Jessop, quite so."

"What is there to discuss?" Temple asked. "It's clear Zack can't continue as he has. He's got to go back to Maryland. He can work for abolition there."

Henley straightened up, alert at last. "He won't go!"

"We've tried to make him," Laurietta added. "Mr Jessop even put him on the train, but he got off again and hid on some farm. We've tried to talk sense into him, but it's like talking to a fence post. He just listens for a while and then starts preaching at us. He says we should free our slaves at once. It's impossible to make him see reason."

"I even gave him money," Henley said.

Laurietta shook her head. "I told you that wouldn't work."

Temple frowned at his uncle. "Do you mean you tried to bribe him into leaving?"

Henley shifted, uncomfortable in his chair. "Well, I figured I could help him set up his law office in Baltimore. Zack's going to be an excellent attorney, and he wouldn't be so far away that we couldn't visit him. But Zack said if I gave him money he'd use it to free Negroes." Henley's eyes widened at the thought. "I couldn't allow him to do that."

"We're at a loss, Temple my dear." Laurietta lifted her china cup and sipped her coffee. "You would be doing us a great service if you'd talk to him. Make him understand how he's ruining our lives. His sister is desperate. As you may know, she hasn't had much success in gaining the attention of a suitable gentleman. The poor girl continues to hope, and this scandal is driving her to distraction. And you know how resentful Hezekiah and Oram are. The situation is unbearable."

"Besides," Henley said, giving his wife a sheepish glance, "I – I gave the mayor my word that Zachariah would leave tomorrow morning. Temple, my boy, could you possibly take him back to Texas with you? Like you said, there are fewer Negroes where you are. He can do less harm among the Indians and Spaniards."

That's how Temple found himself mounting the stairs on his way to Zack's sick room. "Should never have stopped here. Shoulda gone right to Norfolk and sailed for Galveston."

Outside Zack's door Temple met Aunt Matilda, who bore a tray with fresh bandages and bottle liniment. Matilda was a fixture in the Jessop household. Her mother and grand-mother had been with the family before her, and Matilda's three sons and her daughter all remained with the Jessops as well. A tall woman with a wide streak of practicality, Matilda was the one person to whom everyone came for comfort and advice in troubled times. Temple wondered what she made of Zachariah's abolitionist sentiments. But then, he always figured you couldn't tell what a slave was really feeling 'cause they weren't in any position to give their real opinion. If they were smart, they learned real fast not to let on to white folks what they were thinking.

"I'll take that tray for you, Aunt Matilda."

"Don't be foolish, child. I can carry it. I ain't that old."

Indeed, like all her family, Matilda was long-limbed and possessed of a hearty strength that carried her through long work hours and tasks requiring the strength of a man. Temple opened the door for her, and followed her into the sickroom. Zack was propped up in bed as they entered. He was in the act of handing something to a young footman, who pocketed the object, bowed and left. Matilda glared at the young Negro as she set her tray down beside the bed.

"No need to give that boy any extra, Mister Zack. He just spend it on fripperies for a little gal down the road. She don't need no more from my Benjamin. I don't approve of fripp-eries."

"It wasn't for that, Aunt Matilda." Zack winced at she began removing the bandages wrapped around his head.

"You get on out, Benjamin." Aunt Matilda pointed at the door. "And tell brother Rawley I said you boys ain't to come up here an' pester Master Zachariah."

"Yessum." Benjamin backed out of the room with speed as his mother continued to grumble.

"Them boys get into mischief, Mister Zachariah. Can't be having 'em misbehave. They gettin' too big for that. Benja-min think he a man 'cause he's seventeen. Lord help me."

Temple found a chair and drew it up beside the bed as Matilda's complaints faded. "How are you feeling, Zack?"

"Like devils are pounding my skull. If you've come to convince me to give up my abolition talks, spare me."

"I'm not gonna try to convince you of anything," Temple said. "It appears to me that neither side is listening to the other anyway. You can't persuade somebody who isn't even listening. Seems you ought to have realized that by now." Temple held up his hand. "Now, don't start arguing. It'll just make your head hurt."

"I'm right!" Zack snapped. Aunt Matilda placed a new bandage over the stitched cut on his forehead, and he gasped. "Ow! Please Aunt Matilda."

"Hush up."

Temple sighed. "Look. I know you're right. Aunt Matilda knows you're right."

"Don't you be haulin' me into this. I ain't sayin' nothin' 'bout no abolition."

"Sorry," Temple said, giving his cousin a hard stare. "Anyway, Zack, you're right, but it doesn't matter 'cause you're leaving tomorrow with me. You're coming to Texas for a visit."

Zack sat up. "What? Ouch!" He pressed his fingers to his temples, but Aunt Matilda knocked them out of her way as she wound a bandage around his head. "I'm not going to Texas."

"You're going because the mayor and a battalion of policemen are coming to see that you leave Richmond by ten o'clock. If you're still here, they're going to lock you up. If they put you on trial, you know what kind of verdict you'll get."

Zack shoved back the bed covers. "I'm getting out of here."

Aunt Matilda stepped back as he swung his legs around and tried to stand. Temple was on his feet as his cousin started to sway, but Matilda pushed his shoulder, and Zack toppled back into bed.

"You ain't goin' nowhere, Mister Zack. Not tonight. Mister Temple might even have ta carry you out o' here in the mornin'."

"I'm not going," Zack muttered as Temple threw the covers back over his legs.

"You is too," Matilda said. "Now I'm goin' ta bring you a

cup of chamomile tea to help you sleep. You stay in bed and don't be messin' with them bandages." She stalked out of the bedroom without another word.

Temple was on his way out as well. "Get some rest, Zack. We're leaving in the morning." He shut the door before his cousin could protest.

He went downstairs to tell his aunt and uncle that Zack would be on his way to Texas early the next morning. He was on the threshold of the drawing room when Clemency rushed past him in furious tears. Temple watched her stomp upstairs, then delivered his message and retired for the night before anyone else made a scene. He was lucky, for as he gained the second floor, Hezekiah, Oram and their wives arrived with grim, determined looks on their faces. Temple pitied Henley and Laurietta, but not enough to go back downstairs and listen to more arguing.

It was only ten o'clock, but he was exhausted from all the scenes and conniption fits. Opening all the windows in his room, Temple got ready for bed. It was too hot for covers, so he lay down on top of them and waited for the night breeze to cool his body. He drifted off to sleep with the sound of waving live oak branches and the scent of azaleas and magnolias.

It was still dark when Temple awoke to the sound of footsteps rushing back and forth in the hall outside his room. He peeked outside to see Aunt Laurietta in her dressing gown hurrying toward Zack's room with Aunt Matilda close behind. At the door Henley and Augustus waited, both gazing anxiously inside. Dressing quickly, Temple joined them.

"Something wrong with Zack?"

Henley nodded. "I fear that head wound was more severe than we thought. Augustus fetched Doctor Benson."

Beyond his uncle Temple glimpsed Zack in his bed groaning. The smell of vomit wafted out of the room as the doctor examined his patient's pupils.

"How long has he been like this?" Temple asked

"Aunt Matilda says he rang for her a little after midnight." Henley looked at his pocket watch. "It's near five, and the doctor says he's getting worse. Says it sometimes happens this way with those who've been in a fight. They seem all right, then suddenly take a turn for the worse."

Night passed into day with no improvement. Temple and Henley met the mayor's delegation and let them know that there was no possibility of moving Zack. They went away more irritated than sympathetic, but at least they promised to wait until the doctor said his patient was well enough to travel before they tried to eject Zack from the city.

Temple saw little of his aunt or Clemency that day. They and Aunt Matilda took turns nursing Zack, but as the hours went by, he got worse. By dinner time the whole family had gathered at the house again, hoping for some improvement. That evening Temple went to the sickroom, having convinced Laurietta to allow him to sit with his cousin while she rested. In spite of the doctor's care, Zachariah was unconscious. Temple was talking to the physician when his cousin seemed to pass into some kind of fit, then suddenly lay still. The doctor bent over him, listening with his stethoscope.

"Doc?"

Benson straightened, his face expressionless. "Temple, would you please fetch the family. Quickly."

"Aw, Doc . . ." Temple looked down at his cousin's pale face in disbelief. Zack couldn't be dying.

"At once, please, Temple."

Zachariah Jessop died shortly after eight o'clock that evening. Stunned, the family had trouble absorbing the fact that Zack was gone. Laurietta refused to leave her son at all, and Henley wouldn't leave his wife alone. The rest of the family wandered downstairs, dazed and silent, and Temple followed them. Gathering in the library, they sat quietly while Augustus served brandy. Temple downed his in one gulp and immediately regretted it. As he gasped, a long, frightening scream came from upstairs. Aunt Laurietta had finally come out of her daze. The sound of her grief echoed through the old house. Clemency burst into tears and rushed out of the room. Hezekiah lowered his face to his hands, and his wife pressed a handkerchief to her lips as she patted his arm.

Oram stood abruptly. "It's God's judgment."

"Indeed," his wife said with a sniffle into her lace handkerchief.

Hez lifted his head, scowling. "Shut up, Oram."

"Well, it is!" Oram replied. Laurietta's screams cut off what he was going to say next.

Temple jumped in before the two could go at it again. "Say, Oram. Your wife doesn't look too well. This has been too much for a delicate lady like her."

Flattered that Temple had recognized her fragility, Odette nodded and fanned herself with her handkerchief.

"Come, my dear," Oram said. "I'll take you home."

On the third morning after his death Zachariah Jessop was burried after a short service in the First Methodist Church. The family held a reception after the burial according to custom, but few of their acquaintance attended. Zack had horrified too many people in his last weeks on earth. Temple was standing next to an open window in the drawing room, having done his duty by visiting with the minister and a couple of distant relatives who'd come into town for the funeral. He looked out into the front garden in hopes of a breeze. The humid heat was making him perspire, and his wet hair was clinging to his scalp.

He noticed Dr Benson, Henley and the mayor huddled together by a pink oleander bush. Voices rose, but he couldn't make out what was said. Finally the mayor stalked off to find his carriage. Dr Benson was shaking his head at what Henley was saying, then, after a few rapid sentences from Henley, he nodded slowly.

Temple closed his eyes, wondering how long he would have to wait before he could leave without causing offense. Zack had been a lively, amusing friend, intelligent and easygoing. At school he'd put on a front of bravado, but he'd been compassionate and shared intensely in the feelings of others. Temple was beginning to feel guilty for not having supported his cousin's efforts, but logic said that Zack's methods had done more harm than good. But Temple could have persuaded him to use more caution. He should have given him better ideas, clandestine ways to help Negroes escape slavery. Yet something in Zack had insisted on confrontation with his white peers. Sighing, Temple turned from the window to find Henley Jessop approaching.

"A private word, if you would, Temple."

They went outside and stood under an ancient magnolia in the front garden. Henley glanced around as if afraid someone might be near enough to overhear.

"My boy, your aunt is convinced that Zachariah's death wasn't natural."

Furrowing his brow, Temple said, "The doctor said it was his head, an injury to the brain."

"Well, as to that, Dr Benson admits that the symptoms were ambiguous. Many things can cause nausea, fits and a coma. But since Zack had an head injury, he felt that was the most likely cause. Mrs Jessop refuses to accept his decision, however. She says the wound wasn't deep enough. Dr Benson says that without cutting open Zack's skull . . ." Henley wiped damp palms on his pants. "The very thought makes me ill. My poor boy. And you know how hard it is to get Mrs Jessop to leave Zachariah's room. She won't let Aunt Matilda and the maids clean it. She insists it must remain as it was when he died, as a memorial, which would be fitting if she'd allow it to be cleaned, but . . ."

Temple put his hand on Henley's shoulder while the man fought back tears. "Look, Uncle Henley. There's no need for you and Aunt Laurietta to suffer like this. If you want, I'll look into things, just to satisfy her that nothing else went wrong. Once she sees that every possibility has been taken into account, Aunt Laurietta will be able to accept Zack's death."

"It would be a blessing. Thank you, my boy."

After most of the guests left, Temple went upstairs and found Aunt Laurietta in Zack's room. She was sitting in an armchair holding the torn coat his cousin had been wearing at the slave markets. Making no sign that she'd noticed Temple, she put a sleeve to her cheek and rocked back and forth.

"Aunt, I've come to look into what happened to Zack."

Without looking at him she said, "Oh, that's good. Please go on."

Temple thought about offering to send for coffee or tea, but decided Laurietta would refuse. He might as well look around. The main thing was to be seen examining the room thoroughly so that she would be satisfied. Zack's bedroom remained as it had been after the mortuary assistants had removed the body. The bedclothes were disarranged, chamber pots remained beneath the bed, some still full. A bedside table bore medicine bottles, papers once filled with powders, and several glasses and cups. Used bandages had been dropped on the carpet. A small tray bearing a teapot, cup and saucer sat on a bureau, and another had been put on the floor beside the door, ready for removal. The room was growing warm, and Temple went to the window. It was unlocked, and he raised it easily to let in cooler air.

Returning to the bedside table, he picked up a powder packet and sniffed it. It was a harmless mixture used to settle the stomach. One of the bottles contained rosewater, while the other held liniment. The glasses had once contained water, the cups bore the dregs of coffee. Temple was careful to examine and sniff each container so that Laurietta would be satisfied. He glanced around the disordered room, his heart heavy with the knowledge that Zack was never coming back to it. He picked up the empty medicine packets and the bottle of liniment. She didn't seem to notice what he was doing until he went to the tray on the floor, placed the items beside the teapot and lifted the whole thing.

"Please don't remove anything," she snapped.

"Now, Aunt Laurietta, these things don't belong here, and you know Zack liked his room neat. He wouldn't like to see it in this state."

Hugging the coat closer, Laurietta regarded him for a moment, then nodded her consent. Temple left with the tray, leaving the door open to facilitate a breeze through the stuffy room. Immediately a gentle wind came up the stairs and wafted past him. An acrid odour reached him, and he sniffed. It was coming from the porcelain cup on the tray. The dregs of some concoction had thickened in the cup. The smell was strange, bitter and more like someone had steeped tree leaves. There was a hint of black tea to the scent as well.

Ordinarily Temple would have thought nothing of a home remedy, for every family had a collection of them, old tried concoctions that had gotten its members through generations of illness. But this stuff was different. It didn't smell like any remedy his mother had ever employed. Still, he could have missed some seldom-used mixture.

On an impulse, Temple set the tray down on a table that stood beside Zack's door and returned for the one on the bureau. As he passed his aunt, he stopped.

"Aunt Laurietta, may I have your key to the medicine cabinet?"

Giving him a dazed look, Laurietta pulled a ring of keys from her pocket and removed one. Handing it to him, she resumed her silent rocking.

He picked up the second tray and left. Outside, he sniffed the contents of the second cup, which was almost full, and smelled of chamomile and spices. Leaving this tray on the floor in the hall, Temple retrieved the first tray and went down the back stairs to the warming kitchen.

The main kitchen was across the back garden, separate from the house to guard against fires, but the smaller one in the house served as a preparation area. In it were various warmers, large tables, and storage areas for kitchen linens, china and serving pieces. The servants were busy cleaning up and putting away food in pantries, and Temple found Aunt Matilda directing two maids who were washing the Jessop china.

"Aunt Matilda, do you know what this stuff is?" Temple set the tray down on a table and held out the cup.

Matilda looked at it, then sniffed. "Pheew! No, sir. What you put in there?"

"I didn't put anything in it. I got it from Zack's room."

"Must be some medicine the doctor gave that poor boy," Matilda said sadly. "Just leave it be, Mister Temple. The gals will wash it up real good."

Temple had plucked the lid from the teapot and was eyeing the sludge inside. "There's more in here. No, Aunt Matilda. I'll take the pot and the cup. I'm curious about what this is."

"Don't you go breaking Miz Jessop's fine pot there."
Matilda reached for the vessel, but Temple held it away
from her.

"Never mind. Give me a jar." Temple quickly transferred
the contents into the jam jar Matilda fetched, and screwed
the lid on. By now, everyone in the warming kitchen was
watching. Temple glanced around at the silent, black faces.
"Nothing is wrong. I'm just curious about this medicine."

The servants resumed their work, and Temple strolled
over to a tall cabinet set against one of the walls. In an
unlocked lower shelf were homemade headache remedies,
smelling salts, and other mild remedies. Opening the top
door with a key, he carefully examined his aunt's store of
more potent medicines. He found the usual belladonna,
tincture of opium, calomel, arsenic, some turpentine and
aconite. He sniffed each, even though he was sure he wasn't
looking for something that would be found in the cabinet. He
was right.

Ignoring the curious glances of the slaves, Temple locked
the cabinet and left the warming kitchen by the door to the
garden. Before him lay beds of roses, late columbines,
lavender and rosemary. There must have been abundant
rain this season, for the azalea bushes and the old crape
myrtle trees that surrounded the kitchen were heavy with
flowers. Inside, Temple asked Cook what the mysterious
concoction was, but neither she nor her assistants could
identify it.

Temple thanked Cook and wandered outside to lean
against the crape myrtle. He raised the jar and stared at
the mysterious brown mess. Maybe he was being overly
suspicious. Aunt Laurietta's worries were making him imagine things. Dr Benson probably had given this stuff to Zack.
Perhaps the doctor was still here.

He was in luck. He caught the physician as he was getting
into his carriage out front, and submitted the jar for inspection.

"Good Lord, what is that stuff?"

"Don't know. Nobody does."

The doctor sniffed again and frowned. "There's some

kind of plant mixture in here, but it's nothing I've ever come across." Benson handed the jar back slowly, and the two men exchanged brooding looks. "Say, Temple, I don't like this . . ."

"Uh-huh. I know."

"Perhaps I should —"

"No, Doc. I'll look into it. Nobody in this town is going to want to deal with any suspicions about Zachariah's death. Not the mayor or the police, or anyone in authority. Don't you be getting on the wrong side of folks by stirring things up. You do that and you could ruin yourself. Let me handle it. If there's something wrong, I'll find it. Then we can figure out what to do."

"Very well. Please let me know if I can be of help."

"Thanks, Doc."

Since there wouldn't be a reason to worry if the mixture wasn't harmful, Temple's next move was to feed it to a rat. He performed his experiment alone, behind the stable where he'd found the rat. The rat went into violent spasms and died immediately.

Temple crouched beside the carcass under a magnolia tree. "Aw, Zack." His eyes smarted with tears, but he started cussing to prevent them from falling. The cussing released anger he'd hidden from himself and that had been building since he found the poison. He remained under the magnolia tree for a long time before he went back to the house.

Summoning his nerve, Temple took the poison to Henley and explained what he'd done. Looking grim, Mr Jessop gave him permission to search for the source of the poison. It took Temple the rest of the day to go through the house and service buildings. The only person to object was Clemency, but Temple was in no mood for ladylike modesty, and he went through her room anyway. He found nothing suspicious.

He also pestered Clemency until she gave him a tour of the herb garden behind the kitchen and explained the uses for each plant.

"You're wasting your time," Clemency said. "We don't

grow nightshade or monkshood or hemlock, Temple. These are cooking herbs."

"What about the plants in the large garden?"

"Really, Temple, don't you think someone would notice if you tried to feed them mashed rose leaves?"

"Not if you'd already had a lot of medicine to begin with. Aunt Matilda gave Zack chamomile tea."

Clemency snorted and left him in the herb garden. The sun was casting long shadows and golden light by the time he finished looking at all the bedding plants. The heat of the day was just fading, and Temple sought refuge on a bench under the magnolia tree. He'd left the jar of poison in Henley's keeping. It was locked in a deep drawer in his uncle's desk in the library. Temple propped his forearms on his knees and watched a blue jay sweep across the garden. The scent of roses reached him. Mashed roses indeed. The poison could have come from anywhere, not necessarily the plants around the Jessop house.

He seemed to be at an impasse. Someone had given Zack poison, and the most likely person to have done it was a member of the household. Temple couldn't imagine anyone in the family doing such a thing, and certainly the slaves had no reason to kill an abolitionist. He could see Tobias Coutts wanting to do away with Zack, perhaps even one of the slave traders. But would they have gone to the trouble of sneaking into the house and administering poison? Perhaps, if they wished the death to seem natural. Some time during the night, someone had slipped the stuff into that teapot. He'd asked who had brought it, but no one remembered. Zack's sudden illness had confused everyone. Aunt Matilda said most likely it was one of the housemaids. She'd seen the tray resting on the table beside the bedroom door the evening before Zack died, and early the next morning it had been in the room. In between, someone had brought it in to Zack.

Temple realized that lots of people had gone in and out of Zack's room, so anyone might have slipped the poison into the pot. Come to think of it, he supposed an outsider could have come up the outside stairs, walked along the veranda and slipped through the open window in Zack's room. If he'd waited until everyone was asleep, he could have slipped the mixture into the teapot in darkness. He might even have awoken his victim and fed the stuff to him, pretending to be Dr Benson or Henley, or one of the brothers.

"Mighty unlikely," Temple said to himself. He could see Tobias Coutts taking a bullwhip to Zack, but not sneaking around with poison. But how could he know for sure? Those slave traders had been furious enough to try to beat Zack to death, so maybe one of them decided to get rid his tormentor for good. There was no help for it. He would have to visit Coutts and the traders and see if he could weasel out of them where they were when Zack got sick. He didn't hold much hope of success, because even the dimmest of them would have enough sense to claim that he was home in bed. Temple was getting to his feet when Clemency came out of the house and marched over to him.

"Have you finished prying into everyone's affairs?" she asked. Her normally pale skin looked paper white against the black bombazine of her mourning gown.

"Now, Cousin Clem. Your pa asked me to look into things."

"It's absurd! No one killed Zachariah. It was the head wound that did him in."

"I don't think —"

"Indeed," Clem snapped. "You don't think. If you continue to root around and ask offensive questions, you'll cause talk. I'm sure the servants have already gossiped about your suspicions to the neighbours' help." Clemency's voice rose. "Haven't I suffered enough what with Zack causing a scandal and then dying? Now I'm stuck in black for months and months, and I won't be able to have a season in Washington like Mama promised."

She stopped, having run out of breath, and glared at Temple.

"Hellfire, Clem. I never realized what a selfish little ninny you are."

Clemency narrowed her eyes and poked him with a forefinger. "It's all right for you to talk, Temple Forbes. You have a place in the world. If I don't get a husband, I have no place. There's no choice for me. You hear? You had a choice." Clem sneered at him. "Let me see. Shall I be a planter, a lawyer, a merchant? No, I think I'll be a rancher. Good for you. But how many choices do I have? One – to get married. And nothing is going to stop me from doing it!"

Whirling around in a cloud of black skirts, Clem stalked back to the house. His mouth open, Temple watched her leave. His cousin seemed possessed, as fanatical about getting herself married as Zack had been about abolition. Not having a beau must be driving her crazy.

"How crazy?" he muttered. Glancing around, Temple found that the sun had almost set. Time to get ready for dinner.

Early the next morning Temple rode west of town several miles until he came to the Coutts farm. The big house was a ramshackle clapboard affair with a front porch, a poor relation to the grand, classically inspired plantation houses of more fortunate Virginians. Temple knocked on the front door, but there was no answer. He glanced around at the well and the sparse lawn. To his left lay a fenced chicken house, but no chickens pecked in the dirt outside. In fact, the whole place was eerily silent.

Leaving his horse tethered in front, he strode around back to the barn. The doors were closed, but not barred. Temple shoved one aside and entered into darkness. There were no animals inside; the cows must have been let out to graze.

"Hello?"

Silence reigned, and nothing moved. There was hay in the loft, and wooden storage boxes. Beams of sunlight shone through a high window. Temple walked to the ladder up to the loft and paused to see if he could hear anything, but there was nothing to hear. He'd never heard such silence on a farm. It was beginning to make him edgy. No chickens, cows, horses, not even a dog. He was about to return to the house when he heard a faint squeak. Turning sharply, Temple searched the darkness beyond the ladder. He wished now he'd brought his gun, but there was no help for it. He edged into the shadows and stopped to give his eyes a chance to adjust. There it was again, a faint but unmistakable squeak. Then he saw it. The body hung from a rope thrown over the rafters and was swinging gently.

"Damnation!" Temple rushed to it and tried to lift it to relieve the weight on the neck, but he quickly realized that it was too late.

He struck a match and stepped back. The unsteady light revealed the swollen features of Tobias Coutts, his neck snapped. The beam from which he'd leaped rested far above Temple's head. A quick inspection of the area around the body revealed no traces of anyone but Coutts, and it seemed obvious that the man had done away with himself. Yet there was no note from him. Temple left the barn and shut its doors, then went back to the house. This time he tried the door, but it wouldn't open. He looked inside through a window and saw a cold hearth, rough wooden chairs and a table. There was no sign that Coutts had left a note.

It took him several hours to report to the authorities and make a statement to their satisfaction. By the time he finished it was well after closing time at the slave markets, and he was starving. Temple went back to the Jessop house, scrounged something to eat from Cook and then joined the family for lemonade in the garden. He took Henley aside and told him about Tobias Coutts.

"Dear God. The bastard killed my Zachariah and then himself." Henley sank to a chair beside a bed of roses. "Dear God."

"Now, Uncle Henley, I'm not sure that's what happened."

"Of course that's what happened. He hated my son and killed him. Then he was overcome with guilt and did away with himself." Henley kept shaking his head over and over.

"It looked like he was selling everything he had," Temple said. "Maybe he just couldn't face ruination."

"And he wanted to take Zack with him."

"Maybe."

The two of them contemplated the idea while they watched the family. Laurietta, Clemency and Odette were cutting flowers. Ensconced on a quilt beneath an oak tree,

Hezekiah read aloud to his wife and Oram from the Richmond newspapers. Temple could hear a scathing condemnation of Abraham Lincoln. Old Hez never read proRepublican articles. Beyond the oak tree and a border of oleanders the gardener was trimming bushes. Smoke rose from the kitchen where dinner was being prepared.

"Joshua Pendleton and Langdon Shaw came by this afternoon to pay a condolence call," Henley said. "Of course, they weren't really sorry Zachariah was dead."

"I'm going to talk to them tomorrow."

Henley left his chair and went over to the group on the quilt. Temple seated himself in the vacant chair as his uncle told the family about Tobias Coutts. Soon the ladies left their flower cutting and joined them. Temple was deep in thought, wondering if the farmer's death was connected to Zack's. A shadow fell over him, and he looked up to see Clemency standing before him with a basket of roses and azaleas. The perfume of the blossoms was heavy in the warm air.

"Well, Temple. Looks like all your interfering was useless. Tobias Coutts killed my brother." Clem's pale eyebrows were arched, and she pressed her thin lips together.

"I'm not so sure," Temple said as he rose and offered his cousin the chair. The scent from her basket grew stronger, and his gaze fixed on it.

Shaking her head, Clemency went on. "You're just mad because you don't get to snoop around any more. Hez said you'd probably be leaving soon. Why don't you go tomorrow?"

"Now, Clem, that's not nice, trying to push a fella out of the house he was invited to stay in." Temple took her basket and toyed with a rose. "Besides, I'm not done inquiring into things yet."

Odette and Hezekiah joined them in time to hear Temple.

"Not done?" Odette said. "If you don't quit prying, the whole town will discover what happened to Cousin Zachariah."

Hezekiah stuck his hands in his pockets and frowned. "She's right, Temple. Justice has been done, after a fashion. There's no sense in exposing the family to ugly gossip."

"If the truth gets out, my future is doomed, and I shall die of shame!" Clemency fled, leaving everyone embarrassed at her outburst.

The rest of the family was heading his way, so Temple excused himself quickly and retreated to his room, carrying the basket with him. He set it on the bed and lifted first one rose and then another, smelling each blossom. Once all the roses were out of the basket, he sniffed again. This time he picked up a few crushed leaves that had fallen beneath the azalea branches that remained in the basket. Holding the leaves to his nose, he inhaled, swore and dropped them. Then he began to pace. He had to think. Who would have thought about azaleas? Pretty, pink, innocent, they were all over the south. They'd been right in front of him the whole time, only he had been looking for a plant, not a bush.

"Azalea leaves, damn it to hell."

Now that he knew the source of the poison, Temple spent the remaining time before dinner trying to sort out what else he knew about Zack's death. It wasn't much, and he was afraid whoever killed his cousin was going to get away with it. The thought sent him into a black, foul mood that lifted only when Aunt Laurietta sent a maid up with a dinner tray and a note. It said that she thought he would better enjoy his meal away from her anxious and contentious family. Silently thanking his aunt, he ate his meal in peace.

Although he was spared the ordeal of facing his cousins' ire, Temple remained sleepless far into the night. He went over and over the events of the last few days – hauling Zack away from the slave market, suddenly finding his cousin deathly ill, the family rushing in and out of the sickroom. The only people who hadn't gone near Zack were Odette and Hez's wife. The parents were hardly under suspicion, but Temple wasn't so sure about Oram or Hezekiah. Like his wife, Oram was extremely fond of social acceptance and had a morbid fear of appearing unusual. Clemency was even worse with her extreme fear of spinsterhood. Hezekiah had always been jealous of Zack, and his antipathy toward his younger brother had increased the more Henley tried to rescue his youngest son from his follies. The fact that his father had done everything he could for Zack in spite of his scandalous conduct had only fed Hez's anger. Could he believe that Hez or Clem would kill Zack? Then there were the outsiders, Coutts, Pendleton and Shaw. Temple still thought it unlikely that any of them would have done away with his cousin.

Temple finally fell asleep contemplating his next course of action. He would go over the house and garden looking for traces of the azalea preparation. Then he'd go and talk to the slave traders, but he didn't think that would do much good. The answer to this miserable puzzle was somewhere close by. Temple suspected he'd missed something important in spite of his discovery of the azalea poison. But no matter how hard he tried, he couldn't think what that might be.

He dreamed that Zack was standing at the foot of the bed preaching at him. Then Uncle Henley and Aunt Laurietta appeared, pleading, scolding, begging him to do something. Unable to bear the torment, he rose from the bed and floated out the window, hiding behind an oleander bush while everyone tried to find him. The slaves joined in the hunt, and suddenly Augustus turned and pointed at the oleander.

"There he be, Mister Hez!"

Possessed with a strange and unreasoning fear, Temple watched the family and slaves alike come running for him. Suddenly he knew he had to get away. He'd hide in the kitchen! Temple woke abruptly to find that he'd somehow jumped out of bed. He stumbled and dropped back onto the bed, gasping for air. He was perspiring, and his hands were shaking. Why? He sat still, recalling the images that had forced him from sleep.

"Oh. Oh, Lord Almighty." He wiped his forehead with the back of his hand as he finally realized what his mind had been chewing on for days. "Oh, no."

A few minutes later Temple had washed and dressed and was moving quietly through the dark house. He descended the stairs and paused as he noticed that a stiff wind was blowing through the open windows in the drawing room. The white, frothy curtains billowed and danced. The whole house had cooled down, a welcome relief from the constant

heat. Closing his eyes for a moment, Temple turned his face
to the breeze and heard a faint sound. Turning quickly, he
searched the black shadows. He decided the noise had come
from the warming kitchen.

He was grateful for the carpet that ran down the long hall
toward the back of the house. It enabled him to slip quietly
up to the door to the warming kitchen. He listened for a
moment, then opened the door a crack. The place was empty.
Temple went in and glanced around, noting that here the
windows had been left open too. He was going to leave when
he spotted the door to Laurietta's medicine cabinet. It was
hanging ajar. Drawing closer, Temple could see in the dim
moonlight that the lock had been forced. He looked inside,
one of the bottles was missing, but it was too dark to see
which one.

A creaking sound drew him across the warming kitchen
and through a side door. A short passage led to a bedroom,
and the door there wasn't shut and was swinging in the
breeze. Temple shook his head, dreading what he would find
beyond that door. He gave it a push and stepped into the
room.

"What did you take?" he asked

"Belladonna and some other things."

Temple glanced down at the floor and saw a medicine
bottle.

"I'll get the doc –"

"Too late. No use."

Drawing closer, he felt his heart nearly break. Aunt
Matilda was fully dressed and laying atop her narrow bed,
hands folded across her chest. She was watching him calmly
by the light of a candle beside her bed. He sat on a stool next
to her.

"Why did you do it?" he asked quietly.

"You was goin' ta figure it out soon. I knew the Lord
would send someone to make a reckoning. I just didn't know
it would be you, child. How you find out it was me?"

"This evening I smelled the azalea cuttings in Miss
Clemency's basket and realized they were the source of
the poison. But that got me no closer to figuring out who

killed Zack. Until I finally realized there were plenty of more efficient poisons than azalea for the killer to use. Unless the killer didn't have access to them. The only people who couldn't get hold of something from an apothecary would be a slave. It's illegal for slaves to have poisons. I wasn't sure it was you until I came downstairs and found . . ."

"You a smart boy, Mister Temple."

"But why, Aunt Matilda?"

"That Zachariah was gonna get my boys to run away. Can't have my boys run off and get caught by the patrollers, maybe get kilt. Patrollers chasin' my babies, and them dogs tearing at 'em. What happens when they's caught? Whipped to the bone. Whipped to the bone. And Master Zachariah wouldn't listen to me when I tole him to stop giving my boys money so's they could sneak off." Matilda's words were beginning to slur. "Keep my fam'ly together. Fought my whole life to keep 'em with me. Not like when I got sold away. Jus' a little girl. Sold away from my mamma and papa. Cried 'til there weren't no more tears." Matilda's eyes closed.

"Oh, Aunt Matilda, you should have gone to Mr Jessop."

"He never did no good when it came to Master Zack. Only way to be sure. Keep my boys safe 'til freedom come. Ain't long now. The Lord will see us free. He gonna forgive this sinner. Ain't he?"

"Yes, he will," Temple said. Aunt Matilda smiled and took a deep sighing breath. It had been no more than a few minutes, but Temple was sure she was now in a deep sleep from which she would never awaken.

He was never sure how long he sat beside Matilda before he discovered she was no longer breathing, but eventually he left the room and closed the door. He went back to his own room and undressed. He lay on the bed, eyes open, staring at the ceiling.

In the morning someone would discover Aunt Matilda, and there would be shock and confusion again. He hoped no one would connect her death with Zack's. Knowing the Jessops, Temple doubted if they would inquire too closely into the matter. If he told the truth, he would only make things harder for the other slaves by sowing distrust between them and the Jessops. Henley might panic and sell them. The Jessop slaves had lived in Virginia all their lives. It was their home.

What a horror. To have to choose between murder and losing one's children. Sinful, that a good woman like Matilda should be placed in a position like that. Slavery did that. It corrupted and destroyed.

"I'm going back to the ranch," he muttered. If he pushed it, he could be home in a little over two weeks.

Running away wouldn't do much good, though. The election was coming up, and with it a showdown between north and south. And then slavery would do its work again – corrupt and destroy – only this time it would be a nation.

# Poisoned with Politeness

## Gillian Linscott

*Gillian Linscott is the author of the much applauded series featuring suffragette and amateur sleuth, Nell Bray, which began with* Sister Beneath the Sheet *(1991). The eighth book in that series,* Absent Friends *(1999), won both the Ellis Peters Award and the Herodotus as that year's best historical mystery novel. But Gillian, a former journalist and BBC Parliamentary reporter, did start another historical series which, for pressure of other commitments, she did not continue and completed only two stories. It featured the journalist Thomas Ludlow and his less than reputable horse trader Harry Leather. The first of the series was "Wingless Pegasus" (Ellery Queen's Mystery Magazine,* August 1996). *Here's the second.*

"Mr Leather sends his respects to Mr Ludlow and wonders if he could assist in the matter of a young woman who has done a murder."

Harry Leather's laborious writing dinted the page like hoofprints in mud. His note arrived on a windy afternoon in the April of 1867 at the offices of the newspaper where I was earning my blameless living as a subeditor. The messenger who brought it to my desk had the air of a man who'd rather not be responsible for a communication smeared with mud and various other stains that included, from the smell, neat's-foot oil and strong porter. The wonders of the penny post had made no impression at all on Harry Leather. A man who, without blinking, would bid fifty guineas he hadn't got for a horse he fancied, grudged expenditure on stamps. A groom taking a cob to market might hand his message to a carrier who'd pass it to a gentleman's coachman whose second cousin delivered turnips to Covent Garden and so, in the fullness of time, it would get to me. The address at the top of the note was a livery stables in Buckinghamshire. Luckily, several men in the subeditors' room owed me favours, so by the following afternoon I was walking from the railway station along an avenue of budding elm trees, with an assurance from the porter that I couldn't miss the stables.

It was pleasant country and, although no more than twenty miles from London, the spring seemed to be coming in earlier and more softly there. Blackbirds sang and primroses gleamed as bright as pieces of china in the grass by the roadside. After a mile of road muddy enough to make me wish I'd worn stouter boots I came to a public house called The Woodman's Rest and a knot of cottages. Between the public house and one of the cottages was the entrance to a driveway, flanked by stone pillars with gates of elaborate ironwork closed across it. Squire's place, I thought, but not your hospitable hail-fellow country squire of the old school. Those firmly closed gates said that visitors were not welcome and the entrance to the drive, which you'd expect to be churned up with carriage tracks, looked as if no hoof or foot had fallen on it for weeks. On the opposite side of the road a board advertising horses kept at livery and hacks for hire marked my destination and my friend's latest place of business. Harry is a groom, horse breaker, jockey, dealer – anything you care to name to do with horses, with a few chances on the side to earn an extra guinea that doesn't necessarily have the word honest attached to it, and he seldom stays in one place for more than six months at a time. He was at me as soon as I'd set foot in the yard.

"What's been keeping you Mr Ludlow? This rate, they'll have her sentenced and hanged before you get a look in."

He led the way through the tack room to a smaller room crammed with sacks and feed bins, dusted off the top of a bin with his handkerchief, and invited me to take a seat, then settled himself on another bin, empty pipe in his hand.

"Why the hurry? If this young woman who's done a murder is going to be hanged in any case, I don't see why they need my help to do it."

Harry knew very well that my amateur interest was in cases that had a flavour of the extraordinary about them. I was annoyed to be classed with the sort of ghoul who'd come to witness the downfall of some hapless country girl.

"It's not your help in getting her hanged that's wanted. It's getting her off being hanged."

"But you said in your note she'd done a murder."

He nodded.

"And you want me to get her off? Why?"

"Because she's not a bad young woman and the one she killed was as spoiled and cussed a creature as you'd find in a long day at a bad market."

A ray of sunshine, flecked with motes of bran, shone through the window on Harry's lined and weather-beaten face. I knew that his morality seldom coincided with a preacher's, but this was a staggerer even from him.

"If I understand you aright, you're asking me to be an accessory in perverting the course of justice."

He looked at the ceiling. "I knew a racehorse once named Course of Justice. Never won anything to speak of."

The story he told me had its origins in the big house behind the locked gates. I'd been right in thinking it was the local squire's mansion, also that its squire was not of the old sporting kind.

"Mr Haslem. He's thirty or so, but the sort that's never been young. Thin, fidgety kind of a man. Plenty of money from his father, but leaves the estate work to a bailiff. They say he's writing a book about something in Latin. Goodness knows how he came to marry her, except I suppose she wasn't a bad-looking woman on her good days, but a temper on her like an army mule in a thistle patch."

"Are we talking about the person who was murdered?"

"Yes, we are. Veronica, her name was."

"You met her?"

He sucked on his pipe.

"I quarrelled with her."

"Over a horse, I suppose."

"What else? One day at the start of March, about two weeks before it happened, she came down the drive in her victoria, going visiting. Two bays she had to pull it. I was outside the gate here and I could see one of the bays was lame. Her coachman knows me, so he pulled up without asking her first and said would I have a look at it, see what was wrong. Well, madam sticks her head out of the window and starts screeching at him for stopping without her permission. I take no notice of her and start feeling the bay's leg. Off fore, swollen like a puffball and hot as a boiling kettle. I say to the coachman he shouldn't be driving a horse in this state, and he looks back over his shoulder at her and whispers to me that she insisted because she had to go visiting. So I take my hat off and go up to her and say, civil enough, that the horse isn't fit to be driven and I'll hire her another. She curses me up hill and down dale and tells the coachman to drive on or she'll dismiss him on the spot. So off they go with the bay limping like a man with a wooden leg. I'd have taken the whip to her first, but the coachman's got a family to feed."

"And two weeks after that she was dead?"

"Yes, two weeks after that she was dying of convulsions in the house of a lady she was visiting, after she'd stepped out of that very same victoria she cursed at me from."

"And from that incident, you conclude that Mrs Veronica Haslem deserved murdering."

"There's a curse on the man or woman that drives a lame horse. It says so in the Bible."

I'd heard him quote that text before but have never met the Biblical scholar who could find it anywhere from Genesis to Revelation. But to tell that to Harry would make a very atheist out of the man, and the swarm of sins clustering round his head is black enough without that. Instead I asked him to tell me more about Mrs Haslem's death.

"She was going to pay an afternoon call on a lady that lives a good two hours' drive away. She has her lunch in her room, changes into her costume for paying calls, and gets into her victoria with the hood up and my friend driving from the box, as usual."

"Travelling alone?"

"Yes. The coachman swears that they didn't stop anywhere along the way, nobody got in with her and she never called out to him or said anything the whole journey."

"What was the weather like?"

"Nasty biting wind. She was all wrapped up in rugs, of course, so she was all right, at least she should have been. Anyway, they arrive at the house, the coachman draws up and goes to help her out. He notices she seems a bit unsteady on her feet and her voice is croaky but there's nothing new about that. He watches her go up the steps to the door, the butler opens it, and she goes inside. The coachman drives round to the stables, sees to the horses, then goes into the kitchen for a cup of tea. But he's no more than taken a gulp of it when there's this confloption upstairs and a maid comes flying in to say get the doctor because Mrs Haslem's taken ill in the drawing room."

"What were the symptoms?"

"She said she felt her throat burning and asked for water but she couldn't keep it down. She was groaning and clutching at her stomach and shouting out that she'd been poisoned. All this in the drawing room with a lot of other ladies there."

"Did she say who she thought had poisoned her?"

"She did, several times over. She said Miss Thorn had put poison in her travelling flask because she wanted to get rid of her and marry her husband."

"Miss Thorn being . . . ?"

"The governess. Anyway, they carried her up to the bedroom. The doctor was out on his rounds, and by the time he got there she was in convulsions. She was dead before they could get word to her husband."

"Where was he?"

"Up in London all day, buying books."

"Was there any evidence for this business about poison in the travelling flask?"

He looked ill at ease.

"Well, there was a flask and Miss Thorn did have it in her hands. There's no getting away from it."

I said he'd better tell me the worst of it and get it over. On that cold March afternoon, at two o'clock, the victoria was drawn up and waiting at the front door. Mrs Haslem came down the steps. Behind her Miss Thorn, holding the Haslems' eight-year-old son by the hand. The boy, she said, wanted to see his mother driving away. The coachman settled Mrs Haslem in the victoria, positioning the foot warmer for her, tucking a blanket round her. While this was going on, the boy was on one side, talking to his mother, Miss Thorn on the other.

"The coachman's just getting up on the box, ready to drive off, when Mrs Haslem says, quite sharply, 'Have you taken my flask, Miss Thorn?' At first the governess looks as if she wants to deny it, but Mrs Haslem says, 'Don't try to lie to me. You've got it there behind your back.'"

"And had she?"

"She had. So she has to hand it over, looking shamefaced."

"What sort of flask?"

"Flat silver one. The sort a gentleman would carry in his pocket out hunting."

"Did the coachman see Miss Thorn put anything into it?"

"No."

"She'd have had a chance, though, wouldn't she, while Mrs Haslem was talking to the boy?"

"She'd have had to be quick about it, but yes, I suppose she would."

"What did Mrs Haslem have in the flask? I suppose it would be something to keep out the cold on a long journey."

"Short or long journey, summer or winter, it was all the same to her. Brandy."

"In other words, Mrs Haslem was a habitual drinker?"

"Habitual! She drank the way a horse eats grass. That time I had that argument with her, I could smell the brandy coming off her breath."

"Did anybody else touch the flask?"

"There was only the boy and the coachman there. The coachman says he didn't, and I don't suppose the boy would poison his mother."

"And you've told me they didn't stop on the journey. Where did the brandy in the flask come from?"

"Mrs Haslem's own bottle she kept in her room. She'd sent her maid to buy a couple of bottles the day before."

"Why did she have to do that? Surely her husband would keep brandy in the house."

"Only under lock and key. He was driven distracted by her drinking."

"You say she had lunch in her room?"

"Chicken in aspic, bread and butter, China tea. And in case you're thinking the poison might be in that, she didn't finish her lunch so the maid did after she'd gone and she was as fit as a flea."

"It looks like an open-and-shut case against Miss Thorn. What happened at the inquest?"

"Open verdict."

"Astounding! Didn't it come out about Mrs Haslem accusing the governess?"

"Oh yes, it came out, in a manner of speaking. Only everybody round here knew the wicked tongue she had when the drink was in her. They felt sorry for her husband and anybody else who had to do with her."

"What about the symptoms? What did the doctor say?"

"That she'd been very sick, had convulsions, and her heart had stopped – which it tends to do when you die."

"Is this whole countryside in a conspiracy to protect the governess? It can only be a matter of time before she's under lock and key."

"You could think of something, though, couldn't you, a gentleman of your experience? Just enough to give everyone an excuse for pretending to think she didn't do it."

His tone, soft as any sucking dove, was the one he used to get scared colts to come to his hand.

"Where is this paragon of a poisoner?"

"Still up at the hall."

"What!"

"Mr Haslem has kept her on. After all, someone has to look after the boy."

I sat and thought for a while.

"If you want me to take any part in this, you must arrange for me to speak to the governess. Can you do that?"

"Yes. Give me a few hours."

"Mr Haslem too."

"He's not seeing people. Hasn't been out of the house or had anyone calling since the inquest."

"What about the doctor and the maid?"

"Dr Gaynor's easy enough, he's just up the road. The maid's gone back to her parents ten miles away."

"Didn't Mr Haslem keep her on?"

"The fact is, she bolted straight after the funeral. The gossip from the hall is that some of Mrs Haslem's diamonds had gone missing."

"Is the maid suspected of stealing them?"

"I don't know, because Mr Haslem wouldn't have any inquiries made. I had that from the solicitor's clerk."

"But this is incomprehensible. The man's wife is poisoned and he keeps the woman suspected of it in his household. Her jewellery's stolen, he does nothing to recover it and lets the maid run away. Isn't it more likely that the maid poisoned Mrs Haslem to save herself from being found out about the jewellery?"

"It wasn't the maid she accused."

"Accused or not, I want to speak to the maid before anyone else."

He lent me a cob to ride and a boy on a pony to show me the way. As we trotted along together under the green leaves I thought it was a poor thing if I could only lift the noose from one young woman's neck to drop it round another's, but Harry as usual had me caught and bitted whether I liked it or not.

Susan was the maid's name. When we got to the cottage, which looked as if it hadn't had a lick of paint or dab of plaster since Queen Anne's time, she was in the kitchen with her mother making pies. There was a clutch of children toddling, crawling, and bawling round the open door, scrawny hens pecking unhopefully, their skin pink and shiny in patches where feathers had been scratched away. For a daughter of such a place, the position of lady's maid must have been a considerable prize. When I came to the door she was laughing at something one of the children had said, a pretty, plumpish girl in her twenties, neater than you'd expect from the confusion round her, her dark hair tucked under a clean white cap. The laughter died away when she saw me, turned to misery when I introduced myself and asked if I might have a word about the late Mrs Haslem.

"Would you come with me, sir, where we can be quiet."

Mother, brothers, and sisters watched open-mouthed as she led the way up the stairs that rose straight from the kitchen, little better than a ladder. If I say we talked in her bedroom, I wouldn't wish to impute to her a lack of propriety. The place was no more than a kind of open cabin at the top of the stairs with one wide bed that almost certainly accommodated several sisters as well as herself. All the time we talked I was half aware of her mother's worried murmurs from below, trying to keep the children quiet. I asked her about the brandy.

"Every week, sir. She'd give me the money and I'd go into town without letting anyone know. Two bottles a week it was, three sometimes."

"That last day, she had her lunch in her room?"

"Yes, sir, but she hadn't much appetite. She never had these days."

"Was there any sign that she was ill?"

"None at all, sir."

"Did she fill the brandy flask while you were there?"

"Yes, sir. She rinsed it in the water from her ewer, then she opened the new bottle I'd bought from the shop and filled it up over the basin."

"A new bottle, you're sure of that?"

"Quite sure, sir. She had to break the wax seal on it."

"And did she, or you, put anything else in that flask except brandy?"

"Oh no, sir."

Her eyes met mine. Scared eyes, with tears beginning to wash over them but not, I thought, guileful.

"You know Mrs Haslem died, almost certainly, as a result of what was in that flask."

She looked down at her lap and nodded.

"Have you any idea how poison might have been introduced into the flask?"

"No, sir. I know what was said, but I don't think she would. She was always kind to me."

"Miss Thorn?"

Another tearful nod. I didn't care for the situation at all, but there was no going back.

"There's another matter. Did you know that after Mrs Haslem's death, some possessions of hers were found to be missing?"

An intake of breath. Her hands, which had been lying motionless in her lap, began twisting together.

"Do you know anything about them?"

She was crying in earnest now. Her hands came up to cover her face and a few muffled words squeezed out through her fingers.

". . . didn't mean any harm . . . gave them to me . . . for going to buy the brandy for her . . . because she didn't need them any more."

I stood, taken aback by the speed of her collapse, pitying her and thinking of the temptation it must have been.

"Don't you think it might be a good idea to give them to me and I can take them back to her husband?"

I could make no promises about there being no prosecution, but I was inwardly determined to urge mercy on Mr Haslem. She drew her fingers down just enough to look at me.

"You have them still?"

"Here, all of them."

She looked over at a battered wooden chest on the other side of the bed.

"I'm engaged to be married, you see, sir. I was saving them for my wedding."

The thought of a rustic bride glittering with Mrs Haslem's

diamonds was almost ludicrous enough to force a smile, even in those circumstances. But I kept my face grave as she went heavily round the bed and threw back the lid of the box.

"There they are, sir. And these, and these, and these."

They came at me in a soft avalanche across the bed. White silk and satin, cotton and broderie anglaise, pink ribbons, green ribbons, stockings, garters, and a dozen other frills and furbelows that only the goddess of lingerie or her devotees could name. Over them, from the other side of the bed, scared brown eyes looking up at me.

"What in the world are these?"

"Her things, sir. She said I could have them because she'd had new ones made. She told me I could keep them, sir."

When I told Harry he laughed so hard he nearly fell off the feed bin.

"Well, are you taking them back to Mr Haslem?"

"Can you imagine me riding back across country with an armful of lady's cast-off unmentionables? Let her keep them for her wedding day."

"So she didn't take the diamonds?"

"I'm sure of it. The best actress in London couldn't fake such simplicity. And I'm equally sure she put nothing in that flask."

His grin faded. "Still looks bad for the governess, then?"

"Not good, certainly. Still, there's one thing that puzzles me. Why does a lady married nine years or more take a fancy for a whole wardrobe of new underthings? The ones she gave her maid weren't worn out by any means."

"That, Mr Ludlow, is a matter beyond our understanding. Unless . . ."

"Unless."

The word hung there for a moment between us in the bran-flecked air, then he stood up. "Miss Thorn will be arriving any minute. She's bringing the boy down to look at a pony."

A pony phaeton delivered them. A boy got out first, muffled up against the cold, then a young woman in a black coat and hat. I'd imagined that a person who could arouse such concern in Harry would have some special appeal – one of those fragile, flowerlike women. This was no flower. She was squarish in build and broad of shoulder. Her face was attractive in its way, but from an impression of common sense and openness rather than delicacy. Her hair was dark, her eyes a deep grey under straight black brows. If I'd been asked to sum her up in one word, that word would have been honest, the way a rock or a tree is honest because it has no other way to be. But then I'd seen people double-dyed in guilt who had the same air. She looked at me, then towards the boy, who was already well out of hearing, leaning over a stable door with Harry.

"So you're the gentleman who's come to ask me if I poisoned Mrs Haslem? Mr Leather says you'll want to ask me questions. Ask anything you please."

Her voice had a hint of the north country in it. I suggested that we should go into the tack room and sit down, but she wanted to stay outside where she could see young Master Haslem. It was a strange way of questioning. We stood there side by side in the yard as a bay pony was brought out and the boy mounted on it.

"Did you take Mrs Haslem's flask out of the victoria?"

"Yes."

"Why?"

"If I could stop my employer's wife making a scandal of herself before the whole county, it was my duty to do it. Mr Haslem was ill with worry over it. It was bad enough with her friends near here. He didn't want her to call on people who were more in society because the whole world would know, but she was a stubborn woman."

No nonsense from Miss Thorn about not speaking ill of the dead. Her contempt was rocklike.

"So you decided to do something about it?"

"I decided to get the flask away from her. I wanted her to arrive at the house she was visiting as sober as she was ever likely to be."

"Was this your own decision, or in consultation with Mr Haslem?"

"He didn't know what I was going to do."

"Did you put anything in it?"

"No. I didn't even unscrew the cap of the flask. I should have done that – poured it away on the gravel and let her dismiss me if she liked."

"And perhaps saved her life."

She gave me a questioning look.

"If there was poison in that brandy, you'd have saved her life by pouring it away."

"How could I have known that? How could anybody know that?"

"You didn't know?"

She took a step to face me.

"I swear to you, as I'd swear at God's judgment seat if my soul depended on it, that I didn't know."

We followed Harry and young Haslem on the pony to the paddock at the back. All the time that he was walking and trotting the animal I was trying to work up to a question which there was no delicate way of asking. In the end I came flat out with it.

"Do you think it possible that Mrs Haslem had a lover?"

A moment of shock, then anger.

"That's a most improper question to put to me. I have no intention of answering it."

And she moved smartly away to the paddock rail. Back in the yard afterwards she ignored me but smiled at the boy and his babble of enthusiasm for the pony, wrapped his scarf round his neck, and saw him settled in the phaeton. With her boot on the step she turned to me, icily polite.

"I'd offer to shake hands, but you might not want to take the hand of a woman they think is a poisoner."

Then she was in her seat and away.

"Something wrong with your arm?" Harry asked.

He'd caught me with my hand half extended, responding too late to what she'd said.

"That accusation of her wanting to marry Mr Haslem – was there any truth in it?"

"Well, the talk was he spent more time in the schoolroom than with his wife, but so would I have in his place."

"I need to speak to him, whether he likes it or not."

I requisitioned some of Harry's business stationery and composed a careful letter, standing at the old desk in the corner of the tack room where he made up his accounts. The stable boy was sent up to the hall with it. By then it was late afternoon and Harry informed me that Dr Gaynor would be back from his rounds. With the westering sun throwing long tree shadows across the road, I walked the mile to a substantial brick house in a couple of acres of ground.

The doctor was younger and more urbane than I'd expected in a country practitioner, a handsome man in his late thirties. He was working in his dispensary when I arrived but kindly invited me to sit down in his study over a glass of sherry, fastidiously amused by my amateur interest in murder and quite willing to discuss the Haslem case.

"A very sad affair. I take it you've heard the details from Mr Leather."

"You were called to Mrs Haslem?"

"Far too late to be of any use. I was at a confinement on the far side of my practice. When the messenger came I galloped like the devil, but there was nothing I could do."

"Are you in any doubt that she was poisoned?"

He looked at me over the sherry glass.

"Do you want me to tell you what I said at the inquest?"

"I suspect, like other people, you were not anxious to condemn a certain person."

"Unprofessional on my part, if so."

"But human. I think I have my answer."

He sighed. "She was poisoned."

"Did you form any idea as to the poison used?"

He swirled the sherry round in the glass.

"Your knowledge of toxicology is probably as extensive as mine."

"Aconitine?" Another sigh. I prompted. "The symptoms suggest it and there have been a number of cases recently."

"As you say, the burning in the mouth. The convulsions."

"So Mrs Haslem was poisoned with aconitine. And as far as we can tell, that aconitine could only have been administered in the brandy she drank on her last journey. Can you as a medical man see any other conclusion?"

We went on discussing it, in a guarded way, over another glass of sherry. But no other conclusion emerged, beyond my conviction that the doctor too favoured mercy above justice for Mrs Haslem's murderer.

Back at Harry's stables, a curt note had arrived from Mr Haslem to say he'd see me at ten the following morning. Harry offered me the hospitality of his hayloft for the night and I treated him to a supper of chops and claret in The Woodman's Rest. We chose a quiet corner so that I could report progress – or lack of it.

"Aconitine. Does that make things worse for Miss Thorn?"

"Yes. It acts quite quickly, so there's no hope that the poison might have been in what Mrs Haslem ate at lunch or anything before. You'd expect the first symptoms within about half an hour, the tightness and burning in the lips and throat. That fits quite well with her getting out of the victoria and then collapsing in the drawing room. In fact . . ."

"In fact what, Mr Ludlow?"

I sat there with a piece of mutton chop on my fork, staring at his still-hopeful face.

"Harry, this is an odd thing. You said it took her two hours to be driven to the place she was visiting. Now, wouldn't you expect her to be taking nips out of that flask the whole journey?"

"I would."

"And yet if she'd drunk from it at the start of the journey, she'd have been in a much worse state by the end of it. She was well enough to speak and to walk up to the front door. That suggests she didn't drink from the flask until near the end of the journey. Is that likely?"

"It doesn't help, though, does it? It's still the flask we're looking at."

"I need to talk to the coachman. Early tomorrow before I see Mr Haslem. Can you arrange that?"

"Sure as sunrise."

★    ★    ★

Mr Haslem's coach house was a shadowy building with a few shafts of morning sunlight coming through narrow windows. The dark bulk of an old-fashioned closed carriage took up a lot of the space. Beside it were the pony phaeton and a victoria with the hood up. The coachman was polishing the phaeton but straightened up when he saw us. Harry introduced me after his fashion.

"This is Mr Ludlow. I don't know what he's going to ask you, but you tell him what he wants to know."

The coachman stood like a man on trial.

"What happened to the victoria that day Mrs Haslem died?"

He swallowed. "I drove it back, sir."

"It must have been dark by the time you got it back here."

"Pitch. It was past midnight."

"What did you do with it?"

"Backed it into the coach house and left it. Next day I had it out to clean it and put it away again."

"Has anyone used it since?"

"No. The victoria was hers. Nobody else seems to have cared to use it."

"What happened to the rugs and the foot warmer and so on?"

"They're still in there."

We all three poked our heads under the hood. On the seat, a dark wollen blanket and canvas cover. I plunged my hand into the darkness beside the folded blanket. It touched fur.

"Ah." I drew it out so that they could see it, the thing flopping heavily in my hand. Harsh fur, wolf's or bear's probably. "This is the fellow I was looking for."

Harry moved in to look and drew back, disappointed.

"It's only her travelling muff."

"It was a cold day and she'd be wearing light gloves with her best visiting outfit. Naturally she'd have a muff for the journey."

I slid my hands inside the fur's silk lining. "Let's have some more light here. One of the carriage lamps."

A scrape of flint, a flare of light. I waited until they were back with the lamp then slid a hand out and let the muff dangle. Something small fell to the brick floor and burst open in the circle of lamplight. "Whatever you do, don't tread on them."

On the bricks was an enamelled box of the kind that ladies use to carry pills, with small white globes like chalky pearls scattered round it. Harry knelt, picked one up, sniffed.

"They're only . . ."

If I hadn't grabbed it, he'd have put it in his mouth.

"They're what will keep Miss Thorn from hanging. Get some paper."

We tore the wrapping from a new cake of harness soap, bundled the box and most of its contents together. A few minutes later I was walking up the steps to Mr Haslem's front door.

The butler showed me into a handsome study on the ground floor, with leather-bound books from floor to ceiling and classical texts and dictionaries ranged on a desk by the window. The man himself seemed less substantial than his books, thin and pale, with sunken eyes. He held himself painstakingly upright, like a marionette on a single string that might part at any moment and land him in a disjointed heap on his Turkey carpet. I'd explained myself to him in my letter – as far as a total stranger's interest in a gentleman's affairs can be explained – and came straight to the point.

"I spoke to Miss Thorn. She says she wanted to get the flask away from your wife and hadn't discussed it with you."

"Miss Thorn is trying to protect me. We had discussed it."

"Discussed what exactly?"

His face creased up. He may have been a clever man with his books but he lied clumsily and painfully, like an inexpert angler with a fishhook through his finger.

"Discussed how to prevent my wife obtaining brandy."

"Did you know she was going to take the flask out of the victoria?"

"Yes," he said. But his face winced "no".

"Have you and Miss Thorn ever discussed the properties of aconitine?"

"Aconitine?"

"A vegetable alkaloid. A poison."

"No."

"What happened to the flask Mrs Haslem drank from?"

"I . . . I ordered it to be brought to me."

"Were the contents analysed?"

"It was empty . . . quite empty."

I'd come to him with one doubt left and now it had gone. Like everyone else, with just one exception, he was thinking only of the flask. I was on the point of explaining when he raised his hand to stop me. It was a surprisingly decisive gesture for a nervous man and when he spoke again his voice was firmer than it had been.

"Mr Ludlow, since you have chosen to take an interest in my affairs, there's something you should know. At present I am in mourning. When that period ends, I shall ask Miss Thorn to do me the honour of becoming my wife."

He kept his eyes on me, nerved for my protest. There was a kind of desperate heroism about him.

"In that case," I said, "you will be marrying a brave and loyal young woman. And an innocent one."

Shock and relief together came flooding over his face. He almost collapsed and had to support himself on the corner of the desk. I took my hand out of my pocket and rolled a few of the little white globes across the blotter. He looked from them to me and back again, saying nothing.

"You were all looking in the wrong place. Your wife's last words were that the poison was in her flask. She died believing that. But ask yourself if she might have been killed by a poison that was not in the flask and what's the answer?"

"But she took nothing else since leaving the house."

"Not quite. A lady is going visiting, to a fashionable house where she wishes to make a good impression. She won't do that with brandy on her breath. So she'll take the precaution of concealing in her travelling muff a little box of oil of peppermint lozenges. Those were the last things your wife took, not the brandy."

He stared at them, still not speaking.

"My friend Mr Leather is taking the rest to London to a

laboratory that I know. If my suspicion is right, they will indeed contain oil of peppermint – and aconitine."

"Then he killed her. Stole her jewels and killed her."

The relief was there, but pain too. I didn't say to him that there were more ways than one of stealing a woman's jewels. *Take them and sell them, my love, and with the money we shall run away together to that warm sweethearts' nest in Paris*. Or Venice, or Timbuktu, or the dreams of deluded women knew where. No part of her lover's plan to take a drinking and demanding woman along with him.

"Yes, he killed her. How long had you known about your wife and Dr Gaynor?"

Two days later I was back with Harry at The Woodman's Rest, thinking I'd earned some congratulations.

"Once I knew about the peppermint pills, there was very little doubt. Getting hold of aconitine wouldn't be so difficult. Making it into pills would be – unless you had a dispensary at hand."

"Pity he got away, wasn't it?"

"That's your friend the coachman's fault, not mine."

The foolish man had flown to the kitchen in high excitement to tell them all about the discovery. From there the news must have come within half an hour to the doctor's ears, because when I went back to speak to him I found only a disordered house and an empty stable.

"Will they catch him?"

"Depends how hard they try, and that will probably depend on Mr Haslem."

"Nothing will get done then. After all, you can't expect a man to parade in front of the world with horns on his head."

"That means Miss Thorn will never be publicly cleared."

"You can leave that to me. I'll see the story's put about where it matters."

And I knew I could indeed leave it to him. The gossip from the stables gets up to the drawing room and down again as quickly as we can put out an edition of our paper. When the governess walked up the aisle with her employer, there'd be nobody whispering murder. I never heard the report of that event because Harry had moved on long before it could happen. Two things, though, I did hear. One was that Miss Thorn came into Harry's yard, looking by his account "like a linnet let out of a cage", and thanked him and me most warmly. The other was that Mr Haslem bought the bay pony for his son at a price ten guineas over what Harry should have had the nerve to ask for it. I like to think that was a sign of gratitude as well.

# Threads of Scarlet

## Claire Griffen

*Claire Griffen is an Australian writer, actress and dramatist who has a special fascination for stories set in medieval Italy, such as "Borgia by Blood" in* Royal Whodunnits *and "House of the Moon" in the previous* Mammoth Book of Historical Whodunnits. *Here, though, she looks closer to home and tells a tale of intrigue in Adelaide just over a hundred years ago. It's closer to home than you might imagine. Claire reveals that it's "based on a mysterious incident in my family history that has never been fully resolved".*

*In the high summer of 1875, the famous French equilibrist Charles Blondin gave a performance in the South Park Lands. It was attended by members of the George Dugald Fife household, whose residence on fashionable Le Fevre Terrace was about to become the most notorious establishment in Adelaide.*

*The colony of South Australia had seen triumph and tragedy since the* Buffalo *dropped anchor in Holdfast Bay in 1836. The first encampment of mud, straw and calico windows was by 1875 a city of gaslight and architecture that had earned it the title of "The Athens of the South". Tents, huts and roughly constructed barracks had yielded to civic buildings of classic style, cathedrals, colleges, hospitals, hotels and emporiums.*

*In the outlying countryside lay the vineyards, sheep pastures, copper mines, railways and paddle boats on the Murray that gave the colony its prosperity.*

*In 1867 there was a grim reminder that South Australia could still be the White Man's Grave when a band playing "The Death March" accompanied Burke and Wills on their final journey. Explorers who had died of deprivation in what to the black inhabitants was a land of plenty.*

George Dugald Fife was first made aware that all was not well at home when he saw the gaggle of onlookers clustered at his front gate. He was further alerted by the distinctive peacock blue Garibaldi jacket, shako and white cotton gloves of the Metropolitan Foot Police and a plain-clothes man invading the premises.

Inspector Toop was a wiry little man with ginger hair and moustache and a fondness for check waistcoats. He was affectionately named Toop the Snoop by his police colleagues, or sometimes Sniffer because of his uncanny ability to sniff out a miscreant. His freckled face and general scrawniness belied his twenty-seven years.

Very few knew he had been a medical student at Edinburgh, forced to give up his studies through lack of funds. To Toop the case about to unfold before him was a boon. The detective branch had been implemented in 1867 mainly to investigate, in the anonymity of plain clothes, sly grog and prostitution misdemeanours. Progression had been made to murder, but usually those committed in drunken brawls. This promised something else.

He approached the victoria as it drew up at the kerb, noting that there were five occupants, including a plump, middle-aged woman huddling with two children under the hood and a young woman with a parasol sitting on the driver's seat beside Fife.

"Mr Fife? Inspector Toop." The detective touched the brim of his derby. "I wouldn't bring the children in if I were you. There's been a rather nasty accident."

A flicker of fear flashed like lightning across the retailer's face as he took in the black ambulance drawn up in the drive. "What sort of accident?"

"Is it the mistress?" demanded the short, plump woman. "I said she oughtn't to be left alone."

"That will do, Mrs Blount. Take the children to Miss Vickers's. Charlie will drive you."

"I can't take another step 'til I find out what's happened to the mistress."

"Nancy, you'll have to go." Fife turned to the young woman.

Nancy closed her parasol with a snap. Toop appraised her. Although he guessed her to be a servant she was fashionably dressed in a gown with tiered skirt and drooping bustle, and an elaborate bodice embroidered in scarlet which matched the roses in her small, tipped-forward hat.

"You haven't answered my question, Inspector," snapped Fife.

Toop took him at a glance: grey curly hair, smooth handsome face, large blue eyes with silver lashes. Dressed for a warm Saturday in tropical helmet, lightweight cream suit and striped shirt.

"Is it my wife? It must be my wife. She was the only one in the house. Has she harmed herself?"

Toop narrowed his eyes, quizzically. "What makes you say that, sir?"

"I don't know why I said it. What's happened to her?"

"I think you should come inside, sir." Toop stood back, respectfully, allowing Fife to enter by a door guarded by two foot police.

"Which way?" Fife glanced through double doors into an ornately furnished drawing room.

"Straight ahead to the kitchen if you please, sir."

The kitchen was a large, sunny room with scrubbed wooden table, a cupboard from floor to ceiling in lieu of a pantry and coconut matting on the floor. Lying between the table and stove was a body covered with a sheet. There was an acrid smell of singed flesh. A small, thin man somewhat overwhelmed by his luxuriant mutton chop whiskers rose from a chair.

"What, Sandow, you here?" Fife seemed surprised.

"Mrs Fife sent me a note earlier today to say she felt unwell. I arrived to find *this*."

"I'd like you to prepare yourself, sir." Toop grasped the

corner of the sheet. "She's not a pretty sight." Toop was master of the understatement.

Ada Fife lay on her back, what had once been a morning dress of muslin black shreds on her darkly encrimsoned body. Her hair was singed off, her face a mass of blisters from which her eyes glared at them in stark accusation. Only her arms were untouched and lay pale and limp by her sides. The housekeeper gasped, then burst into tears. With an expression of distaste, Fife took a handkerchief from his pocket and held it to his lips.

"Is this your wife, sir?"

"Yes, this is Mrs Ada Fife. What happened?"

"It seems she lit a fire in the drawing room, her dress caught fire and in her panic she ran into the kitchen where she collapsed and died, her flight having fanned the flames. Would you concur, doctor?"

Sandow nodded ponderously as if weighed down by his whiskers.

"I must go and pour myself a whiskey," said Fife, abruptly. "I'll be in the drawing room if you need me."

"It's as well the coconut matting didn't catch alight, there could have been quite a conflagration," observed Toop. "Curious, though, don't you think? That she fell on her back. Did you turn her over, doctor?"

"No. I ascertained she was dead by checking the pulses in her neck and wrist. Otherwise, I did not touch her."

"One would have expected her to fall face down."

The doctor shrugged, non-committally.

"What were you treating her for?"

"She had a nervous affliction which affected her digestion and caused her hair to fall out."

"Was there anyone else in the house when you arrived?"

"No, the front door was locked. I came around to the back door and let myself in. She was already dead. Even if I had found her alive she could not have long survived with burns of that magnitude."

"Why would she light a fire on such a hot day?"

"I couldn't say, Inspector. Maybe she was feeling poorly and looking for a little comfort."

"If she was in ill health why was she left alone?"

"She was a highly strung yet introverted woman, who shunned society. Her disorder was more of the mind than the system. One often sees poor digestion and loss of hair in a highly nervous patient."

"How was her relationship with Mr Fife in the marital sense?"

"That I cannot comment on," replied Sandow, primly.

Toop left the kitchen and went along the passage, turning up the gaslight to observe the track of cinders on the runner. When he entered the drawing room Fife was standing with a glass of whiskey in his hand, surveying the damage done to the Indian rug before the hearth.

"Only laid this week," he remarked, then glanced swiftly at Toop. "I don't know why I said that. It must be the shock."

"Shock does funny things to people," said Toop, soothingly. "Believe me, I've heard it all. Why don't you sit down, sir?"

Toop too examined the hearth, the still glowing embers, the soot and ashes scattered thickly about and one shoe print.

"My wife must have lit the fire and then lost her balance and toppled into the flames. It was typical of her to be careless, I'm afraid."

Toop examined the room with its ornate furnishings, plush chairs with lace antimacassars, a mantlepiece crowded with ornaments and framed photographs, heavy velvet curtains, a whatnot supporting a jardiniere filled with dried flowers, and a sideboard with crystal decanters.

He then turned his attention to the retailer. George Duguld Fife was in many ways typical of the new colonial gentry, either a wayward youth who had been paid off by his family to quit England and stay abroad or someone of lower class whose good looks, ambition, and acquired polish had allowed him to achieve a status he would never have attained in his native land, someone who had started small, worked hard, invested well and was now the owner of Fife & Robertson, a large emporium on Rundle Street.

As Toop had implied, he had seen many and varied

reactions to shock from hysteria to stern self-restraint, but
Fife's demeanour intrigued him. He saw no evidence of grief,
he seemed rather to be – Toop searched for the word –
*inconvenienced*.

"May I ask where you were this afternoon, sir?"

"I took the children to see Charles Blondin."

"The famous equilibrist?"

"Yes, he was performing in the South Park Lands."

"Who accompanied you?"

"A friend of my wife, Miss Emily Vickers and Mrs Blount,
my housekeeper."

"And the maid?"

"No, Nancy had an engagement of her own. We met by
appointment in the city. To walk home she would have had
to cross the Adelaide Bridge, where too many Larrikins
congregate. It's a pity the Commissioner doesn't employ
more foot police to control the Larrikin element. Still, what
can one do when George Hamilton's an ex-pastoralist and
horse breeder and whose pride and joy are the Mounted
Police."

Toop had similar views on that subject, but remained
silent.

"How many in your household?"

"Two others. Charlie, the stable boy and Miss Ivy Amory.
She was visiting her sister, who's been taken ill."

"And no-one stayed at home with Mrs Fife?"

"I urged her to accompany us, but she preferred to stay at
home enjoying a solitary state. My wife had a fragile toler-
ance level, Inspector. People got on her nerves."

"Where does Miss Vickers reside?"

"On Robe Terrace, Medindie within walking distance.
She lives with her father and is a spinster lady devoted to the
children. It's she I've sent them to now."

Toop knew of Halliday Vickers, who had made his fortune
in the East India Company and retired to South Australia to
build an eccentric mansion of domes and minarets.

"We'll speak to Miss Vickers later."

The silver lashes fluttered. "Whatever for?"

"To verify your whereabouts this afternoon."

"There's no question my wife's death was anything but an accident, is there?"

"Just routine, sir. We need to get a clear picture of events and of your wife's state of mind."

"You're not suggesting she committed suicide! Would you choose that way?" Fife looked at the hearth and shuddered.

"We'll be taking the body away now, sir, to be examined by our own surgeon."

"Not to an hotel, I hope. I know it's customary, but . . ."

"No, the West Terrace Cemetery mortuary is operational now. We'll advise you when her body can be released for burial."

Fife ran his hair distractedly through his silver curls. "I suppose I shall have to send a note to Canon Dove of St Andrew's."

"Is that where you worship, sir?"

"Yes, I have a box there." He made it sound as important as having a box at the opera.

"And the undertaker of your choice?"

"I have my own establishment on Rundle Street East."

Toop digested this information as he returned to the kitchen. Kneeling beside the corpse, he lifted the untouched arms and examined the hands and fingernails, and the soles of her slippered feet.

"Have the morgue attendant carry out Mrs Fife's body," he ordered the sergeant, tersely.

Sandow rose. "How is Mr Fife?"

"I'm sure he'd be happy for any assistance you might render him." Toop was anxious to question the housekeeper alone.

"The poor master." Mrs Blount dabbed at her eyes with the hem of her pinafore. She had removed her hat and now that the impediment to the approach to the stove had been removed set about boiling the kettle. "First the loss of his good friend, Mr Robertson, now his good lady."

"Robertson – that would be Mr Fife's partner."

"Yes, sir. He died quite recent. He was a bachelor, always in poor health, a bit consumptive like. He lived here in this house, had no family of his own, devoted to the children, a sad loss."

"Who inherited his share of the house and the retail store?"

"Mr Fife naturally, but I'm sure he would rather have him alive, they were such good friends."

"What can you tell me about Miss Emily Vickers?"

"The master met her at the Archery Club and introduced her to his wife. She was really madam's friend. A kind lady, not handsome but kind."

"And a spinster. One would think that a wealthy heiress, even one who is not handsome, would have suitors."

"Any aspiring suitor would be chased away by her father. A regular old devil is Halliday Vickers. You know he kept the master out of the Hunt Club, said it was only for the elect, and with the master a member of the Adelaide Club, too!"

"I understand your master has an interest in an undertaking establishment."

"Yes, he once managed a block of shops consisting of a chemist, imported glass and china, a milliner's, a dressmaker's, and Indian rugs and carpets. Ironic, isn't it, he was at the undertaker's this very day, collecting rent."

"He wasn't with you at the Charles Blondin exhibition?"

"No, he escorted us there, dropped us off, went off to collect his rents, and then came back to pick us up."

"Strange for a gentleman in his position to do that when he could employ someone to be his rent collector."

Mrs Blount smiled mysteriously and glanced along the passage before closing the door. "That was his excuse, but I suspect he had other business." She paused obviously expecting the Inspector to bite and Toop obliged.

"What sort of business?"

"He's a bit of a ladies' man, if you know what I mean. And who can blame him with the mistress the way she was. Not that he'd patronize the Saddling Paddock at the Theatre Royal, but it's my guess he had an *assignation*." She hissed the last word as gleefully as a cat who'd caught sight of a mouse.

"Would you know with whom?"

"All the ladies dote on him, even those who shouldn't."

"Like . . ." prompted Toop.

"Like Nancy for one. She's got an eye for the men, that one. Off she went today done up like the Queen of Sheba. *You're up to no good, my girl*, I thought to myself." She looked suddenly anxious. "The master didn't say he'd gone to see Charles Blondin today, did he? Have I put me foot in it?"

"Not at all. You've been most helpful."

"He's so daring, so acrobatic."

"Mr Fife?"

"Lawd luv you, sir. *Mr Blondin*. Even made an omelette on a spirit stove on his tightwire and passed it down for some of us to sample, good as I could make meself."

Toop found the master of the house in his study scrawling a letter, which he covered with a blotter when the Inspector entered.

"One more word before I leave, sir. I understand you were not at the performance given by the magnificent Charles Blondin."

The large blue eyes took on a cold, shallow look. "Did I gave you that impression? I didn't mean to."

"Where were you, sir, if I may be so impertinent?"

"I do find you impertinent, sir. If I had been in the house I would have made every endeavour to save Ada's life. Since she is dead you may presume I was not here and *where* I was is of no consequence."

"Collecting rents from your tenants, were you, sir?"

A flash of irritation quivered over Fife's features. "Damn that woman and her runaway tongue. She'll lose her place if she's not careful."

"Was your marriage with Mrs Fife happy?"

"Do you mean am I involved with another woman? Yes, but not one I'd care to kill my wife for."

"That's plain speaking, sir. Would she be willing to alibi you?"

Fife's irritation exploded into anger. "Do you think I'd be willing to betray her name and then expect to read it in the *Midnight Rambler* column? Any more of your insufferable snooping and I'll complain to the Commissioner about you."

A low tap at the door interrupted them. At Fife's brusque

answer, the maid Nancy appeared. She had removed her hat, but was still wearing her elaborate dress and blonde ringlets. She was of the type commonly described as saucy, all dimples and blushes, though some of her colour owed more to the cosmetician than to nature. "Did you deliver the children safely to Miss Vickers?"

"Yes, sir. She was ever so sorry, shocked you might say . . ."

"Yes, all right. What do you want?"

"A boy's just come to the back door with a note from Miss Amory, sir."

Fife took the note from Nancy, read it swiftly and crumpled it in his hand. "Tell Mrs Blount Miss Amory will not be returning tonight. And, Nancy, take some of that rouge off your face. This is a house of mourning."

"Yes, sir," her tone was submissive, but her glance smouldered with resentment. Or passion.

"Miss Amory being . . . ?" Toop raised his eyebrows.

"The children's nurse-cum-governess; she's visiting her sister in Walkerville, who's been taken ill. It appears her condition has worsened."

Toop nodded. "I won't trouble you any further, sir." In the doorway he paused. "How would *you* do it, sir?"

Fife needed no qualification of the question. "With the Smith & Wesson I keep in my desk drawer, I suppose."

Toop found Dr Sandow and Mrs Blount consoling each other over tea and cakes.

"How were you made aware that Mrs Fife required your attention, Dr Sandow?"

"She sent a note by Charlie, the stable boy."

"Would I find this youth on the premises?"

"He's probably unharnessing the horse," volunteered Mrs Blount.

Toop gave a nod to Constable Jessup, who disappeared through the back door.

"By the way, Doctor, did you treat Hamish Robertson?"

"I treat all the members of this household," said Sandow, primly.

"What were his symptoms?"

Sandow hesitated. "He was of a delicate constitution, consumptive, and towards the end his digestion was poor."

"Did he suffer any hair loss?"

Sandow looked startled. "We of the male gender are prone to baldness, I'm afraid." He preened his own luxuriant hair and whiskers as he spoke.

"And what of his state of mind?"

"He became irrational, even deranged."

"But not deranged enough to be committed to the Lunatic Asylum at Parkside. Or to have his will contested."

"What are you implying, sir?" asked Sandow, huffily.

"Was he admitted to the General Hospital?"

"No, he died at home."

"And no doubt was cared for by Mr Fife's own undertaking establishment. What was the certified cause of death?"

"Consumption and decline."

"Wouldn't you concur that his symptoms were similar to those of Mrs Fife?"

Sandow coloured to the roots of his mutton chops. "Mrs Fife didn't have consumption, sir."

"And neither in all probability did Mr Robertson," said Toop to Jessup as they returned to the Gilbert Street branch through the gathering dusk. "The results of a post mortem might prove interesting if we could get an exhumation order from the coroner."

"I thought we wuz investigating an accident." Jessup was surprised.

"So we are, but there are some peculiarities which I'm sure you noticed." When the sergeant failed to volunteer any observations Toop continued. "I don't believe Mrs Fife ran into the kitchen. I believe she was dragged there, hence the black track marks in the drawing room and the passage."

"Why would anyone do that?"

"To make it look as if the flames were fanned by her flight. Her hands and arms were relatively unscathed. Why didn't she attempt to beat out the flames? Her fingernails tell a different story, Alby – traces of skin and blood and something totally unrelated – a bluish tinge."

"Oh, yeah."

"Ada Fife has some of the classic symptoms of arsenic poisoning – poor digestion, hair loss, irrational behaviour and a bluish tint to the nails. The same symptoms were exhibited by Hamish Robertson. That doctor is either a fool or an accomplice."

"Aren't you jumping to conclusions, Mr Toop?"

"Better to jump when the trail's hot than drag one's feet when it's cold. Observe, Alby, that both deaths are advantageous to Mr George Duguld Fife. The first made him full owner of a large emporium on Rundle Street and of a terrace house in the fashionable district of North Adelaide. The second rids him of a neurotic wife and allows him to make a more satisfactory marriage. And think of the convenience of having one's own chemist shop next door to one's own undertaking establishment."

Unfortunately, Coroner Thomas Ward, JP did not concur that there were suspicious circumstances in either case and refused the application for exhumation. Ada Fife's body was released for burial. What if Fife had purchased arsenic and signed the poison's ledger? Had Toop never heard of rats in the cellar? Or Jessup sniggered to Toop, gentlemen who took small amounts as an aphrodisiac? Or women using arsenic as a cosmetic?

Not only, thought Toop bitterly, to add that George Duguld Fife was a respectable member of society, a member of the Adelaide Club and the coroner had no wish to offend him by insinuation that all was not right and proper in his household.

Toop attended the funeral officiated at St Andrew's Church by Canon Dove and the burial in the nearby Wesleyan cemetery. He was mainly interested in the person of Miss Emily Vickers, the family friend described by Mrs Blount as not handsome but kind. She was a woman over thirty, with frizzy hair and a muddy complexion not enhanced by the unrelieved black of her moiré dress and the plumed hat tilted over her forehead. She had charge of the children and seemed very fond of them. George Fife's face was devoid of expression, his eyes opaque as blue ice within their silver lashes. He wore a long black coat and top hat.

"Ain't he a handsome one, though?" whispered Mrs Blount, as Toop slipped into a pew beside her.

Nancy also attended and managed to look voluptuous even in a plain black dress. Charlie was suitably sombre in dark-grey knee britches and jacket, woollen stockings and elastic-sided boots. The only member of the household missing was Ivy Amory.

"She hasn't been to the house since the mistress died," informed the housekeeper. "Right poorly she is, so Dr Sandow says. Must have caught what her sister had."

Toop frowned, but said nothing. He managed to collar the doctor as he was following the coffin out of the church. "I understand you are treating Miss Amory. May I enquire of you your diagnosis?"

"No, you may not," snapped Sandow. "That is a confidential matter between doctor and patient."

*There's nothing to prevent me from paying her a courtesy call*, Toop said to himself, *once I've obtained her address from the indefatigably loquacious Mrs Blount.*

Miss Amory's sister, whose name was Mrs Ramsey, lived in one of the double-fronted cottages along Williams Street, Walkerville, where one opened the wicker gate and was almost immediately on a shallow verandah confronting the front door.

Mrs Ramsey showed no signs of ill health. She was a tall, dark woman with high cheekbones set between sunken eyes and sunken cheeks. Her sister was a younger, rounder version with the same dark hair and fierce black eyes. Her complexion was sallow, she looked ill and despite the heat of the summer noon she had a shawl drawn close about her throat. She was propped high on lace-trimmed pillows on a white-painted iron bedstead. Everything was white including her night-dress and the quilt, but for the scarlet embroidery on her shawl.

While Mrs Ramsey fussed over her, Toop wandered to her dressing table and examined her hairbrush. It was thickly entangled with hairs.

With Mrs Ramsey standing disapprovingly in the doorway, Toop sat gingerly on the end of the bed and fixed Miss Amory with a sympathetic but intent eye. She in turn studied his freckled face and shrewd hazel eyes with an expression bordering on fearful suspense. Toop would have liked to catch a glimpse of her fingernails, but she kept her arms under the quilt.

"I don't understand why you wish to question me. Wasn't the coroner's verdict death by misadventure?"

"So it was, but I'm not completely satisfied. When a doubt gnaws like a rat in my brain I have to harry it like a terrier."

"And you smell a rat?"

"Yes, when Charlie returned on his pony from his visit to Dr Sandow he thought he heard the front door slam. Was it you leaving the house?"

"No, I spent all afternoon with my sister."

"That's right," said Mrs Ramsey, staunchly.

"Miss Vickers, Mrs Blount and the children were watching Charles Blondin teetering sixty feet above the ground, Mr Fife and Nancy can alibi each other . . ."

He had taken a wild shot, but the shaft struck home. Her face took on a yellow hue. "What do you mean?"

"Surely you suspected your employer and his maid of having a clandestine affair. I've made enquiries at his millinery establishment. They spent the afternoon together in an upstairs room."

She made a choking sound and slumped forward. Her sister was instantly by her side, patting her back soothingly and glaring fiercely at Toop. "If you've no real business with my sister I suggest you go."

"One last thing. Would you be kind enough to show me your hands?"

She gasped and fell back against her sister's supporting arm. Toop felt it was time to make his presence scarce. Since the case was officially closed, he had no business to be there and it would be difficult to explain his conduct if the Commissioner received a complaint via Fife.

As he was leaving he saw a woman alighting from a victoria. She was wearing grey, was heavily veiled and carried a basket over her arm. As he watched, she knocked on the front door, exchanged a few words with Mrs Ramsey and passed her the basket. When she turned back she saw Toop standing by his horse. She halted mid-stride, her head turned in his direction. He caught the gleam of her eyes behind her veil before she climbed into the carriage. Toop went thoughtfully on his way. He had recognized the driver as Charlie, Fife's stable boy. Before returning to Gilbert Street, he called in at the telegraph office.

Several other cases demanded the detective's attention over February, but when he was free to pursue the Fife affair he made his first port of call the chemist on Rundle Street East to examine the Poisons Register. While he was wading through the pages, the chemist whispered something to his boy, who went into the back room to fetch a ladder.

"I apologize," the chemist pointed to an unsightly strip of fly-paper clustered with tiny black corpses hanging from the ceiling, "but the hot weather do bring in the blowies."

Toop watched idly as the boy climbed the ladder and replaced the strip. "Lured by molasses to a sticky fate, eh?"

"It's the arsenic that does 'em in."

"Arsenic." Toop's hand jerked, inadvertently tearing the page he was studying.

"Yes, sir, fly-paper is impregnated with arsenic." He eyed the Register. "Look what you've gone and done, sir."

"My turn to apologise. Of course, no-one would have to sign the Poisons Register to buy fly-paper."

"No, sir. No way anyone could murder anyone with fly-paper. How'd you do it? Serve it up with the tea and scones?"

Toop stared thoughtfully at the glass amphorae of coloured tinctures on the top shelf, reminding customers that the profession of the apothecary was among the oldest in the world.

On his return to Gilbert Street, he collared a passing constable. "Harris, I want you to go and purchase some fly-paper and arrest any stray moggie you see lurking about."

Constable Jessup looked up from a copy of *The Register* with a wide grin. "Here's sumpthin' you might be interested in, Mr Toop. The recently bereaved Mr George Duguld Fife has announced his engagement to Miss Emily Vickers. Not wasting any time, is 'e?"

Toop was silent for a few minutes.

"Alby, you and I are going to visit the Fife household in the presence of two constables. We'll call by the telegraph office on our way."

Although he expected George Fife to be absent at the Emporium, Toop examined the elegant facade of local lime-stone and imported ironwork and decided to take the pre-caution of entering by the back door. He found Mrs Blount drinking tea while she poured over the social pages in *The Register*. Her eyelids looked swollen; she had obviously been crying. She evinced no surprise at his intrusion; she looked beyond that.

He sat beside her and sipped the tea she provided for him. She seemed grateful for his company.

"Momentous news, hey?" He glanced at the newspaper.

"With the mistress not cold in her grave and Mr Vickers at death's door, so they say."

"Oh they do, do they?"

"Well, Dr Sandow says. Still, the children need a mother. And Miss Vickers is a very kind woman. At least I used to think so."

"What's happened to change your opinion?"

"Been given me notice, haven't I? Miss Vickers wants to bring her own cook into the household once she's married."

"What about Nancy?"

"She's going, too, but the master's got her a position in that millinery shop he owns, so she'll be all right."

Toop hid a smile. Fife was certainly not going to let his new marriage interfere with his amours with the fetching Nancy.

"And Miss Amory?"

"She's right poorly, the poor dear."

"Yes, I know. I went to see her. I think I saw you arriving in Mr Fife's victoria. You were carrying a basket."

She opened her eyes as wide as her puffy lids would allow. "Not I, sir. If I want to visit Miss Amory I have to walk."

"Perhaps it was Nancy. The lady wore a veil."

"More likely Miss Vickers on one of her errands of mercy. She likes to visit the sick with dainties from her own kitchen to tempt their appetites."

Toop nodded, looking a little bored. Rising, he glanced around the kitchen. From the ceiling hung a strip of flypaper with its cargo of dead flies. She followed the direction of his gaze.

"Not a pretty sight, but what can one do in the summertime? Where do all the flies go in the winter, that's what I'd like to know."

There was a sharp *rat-tat-tat* at the front door. "That will be the doctor," said Mrs Blount.

"Someone in the house is sick?"

" 'Nancy's feeling a bit queasy.' She dropped her voice to a confidential whisper. "If you ask me she might have to pay the piper for the jig she's been dancing."

Jessup's craggy face split into a grin as he realized the inference of her words.

Sandow greeted Toop sombrely, without surprise or rancour. His face looked hangdog, drooping between his whiskers.

"I'm glad to see you here, Inspector. It saves me a trip into the city. Miss Amory has expressed a wish to speak to you. I'm afraid that young woman is not long for this world. Will you accompany me back to see her?"

"Miss Amory dying!" gasped Mrs Blount. "Am I permitted to visit her?"

"She's had too many visitors," said the doctor grimly and went out the back door to the tiny cottages that housed the servants.

"I wonder what he meant by that," said Mrs Blount.

Toop said nothing, but drank a second cup of tea with the housekeeper while awaiting the doctor's return. He asked with his eyebrows an unspoken question. Sandow shook his head. "Nothing lethal. She's suffering nausea from quite a natural cause."

Mrs Blount sniffed.

Toop and his companions followed the doctor's trap the

short distance to Walkerville and along Gilbert Road, past the Buckingham Arms, across Stephens Terrace past the shops, the paddock where the boys played quoits and skittles, past the Sussex Arms to Mrs Ramsey's cottage. The day was hot, the sun a ball of fire in the sky. Jessup took off his shako and mopped his face before he entered the house, where the gloom occasioned by the drawn curtains gave an illusion of coolness.

Toop recognized the smell as soon as he entered the bedroom. Ivy Amory was sallow and feverish, her arms lay on a sheet spread on top of the coverlet. Her hair had been shorn away in a belated remedy for fever. Several healing scratches were now visible on her neck. Her sunken eyes were alert and held a rush of relief when she recognized Toop.

"Gangrene," Toop grunted. "She should be in the General Hospital."

"It's too late. I was called in too late. Not even amputation can save her now."

"Don't blame Dr Sandow," whispered Ivy. "I refused admission. What would it have led to? The realization that I was involved in Ada Fife's arrest, trial and death at the end of a rope in Adelaide Gaol."

"Were you involved?" he asked, gently.

Her face was suddenly Medusa-like, viperish and gloating. "I thrust her into the fire and held her there. She fought like a wildcat, but I was stronger. When she stopped struggling I dragged her into the kitchen . . ."

"To make it look as if she had run in panic and fanned the flames."

"Yes. When the exhilaration of killing her was gone, I realized the extent of my burns. I ran upstairs and changed my dress and shoes – I had scorched one shoe on the hearth. From the window I saw Charlie riding in on his pony. I knew I had to leave before the doctor arrived. I ran out the front door, slamming it in my haste – that's what Charlie heard. I went to my sister's and she put butter on my burns, but it didn't help . . ."

"Why did you kill her?"

"Because George told me that he loved me, that if it wasn't for his wife he would marry me. What a fool I was to be seduced by the promise of a marriage that would never be. He's going to marry an heiress and all the time he's been bedding that little slut Nancy," her voice trailed away with exhaustion, but after a moment she rallied. "I can't sign your statement, but I want everyone in this room to bear witness to my confession. Now I can die with a clear conscience."

"You have a lot to answer for, Sandow," Toop said, sternly, as they stood on the shallow verandah. "You surely must have had your suspicions, but then these people are the top drawer, the *crème de la crème*, so how could they possibly be guilty of murder? You'll have to appear at the inquest and the court will make of you what it will."

"Dr Sandow, come quickly." A distraught Mrs Ramsey was at the front door.

"She's snuffed it," Jessup said, lugubriously. "May she find forgiveness in Heaven, but I doubt it."

"Though her skins be as scarlet, they will be as white as snow," misquoted Toop, softly.

"You reckon so?" Jessup looked dubious.

"If she had lived I doubt whether she would have hanged. Rather she would have been committed to the Parkside Asylum, driven mad not by love but by arsenical poisoning."

"What! You still harping on that?"

"Oh, yes, Alby, I am indeed."

"Well, we goin' back to Gilbert Street to make our report?"

"On the way I think we'll call on Miss Vickers and congratulate her on her engagement."

Toop stationed the two constables at the front door of Mr Halliday Vickers's ornate Robe Terrace masion. The house had an Eastern influence of minarets and balconies with a weathercock perched incongruously on a dome. He took Jessup with him about the house, pausing to peer through its many windows, until they reached the back door. In a wash house at the end of the verandah a woman was turning the crank of a washing machine, the clothes churning like butter in a wooden barrel. She stared amazed as the two officers opened the kitchen door without knocking.

The room was shadowy, the shades drawn against the hot glare. Emily Vickers stood at the scrubbed wooden table dicing vegetables. A pot containing a fricassee of mutton stood at one elbow. At the other was a bowl, its contents covered with a beaded muslin cloth. She was wearing a pinafore over a grey dress with a drooping bustle in the "elegant fish" style so much in vogue. Toop noticed the scarlet bow between the twin peaks of her collar.

"A hot day, Miss Vickers."

"Not as hot as we were accustomed to in India." If she was startled by their intrusion she did not betray it, but said, calmly, "This is an unsuspected visit, Inspector. May I enquire its purpose?"

"To congratulate you on your engagement and to enquire after your father's health."

"A letter would have sufficed for the first, the second a word with Dr Sandow."

"I'm also the bearer of bad tidings. Miss Ivy Amory, the governess to your fiancé's children, has just died."

Miss Vickers continued chopping the vegetables without a quiver. "I'm sorry to hear that. She was devoted to the children."

"And to Mr Fife."

She flashed a glance at him from eyes of murky brown, but said nothing.

"She confessed on her death bed. No doubt, you wish she'd let Ada Fife die in the natural course of events instead of committing this violent act which has resulted in so many enquiries."

"I'm not sure what you mean. Ada was still a relatively young woman." She scraped the vegetables from the board into the pot.

"Do you do all the cooking for the household?"

"Yes, my father prefers the meals I prepare." She carried the pot to the stove.

"It was a very hot day last year when W. G. Grace led his English Eleven out onto a playing field scorched brown by our pitiless sun and faced South Australia's Twenty Two. I paid 2/6d to stand in the broiling sunshine and watch our narrow defeat. News of the English victory would have been flashed immediately to London."

She raised her heavy brows in an hauteur tinged with contempt. "How does this little anecdote concern me?"

"Oh, but it does, Miss Vickers. A wonderful invention, the electric wire. Don't you remember the rejoicing in the streets in '72 when the Darwin to Adelaide Overland Telegraph was officially opened? Or were you still in England then. You lived with an aunt, didn't you? Not with your father in India. A maiden aunt who left you well provided for when she died after a lingering illness. Her death caused suspicion in a certain housemaid, who reported her suspicions. Scotland Yard was very informative. You were never charged because of insufficient evidence and the accusation of the housemaid was put down to envy. Nevertheless, you decided it was politic to quit England and join your father. How unfortunate that he turned out to be such a martinet, treating you like a servant and discouraging any suitors, until he became too ill to interfere. So many ailing people about you and you nursed them all devotedly."

He whisked off the muslin cover from the bowl. "You've forgotten one ingredient in your stew." A strip of fly-paper lay soaking in water. "So that's how it's done, the liquid drained off and added to the stew."

She reacted then, her face as ugly and Gorgon-like as Miss Amory's had been. "Damn you, you meddling snoop. And damn that lovesick governess for whom George never had so much as a glance. If she hadn't murdered Ada all would have gone well. You think me a cold-blooded woman, but everything I did I did for George so he could have wealth and esteem and love."

Toop shook his head, his eyes flint-hard. "Everything you did you did for yourself. From jealousy and desperation that you'd never have a husband, never have children, and you took what belonged to another woman. Who would have been next? Nancy? Did you know she is pregnant with Fife's child?"

She fell back against the dresser. A plate crashed to the floor beside her. It must have sounded to her like the smashing of her life.

"Constable Jessup will remain with you and I'll leave two constables stationed on the verandah. I'll return with a warrant for your arrest for the murder of Hamish Robertson, the attempted murders of Ada Fife, Ivy Amory and Halliday Vickers. I think the court will be impressed with an experiment I intend to conduct with fly-paper and a stray cat."

On his way back to the city, Toop deliberately took a route along Le Fevre Terrace. Arrangements would have to be made for the Fife children to be collected from the Vickers household. He doubted whether Mrs Blount would now have to find a new position.

Along the Terrace he passed the man himself, driving his handsome equipage and spanking thoroughbred. Toop hid a smile as he raised his derby.

For years the ambitious George Dugald Fife had fought and charmed his way into the elect of Adelaide society. Now he would have the most unenviable reputation in South Australia, that of having two women commit murder for him.

# The Gentleman on the Titanic

## John Lutz

*John Lutz has been writing short stories for over forty years and has a shelf full of awards, including the Lifetime Achievement Award from the Private-Eye Writers of America. He's probably best known for the novel* SWF Seeks Same *(1990), which was made into the highly-charged film* Single White Female *(1992). He's also written a long series about St Louis PI Alo Nudger and an even darker series about Florida ex-cop-turned-PI Fred Carver who in* Scorcher *(1987) has to cope with a maniac with a flamethrower who murders Carver's son. For the following story, though, Lutz takes us back to arguably the most famous ship in history, the* Titanic. *The sinking of the* Titanic *brought to an end a Golden Era and is a suitable point at which to bring to a close our travels through the crimes of the centuries.*

The handsome young English gentleman boarded the *Titanic* shortly before she sailed. Instead of staying up on deck to watch Queenstown and the Irish shore recede, as did most of the other passengers, he retired to his first-class cabin on C-deck.

He looked to be about thirty, and everything about his dress and demeanour suggested he was of high birth. His well-tailored grey suit flattered his slim but muscular build, and at lunch he demonstrated flawless social skills. His features were lean, somewhat bony, his eyes hooded and blue, his thin lips almost always arced in a pleasant near-smile that never quite took form. Accompanying these other attributes was his modulated voice and accent of the ruling class, suggesting wealth, education, and connections. The single women in first class were keenly interested.

They weren't alone in their curiosity. "Do you know the chap?" asked retired British Army colonel Roger Brookes, watching the gentleman walk away from the table.

"He didn't give his name, I'm sure," Alma Clinkscale, one of two marginally attractive but wealthy twin sisters at the table said.

Her sister Vera, identically blond and bland except for a dark mole beneath her left eye, looked up from stirring her tea. "I'll bet you were listening closely for it."

"As if you weren't."

Vera glared across the scones at her sister, the mole lending at least some intensity to her expression.

"Extraordinary, hey?" the colonel mumbled from beneath his grey hedge of a moustache. Though in his sixties, he had a military carriage that made his ordinary brown tweed suit seem a uniform despite the bread crumbs flecking his jacket and vest. Colonel Brookes had served the Empire long and well, and his doddering manner and etiquette lapses such as crumbs at table were willingly overlooked. His devoted and accommodating wife Maude reached over and brushed the worst of the crumbs away.

"Wick is his name," said a deep voice from across the table. It belonged to British financier Donald Braithwaite. As usual when he spoke, all other conversation ceased. Large, broad-shouldered, and imposing, with a jutting jaw and fierce dark eyes sunk deep in their sockets, he would have been a man to listen to even if he didn't own much of England. "Bloke's name is Ashton Wick."

"Affable chap, but a bit vague," the colonel remarked, reaching for what was left of a hard roll. "Fine posture. Well set up, as if he's been in one of the services."

"No, I don't think he's ever been a military man," Braithwaite said. He lifted glittering stemmed crystal and took a sip of his port wine.

"He *is* English, isn't he?" the colonel's wife asked.

"Oh, yes," Braithwaite said, "though he was educated in France. I met him a few years ago when I was in Paris on business. He's some sort of artist. A sculptor, I believe."

"An artist!" Alma Clinkscale said. "Isn't that sensual and wonderful!"

The colonel gazed at her with disapproval.

"He was rumoured to have talented hands," Braithwaite said.

Vera Clinkscale sampled her tea, apparently found it to her liking, and smiled without looking up.

Woolgathering, no doubt, the colonel decided.

Later that afternoon, as Wick was taking the air on the main promenade deck, a woman's voice made him pause and turn. More than the voice, it was what the woman had said that brought him up short: "Bertie!"

He stood casually, with one knee slightly bent and a hand in a pocket, and watched her approach. Recognition flooded into him. He knew her, but she was greatly changed.

"Why, Bertie Wicker!" she said more softly, smiling as she drew near. She was wearing a high-collared cotton dress with a billowing grey skirt, cinched tightly at the waist. No jewellery glinted in the sun, and her dark hair was mussed and hanging over one of her startlingly bright violet eyes. Wick sized her up immediately: She would be twenty-one now (he had known her in the slums of London six years ago when he was a twenty-four-year-old destitute art student), she was traveling third class, and she was beautiful. Her smile grew even broader. "Do you remember me? I'm Lorna Palin."

"Yes, Lorna . . ."

"My, my, don't you look as if you're doing well?" Then she seemed suddenly ill at ease. "You might not know it, but I, uh, used to have a terrible crush on you."

Wick knew and had known at the time. If she hadn't been so young . . .

"I was but a girl then, Bertie. Now I'm much older."

"As I am," Wick said. She was gazing at him the way the

younger Lorna had those years ago. He realized he was returning her frank and somewhat confused stare. Their attraction still held, after so much time. "You've become quite beautiful," Wick stammered.

"So have you, Bertie." She winked.

He studied her, gnawing his lower lip. Then he gripped her elbow and steered her toward the rail. She didn't seem to mind. "Lorna, I'm going to have to take you into my confidence."

"Please do, Bertie."

"It isn't Bertie anymore," he said. "It's Ashton."

She took him in with those marvellous violet eyes. "Are you putting on airs, Bertie?"

He smiled. "Not exactly." His face grew serious. "I could always trust you as a child, Lorna."

"And you can trust the woman," she told him, somehow closer to him without seeming to have moved.

"On this ship, I'm not Bertie Wicker, I'm Ashton Wick."

"Bertie, are you on the wrong side of the law? Did the art not work out?"

"I'm on the right side of the law, Lorna. Would you believe me if I told you I'm with British Intelligence?"

"If you need me to believe you, then I do believe."

"No one else is to know. To you now, as to everyone else on board, I'm Ashton Wick."

"Then that's how it will be . . . Ashton. Though I do like Bertie better."

"Lorna, please!"

"All right, Ashton," Lorna said firmly.

"And we mustn't seem to know each other while on board. We must stay apart."

"Ah, I don't like that part of it, Ber – Ashton."

"It's tremendously important, or I wouldn't ask. War with Germany is in the wind, and I have a sworn and secret duty on this vessel."

"Yes, I saw a cartoon in *Punch*, and there were Germany, France, and England, sitting all together and chatting on a powder keg with its fuse burning."

"That's what makes this so important," Ashton said urgently. "It's for all of Europe."

"Then I'll do as you say," she told him, "but I do have a question. What's British Intelligence?"

Shortly after leaving Lorna, Wick met, as planned, with Braithwaite in Braithwaite's first-class stateroom at the opposite end of C-deck from Wick's own. Braithwaite was waiting for him and opened the door on the first knock.

"Good afternoon, Herr Braithwaite," Wick said as the door closed behind him.

Braithwaite waved an arm toward a red velvet wing chair, and Wick sat. Braithwaite continued to stand, crossing his beefy arms. He said, "For the purposes of this operation, remember that I outrank you. But on this ship, I will be Mr Braithwaite and you will be Ashton Wick."

"Of course. That's as headquarters instructed." Wick knew that Braithwaite was one of those English who were German sympathizers banking quite literally on war and on Germany's victory. A genuine British-born citizen, he was one of the more highly placed and valuable German agents. Wick sat calmly, waiting for his briefing. German intelligence operated on a strict need-to-know basis, and for the first time he was to learn the details of the mission.

Braithwaite uncrossed his arms and began pacing as he spoke softly and conspiratorially in his gruff voice. "One of the Englishmen traveling first class on the *Titanic* is transporting plans for a radio-controlled torpedo-guidance device to an American corporation for development and manufacture. Once we learn who has the plans, our object is to photograph them, then leave them undisturbed."

Wick understood why the plans weren't simply to be stolen. This way the Germans could develop a counter-device while the Americans and British continued wasting their time and resources on a guidance system vulnerable to interference.

"We have also learned," Braithwaite said, "that the courier is one of those seated at our table in first-class dining." He smiled. "The seating arrangements were not an accident."

Wick also smiled. Berlin was thorough.

"When we decide on those of our fellow diners most likely

to be the courier, we will search their staterooms, find the plans, and take our photographs. The problem, of course, is that this must be done within a limited amount of time."

"I'm sure it will be accomplished," Wick said.

He rose from his chair, as Braithwaite had gone to the stateroom door, indicating the briefing was ended.

Wick had considered, then rejected, the idea of telling Braithwaite about Lorna Palin. He was sure that problem could be held in check. And he *wasn't* quite sure how the ruthless Braithwaite might react to the information.

What Braithwaite hadn't told Wick was that there was another German agent on board, travelling third class as a Swede under the name Nels Svenson. Svenson had witnessed the meeting between Wick and Lorna on the promenade deck, but as yet it hadn't aroused his suspicions.

At dinner that evening, Wick was his usual charming and casual self, but through all eleven courses he was sizing up his fellow diners. Their table was actually two square tables butted together, so that twelve were seated rather than the usual eight. Who among those present possessed plans that could determine the course of history?

The twin sisters, Alma and Vera Clinkscale, he thought could probably be ruled out. But only probably. They might not be as airheaded and flirtatious as they seemed.

Next to the Clinkscales sat sardonic American playwright Charles Minheart, author of the recent Broadway and London hit musical *Around the Maypole*. He was a definite possibility.

Also at the table were the bumbling Colonel Brookes and his wife Maude, a typical ex-military couple. The colonel liked to recount old war adventures while his wife tolerated and tried to moderate his boorish behaviour.

There were also *noveau riche* American hardware tycoon Ernest Walker and his dour wife Jane, from some place called Indiana; young British bachelor Drake Manningly; Lucy Burnwright, a fading but flamboyant American actress who spent most of the evening flirting with Wick and Manningly when she wasn't obviously trying to manipulate Minheart into giving her a role in the touring production of *Maypole*;

and popular British journalist Rob Coyle, on board to write an article for the *London Times* about the great ship's maiden voyage.

There were, Wick decided, too many possibilities. He had to tackle them in order of priority.

From a port to the east, another ship had set to sea. The German submarine *SM U-7* was several days out in the Atlantic when its sternly handsome and stoical commander, Hermann Geerhauser, informed his officers and crew of the sub's mission. His briefing was characteristically terse: "We are going to a point in the Atlantic where we are to shadow an ocean liner." He did not tell them why.

First Officer Willi Rendt, a bearlike but peaceable man, asked no questions, but he pondered possible reasons for the mission. The sub wasn't armed with torpedoes and was carrying only the minimal amount of ammunition for its deck gun. That boded well.

Doubting that *U-7* was about to engage in an act that might precipitate war, Rendt waited patiently for further instructions from his commander.

Wick and Braithwaite's suspicions centred on Manningly, the dashing bachelor, and journalist Rob Coyle. But Braithwaite did remind Wick that Lucy Burnwright was an actress. British Intelligence might think her eminently capable of deception and might have entrusted her with the plans, appealing to her romanticism as well as patriotism.

While Braithwaite concentrated his attentions on the attractive Lucy Burnwright, Wick managed to become involved in a poker game with Coyle, Manningly, and several other men in the Gentlemen's First-Class Lounge. Deliberately losing early, he excused himself from the game and left to search the cabins of both men as well as that of Lucy Burnwright, who was being kept occupied by Braithwaite. He had told her he was toying with the idea of financing a play.

After stopping at his cabin to get the small Leica camera

Braithwaite had given him, Wick stepped out into the passageway and was confronted by Lorna Palin.

She smiled and kissed his cheek. "I snuck up here with the rich folks to see if you wanted to stroll on the deck."

He couldn't help catching the sweet scent of her perfume, feeling the warmth of her closeness. Couldn't help touching her cheek. "I, uh, told you that wasn't possible, Lorna."

She glanced down at the camera he was carrying. "Isn't it too dark to take pictures?"

"Yes. I'm on my way up to the Gentlemen's Lounge to show someone how this works." He knew she couldn't follow him there.

"Ah! Is it part of your work then?" she asked, grinning at the delicious adventure of it.

"Please, Lorna, don't even mention that. Only trust me. I don't want you to be in danger."

"I don't care —"

"Or to put me in danger."

She paused and stared up at him, then kissed him again, this time gently on the lips. He couldn't help it. He held her close and kissed her back.

When they separated, he whispered, "Please, Lorna!"

"I understand, love," she said. "But later . . . ?"

"Later," he promised.

She hesitantly took her hand away from his arm. Smiling, she left him.

Minding his mission, Wick hurried in the opposite direction, toward the first of the cabins whose door he was to open with the master key Braithwaite had mysteriously procured. It was all enough to make one have complete faith in Berlin.

But after thorough searches, Wick had found nothing suspicious in the cabins of Manningly, Coyle, or Lucy Burnwright.

"We must extend our searches," Braithwaite told him later that night. "And soon."

The next morning, as Colonel Brookes strolled on deck for his daily exercise while his wife reclined in a deck chair and read a Jacques Futrelle novel, Wick found the plans hidden in a false bottom of the colonel's suitcase.

He was waiting for the colonel when he returned to the stateroom to change from his walkers.

Brookes stood motionless while his glance shot to the still-open suitcase then back to Wick.

"Mrs Brookes still reading?" Wick asked.

The colonel didn't blink. "You know she is, or you wouldn't be here. A Futrelle novel. Chap's on board, you know."

"The plans are gone," Wick said. "I'm putting them in a safe place."

"And where would that be?" the colonel asked. His bearing was much different now. The doddering, kindly military fossil was suddenly vital and sharp-eyed.

"My stateroom, one of the last places Braithwaite would search." Wick stood up from his chair and extended his hand. "I'm Captain Evan Wick, British Intelligence. I'm also a German double agent. They think I'm working for them."

Brooks hesitated before shaking the hand, then said crisply, "Explain."

Wick did.

The *U-7* had reached its destination 370 miles off the coast of Newfoundland.

"We will soon be engaged in a recovery operation," Captain Geerhauser told his officers. "An object in a water-tight container will be jettisoned from the ocean liner we are to shadow. It will float a few feet beneath the surface and emit a radio signal, and fifteen minutes later a stream of yellow dye. The U-7 will home in on the signal, then visually on the dye, and recover the container."

He then turned command over to Willi Rendt and retired to his quarters. When it was dark, the *U-7* was to surface and lookouts were to be posted. Neither Rendt nor any of the other officers had asked what was in the container they were to recover. Geerhauser would have informed them if he'd wanted them to know.

On the fourth day at sea, Braithwaite answered a knock on his stateroom door to find the six-foot, hulking form of Nels Svenson looming in the passageway

"You'd better have good reason to be here," Braithwaite said, grabbing the man's arm and pulling him inside before anyone saw him.

"I've been watching Wick, as instructed," Svenson said. "He's been secretly seeing a woman on board."

Braithwaite stared at him, then sneered. "One of those idiot twins?"

"No, a third-class passenger."

"That's absurd. He's a loyal German agent with a mission." But Braithwaite knew Wick was also a man.

"They try to look casual or stay out of sight, but they act like newlyweds. They sneak kisses and pose for pictures. They make love in dark places. And I saw them talking the day we sailed, as if they already knew each other."

Braithwaite jammed his hands in his pants pockets, paced a few steps this way and that, then stood still and looked calmly at Svenson. "She's an unacceptable security risk."

"You mean she won't reach New York?"

"I didn't say that."

"Of course you didn't," Svenson said. "And there's something else. That fellow Rob Coyle's seen them together, too. I saw him watching them."

"He's a journalist snooping for a story," Braithwaite said. "We'll make sure he doesn't get one."

Svenson kept an eye on Lorna Palin as the journey progressed. On the third day at sea, he followed her up on deck after supper, thinking she might be on her way to meet Wick. The evening was cool, Rob Coyle was safely located in the lounge playing whist, and the part of the deck where the woman walked was deserted except for an elderly British gent with a bushy moustache, stubbornly trying to get a pipe lighted.

Svenson nodded to him as he crossed to the other side of the deck, still watching Lorna. He was lucky to notice her pause, then veer toward a ladder. Her pale skirt whipped briefly in the wind like a signal flag as she climbed to the deck above. Svenson glanced around to make sure he wasn't being observed, then followed.

It took him a few minutes to locate her. She was still alone, leaning with both hands on the rail and looking out to sea. She was beautiful, all right, Svenson thought, with her chin raised high and her hair blowing. He could understand how Wick had fallen.

Quietly, he walked to a spot a few feet behind her. She hadn't noticed him.

Didn't notice him until he had one huge hand at the nape of her neck, the other gripping her skirt that he'd bunched between her legs. He was hoisting her high to hurl her over the rail. "I hope you can swim, dear," he told her, as if it were all a joke.

Then they were both yanked backward. The tall man who'd had her staggered to keep his balance. Wick was there to punch him in the jaw.

But the man didn't fall. Instead, he shook his head, grinned, and grabbed Wick by his collar.

That was when the elderly gentleman she'd noticed on the deck below stepped from the shadows and struck the tall man on the head with what looked like a leather sap. The man still didn't fall, but stumbled and slumped against the rail. He reached again for the paralyzed Lorna. Wick punched him again, and the elderly gentleman, still with his pipe clamped firmly in his jaw, quickly stepped forward and pushed the man over the rail.

Just like that, simple, fast, unreal. But it had happened, she knew. There had been no scream, and they were too high even to hear a splash. But the tall man had been there, and now he was gone.

Then Wick had her, holding her close, asking if she was hurt.

When he was sure she wasn't, he walked with her to her cabin. Glancing back, she noticed the elderly gentleman pick up a shoe the tall man had lost in the struggle and casually toss it out into the night.

"How will you deal with Braithwaite?" the colonel asked Wick when he'd joined him later in the Gentlemen's Lounge.

"As of now," Wick said, "he still regards me as a loyal, if love-struck, German agent, and he needs me to help him find and photograph the plans. He'll play dumb about the Swede's disappearance from the ship, and so will I."

Colonel Brookes drew thoughtfully on his pipe, then exhaled a great cloud of smoke that smelled like dry pine needles burning. "Do you know yet how he plans to transport the photographed plans to Germany once he has them?"

Wick shook his head. "The Germans never reveal any more information than is necessary."

"I dare say that's so you can't answer if a British agent asks you," the colonel told him.

"I dare say," Wick agreed.

Later that evening, Lorna surrendered to her emotions and decided to go to Wick in his stateroom. He didn't answer when she knocked, but he'd given her a key in case she needed some place to hide. She used it to let herself in, then looked around at the unsuspected luxury.

As she stood motionless on the plush carpet, she heard another key grate in the lock, and she decided to conceal herself behind a Chinese folding screen with a dragon design and surprise Wick.

Staring through the vertical crack between the screen's panels, she drew in her breath. The man who entered wasn't Wick. It was the large, bullish man she'd heard the stewards refer to as Mr Braithwaite.

Now she had a problem. She considered simply stepping out from behind the screen and telling the truth, then thought better of the idea. Braithwaite probably wouldn't stay long in another man's stateroom. Besides, what *was* he doing here?

He wasn't acting as if he were looking for something. Instead, he sat in a chair that appeared too dainty for him, crossed his legs, and peered at a pocket watch on the end of a long silver chain.

Which was when the door from the passageway opened again and Wick entered the room. Lorna remained still and silent behind the screen, peeking through the narrow space where the panels were hinged. Though Braithwaite remained seated, something in his demeanour made it clear that he was Wick's superior. "Considering your history," he said in an irritated voice, "I expected that by now you would have located the plans."

"What do you know about my history?" Wick asked.

"Oh, I know much about you. Your real name is Erik Kolb, and you're considered one of the most efficient agents in the organization. You scored high when you were in London six years ago on an industrial espionage mission, posing as a young British sculptor named Bertie Wicker. Berlin also described you as a bit of a rogue. At times you tend to digress from orders and work your own strategies."

"That last is because you can trust no one in our occupation."

"You needn't trust me, completely," Braithwaite said. "In fact, I'd be disappointed in you if you did. What you must do is obey my orders to the letter."

"As I do."

"It's a changing world, and some men have wavering loyalties."

"I am not one of them, Herr Braithwaite."

Lorna felt her shattered heart continue its plunge. Wick wasn't pretending – he actually *was* a German agent.

"There's still plenty of time before we reach New York," Wick – or was it Erik Kolb? – assured Braithwaite.

Braithwaite stood up and went to the door. "We need the plans as soon as possible, not simply before the ship docks. Tonight, in fact. It's imperative. I suggest you use your time effectively, or there will be repercussions." He went out.

Wick didn't move for a moment, then locked the door and slowly began undressing for bed. Apparently he was going to disregard Braithwaite's ultimatum.

Lorna waited for hours, trembling and silent behind the screen, before Wick's deep and even breathing assured her he was sleeping and she could creep from his stateroom and return to her bunk below deck.

\*　　　\*　　　\*

On board the *U-7*, which had been running on the surface during the night to intercept, then shadow and close on the ocean liner, Rendt and the rest of the crew were astounded to see the massive, brightly lighted form of the *Titanic* appear in the darkness.

Rendt's voice quavered with awe and alarm. "Captain –"

"Stay calm, I see it," Geerhauser interrupted. The huge ship was moving deceptively fast and he had to act quickly.

"Iceberg dead ahead," the lookout conveyed to the sub's conning tower, and peering through his binoculars, Geerhauser immediately saw the menacing pale form.

He wasn't thrown. "*Titanic* will bear hard to port to avoid the iceberg," he confidently told Rendt. "We will submerge to a shallow depth to remain out of sight and veer slightly in the same direction."

He barked his orders, and *U-7* slipped beneath the dark sea as the towering wall of *Titanic*'s hull approached. The plan was for the sub to pass between the *Titanic* and the iceberg. Geerhauser smiled as he realized the iceberg would reduce the area of ocean where they'd be searching for the container to be recovered in the gigantic ship's wake.

*Who was he, really?* Lorna wondered as she lay in her bunk, finished with her crying. Was Wick really Erik Kolb, German agent? *Did* his loyalties waver? Might he love her enough to consider changing sides in reality?

But she knew she was trying to fool herself. Most likely he'd been using her in some way. She rolled onto her side and was sure she'd begin to sob again, but she found that her eyes burned and were dry of tears.

Beneath the Atlantic's surface, the crew of the *U-7* exchanged horrified glances. The churning sound of *Titanic*'s giant screws continued drawing closer.

"Hold course," the disciplined Geerhauser ordered calmly. He knew *Titanic* would soon veer sharply left to pass the iceberg. She must.

Geerhauser and Rendt looked at each other, each man

waiting for the sound of the *Titanic*'s screws to begin subsiding.

But the frightening sound didn't subside. It grew to a gurgling roar.

The sub began to rock.

Rendt smelled fear.

"Dive deeper!" Geerhauser shouted, his voice breaking. Then he stared at Rendt, his eyes bright with terror and puzzlement. And resignation.

Too late, he'd realized along with Rendt and the rest of the crew that the tiny *U-7* would be crushed between the iceberg and *Titanic's* hull.

Lorna felt the mattress move slightly beneath her, and a slight shudder caused a water glass on a wooden shelf to vibrate and rattle. Then everything was as it had been before. She glanced at the clock on a nearby table. 11:40. Not even midnight yet.

She settled deeper beneath her warm blanket and continued to seek the oblivion of sleep.

The crew of the *Titanic* at first thought the ship had narrowly avoided the iceberg, as indeed it had. No one could guess the presence and destruction of the *U-7*.

Then the rent along the starboard side of the hull was discovered. Water was rushing in below decks, filling watertight compartments one by one.

Wick sat up in bed. Something was wrong. People seemed to be rushing about in the companionway. Voices not usually heard at such a late hour were filtering into the stateroom.

He climbed out of bed, slipped into his clothes and shoes, and left to investigate.

As soon as he stepped into the passageway, he was bumped by a uniformed crewman.

"What's going on?" he asked the man. "What's happening?"

"It's . . . well . . ."

Wick could see that beneath calm, wooden features, the

man was badly frightened. He clutched him by both shoulders. "Tell me," he said, looking him in the eye.

"We've struck an iceberg, sir. The ship is . . . sinking." He started to say something more but seemed to choke on the words.

"What else?" Wick demanded, tightening his grip, shaking the man.

"The ship wasn't supposed to sink. There aren't enough lifeboats." The crewman wrenched himself free of Wick's grasp and hurried away.

Trying to comprehend fully what he'd just heard, Wick noticed for the first time that the passageway floor was tilted slightly toward the bow. He had to see for himself what was happening. Tucking in his shirt, he made his way up on deck.

The night was cool but bright with starlight, and the deck was already teeming with passengers, most of them wearing life jackets. Wick knew the water was too cold to allow survival for very long.

The forward angle of the ship wasn't yet severe, and while there was excitement, there certainly wasn't panic. Even among passengers who knew the lifeboat situation, true realization hadn't yet set in. This, and what must follow, was simply unacceptable. There was no precedent or protocol for such a thing. They refused to believe, yet they knew. The bright, gay, floating city, thought to be unsinkable, would soon be on the ocean floor for all eternity.

A hand touched Wick's shoulder and he turned. Braithwaite, appearing impatient but confident as always, was at his side.

"We're sinking," Wick said.

Braithwaite nodded. "You know the lifeboat dilemma?"

"I've been told." Wick knew something else. Braithwaite had ordered the Swede to kill Lorna because she was a security risk who endangered the mission. Now he wouldn't want her to be one of the survivors. There was a way Wick might protect her. The success of the mission might be enough to make Braithwaite forget her at least for the moment, maybe long enough. The coming war, duty to country, seemed very far away now. Love, and death, were much nearer.

"I found the plans and photographed them," Wick said, and dug into a deep pocket and produced a small and tightly wrapped roll of film.

Braithwaite accepted the film and held it tightly. "This can't be delivered in the manner anticipated. I'll see that a contact in New York receives it and gets it to Berlin."

"If you survive."

Braithwaite smiled. "That's been arranged. There's nothing more for you to do, Herr Kolb. You've performed your duty admirably, and I'll see to it that you receive proper recognition and a medal."

"Posthumously," Wick pointed out.

Braithwaite shrugged. "Perhaps, but I hope not." He turned away from Wick.

Wick immediately began searching for Lorna. She wasn't in her bunk, and none of the third-class passengers knew her whereabouts. And she hadn't gone to Wick's stateroom looking for him.

While he was in the stateroom, he spent a few minutes there, then put on his short grey wool coat and grabbed a life jacket, noticing with a pang of alarm that there were several inches of water in the passageway as he went back up on deck.

Finally he found her, near an entrance to the Verandah Cafe, just aft of the Smoking Lounge. Some of the other passengers, a few of them still in their evening clothes, were seated at the white wicker tables as if confused and awaiting service.

When Wick approached, he was shocked to see her turn her back on him.

"Lorna –"

"I don't want to see or talk to you again, Erik Kolb."

Now he understood, but he didn't know how she'd found out. And now it hardly mattered. "The ship is going to sink, Lorna."

"When the lifeboats are picked up or reach shore –"

"There aren't enough lifeboats. Don't you understand? I want you to go to one of the boats now and –"

But she was hurrying along the sloping deck away from him, wearing slippers already soaked, her long blue robe fluttering about her ankles. When he followed, she broke into a run.

Wick ran after her, around people wearing stunned expressions, through clusters of passengers helping each other into life jackets. Sidestepping an old man trying to comfort his sobbing wife, Wick followed Lorna below deck.

He'd lost sight of her until he turned a corner of a dim passageway, the leather soles of his shoes sloshing on saturated carpet.

Braithwaite had Lorna by an arm and was trying to get his free hand around her throat.

Wick charged and knocked both of them to the floor. When Braithwaite tried to scramble to his feet, Wick slammed him across the back of the neck with the heavy canvas life jacket he was still carrying. The next time Braithwaite attempted to get up, he was met by a solid right cross to the chin and fell back unconsious.

Lorna was leaning against a wall, swaying. Wick supported her. "Whatever my name is, wherever my loyalties lie, I do love you," he told her. She didn't resist as he put his woollen coat on her and led her back up on deck and to the nearest of the lifeboats that were being hurriedly loaded.

As she was about to claim one of the last available places in the boat, she turned and kissed him on the lips, hard. "Come with me, please!"

"I can't. I'll put on my life jacket and wait to be picked up. It shouldn't be long."

She looked out at the calm black sea, then back at Wick.

"Trust me. There's nothing to worry about, Lorna."

"Promise you'll come to me when this is over."

Wick nodded, then urged her into the boat, not telling her that he and the other passengers who stayed on board were doomed.

He knew his duty now, and it wasn't what Braithwaite thought. Wick hurried back to the passageway below deck where he hoped Braithwaite still lay unconscious.

Things had changed. Water was now over a foot deep in

the passageway and rising. Braithwaite was floating face down, and *London Times* journalist Rob Coyle was standing over him, clutching the roll of film.

"There were several German agents on board when *Titanic* sailed," Coyle said with a smile. "It doesn't matter anymore to Braithwaite that with *Titanic*'s passengers abandoning ship, the planned recovery is impossible, and I'll get credit for delivering the photographs to our superiors in Berlin." With the hand not gripping the film, he produced a small revolver.

"I don't know about any planned recovery and I don't care," Wick said. "And what you say might work only if Berlin were at the bottom of the sea. The ship's sinking fast, and the water's too cold for anyone to survive long enough to be picked up. You and I are already as dead as Braithwaite."

"Don't forget to include Colonel Brookes among the dead," Coyle said. "I saw that he went overboard with a fractured skull less than ten minutes ago. And don't concern yourself about me. I've arranged for a guaranteed place in a lifeboat. The only reason you have a little longer to live and I don't shoot you now is that I don't want them to find a bullet hole if your body is recovered. You would have succeeded in your task for the British were it not for the woman. You *are* working for the British, are you not?"

Instead of answering, Wick charged Coyle. But the water slowed his rush, giving Coyle time to react. He sidestepped and raked the revolver across Wick's face, then shoved him into the stateroom where Braithwaite's body had drifted. After closing the door, he grabbed one of the pieces of furniture, a mahogany Chippendale chair, floating in the passageway. Quickly he used it to wedge the door closed from the outside.

From a lifeboat, Lorna watched *Titanic*'s stern rise high into the night sky. Then the great ship slid beneath the surface in majestic surrender. It left a vast blank space in the world, as if a city block had suddenly disappeared. The shrill, distant screams of passengers floating in the water reached them for a while over the calm sea, then there was silence but for the lapping of the waves against the drifting boat.

Lorna knew by now that it didn't matter if Wick was in the water in his life jacket or still on board. It wasn't until later that she found in a buttoned pocket of the coat he'd put on her an oil-skin pouch containing what looked like complicated plans, and brief instructions to turn them over to American authorities as soon as she reached land.

The instructions were signed, "Love eternal, Erik."

As soon as possible after Rob Coyle reached New York with the other survivors, he went directly to his contact on the Lower East Side and had the roll of film developed.

It contained only photographs of a posing, smiling Lorna on board the *Titanic*, the sun and the moment caught forever in her hair and eyes.

She looked young in the photos, and in love, the rest of her life stretched before her like bright possibility.